Hanzel Sventska

A Third Pirate's Tale

Gertjan Zwiggelaar

America Star Books

© 2014 by Gertjan Zwiggelaar.
All rights reserved. No part of this book may be reproduced, stored in a retrieval system or transmitted in any form or by any means without the prior written permission of the publishers, except by a reviewer who may quote brief passages in a review to be printed in a newspaper, magazine or journal.

First printing

All characters in this book are fictitious, and any resemblance to real persons, living or dead, is coincidental.

America Star Books has allowed this work to remain exactly as the author intended, verbatim, without editorial input.

Softcover 9781632495747
PUBLISHED BY AMERICA STAR BOOKS, LLLP
www.americastarbooks.com

Printed in the United States of America

OTHER BOOKS BY GERTJAN ZWIGGELAAR

A Pirate's Tale, PublishAmerica, 2008

Into the Game, PublishAmerica, 2009

A Journey to the Underside, 2013

Marty & Me, Another Pirate's Tale, 2014

Reviews of *A Pirate's Tale* by Gertjan Zwiggelaar

"*A Pirate's Tale* is a fabulous read! There are now four authors who have kept me up all night, John Steinbeck's *Grapes of Wrath*, (had to read for school the night before a test), John Grisham's *A Time to Kill*, (riveting), Kathleen Woodeweiss, all of her books, (ooh-la-la). And now, Gertjan Zwiggelaar. You have made *A Pirate's Tale* come alive for me. Thank you! I love it that the Gertjan Zwiggelaar I know and love has instilled himself in the book, without actually being one of the characters. Magnificent!!! FIVE STARS".

—*Shirley Tipman*

"I have just finished reading, *A Pirate's Tale* by Gertjan Zwiggelaar. I found this book to be an excellent read. The author writes with enthusiasm and is very explicative in his prose. I thoroughly enjoyed the story and easily relate to the characters as the author did an exemplary job of bringing them to life. His description of them superbly portrayed their adventures, their appearance, and very different personalities. This author lead me into the story in a very dramatic way with just the right amount of humour. I whole heartedly recommend this book. *A Pirate's Tale* is an exhilarating adventure which leaves you wanting more. FIVE STARS."

—*Patricia Wangsness*

"*A Pirate's Tale* is as intriguing and dynamic as the author himself. The characters in this book are so vivid, I felt I was living, laughing, and dying with them. The more I read the more I wanted to read. The sudden twists and turns take your breath away. I am sorry the voyage is over! More please!! FIVE STARS."

—*Sharon Sokolan*

"A great story that starts in Halifax, Canada, and takes you on an adventure to the south seas. It is one of those reads that you can't put down. Gertjan has respect for the reader so leaves lots to your imagination. I totally enjoyed this book and it is the first book i have ever read on pirates. FIVE STARS."

—*Karen Galloway*

FOREWORD

Hanzel Sventska is the third of my three pirate tales. *A Pirate's Tale* was the first of this triptych and was published by PublishAmerica in 2008. It is classified as a historic fiction. Of course the writer realizes that all histories are essentially fictions, and his first tale about the extraordinary adventurous lives lived by desperate men and women three hundred years ago is a fiction set in historic times amongst historic characters.

Marty & Me, Another Pirate's Tale was published in 2014 and is a horror pirate story which Star America was kind enough to share with the world in a beautiful soft cover edition; such as the one you are holding in your hands right now.

Hanzel Sventska is a Faustian tale, which will likely be the last of my pirate stories; there being so many other stories clamoring to be told. I am presently at work on what will be my 18th book; it is titled, *WTF?! A Bus Driver's Tale*. This story will be a tragi comedy.

As a writer I am attempting to write in every genre. I have written nine plays, one of which won a literary award and was produced. I also produced several others in my capacity as drama teacher in public high schools. One of my self published productions is a training manual for automotive sales professionals. Many of my letters have appeared in newspapers. I have also been published as a guest columnist. I am a regular contributor to comments sections in blogs. I have enjoyed the act of writing since I was a child.

One of the best presents my parents ever gave me was a beautiful Parker fountain pen with which I filled many pages during my high school years. I am also a practicing visual artist; my first work was reviewed in a public show when I was 18. I entered the University of Regina on that year's B.F.A. Entrance Scholarship in 1970.

Hanzel Sventska, in my opinion, is a masterpiece. The story is rich and filled with colourful characters. I am very proud to have been the conduit for this story, to be brought to this world direct from the Source of All Creation, with Whom I have an Awesome Personal Experience. My Father in Paradise sends me stories from time to time; (not all of my stories); some I make up myself, and basically He looks over my shoulder. In this case, just like, *A Pirate's Tale*,

Hanzel Sventska is an inspired story. *A Pirate's Tale* came in faster than *Hanzel Sventska*, however; the first draft of *A Pirate's Tale* was 400 pages and it arrived in a month and a half and then went through nine drafts before publishing.

Hanzel Sventska was first conceived in September, 2008 and was grown slowly at first, until more concentrated work ensued through the winter of 2012-2013 up to April 20th, a good portion of it during my homeless days. I completed the final draft in April of this year. Writing is an amazing experience. I never know what I'm going to get, especially since I am writing in every genre possible. I love the challenge of writing; to produce something which others will spend their precious time reading. I am so grateful for the many fans who have indicated on lots of occasions, how much they are, or have enjoyed reading what I have written. However, that is not always the case, when it comes to my editorial letters in newspapers or in blogs. I am not afraid to be controversial. I speak my mind. I have opinions and am quite prepared to share them with those who need to hear them. Sometimes politicians do not particularly enjoy my observations. Be that as it may, I am what I am and do what I do; not hurting anyone, but certainly keeping people on their toes, by presenting well written, eloquent critiques, and not just knee jerk reactions, as well as what I hope are, good, books. I want my books to be remembered and shared.

I know that the greatest achievement human kind ever realized is the art of language and her elegant clothing; the written word. Words are mighty creations in any language and must always be used with caution and foresight. Unlike the wounds effected on the body by instruments of torture, the wounds inflicted by words never go away. Hence, it is imperative, in my opinion, that someone engaged in the art of writing down words, which will remain forever, if stored in the correct manner, such as a popular book; a tangible item, and not an electronic collection of bits and bytes, which can be erased at the push of a button, ought to make those 'magical' marks; those incredible letters our ancestors invented to be organized into, what now amounts to over one million different words in English, an enjoyable experience for readers. That is what I am trying to do with my stories. I am attempting to gift my readers with an experience which will keep them reading and wanting more, but also try to enrich my readers by providing interesting details and ideas to consider. We writers of English have over One Million Words! to work with; it would be a worthy challenge, someday, to write a story book that contains all of those words; and make it interesting reading. Come to think of it, there already is such a book; the 21st Century Dictionary of the English Language. Awesome reading! And, also, a great adventure, highly recommended.

It is my sincere desire that you will find, *Hanzel Sventska, A Third Pirate's Tale* to be a good read and a memorable experience. I know this story makes an excellent completion to my pirate adventures. The three separate stories comprise a total of, 540,575 words.

When you think about that, the number of times my fingers have tapped the keys of my keyboard is a huge number. In the case of the three pirate stories it is a total of: 2,996,237 key strokes, give or take a couple of thousand. The reason I tell you this, is to give you, the reader some idea of what writers do. The actual physical work of tapping keys, or for those writers who prefer to write in long hand, is a lot of concentrated work. I thought I'd just give you, dear reader, some idea of what writers actually do. And, if it was not for writers, there would not be much of a civilization for anyone to enjoy. So, here is a toast to my brothers and sisters; my beloved colleagues, giving their lives to the organization of letters into words which bring so much joy to all of us. I am so thankful I can read. Praise God!

Special thanks to my dear neighbour, Shirley Tipman for help with fine tuning the final draft and for an excellent idea which added that extra little spicy touch. She knows what I am talking about.

Also, special thanks to my dear Mother, Ann Zwiggelaar. Always patient and supportive.

Thanks to Jan Zwiggelaar for being a good brother and friend.

A big thanks to my children: Tereigh, Carey, and Michael, just because I am blessed you are in my life. I don't know what I would do without you.

A huge thank you to America Star Books for taking another chance on one of my books. You guys are awesome! I love you!

Thank you to Anthony for another magnificent cover design. You know what I like.

And finally, Thank You! Dear Reader, for buying my book. Bon voyage! Aaargh!!!

Gertjan Zwiggelaar,
April 20, 2014
Red Deer, Alberta

Hanzel Sventska

A Third Pirate's Tale

Chapter 1

An ear splitting thunder clap heralded the arrival of Hanzel Sventska into the world. The storm had rolled over Holland for several days and appeared to be intensifying shortly after the birth; the ninth child of Elizabeth Merkel and Kabel Sventska, a fisherman by trade and occasional privateer. Money was tight. A ninth child was not very welcome. Life was hard. It was April 23rd, 1600.

Kabel was not home when Hanzel was born. He was out to sea with the fishing fleet. However, he would be back next day and then, depending on the catch, there would be hell to pay, or a little less hell to pay. Either way, Hanzel's mother was not looking forward to Kabel coming home and seeing another child he had to feed. Elizabeth knew he wasn't happy about the pregnancy, however, he didn't make much of a fuss because the child was still in her belly. However, now that the child was actually in the world, she didn't know what Kabel's reaction would be. It was hard to tell with him. Her husband's mood shifted like the tide; from moderately grumpy to violently dangerous. He had hit his wife and children on more than one occasion. The children were all scared of him. Elizabeth, too, if truth be known. However, she hid it well in front of the little ones. Alas, on more than one occasion the children witnessed their mother being beaten for standing up to Kabel.

So, there he was, little Hanzel, born into a troubled family and contentedly sucking on his mother's breast when his father came home. Kabel didn't notice right away, that little Hanzel was in the house; since he was contentedly suckling on his mother's breast, in the bed in the other room. The children immediately sensed the mood their father was in. He was drunk and not happy. There were hardly any fish to be had. The catch was mediocre, at best.

Kabel stared at his cowering children and yelled. 'ELIZABETH!"

The sound of Kabel's voice startled little Hanzel, who pulled away from his mother's breast and started to cry. The sound stopped Kabel in his tracks for a moment. Then he rushed to the bed room and beheld his youngest son; Hanzel.

'MY GOD!' shouted Kabel, staring at the baby.

Chapter 2

By the time Hanzel was nine, his siblings were not at home much, anymore. The next youngest was a sister named Marika, and she was fifteen, and already working in a laundry. The rest were either married, or out with Kabel, fishing for herring. They were all too afraid of Kabel to do otherwise. Hence, with more fishermen working for the family, their fortunes were much improved, notwithstanding Kabel's cruelty. By the time Hanzel was twelve years old he had enough of his father's sociopathic behaviour. The regular beatings and deprivations had become unbearable. He tried to convince some of his brothers and sisters to leave home, but none of them came with him. Kabel's attitude had remained the same towards Hanzel; whom he didn't like from the beginning. Hence, the young boy had no choice but to remove himself from that unhappy abode.

One day in July, 1612, Hanzel left. A boy could easily do that back then. A precocious boy especially, could easily make his way to Amsterdam and disappear in the milling throng of the busy port. He left his home, when his father and brothers were out fishing and he had been left to tend the family's five goats and three sheep, which provided milk and wool for the family. His mother had gone to visit a sick friend. So, when nobody was looking, Hanzel wrapped some goat cheese in an oil cloth and grabbed a loaf of bread from the pantry. He stuffed the food into a small leather bag. As he was preparing his bag of food, he remembered seeing his father putting some coins inside a jar, which was sitting on a high shelf above the hearth. By shoving the table beside the hearth, and placing a chair on the table, he was able to reach the jar. Inside was a goodly sum in silver and small gold coins. Hanzel's eyes widened. He knew what money was and there was a goodly sum, as far as he could tell. It was the perfect thing to help him escape his miserable life.

Hanzel quickly climbed down from the chair, gingerly holding on to the jar. It was heavy and he had to be careful. He set the jar on the table and quickly poured the coins into his bag. He returned the jar to its place above the hearth and then replaced the table and chair to their former location. Satisfied that everything looked normal, he left that place, never to return.

The day was warm and a gentle breeze came in from the north. The fishing village, in which Hanzel lived, was quiet and peaceful. It was a Sunday. Not too many people were about. Hanzel was not noticed as he quickly walked away on the dirt road which led to a bigger road six kilometers away. It was that bigger road which led to Amsterdam.

When Hanzel reached the main road, it was mid afternoon. He was hungry and thirsty. Fortunately, he was able to obtain water from a rain barrel, which sat beside a dilapidated house at the crossroad. When he had drunk his fill, he ate some bread and cheese and watched as a steady flow of wagons, carts, and people headed to and from Amsterdam, twenty kilometres distant.

While he was thusly sitting by the water barrel, watching the traffic and eating his lunch, a man, driving a mule cart, stopped beside the old house. The man was quite fat and had some trouble climbing down from his conveyance. The old mule looked back at its master and snorted. The fat man didn't notice Hanzel right away and quickly stepped over to a large tree nearby. Hanzel watched as the man undid his cod piece and relieved himself against the tree, sighing with great relief.

While the portly man was thusly standing there, relieving himself, Hanzel grabbed his bag and climbed into the cart. The man had left the reins, trusting his mule to stay put. Fortunately for Hanzel, the mule did not distinguish who was pulling the reins and quickly trotted off at Hanzel's commands.

The pissing man, realizing what was going on, dribbled all over his breeches and hose, as he ran after the quickly moving cart, but, being as he was so fat, he couldn't run very fast, nor did he have the breath to sustain a prolonged trot. Hence, Hanzel managed to make off with the fat man's cart and mule. The rest of the trip to Amsterdam was much more pleasant as a result. It did not occur to anyone on the road that the twelve year old boy had no business driving that mule cart. Twelve year olds were not uncommon in the work force.

Hanzel felt good as he ate some more cheese, happily sitting in the driver's seat. The old mule just walked on and on, as the kilometers passed by. When he was finished eating, Hanzel reached into the bag and felt the coins slip through his fingers. He frowned. *It's too bad I had to steal it from my family. I'm sure, when father discovers the missing jar, all hell will break loose. I pity my siblings. And mother. Oh, dear God. What have I done?* Hanzel sighed. *It couldn't be helped. I had no choice.* Hanzel shrugged his shoulders. It was a matter of survival. He knew that he would be alright as long as he kept his wits about himself. He wouldn't let anyone know about his money. With a cart, he could earn more money.

As he traveled along the well trodden road, the sky began to darken as clouds rolled in from the sea. Soon it would rain. However, Hanzel wasn't concerned. He would find an inn. Surely, with the money in his bag, he would be able to get a room and a meal at least. Hanzel grinned as he drove through the city gate and entered the bustling metropolis. A flash of lightning lit the sky and illuminated the runaway in a blue light of great intensity. However, the guards took no notice of him as he drove past. A split second later an ear splitting crack of thunder reverberated off the buildings and through the cobbled streets. Rain began to fall in torrents.

Hanzel started to shiver as his clothes became sopping wet. He had to find shelter immediately. Fortunately, the friendly light of a boisterous inn was within a short distance of the gate. Several other hapless beasts of burden were standing outside, tied to brass rings set in posts in the courtyard. Hanzel quickly tied the mule to an available ring. Then he grabbed his bag and ran to the door to let himself in.

The door opened onto a small landing, which led to short, wooden staircases leading to the lower level eating hall and the bedrooms upstairs. The place was filled with noise, smells, and smoke. It took young Hanzel a moment to adjust to the hubbub. Only three men took notice of him, as he stood there on the landing, dripping and blinking, while adjusting to the new experience. Hanzel had never been in an inn before. The place was filled mostly with men. He knew he had to act as manly and mature as possible and try not to attract attention to himself.

As he stood there, adjusting to his new circumstances, a pretty blond haired wench walked up the steps and addressed him.

'What do you want here, boy?'

Hanzel regarded her for a moment before answering.

'Well? What is it you want here?' asked the wench again. 'Are you lookin' for your papa?'

Hanzel's eyes widened and he shook his head. 'N, no,' he stammered. 'I just want to get out of the rain and get warm.'

The girl looked at young Hanzel, shivering on the landing.

'Then you better come and sit by the fire and dry off. Are you hungry?' The wench led Hanzel down into the eating hall.

Hanzel nodded. 'Y,yes. Yes, I am hungry.'

'Well, we'll see about getting you something to eat and drink. Do you have any money?'

'Yes, I have money,' answered Hanzel, just as they walked past the three men who had been watching him from the moment he set foot on the landing.

The young woman led Hanzel to a small bench by the fire. He thanked her and she told him she would be right back with something to eat and drink. Hanzel thanked her again and then turned his face to the fire, rubbing his hands in the warmth.

'The child as money, e said,' muttered one of the three men eyeing the boy.

'Wher'd a young un like im get money?' asked the pale skinned man sitting in the middle.

'Aye. Wher'd e get the money, indeed?' asked the man with the nasty scar running down his right cheek.

'Perhaps we oughts ter investigate?' suggested the first speaker; a man wearing a tattered leather tricorn.

The man in the middle rubbed his fat earlobe for a moment. 'Let's keep an eye on im. If e stays the night, we'll takes a look see. When e's sleepin.'

As the three men sat there watching young Hanzel and discussing the potential for easy pickings, the serving girl walked over, carrying a trencher of food and a tankard of ale for him. She set the food and tankard on a long table, behind Hanzel, where a dozen others were eating heartily, seated on long benches running the length of the table on each side. Happy banter filled the space.

'Your food and drink is on the table,' said the wench.

Hanzel looked up and smiled. The girl was so nice to him. He thanked her and asked how much money she needed from him. He understood the gold and silver disks he had in his bag were money, but, he had never been taught anything about the face value of coins. Hanzel had no idea what coins were what. When the girl told him the amount, he grabbed a palm full of coins from his bag and told her to take what she required. The girl looked at Hanzel and smiled. Then she proceeded to take twice as much as was called for. Hanzel thanked her and returned the rest of the coins to his leather bag. None of this action was missed by the three conspirators watching from the sidelines.

Eventually, as he sat there eating and happily drinking the barley ale, he began to notice the three men sitting at their table on the other side of the room. Hanzel quickly sensed there was something insincere about those characters. He decided he would keep an eye on them. As he thusly sat there, eating and drinking the ale, he began to feel warm and slightly wobbly from the strong drink, which began to taste ever more delicious. For a twelve year old boy, not overly used to drinking ale, the heady beverage was having an ever greater effect. By the time he finished the tankard, and eaten his food, he was heading into his cups; enough so, to order an other one. The serving wench happily complied and helped herself to another double portion from his coins; Hanzel not knowing any better.

By the time Hanzel finished his second tankard of ale, he was leaning into the wind. When the girl returned, Hanzel mumbled, 'ish dere shumewhere I can shleep?'

The serving wench smiled. 'Follow me,' she said.

Hanzel regarded her for a moment and then with some effort extracted himself from the table which had been holding him up. The serving girl, realizing the young man was drunk and leaning precariously on wobbly legs, grabbed him around the waist. She picked up his bag from the bench and then half carried him out of the big room into the back of the inn and up creaking stairs to the family wing of the three story building. The girl took Hanzel to her own room and deposited him on her bed. 'You can sleep here,' she said.

'Sank yew,' croaked Hanzel before he passed out.

Hanzel's Good Samaritan watched him for a moment, then quietly took his bag of money and stashed it in her secret place. When she was satisfied all was in order, she left the room; locking the door behind her. She returned to her duties and Hanzel passed into a spinning dream.

Chapter 3

When the serving girl returned to the dining hall, one of the three conspirators signaled her over to his table.

'Another drink, Jurgen?' she asked as she approached.

The man named, Jurgen, adjusted his tricorn. He eyed the bar wench for a moment and then asked her where she had taken the boy they had been watching.

The young woman regarded the three men and frowned. 'I figured you three might be interested in him. I've locked him safely in my room, where you can't get at him.'

'E as money. Wher'd you suppose a kid gits de money to pay fer stayin ere?' asked the man with the scar.

'Maybe ees a thief. Maybe the authorities ought to be appraised,' suggested the third man; the one with the fat earlobes.

The serving wench regarded the three men. 'He's mine. I took care of him. I'll find out about him in the morning. Meantime, I suggest you three don't get any fancy ideas about him, either.'

'We could elp you wid im. Come on, Angela, we'd cut you in,' replied the scarred man.

'I don't need help, especially not from the likes of you, Kees Kleppers.' Angela leaned over the little table and stared into each man's eyes. 'Leave him alone. He's a child. Pick on people your own size.' She paused for emphasis and then asked if they wanted another round of drinks. The three men declined and decided to leave. Angela returned to her work.

The rain was still coming down in buckets. As the three conspirators stepped outside, a brilliant flash of light lit up the scene, immediately followed by a clap of thunder which shivered the very timbers of the inn. Fast asleep on

Angela's bed, Hanzel never heard it. He was deep into a spinning dream about his uncertain future.

The three men found the back door and opened it onto the landing at the base of the creaking stairs which led to the family quarters. No one was there, the family members being busy with their work, tending to their guests in the dining hall and performing in the large kitchen. No one noticed the three schemers as they carefully climbed up the groaning stairs to the family wing of the building. Hanzel never heard a sound.

When the three schemers reached the landing of the second floor, the man with the fat earlobes tugged at his earring. He put his forefinger to his mouth and whispered, 'shhhhh.'

'What room d'you suppose ees in?' whispered Jurgen.

'I don know,' replied the man with the fat earlobes. He tugged at his earring. 'We'll have to put our ears to the doors and listen.'

'Are you sure the family rooms are ere?' asked Kees, the man with the nasty scar running down his wind worn face. 'What if'n we disturb somebody?'

The man with the earring, stared at his companion. 'There you go. Mister Negative. Always, Mister Negative.' He looked at the other man. 'Isn't it true? Mister Negative?'

The other man nodded. 'Yeah, it's true, alright.'

The man with the bulbous earlobes looked back at the scarred man. 'Stop being negative.' He gave his friend a slap on his forehead.

'Yes, boss.'

'Alright. Jurgen, you listen for a kid's breathing at those three doors. 'Kees, you listen at those three, and I'll take those other four.' He pointed out which doors he meant.

The three conspirators did as they planned; each one listening for a child's breathing behind a door.

As the three were thusly engaged, in the kitchen below, the innkeeper, Mister de Fries decided he needed a nap; having been hard at it since noon and it now being eight thirty. He had cooked a lot of meals and supervised a lot of activity, his inn being a busy one, because it was so close to the city's main gate. A lot of travelers stopped at the *Hijlige Frauw*; that being the name of the inn where Hanzel found his place of refuge, and where the innkeeper was about to walk up the stairs.

Mister de Fries was a Friesian; and hence a tall, very blond, and very strong man with piercing blue eyes and a tenacious will. He also knew the three men who were on the second floor, listening at the doors. They never heard the innkeeper coming up the stairs.

He caught them red handed.

'So, I catch the three of you, once again, up to no good in my inn!' he said, with his booming voice.

The three schemers instantly stood to attention and regarded Mister de Fries with fearful expressions. Their knees were quivering.

'What are you doing up here?' demanded the innkeeper.

'Er, ah, well, um, you see,' replied the man with the earring. 'We, ah, well, we have a friend stayin ere.'

'That's right,' agreed Jurgen, nodding his head vigorously.

The other man also nodded his head.

'What's his name?' asked the big Friesian.

The three men looked at each other frantically, but could not agree on a name.

'We've ah, er, forgotten is name,' said the man with the earring. 'We met im downstairs. In the dining hall. We didn't want to disturb anybody, so we were listening at the doors, to see if we could ear im.'

Mister de Fries stared at the three intruders for a moment. 'A likely story it is, Johannes Poort. This floor is not where guests sleep. Therefore, I don't believe you. I want the three of you to get out of my inn, right now. Disappear into the city and don't ever come back here. I warn you. If I ever, ever, see you here again, in my dining hall, in my courtyard, on my streets, I will break each one of you in half and toss you into the canal.' He stared at each man in turn. 'Do you understand?'

'You want us to just leave and go out in that storm?' asked the scarred man, plaintively.

Mister de Fries pointed to the stairs leading to the front door of the inn. 'OUT!' He shouted. He gestured menacingly, scaring the three men, who quickly ran down the stairs, followed by the irate innkeeper. As they ran out into the rain, Mister de Fries managed to land a good kick into the right buttock of the earringed leader of the little band. Then he firmly banged the door shut, leaving the three miscreants standing in the pouring rain.

Hanzel woke up when Mister de Fries's voice boomed through the hallway outside the room he was lying in. The room was dark and it took him a while to adjust his eyes for night vision. He sat up slowly and swung his legs over the edge of the bed. The room smelled nice and appeared to be well appointed. Hanzel could see a large armour on one side of the room and a large chest on the other. A small table with a chair sat against the wall, beside the bed. A window above it was covered with curtains. As Hanzel gazed at the little table he realized there was a candle in a stand, and a flint box. Hanzel knew about lighting a candle and soon he could see much better as the candle helped to bring its warming light into the pleasant bedroom of Angela, the serving wench. He had no idea that the girl was the innkeeper's daughter. Her father didn't know that Hanzel was in her room, which was immediately next to his own. Hanzel could hear him enter the room and walk across the floor. A moment later a thump against the wall indicated the man had fallen into his bed. Soon, Hanzel could hear him snoring on the other side of the wall.

It suddenly occurred to Hanzel he had a leather bag with coins when he came into the inn. At that moment he had no idea where the bag was. In the dim light provided by the single candle, he could not immediately see the dark brown leather bag anywhere in the room. Hanzel slowly got himself out of bed and grabbed the candle, in order to look around. When he realized his bag was nowhere in the room, he lunged at the door. Unfortunately, Hanzel had not completely slept off the effects of the alcohol, causing him to stumble and fall against the small table sitting beside the door, knocking it over as he fell on top of it. The candle fell from his hand and rolled a short distance before snuffing out. Hanzel groaned quietly as he collected himself and stumbled back to bed. A moment later he crawled under the blanket and passed out, once again; returning to another spinning dream.

Sometime later Hanzel heard the door creak open. He slowly opened his eyes and peered out from under the blanket. In the dim light he saw Angela, as she stood with her back towards him as she closed the door, trying to be quiet. She was not aware that Hanzel was watching her. The girl locked the door and quietly stepped over to the bedside table, intent upon lighting the candle. As she approached the little table, she stepped on the candle, causing her to trip and fall against the bed. Expecting Hanzel to wake up, the girl looked anxiously at his face, however, Hanzel thought it better to pretend to be sleeping. The ruse worked because she carefully picked herself up and retrieved the candle, which she returned to its holder. A moment later she struck the flint and lit it, enabling Hanzel to see much better as Angela began to remove her clothes.

First she removed her apron and then pulled her one piece dress over her head. Underneath she was completely naked. Hanzel stirred slightly as he strained to peer through the dim light sensually bathing the pale skin of the naked serving wench. Hanzel had seen naked girls before; they being his sisters; however, he had never seen a strange girl, and never one with such adult breasts and hairy pubis. As he watched, his penis grew and grew into a rocket ten times its normal length. His penis quivered as the girl climbed, naked, into the bed beside him. Hanzel continued to pretend he was sleeping, as he lay on his side, his back toward her. He could feel her moving in the bed, but thought it best to not stir. Gradually the girl moved her voluptuous, naked body against his. He could feel her hard, erect nipples pressing against his back. He was scared and didn't know what to do. Then, without warning, she began to move a hand along his side and around his pelvis. When she grabbed a hold of his erection, that is when he reacted, jumping out of the bed.

'What are you doing?!' he exclaimed. 'And, where is my money?'

The girl sat up in bed, her large, pendulous white breasts drawing Hanzel's gaze. He had never seen such a pair of wondrous tits before. His young hands definitely wanted to touch them.

'What's the matter? Don't you want to play with me?' asked the girl, taking a deep breath and pushing her breasts forward, making them look even bigger and more inviting.

Hanzel nodded. 'Y,yes,' he stammered. 'Of course I want to play with you.' He didn't know what else to say. The thought of touching those big tits was quite overwhelming for the young boy.

'You've never touched a girl before, have you?'

Hanzel nodded. 'Never,' he agreed. Then, to make it sound like he was not totally clueless, he told her he had seen two of his sisters naked, once. When they were bathing. 'They didn't have tits like yours,' he added.

'Oh, so you like my tits, do you?' The girl smiled and gestured for him to return to the bed. 'How old are you?'

Hanzel stared at her for a moment before answering. 'How old do you think I am?'

'Well, I think you are about 14. Why don't you come here and let me touch your penis.' The girl reached out as Hanzel climbed back onto the bed.

'I'm twelve,' he said as she gently touched his quivering phallus.

'That's alright,' she said, as she began to work her magic.

'Where's my money?' he asked, not really understanding what exactly was happening; not having had any sexual experiences before.

'Don't worry about your money,' she replied. 'It's safe. Just lie back and let me play with you. I'm sure you'll enjoy this.'

Hanzel looked at the two magnificent breasts staring him in the face. 'May I touch them?' he asked.

The girl smiled. 'Of course,' she said.

That night, twelve year old Hanzel was introduced to a sweet pleasure he would never forget and always seek.

Next morning, cocks and dogs woke Hanzel at first light. He sat upright in bed and cleared the sand from his eyes with the backs of his hands. Angela was still sleeping, a happy grin on her face. Hanzel smiled as he thought about what she had done with him. He gently touched her hair. It felt like silk, as he let her blond hair glide through his fingers. A moment later, she opened an eye and peeked at Hanzel, gently stroking her tresses. She smiled. 'Good morning, young Hanzel,' she said.

Hanzel smiled and his eyes twinkled. He thought he was in love with Angela. 'Good morning, Angela,' he replied.

A cock crowed again and several dogs barked in response.

Hanzel watched as Angela sat up. She was naked. Hanzel stared at her voluptuous breasts. The room was chilly in the early morning. Hanzel smiled as he watched her nipples become hard. 'Your tits are beautiful,' he said admiringly.

'Thank you. That is very nice of you to say so.'

Hanzel smiled as he looked into her blue eyes. 'How old are *you*, Angela?'

Angela looked at Hanzel for a moment before answering. 'I'm sixteen,' she said.

Suddenly a loud commotion outside alerted the young lovers there was something untoward happening at the stables. They could hear men shouting.

Angela opened the shutter of her window, which faced into the yard, opposite which stood the stables where overnight guests could keep their horses or mules. Hanzel immediately recognized the voices of two of the men. One was his father and the other was the man from whom he had stolen the mule and cart. In the strange circumstances of life, the two men had met each other on the road to Amsterdam and revealed to each other the purpose of going there; to find Hanzel Sventska.

Young Hanzel stared at Angela and revealed whose voices those were, yelling at the groom and stable hands.

'Where is the boy who rode this cart and that mule to this inn?!' shouted their owner.

'Ya! Vere iz my zun?!' shouted Kabel.

'They musn't find me,' said Hanzel. 'If they do, that'll be the end of me. They'll tear me to pieces.' His frightened eyes told Angela everything.

'Don't worry,' she said reassuringly. 'I won't let them know you're here.'

'What should I do?'

'Stay here. Don't make any noises. I'm going to get dressed and go down there. My dad will be there right away, I'm sure. If your father or that man ask about you, I'll tell them that you went away with those three rogues my father booted out last night.

'Where is the boy who brought this cart here!' shouted the fat man again.

A moment later, Hazel could hear the booming voice of the innkeeper, 'What is all this commotion?! What is the big idea making so much noise in my courtyard?' he shouted at the two men standing beside the stolen cart and mule.

Hanzel carefully peered from behind a shutter. It was overcast and gloomy outside. A thin haze of icy moisture hung in the air. He could see his father and the man from whom he had stolen the cart standing shivering on the bepuddled ground of the inn's courtyard. Mister de Fries was striding towards them, followed by Angela.

'That cart belongs to me,' said the man, pointing at the conveyance in question.

'Vere iz de boy who drove diz cart?' asked Hanzel's father. 'He iz my zun. He escape frum my house an shtole money frum hiz mudder.'

Mister de Fries looked at Angela with a questioning look. 'Do you have any idea which one of our guests drove this cart?'

Angela shrugged her shoulders. 'A boy came into the inn last night. He drank some ale and had a meal. Then he left with those hooligans you kicked out last night.'

'What did that boy look like?' asked the cart's owner.

'He had white hair and large blue eyes. I'd say he was about thirteen or fourteen years old,' replied Angela without a hint of hesitation. She was an expert liar, having learned her art well, looking after customers. Especially the shady ones. Of those types, many of them drifted into *De Hijlige Frauw*. Johannes Poort and his two cronies were no exception.

'Dat zounds like my zun,' replied Kabel. 'Except my zun is twelve.'

'That does describe the boy who stole this cart,' added the man. 'He didn't look much older than twelve or thirteen. The little thief did have white hair. I couldn't tell what colour his eyes were.'

'How do you know this is your cart?' asked Angela. 'There are so many carts in Amsterdam. So many of them look the same.'

'If you look under the driver's seat, you will find an inscription bearing the name, Cornelius Wimpel, that being my name.'

Mister de Fries took a look under the seat. 'Ya, it is dere. That is the name under the seat.'

'You zed de boy went wid zum hooligans?' asked Kabel, eyeing Angela suspiciously.

'Three ner' do wells who come here to drink, once in a while,' answered Angela. 'They mostly linger around the gate, watching for likely victims.'

'De gate, eh?'

Angela nodded her head.

'What did dey look like? Dose hooligans?' asked Kabel, regarding Angela with an icy stare.

Angela looked at her father.

'Those men are a little gang. Johannes Poort is their leader. You will easily recognize him by his fat earlobes. He has a gold ring in one of them. He is short and round.' Mister de Fries regarded his daughter for a moment before continuing. 'The other two are skinny, weasily looking characters. One wears a battered tricorn. The other has a nasty scar on his cheek. You'll recognize them. They're always together.'

Kabel looked at the cart owner. 'Vell den. Ve shuld go to dat gate ant zee if de boy is dere.'

The man shook his head. 'I have other things to do. I have my cart back. That is all that matters to me.'

Kabel scowled at the man and then looked back at Angela. He rubbed his chin and regarded her for another moment before walking off in the direction of the gate, followed by his cronies. The other man took his cart and mule and rode off in the opposite direction.

Mister de Fries looked at his daughter and then up at her bedroom window. He shrugged his shoulders. 'You are sure you saw the boy go off with those ruffians?'

Angela nodded. 'I'm sure they headed off towards the gate.'

'Alright then. We might as well get ourselves to work. Our guests will be up and wanting breakfast.' Mister de Fries gave one more glance in the direction Kabel had gone. Then stepped through the door into the kitchen.

Angela smiled and looked up at her window. Then she followed her father into the kitchen and they set to work preparing breakfast.

Meanwhile, up in Angela's room, Hanzel heaved a sigh of relief. His father had not found him and he did not get into trouble for stealing the cart and mule. He felt blessed and grateful. If his father had found him, he would have been beaten black and blue. Kabel would have broken bones. Hanzel feared for his mother. When Kabel returned home without him, she would bear the brunt of his anger and frustration. Hanzel wrung his hands as he thought of her at the hands of his cruel father. He shivered involuntarily, but did not regret leaving home. He wondered why his mother had not left that terrible place. However, he realized; she had nowhere else to go.

Hanzel looked about the room and wondered if he should stay there or leave. As he thusly sat on the edge of the bed, thinking about his situation he remembered his money. He jumped off the bed and began searching around the room. He looked in the armoire. There were only clothes. Behind the armour there was a wall, nothing more. Hanzel looked behind and under the little table, but there was no bag of money either. Then he looked under the bed. There was nothing there, except the chamber pot. Behind the chair there was dust. In the chest, there were only some more clothes. All there was in the room, as far as Hanzel could make out was; the armour, the bed, the chair, the chest, and the two little tables. He scratched his head. "Where is my money?" was his only thought. 'She's stolen my money,' he muttered out loud as he jumped to action. He quickly gathered up his clothes and put them on. Then he tried the door. It was locked. Hanzel pulled and pushed on the door handle. The door did not budge. Hanzel was not only deprived of his money, but now he was a prisoner, as well. He sat down on the rough hewn chair and stared at the bed, where Angela had picked his cherry.

As he thusly sat there, thinking about his situation, Hanzel began to regard the window. Perhaps he could escape through the window? Hanzel rushed to the aperture and pushed the shutters open. A dreary light filtered into the room. As Hanzel peered outside he noted that the sky was a dull grey. A thin haze of cold, salty water hung in the air, chilling one to the bone. Hanzel shivered as the cold, heavy air crawled into every pore of his body. Looking down, Hanzel noted that below the window stood a cart loaded with straw for the stables. It had just arrived in the courtyard of the inn. The driver had gone inside to find Mister de Fries and to get warm. Hanzel couldn't believe his good luck.

Giving the room a final look, he climbed out of the window and jumped down into the pile of straw. Fortunately, the straw pile was thick enough and absorbed his fall. Hanzel lay back in the soft pile for a few moments, collecting his wits and figuring out what to do next. When he heard Mister de Fries's voice coming from inside, he immediately knew what to do. He climbed out of the cart and quickly made his way into the stable across the courtyard. He opened one of the big doors a crack and slipped inside, closing the door behind him. Two horses whinnied and a mule snorted as he entered the wooden building. The air was thick with the smell of animals. The place was in dire need of cleaning and new straw. Hanzel thanked God it was today, otherwise he wouldn't have had the straw to land in.

Fortunately, the animals settled down and did not consider a twelve year old human, a threat. Hanzel smiled. He loved animals. As he stood there, thinking about petting a horse, he heard Mister de Fries's voice and the crunch of wagon wheels approaching the stable. He quickly looked about for a place to hide. Near the back of the large building was a ladder which led up to the loft. Hanzel ran for it and began to climb, just as the doors of the stable opened.

Hanzel climbed for all he was worth. He had just reached the loft when the straw cart's master pointed to the loft and remarked to Mister de Fries, 'There's someone climbing up in your loft.'

Mister de Fries looked to where the man was pointing and immediately yelled, 'YOU THERE! COME DOWN OFF THAT LADDER!'

Hanzel's heart was pounding as he scrambled into the loft and crawled into the farthest, darkest corner.

Mister de Fries shouted again. 'COME OUT OF MY LOFT! OR I'LL COME UP THERE AND DRAG YOU OUT!'

Hanzel shivered with fear. Mister de Fries's booming voice reminded him of his father's voice. He huddled deeper into the corner and prayed he would not be found. He remained quiet as a mouse. He dared not breathe. Hanzel was scared to his very core and shivered with fright as heavy feet began climbing the ladder. A moment later, Hanzel could see Mister de Fries's head, and then his shoulders. Hanzel closed his eyes, innocently thinking that would help make him invisible.

'I KNOW YOU ARE UP HERE!' shouted the innkeeper. He peered into the darkness of the loft. He was not certain what he might confront in the velvety gloom. The loft of the stable was a sizable place. Light was virtually non existent. Shadows took its place.

Hanzel sneezed. He could not help it. Straw dust had tickled his nostrils.

'Ah, hah,' said Mister de Fries. 'There you are.' He paused for a moment, waiting for an answer. When none came, he continued. 'What are you?'

He waited.

Again, no answer.

'Who are you and what are you doing in my loft?'

Hanzel felt his heart racing in his chest. His mind was reeling. What if the innkeeper returned him to his father?

Suddenly, Mister de Fries disappeared. Hanzel could hear him climbing down the ladder. Hanzel held his breath, wondering what the man might be up to. A moment later he could hear Mister de Fries's voice, but he could not make out what the man was saying. He was obviously talking to someone else. Hanzel could hear an other voice. Hanzel remained quiet as a flea.

After what, to Hanzel, seemed like an eternity, he heard footsteps on the ladder. Suddenly Mister de Fries, followed by the straw cart driver, stomped into the loft. Hanzel's eyes bulged as he beheld the two burly shadows. As his eyes adjusted to the dark shapes moving towards him, he realized that the men were carrying clubs. In an other instant those clubs landed heavily on Hanzel, one after an other, indiscriminately smashing on his head, his shoulders, his torso, his arms, and his legs. Within a minute Hanzel was a black and blue mess.

When the men were done beating little Hanzel, they dragged him out of the loft and threw him down the ladder. Hanzel fell to the stable floor, breaking three fingers as he tried to mitigate the fall. He screamed with pain as he lay on the stable floor.

'I'll bet that's that rapscallion who stole that man's cart and mule. He fits the description,' said Mister de Fries as he climbed down the ladder. When he reached bottom, he stepped over to the crying boy, lying on the floor.

The straw cart driver followed the innkeeper down the ladder and joined the innkeeper, standing by Hanzel, who lay groaning on the hard, clay floor of the stable. He stared up at the two men.

'Your daughter has stolen my money,' blubbered Hanzel.

'And you stole someone's cart and mule,' replied Mister de Fries.

'How do you know it was me?'

'You fit the description.'

'What are you going to do with me?'

'Your father was here, looking for you. I'm sure I can persuade him to offer me a reward for returning you. He seemed quite anxious to know where you were.' The innkeeper smiled. 'My daughter told him you had gone with some miscreants to the gate. I'm sure he'll end up back here, when he can't find you there. He'll retrace his steps to where you were seen last.' He reached down and roughly handled Hanzel to his feet. Then the two men dragged Hanzel across the courtyard to a little shed, next to the cess pit. Mister de Fries took a key from off a protruding brick, next to the lintel, unlocked the heavy padlock and yanked the chain out of its rings. The other man had to push hard on the door to open it. Its hinges groaned and squeaked as the heavy door moved. Then, when the door was open far enough, the innkeeper threw Hanzel into a little, foul smelling room with no windows, except for two vents near the ceiling. The door was groaned shut with a bang. Hanzel lunged at the door as the padlock was being locked. He could hear the key turning in its aperture and the chains rattling against the door. A moment later Hanzel was left alone, in the dark, in a stinking little shed, with three broken fingers and bruises all over his body.

Groaning, he lay down on the cold, damp floor and wondered if he was dying.

Chapter 4

'Where is the money?!' demanded Mister de Fries as he stared at his daughter. They were standing in the kitchen of the inn. Missus de Fries and the cook were busy preparing herring fillets and onions. The place smelled of fish, herbs, spices and fresh bread.

Angela calmly regarded her father. 'What money?'

'The money the boy said you took from him.' Mister de Fries crossed his arms over his chest and stared at his daughter.

'What boy?' Angela looked at her mother peeling an onion. Her mother did not bother to look up. Quarrels between Angela and her father were frequent. She was used to it. And so was the cook.

'What boy? What are you talking about?' Angela did her best to look innocent.

'I found a blond haired boy, like the one you and those men described, in the loft of the stable. The straw cart driver and I beat him black and blue and I threw him into the storage shed beside the cess pit.'

Hearing what had been done to Hanzel broke through Angela's innocence and brought a shocked expression to her face. She couldn't help it. Even though she felt no qualms about taking his money; having given him a pleasant night, so she reckoned, she was not cold hearted towards the little fellow. After all, he was only twelve years old.

'I knew it. I knew you know something about this boy.' Mister de Fries stared at Angela.

'What have you done? He's just a scared little kid.'

'What have you done with his money?'

'What money?'

'The money the boy claims you took.'

'He's lying. There is no money. Where would a little kid like that get any money?'

'He paid you for food and drink, didn't he?' Mister de Fries stared down at his defiant daughter.

Angela paused and thought for a moment. 'That was all the money he had. He had just enough to pay the bill. Then he left with those sleaze bags.'

Mister de Fries looked at his wife and then back at his daughter. He knew, if he wanted to get the truth out of Angela, he would have to beat her. She was such a stubborn wench, he was thinking, as he turned around and began his work; preparing pannekoeken. He did not like beating his daughter. However, he felt it was his duty as a father, to give her a good beating if she did not tell him the truth or was hiding something from him. He knew she was hiding something, from her reaction when he told her what he had done to the boy. No matter how innocent Angela could act, he saw through it every time. He knew her well.

Sometime later, when there was a moment to take a break from the work, Mister and Missus de Fries went upstairs to their room. The morning's breakfast was over and dinner preparations did not start until later. Hence, Angela was able to take a look at the boy in the storage shed beside the cess pit. She prayed the boy was not Hanzel. As she approached the place, the reek of the cess pit was strong in the air. Angela screwed up her nose as she reached for the key to the padlock, which her father always placed on a protruding brick beside the door. The shed was mostly used for isolating an animal in, if necessary. Or a human being who conducted him or herself in an uncivilized fashion on the premises.

The sounds outside the door woke Hanzel from his stupor. Although he was not able to raise himself, he looked up feebly and watched as the door moved slightly in its frame. The sound of the key in the lock made the hairs on his neck quiver. He was afraid Mister de Fries was on the other side of the door. He had no idea it would be Angela.

'Oh my good God!' exclaimed Angela when she beheld Hanzel lying on the floor of the odiferous place. 'What did they do to you?!'

'They beat me with clubs,' croaked Hanzel.

'My father is a brute,' said Angela softly as she kneeled down beside the severely damaged boy. 'Are any bones broken?'

'Three fingers.' Hanzel grimaced as he held up his damaged hand.

'You poor thing,' said Angela, gently cradling his head in her lap.

Hanzel stared into her eyes as he narrowed his. 'Where is my money?'

Angela grinned and stared down at the blond haired boy. 'You don't give up, do you?'

Hanzel nodded. 'Never,' he replied slowly.

'Well, don't worry. Your money is safe with me.'

'I want it back. I need it to live.' Hanzel moaned as he adjusted his body for a more comfortable position. Just as he did so, a loud voice could be heard in the courtyard. Neither Angela or Hanzel could make out what was being said. However, Hanzel had a pretty good idea whose voice it was.

'My father is here,' mumbled Hanzel, his eyes narrowed with pain.

'Your father?'

'He musn't find me. He'll beat me even worse. He might even kill me because the money you have, I stole from him.' Hanzel straightened himself up, grimacing all the while as his broken fingers throbbed with pain and the bruises were beginning to really work their diabolical effects on his body. 'If he finds out that you have his money. You have no idea what he is capable of.'

Angela sprang into action. 'We have to get out of here.'

'How?' asked Hanzel, not seeing a way out but through the door.

Angela opened the door a few inches. She peeked around the door and looked into the courtyard. 'There are four men standing there. They're looking at the main entrance and discussing whether to go in.' Angela looked back at Hanzel who had managed to right himself. He was standing and leaning against the back wall of the room; deep in the shadows of that foul place. Angela returned her gaze to the courtyard. 'Oh, wait. They're going in. All four of them. There they go.' Angela looked back at Hanzel. 'Now is our chance to get you out of here.'

'Where can you hide me?' groaned Hanzel as Angela put his left arm over her shoulder and helped him to the door.

'First I need to hide you in a different place.' She pushed the groaning door open and peered into the courtyard. Seeing that the coast was clear, Angela quickly walked and carried Hanzel out of that smelly shed and closed the door behind them. Then she closed the padlock and replaced the key on the protruding brick. She hurried across the courtyard. Hanzel groaned from time to time, the pain being very intense. As they walked past the main entrance, they could hear voices coming through the door. Angela rushed around the main building to the back door and up the stairs. In her room, she gently deposited Hanzel on her bed and heaved a sigh of relief.

Hanzel sunk back in the soft blankets and stared up at Angela. 'Are you sure he won't find me?'

'Don't worry,' replied Angela reassuringly. She smiled and gently stroked his blond hair. Hanzel smiled weakly. Angela suddenly started. 'Oh dear. I've got to be going. I'm due back in the kitchen. Just stay here and be quiet. Rest. Get well. I will be back tonight.' Angela blew him a kiss and then ran out of the room and closed the door behind her; making sure to lock it. Hanzel did not care.

As he lay there, partially conscious and in great pain, Hanzel felt grateful for Angela having rescued him from being found by his father. He was happy she had let him do things with her in the night. She made him feel grown up and manly. That part he liked about Angela. He wondered why her father felt called upon to brutalize him, just as his father felt it his duty. It made no sense to Hanzel, when he heard the preachers say that God is a loving, merciful Father and yet, on the other hand, rods were often broken to prevent spoiled children. Both Mister de Fries and Hanzel's father followed that admonishment, to not spare the rod, much to the detriment of their children's skins and spirits. Hanzel could not fathom why God did not intervene and let the cruelty continue. Did Hanzel deserve to be so badly treated? Hanzel tried all of his life to be a good boy; honest and helpful to his mother and siblings. However, he was so badly treated by his father and now by Angela's. As he thought of these matters, Hanzel's eyelids began to droop. Soon his eyes were shut and he fell into a deep and troubled dream exploring ideas regarding Angela's hiding place. 'Where is the money?' was the question foremost on his lips as Hanzel explored every possibility. Under the floor. In an other room. Behind a secret door in the huge chestnut tree in the courtyard. Deep in a dragon's liar...

While Hanzel dreamed what he did, Mister de Fries was leading Hanzel's father to the shed. 'So, did you talk to Johannes Poort?'

'Ya,' replied Kabel. 'E told me e never saw de boy leave dis place. E tinks your daughter knows sometin about im.'

"Angela?" Mister de Fries regarded Kabel with a sideways glance. 'My daughter served the kid, that's all.'

'Poort told me e saw my zun in your inn. Described him to a T. Blond, blue eyed, tall, skinny....'

Mister de Fries reached for the key to the padlock. 'The boy I threw in here certainly fits the description.'

'Vhen I get my hands on im, ee'l wish e never lived,' grunted Kabel.

'The things children expect to get away with.' The innkeeper unlocked the padlock and pulled the chain through the rings. Then he pushed the door open and stood aside, not bothering to look into the shed because he naturally expected that Hanzel was there; lying in the shadows.

Kabel stepped into the shed. He looked into the deepest corner. Hanzel was not there. 'Vhere iz dat boy?'

'What do you mean?'

'De boy iz not ere.' Kabel looked back at the innkeeper.

'The boy is not there?' Mister de Fries stepped into the shed and stood beside Kabel. His eyes bulged when he also did not see Hanzel. 'He's gone.'

Both men immediately stepped out of the shed and faced each other.

'That is impossible!' exclaimed the innkeeper. 'The lock was locked. You saw me unlock it.'

Kabel rubbed his chin. 'Dat boy iz frum de Devil. But don yu vurry. I veel find im.' He looked deep into the innkeeper's eyes. His eyes were blazing with a deep, self righteous, Old Testament, rod bearing, psychopathic fire which threw the innkeeper off. Albeit, he did agree it was alright to beat his children, once in a while, but not with the vehemence of Hanzel's father. 'You zed you beat de boy wid clubs?'

The innkeeper nodded. 'Me and my straw man.'

Kabel grunted. 'Dat boy must be in a lot of pain. Seein az how you beat im, en all.' He looked suspiciously around the courtyard. 'Maybe ee iz ere somevhere.'

Mister de Fries regarded Hanzel's father for a moment before replying. 'If you expect me to allow you to turn my place upside down for some boy who has run away from home, I say forget that. I have guests, family, and my staff who live here. Somehow the boy got away. I have no idea how he did it.'

The innkeeper paused and thought for a moment as he regarded the rugged fisherman with the seething rage boiling out of his eyes. 'The kid has probably run into Amsterdam. Maybe he got on board a ship. They're always looking for boys.'

'Ya,' nodded Kabel, frowning. 'Ya zhure dey need boys. Dey don't vant to take girls. Girls bring bad luck on board.' Kabel shrugged his shoulders, pretending he was not suspicious. 'Vhell, I suppoze dat iz vhat happened. Dat boy iz frum de Devil. Zo, if he iz gone on a ship, he vhill get vhat he deserves.'

The innkeeper nodded. 'Yes, I suppose so.'

'Zank you for trying.' Kabel extended his hand, but the innkeeper was reluctant to take it, expecting the man to give him an extra strong grip; intending to crush his fingers. However, he did not wish to be uncivil and took the fisherman's hand. The innkeeper had been correct in his intuition. Kabel grabbed his hand and exerted bone crushing pressure with his powerful right hand. Having been a fisherman since the age of thirteen, he had developed hard, strong hands. The innkeeper was not quite so strong, spending his time cooking and tending to guests. He could not help but grimace as the pain began to register in his brain. 'Vhere is the boy? I know you haf im ere zum vhere. I don't believe for a minute dat ee ran avay, zince you beat im black an blue.'

'Well, maybe it wasn't so black and blue. We only beat him a little bit.'

'Oh, zo now you zay you beat im only a liddle bit?' Kabel stared at the innkeeper.

'Who knows where he is. He was able to walk so he probably ran off to sea.'

Kabel nodded. 'He probably ran off to sea.' He gave the innkeeper a final look and then stormed off. The other men followed him into the street. A moment later they disappeared around the corner of the buildings. Mister de Fries shrugged his shoulders as he rubbed his throbbing hand. He stepped back into the kitchen and observed Angela for a moment, as she filleted herrings. Angela pretended not to notice and continued her work. Her mother was stirring a heavy soup in a large cauldron over the fire. The cook was preparing croquettes. The innkeeper shook his head and returned to slicing a fat sausage he was preparing for a cold cuts tray, before being interrupted by Kabel.

After some minutes had gone by, Mister de Fries looked up from his work and regarded his daughter. 'Do you know anything about that boy disappearing?'

'What boy?'

'The one I threw into the shed.'

Angela shrugged her shoulders. 'Disappearing?'

'Yes, he's gone. The key was where it was supposed to be, but the boy is gone.'

'Who knows, other than you, where the key is?' Angela regarded her father.

Her father thought for a moment and nodded. 'That's right. Only I know where the key is hidden.' He frowned. 'Am I not?'

'Of course you are, Father,' replied Angela, innocently. She smiled as she returned to her work.

'It's most unusual. Maybe there was someone else with him who saw me take the key from its hiding place.' Mister de Fries looked over his shoulder at his daughter.

Angela did not look up. She simply agreed with him as she began to place the herring fillets on a large flat baking tray. She was making roasted herrings; one of the inn's specialties.

Mister de Fries nodded as he regarded his daughter for another moment. He turned slowly, deep in thought about the missing boy, as he returned to his work. They would be busy that evening. The local merchants were getting together for a meeting. He had a lot of sausage to slice, ever so finely. A goodly sum of money was at stake. Sausage like that did not come cheap. And the merchants were very fussy how their sausage was sliced. Slicing sausage was a refined art. People took their sausage seriously. Mister de Fries was no exception. He took pride in how well his inn was regarded. Especially his kitchen.

Meanwhile in Angela's room, Hanzel lay comatose in her bed. He had been badly pummeled and would need days of rest to recuperate. During moments of wakeful delirium, he prayed that Angela would take care of him and that his father would not find him there. When he dreamed, it was of him being ill treated and fighting back. His dreams were of revenge and he in the role of victor. When he dreamed, he did not feel his wounds.

When the workday was over for Angela, she hung her white apron on its hook by the back door to the kitchen. When her father was not looking, she grabbed some food for Hanzel and placed it in a linen cloth, folding the cloth into a small package. Then she stepped outside and walked around the corner of the building. There she stood in the courtyard for a moment; facing the stables. The task had been performed well; the burghers were obviously pleased. They were still in their meeting; but Angela's part in the affair was over and her father had told her she was free to get some air. He and the two regular serving wenches; Kate and Margaret, were able to handle serving post banquet requirements. The meeting would likely go into the early hours of the morning. Since Angela was on breakfast duty, she had to get to bed early. She did not mind. She was anxious about Hanzel and quickly made her way upstairs; to her room, where Hanzel was delirious. The pain had risen up in his body, now showing ugly bruises.

Angela leaned over the young boy and looked down on him with a gentle smile and much sadness in her eyes. 'Poor Hanzel, what have they done to you?' she mumbled.

Chapter 5

Hanzel's mother was worried about him. She feared for his life. The boy had never been far away from home before. His father saw to that. She had watched on more than one occasion as Kabel beat little Hanzel for trying to run away. Now that the boy was twelve, she knew him to be much more determined and capable of looking after himself. Although he was gentle by nature, Hanzel could put up a good fight if challenged. Elizabeth understood why Hanzel had run. She would too, if only she was not held to home by the bonds a woman feels for her children. Hanzel was not her only child. Even though Hanzel was special, she could let go quite easily. Children died at all ages in the 17th Century. If she never saw Hanzel again, she could learn to cope with it. If Kabel found him, he would be good as dead, anyway. She shivered involuntarily as she visualized what Kabel could do to the boy. Kabel, when provoked, became a raging animal. He had done it to her and the other children. But with Hanzel he became Lucifer himself.

Elizabeth wondered where Hanzel had gone to. She reasoned it would likely be Amsterdam. However, knowing Hanzel, he might have chosen a different place; to avoid the obvious. Yet, deep in her heart she knew Hanzel was in the big city. Kabel had gone to Amsterdam, because he would not consider another possibility. "Everyone gravitates to Amsterdam," is what he had said. In his way of thinking it was the natural order of things there in the Netherlands. Amsterdam was the closest big port. Elizabeth thought about all the ships anchored there; from many places in the world. Hanzel could easily disappear on a ship and end up, who knows where? The Indies for example. Or Brazil.

As she sat there thinking about Hanzel, little Piet started crying. He was only three. He was the youngest of what was by now a family of ten. Pietje, as his mother affectionately called him, was born not quite right in the head. The fact that Kabel let him live was a miracle, as far as Elizabeth was concerned.

The child would never be normal and certainly would never be able to help on the boat. Elizabeth shook her head sadly as she got up from the rough wooden chair by the little window which looked out on the garden where she grew vegetables. She sighed as she walked wearily into the bedroom she shared with Kabel. Pietje was lying in a rough hewn box sitting on the floor by the big bed. Hanzel had been gone for three days.

On the morning of the fourth day, Kabel returned home. He had not found Hanzel. The boy had disappeared, he reckoned. 'Probably got hired on a boat. Not any fishing' boat. I asked around. Nobody's seen im.' Kabel regarded his wife for a moment. 'Jus as well. Gute riddance. That boy wud neber have amounted to anyting.' Kabel gestured in the direction of the sea. 'At least his brudders know how to handle a boat und nets. I could neber see Hanzel going dere. It wasn't in im.'

Elizabeth hung her head and looked sadly at the floor. Hanzel had been her favorite. He was the most beautiful of her children. Hanzel resembled her side of the family. Big blue eyes and very blond hair. Kabel's side were dark eyed; like Spaniards. Kabel was dark haired. Hanzel and Elizabeth were blond. The other children varied in shades of brown; most of them taking after their father. 'Are you sure nobody had seen him?'

'A man, frum whom he stole a cart und mule,' Kabel reflected on that for a moment. 'Resourceful liddle bugger, dat Hanzel. I've got to give im dat.' Kabel stared at Elizabeth and gave her a thin lipped smile. 'Hanzel is a resourceful liddle chap, alright.'

'You said he'd never amount to anything,' replied Elizabeth through her tears.

'He knows how to steal,' replied Kabel happily. 'He stole a man's cart und mule. He vent to Amsterdam und ended up in de *Heijlige Vrouw*, an inn near the gate. I haf a suspicion about dat place, but dey claim de boy disappeared from deir clutches. De innkeeper claims he had captured a boy dat fit Hanzel's description.'

'Lots of boys fit his description in this country,' replied Elizabeth. 'Blue eyes and blond hair. It is very common around here.'

Kabel nodded. 'Ya, I suppose so....'

Elizabeth regarded Kabel for a moment and then returned her gaze to the floor.

'I pray that he's alright.'

'He's lucky I didn't find him. I would haf given him a drubbing he would never forget.' Kabel punched the palm of his left hand. 'No son of mine runs away frum home. Especially not at twelve years of age.'

'You never liked him.' Elizabeth regarded Kabel.

'Dat has nuting to do wid it. He was going to vurk on de boat next year und finally earn his keep, even dough he'd be useless at it.'

'Thank God he saved himself from that slavery,' replied Elizabeth sarcastically.

'Oh, so you tink it's slavery, when children earn der keep?' Kabel stood over Elizabeth and stared at her seated figure. 'Do you tink dey shud live for free?'

'We brought them into the world. It's not their fault that they're here.' Elizabeth looked up at her husband. 'I never wanted my children to have to work like slaves.'

'Dey get der room und board!' roared Kabel.

'And nothing else, except hard knocks from you.' Elizabeth regarded Kabel. She could see the fire in his eyes. 'You treat them like a slave driver. You think you can beat them and force them to work for you. Your sons don't like working for you. You are a tyrant! That's why Hanzel left. He couldn't stand to be around you anymore!' Elizabeth stared at Kabel for a moment before she hunkered down. She knew what was coming.

It came as it always did. Kabel smacked her on the side of her head with his hard open hand, knocking her off the chair and onto the floor. 'That's always the way it is with you. When you know I'm telling the truth, you resort to violence because you are a dimwitted brute,' whimpered Elizabeth as she began to stand up.

Kabel regarded her for a moment. He did not say anything but grunted something about her being a bitch. Then he punched her hard in the stomach, knocking her over the chair. Elizabeth fell backwards; hitting her head against the corner of the table. The corner of the table crashed into her temple and broke the bone, before entering her brain. Elizabeth slumped to the floor; blood and brains leaking out of the hole the table had made.

Kabel stared wide eyed at Elizabeth's corpse bleeding on the tile floor of the kitchen. He rushed to the body and kneeled down beside his dead wife.

Touching her neck, he felt for a pulse. Alas, her pulse was waning fast, as her body was shutting down. As he held her, she suddenly shuddered, before expiring in his lap. 'My God, what have I done?' whispered Kabel; staring down at his dead wife. 'What am I going to do now?' Kabel looked frantically around the room, wide eyed and staring. What to do was racing through his mind. He had killed his wife. He would be broken for that.

'I must make it look like an accident,' he muttered as he dropped Elizabeth to the floor and stood up. He ran to the door and looked outside. Regarding the location of the sun through the thick grey sky, he ascertained that he still had some time before his daughters would come home from the laundry. The other boys were out fishing and would not be home for a few more days. He figured the best way to make it all go away is to leave the body and chair as they were and for him to pretend he had not been there. He would leave and return the following morning; just as if he had been longer in searching for Hanzel.

Kabel quickly left the house, just as little Pietje began to howl. Kabel cringed and looked to see if anyone was looking in his direction. It was early afternoon. No one, as far as he knew, had taken notice of him as he came home on the back road. He left the same way. Kabel figured his daughters would simply call the undertaker. People died of accidents all the time in the 17th Century. Others died of executions. Kabel shivered involuntarily as he thought of himself being braided. He never saw the old couple sitting in their garden.

The back road led out of the village and forked into two directions; a trail into a forest and the road to Amsterdam. Kabel chose the trail and quickly disappeared into the woods. He was not really familiar with the trail, having avoided it all of his life. He did not like the forest. That is why he became a fisherman and not a forester. The deep forest was a scary place for Kabel. However, it was a good hiding place he figured. He could find a mossy spot and sleep there. Surely he would be alright in the forest, he reasoned. All of his worries about the woods were probably just silly myths. Surely there really were no dangerous wolves in this little forest. No snarling bears…

As the afternoon crept into evening, the sky darkened as heavy clouds rolled in. The light in the forest suddenly became nearly non existent and Kabel stumbled on the unfamiliar trail.

An owl hooted.

Kabel nearly jumped out of his boots. He looked fearfully about.

Suddenly a brilliant flash of lightning lit up the forest, followed by a massive crack of thunder. Instantly it began to rain. Kabel jumped under a huge oak and sheltered close to the trunk. Buckets and buckets of water poured down around him as the temperature began to drop.

Another flash of light lit up the scene, revealing Kabel huddling fearfully against the trunk of the mighty tree. The thunder clap which followed reverberated through the forest. Wind began to roar through the leaves and the temperature dropped even more. Kabel began to shiver. The cold was going straight through to his bones. His woolen coat was no comfort to him now.

Kabel crouched down and bunched himself up into a fetal position to conserve heat. Horrible thoughts of him being broken and braided on a wheel haunted his mind as the night brought on total darkness in the forest. The only light being provided by the lightning. However, that eventually went away. Alas, the rain did not. It continued to pour. Even the mighty oak was having difficulty keeping the rain off Kabel. Eventually he began to get wet, just as everything else around him. Even the bear; who lived nearby. As the night dragged on, Kabel could not stay awake any longer. He gradually drifted off to sleep, his head under an arm and his body pushed against the trunk. Kabel had a long and nerve wracking day. He was bone tired. He never heard the wolves.

The rain stopped around three in the morning. The gradually diminishing sound of rain pouring into the forest woke Kabel. The heavy clouds were beginning to break and slivers of moonlight began to reveal things to him Enough was revealed to enable him to pick his way back to the trail. He heaved a sigh of relief as he slowly walked along the wet path, shivering in the cold damp.

A branch creaked.

Kabel flinched. He could not help it. The dark, wet forest was even more scary than before. However, breaking and braiding was more scary than that. He had to have a rock solid alibi. He could not be pinned with the death of Elizabeth. Kabel thought hard about whether anyone had seen him come or go. He prayed as he stumbled along the path, that he would be alright.

An hour after leaving the oak, Kabel began to discern a flickering light up ahead. The light was obviously that of a fire. As Kabel came closer, he could see a campfire, around which were sitting several dark figures. Kabel stopped in his tracks and fearfully regarded the flickering fire and the dark figures sitting around it, warming themselves. He was cold, wet, and shivering. The fire was warm and inviting.

A woodpecker rata tatted in a tree nearby.

Kabel ducked behind a tree, thinking the bird had given him away.

Unfortunately it was not the bird which gave him away. It was a branch upon which he had stepped when he ducked behind the tree. The cracking wood alerted the dark figures by the fire. They turned around and looked in the direction of the sound.

'Somepin big there,' muttered one of the figures.

'Maybe it's a wolf?' whispered another voice.

'Maybe you should go haf a look, Leo,' said a third voice.

There was a long pause. Kabel held his breath. He was afraid the men might be highwaymen. Perhaps he had inadvertently stumbled into their hiding place. Kabel was suddenly afraid. His heart pounded in his chest.

'Probably a deer,' said a female voice. 'Nothing to worry about.'

'I don't think it was a deer,' replied another female voice. 'I think it was probably a branch dropping on another branch. After all, we did have quite a wind.'

'Ya,' replied a deep, throaty male voice. 'Blew my blanket into those bushes.'

As Kabel listened to the voices, he came to the conclusion there were four men and two women camping there. Since there were women, he relaxed because he didn't think highwaymen would have women with them. They brought bad luck at sea, so they must bring bad luck on land, as well; where larceny is involved. Piracy at sea, or highway robbery on land. It amounted to the same thing, as far as Kabel was concerned. In either case, women brought bad luck, so therefore these people could not be highwaymen.

Kabel stepped out from behind the tree and boldly walked the thirty paces to the campfire, glowing so invitingly. When he reached the little group, he cleared his throat. The six campers turned around and looked at the bedraggled fisherman standing with his cap in hand, begging to share their fire. The flickering light of the campfire played over Kabel's hardened features. The six campers could see that here stood a big, strong fisherman, who was not accustomed to being in the forest.

One of the campers, a tall, thin man with a nasty scar on his cheek and wearing a battered leather hat, gestured for Kabel to join them. 'Sit, my friend. You are welcome to share our fire.' His voice was authoritative. He was obviously the man in charge. 'My name is Henk de Meer.' He gestured around at his companions. 'These are my friends, Dirk, Leo, Mark, Maarta, and Sophie.'

The five companions nodded their greetings and watched as Kabel sat down on the big log, next to Henk. He rubbed his cold hands near the flame and thanked his host.

'That's alright, friend,' replied Henk. 'We're glad to be helpful to you, in this dark time of need.'

Kabel stared at Henk for a moment with a suspicious look. 'Vhat do you mean, in dis dark time of need?'

'Well, it is rather dark out, and you are in need because you are sopping wet,' replied Henk, wondering why his guest was suddenly suspicious. Henk kept his calm and regarded Kabel, who was leaning closer to the fire. Kabel grunted and rubbed his hands, not looking at the others as he stared into the flames. After an awkward pause, Henk continued. 'Judging from your apparel, I would say that you are a fisherman. What, pray tell, brings you into these parts? The closest fishing village is in that direction.' Henk pointed in the direction Kabel had come.

'I'm looking for my zun, Hanzel. He has run away from home,' grunted Kabel, not looking up. 'Maybe he's here, in de forest. I'll likely find him in de daylight.' Kabel looked up, through the canopy of leaves. The sky was still thick with cloud. What moonlight there was, had to battle its way through the dense haze.

A wolf howled, startling Kabel. He looked fearfully in the direction of the sound.

'Don't worry, my friend,' said Henk. 'They won't bother us here. As long as we have the fire going.' He looked around at his companions. 'And, we always have a fire going, don't we?'

The others agreed in unison and reassured Kabel, not to worry.

'Besides, we have pistols and swords,' said Mark, the man with the deep voice.

'Not to forget the dirks in my stockings,' laughed Sophie.

'We're not afraid of the big bad wolves,' added Maarta, laughing. 'They're no match for us.' To emphasize the matter she brandished a flintlock pistol and waved it in the direction of the howling.

Henk reached over and grabbed a dark, glass bottle. He handed it to Kabel. 'Here, friend. Drink this. It'll calm your nerves.'

Kabel looked over at the bottle and then at Henk's smiling face. Then he reached for the bottle and grunted, 'thanks.' Before drinking, he sniffed at the mouth of the bottle. The drink was rum. Kabel liked rum. He drank a hearty drought. The liquor warmed his stomach. When he handed the bottle back to Henk, his mood had softened. He thanked Henk, once again. The rum lightened his spirits. He suddenly felt more comfortable with his new companions. However, it did not make him any more talkative. Kabel was a man of few words and simple brain.

The rum bottle was passed around a few more times until it was empty. However, there was a second bottle of gin, which was also passed around. Kabel, being quite addicted to hard drink, greedily drank hearty droughts. He never noticed that his new companions hardly drank anything. Eventually Kabel decided he was too tired to continue and with his host's permission, curled up on the ground, next to the fire and promptly fell asleep. When the six companions were sure that he was fast asleep, they searched his pockets and relieved him of his purse, which really did not amount to anything; he having spent most of what he took with him to Amsterdam to search for Hanzel.

'A couple of pennies and a half daalder,' mumbled Henk, as he examined the contents of Kabel's purse.

'What do you expect? He's a fisherman. They don't have any money,' replied Maarta, sarcastically. 'You spent our good rum and gin on that lump. All for what?'

Henk looked at Kabel. 'Well, we can steal his clothes. Mark can use a new coat. That coat looks in good shape. He's about your size. Wouldn't you agree, Mark?'

Mark looked down at the sleeping fisherman. He nodded. 'Ya. I think he's about the same size.' Mark stepped over to Kabel and began to remove the coat. This woke up Kabel. He noticed Henk was holding his purse. He immediately realized what was happening. As he started to get up, he mumbled drunkenly, 'so you are robbers, after all...' When he had righted himself he lunged for the purse. Unfortunately for Kabel, Henk was also holding a loaded flintlock pistol. Before Kabel could reach the purse, Henk discharged the pistol and put a ball of lead directly into Kabel's chest. The ball pierced the flesh and smashed against a rib, and came out of his back. Kabel fell to the ground with a heavy thud.

'Quick, take his coat before it becomes blood stained,' said Henk as he began to help Mark with removal of the garment. A moment later, the others were busy helping, as they removed every stitch of Kabel's clothing; finding another small purse containing three golden ducats.

'I knew he was worth more than those measly pennies and that single daalder,' said Henk, happily. As he held the golden coins before the fire, making them sparkle and glint, 'These little babies will buy us a week of pleasure in Amsterdam, my friends.' He laughed.

His friends laughed with him. When they were done laughing and celebrating their good fortune, Leo asked what they should do with the body.

'Leave him to the wolves,' replied Henk, prodding the body with the toe of his right boot.

'It looks like it will be dawn, soon,' observed Sophie, looking at the sky. 'We should pack up our stuff and get out of here. Who knows, someone might come down that trail and find us with this dead body.'

Henk pointed to some shrubs. 'Stuff him behind those bushes. People coming down the trail won't see him there.'

Leo and Dirk began to drag the body to where Henk had indicated, while the others began to gather up their things. When all was ready, the four men pissed on the fire. A few minutes later they left the scene and headed in the direction of the road leading to Amsterdam.

Chapter 6

When Marika came home after her work in the laundry she found her mother dead on the floor of the kitchen and little Pietje sitting nearby, playing with a spoon. He was in bad need of a diaper change.

'Oh my God!' shrieked Marika, as she kneeled down beside her mother's corpse. Tears were streaming out of her eyes. 'Oh, mother, what happened to you?' When Marika noticed the hole in the side of her mother's head, she recoiled in horror. The sight of the horrible wound made her instantly nauseous. She immediately ran outside and threw up beside the door. Just as she did so, her neighbour, Johannes Sintjans walked by. He noticed Marika throwing up and walked over to her to see if she was alright, or if he should fetch the apothecary.

'My mother....it's my mother...she's dead.....' sobbed Marika; pointing to the door. 'She's in there.' Then she threw up the rest of what was left in her stomach.

Mister Sintjans ran into the house and found Elizabeth, dead on the floor. As he looked down at the neighbour he had known for many years, he noticed a large welt on the side of her face. He realized that she had been hit. The only person who could have done such a thing would be Kabel, he figured. However he was not there. As far as Mister Sintjans knew, Kabel was looking for his son in Amsterdam. He scratched his head and found it to be a strange circumstance. As he looked around he noted the chair over which Elizabeth had fallen. He also noted the blood on the corner of the table. As he looked over the scene it occurred to him, she had been knocked over the chair and hit her head. The evidence was quite obvious. The only one who could have done such a thing would have been her husband. There were no brigands in town, who would have broken into the house. Mister Sintjans resolved to involve the authorities. There was something very suspicious about Elizabeth's death.

Stepping outside the house, Mister Sintjans touched Marika gently on the shoulder. 'It looks like your mother was pushed over a chair and she hit her head on the table.'

'Who would have done that? My father is in Amsterdam.' Marika looked at Mister Sintjans. 'Are there brigands in town?'

Mister Sintjans shook his head. 'I don't think so. I think the authorities should be notified.'

Marika stared at Mister Sintjans. 'Shouldn't we wait until my father comes home?'

'We should at least notify the magistrate,' said Mister Sintjans.

Marika nodded slowly and burst into tears, just as Pietje began to howl inside.

Meanwhile, in Amsterdam, at the *Hijlige Vrouw*, Hanzel was still lying in Angela's bed, unbeknownst to Mister de Fries. Hanzel made certain to make no noise. Fortunately, Angela did not mind emptying the chamber pot. Thanks to it, Hanzel did not have to venture out of the room and could just lay there and recuperate. Angela had reset the bones of his broken fingers and bound them to splints she had fashioned from flat slivers of firewood. When she reset the fingers, she had made certain nobody was around. Her mother and father were in the kitchen and she was on a break. She placed a rolled up tube of cotton cloth between his teeth. Needless to say, Hanzel grimaced with intense pain as his teeth bit deep into the cotton roll. The pain was so intense, that Hanzel passed out and Angela went back to work in the kitchen. No one was any the wiser that there was someone staying in her room, besides herself.

The six brigands, who stole Kabel's purse, arrived in Amsterdam. They were feeling good, having had a pleasant walk through the forest and having met people they knew, on the road to the incredible city. They smiled at the guards as they passed through the city gate. Noticing, *De Hijlige Vrouw*, they decided to stop in and have themselves a good meal. 'Now that we have some money, it's high time we ate and drank at a decent place.' Henk pointed at the inn. 'This here inn has a good kitchen. I've eaten here before.'

Henk's companions heartily agreed that a good meal and drink was in order.

'It's a good thing that fisherman happened along,' remarked Sophie, happily.

Henk stared at her. 'Shh,' he said. 'Don't be saying things.' Henk looked about to see if anyone might have overheard her.

Sophie looked down. 'Sorry, boss.'

Henk nodded. 'Alright, let's go in.'

The six brigands entered the inn and were soon served by Angela.

In the forest they had just left, the fisherman, whom they thought they had killed, opened his eyes. He was staring at an ant, which had crawled onto his nose, which was firmly implanted in a pile of shriveled leaves behind a prolific shrub, not far from the trail. He groaned as he felt the pain in his chest. The ball had broken a rib, but had not damaged any vital organs; passing neatly out of his back. It was a miracle he lived.

As Kabel lay there ascertaining his circumstances, a raven croaked nearby. Kabel looked up out of the corner of his eye in the direction of the sound. The raven croaked once more. Kabel could not see the croaking bird from his position. As he slowly adjusted his body, he groaned. The pain in his chest was intense. He felt weak, having lost a lot of blood, as well. As he attempted to right himself, he nearly passed out. Kabel felt woozy. The trees moved in front of his eyes. Suddenly he threw up, spraying the bushes and trees with what was left of the contents of his stomach. Then he fell backwards, hitting his head on a log. The bump knocked him out.

And so they found him; three people taking a shortcut to Amsterdam.

'What is this then?' asked the tall, skinny man. He pointed to a pair of feet sticking out from behind a bush.

'Those look like feet,' replied the short, fat woman.

'Human feet!' shouted the boy, as he quickly walked to where Kabel lay. 'There's a man lying here! He looks like he's dead!'

The short, fat woman and the tall, thin man quickly joined the boy and peered down at the naked man, lying on his back behind the shrubs.

'Looks like someone got to him. Shot him, robbed him, and took all of his clothes.' The tall man prodded Kabel with the toe of his boot.

Kabel groaned.

'He's still alive!' shouted the boy. He looked at the tall man. 'He's alive, father!'

'So he is,' replied the tall man.

'What should we do with him?' asked the woman.

'Water,' croaked Kabel, as he attempted to lift his head.

The three travelers regarded Kabel for a moment; surprised to see that the naked man was still alive.

The tall man took a flask of water from his bag and knelt down beside Kabel. He gently lifted the fisherman's head and let him take a sip from the flask. Kabel nearly choked as he swallowed the water; his throat being very dry. 'Easy, there,' said the tall man, soothingly. 'You must take very small amounts.' The man looked at the wound in Kabel's chest. 'You've been shot. We've got to get help.'

Kabel groaned and passed out.

'Is he dead, father?' asked the boy.

'I don't know. Whatever the case. We must alert the authorities.' The tall man stood up and regarded his wife and son. 'One of us should stay here and guard the body, so that the wolves don't get him.'

The woman looked down at Kabel. 'What's it got to do with us? Just leave him. The wolves will take care of him.'

The tall man knelt down and felt Kabel's chest. 'His heart is still beating. And, he's still breathing. The man is alive, Alice.'

'We're late as it is. It'll be dark by the time we get to the city.' Alice was impatient. They were on their way to visit relatives, whom she had not seen in three years.

'Alice, remember the story of the good Samaritan? About helping someone who has fallen and is hurt.' He pointed to Kabel. 'This man has been shot and his clothes were stolen; even his cod piece.' He looked at the fallen fisherman. 'He's still alive, Alice. We can't just leave him.'

'Ya, mother. We can't just leave him. He's still breathing. If the wolves get him, he would be eaten alive.' The boy looked deploringly at his mother.

The woman stamped her feet impatiently and stared off in the direction of Amsterdam. She turned back to face the man and the boy standing beside the naked man. She nodded. 'Alright, William. Kareltje and I will alert the authorities in Amsterdam. Then what?'

'You come back here with help.' The tall man stood up. 'Don't worry, I'll make a fire, when it gets dark. So, just hurry and get going. The sooner you do, the sooner help comes.'

'Well, alright, then. I suppose we would want someone to do that, if it was us, wouldn't we?' Alice stared down at Kabel. 'Yes, I suppose we can't let a live man be eaten by wolves. That would be inhuman and unChristian.'

'Exactly, Alice.' William smiled at his wife. 'Alright, then. You had better get going. The sooner you go and fetch help, the sooner we'll be together again.'

Alice hugged her husband briefly. 'I have a bad feeling about this, William.'

'Do not worry, Alice. You'll be fine. Now hurry. It's best you get to Amsterdam before dark.'

Alice nodded and then mother and son hurried off in the direction of the great port city, leaving William guarding Kabel.

Mother and son reached Amsterdam around seven o'clock. The sky was overcast. The air was cool and filled with moisture. Kareltje shivered in his sparse coat. Winter would not be long in coming. When they reached the city gate, Alice approached one of the guards. 'Can you tell us where we can find help.'

The guard regarded the short, fat woman for a moment. 'What kind of help?'

Alice pointed in the direction she had come. 'In the forest, back there, is a naked man who has been shot.'

The guard looked at his companion, who shrugged his shoulders, before returning his gaze at a voluptuous young woman walking by with a small herd of goats. 'If he's been shot, he's probably dead already,' said the guard. 'Not much we can do.'

'Leave him for the wolves,' grunted the other guard. He regarded Alice and Kareltje for a brief moment before returning his gaze at the young woman, whacking a surly goat on the rump with her cane. The goat bleated.

Alice looked at her son, who shrugged his shoulders. 'I don't know, ma.'

Alice looked up at the guard. 'What about the police?'

'The police?' asked the guard.

'Yes, the police,' repeated Alice.

'Good luck,' chuckled the guard. He looked over at his companion, who also chuckled. He pointed to the street leading from the gate. 'Down there. You'll find them in a building down there. You can't miss it. Says, "POLICE" on it.'

'Thanks,' replied Alice. Then she took Kareltje's hand and walked off to the police headquarters, where she reported the situation concerning Kabel.

'That's not our jurisdiction,' replied the sergeant. 'The man is lying in the forest. We don't cover the forest. We just patrol Amsterdam, that's all.'

'Who patrols the forest?' asked Alice dumbfounded.

'The forest warden. You'll find him in his hut, which sits beside the road leading past the forest, unless, of course, he's out patrolling. They've had some problems with wolves out there.'

'Wolves?' asked Alice, nervously. 'My husband is with the man.'

The sergeant pointed in the direction Alice had come. 'Go talk with the forest warden. He can probably help you.'

Alice nodded slowly. 'Alright,' she sighed.

On their way back to the gate, Alice decided to stop at the *Hijlige Vrouw* for a meal. She and Kareltje were tired. A long trek back to the forest, hoping to find the forest warden, was not something Alice was looking forward to. She wanted to visit her relatives, not engage in good Samaritanism. However, her sense of humanity compelled her to do what was right. The man could not be left lying in the forest with no one to help him. She wouldn't want to be treated that way, either. The Golden Rule did matter to Alice.

When they stepped into the dining hall of the inn, Angela was busy serving Henk and his gang, who had decided to take rooms, since they were available, and they had gold to spend. No one in the group took notice of Alice and Kareltje.

Alice and Kareltje sat down, side by side, on an empty bench, at a table at the far end of the large room. The place was full of people, filling the place with a hearty hubbub. Happy conversations and rousing songs bounced off the walls and ceiling. The place smelled of tobacco, ale, rum, wine, herbs, spices, and good cooking. A few minutes later, Angela came over to ask if she could bring them something to eat and drink.

Alice smiled as she looked up at the happy serving wench. 'We can afford some of your stew and a tankard of ale.'

Angela smiled. 'I will be right back.'

Alice and Kareltje looked about, as they sat on their bench. The people across the table from them were busy in animated conversation. The people on the bench, beside them, were eating their dinner and not saying very much. Alice attempted to make a conversation with them.

'We found a body,' she said.

The man sitting next to her turned to look at her.

'You found a body?' he asked, perplexed she would approach him with such a topic.

'Well, we thought it was a body. But he's still alive. He was shot. In the forest.' Alice regarded the man. She hoped, perhaps he might have an idea what to do.

The man looked at Alice for a moment and then turned to his companion. 'The lady says she found a man that's been shot. In the forest.'

As he said the words, Sophie, who was sitting at a table behind Alice and Kareltje, overheard him. She turned to Henk and, indicating the people at the table behind them, told him what she had overheard. Henk regarded the people and scratched his chin. 'Do you suppose they're talking about the fisherman?' he asked.

Sophie turned around and studied Alice and Kareltje. 'It's those two,' she said. 'They're the ones with the information. I heard them mention the forest warden.'

Henk looked calmly at Sophie. 'Don't worry. They can't pin a thing on us. Just don't tell anybody.'

'I heard her say the man's still alive,' whispered Sophie.

Henk's jaw dropped. 'Still alive?'

'If he's still alive, we could be in deep trouble. He would identify us.' Sophie looked fearfully at Henk.

'We'll have to go back,' he replied, frowning.

'And do what?' asked Maarta.

'We'll have to kill him,' replied Henk. 'We have no choice.'

Maarta gestured towards Alice and Kareltje. 'What about them? They're off to find the Warden.

'They're not likely going to go out tonight. Perhaps they'll stay here overnight. We'll just have to keep an eye on them,' said Henk, stroking his chin and eyeing Alice. 'They don't look much of a threat. A couple of balls will do it.' He fingered the pistol in his belt; an evil glint in his eye.

Meanwhile, in the forest, light was becoming scarce. William was getting cold and decided to make a fire. He gathered up some dry wood and soon had a nice little fire keeping him and Kabel warmer. An owl hooted nearby. Somewhere else a crow cawed. Otherwise the forest was quiet like a grave, except that Kabel grunted and groaned with pain, every now and then. William regarded him with a concerned expression, however, there was nothing he could do.

The night became colder. All that William had with him was his blanket. He put it on Kabel and did his best to keep him breathing. Whenever Kabel croaked for water, during one of his wake moments, William would give him some from the flask. As night wore on, eventually William fell asleep beside his fire. Gradually it dwindled and was reduced to glowing coals. Neither Kabel nor William saw the first flash of light. Neither one heard the first roar of thunder. They did, however, feel the first drops of rain.

'Oh, no, it's raining,' mumbled William, opening his eyes. He looked at the fire and realizing that it had gone out, he quickly righted himself and looked for a suitable tree under which to take cover. The best one was a tall spruce, a few yards distant. He made for it in the nick of time, just as the sky opened up and a torrent of rain pelted the forest. As William crouched, shivering under the spruce tree, he could see Kabel lying under the blanket and being soaked with icy cold water. The temperature dropped twenty degrees. Hypothermia loomed its ugly head. William was cold to the core. He could not imagine what Kabel must be going through.

When morning came, the sun had a terrible time trying to break through the clouds. Eventually the sun won the battle and a glorious heat dried up all the rain, which evaporated in a thick steam off the forest floor and the leaves above. William crawled stiffly out of his shelter. Having sat crouched under the tree for so long, William's joints were not functioning so well. He was in some considerable distress trying to right himself. 'All for what?' he mumbled, as he stared at Kabel lying under the blanket. 'A corpse under an old blanket.'

As soon as William had righted himself he stepped into a circle of sunlight coming down through the canopy. He warmed himself in the glorious rays. He was thankful to be alive. It had been a harrowing night. William had never spent a rainy night under a spruce tree before. As he straightened a leg, his joints cracked. 'Aaahh,' he moaned. 'That hurt.' As he stumbled over to Kabel he muttered, 'I'm getting old.' William bent down over Kabel and gently shook his shoulder.

William waited.

He shook harder.

William waited.

He shook harder still. Then, to his utter amazement, Kabel groaned.

'You are some tough character,' muttered William.

'Water,' croaked Kabel. 'I need water.'

'Just a minute,' replied William. He grabbed his bag and retrieved the flask. Then he carefully poured some water into Kabel's mouth. Kabel coughed, but managed to swallow the water. He opened his eyes and looked at William. 'Thank you,' he said.

'Who shot you?' asked William.

'A scoundrel who introduced himself as, Henk de Meer,' croaked Kabel. 'He stole my purse und my zun shtole my savings.'

'You are in a sorry state,' replied William, not knowing what else to say. He felt awkward. He was not certain if the man might be dying. William had never been with a dying person before. Especially not in a forest, where there might be wolves, or even a bear. William shivered and looked around, to see if there might be dangerous predators about. Suddenly a woodpecker tapped on a tree nearby. William nearly jumped out of his boots. The forest became a scary place in the hazy mist rising from the heating ground.

Meanwhile in Amsterdam, Alice and Kareltje got an early start. So did Henk and his crew. Henk and his gang followed Alice and Kareltje as they hurried off to find the forest warden; the very warden who discovered Kabel and William, while out looking for poachers. Alice and Kareltje never made it to the Warden's house. Henk and his gang of cutthroats made certain of that.

Their bodies were dumped down an old well on a dilapidated farmstead from ages ago. It lay along the road which led out of Amsterdam towards the forest, whose jurisdiction it was of the warden in question. This warden sent his able assistant for help from the fishing village nearby, while he stayed with Kabel and William. He placed his musket against a tree.

Three hours later, Henk and his friends arrived in the forest. They were approaching the place where they thought they had made camp and where they had hidden the fisherman. William was the first to hear them approaching down the trail. They were talking animatedly. They had no idea there was anyone in the forest but themselves. William peeked carefully out from the shrub. He could see several people walking in his direction along the trail.

'I think it's around here somewhere,' said Maarta. 'I think I recognize that tree over there.' She pointed in the direction of a massive oak. 'That one looks really familiar.'

'Look, there,' said Dirk. 'Isn't that pile of rocks our fire pit?' He pointed to a small circle of rocks.

'Could have been someone else's,' said Mark.

'Possibly,' replied Leo. 'But judging from that tree and those bushes, I would say we have arrived.'

'I think you're right,' said Henk. 'Let's go find our fisherman.'

William realized that the people were those responsible for shooting Kabel. He quickly stepped back from the shrub. 'Those are the people who likely shot that man,' he whispered to the warden, who was readying his gun.

'Are they armed?' asked the warden.

'I think so,' replied William. 'I couldn't see exactly.'

The warden stood beside Kabel and pointed his musket in the direction the voices were coming. William stepped behind the warden. A moment later Henk and Dirk stepped from the trail.

'That looks like the shrub,' said Dirk.

'Ya, I think so, too,' replied Henk as he stepped toward the shrub. 'It's over here!' he shouted.

A moment later he and Dirk, stepped around the bush and faced the warden, pointing his musket.

'Whoa, there warden,' said Henk. 'There is no need to point that gun.'

'What do you want here?' asked the warden.

Henk looked at Dirk. Dirk stared back with a vacant expression. Henk returned his attention to the warden. 'We've come to collect our friend.' Henk pointed at Kabel lying on the ground. 'He was shot. We had to get help.' Just as he said the words, Sophie, Maarta, Leo, and Mark stepped around the shrub.

'What's going on?' asked Sophie.

'Who are they?' asked Maarta, pointing at the warden and William.

'I am the warden of this forest. We are guarding this corpse to protect it from wolves.'

William looked at the warden and then down at Kabel. He was about to say that Kabel was alive, but quickly realized what the warden's game was.

Henk smiled and looked at his companions. Then he regarded the warden. 'Well, I guess you won't need us then. I suppose you have taken control of the body?'

'That I have,' said the warden. 'Help is coming, so that the authorities can ascertain what happened. They will want to question you, as well.'

'Question us?' Henk stared dumbfoundedly at the warden. 'What do you mean, question us?'

'You obviously know about this body,' replied the warden. 'You called him your friend.'

'Well, not really a friend. We just happened by when we heard the shot. When we got to the body,' he gestured towards the trail, 'whoever shot him and stolen his clothes, rode away on a horse. Dirk and I couldn't carry him by ourselves. So we got help.' He indicated the other two men and the women. As he said the word, "help," a horse's neigh drifted into hearing.

Kabel groaned.

Henk stared down at Kabel and reached for the pistol in his belt. 'He's alive!'

He looked at his companions and then back at the warden as he and his friends began to draw their weapons.

The clip clop of two horses could be heard coming up the trail from the direction of the village. Voices could be heard conversing.

Henk looked wild eyed at the warden. He did not know what to do. Shoot Kabel or the warden? His friends were looking at him for guidance. The warden kept his musket firmly pointed at Henk.

'It's by those trees, over there,' said the warden's apprentice over the clip clop of the horses, still some distance away.

'What should we do?' asked Dirk anxiously, pointing his pistol at William.

Henk looked at his friend. He pointed his pistol at the warden and cocked the trigger. 'Get down and hide behind those trees,' he whispered to his companions.

'If you shoot us, they can catch you real quick with the horses,' said the warden.

Henk smiled. 'Not if we don't use the trail.' He indicated the forest. 'We'll just disappear into there. The horses can't follow in there.'

'We can't leave him alive,' hissed Sophie, indicating Kabel. 'He'll identify us.'

Henk looked at Sophie. He pointed his pistol at Kabel and shot.

In his haste he did not aim very well. The ball hit Kabel in his left buttock. The pain woke him out of his stupor. He groaned with intense pain as the hot ball seared his quivering flesh. The warden discharged his musket and hit Henk in the right shoulder, making him drop his pistol as he fell backwards into the shrub. Dirk discharged his pistol at the warden, the ball slicing through the shoulder of his leather coat and thudding into a tree, right next to William's head. As he looked fearfully about, the other members of Henk's gang began to discharge their pistols.

Meanwhile the people with the horses heard the shots and galloped down the trail, arriving at the scene a moment after Maarta shot her pistol and hit the warden in his left leg. He went down, groaning with intense pain. A shot fired by Mark sliced through William's hat, missing his head by half an inch. He fell flat on the ground, as two other balls went whizzing through the trees. The horse riders arrived, followed a moment later by five soldiers. On the horses were the warden's assistant, Franz and the sheriff. They immediately drew their pistols.

'Round up those men and those women!' shouted the sheriff to the soldiers as they arrived at the scene. Two of them were carrying a litter, which they set down beside Kabel before joining the other soldiers, who immediately ran off after the fleeing gang members.

Henk was lying on the ground moaning, next to Kabel who was staring at him, wide eyed and alert.

'You bastard,' moaned Kabel. 'I will now get even with you. I'm going to tell dem how you shot me und left me for dead. How you robbed me.'

'You'll be dead before any of this comes to trial. My friends are very resourceful. I doubt if those soldiers will catch them in this forest,' replied Henk. He chuckled. 'They won't let you live. Trust me.'

When the sheriff stepped over to join Franz, who was examining the warden's leg, he overheard Kabel and Henk muttering at each other. He perked up his ears and listened as he examined the warden's leg. He patted the warden on his shoulder. 'You'll be alright, Hans. It's not a serious wound. The surgeon will have you fixed up in no time.' He gestured toward the two men on the ground. 'Franz told me you found that man, naked and shot. What's the story with the others?'

'I think they're the ones who did it to the naked man. The other one stayed here with him, when they discovered him lying there. His wife and son went to Amsterdam to fetch help.' The warden looked down at his wound and gingerly touched the hole in his breeches. 'I think they must have learned that he was still alive and had come back to finish him off. They must have been tipped off. Perhaps they learned it from William's wife and she sent them, thinking they were trustworthy helpers to take care of the matter.' The warden looked at Henk. 'He's the leader.'

The sheriff looked over at Henk and Kabel. He stood up and walked over to them. When he looked at Kabel's face, he recognized him. 'So, it's you, Kabel Sventska. I am not surprised that Almighty God has finally struck you down for your evil ways.' Kabel grunted something under his breath. The sheriff did not respond as he examined Henk. 'So, what's your story? What's your connection with that fisherman?'

Henk stared at the sheriff. 'Me and Dirk found im ere in the forest. E was naked and lying there. So me and Dirk we went to Amsterdam to fetch help. That's them, who ran off.'

'Why were you shooting at the warden and that man over there?' The sheriff gestured toward William who was attending to the warden.

'They shot first.'

'That's a lie,' mumbled Kabel. 'You shot me in the arse, you bastard.' Kabel lifted his head and stared with wide eyed pain at the sheriff. 'He shot me the first time, as well. Stole my purse and my clothes. Left me for dead to be eaten by wolves.' Kabel grimaced as a jolt of searing pain traveled up and down his body. He lay back and moaned.

'Getting shot is no laughing matter. However, it looks like the both of you will heal. The wounds are not life threatening.' The sheriff stood up just as the soldiers returned with, Sophie, Leo, Mark, and Dirk.

'Where's the other woman?' asked the warden.

'Musta got away,' answered a soldier. 'These four is all we found.'

'Alright, tie those four behind the horses. Put that man on the litter.' The sheriff indicated Kabel, 'and put the warden on my horse.' The soldiers dutifully followed the orders and soon the four captives were tied up in pairs behind the two horses. Pointing at Henk he added, 'that one too. He can walk. He only has a shoulder wound.' He smiled at the warden, sitting up against a tree.

The warden looked up at the sheriff. 'Thank you Steven.'

When everything was ready, four soldiers carried the litter behind the two riders. They set off in the direction of the village, only five kilometres away. The other soldier followed along behind with William and Franz. An owl hooted nearby. The forest was beginning to get dark.

'I must needs be in Amsterdam tomorrow. I must find out where my wife Alice and son are. I don't believe that she would have sent the likes of him and his gang to come and help that fisherman.' William looked at Franz.

Franz regarded William for a moment. 'I'm sure the sheriff just wants to hear your story in front of the magistrate. There is something very strange about all of this. Especially since he was in the village to investigate the murder of that fisherman's wife.'

'His wife is dead?' William looked at the ground. 'Poor man. Not only has he been shot and robbed, but his wife is dead? That's awful.'

Franz nodded. 'Isn't it so?'

When they reached the fishing village, it was late. The sheriff had Henk and his gang locked up in a cell. Then Kabel and the warden were taken to the doctor's house. It was nearing two o'clock before the sheriff fell asleep in his room at the inn.

Meanwhile, at the same time in Amsterdam, Hanzel woke up suddenly. He looked at Angela contentedly sleeping beside him. Her long golden hair lay strewn about on the pillows. He gently stroked Angela's hair and smiled. Angela was becoming a very good friend. He owed her a lot, he thought. Once she gave him back his money, he vowed he would give her her some of it. How she had managed to keep him a secret, so far, was a wonder to him.

Hanzel stared at the sky through the open window. It was overcast and gloomy. He thought of his family and wondered how they were faring without him there. He wondered how his mother was feeling about him being gone. Hanzel knew that he was her favorite son. The older boys, Wim, Paul, and Henrik were rarely home, except for stretches in the winter. They were rough, tough men; fishermen like their father; with similar dispositions. Hanzel's older brothers were mean spirited bullies too. Hanzel's two oldest sisters, Miep and Kate were already married and Marika worked at the laundry. She never did have much to do with Hanzel, being four years older.

Some dark clouds scudded across the sky. The wind had picked up. A shutter began to swing slowly; squeaking in its hinges. Hanzel thought about his father. He was glad his father had not found him. He again thanked God for Angela. Without her he would have had to go back to a life of more hell. Hanzel knew that Kabel would have beaten him to an inch of his life. He well knew his father's rages and what that meant for his mother and his siblings. Him not finding Hanzel would certainly result in violence at home. He prayed his mother would be alright. When he finally drifted back to sleep he dreamed of horrible things; his mother and father being murdered in numerous nasty ways by all kinds of other people. When the dream showed his father doing the killing he woke up in a cold sweat.

Suddenly, a brilliant flash of light lit up the room. In the blinding light Hanzel happened to look up at the ceiling. The open beams stood out in stark contrast. A familiar shape was sitting on top of one of the beams, above the chair. It was his leather bag! A earsplitting clap of thunder reverberated through the room. Hanzel had located his money. He looked at Angela peacefully sleeping. Hanzel decided he would wait until next morning when she was back to work, and he, supposedly recuperating in bed. He lay back in bed and planned how he would get the bag down. Gradually he drifted back to sleep. He never saw the second flash of lightning, nor did he hear the thunder.

Next morning, after Angela had gone off to work in the kitchen, Hanzel painfully got out of bed. His bruises were hurting him tremendously and his broken fingers throbbed. If he ever would have the opportunity, he would revenge his wounds on Angela's father. He was a brute, just like his own father. Hanzel listened against the wall to hear whether anyone was in the room next door. Hearing no sounds, he climbed up on the chair and reached for the bag. Alas, it was just out of reach. No matter how far he stretched, he just could not reach the bag, sitting on the beam above the chair. He looked anxiously around the room for something to extend his reach. There was nothing he could see that would do it. He needed something to prod the bag to fall off the beam. He stared at the armoire and decided to have a look inside. He opened the door and peered inside. To his utter amazement, the perfect tool to help his cause was there, in a corner. He quickly took the broom out of the armoire and prodded the bag off the beam. He caught it before it hit the floor, nearly dropping the broom and making a noise. Hanzel set the bag down on the bed and returned the broom to the armoire. He closed the door and returned to the bed. When he looked inside the bag, his money was not there! The bag was empty.

Chapter 7

Kabel lay face down on Doctor Pizarro's operating table. He was wearing a fisherman's sweater but nothing else. The doctor was preparing to remove the ball from Kabel's left buttock with a heated knife and tongs. 'These weel hurt, a leetle beet,' said the good doctor. He placed a wooden dowel into Kabel's mouth. 'Eer. Bit on dees steek.' Kabel took the wood between his teeth and bit down. 'Alright den.' Doctor Pizarro grabbed the heated knife and began to dig into the wound with it. Kabel flinched and bit hard into the spindle. A moment later Doctor Pizarro reached into the wound with his little tongs and pulled the bloody ball out of the hole. He dropped the ball into a pan. 'Dat ball made a nice clean ole. I theen all de dlot of yor pantaloons is a ere, as a well.' Doctor Pizarro examined the piece of cloth which came out of the hole, along with the ball. He placed it against the hole in Kabel's pantaloons and nodded; smiling. He swabbed the bleeding hole with a cloth and then proceeded to pour some alcohol into the wound making Kabel bite the spindle even harder. 'Now we steech up de ole an you'll be good dere.' Doctor Pizarro threaded some silk into a surgical needle and proceeded to stitch the hole closed. By the time he was done, the spindle was nearly bitten through. 'Now we haf to see about de odder oles.' The doctor gestured for Kabel to roll over. Seeing that the entry and exit holes were clean, the doctor swabbed the wounds with alcohol and stitched them closed, as well. When he was done he told Kabel about his fee.

'I will haf to pay you wid fish,' replied Kabel. 'My money waz shtolen, as you know.'

'Don vorry, Kabel Sventska. You can pay me wen you haf the moneey.' Doctor Pizarro handed Kabel a note on which his fee was written. 'Joost sign dis.' He handed Kabel a quill. When he saw Kabel hesitate, he added, 'joost make your mark.'

Kabel reluctantly took the quill and dipped it into the proffered ink bottle. Then he marked a jiggly squiggle, that having been the mark he had made since he first entered into a contract upon his marriage to Elizabeth. When he was done, he hobbled out of the doctor's house and made his way home. Unfortunately for him, he never made it there. He was arrested by two of the sheriff's men.

'Vhy are you arresting me?' asked Kabel, not suspecting anything unusual.

'For the murder of your wife,' replied one of the men.

'M, murder? Of my wife?' Kabel looked dumbfounded.

'Yes. You are charged with murdering Elizabeth Merkel, your wife of twenty five years.

Kabel stared at the two men. He acted as if he did not have the slightest idea what they were talking about. 'My wife is dead?'

'The sheriff wants to see you,' said the other man.

Kabel looked about himself to see if he could run away. However, given his condition, he was in no shape to run anywhere. He could barely hobble as it was. Kabel decided it was best to act innocent and go along with the sheriff's men. Pretending that he knew nothing of the affair was the best way to act. However, no matter how calm he tried to appear on the surface, his heart was pounding in his chest as he let the two men lead him back to the magistrate's office.

When Kabel arrived at the magistrate's office, Henk was there sitting on a chair and nursing his bandaged shoulder. William was sitting with the warden, on a bench against the west wall. The magistrate was sitting behind a massive, carved mahogany desk from the East Indies. He stared at Kabel as he was led into the room. The sheriff stopped pacing and regarded Kabel with a piercing stare.

'Sit there,' said the magistrate sternly. He pointed to an empty chair in front of the desk, facing him.

Kabel hobbled to the chair and slowly sat down. He looked quizzically at the magistrate.

The magistrate looked sternly back at Kabel and did not say anything for some time as he regarded Kabel, fidgeting in the chair, trying to find a comfortable way to sit, given the wound in his buttock.

'We have good reason to believe that you killed your wife, Elizabeth Merkel and are therefore, formally accusing you of her murder.' The accusation was direct and to the point. The magistrate stared deep into Kabel's eyes and noticed them shifting back and forth.

Kabel fidgeted in the chair but tried to remain calm. It was difficult to sit still because of his wounds. His mind was racing. *How could anvone know? Nobody saw me come und go, did dey? I came und vent by de back vay. Dey don't haf anyting on me.* 'No, I didn't,' he said in as steady a voice as he could.

The magistrate regarded William. 'Who are you? And what is your connection to this man?' He pointed at Kabel.

William stood up and regarded the magistrate for a moment as he collected his thoughts. When he was ready, he told him his story. How he came upon Kabel, shot and naked in the forest. He told how he sent his wife and son into Amsterdam to send help. In the meantime the warden came along on his patrol and found him and Kabel. So the warden stayed while his assistant went for help. Then, that man,' he indicated Henk, 'came along and he and his gang tried to kill that man.' William pointed to Kabel. 'Then the sheriff came and here we are. Is there any news of my wife, Alice and my son Kareltje? They went to Amsterdam to fetch help, as I told you.'

The magistrate looked at the sheriff. The sheriff shrugged his shoulders. 'We have no word of his wife or son. Perhaps, finding the warden not in his cottage, returned to Amsterdam, or the forest to find William.' The sheriff looked at William.

'That man knew about the fisherman in the forest and came with five others to kill him. The only way they must have known that he was alive is from my wife and son.' William stared at Henk, who began to look very concerned all of a sudden. He sat up in his chair and stared at William. 'He must have overheard them and therefore he should know something. I instructed my wife to return with the helpers, so we could be found in there in the woods. That man could not have known the exact location where the fisherman was lying unless, either they came with my wife and son to the place, or they had prior knowledge of the place, having shot him and dragged him behind a big bush.'

'That's right,' grumbled Kabel. 'He knew where I was lying because he shot me the first time and left me for dead.' Kabel stared at Henk.

'That's a lie!' shouted Henk. 'We were coming to help. Your wife told us exactly where you were and she and your boy left us.'

William regarded Henk coldly. 'I told her to come back with you. What did she tell you that was so important in Amsterdam that she felt it unnecessary to accompany you back to me?'

Henk looked at William and then back at the magistrate. His eyes were staring wide as he tried to figure out what the story could be. Unfortunately for him he chose the wrong one. 'She had to take the boy to the doctor in Amsterdam because he was feeling very poorly and she was afraid he was going to die.'

'That's a lie! That's a bald faced lie. There was nothing wrong with my son.' William looked at the magistrate and then back at Henk. 'What have you done with my wife and son?'

'Nothing,' replied Henk. 'We did nothing to her. I'm sure she is fine, somewhere in Amsterdam.'

'I don't believe you,' replied William.

'Alright, alright, gentlemen, please. We are here to see if it is possible that this man, Kabel Sventska caused the death of his wife. That is the first order of business. We will deal with that man, later.' The magistrate looked at the sheriff. 'You told me you have witnesses who say they saw that man,' he pointed at Kabel, 'coming and going from the village around the time that his wife was killed?'

'I do have witnesses. They came to my deputy while we were here on a routine visit to see that all is in order. They told my deputy they saw that man come and go.'

'Where are these witnesses?' asked the magistrate.

'Here. They're waiting outside,' replied the sheriff, looking at a deputy standing by the door. 'Fetch them, if you please,' he said to the deputy, who immediately left the room.

Moments later two ancients of days wobbled into the room and stood hesitantly at the door. The magistrate looked at them quizzically.

'Mister and Missus van den Tuin,' said the sheriff.

The two ancients looked at the magistrate and nodded and bowed.

'So, you say you saw that man coming and going in the village during the time that Elizabeth Merkel was killed?' The magistrate folded his hands on the desk and leaned forward to hear the old folks croaking out their story.

Mister van den Tuin looked over at Kabel for a moment before speaking. 'We've known that man since he was young; when his family first moved here. His parents died and he was left an orphan. We know his whole story. He's been a trouble maker from the beginning. It wouldn't surprise us if he killed his wife.'

'He beat her, he did. We know that for certain,' added Missus van den Tuin.

'So it doesn't surprise us that she is dead. He finally killed her,' said Mister van den Tuin authoritatively.

'That's a lie,' said Kabel firmly. He sat up and looked back at the old people standing by the door. 'Those old people are deaf and blind. They don't know anything.'

The old couple stared at Kabel. Then the old man related the tale. 'We saw him come to his house. It was early in the afternoon, two days ago. We were sitting on our bench in our little garden. We both saw Kabel coming home through his yard from the back road. We heard noises coming from his house and saw Kabel leave the house in a hurry. He left as he came. He never saw us sitting there.'

Kabel stared bug eyed at the old couple. He did not know what to say. Kabel stared wildly at the judge. 'It's a lie! It's all a lie! How could I haf been here, ven I vas shot in de forest, vay over dere.' He pointed in the direction of the forest.

'We saw him with our own eyes,' said the ancients of days in unison.

'Vell, your eyes are old, blind eyes!' shouted Kabel desperately. 'You're a hundred years old! Vhat can hundred year old eyes see anymore?'

'We can still see plenty, we can,' replied the old lady.

'You say you have other witnesses?' asked the magistrate, looking at the sheriff.

'Two of his daughters and their neighbour,' replied the sheriff.

'My daughters?!' Kabel stared at the sheriff. 'My daughters vill testify? Dey'll tell you dat I'm incapable of killing my wife.' Kabel looked anxiously at the door.

'Are the daughters here?' asked the magistrate.

'Waiting outside,' replied the sheriff, nodding to his deputy.

A moment later, Mister Sintjans, Kate, and Marika stepped into the room. The girls looked nervously at their father sitting in the chair in front of the magistrate. They were good girls who knew whose hands wielded the rod. The magistrate regarded Mister Sintjans. 'What is your story regarding that man and allegations that he killed his wife?' He pointed at Kabel.

'Don't believe him. He's a liar. I vuldn't believe a vurd he says,' grumbled Kabel.

The magistrate stared at Kabel and pointed his right index finger at him. 'You be quiet. Don't speak unless I tell you to.'

Kabel stared at the magistrate. But he, Kabel was just a simple fisherman and the magistrate was who he was. Kabel knew it was best to be quiet if he wished to save himself. He nodded.

The magistrate looked at Mister Sintjans. 'Go ahead. Tell me your story.'

'I've known Kabel Sventska to be a hard man, especially where his family is concerned. I've lived next door to him for twenty three years. I was the second person on the scene of Elizabeth's death. Marika had found her mother and came outside just as I was passing by. When I went inside the house, I noticed her lying on the floor and that she had a massive bruise on the side of her face. She must have been knocked over a chair, because there was an overturned chair in the room. I think she must have been pushed over that chair and smashed the side of her head into the corner of the table.' He grimaced. 'It was an ugly scene.'

'Where are Elizabeth's remains?' asked the magistrate.

'Mortuary,' replied the sheriff.

The magistrate nodded and then turned his attention to Kate and Marika.

'Is that man your father?' The magistrate looked intently at the two young women.

The girls nodded. 'Yes, he's our father,' they replied in unison.

'Do you think that your father might have killed your mother?' The magistrate regarded the girls with an empathetic expression on his otherwise, stern face. He stroked his van Dijk beard and waited for the girls to reply.

The two girls looked at each other and then at their father, knowing there would be hell to pay if they told the truth. They both looked fearfully at the magistrate.

'Do we really have to answer that?' asked Kate, who was 20. Her eyes told the magistrate of her fear. That look was enough to convince the magistrate that Kabel was guilty. However, he was merely seeing if there was enough evidence for a trial in Amsterdam. The magistrate, Jacob van Ruiter knew his work very well. He had done the job for many years with great success. He could clearly see that there was significant evidence to send Kabel to trial. Hence his verdict was, 'that you be held in confinement and transported to Amsterdam and there held in prison until such time that a trial will take place where you can plead guilty or not guilty before learned judges and a jury of your peers.'

Kabel jumped up. 'I am to go to prison because you suspect me of murdering my vife? There is no real proof. All you have is de hearsay of a couple of old people, who are nearly blind und deaf. As you know, I vas lying in de forest, shot through de body und in my arse! It is somevun else! Not me!' He pointed at the two ancients of days. 'Look at dose two. They can barely see you, let alone a person walking in und out of my house at a distance. They might have seen somebody, who looks like me, my height, my build, perhaps with dark clothes, such as I vear. I vas in de forest, on my vay home from Amsterdam. I vas looking for my zun Hanzel, who ran away from home.'

The magistrate stared calmly at Kabel. 'Why would your son run away from home?'

Kabel clenched the arms of the chair and stared at the magistrate. *Because of you, Kabel. You alone are responsible. Your son, Hanzel ran away because of your ill treatment of him. How can I hide dat fact? Everyone but my daughters will likely testify to that. Better play dumb, Kabel.* 'I don't know. He ran away because he tinks he can go out on his own at de age of twelve. Hanzel is very smart. Much too smart for his own good, I reckon. Now he's somewhere in Amsterdam, or maybe jumped on board a ship und vent to sea, just like I did at dat age.' Kabel looked at the floor with a sad expression on his haggard face. 'Just as I did at age twelve,' he mumbled. 'Just like I did....' Kabel stared at the floor and leaned forward as he began to reflect on what happened with Hanzel and what he had done to Elizabeth. *I did not mean to kill her. It was an accident. Wasn't it?'*

The magistrate stared at Kabel, 'Why did you come through the forest when the road is a much shorter route? You know the forest is home to robbers and villains. Why come home that way? It makes no sense.' The magistrate looked at the sheriff who shrugged his shoulders.

'Makes no sense to me, either,' replied the sheriff, staring at Kabel.

'Take him away,' said the magistrate coldly. 'I will hear your case next.' The magistrate pointed to Henk, who was watching Kabel squirming in the chair.

Two of the sheriff's men stepped over to Kabel. Kabel regarded them for a moment before reacting. Without warning he punched the man on his left, sending him backward against the sheriff and knocking them both into William and Mister Sintjans. Then Kabel turned and spun the other deputy over the desk into the magistrate. As he spun around he knocked over a chair and flew for the door. Kate and Marika, who were standing by the door were knocked over in the rampaging escape.

Kabel swung the door open and ran down the five steps to the street.

The two deputies and the sheriff recovered themselves and ran after Kabel, who was not able to continue the effort, due to his wounds. He was standing, panting in the middle of the street when the two deputies tackled him and threw him onto the ground. He landed with a thud.

'Put him in irons,' demanded the sheriff, handing the heavy shackles to one of the deputies. A moment later Kabel was led off to a cell in the basement of the building.

Kate and Marika, who had come outside, and were standing on the steps, watched their cruel father being led off. Tears stained their cheeks. Neither one spoke a word.

Chapter 8

Hanzel woke up with a start. He had been dreaming unsettling scenes involving death and mutilation. It was not something Hanzel was willing to continue dreaming about. The dark visions were too real. He did not like those dreams. His spirit was repulsed like a wrong poled magnet. As he sat there, upright in bed, he realized that his bruises were hurting less, but his fingers still throbbed with intense pain. He looked at Angela peacefully sleeping. Light from a full moon trickled through the clouds and into the room through the open shutters. *When did she come to bed? I never noticed her getting into bed.* He looked up at the beam where he had returned the bag, so as not to alert Angela that he was on to her. *I will trick her into revealing where my money is. I know it has to be in this room, somewhere. The question is how do I trick her into revealing its location?* Angela turned over and faced Hanzel who looked down at her pretty features. She was breathing evenly, with her full lips parted and revealing her slightly crooked teeth. Hanzel liked kissing that mouth. Angela liked it too. Hanzel smiled. He liked Angela, but he did not trust her.

Eventually, Hanzel became tired again and lay down. He soon drifted into more pleasant dreams and woke up refreshed in the morning. He faintly remembered Angela touching his privates in the night, but that was about the only memory he managed to hold onto for three seconds after he woke up. Then he no longer knew whether Angela had actually touched him or if it had been a dream. Hanzel opened his eyes. Angela was already up and was standing by the armoire. She was not aware that Hanzel had woken up. He remained lying on his side, his eyes open and watching what she was doing. The tiny clink of coins trickled into Hanzel's ears. *She is counting money. I won't need to trick her. She is showing me where the money is.* When Angela was done, she could be seen tying the leather laces of her money bag, which she replaced in its hiding place in the ceiling of the armoire. Hanzel watched intently as Angela reached up into the armoire; her strong, fleshy buttocks pinched tight against the white cotton of her night dress. Hanzel began to get an erection. The girl was definitely pleasant to watch. When she was done, she turned around. Hanzel had to quickly close his eyes, so that she would not suspect him of having seen where the money was hidden. He did get a tiny glimpse of her, as she turned around, which added to his blood pressure.

When Angela finished dressing, Hanzel pretended to wake up just then. 'Oh, so you're awake at last,' said Angela, looking affectionately at Hanzel. 'How are you feeling? You had a restless night.'

'I'm alright,' replied Hanzel bravely. His face showed the pain he was feeling from his broken fingers. 'I just had some bad dreams.'

'Your fingers are paining you, aren't they?'

Hanzel nodded.

'Well, today I'll go see the apothecary and get you something for the pain. I promise.' Angela opened the door. 'I have to go. I'm probably already late. Don't worry, I'll bring you something when I see you next.' Angela blew Hanzel a kiss and left the room. She locked the door as per usual; leaving Hanzel alone to recuperate in her soft bed. *I wonder how much longer I can stay here? Surely her parents are going to discover me. If her father catches me here, I'd hate to think what else he would do to me. I need to get out of here.* Hanzel looked at his clothes on the chair. He stepped out of bed and quickly dressed. When he was done he brought the chair over to the armoire and used it to gain easy access to the wooden ceiling. Feeling around he located a loose plank and discovered the money bag. He carefully lifted it out of its hiding place. The bag was heavy with coins. Hanzel set the bag on the bed and then returned the chair to its place. He closed the door of the armoire and then returned to the bed to feel the weight of the bag of coins. It was considerably heavier than the bag of coins he came there with.

Hanzel looked up and realized he needed his leather bag. He quickly placed the chair under the beam and retrieved the bag into which he deposited the leather bag of coins. He returned the chair and looked around the room to see if there was anything he had forgotten. Seeing that all was well, he opened the shutters and looked outside. It was raining. Nobody was in the courtyard below the window. However, there was no hay or straw cart. *How am I going to get down without hurting myself?* Hanzel saw the only way down was by inching his way along the overhang below the window; praying he would not slip on the wet tiles. He would have to lower himself onto a wall which brought him closer to the ground. Then he would have to lower himself down from there. *In the rain nobody will see me. It's good and misty. I pray that I won't slip.* Even though his fingers were paining him tremendously, Hanzel managed to climb out of the window. Rain was pelting him but he gritted his teeth and bore the cold. *I have to get out of here. As good as Angela is to me, if her father catches me here, I'm as good as dead.* Hanzel reached the place where he was able to lower himself onto a short wall that formed the enclosure of the inn's courtyard.

Fingers throbbing, he managed to hang onto the roof and lowered himself onto the top of the wall. The wall, being only eight feet off the ground made it possible for Hanzel to lower himself onto the top of a barrel, from where he jumped down to the ground. Then with a furtive look at the main entrance to the inn, to see if anyone had seen him, he darted off into the street and quickly disappeared into the rain. Fortunately, he did not have to walk far before locating a public house in which a blazing fire warmed the room. This time he was more discreet about his money.

The inn where he found himself had a friendly atmosphere. People were happily talking and singing in groups around rectangular tables. The place smelled of alcohol, tobacco, and good food. *Hmmm, this place smells great! I hope they have a room available. With this bag of money I should be able to stay here for a while and find my way in Amsterdam.* While Hanzel sat on a bench near the fire, he looked around and noted that the place was decorated with all manner of exotic weapons from; Africa, Brazil, the Caribbean Islands, China, the East Indies... *The owner must be a collector. There sure are a lot weapons. Oh, look at that one!* Hanzel stared at a strange club from Tasmania. As Hanzel sat there, warming up, he stared, wideyed at the weapons on the walls. He saw a Javanese Kris for the first time and a Ghurka kikri. He also saw a blow pipe and poisoned darts from South America and small bows with beautiful arrows whose fletching was made from parrot feathers. There was also a shield and several spears from South Africa.

A serving wench approached. She asked the man, who was sitting on the bench to Hanzel's left, if he was Hanzel's parent. The man looked at Hanzel and then back at the girl. He shook his head. 'Never seen im before,' he said. Hanzel was not paying any attention, having his back turned in order to look at the fascinating collection of weapons on the walls. *No wonder that this place is called, Armory Inn.* The serving girl tapped Hanzel's shoulder, startling him. He turned around and regarded her.

'Are you here with your parents?' asked the girl.

Hanzel shook his head. 'No,' he said. 'I had to come out of the rain to dry off. And I am hungry and thirsty. I need something to eat and drink.' He winced as he moved his damaged left hand. 'And a place to sleep.'

The girl's eyebrows lifted, 'and a place to sleep, is it? And how do you propose to pay for all of that? We don't serve urchins.'

Hanzel looked up at the girl. 'Just tell me how much that will cost and I will pay you. In advance if I have to.'

The girl eyed the boy sitting there confidently staring back at her. 'Alright, I'll tell you. For a meal, a tankard of ale, and a place to sleep will cost you one guilder.'

Hanzel smiled. 'I have that.' He reached into his bag sitting on the bench beside him and discreetly extracted a guilder from the purse. He handed the guilder to the girl. 'Here,' he said. 'Will that do?'

The girl smiled as she took the coin. 'That will do just fine,' she said, happily. 'What would you like to eat, pork, beef, or fish? We have really nice haddock tonight.'

Hanzel smiled. 'I'll have the haddock. With a tankard of ale, please.' He looked down at his broken fingers. 'Do you have anything to kill pain?'

The girl looked at Hanzel's splinted fingers. 'What happened?'

'I fell.'

'Oh,' said the girl. 'That's too bad. Does it hurt a lot?'

Hanzel nodded.

The girl's maternal instinct came out. Especially for such a handsome young man, who she reckoned to be a young looking fifteen year old, judging from his demeanor. He was much too confident to be any younger. And, to her way of thinking, he was so good looking that he deserved her compassionate side. 'I'll see what I can do. I believe the local apothecary is having his dinner here.' The girl smiled. 'I'll be back with your food and drink.' Then she turned and walked off to the kitchen. Soon she returned with a plate of delicious haddock with lemon potatoes and onions, and a tankard of ale. 'There you are, young man.' She set the food and drink on the table. Hanzel thanked her and she walked off.

Hanzel stared at the food for a moment and then immediately began to eat. He was very hungry for a full, hot meal. The fish was perfectly battered and fried. The potatoes were unlike any he had ever tasted and the onions, boiled and buttered like no onions he had ever savored. Hanzel thought he had gone to heaven as he hungrily chowed down. When he was done, he drank the tankard of ale. When he was done with the ale, he set the tankard down on the table and let out a long and contented sigh. Then he burped. He looked around to see if anyone took note, but nobody did. People burped and farted, snorted and spat; that was life and there was nothing anyone could do about it, so nobody in that happy inn could care less.

Hanzel felt good as he turned around and leaned back against the table. He made certain to keep the strap of his bag firmly around his neck and shoulder. For extra security he placed his right hand on the bag to make sure he could feel the money bag inside. After all he had gone through, he had become much more cautious. None of the adults around him took any notice of him. He was just a child in the crowd. Hanzel felt perfectly content. He wanted to be left alone. He was having to contend with three broken fingers and a lot of pain.

The fire was stoked up and filled the place with a good heat which, in addition to the ale, warmed Hanzel. He was gradually beginning to glow happily. *I will not drink any more ale. There is no way I ever want to get drunk, like I did at the other place. Just that one tankard alone and I already feel whoozy. That's strong stuff. I'll just sit here and look at the weapons and soak up this warmth. I'll go and sleep and hope it doesn't rain in the morning.*

Hanzel contentedly sat there by the fire, thinking and dreaming of a better future; about how he was going to prosper in Amsterdam and about how much better he felt away from his unhappy home. *The best way is for me to stay sober. From now on I vow to never touch too much alcohol again. I don't like how it makes me feel. I don't want to be poor, ever again, either. I will become a rich and famous person.* Hanzel was staring at a massive claymore attached firmly to a solid square pillar at the far end of the room. 'Someday I'm going to have a collection of weapons,' he muttered. 'Without weapons you can't protect yourself.'

The man on Hanzel's right overheard Hanzel muttering. He turned to look at the handsome young boy sitting on the bench beside him. 'I agree,' he said.

He smiled at Hanzel. 'Without a weapon a person can not defend himself against those intent upon stealing his purse, or his life.'

Hanzel regarded the man for a moment before replying; having to come out of his deep meditations concerning his circumstances. 'What did you say?'

'I said that you are correct. You need weapons,' replied the man.

'Oh, yes, weapons.' Hanzel smiled. 'Of course, weapons. I don't have any. I wish I did. I could use a weapon. Of course I would have to learn to use it. I mean, I'm not that old.' Hanzel looked into the fire.

'It doesn't matter how old you are,' said the man. 'A young man, such as you, alone in this town, a port where all manner of villains are plying their trade, ought to have a weapon.' The man paused for a moment as he regarded Hanzel with a friendly smile. Hanzel could tell that the man was sincere and meant him no harm. 'You need at least a dirk.' He reached into his boot and extracted a dirk in a sheath. He handed it to Hanzel. 'Here,' he said. 'Take this. It's good and sharp.'

Hanzel gratefully received the dirk and regarded it for a moment before extracting the eight inch blade from the leather sheath. The knife had a bone handle and a blade of blue steel with a razor sharp point and an edge that could slice a hair. The dirk was perfectly suited for his hand. The knife felt good. It was as if it was made for Hanzel.

'Thank you. I've never received such a fine present before.' Hanzel extended his right hand. 'My name is, Hanzel Sventska.'

The man took Hanzel's much smaller hand and introduced himself as, Gerritt de Witt. 'I am a dealer in weapons, armour, and oddities from around the world. That is why I come to this place from time to time. Geert, who owns this place is my brother.'

'Ahh, now I see how all of these weapons came to be here, I suppose?' Hanzel indicated the weapons on the walls.

'He started his collection before I became interested in the business. He inspired me to it. Now I handle all kinds of weapons.' Gerritt smiled and put his hands on his ample stomach. 'Now I can afford to eat and drink well.'

'So, why are you giving me, a total stranger, who is still a boy, an expensive knife like this?' Hanzel indicated the dirk.

'Because I am looking for a young man who I can train in the business. For some reason I felt compelled to give you the dirk from what you said. Looking at you, you appear to be the perfect candidate.'

'The perfect candidate?'

Gerritt nodded. 'You are young enough to be teachable. You obviously have an interest and an understanding about weapons. And, there is something about you that I like. I think I would like to help you. You obviously look like someone who could use some help.'

Hanzel could not believe what he just heard. Someone was offering him a job. Actually what Gerritt was proposing was an apprenticeship. He was elated and accepted immediately. They shook hands and became instant friends.

'Where is your home?' asked Gerritt.

'I don't have a home. I ran away because my father is a tyrant.'

Gerritt regarded Hanzel's damaged hand. 'What happened to your hand? Did he break your fingers?'

Hanzel shook his head. 'A brutish innkeeper thought I was up to no good. He and his friend beat me and when I fell from a ladder, these fingers were broken. A friend of mine set the bones for me and put these splints on.' Hanzel showed Gerritt his splinted fingers.

'I think it would be wise to let my doctor take a look at those fingers. We will visit him first thing in the morning.' Gerritt looked at a short, bearded man, who was sitting on the far side of the room with a group of other men and a couple of women. They were singing and having fun. 'I see that the apothecary is here.'

'Ya, that's what the serving wench said. She said she would try and get me something for the pain.' Hanzel looked at the serving girl, but she was being kept busy and did not appear to have time to talk to the apothecary at the moment.

Gerritt smiled. 'He's a friend of mine.' He patted Hanzel's shoulder. 'Wait here. I'll take care of it.' Gerritt stepped over to the apothecary and when he had gotten his attention, the singing stopped while Gerritt spoke with his friend. Hanzel watched from across the room as his new friend pointed towards him and continued to speak with the apothecary. A moment later, he and Gerritt returned to talk with Hanzel.

'This is young Hanzel Sventska,' said Gerritt. 'As you can see, he has three broken fingers.' Then, gesturing to the apothecary, Gerritt introduced him as, Jakop Zuiterman.

Hanzel shook hands.

'You must be in quite a lot of pain,' said Jakop as he sat on the bench where Gerritt had sat. 'Let me see those fingers.'

Hanzel gingerly held up his left hand for Jakop to have a good look. Jakop held Hanzel's hand, ever so gently and examined the fingers and splints. 'These splints are reasonably well done, but will need a doctor's attention. As for soothing the pain, I do have something which will help you. I carry some with me wherever I go.' Jakop reached into a pouch he carried on his belt. He extracted a small bottle and pulled the cork out. 'This is something Paracelsus was working on. It is laudanum. A tincture of opium. You should take this an hour before you want to sleep. You can take another small amount in the morning.' The apothecary took out a small silver spoon and showed Hanzel how much to take. 'You will not feel your pain quite so much.' He held the bottle under Hanzel's nose so he could smell the elixir. He crinkled his nose as a vapour of pure alcohol drifted into his nostrils. Hanzel sneezed. Jakop pulled the bottle away just in time. He smiled at Hanzel as he stoppered the little flask.

'How much do I owe you?' asked Hanzel.

'Nothing,' replied the apothecary. 'It has been taken care of.' He smiled. 'Remember, a spoonful an hour before bed and in the morning. You may take a half spoonful in the late afternoon if the fingers are bothering you.' He looked at Gerritt. 'I recommend that Doctor Tulp takes a look at him.' Gerritt nodded.

'Thank you Jakop. I will call on you in a day or two and we can have that game of Klaver Jassen.'

'That would be fine,' replied Jakop. 'Now, if you will excuse me, I must return to my group. They are expecting me to lead in a joyful melody in praise of Bacchus.' Jakop chuckled as he returned to his friends, leaving the little bottle on the table beside Hanzel.

'Do you have a place to sleep?' asked Gerritt.

'I gave the serving girl a guilder. She assured me that included a place to sleep.' Hanzel looked up at Gerritt, who was standing over him.

'Let her keep it. We will go to my house. I have a spare room that you may use as your own. You will be comfortable there.'

Hanzel stared wide eyed at the man standing there. He could not believe his ears. His new friend was giving him a place to stay. Hanzel looked up for a moment and thanked God for his good fortune. 'Thank you,' replied Hanzel. 'I hope that I can be worthy of this honour.'

Gerritt smiled and put his hand on Hanzel's shoulder. 'Don't worry, my young friend, you will earn your keep and provide good company I am sure.' He looked towards the door, then back at Hanzel. 'Come, Hanzel. We will go now and you can take your laudanum at my house. Then you will have a good sleep before we see Doctor Tulp in the morning. He will make you good as new.'

Gerritt helped Hanzel to his feet. He waved to the serving girl, who walked over to see if any change was required. Hanzel regarded her and smiled. 'It's alright. You may keep the change. I won't be needing a place to sleep, after all. Thank you for your hospitality. Your food and ale is excellent.'

'Thank you for saying so,' replied the girl. She smiled at Gerritt. 'Are you going to teach him how to make swords?'

'He'll learn a lot more than that, my dear Grechen. He'll learn a great deal more.' Gerritt laughed and then led Hanzel out of the inn to his waiting carriage. They drove in silence through the rain for twenty minutes; arriving at the home, workshop, and storefront of de Witt & Zoon, Purveyors in Arms, not far from the port of Amsterdam, where hundreds of ships lay at anchor in the harbour or beside dozens of piers and docks. 'I have a nice little sloop tied up over there,' said Gerritt, pointing in the direction where the ships lay. But, come, Hanzel, walk quickly so you won't get very wet in this rain.' Gerritt led the way and the two new friends walked up ten steps and entered the front door of the storefront. They arrived in a small foyer. Gerritt took out a key and unlocked the other door. Then they stepped into the shop. Gerritt lit some candles so that Hanzel could have a cursory look.

What Hanzel saw was incredible. In the flickering light of the candles, Hanzel saw more swords, halberds, bows, crossbows, spears, pikes, helmets, cuirasses, and the like than he had ever seen before, notwithstanding the *Armory Inn*. Racks of swords, short swords, claymores, sabres, rapiers, knives, and stilettos lined one entire wall. On stands various components of body armour and chain mail was displayed. In other racks stood spears, halberds, and pikes. Assorted shields hung from the rafters.

'This is even more of a collection than at the inn,' said Hanzel enthusiastically.

'Just wait until you see all of this in the daytime,' enthused Gerritt. 'But come. We must go through the back, to the stairs which lead to the living quarters. You will meet my dear grandmother, my wife, and our housekeeper.'

'What about your son?' asked Hanzel. 'It said, de Witt and Zoon on the sign out front.'

Gerritt turned to Hanzel. 'My son died in an accident. My wife is very sensitive about it. I appreciate it if you don't mention it with her.'

The two new friends stood on the stairs for a moment before climbing up to the living quarters where the three women were playing cards. Plenty of candles lit the room.

'We were waiting for you, Gerritt,' said an attractive woman, whom Hanzel assumed was Missus de Witt.

'My love, I bring you, Hanzel Sventska.' Gerritt indicated Hanzel with a flourish.

Gerritt's wife looked Hanzel over but did not say anything, except that her eyes opened wide, as in she was greatly surprised and somewhat shocked. Then she looked at the older woman, who looked at her at the same time. They exchanged a look and then Gerritt's wife said to the older woman, 'It's unbelievable.'

'I know,' replied the older woman. Then they both regarded Hanzel with wide eyed expressions. 'He's the spitting image.'

'I know,' replied Gerritt's wife, smiling. 'Welcome, young Hanzel Sventska.' She put out her hand and Hanzel took it. Her hand was warm and gentle. 'And what brings you here?'

'He is my new apprentice. I knew he was the one the moment I heard him speak and took a good look at him.' Gerritt regarded Hanzel and put an arm over his shoulders. 'This young man is going to learn the art of weapons making.'

Hanzel nodded and smiled.

'But first we must nurse him back to health. He was badly beaten and three of his fingers were broken.' Gerritt pointed to Hanzel's damaged hand.

The ladies were shocked to see the young man damaged so. 'Oh, my goodness!' they exclaimed.

'You must be in great pain,' said Missus de Witt.

'Oh, you poor young man,' said the older woman.

'What happened?' asked the housekeeper.

Gerritt looked at Hanzel and noted that the young fellow looked tired and in pain. 'It is better he get to bed and rest. Jakop gave us some medicine for him. He is going to take some and then we are going to show him his room.' He looked at his wife. 'Is the room ready to receive a guest?'

'The room is always ready,' she replied. 'By the looks of him, he should get into bed, the sooner the better.'

'Thank you,' said Hanzel. He bowed to the ladies and then followed Gerritt, who showed him the room, at the back, behind the kitchen. On the way Gerritt had picked up a small spoon from the counter they passed by. Gerritt lit the three candles in the room from his own, and then reminded Hanzel to take the medicine as he gave him the little spoon.

'We'll talk more in the morning,' said Gerritt gently. 'Have a good night, young Hanzel Sventska.'

'Thank you, Gerritt,' replied Hanzel. 'And a good night to you too.'

When Hanzel was alone he decided the first thing to do was to take the Laudanum. His fingers were throbbing. Since the pain was quite intense, Hanzel decided he would double up the amount of the medicine, licking the spoon clean. He put the cork back into the little bottle and set it down on the table beside the bed. The candle holder stood on this table, as well.

Hanzel sat on the edge of the bed and felt the mattress. It was basically a sack filled with cotton and quite comfortable. Several large pillows and plenty of blankets covered the bed. Hanzel knew he would be happy sleeping on that bed. He lay back and relaxed. He let out a long sigh. *This is incredible. Who would have thought it possible? I'm a swordmaker's apprentice and this is my room.* Hanzel could not believe his good fortune. He was free of his father and a life of oppression and suffering. He could already tell that the people, into whose household he had landed, were kind, gentle folk.

As he thusly lay there thinking about what a wonderful new life he had landed in, the opium began to work its magic and he drifted off into a pleasant euphoric sleep, where he felt no pain and dreamed only of happy futures. He never noticed his damaged fingers as he slept with a smile on his face.

Next morning Hanzel woke up refreshed and energized. He had completed an excellent sleep, the like of which he had not experienced since he could ever remember; not even in his mother's womb; where he was traumatized by his father's yelling and beatings of his mother. He looked around his new room. *I actually have my own room! My own bed which I don't have to share. And my own chair and a table with a candle stand. My very own candle stand!* As he thusly thought about the candle stand he looked over at it and noticed that the candles had burned down through the night and made a beautiful waxen sculpture of drippings. As he stared at the wax he could see it move and form all kinds of things; from dragons to people.

He slowly sat up in bed and stretched luxuriously. Hanzel felt he was in heaven.

Chapter 9

Kabel stood staring through the bars of the tiny window of the cell he shared with twenty others. The place was a hell hole and smelled worse. The only inmate with whom he was acquainted was Henk, however he was being held in an other cell on account of Kabel threatening to kill him if he could lay his hands on him. Kabel and Henk had been there for three weeks by this time and smelled like it too. Kabel was miserable.

As he was thusly standing there, staring out of the little window of the cell, a man with a nasty scar running down his face came over to him. 'Ay. Don I know you from somewhere?'

Kabel looked at the man for a moment and returned his stare out of the barred little window. 'Never seen you before.'

'Ya, ya, I have seen you before.' The man thought for a moment while gesturing with his right hand. 'Sure, how can I forget such a big man, like you. Especially one with such a voice.'

'I never seen you before, now piss off,' replied Kabel not bothering to turn around to face the man.

'My name is Kees. You must remember me. Weren't you the one who came looking for your son? At the city gate.'

'Vhat zun?'

'The one you said had run away.'

'Vhat concern is dat of yours?' Kabel continued to stare out of the window, wishing the man would go away. He was feeling irritable. His wounds were bothering him and Laudanum was non existent there in jail. He was awaiting trial, which was upcoming in a week. He and Henk were both being tried for murder, along with several others. Henk was allegedly guilty of murdering William's wife and son, who were found in the abandoned well. Both Kabel and Henk claimed innocence. They would likely be tortured to extract the confessions. Kees was there on thievery charges. It was his tenth time and could be his last, he figured. Kabel regarded Kees. 'So what if you have seen me before?'

'I have news about the boy,' wheezed Kees. 'At least, I think I do. The boy I am thinking of surely fits the description you gave us; white blond hair and big blue eyes...'

Kabel regarded the man; slight interest registering in his black eyes. 'Vhat of him?'

'I saw him.'

Kabel's interest was piqued. 'Vhat do you mean, you saw him?'

'I think it was him. Sure looked like the kid you described. Skinny kid, about twelve or thirteen with really white blond hair and blue eyes.'

Kabel nodded. 'Ya, that describes him, alright. Vhat vas he doing?'

'He stepped out of a carriage and carried a long package into a fancy house me and my friends was keeping an eye on, before we were caught.'

'Is dat it? Is dat all you have to tell me?' Kabel grabbed the man by the front of his torn old coat.

Kees looked at Kabel's big hand on his lapel. 'Hey! There's no need to get violent.' He tried to push Kabel's hand away. Seeing that was impossible, he sighed. 'At least it shows that the kid is alive and obviously doing alright.'

Kabel pushed Kees back as he released his hold on his coat. He grunted and returned his gaze out of the little barred window. 'Dat zun vas never any good. I don't care about him anymore. Dere are odder mouths to feed.'

Kees stared at Kabel's back for a moment. Then, seeing that Kabel was not socially inclined, he slunk off to talk with another prisoner.

Meanwhile, Hanzel had already been in the employ of Mister de Witt for four weeks. He was enjoying his work. There was always something new for him to do. Sometimes it was counting and placing weapons in their racks. Other times he polished steel. Every once in a while, Gerritt would show him some aspect of the art of weapon making. He would show Hanzel the forge in the blacksmith's shop and how they made the steel for the weapons and armour they made there. Hanzel met all of the workers, who either fashioned chain mail to order, or sharpened steel blades until they could cut hairs. Hanzel especially liked it when one of the masters demonstrated the sharpness of a blade by neatly slicing through a thick bundle of straw made to look like a man. The man was cut in half. Hanzel grimaced involuntarily as he thought of someone being cut in half. He cringed everytime the test was done. The best times were those when Hanzel got to go out in the company's carriage and deliver an item. He felt important. It was on one of those occasions when Kees saw Hanzel.

Eventually, after two more weeks, Kabel was brought up on trial before three judges and a jury of twelve. It did not take very long for him to be found guilty of murdering his wife and sentenced to breaking and braiding on the wheel. Henk was found guilty of the attempted murder of Kabel and the murder of William's wife Alice and their son. He was sentenced to the same fate. The executions were set for a week hence.

There had not been a good double breaking in a while. People were quickly spreading the word. The public murder of two men on wheels was a sight to behold. The topic of conversation amongst those who took an interest in executions was whether they would do them at the same time, or one after the other. One after another would prolong the show. Although hearing two different men screaming at the same time would also be very entertaining, for those so inclined.

Executions were also good for the business of pickpockets and food vendors. People came to be entertained and they grew hungry during the several hours a good breaking could take. Knee bones alone could take twenty minutes to break through. It took time to break a man properly.

News of the execution of two murderers came to Hanzel's ears three days before the event. The names of the unfortunate victims was not made known to him as he helped to polish the steel instruments the executioners were going to use. The bars were heavy two inch square bars, four feet long with a round handle for two hands. The handles were wrapped with leather. Hanzel was also given the job of oiling the leather handles. He wondered who would wield those lethal bars. *Whoever they are, they have to be pretty strong. These things weigh a ton.* He grinned at the master chainmailer. 'Can you swing one of these, Master Wenders?'

'No, those things are pretty heavy alright,' he said. 'I can't swing one.'

'Who are the executioners?' asked Hanzel.

'Some no neck giants, I should think. It amazes me that those fellows can use those things on living human beings.' The master chainmailer grimaced. 'I don't like killing and maiming. I don't find much joy in it, like some folks. That is why I make chainmail, to at least do what I can to protect people. I make some of the best chainmail in this part of the world. People come from all over the place just to buy chainmail and weapons here. Master Gerritt is a first class weapons maker. A sword which he made was presented to the emperor, Rudolf three years ago.'

'Impressive,' replied Hanzel. 'I am still amazed that he took me in. He didn't even know me. We just met at his brother's inn.'

'Young Hanzel. I will tell you something.' Master Wenders leaned closer. 'You are the spitting image of his son, Charles, who was killed in a tragic accident.'

'What happened?' Hanzel stopped rubbing oil and listened intently.

'Master Gerritt does not want to talk about it and neither does his wife.'

'Yes, I know. I have never brought it up because Master Gerritt told me not to ask about Charles.'

'They don't want to be reminded. It was a tragic accident which nobody foresaw was even possible.' Master Wenders pointed to a crossbow hanging on a ceiling beam. 'See that crossbow?'

Hanzel adjusted his position in order to take a better look. 'Ya, I see it. What about it?'

'That's the crossbow that killed Charles.'

'The crossbow that killed Charles?' Hanzel regarded Master Wenders and then looked back at the weapon, hanging on the crossbeam.

'It was resting in that vise over there. It was on the vise because someone, who isn't here anymore, was working on it. He was adjusting various things and had a dart in the thing to test how smoothly it could fly out of the weapon. There was supposed to be a target at which it was directed. The dart flew out of the crossbow and hit Charles square in the heart. He died right there.' Master Wenders pointed to the place where Charles spent his last seconds on earth.

Hanzel stared at the place where Charles met his demise. He shivered thinking of a lethal dart hitting his own heart. 'Those things are dangerous.'

'They certainly are. Especially in the wrong hands,' replied the chainmailer.

'What hands are those?'

'The ones intent upon killing you.' He pointed to the chainmail shirt he was working on. 'That's why you wear one of these. It will at least give you a chance.'

'Will it stop one of those crossbow darts?' Hanzel touched the steel shirt and admired how precisely each link fit to make a tight mesh of hardened metal rings.

'Those darts are very lethal. They can penetrate this mail shirt, depending on the crossbow's strength and the type of head on the dart. Distance is also a factor.' Master Wenders looked lovingly at the shirt he was making. 'This is more for thwarting sword thrusts. These mail shirts are really not that much in demand anymore. Most now prefer a steel cuirass, such as that one, over there.' He pointed to a magnificent piece of steel armour to protect a man's chest. 'That'll stop arrows, darts, swords....'

'What about a heavy calibre ball?' asked Hanzel, examining the cuirass.

'Depends on the charge used and the distance the ball has come. At close range, a heavy calibre ball, say one of 50 millimeters, with a maximum charge using fine grained powder, could penetrate it.' Master Wenders came over to stand beside Hanzel who was examining the breastplate.

'So, tell me more about Charles. You say he looked like me?' Hanzel regarded the chainmailer.

Master Wenders looked directly into Hanzel's eyes. 'Same slim build as you. Your white hair and your big blue eyes. The shape of your chin. It is all pretty uncanny, really. He'd be about your age, now. If none of us around here didn't know any better, we would all agree that you were Charles and not Hanzel Sventska.'

'That's very interesting. Too bad his son had to die in order for me to find a place in the world. However, I am grateful and bless Charles, who I am sure is in Paradise with the Father.' Hanzel looked up for a moment and then crossed himself.

'You better finish up those handles,' reminded Master Wenders. 'They're coming to pick those up first thing tomorrow morning. The oil must soak into the leather and not be slippery for the executioners.'

Hanzel nodded thoughtfully and quickly returned to his task. *So, Charles actually looked like me. I wonder if Master Gerritt has any intentions of adopting me? That would be alright. He and his Missus de Witt are so good to me. Everyone is so good to me here. Now I understand. I look like their son.*

Master Gerritt stepped into the room and examined the chainmail shirt Master Wenders was working on. 'Nice work, Wenders. You haven't lost your touch.'

'Thank you, Gerritt. I knew you'd be pleased.'

Master Gerritt regarded Hanzel, who was sitting on a bench with his back to the two men. He was carefully oiling the handle of the second bar. 'How are the two of you getting along back here?'

'He's a good boy,' replied Master Wenders. 'He is doing good work. Look how well he has polished the executioner's instruments.'

Gerritt grimaced. 'A grisly business. Every time those things are brought out I feel a great sadness.'

'Two murderers, they say. One killed his wife and the other killed a mother and her son,' replied Master Wenders. 'The one smashed his wife's head on a table and the other shot and strangled the mother and son and then threw them down a well. It's a terrible thing. Both men confessed under torture.'

'How do you know so much about this?' asked Master Gerritt, regarding the chainmailer.

'My friend, who works at the courthouse, told me over a glass of Jenever last night.'

'Do you know the names of the miscreants?' asked Master Gerritt.

Master Wenders shook his head. 'No names. Just the crimes.'

Gerritt stroked his beard. 'A nasty business. A very nasty business, indeed.' He regarded his chainmailer. 'I suppose you'll be going to see it?'

'What? The execution?' Master Wenders grimaced. 'No, thank you. I don't enjoy that sort of thing.'

'What about you, young Hanzel? Do you want to go to see an execution?'

Hanzel stared at Master Gerritt. 'I've never seen an execution.' He shook his head. 'I don't know if I have the stomach for such a spectacle. It's pretty gruesome, I understand.'

Gerritt nodded. 'It is that, most definitely. A public execution serves an important function. It shows the people what the consequences are for murder, most abominable.' He pointed to the heavy steel bar Hanzel was working on. 'Those things are very effective in persuading people to keep within the law.' Gerritt raised his right index finger and pointed up. 'The law says, thou shalt not kill.'

'And yet, here we are making armour and weapons,' replied Hanzel.

'Indeed we are,' replied Gerritt sadly. 'We live in an imperfect world. There are still those who are intent upon murder and mayhem. There are still those who have their greedy eyes on our success. They do not want us Netherlanders to be too rich and too powerful. They cast covetous eyes in our direction and we must defend ourselves. We need good weapons to do that. What we do here is of major importance to the welfare of our city and our country. Because of what we do here, the city fathers gave me their seal of approval for ten years in a row. My weapons are some of the very best in the region. Did I ever tell you about one of my swords going to the emperor?'

Hanzel smiled. 'No, you *never* told me about that.'

'A beautiful sword it was. The pommel was of chased gold with filigree and the head of a dragon. The grip was of Italian leather and cherry wood. I will never forget how magnificent the quillian complimented the hilt. For the blade we chose a straight long shaft of choice steel, polished until it was a mirror. Into the blade we incised the Emperor's name and titles.' He turned to Master Wenders. 'Wasn't that a fine blade, eh, Wenders?'

Master Wenders nodded. 'Ya, Gerritt, it was a magnificent blade. The Emperor was very pleased with it, I'm sure.'

Gerritt was beaming. 'So, Hanzel, are you curious, even a little bit, what those bars can do to a man. I mean, you have polished them and are making them ready.'

'I really haven't seen any weapons used against anybody,' replied Hanzel. 'I suppose it is all very grisly.'

'Yes, it is that. However, you are old enough to see such a thing, and it will harden you to understand that there are consequences for breaking our laws.'

Hanzel regarded Master Gerritt. 'So, I take it that you are going?'

'Of course I am going. I don't know these poor fellows. However, I trust they were properly tried and found guilty of murder.' Gerritt shrugged his shoulders. 'I suggest you bring something to plug your ears, if you can't handle the screams.'

'Screams?' Hanzel looked at Master Wenders, who shrugged his shoulders.

'That's mostly why I don't go,' said Master Wenders, returning to his work. 'I can't handle the screaming.'

'Well, I am going. The event happens in three days. The show begins at ten o'clock in the morning. Better get there early, in order to get a good view. They've already built a platform in front of City Hall. For ten florins one can sit on bleachers. I'm tempted, but that's a lot of money.' Gerritt held his purse open, to suggest there was nothing in there. Of course he was fooling nobody. Gerritt de Witt was loaded; just very frugal.

Over the next two days Hanzel struggled with his conscience. *Should I go or not? Can I handle the horror? And, yet, it's something I will always remember and perhaps will serve me for a lesson, although it is very gruesome. I think I should take the opportunity to see something I may never see again, hopefully. I am curious. I think I will take Master Gerritt up on his invitation. I think I can handle it.*

He told Master Gerritt after supper, when Hanzel and he were sitting in his library, that he would like to accompany him to the execution the following day.

Master Gerritt smiled. 'Excellent, my boy. I had a feeling you might want to come. I took a chance and bought you a seat on the bleachers. We'll have an excellent view and see how those steel bars are made to work.'

Hanzel stared at Gerritt and slowly nodded his head. 'Yes, I'll see it for myself.'

There was a long pause as the man and the boy stared off into inner space and thought about what they were going to witness the next day.

Chapter 10

Hanzel woke up not feeling particularly spry. His limbs felt heavy and his head hurt from a night of unsettling dreams. It was the morning of executions in front of City Hall. There were to be several hangings and two breakings on the wheel. Hangings were commonplace and used for highwaymen, pirates, witches, sometimes homosexuals, that sort of person. Sometimes the trials were fair, sometimes not. Such is the judicial system. It is not perfect. Neither were hangings. Sometimes the results were quite horrific. For some, that potential for the horrific and macabre drew them out for the show. Executions were an entertainment. Breakings and braidings were not so common anymore, and were reserved for loathed individuals, wife killers, and those who kill innocent women and children. Wife killers were definitely not tolerated. And people who practiced paedophilia. Someone who was both a wife killer and a paedophile, such an one was loathed especially. Their executions could take a lot longer.

Unknown to Hanzel, his father Kabel had molested all of his daughters at one time or another. Kate was the first to confess to the suspicions which were brought forth in the trial. Once Kate had come forth, Miep and Marika also came forward and confessed that their father not only beat them and their mother, but he had also had sexual intercourse with the girls. Miep remembered it started as far back as her toddlerhood. When she confessed that, the court went silent and then an audible sound of revulsion filled the space. The judge had to call for order before the trial could continue.

Kabel never touched the boys, other than to lay a good belting on them from time to time. Those boys, who were able to be at the trial, Wim and Henrik, told the court how their father had used the buckle end of his belt on many occasions; to teach them lessons. It was obvious, from the way the boys regarded their father, the man had not won the hearts of his children. They loathed him and now that he had killed their mother, they hated him even more.

Every time one of the children confessed some horrible truth, Kabel flew in a rage, jumping up from his bench in the dock, accusing the children of all manner of terrible things; even suggesting that the girls came on to him at an early age. That his molestations of them were brought on by the girls being provocative. There were audible gasps in the audience.

Hanzel knew about none of it. He did not know about his mother's death. He never knew about his father's crimes. And, he never heard anything about the court case and his father having been found guilty and sentenced to a horrible death. When Hanzel set out, with Gerritt de Witt, in the company's carriage, accompanied by Missus de Witt, her mother, Master Calponi, and the other apprentice; Steven Pedersen, he had no idea who he was going to see executed. According to the proclamation, there were seven names. Hanzel never saw the menu. Even if he did, he could not read it. Hanzel had yet to learn that skill.

When they arrived at the City Hall plaza, there were already hundreds of people milling about and hundreds more standing in their places, to get as good a view as possible. Those who could afford to sit in the bleachers were already beginning to arrive, as well. There was an excitement in the air, like a carnival. Vendors were hawking: salted or pickled herrings, breads, buns, sausages, onions, boiled eggs, ale, Jenever, rum, miniature scaffolds, dolls from which entrails could be extracted, little hangman's nooses, and wheels with dolls strapped to them, plus more mundane things such as: new clothes, shoes, pots and pans, that sort of thing. The place was already a circus. The air smelled of people, food, tobacco, ale, and all manner of subtle whiffs containing hints of piss and excrement. An excited hubbub filled the space, as people shared stories of previous executions, family and friends, business and pleasure, and of course, what the menu was for this day.

Several crows cawed overhead; looking forward to what delicious food things might come their way at some point in the day. Gulls filled the remaining space with their screams and laughter. The overall cacophony necessitated speaking at higher volumes than normal.

Gerritt de Witt and company had bought excellent seats in the middle of the bleachers, near the top. They had a perfect view of the scaffold which consisted of a floor of planks, eight feet above the ground. The entire space was about 15 by 20 feet. A set of steps led up to it from the City Hall side. At the back of the platform was a sturdy beam set on three uprights, about eight feet off the platform. Five hangman's nooses hung from the beam, evenly spaced, two on one side of the centre upright and three on the other side. At the front of the platform, exactly in the centre stood an upright short, steel axle, firmly bolted to the platform and reinforced. Two large wheels lay on either side. To one side stood a small table with assorted objects covered by a black cloth. Hanzel could not tell what was on the table, other than the two steel bars, which he had polished and prepared, because they stuck out of the cloth on each side.

'What's under the cloth on the table?' asked Hanzel.

'The executioner's instruments,' replied Steven. 'You'll see.'

Hanzel could feel his heart beating as the excitement was building in the crowd. By this time, several thousand people were standing or sitting in the plaza. People had come out on their balconies, or were standing at their windows in the buildings around the square. The noise was becoming quite deafening, as hundreds and hundreds of people carried on conversations over the yells of vendors hawking wares and screeching gulls. As Hanzel watched, he noted a small group of urchins scouting out a prize; a fat burgher with a purse. He smiled as he watched two of the young boys distract the man, while two others lifted the man's coat, and another, a girl, stole the purse and ran off with it. Hanzel laughed.

As Hanzel scanned the crowd he saw a girl he recognized. It was Angela. *She's probably wondering where her money is.* He laughed. *I'm not going over there to tell her, either. She's looks like she's put on some pounds. Could it be that she's pregnant?*

'What are you laughing about?' asked Steven. 'This is not a place to be laughing. This is an execution we are attending.'

Hanzel stopped laughing, as he turned to face his friend. 'You're right, Steven. This is a solemn occasion. However, I couldn't help but laugh when I saw some urchins pickpocket that fat man, over there.' Hanzel indicated the man. 'And I was thinking about that girl, over there.' Hanzel pointed to Angela. 'I think I know her.'

'You have to be so careful at big events where there are a lot of people. Executions bring all kinds out, trust me. I've been to two others. Nothing as dramatic as this, though. Seven in one day. That's a lot.'

Hanzel gazed out over the crowd and the scaffold. 'Those who are about to be killed, I wonder what they're feeling right now. Knowing within a few hours they'll be dead.'

Steven regarded Hanzel with a sideways glance and then returned his gaze in the direction of a buxom young wench who was serving ale off a tray she carried over her head. 'I would think they're scared shitless.' Steven looked back at Hanzel. 'Wouldn't you be scared shitless? I mean, here you are, facing death. You actually know it's coming. It's waiting for you, right there on that scaffold. And, maybe you've seen it before; an execution, that is. And therefore you know what's coming. I would be scared shitless because I can guarantee you my brother, it will hurt. Especially for those two unfortunate ones they saved for last.'

'You mean the breaking and braiding?' Hanzel clenched his teeth.

'Especially those two. If I was one of them, I would want to be poisoned before it begins. Hopefully you're dead before they go too far.' Steven grimaced. 'You have no idea, Hanzel. The horror. It's unbelievable. You will hear screams like you have never heard before. Even the toughest men scream like women. It's inevitable. I mean, think of it. You've bumped your shins or your knees before. You know what that feels like. Now imagine one of those steel bars smashing down on those bones.'

Hanzel shivered. 'I'm beginning to think, perhaps I shouldn't have come.' He looked at Gerritt, merrily conversing with some friends sitting on the tier below them.

Steven put his hand on Hanzel's forearm. 'Don't worry, Hanzel. I think you can handle this. It'll make you into a man. It'll toughen you up.' Steven grabbed Hanzel's shoulders and gave him a little shake. He grinned at Hanzel and then returned his gaze toward the crowd gathering in ever increasing numbers.

'People have come from all over.' Hanzel pointed to a man and woman. 'Look, people from Vollendam. I know their costume.'

'How so?' asked Steven.

'My father is a fisherman. Vollendammers are fisher folk. My father has a friend, if you can call him that; someone he does business with; who came to our house a couple of times. He was dressed like that.'

'I see,' replied Steven, offhandedly, not really paying close attention to what Hanzel was saying. Steven was more intent on the girl and was trying to signal her to come over. 'I'm going to buy an ale from her. Do you want something to drink, Hanzel?'

'Oh, er, sure. Ale will be fine. Thanks.'

'Oiy guvnor!' shouted a voice. 'Guvnor! D'you an your pahty care for sum fresh errings? Jus of'n the boat.' An ill dressed, odiferous fishmonger was standing at the bottom of the bleachers and shouting up at Gerritt.

Gerritt recognized the fishmonger's voice. He looked down at the short, fat man. 'We'll have,' he looked around at his group and counted, and then addressed his friends on the seats below, 'Alexander, what about you? And you, my dear Martha? A herring?'

Of course, everyone wanted a fresh herring so Gerritt ordered seven herrings.

The fishmonger handed the herrings up. They were nicely placed on oiled paper and were accompanied with a generous amount of chopped onions. Gerritt paid the fishmonger and thanked him for bringing them.

The herring was fresh and perfectly salted. Hanzel gratefully ate the fish and onions. It was the perfect snack before the show.

A moment later the bell on the City Hall clock counted the tenth hour. A great cheer rang out from the crowd. What they had come all that way to see, some for hundreds of kilometers, was about to take place; the execution of seven criminals in one day. The excitement was building. The crowd was ready for a show.

Several dignitaries stepped up onto the platform. One of them was carrying a big Bible. He was dressed all in black except for a white collar. The next dignitary was dressed in blue. He was carrying a device for listening to a man's heartbeat. Another man was carrying a scroll. He was also completely dressed in black, except for a different white collar to that of the priest. Edward van Sullivan was a doctor of law and the director of affairs. The other dignitaries were the mayor, with his golden chains, the three executioners in their leather hoods and aprons, and their three assistants in aprons but no hoods. When

Edward van Sullivan held up his right hand a great hush went through the crowd and within a minute, stillness prevailed.

A crow cawed.

'Ladies and gentlemen, you have all come here to witness what is done to those who will not obey our laws. This is an auspicious occasion, seeing as that we are teaching lessons to seven villains. Seven vile, dastardly villains who have taken it upon themselves to defy our rules; to not do unto others as they would see done to themselves. NO! They chose to rob, steal, pillage, and plunder. They chose to defile their daughters and murder their wives. Yes, such are those who you will see dance into the halls of perdition today!' The speaker paused for effect.

The crowd went wild with hoots and howls. A great applause expressed the crowd's appreciation for the words. The crowd loved seeing villains dancing into the halls of perdition.

Edward van Sullivan raised his hand and the crowd fell quiet, once again.

'Before we begin with this really big show, the mayor would like to say a few words of welcome.' He gestured for the mayor to step forward. 'Ladies and gentlemen! Your mayor, Jacob Witsz!'

Most people clapped. Some did not.

'Ladies and gentlemen. Thank you for coming out today in such large numbers. We appreciate your business and pray you will respect our rules. Please clean up after yourselves. Last time there was quite a mess left behind. It is not the city's job to clean up after you. We are providing you a day of entertainment, the least you can do is take your garbage with you, or dump it in the bins we have set up. And, please refrain from throwing things up here, such as rotten fruit and vegetables. If we have to keep cleaning up the scaffold it will only slow things down.' He looked up at the sky. 'You don't want to be here until night fall, do you?'

'We'll be here until night fall if you keep talking!' shouted a voice.

'Yeah, get on with it!' shouted another.

Jacob frowned, but kept his composure. He was used to hecklers. After all, he was a politician. 'I understand you don't want to hear long winded speeches. As your mayor, I know what you want. You want action. You want decisiveness. You want...'

'Come on! Stop talking you old windbag!' shouted an impatient voice.

'Stop stalling!' shouted a voice near the bleachers Hanzel was sitting on.

'Yeah, stop stalling! shouted a third voice, which started the crowd chanting. 'Stop stalling! Stop stalling! Stop stalling!'

Edward van Sullivan held up both of his hands, bringing them up and down several times to quiet the crowd. When they were sufficiently still he told them to have some respect for the mayor and let him finish his speech.

'Allright, let him finish!' shouted a woman near the front of the scaffold.

Jacob nodded thanks to Edward and then thanked the crowd for letting him finish what he had to say, which actually wasn't anything, really. But, like all politicians, Jacob Witsz was no different. Even if he had nothing to say, he still wanted to say it. 'So, without further ado. Enjoy the show!' The mayor waved as a few people clapped and hooted. The people loved it when politicians made short speeches. That meant show time was closer.

Edward van Sullivan unrolled the scroll and held it up. 'The first person who will hang today is, Bart from Rotterdam, an itinerant laborer who raped one Katerina van Kelt within the perimeter of the city. The High Court has sentenced him to be hanged. Bring forth the prisoner!'

A homely, 20 something, with a mop of course brown hair; obviously not entirely one hundred percent in the cranium, was hauled out of a tumbrel at the back of the platform. He was led up the stairs by two of the sheriffs. When Bart reached the top, Hanzel could see that his hands were tied behind his back. The chief executioner pointed to the rope he wanted to use for Bart. The two men who brought him up to the platform led the young man to his rope. Then they returned to the prisoner's cart.

The executioner placed the noose around Bart's neck and tightened it. Then he stepped back in order for the doctor of theology to say a few words. As the learned doctor approached Bart, the condemned man began to piss in his britches. He was obviously scared shitless, as Steven identified, otherwise Bart might have moved his bowels into his britches as well. When the theologian was finished, he nodded to the executioner who looked to the director of affairs.

'Do you have anything you wish to say, Bart of Rotterdam?' asked Edward van Sullivan.

Bart stared dumbfoundedly at the crowd assembled on the three sides of the platform. He was obviously embarrassed at having pissed himself. He nodded to Edward. Then, in a scared, shaky voice he said, 'I didn't mean to rape er. It just sorta happen like.'

'Like that broken arm just happened to my daughter!?' shouted a woman from the crowd.

'And what about her broken ribs?! You bastard!' added a man's angry voice.

Bart stared at the woman. 'I didn't mean for it to happen...'

The crowd booed. Some hissed. Others yelled, 'HANG HIM!'

Bart stood there and did not say anything more.

'Is that it?' asked Edward.

Bart nodded. Tears were streaming from his eyes.

Edward van Sullivan nodded to the executioner, indicating he was good to go. And go he did. The exectioner's assistants tied Bart's ankles together and held him six inches off the floor of the platform. Bart wriggled, but it was to no avail. The two assistants were very strong men.

While the two assistants held Bart above the platform, the executioner pulled on the rope which was passed over the crossbeam. When the rope was tight, he tied it off on a cleat. Then he signaled to the assistants to let Bart swing. They gently let him go and Bart from Rotterdam was hanging by his neck, his legs in space, about six inches above the platform.

Bart dangled on the end of the rope and began to choke and wiggle. As he wiggled, the rope tightened ever more over his windpipe, making his tongue stick out of his mouth; quickly becoming blue and swollen. Hanzel could see that Bart's eyes were bugged out as he wiggled and wriggled. After nearly four minutes Bart could dance no more. He gave a final kick and was dead.

The doctor with the listening device checked Bart's breathing. He nodded and Edward van Sullivan noted the time in a small book.

The crowd was murmuring. 'Come on! Get on wid it! Bring on the nex one! Stop yer stallin! ...'

'Boy, they're impatient,' observed Hanzel.

'It's always like that,' said Master Calponi, who was sitting on Hanzel's left. 'They've come for the big event. Hangings are common place.'

Hanzel stared at dead Bart dangling from his rope. 'I'll bet that Bart wishes they were not so commonplace.'

'Yes, I suppose so,' replied Master Calponi with his unusual Italian accent.

Edward van Sullivan raised his hand and the crowd calmed down. 'Next! We have a villain so foul and dastardly you will be happy to see him dance. This monster robbed people at gun point!'

'He robbed my mother!' shouted a voice from the crowd.

'He stole from my cousin!' shouted another voice.

'Hang im!' shouted a third voice.

'HANG HIM!' shouted the crowd.

Edward van Sullivan raised his right hand. 'Quiet! he shouted. 'Let me finish!'

The crowd quieted down.

'The man who is about to be hanged is known by the names of: Harmon Steek, Hans van Sloot, and Harmon the Terrible.'

'Hang im!' shouted another voice.

'Come on, get on with it. We haven't got all day!' shouted the crowd.

'Be quiet, you riff raff. This is a solemn occasion. I must read the charges.' Edward stared at the impatient crowd.

'Well get on with it then,' replied an old crone near the front of the scaffold.

'This man!' Shouted Edward above the crowd. 'This man, Harman van der Loos has been charged with highway robbery. He has been repeatedly caught red handed in the act of stealing people's valuables at gunpoint. The high court has sentenced him to hang.' He regarded Harman. 'Do you have anything to say?'

Harman looked out over the crowd and began to speak.

'Hey, come on! Get on with it! We don't want to hear no speeches!'

'Make im dance! Make im dance!' yelled the crowd. They had been waiting too long and were not interested in speeches from low lifes like the highwayman. However, for some, that was the entertainment. There were people in the crowd who wrote the words of condemned people on paper and published them. They were the ones yelling, 'Quiet! Let him speak!' Hanzel watched as a scuffle broke out between opposing camps near the bleachers.

Eventually, order prevailed and the crowd became quiet as the highwayman stepped forward. He was a tall, lanky character with a large golden earring in his left earlobe. He was unshaven but ruggedly good looking. He was dressed like a gentleman, except for the fact his shirt was open, revealing a fine golden chain and a medallion.

'Oh, he's a handsome one,' remarked Missus de Witt to her friend.

'Isn't he, though. He's scrumptious. If I wasn't married, I'd want a one such as he.' The friend tittered into her fan.

'Don't let your husband hear you talking like that,' reminded Missus de Witt.

'I already heard it,' chuckled the husband. 'If she wants to go running after highwaymen, she can be my guest.'

His wife regarded him for a moment and gave him a poke in the ribs. 'Oh, you....' she said. He and Gerritt laughed.

'Shhh,' he's about to speak, said Gerritt.

'I expect you all have come here to have some fun. Some entertainment. Well, I sure hope I can provide it for you. At least I go out having given something back, in addition to the thousands of florins I have contributed to help my friends, who are poor, struggling people, living on potatoes, while most of you eat far better here in the fair Port of Amsterdam. I am a highwayman because there was no other place for me to do what I believe in, to redistribute wealth to those who need and deserve a better life. You, rich burghers, sitting there up on your bleachers,' he pointed directly at Hanzel. 'And those of you in the crowd who eat three times a day, you have become fat off the backs of others. I believe I did God's work here on earth and am not afraid to die. I hope you will all wake up some day and realize that your unbridled greed will lead you to the GATES OF HELL!' He made a grand gesture and waited for a reaction from the crowd.

'Come on!' shouted someone with a high pitched voice.

'That's enough!' boomed another.

'Get on with it!' shouted a third impatient voice.

'You're not our preacher!' shouted several voices at the same time.

The highwayman looked out over the crowd. 'May you be enlightened someday.' Then he nodded to the executioner who placed the noose around his neck and tightened it. Edward, sensing the impatience of the crowd and their desire for a show, said something into the executioner's ear. The executioner nodded. He gestured to his assistants, who were about to tie Harmon's ankles together, not to do so. Harman smiled. He knew what was coming. 'You'll get the show you want! YOU SPIRITUAL CRIPPLES!'

The executioner, with the help of the assistants, hoisted Harman a few inches off the floor, cleating the rope so that he hung just high enough to be able to touch the floor with his toes. This type of hanging resulted in Harmon doing a choking man's dance on the platform, much to the delight of the crowd, which hooted and hollered as Harmon's face contorted and his blue tongue began to stick out of his mouth; all the while that his feet tried desperately to find a place to touch down and lessen the tension on the rope. The crowd loved it. Edward was pleased. He knew how to put on a really good show.

Hanzel watched in horrid fascination as Harman finally gave his last kicks and choked to death. The doctor inspected the body and indicated that breathing and heartbeat had stopped. Edward again noted the time in his little book.

The crowd applauded. The hanging of the highwayman was the sort of thing they wanted to see. Watching villains dancing, that is what entertained the crowds. Just hoisting them up and watching the hapless victims wriggle a little bit was too lame. The people wanted to watch the condemned dance a jig or a passpied.

Edward stepped forward, scroll in hand. 'The next person condemned to hang on our gallows is a dangerous witch!'

'A WITCH! A WITCH!' shouted the crowd as the unfortunate woman was taken from her tumbrel and pushed up the stairs. Hanzel noted that her clothes were torn and filthy. Her long, dark hair, was matted, and bits of straw were sticking out of it. She had bruises on her cheeks and a black eye. Her fingers appeared to be broken, as were her arms. Hanzel noticed that she could not move them.

'Someone beat her really badly,' remarked Hanzel.

'They do that to witches,' replied Steven matter of factly. 'It's to beat the Devil out of them.'

Hanzel stared at the woman. She did not appear to be completely conscious.

The two sheriff's men led the woman to the front of the platform. The crowd jeered and threw rotten food at her. A tomato splattered on her belly, pieces of it spurting out at Edward, who jumped back. He frowned as he brushed the goop away.

'Stop throwing things!' he shouted. 'You could hurt somebody!'

The crowd laughed.

'This is Maddie van der Sluis, and she is a witch!' began Edward. 'She mixed potions and healed the sick!'

'Ooooh!' yelled the crowd.

'BURN ER!' shouted a voice with an odd Eastern accent.

'Yeah, shouldn't she be burnt?' shouted another voice.

'We want to see a burning!' shouted some others.

Edward van Sullivan stared out over the crowd. 'We are hanging her! So, shut up and listen!' He looked at the disheveled woman and crinkled his nose. She obviously stank. 'Not only did she heal the sick, she did it without advice from learned doctors of medicine and theology. She practiced without a license. And, she kept cats. Black cats! Sinister cats with yellow snake eyes!' Edward was warming up as he continued with a dramatic voice. 'She was seen in the company of others, dancing to a full moon, NAKED!'

The crowd went wild. 'NAKED! She was NAKED?! UNDER A FULL MOON! HANG ER! BURN HER!'

Edward held up his hand and the crowd, now in his control, settled down. 'Because we are a benevolent people, we will not burn her, but we will hang her and make her DANCE HER WITCH'S DANCE FOR YOU!'

The crowd exploded. The people applauded and cheered; whistled and hooted, all the while throwing rotten cabbages, onions, and garlic at the unfortunate woman trembling on the platform and regarding the delirious gathering through half closed eyes.

Edward turned to look at Maddie. 'Do you have anything you want to say, Witch?!'

Maddie slowly opened her eyes and looked defiantly out at the crowd. She took a long breath and straightened herself up as best as she could. Then she began in a voice which surprised Hanzel, it being strong and unwavering. 'You bet I do, Edward van Sullivan. I have plenty to say. You gave me plenty of time to think in that hell hole you threw me in. Even though your people have dislocated my shoulders and broken my arms and fingers, beat me unconscious, and done abominable things to me, I am not dead yet. I still have a voice and I thank you for giving me an opportunity to speak.'

The crowd went dead silent. There were a whole lot of guilty faces in the crowd and relieved ones also, glad it was not them, or a daughter, sister, or a wife up there on that stage of death. The witchcraft issue was a divisive one, however, it was not much discussed in public lest the same fate as that of poor Maddie van der Sluis befell the speakers.

Maddie continued. 'I am thirty four years old. I was born in Amstelveen. Since I was young I have always been interested in healing people. I sought out learned teachers, women and men, who understand how nature works to heal people.'

'Only God heals! shouted a strident voice.

'She's a blasphemer!' She's a pantheist! She's a NATURE LOVER!!!' shouted the maddened crowd.

Hanzel regarded his friend. 'I love nature.'

Steven frowned. 'Yes, so do I, but that is different. She loves nature differently, in that she hugs trees and has conversations with mushrooms.'

'Ah. I see. That's the difference. She's an unnatural nature lover,' observed Hanzel.

Steven nodded. 'That's what makes her a witch.' He put his right index finger to his lips. 'Shhh. She's going to continue. I want to hear what she has to say.'

The crowd had settled down, but was restless.

'When I was older I wanted to study medicine,' continued Maddie bravely.

'Yeah, yeah! Come on get on wid it!' shouted several voices. 'We're not interested in biographies!'

'We eard it all afore!' shouted others. 'If we want biographies, we can go to the library!'

Maddie stared out at the crowd and then looked exasperatedly at Edward van Sullivan, who held up his hands.

'Shut your pie holes you uncivilized scum!' shouted Edward.

'Yeah, let er speak!' shouted a number of supporters.

The crowd quieted down.

Maddie looked at Edward, who nodded for her to continue. 'I am from a poor family and am not a man. They wouldn't let me into the school for medicine.' The man in blue fidgeted. 'I was not allowed into the school for apothecaries, either. So, I learned healing arts from those who practiced them and helped a lot of people. Some of you are here.'

'Yes, it's true! She healed my husband of warts!' yelled a woman.

'My uncle was saved from skin lesions by her,' said someone on the bleachers, near where Hanzel was sitting.

'I am living proof she can heal!' shouted an old man near the front of the crowd. He was leaning on a cane. 'I'd be dead today, if it wasn't for her.'

Edward van Sullivan raised his hand. 'Quiet! Let her continue.'

Maddie looked out at the crowd. 'Thank you, my dear friends for your support.'

The people, to whom Maddie addressed her words were tearful and lamenting the decision of the judges.

'Medicine is a profession of men. When a man gives you medicines he is an apothecary. When women do it you call it witchcraft. You, who think like this are HYPOCRITES! YOU WILL MEET YOUR MAKER FACE TO FACE AND YOU WILL FIND THAT HE IS THE DEVIL!' she screamed.

The crowd instantly reacted. 'SHE INVOKED THE DEVIL! SHE'S A WITCH! HANG ER! STRING ER UP! FOUL WITCH! MAY SHE BURN IN HELL!'

'Are you done, Maddie van der Zluis?' asked Edward van Sullivan.

'There is nothing more to say,' replied Maddie. 'Let the Father's Will Be Done.'

'Amen,' intoned the learned doctor of theology, whose name was, Isaac van Damm. 'May God have mercy on your miserable soul.' He handed the Bible to Maddie to kiss. She kissed the book and then spat on it.

The crowd went bezerk. 'SHE SPAT ON THE BIBLE! HANG ER! HANG ER!'

Edward nodded to the executioner who nodded to his assistants. They led Maddie to her rope and tied her ankles.

'LET'S SEE ER DANCE!' screamed the banshee crowd. 'LET THE WITCH DO HER WITCH'S DANCE! LET HER DANCE INTO THE HALLS OF PERDITION!!!'

Edward looked out at the sociopathic mob as they threw more rotten food. 'ALRIGHT, ALRIGHT! STOP THROWING THINGS! WE'LL LET HER DANCE.'

The people cheered and applauded. They liked to get what they wanted; spoiled burghers that they were; those 17th Century Hollanders. As the assistants untied Maddie's ankles she looked up at the sky. 'Forgive them, Father. They don't know what they are doing.'

The executioner placed the noose around Maddie's neck and made it fast. Then he and his assistants hoisted Maddie off the platform a few inches, where she danced and danced for the ignorant masses until she was dead, dead, dead.

Hanzel wiped tears from his eyes. Watching Maddie swing had a profound effect on him. He thought of the apothecary, Jakop Zuiterman, who had helped him alleviate the pain of his broken fingers. He looked down at the fingers of his left hand and felt them moving much better, already. It being more than a month later, the fingers were healing nicely. He thought about what Maddie had said. She could have helped him and there she was, a dead witch. *The world is screwed up. People have things figured out all wrong. Poor Maddie.* Hanzel stared at the three dead people hanging from the gallows and shook his head sadly.

'Next, ladies and gentlemen, boys and girls,' said Edward, holding up his right hand. Next we have a dastardly young one. A boy of ten, who should have known better. Even young ones fall into the pit of perdition.' He leaned down and waggled his right index finger at some youngsters sitting on top of their father's shoulders. 'This one was caught on more than one occasion, stealing bread from a bakery. A little thief who will pay in Hell for his indiscretion.' Edward looked at the boy standing between the sheriff's helpers. 'Do you have anything to say?'

The boy shook his head. He was trembling. Tears filled his eyes. He looked up at the sky as several white pigeons flew overhead.

Edward signaled the executioner to proceed.

They tied the boy's ankles and hoisted him up. He was dead in two minutes. The crowd remained silent. They never liked seeing children hung. It took Edward a moment to collect himself. He was no supporter of child hangings, either. Anyone under 12, in his opinion was not capable of making life and death decisions, such as stealing bread. Edward considered himself a more enlightened soul in that second decade of the 17th Century. He continued in a somewhat subdued tone; which took a few seconds to regain its former majesty.

'And finally, to complete the day's hangings we have a pirate most scurvy!' shouted Edward van Sullivan. The crowd went completely still and gazed intently at the director of affairs. 'This dastardly pirate robbed seven fishing vessels off the north coast and impeded the herring supply for Amsterdam FOR THREE DAYS!'

The crowd went crazy. 'TEAR HIM TO PIECES! PULL HIM APART! STAKE HIM! CUT HIS HANDS OFF! BATTER HIM AND FRY HIM IN OIL!'

Edward van Sullivan paused as he looked into the crowd, wondering who had shouted that last remark. *Blood thirsty cannibal.* Not able to discover the speaker, he put up his right hand. The crowd slowly calmed down. 'This pirate, known as, the Scourge of the North Sea,...'

'Oooh!' went the crowd. 'The Scourge of the North Sea!' Silence descended like a velvet blanket. People were interested in pirates; especially, "Scourges."

'Ya,' continued Edward van Sullivan with his powerful voice. 'This scourge will scourge no longer.' He looked towards the stairs. 'Bring the pirate!'

Hanzel could see the man being taken from the tumbrel. The pirate was wearing a tricornered hat. As he was being led up the stairs, Hanzel could see that the man was covered in gold jewelry; golden earrings, numerous golden chains, a large gold medallion, gold rings with jewels, and golden buckles. He walked up the stairs with a swagger, not at all scared of his future.

'I present to you, Kurt Zummer, the Scourge of the North Sea!' shouted Edward van Sullivan.

The crowd applauded, hooted, and hollered. Women swooned. Men prayed some gold would come their way. Others in the crowd admired the pirate and were in full support of his agenda.

Edward regarded Kurt as he stepped bravely forward. He shrugged off the two sheriff's men. 'Piss off!' he hissed.

One of the deputies wanted to draw his short sword, but his partner stopped him. 'Let the executioner take care of him,' he said.

Kurt faced the crowd. 'Hello my friends!' he shouted.

'Hello Kurt!' shouted a number of people.

'So, here we are. It's my last day on earth.' Kurt paused for effect.

Some people in the crowd were visibly shaken. Most of them were women.

He took a gold chain and lifted it over his head. 'So, I no longer have need of this gold chain.'

'I'll look after it for you, Kurt!' shouted a woman near the front.

Kurt tossed it into the crowd. 'There you are!' He watched as an agile youth jumped up and caught the chain in mid air. The crowd applauded. Kurt smiled. 'Good going, young man. May that chain bring you good luck.'

'Like what it brought you?' shouted another man; this one was wearing a large red hat with a feather. He laughed. Several others joined him. A second later the entire crowd joined in, greatly relieving tensions which had built up; especially after the boy was strung up.

The crowd laughed and laughed. Kurt smiled, happy to be so entertaining. He slowly removed his remaining chains and tossed them, one after the other, in various directions into the crowd. Then he tossed his rings and buckles. Each time the crowd went wild as they jumped for the gold and fought over who had it first. When Kurt was finished throwing golden jewelry he pulled a heavy purse from inside his shirt and tossed gold and silver coins until the bag was empty. The crowd applauded and thanked, the Scourge of the North Sea.

'Well, my friends. That's the extent of my wealth. I hope, that for those of you who got a piece of it, that it brings you some happiness for a time. In these troubled times, a little happiness is what we all deserve.' He gestured to the crowd. 'I have attempted to live a decent life, even though I am a pirate. I never knowingly hurt anybody. We never killed the sailors of the ships we captured. I shared my wealth, whenever I had any. Not like the kings of this world.' He pointed to the City Hall. 'They can kill and loot when they want. However, now I am judged a bad man and am to be hanged. Don't worry, my friends. I am not afraid to die. I know that My Father in Heaven will take me into His bosom and I shall live in Paradise for ever and ever. Amen.'

The crowd was still for a moment as they thought about what Kurt had said. Then they broke out in spontaneous applause. Kurt bowed. Then he nodded to Edward, who nodded to the executioner, who nodded to the assistants. The assistants led Kurt to his rope and the executioner fastened the noose, while the assistants tied Kurt's ankles. When they were ready, they hoisted Kurt up and the rope was tied to the cleat. Kurt was released into the air. After wiggling for five minutes he was dead and off on a different adventure.

Edward stepped to the front of the platform. 'That's it for the hangings today. We will take a recess for an hour, in order for you to refresh yourselves. The program will continue at one o'clock.'

The crowd applauded and then started milling about, in search of victuals, libations, places to expel bowel contents or empty bladders. The noise of the crowd's hubbub overcame the screeching of gulls, which were appearing in greater numbers now that more food was coming out and more of it ended up on the ground. Hanzel watched as two gulls fought over a morsel behind the bleachers. A crow landed on Bart's head.

It was time for bladder functions so Hanzel, Steven, and Master Calponi climbed down from the bleachers and set off to find the facilities. As they walked, they discussed the morning's events; what each person had said and how they had died at the end of their ropes.

'I'm glad they've saved the best for this afternoon. I wouldn't want to have to go to the can when the breakings are going on,' said a man standing at the urinal next to Hanzel.

'They'll have an intermission between the two,' replied Master Calponi, standing on Hanzel's left. 'They wouldn't do them right after the other. Each breaking will take at least an hour, or more. My guess is that there will be another hour, or so, between shows.'

Hanzel nodded. 'Makes sense.' He was already becoming somewhat hardened to the execution scene, having just watched five brave people put to death. By the time the pirate was hung, Hanzel no longer felt anything, really. It was just a show. As he thought about that, it bothered him that he was already becoming numb to people's suffering. Hence, he was confident that the afternoon's proceedings would not affect him too badly. Of course, Hanzel had no idea what was coming.

When they returned to the bleachers, Missus de Witt had a picnic spread out on the empty benches. There was sausage, bread, butter, herrings, onions, and wine. The little group ate ravenously. The morning's proceedings had made them very hungry for some reason. As Hanzel bit into a piece of sausage he looked over at the gallows, where the five bodies were gently swinging in the light breeze that had blown in from the sea. As he looked around the square he saw that most people were having something to eat, it being the dinner hour, normally. Several people were already quite drunk and sloshing about. Pickpockets infested the place, along with the many vendors yelling to advertise their wares. The place was a carnival, which Hanzel was beginning to enjoy. Throughout the time of the lunch hour, ever more people were arriving; attracted to the next order of business; the breakings and braidings on the wheel. People had not seen a good one of those for a while. They were ravenous to see and feel real pain. The electricity in the air was tangible.

Just as Missus de Witt and her friend were clearing up the luncheon, Edward van Sullivan stepped up on the platform and shouted to people to take their places because the show was about to begin. Just as he said it, a small, noisy group of gulls flew overhead and deposited a package on his shoulder. The crowd roared with laughter as the dignified official grimaced at the disgusting slime on his expensive clothes. One of the executioners stepped forward with a rag and offered it to Edward, who took it gladly. He wiped the goop off as best he could. Hanzel and Steven were roaring with laughter. When Edward van Sullivan finished wiping the goop, he pulled his scroll open with a dramatic gesture. The crowd applauded. They loved it when politicians can keep a straight face in times of adversity. It inspired confidence. They certainly had confidence that Edward van Sullivan could put on a really big show.

'Ladies and gentlemen, you are now going to witness what we do to those who kill a mother and her child in cold blood. The man you are about to see justice done to is a known criminal. He has many names. Some of them you might know, they being: Renee or Henk de Meer, Pieter Hedricksen, or Jake the Fox, amongst several others. While using the name of Henk de Meer, this villain shot a man and left him for dead in a forest; the very man who is also here to meet his Maker.' Edward paused for a moment, a thoughtful expression on his face. 'Is it not strange how people's paths cross? How, one minute people are complete strangers and next minute they share a cell to meet Saint Peter at the same time...'

'Come on! Quit yer stalling!' shouted a voice.

Immediately other voices joined in:

'Ya, come on! We've got no time for philosophy!'

'Ya, get on wid it. We din come ta hear no filosofeeeee!'

'We wanta see a breaking!'

'We wanta breaking!'

'Breaking!'

'Breaking!'

'WE WANTA SEE A BREAKING!!!'

Edward van Sullivan held up his right hand and the crowd quieted down. When they were sufficiently settled, he continued. 'Bring forth, the prisoner!'

The crowd applauded and cheered as Henk was led up onto the platform and made to stand, facing the raving mob. His hands were tied behind his back. He looked the worse for wear. His clothes were filthy. Several people pelted him with rotten Brussel's sprouts and slimy onions. Edward pointed to him and shouted over the crowd; which quickly settled down, once again, in order to hear what Edward was saying.

'THAT MAN KILLED A MOTHER AND HER CHILD!'

The crowd erupted like a volcano. More rotten vegetables and moldy fruit was thrown up on the platform, making Henk and the other people on the boards step backwards, until several of them bumped into the dangling corpses. Edward stepped forward and frantically waved his arms to get people to stop; all the while a great merriment broke out in the crowd as they watched the chaos on the scaffold.

When the crowd was again sufficiently under control, and the platform swept off, directly into the crowd standing in front, much to their chagrin; Edward continued, trying to be reasonable. *It's like talking to children.* 'The mayor asked you not to throw stuff up here. Please stop doing that. It just slows things down.'

Several people agreed with Edward; shouting in unison, 'Stop slowing things down!'

'Alright then,' continued Edward. He pointed to Henk, who had been returned to his place down centre stage by the executioner's assistants. 'This man. This, horrible man. This, this, murderous son of a succubus and Satan himself; spawned in the pits of perdition MURDERED A WOMAN AND HER CHILD!!!'

The crowd went ballistic. People booed and hissed, cursed and swore their vengeance with fists raised. They refrained from throwing things this time, since, the people mostly responsible were those in the front rows and they did not appreciate the filthy stuff coming back at them when the executioner's assistants violently swept the rotten, slimy garbage off the stage. Edward smiled inwardly. *I guess they can be taught, after all.* When the crowd was settled, he continued, all the while pointing at Henk, 'After he killed those poor innocents, who happened to be on a Good Samaritan mission, HE STUFFED THESE PEOPLE DOWN A WELL!'

'Which people did he stuff down a well?' asked a woman standing in front of the crowd.

'The woman and her child,' replied Edward.

The crowd exploded.

'HE KILLED A MOTHER AND A CHILD?! HE STUFFED EM IN A WELL?! TAKE HIS EYES OUT! CUT HIS HANDS OFF! PULL HIS INNARDS OUT!'

'I had help!' shouted Henk 'I had help! I was not alone!'

'He killed my wife and son!' shouted William, who was standing in the crowd with the warden and his assistant. Several people turned to him and offered their condolences.

'Break im!' shouted a voice.

'Into pieces!' shouted another voice.

'BREAK IM!, BREAK IM! BREAK IM!' chanted the crowd.

Edward van Sullivan raised his right hand and quieted the crowd. 'Let him speak! QUIET!'

When the crowd had stopped yelling, Edward asked Henk if he had anything to say.

Henk looked sadly at the crowd and then, as one of the wheels was rolled across the platform to the axle, he completely lost all heart and feebly said, 'I was not alone. I had help.' Then he fainted. One of the assistants dragged Henk aside, in order to make room for the wheel to be placed onto its axle. They rotated the wheel to make sure it was seated correctly. When it was ascertained that all was well with the wheel, the three assistants and one of the executioners, upon a nod from Edward, lifted Henk onto the wheel and laid him on his back across the spoked torture instrument, the back of the hub digging into the middle of his back. Henk woke up from his faint and began to struggle, however, the four strong men held him firmly in place as the other two executioners tightly fastened Henk to the wheel with strong leather straps. When Henk was firmly strapped down. The crowd applauded and shouted. They were ready for a really big show. They could tell that it would be one to remember.

Edward van Sullivan stepped forward. 'Now, ladies and gentlemen you will see what we do to those who kill women and children. Behold, the tools of execution!' As he said the words, he gestured to the little table. One of the assistants removed the cloth with a flourish to fully reveal the two glistening steel bars that Hanzel had prepared for the occasion. On the table were several other items, some knives and hooks, to facilitate the braiding. When Henk regarded the torture instruments he started to yell, 'Mercy! Oh, God, please have mercy!'

'Like the mercy you showed my wife and son?!' shouted William.

'Ya! Like what you showed his wife and son!' yelled the crowd.

Henk stared up at the sky where several crows were circling. 'Oh my dear God help me!' he shouted.

Two of the executioners took the bars in hand and stood on either side of the spread eagled murderer. Then, upon a signal from Edward van Sullivan, the two executioners raised the bars over their heads. Upon a nod to each other, the two executioners brought their heavy instruments down hard on Henk's hands, totally pulverizing most of the bones with one blow. Henk screamed and twitched with pain. The crowd cheered. The really big show had begun.

The next blows totally obliterated the rest of the bones in Kabel's hands and wrists. Pieces of bone tore through flesh and could be seen flying about. After each blow, Henk screamed and screamed, as the executioners smashed his feet and ankles. When they were done with the hands and feet, they started on the shins and slowly worked their way up to the knees. Slivers of shin bone flew out at the crowd, striking one man in the cheek. The screaming was so intense, Hanzel didn't think it possible for a man to be able to scream any more.

He was wrong.

After a little rest, the executioners continued their grisly work on Kabel's knees. These bones being the largest and densest bones, took nearly twenty minutes each to break through. When they were good and pulverized the executioners had to take another break. It was hard work breaking those knee bones. Henk was unconscious by this time.

After a ten minute break the executioners' assistants refreshed Henk by pouring ice cold water on him and shaking him awake. He screamed immediately as the bars began to land on his thighs, smashing his femurs to pieces. Then they totally smashed his hips with four blows. When the hips were good and pulverized they worked their way up the arms, pulverizing every bone into many, many splinters. Spatters of blood and fragments of bone littered the platform and the executioner's aprons. Breaking through the elbows took a few minutes each. After that they broke his shoulders, expertly smashing through the clavicles. Then, when Henk's shoulders, hips, and appendages were totally malleable, they resembled more the tentacles of an octopus, which, with the help of the knives and hooks, were braided through the spokes of the wheel. When Henk was thusly affixed to the wheel, the assistants lifted the wheel off the axle and set it upright, in order to display Henk braided into its spokes. The crowd cheered and applauded. Henk stared bug eyed at the crowd, emitting incoherent noises through blood and foam dribbling from his mouth, the veins of his neck bulging.

The breaking of Henk de Meer took just over two hours. The crowd cheered and hooted. Breaking Henk had been a big show; a really big show. Many people threw rotten vegetables at the hapless victim hanging in his wheel; like some anthropomorphic octopus. Most of the vegetables bounced off the tortured victim, back into the crowd. When they were done with Henk, he was rolled away to make room for the next act. Henk's wheel was bounced down the stairs, and set against the tumbrel which had brought him to his fate, to await the next stage of his misery. Nobody bothered over the fact he was upside down. It was just how the heavy wheel came to rest.

Hanzel's face was white as a ghost. He was feeling nauseous and about to vomit.

Steven did throw up.

'Hey, watch it!' shouted a voice below the bleachers.

'That was quite a show,' enthused Gerritt. 'I'm glad it wasn't me.'

'It's the screaming I find terrible,' said Missus de Witt. 'It all wouldn't be so bad if they would just gag them.'

'The screaming sends a strong message,' replied Gerritt.

Missus de Witt thought for a moment and then agreed, the screaming did indeed send a potent message to those contemplating homicide.

'We will take a half hour break,' shouted Edward van Sullivan. 'We need some time to clean up our work area and for our able bodied executioners to have a rest, and for the assistants to clean their tools. I suggest you take advantage of the many vendors selling everything you may require to refresh yourselves. And, again, thank you for coming to spend you money in the Port of Amsterdam.' When he had completed his message, Edward walked down the steps and entered City Hall.

The three assistants used buckets of water and stable brooms to scrub off the platform. Henk's blood and bits of his bones made for a slippery surface. The offal was simply brushed off the platform, some of it splashing those who were standing too close. When they were done, the three assistants sprinkled sand on the boards. Then they cleaned the steel bars, knives, and hooks. Meanwhile, the executioners changed aprons and hoods. Nobody saw them change in the little green room under the stage. Hence, no-one knew who they were. When a half hour had expired, everything was ready to go. Moments later, Edward van Sullivan stepped out of the City Hall and mounted the steps of the scaffold. The crowd softened their hubbub and became quiet. The final show was upon them. They knew that Edward van Sullivan always saved the best for last.

'Ladies and gentlemen, now we come to the final act of today's show. This one we saved for last because this man is a wife killer and a paedophile!'

'A paedophile?!' answered the crowd, incredulously.

'Yes, a knave so villainous that HE FORNICATED WITH HIS OWN DAUGHTERS!' Edward's voice had reached a high note, he had not reached before.

The crowd immediately reacted. They went off like fire works, yelling and shouting, 'BREAK HIM! CUT HIS PRICK OFF! CASTRATE THE MONSTER! PULVERIZE HIM NOW!'

It was obvious to Hanzel, the crowd did not tolerate paedophiles and wife killers. Edward held up his hand. The crowd quieted down.

'This man, a simple fisherman, beat his children, and his wife. And, as I told you, committed the most abominable acts against his young daughters!'

'PULL HIS ENTRAILS OUT!' shrieked a voice.

'Roast his balls and make him eat them!' shouted another.

Edward held up his hand. The crowd went still.

At the words, *Fisherman, who beat his children.* Hanzel's ears perked up.

Edward van Sullivan gestured with his right hand. 'Bring forth the prisoner!' he shouted.

Hanzel stared to get a better look. A large man was being taken from a tumbrel and marched up the steps by two deputies. When the man stood at the front of the platform and faced the angry crowd, Hanzel recognized his father.

'That's my father!' exclaimed Hanzel, surprising his friends.

'I present to you, Kabel Sventska!' shouted Edward van Sullivan. 'A dastardly sinner, who will now atone for the damage he has caused.' He looked at Kabel with a disdainful expression. 'Do you have anything to say?'

Kabel stared at Edward for a moment and then suddenly lunged at him, knocking him over. Kabel ran back towards the steps, trying desperately to get away. Since his hands were tied behind his back, it was difficult for him to do much, other than knock a few people over. He was quickly subdued at the bottom of the steps by the sheriff's men, who immediately marched him back onto the platform.

Edward did not look pleased. The crowd was in awe. They had never seen such a display. Some booed Kabel, and others applauded him, as if he was some sort of favored gladiator. The deputies, with the help of the executioners' assistants fastened Kabel on to the second wheel and spun him around, much to the delight of the crowd, who threw rotten fruit and vegetables. Edward shook a fist at them. 'Stop throwing things!' he shouted.

'He never got a chance to speak!' shouted someone in the crowd. When Hanzel looked to see who it was, to his amazement he recognized his oldest brother, Wim. He was standing with his other brothers and sisters, not far from the bleachers. Hanzel wanted to go to them, to share the grief over their mother's death. And confirm for himself that his father had done nasty things to his sisters. However, Hanzel was too distraught. He had to sit and regain his composure. Steven and Master Calponi tried to comfort him.

'It is not so easy to find out that your mother is dead and your father is the killer,' said Master Calponi. 'I would be upset.' He looked at Hanzel and put a gentle hand on his shoulder.

Edward van Sullivan regarded Hanzel's brother. 'He forfeited his right to speak by knocking me over and attempting to escape! He goes straight to his fate.' He nodded to the executioners, who picked up their bars of steel.

'May God have mercy on my soul!' shouted Kabel as the executioners began their nasty work on his hands and feet. Kabel kept his screams inside and strove to be brave. However, when the steel bars began smashing through his shins he could not help but groan loudly. When the bars began pounding on his knees is when he screamed. It was a scream like none Hanzel had ever heard before. It was primordial. The scream tore into his heart and became a heavy lump which brought tears to his eyes.

'Oh, father, what have you done?' he muttered.

When the horrible work was done, and Kabel had been braided through the spokes of his wheel, most of the crowd began to disperse. Hanzel tried to find his brothers and sisters in the milling crowd. Alas, he never found them and ended up walking home, his friends having left in their carriage.

Kabel and Henk were taken by wagon to a place outside the city where their wheels were put on top of tall poles, which projected them into the sky three meters; easy targets for the crows that infested the place. A few people stayed to watch for a while; taking particular pleasure in witnessing the final twitches and hearing the moans of dying people.

Henk and Kabel were left there as night began to fall. Nobody remained behind to mourn the two broken men. Eventually, night brought rain, followed by lightning and thunder. The air became cold. In spite of his broken state, Henk shivered and moaned. Kabel was quiet. Henk figured he was already dead.

Next morning, a glorious sun warmed the air. Henk and Kabel regarded the sunrise and both men figured it would be their last day on earth. They each hoped it would come that day. The pain tormenting them was so immense it was indescribable. As they both lay there, and the morning made it possible to see, three crows landed on the wheels. Two on Henk's wheel and one on

Kabel's chest. They cawed with delight, having found a feast. Kabel's crow hopped toward his head. He tried to move, to get the crow off him. It was to no avail. The crow stood on his face and to Kabel's utter horror, the crow pecked out his right eyeball. 'AAAAAAAGGGGGHHHHH!' he screamed.

A moment later, a deep moan, signaled that Henk had lost the battle and was dead. Kabel looked over at him with his one eye. A powerful spasm ran up and down his body. Kabel screamed again. However, there was no one there to hear him. Moments later he watched as another crow arrived. Kabel's heart beat harder as the crow cawed twice before hopping onto his face and within the blink of an eye, popped his other one out. Everything went black for Kabel Sventska. The crow flew off with the dripping eyeball in his glistening beak.

'Caw, caw, caw!' shouted three more crows, having come to begin their feast on his bleeding flesh.

That night, Hanzel never slept a wink. He constantly saw himself polishing the steel bars which smashed his father to pieces. It was all so horrible. Every time he tried to sleep, he saw the bars before his eyes and heard the screams; the terrible screams of his father being broken into thousands of pieces; some of which escaped the confines of his tortured skin.

Next morning Hanzel took the day off. Gerritt understood that Hanzel had to be alone, to contemplate the demise of his parents. The day was warm and a glorious sun warmed the air. It would likely be one of the last days of warmth before the cold fall weather really took hold of Amsterdam. Hanzel walked out of the city to the refuse dump, where the broken men were placed to wait out their excruciating deaths. Henk was already gone. Seven crows were sitting on his corpse squabbling over a choice piece of bleeding flesh.

When Hanzel reached the place where the wheels had been placed he could hear a soft moan. It was his father. 'Father!' he shouted. 'It's me, Hanzel.'

There was a long groan before Kabel spoke. 'All,' moaned Kabel. He coughed. Then continued in a voice filled with so much pain, Hanzel could feel some of it. He winced.

Kabel coughed and continued, 'all..... be,' cau....ssse,' he groaned as a spasm of intense pain coursed through his brain. 'All b'coz of you!' Kabel coughed and moaned, the last few words having cost him a major effort. When he stabilized, he continued in a hoarse whisper. 'B c...z you...... I'm... he...re.'

Hanzel paused. 'You killed my mother.'

'Ac..ci..de...nt.' Kabel groaned. Hanzel could not help the tears of empathy for his suffering.

'What about my sisters? Is it true what they claim?'

Kabel did not reply. His breathing was becoming very laboured. Hanzel could hear him wheezing above him, his arms and legs twisted grotesquely through the spokes of the wagon wheel on the pole. The smell of feces and urine permeated the place. The horrific reek of the excrement, urine, vomit, and rotting garbage was beginning to make Hanzel nauseous. He was beginning to feel his stomach rising. 'You will rot in hell, Kabel Sventska. I herby disown you as my father.' Hanzel spat on the ground and turned his back to the dying man. He never heard his father whisper his last words.

'I'....m..... so...rr....y....'

Chapter 11

Over the next couple of weeks, Hanzel's dreams were highly unsettling and his days were spent in deep reflection. He performed his chores around the various shops, comprising Gerritt deWitt's enterprise. He polished blades in the weapons shop. He polished armour in the plate and mail shop. He helped clip horse hair, or feathers, sometimes, in the helmet shop. Other times Hanzel helped out in the store, or delivered packages to valued customers. Unfortunately, Hanzel did not perform his chores with the usual vigour. Having watched the execution of his father with weapons that he, Hanzel, had prepared, and then to learn that his mother is dead and what his father had done to his sisters... It was all too hard to bear.

By the time three weeks had passed, Hanzel was beginning to accept what happened. He vowed he was not going to let it deter him from his path. He was going to learn what he could about armour and weapons. Hanzel realized that he lived in dangerous times and the more he knew about the means and tools one needed to protect oneself and one's loved ones, the better protected he would feel. Hanzel vowed to put his heart and soul into learning what Gerritt's workshop could teach him and that he would put the nasty business behind him. *The past is the past. There's nothing I can do about that. And, there is nothing I could have done to save my mother or my father. We must live with our decisions. I hope I make the right ones most of the time. I sure don't want to end up on a wheel, like my father.* Hanzel grimaced and shivered involuntarily Visualizing the execution still sent shivers up Hanzel's spine. *I hope I never see such a barbaric thing ever again.*

'As for missing my brothers or sisters, I would have to say I don't really. The age differences and the fact that my brothers were on the fishing boats a lot of the time, I hardly saw my siblings, really. It is unfortunate I didn't get a chance to speak with them after the execution. But, with the crowd in the way, by the time I got to where they had stood, they were gone.' Hanzel looked up from polishing the pommel of a fine broad sword. He regarded Master van Dijk, the sword maker. 'So, I guess that pretty much answers your question.' Hanzel smiled. 'I have a new family now.'

Master van Dijk looked up from his work fashioning a beautiful handle for a stiletto for the Marquis de Frontenac. He smiled. 'Yes, you do. Indeed, you do.'

Hanzel smiled at his new friend. Hanzel had come to the decision he wanted to learn how to make swords. Master van Dijk had accepted to teach him. Master van Dijk's wife offered to feed him four times a week. Everyone was happy with that. Molly van Dijk was a very excellent cook. Molly liked to eat her own cooking. It was likely the reason she was so fat. It did not matter to Master van Dijk. He liked her that way. 'More for me to love,' he said on more than one occasion.

When the work day was done, Hanzel and Steven chose to go for a walk to the port, in order to look at the ships anchored there. On the way, they ate a salted herring with white onions and a crusty roll. They washed it down with a hearty pint of ale and then continued their walk, arriving along the roadway around five in the afternoon. The sight, smell, and sounds, which greeted them, were overwhelming. Hundreds of gulls were screeching all at once, the smell of tar, kelp, and rotting things, created a tangible presence. As they came closer to a large East India Trader, the smell of feces and urine added to the mixture.

'D'you ever want to go to sea?' asked Steven.

'My father was a fisherman,' replied Hanzel. 'Going to sea is in my blood.'

'Not me,' said Steven. He was looking up at the tall masts towering above them. 'Storms, pirates, leaks, monsters.....You name it. So many reasons why I don't want to go to sea.'

'You could be hurt or killed here on land, just the same,' suggested Hanzel. 'You could slip at work and fall on a spear, which pierces your heart.' Hanzel stared at his friend. 'You could bleed to death; pierced by an errant dart from a crossbow, just like Master de Witt''s son.'

Steven, who was two years older, laughed. 'Your imagination is a wonder, Hanzel Sventska.

The boys walked past the merchantman and approached a massive pile of oak, lying low in the water.

'What kind of ship is that?' asked Hanzel.

Steven looked up. 'I have no idea. It sure has a nice bow ornament.'

When Hanzel looked up, he beheld a naked mermaid with massive breasts and large, erect nipples. She was pointing out to sea with her hands, on outstretched arms. Her hair was carved in long, undulating curls and painted a bright yellow.

'Have you ever lain with a girl, Steven?' Hanzel looked at his friend.

Steven regarded Hanzel. 'Why do you want to know that?'

'Just wondering,' replied Hanzel. 'I just thought, since you are two years older than me, that you probably had done it.'

Steven smiled. 'Thanks for your vote of confidence. But, no. No, I have never even been really close up to a girl. Where are there girls in our business?'

Hanzel shrugged.

'And, besides. I'm only fourteen. Give me some time.' Steven continued walking. The ship they were looking at had just returned from Sumatra with a fabulously expensive cargo of assorted goods; silks, rare woods, tea, that sort of thing. It was a huge ship, over one hundred and fifty feet long. It was a hive of activity as the precious cargo was being unloaded.

'Aiy! Aiy, you boys! Get outa here!' Before you gets hurt!' yelled a stevedore.

'I think we had better walk around them,' suggested Hanzel. 'They look like they mean business.'

The boys quickly skirted the work crew and continued along the roadway. The day was nice and warm. There were clouds, but they did not impede the sun very much. The air was comfortable, making their walk a pleasant affair. As they looked between two ships, tied to the roadway, they could see other ships anchored beyond. When they came to a pier jutting out into the harbour, the boys walked along it to the very end, where a sleek merchant vessel lay tied. It must have returned from an engagement because there were pieces missing out of the hull and its foremast was gone.

'That's obviously a privateer's vessel,' said Steven, pointing to the damaged ship.

'Could be that Spanish privateers tried to take er,' suggested Hanzel.

'Yes, that's possible, too,' replied Steven. 'Maybe both vessels were privateers. I wonder who got the best of the other?' He stared at a large hole in the port side of the ship. 'I wonder if anyone was on the other side of that hole?'

Hanzel stood beside Steven and looked at the hole. 'If there was, he'd be blown to bits.'

'Ya, that's for sure.' Steven pointed. 'Look over there. Out in the harbour. That black ship.'

Hanzel looked where Steven was pointing. 'Ya, the black ship. Ya, I see it. What about it?'

'Pirate ship,' replied Steven affirmatively.

'How do you know that?' Hanzel stared at the ominous looking ship.

'It's all black. It's out there all by its self. And it looks suspicious. It has a piratical look about it.'

Hanzel regarded his friend. 'That doesn't mean it's a pirate ship. It could just be a merchant ship made to look ominous, to scare pirates away.'

'You do have a good point there.' Steven regarded the ominous ship in the harbour.

'Come on,' said Hanzel, let's go to the end of the pier and sit down. We can dangle our legs over the edge.' Hanzel started to run. 'Come on. Last one there is a monkey's arse.'

Steven immediately reacted and the two boys raced to the end of the pier, Hanzel readily beating the older boy. Hanzel was fleet on his feet. He had to outrun Kabel on more than one occasion. And his older brothers, when they were home. When they reached the end of the pier, they sat down and dangled their legs and watched the ships. Several were leaving port and sailing slowly past the breakwater. They were East Indiamen, headed for Borneo, Java, and Sumatra. Gulls screeched overhead. The air was refreshing and cool. A slight breeze was blowing in from the sea.

'I wouldn't mind going to sea,' said Hanzel, as he stared at the three ships sailing out of the harbour. 'I'd love to go on an adventure to other lands.'

Steven crinkled his nose. 'Not me. No siree. I heard life at sea is pretty hard.'

'I'm tough. I can take it,' replied Hanzel bravely.

'From what I've heard, you have no idea how hard it can be. If you run afoul of an officer, you can be beaten with a cat o' nine tails.'

'What's a cat o' nine tails?' Hanzel looked at his friend.

'A horrible torture device. It rips your back open to the bones.'

Hanzel stared at Steven with wide open eyes. 'To the bones?'

Steven nodded. 'To the bones.'

Hanzel shook his head sadly. 'It's all so horrible.'

'That's human nature,' replied Steven. 'People hurt people. I mean, look at us. We're apprentices in the arms industry. We help make things that are meant to hurt or kill people. What do you suppose a sword is for? Or a halberd?'

Hanzel nodded and stared off into inner space. 'It's all so very, very horrible.'

The two boys sat in a long silence, each immersed in his own thoughts for a while until Hanzel noticed that the sky was starting to become dark. Clouds were rolling in. 'I think it's going to rain soon.'

Steven looked at the sky and frowned. 'Ya, I think you're right. We better get home.'

Hanzel suddenly jumped up and challenged Steven to a race back to the roadway. Steven jumped up and ran after Hanzel, happily laughing and taunting him.

This time Steven won. Hanzel laughed. 'Good job, Steven!'

'Th...an...k..s....' coughed Steven, out of breath.

When the boys returned to the district where the workshops were located, Hanzel and Steven said good night and returned to their separate homes, that being their master's houses. When Hanzel stepped through the door he could smell dinner. He was just in time to join the family at the table where they feasted on roasted goose. Hanzel was happy. He was part of a real family. Life was good.

That night, Hanzel slept with a smile on his face.

Over the months and years which followed Hanzel worked hard in the workshops. His broken fingers had healed well, except for a slight sideways bent in his left index finger. It did not impede him. Over time he got to know all of the masters and apprentices really well, especially the blades specialist, Master van Dijk. By the time his fifteenth birthday rolled around, Hanzel had already become quite learned regarding the making of arms and armour. He made certain to ask many questions and eventually was able to do some of the more specialized work. The families of the masters and apprentices were like one large family and Hanzel became an integral member. Because of his good nature and stunningly good looks, everyone loved him.

'And, because he is smart,' said Master van Dijk to his friends over a glass of wine after a day in the workshop. 'Hanzel is a very smart boy. That apprentice of mine will become a great sword maker, someday. Or whatever he chooses. The boy is smart. Mark my words.'

'Maybe he'll outsmart you, van Dijk,' laughed Gerritt.

'Ya, and then he'll take over your shop. And you will be *his* apprentice.' Master Calponi roared with laughter and slammed his stein down on the table of the public house, where they had gone for a pint after work.

'I knew there was something special about that boy when I first met him three years ago,' said Gerritt. 'I'm glad I took him in.'

'Ya, me too,' agreed Master Wenders. 'Hanzel is a hard worker. He will go far in life.'

The others agreed, Hanzel would go far in life. Then they drank a toast to the excellent apprentice.

By the time Hanzel was sixteen, he had become very knowledgeable in the arts of weapons and armour making. He still had some years to go, before he would be a master, however, given his early start; two years before most apprentices, his mastership would come early in life. *Someday I will be a master armorer. I sure do love this work.* Hanzel was fastening a pommel to the hilt of a beautiful short sword he had made. It had the appearance of a Roman gladius. The blade was well forged and tempered. Hanzel had worked with the smith himself, turning the molten steel and hammering it out. The grip was fashioned with cherry wood and fine leather, with blue steel ferrules. The guard was made of the same steel as the blade, as was the pommel, into the faces of which he had carved a phoenix on one side and a tiger on the other. He was very proud of it. It was the first project he was given to do from start to finish. Master van Dijk often expressed his admiration during the process.

'You will become a great master of the art, my young Hanzel,' said Master van Dijk on more than one occasion. 'But, remember, dear Hanzel. Do not let the praise you receive, go to your head. Remain humble and always a student in your heart. That way you will always learn and progress.'

Hanzel smiled as he thought about the master's words. He was right and Hanzel knew it. He knew he could do whatever he set his mind to. All he had to do was to learn the skills. He had to master the craft. *I will make the finest swords in the country. I can hardly wait to have my own workshop. Yes, but first you must earn the money to make it happen. Soon I will be receiving a wage for the work I do. I will save and save.*

'What are you daydreaming about, young Hanzel?' asked Gerritt when he entered Master van Dijk's workshop.

Hanzel snapped out of his ruminations and regarded Master de Witt. He smiled. 'Oh, I was just thinking of how grand it will be when I have my own shops, someday. I really want to be the best blades maker in the country. Next to Master van Dijk, of course.'

'Of course,' agreed Gerritt, smiling. He regarded Hanzel for a moment and then looked at the beautiful gladius Hanzel was putting together. 'It is a marvelous piece of work, Hanzel. I am proud of you.'

'Thank you, Gerritt. It's all because of you. I am very grateful.'

'You are welcome, Hanzel.' Gerritt smiled. He loved Hanzel like his own son. 'So, my fine young man, I have come to bring you news. You are coming with me to England. We are sailing to London in order to deliver those special orders we have been working on. The cuirasses, swords, and helmets are for an English nobleman. I think they are meant to be gifts for his friends and family.'

'He lives in London?'

'Actually, we'll sail up the Thames River a ways north, where we will meet Lord Chesterton's men, who will take delivery. I thought you would like to come along, since you have never made a sea voyage and you have expressed a desire to go there.'

Hanzel's eyes lit up. 'Oh, Master, that would be grand. I would love to come for a sea voyage. When are we leaving?'

'We will leave on Thursday, early in the morning. Master van Dijk will accompany us.'

'Thank you for including me. I know this is going to be a great adventure.' Hanzel stood up and clasped his Master's hand.

'Well, then. I will let you get on with your work. You might have that ready in time and wear it on your belt by the time we leave.'

'I hope so.' Hanzel regarded his gladius and smiled. 'I'll have it ready. Even if I put in extra hours. It will be ready, sharpened and polished and with a scabbard.'

'Excellent, Hanzel.' Gerritt paused for a moment to examine the gladius one more time. Then he excused himself because he had business to attend to.

'I can't wait until Thursday.' Hanzel smiled and was already looking forward to the voyage. He had never been to sea. Now at sixteen, he finally got his wish.

The next three days dragged slowly, as Hanzel worked on his chores and short sword. His nights were filled with dreams of sailing on the sea and of adventures with sea monsters and giant fish. Eventually, Thursday morning arrived. The sun would not be up for two more hours. It was three o'clock when they rode in the company carriage to the docks where a fine sloop awaited them. *Independence* was the name on her transom. The wagon, carrying the armour and weapons, which had followed them, was quickly offloaded by four stevedores, with the help of the lighted ship's lanterns. Gerritt and Master van Dijk spent some time with the captain, before Hanzel was allowed on board. Hanzel assumed they were negotiating a price, or something to do with him.

As it turned out, the captain demanded an upfront payment of the entire amount, in order to take the weapons shipment to England; especially since there were all kinds of nasty things going on there. 'What with them Papists and the hostilities between them and King James. How do I know those weapons aren't meant for Papists? What you are proposing is a dangerous business,' said the captain. 'My asking for my fee up front, is not unreasonable, under the circumstances.'

Gerritt and Master van Dijk deliberated but for a few moments. When they were done, Gerritt addressed the captain.

'I was hoping to pay you half now, and half upon our return. However, we understand your position. Do you want me to write you a bank draft?'

'I prefer silver,' replied the captain.

Gerritt looked at Master van Dijk. 'Silver.....?'

'Ya.' He shrugged his shoulders. 'Now what?'

'I have to go to my bank,' replied Gerritt. He looked at the captain. 'That would mean we can't sail now and have to wait until I get back from the bank.'

'How long will that take?' asked the captain.

Gerritt thought for a moment. He looked at Master van Dijk. When he again looked at the captain, he replied. 'About an seven or eight hours, tops.'

'Isn't the bank open all hours?' asked the captain.

'No,' replied Gerritt. 'The bank opens at ten.'

'Too late,' said the captain. 'We'd have to wait here until the evening tide.'

'Does it matter?' asked Gerritt.

'We have a rendevouz. It takes so long to get there,' suggested Master van Dijk.

'If we leave later...'

'It's only twelve hours. They know there are contingencies at sea. They will wait for a week, or more, if necessary. They need the arms.' Gerritt shrugged his shoulders. 'So, if you want to wait for silver, I am glad to oblige.'

'Excellent,' replied the captain, smiling. 'Silver is so much better. I can see it and feel it.'

'Ya, I understand,' replied Master van Dijk, who also made silver weapons for wealthy noblemen.

Negotiations done, Gerritt and Master van Dijk informed Hanzel that he would have to wait until this afternoon, before they would leave for England. Hence, they rode back home, where Hanzel went back to bed. He was very tired anyway. Deep asleep, Hanzel dreamt of sailing.

When he awoke it was noon. Gerritt had gone to the bank. Only Missus de Witt and her mother were home. They loved Hanzel and doted on him with a fine luncheon they had prepared. Hanzel was very grateful. *They are like the parents I never had.* He smiled and felt overwhelmingly grateful. *God is good. He has blessed me, to make up for the years of pain I've had to put up with. This is all so good.*

At two o'clock, Gerritt returned. Hanzel quickly joined him in the carriage, along with Master van Dijk. They returned to the sloop, where the captain waved them aboard; a broad grin on his bearded face. Hanzel watched as Gerritt handed the captain four heavy leather bags of silver. The captain smiled broadly and had the bags carried to his cabin. 'Thank you,' he said. 'Alright boys!' he shouted. 'Let's get underway!'

By four twenty three they were ready to sail for England. Ropes were cast off and sails unfurled. Gradually, as the wind began to fill the sails, the sloop headed away from the pier. As they sailed into the late afternoon, gulls followed them for awhile, screeching goodbyes and bon voyages. Hanzel stood on the afterdeck and watched Amsterdam disappear. It was a great day for sailing! The sea was calm and the weather fair. A goodly breeze filled the sails and the sloop was soon into the English channel and headed south for London.

Hanzel walked from the back to the front of the ship. He held onto a rope and stood near the bowsprit, looking ahead. The occasional spray of salt water freshened his face. Having never been on a ship before, the experience was both interesting and invigorating, at first. The fresh, salty air felt good on his skin. The breeze blew his long hair about his face, but he did not mind, it all felt so good. When it came time to eat, he was treated to a wonderful meal of seafood chowder, fresh bread, and butter. Friendly banter livened up the meal. Gerritt and Master van Dijk were in excellent spirits.

That night, Hanzel slept well, until early the next morning, when a squall blew up and began to toss the sloop up and down and sideways and up and down and the other ways. As the sloop tossed, so did Hanzel's stomach. The dreaded seasickness had come upon him and he was not well. By four in the morning he had to stumble out of his hammock and attempted to make it topside before evacuating the contents of his stomach, which was now roiling. His skin felt clammy. When he opened the hatch, a wave of cold water washed over him. He instantly shut the hatch and ran for the head.

Fortunately nobody was using it. Unfortunately, someone had recently used it and had left a nauseous odour behind. The smell made Hanzel instantly vomit into the hole, splattering disgusting bits of acidified food here and there. 'AAAAhhh,' moaned Hanzel, feeling completely at the mercy of the illness which was beginning to make him prefer death as he poured another burning punch of half digested food into the stinking hole. *Why does this have to happen to me? I feel horrible. I've never been this sick...*

'Braaaaaaaghck!'

Hanzel prayed it was his last heave. His stomach and esophagus were starting to hurt. After fifteen minutes in the head, Hanzel stumbled back to his hammock and fell into a miserable sleep for about ten minutes, when he had to get up and visit the head again.

And so it went, until Hanzel had nothing left to regurgitate. All he could do was dry heave; which eventually became a very painful abdominal problem. Hanzel was in so much misery.

When morning came, the sun's rays gloriously lit the waves, and made them glisten with golden light. The winds died down, when Hanzel finally fell asleep. He lay curled up in his hammock and remained there throughout the day. He woke up twice to empty his bladder and take a drink from the water barrel. The rest of the time he slept. No one on board questioned it. Hanzel had never been to sea before. Everyone sympathized.

On the second night out, when Hanzel was curled up in his hammock and oblivious to anything but his dream about Angela, several yawls came out of nowhere and were rapidly catching up with the sloop.

'What in the blue blazes?!' shouted the captain, looking through his telescope.

'We're being overtaken by Spanish privateers!'

'They must have been hiding in one of the inlets along the English coast. They came from starboard,' said the first mate, looking through his spy glass.

'We'll outrun em,' said the captain. 'Call all hands, Mister Spier. Put out more sail.' He looked at the helmsman. 'Hang on, Albert. This is going to get interesting.'

Within minutes every inch of sail the sloop could handle was filled with wind. The sloop surged ahead.

'Stay on course,' said the captain. 'I will tell you when to change it. Don't worry about the pirates.'

'I thought you said they were privateers?' asked the first mate, looking at the captain.

'Privateers, pirates, what's the difference?' The captain shrugged his shoulders. '

'The yawls are putting out more canvas,' said the first mate, looking through his spy glass.

'Let's hope we get to London before they do,' replied the captain, lifting his telescope to his eye. 'Pretty soon it will be pitch black. We'll have to be really quiet and change course. Maybe by morning we'll be away from them.' The captain pointed to the lamp. 'Don't light the lamps. Have the men eat cold rations. And no pipes!'

'Aye, captain,' replied the first mate who set about channeling the commands.

When night was fully upon them, the captain had Albert change course, which would take them closer to Oostend. 'We'll lose some time, but we have no choice.'

'I just hope that the English Lord's men will wait,' replied Gerritt. He had a worried look on his face.

'Do not worry, my friend,' said the captain reassuringly. 'They want the arms, they'll wait.'

The first mate nodded.

'Ya, I suppose you're right,' replied Gerritt. 'However, in these uncertain times, with privateers, and hostilities between countries, one has to be so careful.'

'That's the truth,' agreed the captain. 'What can we do?'

'We must do what we must do, each in his own way,' suggested Gerritt. 'I make and sell arms and armour. That's all I'm really concerned about. I want to make sure my commerce is not impeded.'

'Don't worry, we'll get you to Wolwich. I don't think those privateers are aware of what we're doing.'

Indeed, by morning, when the sloop was skirting the Belgian coast, the Spanish privateers were nowhere to be seen.

'Set a course for the River Thames,' ordered the captain.

'Aye, aye, captain,' replied the helmsman.

Chapter 12

Hanzel felt much better by the time they arrived in Wolwich, just east of the City of London. As they sailed to their rendevouz location, they could see the massive navy shipyard, where several large ships of the line were being refitted. The sound of saws and hammers was clearly audible over the screeching gulls. The river Thames was full of boat traffic, which made standing on deck very pleasant for Hanzel. He had never seen so many different boats and ships.

The rendevouz location was just west of Wolwich, about three miles. The exact place was indicated by a large flag with the coat of arms of Lord Chesterton. The pole was stuck in the river bank, where a landing place was available. Several armed men could be seen on the bank watching as the sloop's anchors were dropped and a boat lowered. Then the two masters supervised the loading of the first batch, of what would amount to seven boat loads of armour and weapons.

'What's he need all those weapons for?' asked Hanzel, as he watched two sailors handling a crate of swords.

Master van Dijk looked around to see if anyone would overhear them. Noting it was alright to speak, he informed Hanzel that Lord Chesterton was a Papist.

'What's that?' asked Hanzel.

'A Catholic believer,' replied Master van Dijk. 'Someone who believes that the Pope has supremacy over the king. King James sees things differently.'

Hanzel stared toward the shore and to the left and right. 'Isn't this kind of dangerous, then? We being here, bringing that nobleman these weapons. What if the King's men discover us?'

'We would be hung for treason,' replied Master van Dijk.

'Or, drawn and quartered,' laughed Gerritt, as he put his hand on Hanzel's belly and pretended to pull his entrails out. Hanzel did not think it was so funny. Gerritt ignored Hanzel's frown and continued, 'Well, I must accompany the boat now and accept payment for our shipment. Do you want to come along, Hanzel?'

Hanzel, realizing the implications if they were caught on land by the King's men, preferred to stay on the sloop. *Call me a chicken, I don't care. I am keeping my intestines inside my body. Something tells me there is something amiss.* Hanzel had learned to trust his intuition. The thought of being drawn and quartered did not sit well with Hanzel. He watched from the rear deck as Masters Gerritt and van Dijk were rowed ashore by four sailors.

Some time later several gun shots rang out from shore, followed by the clash of weapons and shouts of men's voices. As Hanzel watched, to his horror, several soldiers came to the shore and removed the banner of Lord Chesterton. They stared out at the sloop. We heard one of them shout something. A moment later, several harquebusiers arrived. They aimed their weapons in the sloop's direction and fired. An instant after the blast, several balls came whizzing through the rigging.

'They're shooting at us!' shouted the captain. 'We are getting out of here. Something has happened. Weigh anchors!' he shouted.

'What about Master de Witt and van Dijk?' asked Hanzel anxiously.

'We have to leave them. We can't get caught up in this. King James is not a nice man. He would not look kindly on us bringing arms to his enemies.'

'Yes, but, doesn't my master have an agreement with you?' asked Hanzel desperately.

'Not for something like this,' replied the captain. He stared at a sailor working a rope. 'Come on there, Renée! Make haste!'

Several more shots rang out. Two balls buzzed through the sails.

Hanzel noted the anxiety in the captain's eyes and the fearful expressions in the sailors' faces as they rushed to obey orders. Several more gun shots encouraged them to work even faster. The sloop was quickly turned and, given a fair breeze, managed to sail away before the king's men could launch a boat. *I knew it. I knew there was something wrong.* Hanzel looked back to the place where the arms were delivered. *I hope Gerritt and Master van Dijk are alright. What will I tell Missus de Witt?*

By the time the sloop returned to the English Channel it was well into night. Stars filled the sky. A fair breeze filled the sails. Hanzel sat on the fore deck and stared at the water passing by. He was thinking about the two masters whom they had left behind. *But, what could I have done? Not much I could have done. Master de Witt set it up for himself. However, there surely must be some way for me to get them back. A ransom is the likely way. The King will likely ask a ransom. I can't see him executing them. They're too valuable alive. King James would likely try to employ them.* Hanzel smiled at the thought because it was a good, positive thought which led him to believe his friends would be safe.

The following afternoon, as they were beating up the east coast of England, Hanzel was sitting on deck and staring off to port. In the distance, he could make out the shoreline, about two miles away. As he sat there staring over the water he suddenly noticed several white shapes off the port bow. Hanzel pointed. 'Do you see those white shapes?' he asked of a sailor who was cleaning the deck. The sailor looked to where Hanzel was pointing.

'I think they're sails,' said the man. 'Run and tell the captain to take a look.'

Hanzel did as the sailor suggested and ran off to tell the captain. When the captain looked in his telescope he immediately told his first mate to put out more sail. 'I think we have company again. This time they're heading right for us.'

As Hanzel watched the distant sails take shape he could tell that there were five boats heading for them.

'All hands on deck!' shouted the captain. 'Man the guns!'

Hanzel watched as the six deck guns were loaded and rolled out on either side of the ship.

Moments later, several guns boomed.

'DOWN! EVERYBODY DOWN!' shouted the captain, as he fell flat onto the deck.

An instant later, several five pound cannon balls came whizzing over the deck of the *Independence* and smashed through the legs of a hapless sailor who was not quick enough. Another ball took a chunk out of the mast.

'Bring her up for a broadside!' shouted the captain to Albert, who was manning the helm. 'Gunners! As soon as you have a good aim on those pirates, let er go and reload as quickly as you can.'

'Aye, Captain!' shouted the sailors, manning the guns.

When the sloop was turned, so that her guns could shoot at the oncoming ships, the gunners let their volleys go. Boom! Boom! Boom! Then they set about reloading as rapidly as they could. Two of the balls hit their targets; a piece of the oncoming ships. The second round did more harm as a ball miraculously smashed through the helmsman of one of the pirate vessels, taking the tiller with him. The yawl veered to starboard and cut in front of a sloop which rammed into the yawl's port bow. The sound of splintering boards and screams of men carried across the water. The other three boats kept coming.

To Hanzel's utter horror, within minutes, the three remaining privateers pulled alongside and began lobbing cannonballs into the sloop.

'Run up the white flag!' shouted the captain.

A sailor rushed to obey.

A moment later the bombardment stopped. Several sailors lay mortally wounded on the deck; their red blood staining the planks. The sudden stillness seemed strange to Hanzel, who gazed anxiously at the yawl off their starboard side.

A voice cut through the silence.

'We obviously have you surrounded, gentlemen!'"

'English!' exclaimed the captain. 'They're English privateers!'

'There is no way that you can escape. We suggest you give up your ship and its cargo. We prefer to avoid bloodshed.'

Hanzel watched as the captain deliberated with his first mate. When he reached a decision he told the boatswain to use the speaking trumpet and tell the English that he was capitulating. 'There's no use trying to outrun them. We'll only be shot to pieces.' The captain sighed.

The boatswain did as ordered.

The reply was, to send a boat over, with the captain and first mate.

'Lower the boat,' sighed the captain. 'Looks like we're going to visit with some English privateers. What an insult.'

Hanzel watched as the boat was lowered. It landed with a splash. Six sailors climbed down and manned the oars. 'We'll be back shortly,' said the captain, as he began his climb down the ladder, followed by the first mate. Soon they were making their way to the pirate sloop.

'Privateers, indeed,' said a sailor standing beside Hanzel. 'Just legalized pirates. But, the question is, legalized by whom?'

Hanzel regarded the sailor, who was obviously a philosopher. 'It's a good question. The English King, I guess.'

'Yes. But, we are Hollanders, not Englishmen. The King of England has no rights over us.' The sailor smiled. 'But, so what, eh? He gives those characters a piece of paper with some legal scribble and they think they can steal our ships and our stuff. It just isn't right, is it?'

Hanzel shook his head. 'I guess not,' he replied. 'But, what's the point. We don't have any cargo.'

'There you have it. What's the point? And, who in the blue blazes does the King of England think he is?'

'I don't know,' asked Hanzel. 'Who do you think he thinks he is?'

'God!' The sailor exclaimed. 'That's who he thinks he is. Although he won't admit it in public. He likely is thinking it in private.' The sailor tapped his left temple. 'Deluded like all of em. All kings and queens are delusional beings. They think they have a God given right to lord it over the rest of us. I just don't believe it.' The sailor laughed. 'It's just their opinion and I don't agree with their opinions.' He laughed louder as he walked away. Hanzel watched him for a moment before returning his gaze to the privateer sloop.

A half hour later, the captain returned without the first mate. 'Thieves! Rogues and thieves, they are, those English pirates! They're keeping my first mate for a hostage until we get to shore. The privateers are taking this ship for a prize. We are to follow them to the Norfolk coast.'

'What happens to us?' asked Hanzel.

'I told them that we have no cargo. They just want the ship and what gold and silver we have on board. Those dastardly thieves!' The captain shook a fist in the direction of the pirate sloop. When he had expended his anger, he lowered his arm and continued. 'So, we'll be put ashore and will have to fend for ourselves.'

'Put ashore? Where?' asked one of the sailors, a man named Jake Putt.

The captain pointed west. 'There,' he said. 'Somewhere over there.'

Hanzel looked toward the place the captain was pointing. He could just make out the shore line, appearing like a continual undulating, thick grey line on the horizon. 'There's nothing there.'

'And, night's coming,' added the boatswain, looking up.

'It's quite a predicament,' replied the captain. 'However, I'm confident we'll be alright. We'll just have to walk along the shore until we come to a village, or a town.' He looked up. 'For tonight we'll just have to sleep in our coats.'

A voice from the privateer's sloop told them to make sail.

'I guess they're impatient,' said the captain. 'Alright boys, let's make sail and follow them to shore.'

An hour and a half later, Hanzel and his shipmates were rowed ashore and deposited on the sands of a deserted beach on the coast of Norfolk. He watched as the privateers sailed off with their sloop; a new pennant flying from her mast head. He could hear them laughing as they sailed off. He could clearly hear a laughing voice shouting through a speaking trumpet. 'We gave you orange peeling herring eaters something to remember!'

'Something to remember, alright,' grumbled the captain. Then he shouted back. 'WE'LL FIND YOU!! I WILL BE AVENGED!! YOU ENGLISH DOGS!!!' He had to stop because he began to cough

Hanzel watched the captain, whose face was red with the exertion. 'You should be careful, shouting like that. You could have a heart attack.'

The captain looked at Hanzel with tragic eyes. 'They took my ship and my silver, those bastards.'

The boatswain shook his head sadly. 'She was a good sloop.'

Hanzel looked up and down the beach. 'At least we have a nice sandy beach. And, judging from the number of shore birds, there is a goodly supply of food. Did those English leave us a flint? So, we can make a fire?'

'Those lousy English bastards! They took our flints, our knives,..... everything,' replied the captain. 'All we have is the clothes on our backs. That's it.'

Hanzel smiled. 'Not to worry, my friends. They never looked in my boot.' He pulled out the dirk Gerritt had given him when they had first met.

'So what? So we have a knife,' grumbled the quartermaster. 'What do we use it for? We've got no flints to make a fire. So we kill something. So what? We can't cook it.'

'I'm not hungry, anyway,' replied another sailor; a man with a heavy beard and totally bald head. 'The night is warm and the sand is soft. Why not just lie down here until morning?'

The other sailors all agreed, it would be better if they slept. They were tired and would need their strength. 'Perhaps in the daylight we'll see a village, or other sign of habitation,' suggested Jake Putt.

'I think he's right,' agreed the captain. 'There is little we can do in the dark. Walking on a beach in the dark is not a good idea. There are things one can trip over and one never knows what lurks there.'

'I agree with the captain,' said the first mate. 'Does everyone agree that we stay here?'

'Aye!' came the unanimous reply.

Hence, the twelve sailors, the boatswain, quartermaster, first mate, the captain, and Hanzel lay down on the sand and huddled into their coats. The sky was clear and filled with stars. The only sounds were those of shore birds pecking about, waves crashing on the beach, and men snoring. The smell was that of sand, dead marine creatures, and kelp. All of it was far from Hanzel's consciousness shortly after he lay down. Instead, Hanzel dreamed about being a sea captain and successfully overcoming sea scum, such as the privateers who stole the sloop he had been sailing on.

Next morning, everyone woke up hungry and thirsty. The privateers had not left them with water to drink, nor food to eat. 'They likely meant for us to die on this beach,' grumbled one of the sailors. 'In every direction you look, you see sand and rocks.'

'Don't despair,' replied another sailor. 'On a coast this good, there is bound to be, at least, a village.

'I agree with Nick. Why don't we just walk in a direction? Surely there's got to be a village along this coast. It's too nice for there not to be habitation along this shore,' said the first mate.

'Why don't we walk in that direction,' suggested Hanzel, pointing north.

'Or, we could go that way,' suggested Jake. He was pointing in the opposite direction.

'We could toss a pointed stick,' suggested the boatswain.

Everyone agreed the pointed stick was a good idea. Hence, when the stick pointed north, that is the direction they walked. Eventually they did come to a village, where people spoke a very different dialect of English. The people were not overly friendly and stared, hard eyed at the intruders in their midst.

'What'll ye be wantin ere'?' asked the mayor, when the group found themselves in the middle of the little town. He was standing on the steps of the town office and did not appear overly welcoming.

'We need a ship to take us back to Amsterdam,' replied the captain. 'Privateers took our sloop.'

The mayor nodded slowly. 'Privateers, eh?' The mayor cleared his throat. 'Them damn pirates, they's makin' a bad name fer us.' The mayor suddenly stared straight at the captain. 'I'm assumin' dem privateers was Englishmen?'

'Ya,' replied the captain.

'I kin ere yous is a Ollander?'

The captain nodded. 'Ya, we are all Hollanders.'

The sailors all nodded and said, 'Ya, ya.'

The mayor looked at the captain with a sideways glance. 'Ye say, ye be wantin' a ship to take yous to Amsterdam?'

Everyone nodded vigorously.

'I have a boat,' replied the mayor. 'When do ye wan a go?'

'As soon as possible,' replied the captain.

'Do ye haf money?' asked the mayor.

'In Amsterdam,' replied the captain. 'The privateers stole our money.'

The mayor stroked his chin. 'Oh, I see.....' He looked at the sky for a moment. 'Ye haf no money ere?'

'I told you, the privateers took it along with my sloop.' The captain stared at the mayor, wondering what his problem was. 'I told you, I'll pay you when we get to Amsterdam. Just name your price.'

The mayor looked our group over. 'There's seventeen of youse. That's a goodly number.'

'It's not that big a number. It's less than twenty,' replied the captain. Then he added, 'How big is your boat?'

'Big enough.'

'So, will you take us? It's not a long journey. Amsterdam is just across the channel,' said the captain.

'Water's dangerous,' replied the mayor, looking out to sea. 'Choppy waves. Heavy cargo...'

'I thought you said your boat's big enough,' said the captain.

'All the things I named are factors to determine a price,' replied the mayor stroking his chin. 'As I see it, ye are desperate to get back to Amsterdam. Ye want that I take ye in my boat, which will put a strain on my vessel crossing the channel. Then I have to trust that ye will pay me when we gets there.' The mayor paused for effect. 'That's all worth somethin', doncha think?'

Hanzel and his group had to agree that the mayor was reasonable in his request. However, what was it going to cost to get them all back?'

'I'll charge ye a crown a head. That's seventeen crowns, altogether. And I'll charge ye seventeen crowns for wear and tear on my boat. So, altogether, thirty four crowns.' The mayor looked down at the captain and the little group gathered below the steps.

The captain looked at each member of his group and asked them if they could come up with some of the money. Everyone agreed that they could come up with two crowns in Amsterdam.

The mayor eyed the little group. 'Ye expect me to believe that ye will scatter about in Amsterdam and that each one a ye will return with two crowns?' He laughed. 'I was not born yesterday.'

The captain looked at his crew. 'Alright boys, I'll go to bat for you.'

The sailors and the officers thanked their captain. Hanzel also thanked him. They all agreed to repay the good man.

'Alright, I'll pay you from my purse,' said the captain. 'In Amsterdam.'

'Yes, in Amsterdam,' agreed the mayor.

Agreement sealed, they journeyed across the channel that night. The crossing was uneventful. Hanzel slept most of the way. He dreamt about Gerritt and Master van Dijk. He saw them in an intense battle with royal forces. They were taken captive. Hanzel watched the entire affair from behind the bushes. *I should have helped them. But what could I do? I don't know anything about sword fighting. I only know how to make them.* Hanzel watched as Gerritt and Master van Dijk are taken prisoner and thrown into a dungeon. Horrible things happen. Hanzel tossed and turned. The visions were macabre and horrific. He woke with a start. A loud creak made him stare into the darkness of the hold where his hammock was slung. Another creak completely woke him up. *Where are Gerritt and Master van Dijk?*

Chapter 13

'At least the cell is reasonably appointed for gentlemen, such as ourselves. At least the King recognized our status as master craftsmen,' said Gerritt as he regarded his friend Markus van Dijk sitting in his chair by the window, reading a book. 'What is that you're reading?'

'I'm reading Dante. There was a copy of his, *Divina Commedia* on the table. It was lying on top of that Bible.' Markus turned a page.

'What's it about?' asked Gerritt, gazing out of the window at a gallows set up in the courtyard below their room.

'As far as I can make out, it's the story of a Roman poet named Virgil who goes into a scary forest.' Markus looked up at Gerritt standing by the window. 'My Italian is not so good. I suppose, since they've included a Bible, as well, they must think we'll have enough time to learn Italian in here.'

'That could be a long time,' observed Gerritt wryly. He began to pace. 'I wonder how long they plan to hold us here without a trial, or a ransom request, or something.'

Henrik watched Gerritt pacing. 'You're going to wear out the floor with your pacing, Gerritt. Or is it that's how you get your exercise?'

Gerritt stopped pacing and looked at his friend. 'I'm just bored living in this prison, if you can call it that. A room, I suppose.' He looked around the room where two comfortable beds, with side tables, candelabra, and chamber pots, a big armoire, a table with four chairs, a dressing table with chair, and a WC. 'It is civilized, I must admit. However, being in this space for as long as we have, and not being allowed to walk around outside, is getting to me.' Looking out the window he could see a scaffold with a gallows, a block, and a torture device; a horizontal cross upon which a human body could be poked and proded, burnt, and disembowled. Geritt shivered involuntarily. 'It's not a pleasant sight, looking out of this window. It gives me very bad feelings, Henrik.'

'I'm trying not to think about it,' replied Henrik. 'I'm just trying to forget about it. Thinking about what may be in store for us, makes my heart stop. Therefore I'm trying not to think about it. It is much too depressing.'

Gerritt frowned and nodded his head. 'I'm trying not to think about it.' Then he returned his mournful gaze at the scaffold below his window. Tears formed in his eyes.

Meanwhile, back in Amsterdam, Hanzel had long ago returned to his new family and had to inform Gerritt's family about his circumstances. At first she was very upset, but after some days of reflection, she decided to raise money to send Hanzel to the King of England with a letter pleading for her husband and Master van Dijk's lives. She figured, since Hanzel was very good looking and amiable, that he would make an excellent representative. Since he was but a young man, of only 16 years, he was harmless, therefore, she figured, Hanzel would be safe. A few days later, she had the money to pay for Hanzel's voyage to England and provide him with room and board money. She also sent an exquisite stiletto knife with an ornate scabbard in a beautiful wooden box. The King's name was inscribed on a highly polished plaque of silver on the lid.

'I pray you get to the king. Surely King James will be reasonable. Gerritt and Markus had no idea the weapons were going to these Papist people. He went there in good faith intending to sell his wares to an English nobleman. What the nobleman does with the goods is his business. We are just craftspeople, who provide an excellent product. We have no political opinions regarding what goes on in England. That is their business.' Missus de Witt had tears in her eyes. 'I wish you God speed, my dear Hanzel.' Then she gave him a kiss and sent him on his way.

The carriage ride to the ship was a blur to Hanzel. He had so many thoughts going around in his head. He was not sure which one to hold on to first. *What if I'm not successful? What if the king doesn't like me and throws me in gaol as well. What if he hates this stiletto? What if we are captured by privateers again?' I really wish I didn't have to make this trip. Something doesn't feel right about it. I have a bad feeling in my gut.*

By the time Hanzel arrived at the ship his head was spinning. He walked up the gangplank in a daze. The ship was a regular packet which operated between Amsterdam and London, carrying passengers and goods. Hanzel was one of twenty passengers. He did not know any of them. Since his mind was in a turmoil, he decided to retire to his little stateroom; number 3B, a cramped little space with a bunk, a small table, a chair, a few hooks to hang clothes on, a small mirror, and a chamber pot. Hanzel was grateful for that and used it right away to empty his troubled bladder. When he was done, he closed the lid on the pot and put it back in its bracket under the bunk. *I'll empty it later.* Then he lay down on the bunk with his hands behind his head thinking about his upcoming adventure to see the King of England. He never noticed the ship getting underway because he had drifted off into an unsettling dream about his future.

Hanzel woke three hours later. They were some distance north on the Zuider Zee and headed for the North Sea. The water was relatively calm, so that the ship did not rock too badly. Hanzel climbed out of his bunk and straightened out his clothing. He looked into the little mirror and saw a much older face than the one he last saw in the mirror at home. He felt burdened with a great responsibility.

At dinner he met some of the other passengers; a Mister Gelder from Delft and his wife, Abigail, a charming young woman, who took an immediate liking to Hanzel. He also met the Porters, Mister and Mister; they did not share their Christian names and Hanzel did not ask them. They were both portly and obviously related. Hanzel did not find much to discuss with those two gentlemen, they being mostly interested in only one thing; each other. The fifth person with whom Hanzel had conversations was, Miss Jeanie Pettigrew. She was nearly 18, and a very fine looking young woman with light brown hair. She was traveling with her aunt and uncle, who was a wealthy cloth dealer. They were enroute to England for business purposes and, 'a little sightseeing,' she said. After dinner, Jeannie invited Hanzel to join her and her relatives to sit on the after deck for polite conversation over coffees. Jeannie was an intelligent conversationalist, full of humour. Hanzel took a real shining to her. Talking with Jeanie made the dreary voyage more bearable and helped him forget about the nasty business in London .

Hanzel and Jeannie became constant companions, under the watchful eyes of her aunt and uncle. By the time they reached London, they had become very good friends. When the relatives were not looking, Jeannie gave Hanzel a kiss on the cheek, before they went their separate ways. Hanzel remembered that kiss for a long while afterward. They lost sight of each other when they set foot on shore. She went with her relatives and Hanzel stood there by himself, facing the city. Since it was early in the afternoon, when they arrived, he had lots of time to find his way to the king. *I wonder where he is. I'd better ask someone.* Hanzel spotted some stevedores standing by several large barrels. 'Good day,' said Hanzel, pleasantly.

The stevedores looked at young Hanzel.

'Can you tell me where I might find the King?' asked Hanzel, as if that was the most ordinary of questions to ask a group of stevedores.

The three stevedores looked at each other and then suddenly burst into raucous laughter. It was as if, what Hanzel asked was the funniest thing ever said in the history of the spoken word. Hanzel was perplexed.

When the three stevedores settled down, one of them; a man with thin lips asked his friends, 'ee wantsta kno, whar's de King.' Then they burst into laughter again.

'Look, I need to find the King because he has jailed my friends and I must get them free.' Hanzel looked at them with a pleading expression.

The men stopped laughing. The man with the red shirt looked at Hanzel and pointed towards the Tower of London. 'Do you see that fortress over there?'

Hanzel nodded.

'Go there and ask, "where's the King." They'll know where ee is.'

'Aye, they'll know,' added the other men, nodding.

Hanzel thanked the stevedores and headed off in the direction of the infamous Tower. He could hear the stevedores laughing uproariously behind his back. *Why are they laughing? There's nothing funny about this, is there? I'm dead serious. Silly fellows.*

As Hanzel walked he thought about stories he had overheard in Amsterdam about the Tower of London. The things he had heard made him feel very unsettled. He envisioned strange tortures and beheadings. *And they call it civilization. People are still barbaric, even back home.*

The city was teeming with people, not much different from Amsterdam. High life and low life abounded. The place smelled of some sort of exotic stew made of rotting things, mildew, body odours, moss, piss, feces, perfumes, and offal. As Hanzel walked towards the Tower of London he got a good look at abject poverty as well as extreme riches, as a gentleman and three ladies rode past in a coach, attended by liveried servants. *Someday I'll own one of those.*

Hanzel had to snap out of his euphoria. He was in London and also had to find lodgings. He only had so much money to spend and had to make it last. Neither he, nor Gerritt's wife had any idea how long it would take before he was allowed an audience. She reasoned that some of the money would likely have to go to bribes. She was under no delusions regarding how things worked.

He reached the Tower at seven o'clock. Darkness was already starting to arrive making the place look even more ominous and formidable. He prayed Gerritt and Master van Dijk were alright. He stood for a long while examining the foreboding structure. *Is that where the King lives?* Hanzel shivered. He realized it was getting late. He still had not found an inn. *At least I know where the Tower is. Now, I'd better find a place to eat and sleep.*

Hanzel was very tired by the time he stepped into the *Tower Inn*, a friendly place with macabre decorations; hangman's nooses from actual hangings, a jar of pickled entrails from a tragic traitor who was drawn and quartered, a dozen or more blood soaked handkerchiefs; the blood long ago having turned brown, with the names of the persons providing the precious body fluid under extreme circumstances written with black ink. There were also: six shriveled hands, five noses, ten ears, and an entire arm, which had been provided by another hapless soul who was drawn and quartered ten years ago, all of these items were attached to the walls with nails. There were also a number of human heads, mounted on polished boards; just like deer and antelope heads prepared by a taxidermist. The jar of entrails was prominently displayed on a shelf. On one wall hung a broken headsman's axe and other tools of the executioner's trade. The place was filled with a noisy hubbub, and the aromas of soups and stews cooking. No one paid the slightest attention to the macabre display; it being, merely thematic decorations, and relatively commonplace. Nobody paid any attention to Hanzel, either. Finding a bench free, he sat down and put his bag on the floor by his feet. Then he watched and waited until a serving girl came to take his order.

Hanzel ordered stew, bread, and ale. As he sat there, waiting for his food and drink, he began to look at the people who were eating, talking, drinking, smoking... *Oh my goodness, look at her. How did she get so fat? And him? That can't be her man, he's way too skinny. She'd crush him. I've never seen a nose that big before! That woman has to be one of those ladies. My goodness, her bosom is practically protruding out of her bodice! He doesn't seem to mind it though. Oh, my God.... what happened to him? He hasn't got a nose. Euw, that looks horrible. Hmm, sure smells nice in here. I hope my food comes soon. I'm starved. I wonder if they've got a room for me.....* Hanzel looked in the direction the serving girl had gone. As he did so, he saw that she was returning with his food and drink. *Excellent.* She set the bowl of stew, two thick slices of dark rye bread, and a tankard of ale on the table in front of him. 'That'll be thropence, hay penny.'

Hanzel looked at her. 'Thropence, hay penny?'

'Three and a half cents,' she replied. 'You can make it four pence, if you like. For a tip, like. People do that around here.'

Hanzel looked in his purse and pulled out three copper coins. 'These are stuivers. They're from Holland.'

'We get those here all the time. I only need two of them, if you are giving me a tip, that is.' The girl smiled. 'They're worth the same as our pence.'

'Of course, of course, I'll give you a tip.' He handed two stuivers to the girl.

'Thank you. Is there anything else you need, before I go?'

'A place to sleep. Do you have a place for me to sleep?'

'I'm not sure, but I'll ask and let you know.'

'Thank you.' Hanzel smiled at the girl. He obviously impressed the girl, because she smiled and smiled; her eyes sparkling. Hanzel's good looks did it to her. He was beginning to understand that girls liked him.

'I'll come back and let you know,' she repeated and walked off. Hanzel watched her go; admiring her from behind. She looked over her shoulder to see if he was looking. His stomach alerted him that he was ravenously hungry. The aromas coming from the stew had wafted into his nostrils. He turned, and putting his face over the bowl, sucked in the delicious smells. Then he picked up the spoon and began to eat, and eat, and eat. *This stew is fantastic! Oh, yummmm. Hmmmmm.*

Halfway through his meal, the girl returned and informed Hanzel that he would be welcome to sleep in her room because there was no room at the inn available. *Sleep in your room? She's not bad looking, Hanzel. It might be alright.* 'Where is your room?'

'Just a couple of streets away. I rent a room above a butcher shop. I'd let you stay for free.'

Ya, so you can steal my money, just like Angela. 'That is very kind of you,' he replied. 'When are you going home?'

'Not until I'm done work.'

'I'm very tired after my long journey. I'm sure I could find another inn.'

'Suit yourself,' replied the girl. 'But, you'll find most of the inns around here are full.'

'Why is that?' asked Hanzel.

'Execution,' she replied. 'Some Papists are being drawn and quartered. I think a couple of others are going out on the end of a rope. There have been several attempts on the king's life. I think he wants to set an example.'

'When are the executions to take place?'

'Two days, I think.' She looked over at a fat man drinking from a large tankard. 'Eh, Joe, when's the execution?'

'Sa ur doiy,' came the reply.

'What time?' asked the girl.

'Aye nuun,' replied the man.

Hanzel stared at the girl for a moment; a rush of thoughts going through his head. *What if the Papists include Gerritt and Master van Dijk? My God, maybe I'm too late. I have to get to the King before Saturday.* 'Do you know if they have posted the names of the condemned?'

'I have no idea,' replied the girl. 'Besides, I don't really care. I've no interest in seeing an execution. Especially a drawing. Too horrid. I don't care for that kind of entertainment.' The girl indicated her disgust with a grimace. 'Well, I've got to get back to work.' She scooted off to take an order from a group of laughing topers sitting at a table next to Hanzel. He watched her to assess whether she appeared honest, or not.

She doesn't look like Angela and she has a nicer smile. But, then, Angela didn't appear particularly dishonest. It's so hard to tell with people. Hanzel took a long drink of his ale. His mind was racing. He had to find a place to stay. For some strange reason a nice looking girl offered him a place to sleep because the inns are full. Now he was in a quandary. *What harm can there be in it? She seems nice enough. I really have no choice. Then, I have to find the king tomorrow. The question is, where is he?*

The man sitting on Hanzel's left turned to him. 'Yur kinda yung aintcha?'

'What do you mean?' asked Hanzel.

'Whut yu doin out n' aboot dese ere pahts? Yu ere fer the enertoinment? On Saturdoiy?'

'I'm here to see the king,' replied Hanzel. 'I have to find him before Saturday.'

'An whoi duz a yungn' loik youse av tu soy ta is Majestie de King?' asked the man, surprised at Hanzel's reply.

'I've first got to find him.'

'Ees not ere, as yew can see.' He laughed uproariously and repeated what he just said and laughed all the louder. 'Eh boys. Whot do yew soy? Is is Majestie King Joimes ere?'

'Eer oi am!' shouted a voice from the other side of the room. Then the entire room burst out laughing. When the laughing slowed down, many people in the crowd broke out in a funny song.

'Good King Joimes,

e spoke ta God,

one doiy in da mohnin,

Seein as ow es one wid de odder

Good King Joimes thinks Him a brodder.

So talk ee did, an scribble, scribble...

Days on end, it's all so boring

An now e puts a Boible in yur ans,

before e stretches yur neck for snorin.'

When the singing was done everyone broke out in another raucous bout of laughter.

Hanzel couldn't help but laugh with the people. The energy was so happy and good there at the inn, notwithstanding the macabre embellishments on the walls. Hanzel felt so good, he decided, since he was now 16, he could handle another pint of ale. *Since I've got to wait for her anyway, I might as well enjoy myself. Not much I can do now, anyway. I just pray the execution doesn't include Gerritt and Master van Dijk. I hope I can get to the king tomorrow.*

As Hanzel sat there, deep in thought, it occurred to him that he had no idea what day it was. He looked at the man on his left. When he got his attention, he asked him what day it was.

'Thoisdey,' replied the man smiling and revealing several missing teeth.

'Thursday? You mean to say, tomorrow is already Friday?'

The man nodded and smiled. 'Oi lose trek o' doiys, me sef, guvnu. Nutin' te wurrie aboot.' Having said that, he returned his attention to his drinking partner; another fat, jovial man, with glowing red cheeks and a bulbous red nose. His eyes twinkled merrily. Hanzel noted the man was leaning a little to one side. *Deep into his cups, that one....*

When the girl returned, Hanzel asked her if her offer was still open. She smiled happily and agreed it was. Then he requested another pint of ale. 'Since I have to wait for you, I might as well enjoy myself. How much longer will you be?'

'Three hours, or so. It all depends on how busy we are. By the looks of things we will be very busy in another hour, when people come to eat. Then this place really fills up.' The girl looked at Hanzel and held out her hand. 'My name is Jane.'

'I am Hanzel Sventska.' Hanzel smiled at her and shook her hand.

'That's a very unique name,' replied Jane.

'Are these people from out of town and staying here at the inn?' asked Hanzel indicating the people sitting about the room.

'Some of them have come from out of town on business, others are here for the big event on Saturday. They are the demented ones, as far as I am concerned. I mean, why would anyone come from out of town, spend money to stay here, just to see some people officially murdered in gruesome ways.' She looked directly into Hanzel's eyes. 'Don't you think so?'

'Oh, er, yes, of course. I don't like seeing executions,' replied Hanzel. 'It's all so horrible.'

Jane smiled, obviously pleased with his answer. 'Alright, I'll go and fetch you another ale.' Then she walked off. Hanzel watched her go and kept his eyes on her for the rest of the evening. He drank one more pint after his second one, however, by the time Jane got off work, it was well after midnight. Hanzel was pleased that he was happily affected by the ale but not drunk and leaning precariously. He smiled because he knew he would not be sick.

As they walked along stinking streets with all manner of disgusting refuse sitting along the sides; Hanzel saw some of the dregs of English society. Horrible poverty in all its ugly manifestations sat hunched against mossy walls, or desperately tried to wreak a living by holding out bony hands to strangers passing by. The streets were dark and gloomy. 'I feel a lot safer walking home with you on my arm,' said Jane. 'I hate it when I have to work late.'

'This is definitely a good reason to live in the country,' replied Hanzel. 'I come from a village. The city is actually still kind of a strange place for me. I don't think I could live here.'

'Have you come to take me away, Hanzel?' asked Jane. She laughed.

'I thought I was just going to sleep at your place and then go to find the king tomorrow. I can't take you with me.'

'I have to work anyway.' Jane pointed. 'That's my building. I live on the third floor.'

'I'm so glad we're here,' replied Hanzel. 'I'm bone tired.'

'Me too.' Jane opened the front door and held it for him. 'Don't worry, Hanzel. You'll sleep well, I'm sure.'

The lobby was lit by a single candle, sputtering in a holder on the wall. The stairs were dark and foreboding. When they approached the steps, a rat scurried off.

'Nasty things, them rats,' said Jane as she began to climb.

'Yes, they are,' agreed Hanzel, wondering what sort of place he had come to.

They climbed the stairs in silence. The stairs creaked and groaned. The building was obviously ancient and decrepit, like an old person. Jane's rooms were at the end of a long corridor. She unlocked the door with a key she kept on a ribbon around her neck. When they entered the room she immediately struck a flint and lit a candle in a stand on the little table beside the door. The room revealed a little of itself in the tiny light. 'I'll light some more candles over there.' She picked up the candle stand and walked to a larger table in the middle of the room, where a candelabra stood with six candles waiting for fire. Jane lit the candles which immediately lit up the room nice and cozy.

'This is a nice place, Jane. Can I set my bag down here?'

'Oh, no,no. Follow me.' Jane picked up the single candle stand and led Hanzel into another room, where her bed stood waiting. 'Put your bag down there.' She pointed to the foot of the bed. 'Since we're both tired, I think we should just go straight to bed. I have to work tomorrow and I need my sleep.'

Hanzel agreed it was the best plan. 'Where do you want me to sleep?'

'You can share my bed. It's big enough for two. It'll be nice to have company. It gets lonely here all by myself.' Jane pointed to the bed. 'Go ahead, you can get in and go to sleep. There's a chamber pot under the bed, if you need it.' She pointed to the other room. 'I have to take care of something in there, you can go ahead and take off your clothes and get into bed. I'll be along in a few minutes.'

'Thank you, Jane,' said Hanzel.

Jane nodded. 'You're welcome.' Then she stepped into the other room.

Hanzel was too tired to argue and quickly took off his shoes and clothes, leaving his underclothes on. Then he climbed into the bed and pulled the blankets over himself. Hanzel never felt Jane getting into bed. He was far into a dream by the time she climbed in, a few minutes later.

Next morning Hanzel woke up first. A dreary light was filtering in through cracks in the shutter. He stepped out of bed and pushed the shutter open to light the room. Jane stirred. Hanzel quickly put on his good clothes and shoes, trying hard not to make a noise. He took a small silver coin from his purse and left it on the night table beside the bed. He took a long look at Jane, still peacefully sleeping; her long brown tresses strewn over the pillow. Hanzel smiled as he rushed off, closing the door quietly behind him. He had to find the king, there was no time to waste.

With his bag slung over his shoulder he headed off in the direction of the Tower of London. On the way it felt like he was walking through a gauntlet. Everywhere there were bawds and pimps, beggars and thieves, pickpockets, pock faced poverty cases dressed in rags, and filth and slime. *Not a place I want to live, that's for sure.* Being nearly six feet tall, by this time; and with his striking good looks, Hanzel presented an imposing figure. Hence, he was generally ignored on his way to the Tower.

When Hanzel arrived at the front gate of the foreboding fortress, Beefeater guardsmen were standing in groups of three on either side. They were dressed in splendid livery and wielded halberds. He approached the group on the right.

'Excuse me. Can you tell me if your king is personally present here in this castle?'

The three guardsmen stared at Hanzel.

Hanzel stared back.

He waited.

When no answer came, he repeated his question.

The three guardsmen looked at each other in dumbfounded amazement. Then they returned their gaze to Hanzel.

'Are yew askin' us? Wedder is Majestie, King Joimes the sixth of Scotland an Joimes the Foist of England is wid in?' The man had the appearance of a bulldog; broad shoulders, big jowls; all upper body. His voice was more a growl than a human voice.

'Yes,' replied Hanzel, as if it was the most normal of questions.

The guard eyed Hanzel. 'Ooh, are yew? Ur joost a boy? Wha would is Majestie wan wid da loikes oh yew?'

'I am Hanzel Sventska. I am from Holland and I need to see the king. It is a matter of life or death.' Hanzel indicated the bag over his shoulder. 'I also have a present for the him.'

The bulldog guard looked at his colleagues. 'Shud we tell im?'

The other two guards regarded smiling Hanzel for a moment and nodded consent.

'Ohlroight, we'll let youse tru de gate. Yew're in luck. De king is in. On accounta da executions. It's not easy ta see de king. Once yew're in, den yew'l av tu deal wid de courtiers.' The guard smiled, revealing a golden tooth. 'Good luck.'

'Yeah, good luck,' chorused his colleagues.

'Thank you,' said Hanzel. He smiled as he stepped past the guards and through the gate into the grounds of the grim palace.

When he reached the main door to the imposing building he was stopped by more Beefeaters. The one with the double chin spoke first.

'Ou let yew in ere?' asked the chubby guard.

Hanzel pointed to the front gate. 'They did,' he said. 'I'm here to see the king. I am from Holland. This is a matter of life or death.'

The guard gave Hanzel the once over. 'A mattah of loif or deaf?' He turned to his three colleagues. 'D'yu ere dat? Dis yung gentle mun came aaahl de way frum Olland to see de king, e as. A mattah of loif or deaf e says.'

The tall, skinny guard sniffed as he stared down at Hanzel.

'I have a present for him,' said Hanzel, showing them the wrapped box containing the knife.

The chubby guard pointed to the package Hanzel was holding up for them to see. 'E as a present.'

'For the king,' repeated Hanzel.

The chubby guard regarded the tall guard. 'Wada ye say. Shud we let im in?'

'Please,' pleaded Hanzel. 'My friends' lives are at stake.'

'Alrite,' said the tall guard, nodding his head. 'On accoun a da executions an all.'

'Thank you,' said Hanzel gratefully

'Alroit, Cecil. Look liovly now an open de doh,' said the chubby guard to a shorter Beefeater standing behind him.

The door was opened and Hanzel stepped inside the palace. He shivered involuntarily.

A moment later an officious looking courtier approached him. The man was wearing a pompous wig and expensive silks. He smelled of lavender. 'Yes? Can I help you?'

'I'm here to see the king,' said Hanzel. 'I have a present for him. I came all the way from Holland to bring it to him.' Hanzel regarded the courtier for a moment, sizing the man up. *He likely doesn't know anything about my country. I'll tell him I come from our king. That should impress him.* 'It's a present from my king.' He showed the man the exquisite box but did not open it.

The man looked Hanzel over. *He is splendidly dressed, although a bit conservatively for my taste. He is very polite and poised for such a young man.* 'I will speak with the King's secretary. You can wait here.' The courtier pointed to a bench against the wall beside a door.

Hanzel was glad for the bench, he was suddenly tired and feeling very ill at ease. The place lowered his spirits. It seemed grim and uninviting. Sour faced people walked by, totally ignoring him, as he sat there, waiting.

And waiting.

Hanzel sat with the wrapped box on his lap. He watched busy comings and goings. *This place is a madhouse. Who are all these people?*

After waiting for just over an hour, the courtier, who had set him there, approached. 'The secretary has spoken with the king. You caught him at the right time. He will receive you.'

Hanzel stood up, his eyes beaming gratitude. He shook the man's hand. 'Thank you, thank you,' he said, grinning.

'Follow me,' said the courtier, as he turned and walked in the opposite direction.

Hanzel stood dazed for a moment. *I've got an audience with the King of England. I can't believe it.* Hanzel suddenly realized the courtier was already halfway down the hall. He quickly followed.

The courtier led Hanzel to a door, attended by two guards.

'He has an audience,' said the courtier, when the guards gave him a questioning look.

The guards opened the doors to a large room. Hanzel stood in the doorway beside the courtier, who beckoned to a man with grey hair. He nodded and stepped over to the courtier.

'This is the young man from Holland,' said the courtier in his impeccable English.

'Oh, yes, of course,' replied the man. 'I am George Villiers, the king's secretary.'

'I am Hanzel Sventska, from Holland, with a present for the king,' replied the young Dutchman.

'You wish to speak with the king?' asked the secretary.

Hanzel nodded.

'Alright,' replied George. He turned on his heels and walked to the far end of the room, where a huge table stood, covered with numerous books, maps, pots of ink, pots of quills, and paper, lots of paper. King James was sitting in a chair at one end of the table, reading in a large book. George Villiers approached the king and whispered in his ear. King James looked up and regarded Hanzel, standing by the door. Hanzel could see that the King was not well and appeared frail.

'So, young Hanzel Sventska from Holland, what brings you to this place?' asked the king.

'I have a gift, Your Majesty. It is in this box.' Hanzel indicated the box in his hands. *He talks strangely. I think there's something wrong with his mouth. His tongue is sticking out. Strange. Maybe he's really ill.*

'A gift?' King James smiled. 'I like gifts. You may bring it to my hands.' He beckoned Hanzel forward.

As Hanzel crossed the room, the king watched him intently. However, Hanzel was calm and not at all nervous. He and King James saw something good in each other's eyes.

Hanzel placed the box on the table in front of the king. *His hands are trembling and his fingers are all bent. Poor man.* Hanzel watched as the king read the plaque and nodded approvingly. Then he opened the box and discovered the beautiful stiletto. He carefully took the knife out of the box and examined it.

'Truly magnificent.' He smiled at Hanzel. 'Thank you, young Hanzel Sventska.' The king indicated a chair on the opposite side of the table. 'Sit down there and tell me why you have brought this fine gift.'

Hanzel did as the king directed and sat down in the chair. *I am sitting with the King of England. This is a very singular honour, I think.* Hanzel looked directly at the king and asked him. 'Does everyone, who gets an audience with you, Your Majesty, sit in your presence? I mean, I am just a boy from Holland.'

'I sense something about you, young Hanzel Sventska. You appear to me, to be a remarkable boy. The fact you managed to get past my many gate keepers, into my presence, indicates to me that you are a remarkable boy. I am also amazed at your fine command of the English language. How is that possible?'

'In my trade, we meet many people, from all over the world. In my country, many languages are spoken. I happen to have a good feel for languages. My masters also speak English. Our countries are at peace. We do a lot of trade with English speaking customers.'

'I see,' said the king, smiling and nodding his head. 'You are a remarkable young man, Hanzel. I think you will go far in life.' He turned to one of his servants; a tall, thin man in livery, standing behind and to the left of the King's chair. 'Claret. Bring claret. And bring a goblet for my young friend.'

'Very well, Your Majesty,' replied the servant. He turned and quickly went to fetch the wine. He returned a moment later with a silver jug of claret and two goblets. He set a goblet in front of the king and then stepped around the table and put the other goblet in front of Hanzel. Then he poured the claret, first into the king's vessel and then into Hanzel's. All the while King James regarded Hanzel, who calmly sat back and regarded him calmly. They were smiling at each other. King James and Hanzel liked each other right away.

'Now we can see each other, eye to eye, my young friend. We'll drink a toast.' He held up his goblet. Hanzel held up his goblet. 'Here is to you, my fine young friend from Holland. May you live a hundred years.'

'Thank you, Your Majesty,' replied Hanzel, smiling widely.

Then the king and Hanzel drank a drought and set their goblets on the paper strewn table. King James crossed his hands over his chest and sat back in his chair. He regarded Hanzel for a long while before speaking. 'So, what's this all about, then? Why have you come all the way from the lowlands with such a fine gift?'

'Your Majesty, the stiletto comes with the compliments of the Amsterdam workshop of my master, Gerritt de Witt. That stiletto was made by Master, Markus van Dijk, who works there. I have reason to believe that these fine gentlemen may be prisoners here in England. Without any understanding of political affairs in your Kingdom, Your Majesty, these masters were contracted to produce a number of items for a certain nobleman. I came along on the voyage to deliver these products to a location near Wolwich."

'What nobleman? What is his name?' The king leaned forward and regarded Hanzel closely.

'Chesterton. Lord Chesterton, I think it was,' replied Hanzel.

The King looked at his secretary who responded, 'He's to be quartered tomorrow, Your Majestie.'

'Oh, yes, of course, of course. Chesterton, eh? Hmmm. Terrible thing, that. When a king's nobles plot to kill him. Don't you agree, young Hanzel?'

Hanzel eyed the king. He realized that he had to agree. 'When people plot to kill the monarch, they must be executed. Trying to kill a king is high treason.'

'Indeed, indeed, my young friend. High treason, indeed.' King James took a long drought of claret and thought for a moment before continuing. 'So, what about your story? Please continue.'

Hanzel took a sip of his claret to clear his throat. 'While I stayed on board ship, somewhere up the Thames River, I have no idea where, Masters de Witt and van Dijk went ashore to finalize the transaction and receive their payment. They did not return. I have reason to believe they might have been apprehended by Your Majesty's soldiers. Now that I know about what is going on, with regard to plots against your life, I understand it is highly possible my allegations are correct. If it is indeed the case that these men are in custody here, I have come to plead for their release, since they transacted in good faith with the said nobleman.'

King James regarded Hanzel for a long while. 'How old are you, Hanzel?'

'I am sixteen years old, I think, Your Majesty. My birthday is April twenty third.'

'April twenty third?' The king stared at Hanzel for a moment and his eyes misted over. 'April twenty third...' King James stared through Hanzel and looked to a different time. He recalled his happy times spent with his friend, the amazing poet and playwright. 'That is a date which will live in my memory forever,' he said, looking directly at the handsome boy. King James stared past Hanzel and sat thusly in thought for a moment more. 'Yes, that is the date my dear friend William died. The greatest literary mind England has produced. A man I loved, and whose plays have entertained me all these years... April twenty third... What a loss.' The King sighed and stared for a long while, as he thought about his dear friend, The Bard of Avon.

'I'm sorry to hear that, Your Majesty. You have my deepest condolences.' Hanzel watched the king, who seemed even older and more decrepit after thinking of his friend who had died.

'And now here you are, pleading for people who brought arms to two traitors, to further a plot to kill me.' King James regarded his secretary. ' Are we holding these men? These Hollanders? De Witt and van Dijk?'

George Villiers nodded. 'Yes your Majestie. They are to hang tomorrow.'

King James nodded and looked directly at Hanzel. 'Well, there you have it. They have already been condemned. They were obviously proven guilty.' King James regarded Hanzel coldly. 'They came here to deliver arms to my damned enemies. Men who would have me dead!' King James paused for a moment. 'These men...these detestable traitors....they must be made an example of. If I let these men live, even your masters, it will send a message to others who would wish me dead, that it is a frivolous affair. That, I, King James the First of England, Scotland, and Ireland does not take plots against His Royal Person seriously. That foreigners can come into my realm with weapons to kill me and I will tolerate that and let such abominable men live? They knew full well for what reason those weapons were brought here.'

The King reached out to a small stack of papers and shuffled through them. He pulled out a sheet and regarded it for a moment, reading several lines of text. 'We have their confessions. Your masters confessed, under torture, that they knew why the weapons were purchased by Lord Chesterton and his accomplice, the Earl of Montcarl, who will also pay for his crime tomorrow. Your masters and my nobles were in a conspiracy together to kill the me. I have no choice. Men have been hung for far lesser crimes. Justice must be done. "Vengeance is mine, sayeth the Lord." I am God's agent on earth. There is no pardon for these despicable men. You must understand that, Hanzel Sventska. You agreed, plotters against the King's life are traitors. Our law says, traitors must die. That is it. Pure and simple.' King James regarded Hanzel, his expression, cold, yet, sympathetic at the same time. He reached for his goblet.

Hanzel stared at the King and did not say anything. What could he say? The King was right, and he knew it. *I can't think of a rebuttal. He is right. If I was him, I would have to do exactly the same thing. Poor Gerritt and Master van Dijk. There is nothing I can do. Poor Missus de Witt.....* Hanzel nodded slowly. 'I understand, Your Majesty. I understand, you have no choice.' Tears formed in Hanzel's eyes. 'However, it does not make it any easier. They are my masters and my friends. Master de Witt rescued me and took me in to his home when I was alone and on the street. Master van Dijk is teaching me the art of sword making. I am his apprentice.' Hanzel wiped tears on his sleeve.

King James regarded Hanzel sympathetically. 'I understand that you are upset, young Hanzel. However, you will get over your sorrow. Believe me, I have had many sorrows over the years. You can not dwell on them. Life is not always a bed of rose petals. Sometimes it is a bed of thorns. You must get used to that.'

Hanzel nodded. 'I know about the petals and the thorns, Your Majesty. I have also had many sorrows.'

The King's expression was sad. 'It is a terrible world we live in, young Hanzel. Now I must needs continue with my work and you must now leave me. Thank you for your present. I am sad I was not able to pardon your friends. Good day to you and God speed, young Hanzel Sventska.'

Hanzel nodded and stood up. 'I understand, Your Majesty. Is it at least possible for me to see them?'

The king looked over at his secretary who shook his head. 'They're on death watch. They have to be left to their meditations.'

King James nodded slowly, all the while regarding Hanzel with a tragic philosophical expression on his sad face. 'Well, there you have it. You will have to be content. It is what it is. They must be allowed their prayers and make their peace with God. Now, good day to you, young Hollander. May God bless you and guide you.'

Hanzel tried his best to be brave. 'Thank you for giving me an audience. God Save The King.'

'God Save The King,' repeated the courtiers.

Hanzel bowed and then backed out of the room, as he had watched others do.

The door closed behind him with a hard thud.

Hanzel's audience with King James was over.

Chapter 14

It was raining when Hanzel stepped outside the formidable building. His eyes were filled with tears as he walked across the grounds to the gate leading out of the Tower. The guards asked him if he got an audience, but Hanzel did not acknowledge them. Tears mixed with rain dropped on the muddy ground as Hanzel trudged his way through streets and alleys thinking of his failure to save his friends and benefactors. Tomorrow they would be hanged and become dead. The thought of witnessing their demise was too much for the young man to handle. He sobbed loudly and became exceedingly wet and cold before he came to grips with the unfortunate outcome of his trip to England.

Hanzel realized he was becoming very wet and cold. The light of an ordinary attracted him into a grimy little place in a smelly alley; where the lowest of the low carried on their nefarious schemes and lusty manners. The place reeked of stale ale and unwashed human beings in various stages of inebriation. Fortunately a place on a bench was available. Hanzel was glad to get out of the rain.

A huge, fat woman approached him and asked if he wanted a drink. Hanzel snapped out of his thoughts and regarded her for a moment. She had a huge cleavage which seemed to go on and on. Hanzel had never seen such a huge bosom. He was quite speechless for a moment.

'Oiy, so's yu loikes moi teets?' asked the woman, laughing. 'Ey, Jonas, de boi ere loikes me teets!' she shouted to a fat man with a bottle in his hands.

'If'n yer wantsta fook er, yer gotsta poi fer eet,' said the man she called, Jonas.

Hanzel regarded Jonas for a long while, as he processed what the man had said to him. He looked at the woman and back at Jonas. 'With all due respect, but, no thank you. I just came here for a cup of ale and to get out of the rain.'

'Ah, so's eet's ale ye be wantin. Jes a minute.' The fat woman regarded Jonas. 'Ee jes wantsa cup o' ale.'

'Roight yer are den, Aazel,' he said as he reached for a wooden cup. He poured the ale, until it frothed over the rim. Hazel brought it to Hanzel.

'Dat'l be n' aypenny,' she said.

Hanzel reached into his purse, extracted a copper, and handed it to the fat woman. She gave him a penny in change. Then she waddled off to help another customer. Hanzel drank a deep drought of the rancid ale. He did not care. It brought relief. He drank the entire cup and immediately ordered another. Hanzel burped when he finished his second cup. He did not care. Nobody cared what anybody did in that haunt of conycatchers, trollops, and masterless men; poor folk who lived by their wits to stay alive. There was no other choice for them. It was either a low life, or no life at all. Relief from poverty is what those people needed; those who were sitting there in that grimy ordinary, in that muddy, slimy alley, far from the Tower of London. Three such people were eyeing Hanzel beginning to feel his cups.

'Ees gota poise full a monie,' whispered a deep voice in a dark corner.

'Oiy sow eet, Chaalie. Oiy tinks we ota releeve im of eet, roight awoiy. Afore ee spends eet all ere in dis ordinary,' replied another masculine voice.

'Looks loike ee's de sun of 'n a genelmun, frum a look a is clotes,' said the first voice.

'Ees a fine cony to catch,' said a third voice. She cackled softly. 'Me thinks it's toime to woik.'

'Alright then, let's catch us a cony,' said the first voice. He stepped out of the dark shadows of the room. Light glinted off his tin nose. Grinning, he approached Hanzel. The young Hollander paid him no heed. He was focused on his thoughts. Hanzel was on his fourth cup of ale by this time. The tin nosed conycatcher stood for a long moment watching Hanzel, before speaking.

'Ello me fine fello,' said the man with his sonorous voice.

Hanzel paid no attention.

The tin nosed man regarded Hanzel for another long moment, wondering if Hanzel was deaf. He nudged Hanzel's shoulder. 'Ello,' he said.

Hanzel looked up and regarded the man. 'Hello,' he answered.

'Ye look verrie sad, me fine yung frend. Whoi so glum, chum?' The tin nosed man sat beside Hanzel.

'My friends are going to be hung tomorrow, and I couldn't do anything about it,' replied Hanzel sadly. 'The king thinks they're traitors.'

'I hoid about eet. Two of em traitors is noblemen,' replied the man. 'I reckon ther'll be a large crowd dere. People loikes a good execution.'

Hanzel stared at the man.

The man cleared his throat. 'Not me, of corse. I don't loike executions. Give me an uncomfortable feelin' in me stomach.' He rubbed his neck for a moment, as if he foresaw his own hanging, someday. Conycatchers, when caught, could just as easily face a hanging as the stocks.

'Perhaps a goime of doice moiht be in ohdah; to take yer moind of'n yer problems,' said the man, taking a pair of dice out of his pocket. 'Dese ere doice is moighty locky.' He showed the dice to Hanzel. Then he rolled them on the table. A pair of snake eyes turned up.

The man pointed to the dice. 'See dat. Oi was thinkin' snake oiyes, an dere dey is.'

Hanzel stared at the dice.

'Go ahed, pik em up. Ye can do er,' said the man, smiling. Hanzel noticed he was missing several teeth. Two others were black and rotting. His breath reeked of stale ale, onions, and tobacco.

Hanzel crinkled his nose as he picked up the dice. 'Alright, I'll throw a pair of sixes.' He shook the dice in his hands and tossed the dice on the table. To his astonishment and delight, a pair of sixes did come up.

'See, oi tol ye so,' said the man. He smiled as he picked up the dice. 'Olroight, I'll trow a pair o' sixes.' He shook the dice in his left hand and tossed them on the table. Up came a one and a six. 'Loike all onest doice, dey don always foller yer orders.' He laughed.

Hanzel picked up the dice. 'I'll throw another pair of sixes.' He shook the dice and tossed them on the table. A pair of sixes came up. *Hmm. I seem to have to have a way with these things.*

'Do ye care to moike a liddle waagah? Ter make tings interestin?' said the man, pulling a coin from his purse. He laid it on the table. 'It'll take yer moind of'n yer problems.' He nodded and pointed to the half penny on the table.

Hanzel nodded. 'Alright. Sure. I'll wager one of those.' He reached into his purse and extracted a penny. 'I don't have a half penny. So I'll use this.' He set the larger coin on the table beside the man's coin. 'Since you made the wager first, you can roll first.'

'Olroight, I'll roll a pair o' eyes,' said the man as he shook the dice in his left hand. He tossed the dice on the table. A one and a four came up. The man stared at the dice for a moment and frowned. 'If yer call comes up ye wins de coins. Udderwoise, we keeps go in. If'n yer wanna add more wagers, that is. It's up ter yew.'

Hanzel nodded. 'I understand.' He shook the dice in both hands. 'I'll roll another pair of sixes.' He rolled the dice on the table. A pair of sixes came up. Hanzel smiled. 'It looks like I won.'

The man nodded. 'Aiy, ye won.'

Hanzel took the two coins in hand. Then he smiled happily. 'Do you want to play again?'

Tin Nose eyed Hanzel for a moment. Then he looked toward his friends sitting in the shadows. He nodded slightly. A moment later, one by one, the other conycatchers joined Hanzel and the tin nosed man at the table.

Tin Nose nodded to Hanzel. 'Olroight, I'll gives er anodder troi.' He reached into his purse and extracted another half penny. He laid it on the table.

Hanzel smiled and placed the penny and half penny on the table. 'I'll make it a penny, hay penny,' said Hanzel, feeling very confident.

'Oiy. Yur feelin lucky, are ye?' The man added a penny and a half penny.

'D'ye moind, guvno, if'n me frend an oi plays along?' said the woman to the tin nosed man.

Tin Nose looked at Hanzel. 'What d'ye tink? Lets em ploiy?'

Hanzel regarded the woman and the other man. He shrugged his shoulders. "I don't see why not. The more the merrier.' He took a sip from his fifth cup of ale and was beginning to really feel the effects. *I better not drink more. I am feeling woozy. Boy, oh boy. Those dice sure are rolling well for me. I'm gonna make a lot of money here.*

'De more monie is in de pot,' said the other man; a short fellow with very thin, stringy hair. 'De moh I can win.' He tossed a couple of pennies on the table. They clinked as they touched the other coins. The woman also tossed two pennies, making a nice little pile lying before Hanzel's widened eyes.

'Yew each gots ta trow in a hay penny. On account is, me an Molly each put in two pence.'

The tin nosed man regarded Molly and the short man and then looked at Hanzel. 'Whot yew soi, guvnoh?'

'I don't have any half pennies,' said Hanzel, looking into his purse.

'Yew gots ter trow in a whole penny, on account there be two hay pennies, combined,' said the tin nose.

Hanzel nodded and tossed another penny on the table. Tin Nose did the same.

If I win, that's a nice pile of money to add to my purse. Hanzel regarded the pile of coins and smiled.

'Oil trow in anuddah two pence.' The woman regarded Hanzel and smiled, showing a mouth full of missing teeth. 'Since Oi tinks de boy can not trow anuddah dubble, I'll wager me monie on im not trowin dubbles.'

'Me too,' said the short man. 'Oil wager de same.' He tossed two more pennies on the table.

Tin Nose smiled at Hanzel and gestured for him to add two more pennies. By this time Hanzel was becoming confused with the numbers and who was betting what. He tossed two more pennies on the table; as did the tin nosed man. He pointed to the dice. 'It's your toss. I'll wager ye don trow dubbles agin, as well.'

Hanzel looked at the three people, one by one. He pointed at the pile of money on the table. 'So, if I throw doubles, you are saying that money is mine?'

'Dah's wot we'se bettin on; dat ye not trow dubbles agin,' said Tin Nose.

Hanzel smiled. Even though he was into his cups, he had a good feeling about the dice. He picked up the ivory cubes from the table and shook them in both hands. When he rolled them on the table, they stopped on double sixes. 'Haaa! I did it!" Hanzel laughed happily. He eyed the pile of money. 'So, that's all mine?'

The three people all agreed that he had won and the pile of pennies and half pennies was his.

Hanzel eyed the money and the dice. 'I'll tell you what. If you like, I'll give you a chance to win it back. Do you want to make another wager? I'll bet the entire pile,' slurred Hanzel, greedily.

The three conycatchers eyed Hanzel and acted as if it was a great pile of money to them; however they all felt confident that Hanzel could not throw another set of doubles. Hence, they all three matched the wager, making the pile, 6 Shillings. It was a goodly pile of coins. The three gamblers all bet against Hanzel throwing doubles. However, he again threw double sixes. The three conycatchers bemoaned their losses, however they decided to play one more time. Hanzel agreed and left the coins on the table. 'I'll bet the lot,' he said.

The conycatchers agreed and they each added 6 Shillings in various denominations; now making the pile, one Pound, four Shillings, a very sizable sum already. The conycatchers were sorely perplexed when Hanzel rolled another double six.

Hanzel was grinning from ear to ear. He had won a goodly pile. He decided to be bold and placed his purse on the table. 'Since you all seem to have money to play with and I seem to have a goodly control of these dice. I'll wager my purse that I will throw another set of doubles. Will you bet your purses?'

The three conycatchers looked at each other and entered into a serious discussion.

'Oim gung te wager e trows udder numers,' said the short man. He regarded his purse for a moment. It was not very fat, but it was all that he had.

'Oim gung te wager e trows anudder dubble,' said the woman, putting her purse on the table. It appeared to hold a number of coins. Hanzel smiled at that. He took a sip of his ale and regarded the dice. He concentrated on double sixes. *When I throw another double six, I'll have enough money to buy my friends a decent burial, I hope. Poor Gerrit and Master van Dijk...*

'Oil wager e trows udder numers,' said the tin nosed man. He picked up the dice and placed them into his palm and regarded them for a moment as he rolled them around. Unbeknownst to Hanzel, he changed the dice to those he rolled with his left hand before replacing them on the table. 'What do ye wager, yung fello?' he said as he laid his fat purse on the table.

Hanzel regarded the fat purse and ignored the tin nosed man as he replaced the dice on the table. Hanzel took a sip of his ale. 'I will roll another double,' he said confidently. 'And I am betting my purse against yours.'

'Ow do I knows yer poise is equal to moine?' asked the tin nosed man.

Hanzel eyed the man as he opened his purse. He poured out a sizable sum in Dutch silver and gold. All six eyes of the conspirators opened wide when they beheld the pile.

The tin nosed man nodded his head. 'Ol roight, ye can bet agin me poise.'

Hanzel rolled the dice in his hands. He never thought to ask what was in the man's purse. He was totally intent on rolling double sixes.

'That's the spirit, yung fellah,' said the woman. 'Make it appen, coz oi bet on ye. We'll split the proize. Yew n' me, we'll split the proize, if'n yew trow dubbles. Ye kin do it.'

Hanzel drained his cup. He was beginning to see double, but he did not care. He was about to win a goodly sum of money. 'I will roll doubles,' he slurred, confidently as he shook the dice in his hands. *Please let it be double sixes. Please, please...* He tossed the dice on the table.

The dice rolled onto the wooden table with a clatter. Hanzel watched them in slow motion and through a glass darkly. It seemed like minutes before the dice stopped rolling. When they stopped, the numbers were; six and one.

At first Hanzel could not make out the number of dots on the dice correctly. It was if he was looking through fog. As he stared at the dice he heard the two men laughing and the woman bemoaning her loss. The tin nosed man picked up the dice and helped the short man gather up the money and purses. They quickly disappeared into the shadows, leaving the woman to console Hanzel for a moment, before she also disappeared into the darkness of the room, to join her friends, leaving Hanzel in a daze and unable to pay his ale bill. He tried to explain but it was to no avail. The inn keeper had him tossed into the rainy alley, where he landed with a thud and a splash; drunk and unable to right himself.

Rain pelted Hanzel and further liquified the slimy ground he lay on. Hanzel moaned but nobody heard him. He was alone in his misery. Not even the rats were out in that horrid place.

Eventually, Hanzel began to recover his senses. He vomited the contents of his stomach and felt much better for having done so. The rancid ale had done a nasty work inside his body. *I'm never doing that again....I feel awful...* He vomited again. This time it felt as if his insides were coming out through his burning throat.

He slowly righted himself and looked at his surroundings. He faintly remembered what had happened to him. He felt for his purse. When he realized it was not there, he was suddenly sober and instantly aware of what had happened to him. *I'll find those scum and get my money back. I swear it. Even if I have to sell my soul to the devil, by God.* A sudden flash of lightning lit up the miserable place he was in. Hanzel had to shield his eyes as the intense light destroyed the shadows of the filthy alley, suddenly revealing a dead body lying beside a heap of trash. Hanzel recoiled. *I'm in Hell. I've got to get out of here.*

He stood up and straightened his wet clothes. He looked about himself to see where he was in relation to the ordinary, where he had been robbed. *I'll bet that's their regular hideout. I'll recognize Tin Nose anywhere.* Hanzel realized that he was cold and needed to dry off. He stumbled off to find *The Tower Inn* and the friendly bar wench who let him sleep in her bed.

By the time morning came, the sun merely brightened the thick hazy drizzle through which Hanzel struggled to find his way to the Tower Inn; in hope of finding the girl who might take pity on him, once again.

When Hanzel arrived at the inn, he was soaked through to the bone and shivering. He stepped into the warm common room. There were only a few people sitting about eating an early breakfast. The place was deserted for the most part. When Jane saw him, she immediately recognized the handsome boy from Holland. She greeted him happily.

'What happened to you?' she asked, as she regarded the drenched young man standing there.

'It's a long story,' replied Hanzel, shivering. 'I was robbed.'

Jane looked shocked. Oh, no. Poor Hanzel,' she said, sympathetically. 'Come sit by the fire and dry off. Looking at you, me thinks you could use a bath.' The girl looked at his mud caked hair and face. 'When you warm up, I'll bring you some warm water and a towel.'

Hanzel smiled and touched her hand. 'You are an angel, Jane. Thank you.'

Hanna smiled.

'What time is it?' asked Hanzel, suddenly realizing it was execution day.

'It is but six o'clock, thereabouts,' she replied. 'I am on breakfast duty.'

'I must attend the execution. My friends are to be hanged for treason.'

'Only hanged? They're not to be drawn and quartered?' she asked. 'I thought I heard that these executions were for treason.'

Hanzel shook his head. 'That's what my masters are charged with, but because they're foreign arms makers, they'll just be hanged.'

'Thank God for that. To be drawn and quartered, that would be such a horrible death.' Jane screwed up her face with a look of disgust. 'It is all so horrible. We live in barbaric times.'

Hanzel nodded. 'It is that, alright. Barbaric....'

Jane agreed and paused for a moment as they both reflected on the twisted nature of their world.

Jane was the first to break the silence. 'Well, I should get to work. I'll bring you a hot drink.'

'No ale, please,' he replied with a rueful smile. 'I think I'm giving up on ale.'

'Don't worry,' she said and walked off, leaving Hanzel to sit by the warm fire ruminating about his circumstances.

Jane brought Hanzel a hot rum toddy, which greatly warmed him and helped him to sleep for a couple of hours, lying on the bench beside the fire. She woke him around eight thirty and brought him a bowl of warm water and a towel. Hanzel washed his hands and face. Then he placed his long hair into the bowl and washed the mud away. When he dried himself off, he felt very much better. Jane brought him some pottage for breakfast, which he ate greedily.

Other people had come into the room and were ordering breakfast, so that Jane could not spend more time with him. She invited him to come back after the executions. 'I'll give you a place to sleep and food, if you help out around here, until you can get your money back. If that will even be possible.'

Hanzel narrowed his eyes as he regarded Jane. 'I'll get my money back. I'm sure I can find Mister Tin Nose.'

'A man with a tin nose robbed you?' Jane smiled. 'He comes in here from time to time. A tall, thin man?'

Hanzel nodded. 'Sounds like the same man. Tall, thin, and with a tin nose.'

'He lost the nose because it was cut off in Spain for molesting a virgin and stealing her father's money. He's not a very nice man. He'd sell his own mother.' Jane frowned. 'You should avoid him.'

'I'll avoid him after I get my money back,' replied Hanzel.

'Well, whatever you do, don't get yourself killed. Tin Nose is dangerous,' cautioned Jane. 'Anyway, when it's all over, with the executions, and all, you can come back here.'

'You're very kind to me, Jane. I will always be grateful to you.' Hanzel smiled and touched her hand. Then he turned and left the inn, headed for Tower Hill.

When Hanzel arrived on the infamous hill, the rain had stopped and the sun was beginning to break through the clouds. There were already several thousand people standing by the scaffold and milling about, selling wares, or picking pockets. Dozens and dozens of people were arriving by the minute. Noise and human stench filled the space. It reminded Hanzel a lot of an earlier execution; that of his father. Here too, seagulls screamed overhead and crows were gathering.

The scaffold was somewhat similar to the one in Amsterdam, except there were no wheels, just a large and small table, a glowing brazier, plus a very wide hangman's tree, from which twenty nooses were hanging.

'Dis is going ta be a groit beet o' fun, oi? ' said a man standing next to Hanzel.

'Aye, eet'l be sum gute entertainmen,' replied his companion; a short fat man with stringy hair. Hanzel regarded him for a moment. *He looks like one of the fellows who robbed me. I wonder if it's him.* Hanzel kept an eye on the man. *He sure looks like him. I wonder if Tin Nose is nearby.* Hanzel scanned the crowd.

Drums came from within the walls of the Tower. The crowd started to become quiet. Moments later, Hanzel could see the drum corps and guardsmen, followed by horse drawn tumbrels; behind which, the prisoners were being dragged to the scaffold. The drum corps, with their black velvet draped drums, marched in front of the scaffold and continued their sad rhythm as the executioners and several clerics stepped up on the scaffold. The crowd booed.

The crowd booed even louder when the king's representatives stepped onto the platform. A moment later, the twenty men, who were about to be hanged, were untied from the carts, and one by one, prodded up the stairs. As each man came to stand on the platform, with his hands tied behind his back, the mob jeered and shouted. The noise was deafening.

The executioners led each man to his rope and placed the noose tightly around his neck. When Gerritt and Master van Dijk came to stand on the platform, Hanzel's heart stood still and lodged itself in his throat. *I wish I could have helped them. I feel so terrible.*

When the twenty men were all standing on the scaffold with the nooses around their necks, an official of the court stepped forward and read the various charges for which the men were to be hung. The offenses ranged from treason to cony catching. One woman was being hung for witchcraft.

When the charges were read, the official signaled to the executioners to proceed. Then, one by one, the condemned people were hoisted a few inches off the ground and tied off; to finish their lives doing a dead man's dance, much to the enjoyment of the assembled throng.

The crowd's cheering was deafening, but Hanzel could hear nothing. His ears went deaf as his eyes streamed with tears. He could barely see through the haze, as his dear friends did their dance of death. A few long and terrible minutes later they were hanging lifeless from the end of their ropes. Hanzel vomited.

'Ey, watch it guvno!' shouted the man on whom Hanzel nearly spilled his half digested pottage. 'If'n ye can nay stan de site, stoiy awoiy!' The man glowered at Hanzel, but seeing that the young Hollander stood a head taller than him, he decided to let it go and returned his gaze toward the scaffold, where the executioners were giving each corpse a good yank by the legs, to make sure each man was good and strangled. When it was ascertained each man was dead, they cut Gerritt down and laid his body on the large table. Then they cut off his head and stuck it on a pike. Hanzel nearly fainted. The executioners did the same to Master van Dijk.

'Traitors!' shouted the court official. 'Their heads will be placed at the entrance to London Bridge for all potential traitors to learn a lesson. King James does not suffer the ingratitude of traitors!'

The crowd cheered.

Hanzel cried. It was too much for him. Cutting off the heads of his friends and seeing them stuck on pikes, was too revolting.

Hanzel felt like leaving, and yet, the upcoming event; the drawing and quartering kept Hanzel glued to his place in the crowd. The idea was so revolting, and yet incredible at the same time. Morbid fascination held him rooted to the ground.

The court official stepped forward, as a well dressed gentleman was brought up on the scaffold and made to stand before the crowd.

'For high treason against the King, I present, Lord John of Chesterton.'

The crowd booed. Some threw rotten vegetables.

'Traitor!' shouted several people.

'Hang im!' shouted some others.

'Les see whot es guts look loike!' shouted several more.

'Quiet!' shouted the official. He held up his right hand. The crowd went quiet and the official continued reading from the parchment in his left hand.

'For high treason, you, Lord John of Chesterton are to be hanged by the neck, until you are near death. Then your genitals will be cut off and burned before your face, after which your entrails will be extracted from your body and equally burned before your eyes. When your eyes have beheld your demise, your head will be struck from your body and your body divided into four parts to be displayed outside Chesterton manor, and three other locations within this realm, to educate the people that there is a severe penalty for treason against the King of England, James the First. Do you have anything to say?'

Lord Chesterton, having been tortured in The Tower, appeared weak and greatly distraught. Hanzel could clearly see that the man was not in complete control of his limbs; they likely having been disjointed on a rack. He stared wild eyed at the assembled throng. Then, in a barely audible, croaky voice he delivered his final words.

'People of England,' he stammered, 'There is an Antichrist upon the throne of this realm! Indeed, King James pretends to be holy, and yet, he puts himself above God by denying the Pope in Rome.'

Some in the crowd jeered, hissed, and shouted obscenities. The official in charge held up his hands and demanded quiet. The crowd settled down and the condemned man continued.

'The Pope is the only true representative of Christ on Earth, not King James!' he sputtered.

'Get on wid it!' shouted a voice.

'Papist!' yelled another voice as people began to throw more rotten vegetables onto the scaffold.

'TRAITOR!' shouted hundreds of voices in unison.

'Let im speak!' shouted other voices.

The official in charge held up his hands. 'People! The king has ruled that Lord Chesterton be allowed to have his say. Now, quiet down and let him speak!'

The restless crowd settled down and Lord Chesterton continued his diatribe. He went on at some length, about how Jesus founded his church on a rock named Peter, not some other person, such as Calvin, Luther, or King James. How Satan and his minions ruled the land and permitted such atrocities as the people were about to witness. 'Is this a Christian thing to do?! To butcher me and make of me a spectacle?! To recreate a vision from Hell!?!' He shook his fist in the direction of The Tower. 'You call yourself a Christian King, to allow such as this to happen in your realm!?! I SAY, YOU ARE THE ANTICHRIST!'

Lord Chesterton began coughing and wheezing. The effort was too much for him. Drool seeped from his mouth. He was not a young man. His white hair and beard attested to that. The exertion was too much for him and he collapsed to his knees.

Some in the crowd booed, others threw more wilted vegetables, but many were still and reflecting on what Lord Chesterton had said. Hanzel was one of them.

The official asked if that was all he was going to say.

Lord Chesterton wanted to say more, but his voice would not let him. He stared at the maddened crowd, wheezing and trying to catch his breath; his eyes fearfully regarding the instruments of his impending ordeal.

The official signaled to the executioners. 'Let the execution begin!'

The crowd cheered as Lord Chesterton was led to his rope. An executioner placed the noose around his neck and cinched it tight. Then three men pulled on the rope and hauled the nobleman off the ground. Hanzel could hear the man choking as he danced and danced. When the man's blue tongue began to protrude from his lips, the executioners dropped him. The old man fell down and crumpled, groaning to the boards. Two executioners grabbed him by the arms and dragged him to the table. Two apprentices helped to lift him up and laid him on his back. They spread out his arms and legs tied them with strong leather belts. One of the executioners grabbed a bucket from under the little table and splashed water on the nobleman's face. Moments later Lord Chesterton sputtered and revived.

'Les see whot e's got!' shouted a female voice near the front of the scaffold.

'Yeh, let us see if 'n e's got anyting woith a woman's whoile!' shouted another shrieking voice.

The crowd laughed.

One of the executioners; a tall, muscular man approached the table. He was wearing a leather hood over his face and a long, leather apron. In his hand was a large knife. He proceeded to slice the victim's breeches open, revealing the old man's private parts. The crowd went wild as the executioner carefully cut off the nobleman's testicles and penis. All the while Lord Chesterton stared wide eyed at the crowd and grimaced with intense pain. He did not utter more than a horrified gasp.

The executioner showed the severed penis and testicles to the hapless man and then carefully placed the man's private parts on the brazier. The crowd went wild with horrified pleasure. They cheered and shouted obscenities. Within moments, the smell of roasting flesh permeated the place as the executioner placed a white hot iron on the wound to sear the flesh and close the bleeding vessels. Lord Chesterton screamed.

When Lord Chesterton had stopped screaming, a second executioner; another big man, but with more experience regarding the arrangement of things in a body, carefully unbuttoned the Lord's waistcoat. He did not want to spoil it by cutting it off. Then he carefully removed the waistcoat and handed it to his assistant. He also carefully removed the Lord's shirt, which he also handed to his assistant. Then, with another very sharp knife, he sliced into the Lord's abdomen and opened the wound so he could look to where he would extract the entrails. When he ascertained the correct place, he inserted his hook and began to pull out Lord Chesterton's guts.

The pain must have been immense, for poor Lord Chesterton screamed and moaned as he twisted his head and torso and pulled on his restraints. The crowd cheered and clapped and shouted obscenities; mostly to muffle the awful sounds of the screaming man.

When Lord Chesterton's steaming guts were fully withdrawn from his twitching body, they were shown to him, still conscious on the table and staring with intense pain; his face mad; his eyes bulging. The steaming pile of guts were tossed on the brassier, instantly filling the air with the smell of burnt excrement and quivering flesh.

Then the first executioner, because he was younger and stronger, took up a large axe and with one mighty blow nearly severed Lord Chesterton's head from his twitching body. He had to chop once more to complete what he could do with the axe. The last strings holding the head to the body were cut with a knife and Lord Chesterton's head dropped into the basket held by the other executioner. The crowd cheered.

The executioner reached into the basket and pulled the head out by the hair and showed the head to the body on the table and then to the crowd. Most of the crowd cheered and yelled. Others silently reflected on what they had witnessed. Others were totally revolted. Some were mad as hell.

Hanzel continued to stare at the scaffold, for things were not over for Lord Chesterton's remains. The head was stuck on a pike and his body was quartered with an axe, a saw, and a knife. The pieces were laid down on the scaffold, to be distributed after the horror was done and the executions were over. Hanzel did not stay to watch anymore. He had seen enough. Now that he had seen what the English did to traitors, he did not need to see anymore. *I'll never get myself in a plot against a king. My God they're a ruthless people here too. Breaking people, hacking people, hanging them. it is all so horrible.*

Poor man. To see your own dick cut off. Hanzel shivered as he thought of it. *And to have your guts pulled out. And to be alive and smell your own entrails burning. The smell was disgusting.* Hanzel grimaced and shook his head. The experience had been a terrifying event. *I don't ever want to see that again.*

Hanzel walked off Tower Hill filled with thoughts about what he had witnessed. It was a view of Hell. 'I'm never going to end up there,' he said out loud to nobody in particular. Nobody paid attention, the street was mostly empty on account of the spectacle on the blood soaked Hill.

Hanzel walked back towards The Tower Inn, in a haze. What he had witnessed was very unsettling to the young man. He walked like a zombie, directly to his refuge. It was already late afternoon. *She might have gone home. I hope not. She did say I was welcome to stay with her.*

He arrived at the inn, two hours later, on account of him getting lost in the warren of streets, lanes, and alleys. Hanzel heaved a sigh of relief to find the Tower Inn, at last. His legs were tired and his feet were sore. His heart was heavy and his mood was sad as he stepped into the eating hall. *I have no money. What can I do?' I hope Jane will help me.* She smiled when she saw Hanzel step into the room.

Poor Hanzel, he looks so sad. I'll bring him a toddy. That should cheer him up.

Hanzel sat down on the bench in front of the fire. He was cold and miserable. *What am I going to do now? How will I get back to Holland, if I have no money to buy my passage? I'm stuck here.*

'Hello, Hanzel,' said Jane, approaching him.

Hanzel looked up and managed a rueful smile. 'Hello, Jane,' he said.

'You sound very sad, Hanzel. I guess the executions did not sit well with you.' Jane gently touched his shoulder.

Hanzel hung his head and began to cry. 'It was all so horrible. I have never in my life seen anything more horrible. Thinking of it makes my stomach turn.'

'That's why I never go to them. I went once, when I was a little girl. It was just a hanging, but that was enough for me,' replied Jane. 'I never want to see something like that, let alone a drawing and quartering.'

'All I can say is, whoever can order and have carried out such an abomination, is a very sick individual.' Hanzel paused for a moment to wipe his eyes and nose on a handkerchief he kept in the pocket of his waistcoat. 'What kind of human animals are those fellows who chopped up Lord Chesterton? What kind of human being can open up someone's belly and pull out their entrails? Or cut off their privates and roast them on a fire?'

'There are all kinds of people in this world, Hanzel. Not all of them are as good as you.' Jane moved her hand over his back. 'I'll bring you a hot toddy. That'll help to lighten your spirit.'

Hanzel looked up. 'I have no money, Jane. Tin Nose and his cronies got it all.'

'Don't worry, Hanzel. I'll take care of you.' Jane smiled and then turned on her heels to fetch a toddy for her Dutch friend.

If it's true that Tin Nose comes here. Maybe I can work for my keep and bide my time until he shows up. Yes, but then what? What are you going to do? How am I going to get my money back? If he hasn't spent it already. Can I turn him in and get a reward? Will the authorities arrest him and return my purse? That's a question. I'll ask Jane. Maybe she knows....

Jane returned with a hot toddy in a large clay stein. She set it on the table beside the bench Hanzel was sitting on. 'This will help to lift your spirits,' she said.

'Are there police here?' asked Hanzel.

'Police? What do you want with police?'

'Maybe I can turn Tin Nose in to the authorities and have them get my purse back.' He regarded Jane with a hopeful expression.

'I wouldn't be turning Tin Nose into no authorities. He has a large gang. You for sure would end up dead.' Jane looked up as three people entered the room. She leaned down and spoke more softly. 'Tin Nose has people everywhere around this entire district. It's just your luck you were scammed by one of the best conycatchers in London.'

'Do you think it's possible to get him?' asked Hanzel.

'Like I said. He comes in here from time to time,' replied Jane. 'I have no idea, at the moment, how you can deal with him. I'm not really into that sort of thinking. Especially not with regard to someone like him.'

'Can I work here?' asked Hanzel. 'So I can earn my keep and at the same time be able to keep an eye on Tin Nose.'

Jane paused for a moment. 'We don't want any blood shed in here, Hanzel.'

'Oh, I don't think I will have to kill Tin Nose. I just need to figure out a way to get my purse back. If I don't get my purse back, I won't have money to buy my passage back to Holland.'

Jane smiled. 'Alright. I'll ask Mister Brinker. He's the man who owns this place. It's possible he may have a job for you.'

'Thank you Jane.' Hanzel smiled; a twinkle returning to his saddened eyes.

Jane smiled. 'You're welcome, Hanzel.'

Hanzel watched as she walked off to find Mister Brinker, who was busy preparing dinner pottage and ham in the kitchen. Misses Brinker was cooking eggs. Their daughter, Bess was cutting onions. Hanzel took a sip of the toddy and smiled. *I pray she can convince Mister Brinker.*

It was a good thing for Hanzel that Missus Brinker was in charge. She took a liking to the handsome young man right away. He was put to work the very next day.

Chapter 15

Three weeks later, on a rare sunny Saturday morning, while Hanzel was cleaning a large cooking pot in the yard behind the kitchen, Tin Nose showed up at the Tower Inn. He was accompanied by the same two people who helped him to fleece Hanzel; the woman and the pudgy man. Jane was the first to see them enter the eating hall. She scurried off to warn Hanzel.

In the two weeks, he and Jane had come to live together, she and he had discussed numerous plans, how to bilk Tin Nose out of his money. The best plan they could come up with was to spike his drink.

'Yes, but we didn't count on him bringing two others with him. Do we even have enough powder to make three people drowsy?' asked Hanzel, looking up at Jane standing beside him.

'Well, I'm not really sure. It's really pure opium. That's what my brother said. He should know. My brother is a sailor and he's been to the Indies and back a number of times.'

'Well, I guess we'll see. We may have to buy some extra drink for these thieves,' said Hanzel. 'I'm prepared to spend my passage money that I've saved, so far.'

Jane frowned. 'That'll barely buy two rounds for the three of em.'

'Yes, but look at it this way. I invest that money, to get back that money and the rest of it too.'

Jane smiled. 'You're so clever, Hanzel.' She bent down and kissed him. 'Finish cleaning that pot and help me get things done in the kitchen. I have to go attend to Tin Nose.' She stroked Hanzel's head. 'Okay, my Hanzel, let's hope Tin Nose is planning to stay here for a while.'

Hanzel watched as Jane walked back into the building. He quickly finished cleaning the pot and set it in the sun to dry. He wiped his hands on his apron and then stepped into the kitchen, just as Jane returned from the dining hall. She regarded Hanzel and winked her right eye. Hanzel knew what she meant. Tin Nose had come to the inn because he knew it was going to be busy that day. It was Saturday; and there was to be another execution on Tower Hill. The inn would be crowded with people. Tin Nose wanted to make sure he had a good seat in a place where many people were sure to be that afternoon and evening. The inn was not a cheap ordinary. A more expensive clientele ate and drank there. Tin Nose preferred to fleece the well healed who would come to eat and drink after the spectacle.

'We're in luck. He's here to eat and drink,' she whispered. 'They chose to sit in that dark corner, at the far end of the hall.'

'Where's the powder?' whispered Hanzel. He looked over his shoulder to see if Bess had overheard him. However, Bess was busy cutting up onions. She was humming to her self.

'I hid it over here,' answered Jane, as she opened a cupboard door. She extracted a small jar from behind several larger jars and showed it to Hanzel.

'So, what do we do with it?' asked Hanzel, not having any experience with opium powder.

'We'll put it in their drinks. I think that's likely the best way. It'll dissolve in their ale.' Jane walked to the ale barrel. She set the little jar down and grabbed three clay steins and poured equal amounts of the powder in the three vessels. Then she filled the steins with ale and swished each one to make sure the powder was dissolved.

'Should we taste it to see if they can tell?' asked Hanzel.

Jane shrugged her shoulders. 'I'm sure a little sip won't make much difference.' She held up a stein. 'Here,' she said, 'Try it.'

Hanzel took a little sip and swished the ale in his mouth before swallowing. 'Tastes normal, to me,' he said.

Jane also took a small sip from another stein and swished the ale in her mouth before swallowing. She nodded and smiled. 'I can't tell.'

'Alright then,' said Hanzel. 'Bring them their drinks and let's hope it works. If they fall asleep, we'll just simply pick them clean before many more customers arrive. We're lucky they picked the right place to sit.'

Jane smiled and nodded her head. She picked up the steins and walked out of the kitchen.

If this works, it was well worth spending the money on the powder. I'm sure Tin Nose has my money and more. I have to get home and tell the families what happened. They must be wondering what's going on. Hanzel opened the door to the dining hall and peeked out. However, the far corner of the room was dark and not really visible from the kitchen door, due to the angle of the room.

Jane returned. 'They've ordered food.'

Hanzel stepped back into the kitchen. Jane followed him. 'Okay, let's make them some food.'

'Bess, where are your parents?' asked Jane, as she began to stir the pottage.

'Had to deal with the chickens,' replied Bess, slicing a leek. 'They'll be back before the crowds arrive.'

'What about Robert?' Jane grabbed three bowls from the shelf where they were kept.

'He's gone to the market to fetch some oil. Father forgot when he was there yesterday.' Bess smacked her knife down on the cutting board, cleaving a cabbage.

'So, it's just us, for now,' said Jane. 'No problem. We're not busy yet. That works out best for us,' she whispered to Hanzel. Jane scooped pottage into the bowls. 'Slice three slabs of ham and put them on top of the bowls.'

Hanzel nodded and sliced the ham. Jane cut three slabs of rye bread and placed them on a plate. When the food was ready, she placed the bowls and plate on a tray and brought the meals to the three brigands. When she arrived at the table, the three cony catchers were already half way through their ales.

'I hope the food doesn't lessen the effect of the powder,' said Hanzel, as soon as Jane returned to the kitchen.

'I hope so too,' replied Jane. She looked back into the room, before closing the door. 'Well, I guess all we can do now is wait.' She gave Hanzel a quick kiss. 'I've got to get out there. More people have come in to eat and drink before the executions begin at one thirty.'

'What's it this time?' asked Hanzel sardonically.

'Three hangings, a decapitation, five mutilations, and a drawing and quartering,' replied Jane. 'There's a poster in the market. I read it three days ago.'

Hanzel nodded sadly. 'Such barbarity.'

'That's the truth for sure. But then, what do you do with traitors, murderers, and thieves?'

'Put them to work fixing things. Or have them build roads,' replied Hanzel.

'That makes sense. However, it would take a lot of soldiers to guard so many prisoners.' suggested Jane.

'It's better they guard dangerous prisoners than to use them for war. We would get public work done and soldiers would be doing something constructive rather than destructive. Don't you think?' Hanzel regarded Jane.

'You are so smart, Hanzel. Why the king doesn't think of it, I don't understand. Maybe he thinks barbaric spectacles are entertainment for the people. It keeps them fearful and base.' Jane set a stack of bowls down on the counter by the pottage pot. 'I'm going out to have a look if more customers have come in.' She looked at Bess. 'When do you think Robert will be back?'

Bess looked at Jane and frowned. 'He should be back by now.' She looked at the door. 'Probably taking his time flirting with the vegetable seller's daughter.'

Jane opened the door to the dining hall and peeked out. 'Yep, I knew it. We've got customers. We better get to work.' She smiled at Hanzel, and then walked out of the kitchen to attend to the people starting to drift in for lunch.

For the next two hours, Hanzel and Jane became busy, as the inn filled up with regulars and those who had come to watch the gruesome spectacle. Most of them would return to the inn for more food and drink afterwards. All of the sleeping quarters were booked. Executions were good for business.

As the two friends worked, they kept an eye on Tin Nose and his friends. Hanzel made certain that the villains never caught sight of him. Eventually, as the time neared twelve o'clock it was time for people to start walking to Tower Hill, in order to have a good place to stand. By fifteen after twelve the dining hall was empty, except for Tin Nose and his two companions, who were slumped over their table, fast asleep.

It only took Jane and Hanzel a minute to locate the sleeping cony catchers' purses. They quickly cut them loose from their belts. Tin Nose moaned and moved an arm, startling Hanzel as he was slicing through the leather strap holding the purse to the man's belt. Tin Nose opened an eye. Hanzel jumped back, purse in hand. Tin Nose snorted and turned his head, to rest it on his other arm. He continued his opium dream. Hanzel and Jane heaved a sigh of relief and then quickly disappeared with the purses through the kitchen to the yard. Bess was too busy cutting beets to take notice of Hanzel and Jane's comings and goings. She was used to their shenanigans.

When Hanzel opened Tin Nose's purse, his eyes widened. The purse was full of gold and silver coins. He recognized two of his daalders and a florin.

The other purses together wielded about the same amount as Tin Nose's purse. 'You keep those two,' said Hanzel. 'I'll take this one. There's about the same amounts in them, don't you think?'

Jane looked at the three purses and agreed. 'That's more money than I'd ever be able to save in a life of working here.' She suddenly had a thought. 'Where should I hide it? How do I avoid suspicion? Those people are not stupid. They're going to be questioning Missus Brinker.'

Hanzel shrugged his shoulders. 'You can't run home, because there's no time. The Brinkers and Robert will be back any moment.' Hanzel looked around. He pointed to an empty plant pot, sitting on the ground beside the shed. 'Put the purses in that pot and turn it over. You can retrieve the purses when you finish work.'

Jane nodded. 'Good idea.' She put the purses into the pot, as Hanzel had suggested and then placed the pot upside down between the shed and the wall of the kitchen. 'That's pretty safe. Bess didn't see anything, did she?'

Hanzel looked toward the kitchen door. He shook his head. 'I doubt it.'

'Well, I suppose we should get back to work, clearing the tables,' said Jane, walking back to the kitchen.

'Now that I have my money back, Jane, I have to go. I have to go back to my country and inform the families of my friends who were hanged. They have to know what happened.'

'You mean, you are going, now? Right now?'

Hanzel nodded. 'I think it's best. Leave before the Brinkers get back and before those villains wake up.'

'I'll go with you,' volunteered Jane. 'We can go together.'

'What about the Brinkers? My leaving and then you leaving, too? All of a sudden they have less staff and a busy inn to run. After all they have done for you, you can't just leave with me. They can understand me leaving, but not you too.'

Jane looked at the ground. 'You don't want me to come with you?'

'Of course I want you to come,' replied Hanzel, reassuringly. 'However, it just would not be practical. I have no idea what my future holds, with my masters dead.'

Jane nodded. 'Yes, I suppose there's that, isn't there?'

Hanzel stepped up to Jane and gave her a long hug. Jane was crying. She knew it had to be. Hanzel had to go away.

'So, when is it going to be then?' asked Jane, through her tears.

'Today, tomorrow. I don't know. I have to find a ship. Now that I have the money, I can buy passage.' Hanzel looked toward the kitchen. 'I think I should go now, while those three are sleeping. When they wake up, there are going to be questions.'

Jane looked sadly at the ground.

Hanzel regarded Jane. 'Thank you for everything, Jane. I will always remember you. I hope that money helps you have a happier life.'

'What about the money in your stash, under my bed?'

'You can keep it,' replied Hanzel. 'I don't need it. It's only a few pennies, anyway.' He looked at the door to the kitchen. 'I have to go. The sooner I get to the docks, the sooner I find a ship. I have to take the opportunity now. If those robbers wake up and find their purses gone, they're going to come looking. If they see me, they will suspect me immediately.'

Jane recognized the wisdom in Hanzel's words and let him go. 'Good bye Hanzel Sventska,' she said softly through her tears.

'Good bye, Jane Goodacre,' he replied. He smiled and gently stroked his right hand down the side of her head, touching her silky hair for the last time. Then, taking a deep breath, Hanzel turned and walked out of the back yard.

Hanzel wasted no time and walked as fast as he could to get away from the inn. *I have to get away from there, the sooner the better. The more distance I can put between me and Tin Nose, the safer I am. Taking his purse was so easy. That opium powder works great! Thank God for Jane's brother. That stuff is a useful product. Maybe I should think about getting some more of it. It's an easy way to gather purses and not have to work too hard. I like that idea. Poor Jane. I hope she's not caught with those purses. She was so sad. Well, at least she has two fat purses to make it easier for her. I still can't believe how easy that went.*

As Hanzel was thusly absorbed in thoughts, he walked as quickly as he could, south east towards the River Thames. *I'm sure I'll find a boat there. The river is full of boats.* As he came closer to the Thames, the air began to fill with the smell of the river; a rich, pungent smell of water and dead things; like rotting vegetable matter and fish. Gulls screeched in the air.

When he arrived at the river bank, he stood for a while to get his bearings. He was standing on the east side of London Bridge. He watched as a cleaning woman leaned out of the window of a house on the bridge. She slowly poured the contents of a chamber pot into the rushing waters below. Hanzel wondered how the bridge could remain standing in the river when the water was rushing so fast between the piers. *Surely that water is going to wear down those piers.*

Sea gulls screeched in the thick, moist air, and people, many people were talking and shouting, as they conducted their business on the river bank and in the many boats plying their trade on the dark grey waters. Hanzel watched in amazement as a group of brave individuals shot through the turbulent waters rushing between piers near the middle of the bridge.

'There goes McCarthy, that crazy fool. One a these days he's gonna crash into a pier and that'll be the end of im,' said a man, standing on the bank, not far from where Hanzel was gathering his bearings.

'Ees nay de only fool,' replied a short, bearded man. 'Whot about de ones payin' im ta take em trou?'

'Aye, deys gotta be d' biggest fools of em all,' said a third man; the one wearing a feather in his hat.

The boat shot through the waters and past the place Hanzel stood watching. He smiled. *McCarthy is one brave soul.* He watched the boat shoot off to the east. *He has enough momentum to take him a ways.* Hanzel shook his head. *I wouldn't take the risk. Why risk your life, just to gain some time?* Hanzel regarded London Bridge. *On the other hand, it would take several hours to take a cargo around the bridge. I guess it makes sense.*

Hanzel watched the boat for a minute longer. Then he approached the three men, whose conversation he overheard. 'Excuse me, gentlemen. I need a boat to Holland.'

'To Olland, you soy?' asked the first man. 'As in Olland across the Channel, loike?'

'Yes. I need a boat to Amsterdam. Where can I get one?' Hanzel regarded the three men.

'Well, ye would have to go to Wapping',' said the short, bearded man.

Hanzel scratched his temple. 'Wapping?'

The man pointed east. 'It's down river.'

'Eh, Georgie!' shouted the man with the feather in his hat. He was shouting down to a boat man who was sitting in his rowboat talking to a man with large mustaches. 'Can ye take this lad to Wapping?'

George looked up. 'Ter Wapping,' you say, guvno?'

'Yes. This lad needs to find a boat to Olland!' shouted the man with the feather in his hat. Hanzel noticed that he had rather large ears which wiggled as he shouted.

'As e gots de monie?' asked George.

'How much?' asked Hanzel.

George took a moment to access Hanzel, trying to figure out what he could charge the young, fair haired gentleman. 'Arf a crown,' replied George.

'Half a crown?!' asked Hanzel, incredulously. *I'll lead him along for a bit. Maybe I can get a lower price.*

George did not expect such a young gentleman to question him like that. 'Olroight, not arf a crown. I'll only charge ye tree shillins.'

Hanzel smiled. 'That's more reasonable, I think. How far is it?'

'It'll take him about an hour from here,' said the man with the big ears.

'Thank you for your help,' said Hanzel, as he stepped down the bank.

'God speed you, young Ollander,' said the man with the feather in his hat.

Hanzel stepped into George's boat and sat down on the wooden bench at the stern. He waved to the three men. George stepped in and grabbed the oars. The other man shoved the boat away from the bank. A moment later, George was rowing the boat into the current, where he let the river do most of the work taking Hanzel to Wapping.

The boat ride was uneventful. George did little talking and focused on keeping the rowboat on course. The river was full of traffic, traveling east and west. Those going east had an easier time of it, moving with the current. George and Hanzel moved past large barges and long, elegant pleasure boats. There were other row boats, and freight, lots of freight coming to and from London. The Thames was the main highway for a long way upstream as well as down from the huge metropolis. People, animals, and freight; the commerce of a nation flowed along that incredible river. As they floated along, Hanzel was lost in his thoughts, and praying that he would find a ship to Holland as quickly as possible.

'Oi doubts if'n ye ave much trubbel foindin' a ship ta Olland,' said George as they neared Wapping. 'Los a ships going te Olland frum ere.' George thought for a moment and continued. 'Los a ships, go in ter Danmark an Norway, France, Portugal, the Caribbean, ye name it. Ye'll surely fine a ship ter Olland.' George rowed past a large merchantman. 'Me thinks dat ship's been ter India.'

As they rowed past, Hanzel looked up at the large ship rising above him. A sailor looked down from a yardarm. He waved. Hanzel waved back. The smell of excrement, urine, and tar filled the air at the water line of the hulking ship. A few minutes later, George rowed past the stern of the merchantman and made their way through a maze of ships and service traffic. The smell of rotting sea plants and dead fish added to the redolent air filled with the screams of the ubiquitous sea gulls.

When George pulled up to a landing, he tied his little rowboat to a ring. Hanzel was groping about in Tin Nose's purse. 'Tha'll be tree shillins, guvnoh,' he said, holding his right hand out. Hanzel gave him a half a crown.

'Dah's a arf crown, guvnoh. I don ave de change fer ye.' George looked apologetically at the young Dutchman.

Hanzel smiled. 'I know how hard you work, George. Life is hard. Therefore, since I have what I need, I don't mind to share some of my good fortune. You can keep the change. The half crown is yours.'

George smiled. 'Thank ye guvnoh. I thanks ye. It was a pleasure te ave rowed yer ere. Good luck. If'n yer effer needs anuddah row up n' down dis ere Thames, jes ax fer ol' George.'

Hanzel stepped onto the landing and thanked George for his good service. Then, with a wave of his hand, he was off, walking along the roadway, searching for a ship flying the flag of Holland or that of Amsterdam.

What a lot of ships are here. If I don't find any on this side of the river, I might have to look on the other side. I sure hope someone is going to Amsterdam from here. I'm hungry. I should find something to eat. Maybe there'll be someone to talk to.

The Boar's Head, proclaimed a sign over an eating house along the road. As Hanzel approached, he could smell pleasant aromas of roasting flesh. He licked his lips and followed his nose to the succulent aromas.

Inside Hazel discovered a noisy crowd of sailors and their women, eating dinner. Lively conversations filled the space in between the smells of cooked food. He stood in the doorway for a few minutes, looking for a place to sit. He noticed there was a space on a bench at the long table which ran down the middle of the room. He made for the bench and sat down between a large woman on his left and a sailor with a pungent body odor on his right. Neither one paid him any attention, being engrossed in their conversations and meals.

Hanzel kept an eye open for a serving wench; flagging down Molly McGuire a few minutes later.

'I'm hungry,' he said with his charming Dutch accent. 'What do you recommend?'

Molly smiled. 'Roasted erring wit spring portaters and boiled leeks.'

Hanzel grinned. 'Excellent! I'll have that. And a pint of ale, please.'

'You're a polite young man, aren't you?' replied Molly.

'No sense in being impolite. That just creates ill will,' said Hanzel. He smiled, showing her his straight white teeth.

Molly nodded. 'I'll be right back with your ale.'

Hanzel watched her as she completed her rounds, taking orders. After a few minutes she disappeared into the kitchen. *She's efficient. Looks like she's done this job for a long time.* A moment later Molly returned from the kitchen with a tray full of tankards of ale and goblets of wine. She circulated around the room, saving the last tankard for Hanzel.

'So, I don sense ye's from dese pahts,' said Molly, setting the tankard of ale on the table.

Hanzel nodded. 'I'm not. I'm from Holland. I'm on my way back there and looking for a ship.'

'I thot ye was from Olland,' replied Molly. 'Oi neber been deh. I alus wantad ter go.'

Hanzel smiled. 'How much do I owe you for the ale?'

'Oh, don wurry, aftah ye finish yer meal, we'll tally de bill,' she said. *Ees so ansum. Oi can nay take me eyes ofn im.*

'Eh, Molly!' shouted a voice from the other end of the long table.

Molly looked in the direction of a burly sailor, waving his tankard.

'Can yer fill dis ere tankard?!'

Molly smiled at Hanzel. Then she turned and glared at the sailor. 'Hold yer halyahd, O'leary. I'm comin.' She regarded Hanzel. *Wot oi wold give ta be wid sumun ou looks loik im.* 'Oi've gots ter go. Maybe later we kin tahk a bit moh, wen oi brings yer dineh.'

Hanzel nodded. 'That'll be fine,' he said, reaching for the tankard of ale.

Molly turned and quickly walked over to the sailor wanting a refill. Hanzel watched her. He had nothing better to do with his eyes as he thought about finding a ship home and how he was going to tell the bad news to the families of his deceased masters.

A few minutes later, Molly returned with a trencher on which lay two beautiful roasted herrings, five spring potatoes, and three boiled leeks. 'It smells delicious,' said Hanzel, taking in the aromas of the hot food.

'Ye'll loike eet. Is one o' cook's best,' said Molly. 'Oi loikes er mesef.'

'Do you have salt?' asked Hanzel.

'Salt? Oh shore, we gots salt,' replied Molly. 'Oil git sum.' She hustled off and returned a moment later with a dish of salt. 'Ere ye are, yung Ollander. A dish o' salt.'

She set the dish beside Hanzel's trencher.

Hanzel smiled up at Molly. 'Thank you.'

'So, ye're seekin' a ship, are ye? Ter Olland, loike?' Molly began twisting her light brown hair with her right hand. 'Maybe oi kin ep ye. Oi knows a lot a sailahs. Oi kin ax aroun.'

'Would you do that? That's very kind of you,' replied Hanzel. 'What's your name?'

'Molly. Moi name is, Molly. Molly McGuire,' she said, sticking out her hand.

Hanzel took her hand and squeezed it gently. 'My name is, Hanzel. Hanzel Sventska.'

'Dah's a ineresin noime. Oi nebbah hoid eet bafoh. An oi hoid a lotta noimes aroun ere.' Molly indicated the room.

Hanzel looked at his food and picked up the fork.

'Well, oi suppose oi shud git back ter woik,' she said, sighing. *Oh ees so ansome. Oi cud eat im aloive.*

'Aay, Molly! Whots takin yer so long? We needs refills ovah ere!' shouted a gravelly voice from the far end of the table. The voice belonged to a wrinkled old salt with a short, white beard and massive eyebrows. He was wearing a battered old hat and a dark blue coat. Hanzel noticed he only had one hand.

'You better go, Molly,' said Hanzel. 'We'll talk later.'

Molly smiled and hustled off to attend to the old salt at the far end of the table. Hanzel paid her no further mind as he began to devour his meal. He was ravenously hungry and the food was excellent.

When all that was left on the trencher were the bones of the two herrings, Hanzel burped. *That was really good. Just what I needed.* He drank the last of his ale and burped again.

'Good food they have here,' he said to the man sitting beside him. The man nodded but did not want to engage Hanzel in conversation; preferring to focus on his own meal of roasted pork and potatoes.

Hanzel looked to see where Molly was. She was wiping a table at the far end of the large room. Five sailors and an officer were waiting to sit, and stood patiently waiting for her to finish. Molly looked in Hanzel's direction as the new guests were seated. Hanzel caught her eye, and motioned for her to come over. She nodded, but indicated she first had to take orders from the six new arrivals. When she was done, she quickly placed the orders with the kitchen staff and then attended to Hanzel.

'Oi see yer were ungry,' said Molly as she regarded the two fish skeletons on the trencher. 'Will ye be wantin more ale?'

Hanzel shook his head. 'No, I've got to find a ship. The sooner I do that, the sooner I get home.'

Molly smiled. 'Well, oi av good news fer ye.' She pointed to the six new arrivals. 'It so appens, det dose sailahs is going ta Amburg. Dey has ta stop in Amstehdam.'

'They're going to Amsterdam?! That's great news, Molly!' Hanzel was delighted. *I can't believe it. Everything is just falling into place for me. I prayed to get my purse back and that was so easy. Now I meet another serving wench and she serves me up a ship when I need it. Thank you, thank you.* Hanzel was grinning from ear to ear. 'When are they leaving?'

'Tamorroh. Dey's loadin' cargo an will leave on de tide firs thin in da mohnin,' replied Molly.

Hanzel thought for a moment. 'First thing in the morning? I'm going to need a place to sleep. Do you know if there is a place to sleep nearby?'

Molly smiled. 'Ye kin stay wid me, if'n ye loikes. Oi av a room, upstahs.' *Oi opes, oi opes. If'n eel stoy wid me, oi'd be appy.*

Hanzel regarded Molly and took a long look at her. She was a pleasant, ordinary looking girl. Her blue eyes were sparkling and her manner was friendly and warm. *What harm can there be in my staying with her? She doesn't appear devious. I like her eyes...*

'De ownah, ee don care. Oi'm entoitled te me proivite loife.'

Hanzel nodded. 'What are you going to charge me for sleeping in your bed?'

Molly shook her head. 'Nutin. Oi jes wants a bit o company, is all.'

'Thank you, Molly. I accept.' Hanzel gestured toward the officer and five sailors. 'Will you introduce me when they have finished their meals?'

Molly nodded. 'Oi thinks dey'll take yer.'

'Ayeee, Molly!' shouted a large, muscular sailor. He banged his tankard on the table. 'Where's dat Molly McGuire?!' He banged his tankard again.

Two other sailors began to pound their tankards on the table. Within a few more seconds, twelve more tankards were pounded on the tables and Molly's name began to be chanted.

'Molly! Molly! Molly!'

'Oi've gots ter go,' she said and quickly left Hanzel in order to attend to the thirsty sailors.

Hanzel watched as Molly performed her duties. He was happy. Everything was coming up roses. *I hope I can trust her. I'd better sleep with my purse under my pillow. I don't want to go through another Angela experience. I wonder what she's up to? Probably still at the De Hijlige Frauw. I was so young.* Hanzel smiled. *She did clue me into something. I sure do like girls. This one seems genuine. She seems to like me. That's how it has to be. I never want to force a woman to like me. I guess I don't really need to. I seem to have good fortune with them. They sure have helped me. Even Angela. Although she tried to steal my money. Now, here I am, once again in an inn and one of the girls wants to help me. I am so lucky.*

Molly returned with a full tankard of ale. 'Ere,' she said. 'Oi gots yer anudah tankah of ale.' She grabbed the empty and set the full tankard in front of Hanzel. 'So, are ye plannin' ter stay wid me?' Molly smiled. *Oh, I wants ter touch is blond air and strokes is face, ees so bootifool dis Ollandah.* Molly regarded Hanzel with dreaming eyes. Her expression was not missed on Hanzel. He nodded as he looked into her eyes.

'Thank you Molly. You are very kind. However, wouldn't it be better if I sleep on board ship? If I come home with you, neither one of us would sleep.' Hanzel smiled. 'When those men are done with their meal, please introduce me, so I can make arrangements. I do not want to miss the boat.'

Molly's shoulders sank. She was so hoping that Hanzel would come home with her. She smiled bravely, but with saddened eyes. 'Oi'll interduce yer. Oi'll com n' fetch yer.'

'How much money do I owe for food and drink, Molly?' asked Hanzel, opening the purse.

Molly looked sadly at Hanzel, so wishing she could touch the beautiful young Hollander. 'Er, dat'll be. Let me see…a shillin, thropence.'

Hanzel rummaged in the purse and pulled out another half a crown. He handed it to Molly.

Molly regarded the coin in her hand. 'Oi don gots no change fer arf a crown. Oi'll ave ter git de change.'

'You may keep the change, Molly. Thanks for helping me,' replied Hanzel.

'Wot if'n ye kin nat sleep aboard? asked Molly, giving it one last try.

'If there is no room for me now, there would not be room tomorrow, either. The journey takes a while.' Hanzel looked towards the six men sitting at a table in the middle of the large room. 'Did you tell them about me?'

'No. But, I will. I will go an tahk ter dem.' Molly put the coin in her purse and walked over to the men. Hanzel watched her talking to the captain and gesturing towards him. The captain turned around and gave Hanzel a long look over. Hanzel smiled and appeared harmless. He saw the captain nodding to Molly. She looked over at Hanzel and smiled. Hanzel's heart filled with gladness. He had a ride home.

Chapter 16

At five bells the ship's company rose from their slumbers. It was time to sail.

The commotion woke Hanzel from a deep sleep. He had been dreaming of a dragon attempting to devour him. It was an unsettling vision. He sat up in the hammock and rubbed his eyes. *I've got to wake up. I promised the captain I'd help out. Why did I do that. I could easily have paid for the voyage. Oh well. He needed the help and I need the ride.* Hanzel climbed out of the hammock and stepped onto the boards of a small brigantine, carrying an assortment of cargo, from cotton goods to wool.

He put his shoes on and walked up the stairs to the main deck. A rush of cool, moist air greeted him. A stiff breeze was blowing.

'Aaarh, tis a fine mornin' ta go sailin, eh, lads?' said Captain Bloomingdale, when all hands were on deck. He was clapping his hands together to stay warm. 'We arf a stiff breeze ter battle, so everyone at their stations an let's make dis an enjoyable sail.' He looked at his first mate. 'Alright Mister Swansong, let's take her out.'

Hanzel was assigned to follow a sailor named, Olafson. Together they cast off the ropes. When they cast off the bow lines, the brigantine began to drift away from the pier.

'Quick!' shouted Olafson as he jumped. 'Jomp aboard!'

Hanzel quickly followed Olafson; jumping onto the deck of the *Hamburg Swan. I already feel I'm a sailor. This is great. I can't wait to get off the river and into the Channel. I love sailing.*

Sea gulls screeched overhead, following them for a short distance. Eventually the gulls returned to Wapping as the sloop plowed waves on its way down the Thames to the English Channel. Hanzel was put to work hauling ropes. Olafson showed him how.

Hanzel's hands were not used to the ropes. It did not take long for him to suffer from rope burn. Fortunately, he was no longer needed topside and was allowed to get his breakfast below deck, from the galley amidship. Breakfast consisted of porridge, a piece of boiled beef, and a chunk of tack. All of it washed down with two pints of ale. By the time breakfast was done, and he had drunk the two pints of ale, Hanzel was feeling content. *I'm going home. Yohoho. I'm happy. And, yet, I'm sad. What am I going to tell Missus De Witt? What can I possibly say?* Hanzel climbed the steps up to the deck. Stepping out of the hatch he was hailed by Captain Bloomingdale, who was standing by the helmsman.

'Good work tis mornin' Mister Sventska!' shouted the captain with his jovial voice, full of good cheer.

Hanzel smiled as he stepped toward the helm. 'Thank you captain,' replied Hanzel as he came near.

'Yes, I was watchin' ye. I thinks ye as a natural talent fer sailin'.' Captain Bloomingdale looked at the helmsman. 'Don ye thinks so too, Wim? Don e arf a natural talent fer sailin?'

The helmsman nodded. 'Ya, dat e as, Cap'n'.

'Well, young Hanzel, if ye stays wid us, ere at de elm, ye'll learn a whole lot about sailin.' He looked at the first mate, standing behind the helmsman and watching the mainsail. 'Eh, Mister Swansong. We kin teach dis ere lad about sailin?'

The first mate smiled. 'We been sailing these here waters for many years; Captain Bloomingdale and I.'

'Of course, it all depends on whedder e wans ter learn about sailin,' said Wim.

Hanzel regarded the three men for a moment before replying. 'My father was a fisherman. He sailed almost everyday, from when he was twelve years old. I guess I must have it in my blood. I grew up in a fishing village, not far from Amsterdam.'

'So, d'ye wants ter learn ter sail, or d'ye wanter jus elp out when we needs yer?' asked the captain.

'Yes, of course I am interested to learn. My masters are dead. I can't go back to working in De Witt's shop. The memories are too painful. A change will do me good. I've thought about going to sea. So, why not? I think learning to sail would be good for me,' replied Hanzel enthusiastically.

The captain looked at his first mate and smiled. 'Well, we be needin' an extra hand. Whot's yer business in Amsterdam?'

Hanzel frowned and looked at the boards for a moment as he began to reply. 'I have very sad news to bring to the families of my masters who were hung for treason on Tower Hill. They had brought arms to a nobleman who was drawn and quartered. My masters were arms manufacturers. They had no idea the arms were meant for a revolt against King James. They were caught.'

'So, after ye brings der sad news, den whot? Whot would keep yer in Amsterdam?' asked the captain.

Hanzel looked at Captain Bloomingdale and slowly shook his head. 'I have learned enough about arms making, I think. If a better opportunity presented itself. I'd be prepared to consider it.' *I wonder what he's getting at. Is he thinking of including me on his crew? That would be interesting. I like these men. Sailing on this ship would be a good learning experience.*

'Well, den. Wood yer be inerested ter sign on board wid us. I kin pays yer a decent wage, an ye will learn all der is ter sailin dese ere waters.' He pointed to the bow. 'Ye'll learn ter sail de channel, an der Nort Sea, an de Baltic. Ye'll see a good part o' dis nortern part o' de worl.'

Hanzel smiled. 'So, you'll let me off in Amsterdam and wait for me to return to the ship?'

'I'se gots ter do business in Amsterdam. Dat'll take two or tree days. So's yer gots time ter perform yer sad errand.' Captain Bloomingdale regarded Hanzel and smiled. 'Whad'yer say, young Hanzel? Will yer sail wid us?'

Hanzel nodded. *This is too good an opportunity to pass up. I am going sailing with these friendly men. Most excellent.* 'Alright, Captain, I accept your kind offer.'

Captain Bloomingdale shook Hanzel's hand. 'Now ye are truly welcome aboard, Mister Sventska.'

'Welcome, Hanzel,' said Mister Swansong, the first mate. They shook hands.

Wim smiled and nodded his head. 'I'm shore we'll gits along jes foine,' he said, also shaking Hanzel's hand.

'Thank you,' replied Hanzel, grinning from ear to ear.

'Well, now dat yer officially one of der crew, yer shuld learn all der ropes,' said Captain Bloomingdale.

'My hands are burning from working ropes this morning. They're not used to working with ropes.' Hanzel showed the captain the palms of his hands, which were red and slightly swollen.

'Dey'll git useter de ropes. Jes soaks em in salt water fer a bit. Den jes works em easy. Yur can foller Olafson. Ee'l shows yer wot ter do.' Captain Bloomingdale patted Hanzel on his right shoulder and pointed to where Olafson was already working, tightening the mainsail.

So began Hanzel's apprenticeship in the art of sailing. All the rest of that day he helped Olafson perform his duties. As he worked, he was also able to interact with the other sailors; Ben, Gerald, Herman, Ignatius, Piet, and Patrick, a boy three years younger than Hanzel.

They came into the channel around midnight. The sky was overcast and no moonlight was able to penetrate the clouds. At two bells, Hanzel was roused from his hammock by Olafson. It was their turn to handle the helm and keep watch. When they stepped on deck, a cold, hard breeze hit their faces and instantly caused both men to shiver. Ben and Gerald wished them good sailing and turned the helm over. Hanzel watched them quickly walk to the hatch and disappear below deck, closing the hatch doors firmly behind them.

At three bells the rain began. By four bells, Hanzel was beginning to lose feeling in his cheeks and hands, as they were pelted with the nearly freezing water. When six bells arrived, Hanzel and Olafson were greatly relieved to be able to get warm below decks when Herman and Mister Swansong came to take over.

Hanzel was bone tired. When he lay in his hammock, he was asleep within minutes and dreaming of a warm, sunny place, with flowers and birds twittering in the trees. The sky was a gentle azure and the clouds, white and fluffy. Little rabbits played in the grass and he, Hanzel was kissing a pretty girl.

The rain eventually stopped and the seas became more calm and pleasant to sail. When Hanzel next woke up it was high noon; time for a meal before his duties started on deck.

They reached Amsterdam four and a half days later under blue skies. The sun was able to present his full glory to the low lands. The air was warm and tulips were blooming. In spite of the beautiful weather, Hanzel's heart was heavy. The time had come for him to return to the workshop and report the news. The crew knew what Hanzel had to do and they all wished him courage and strength.

'Tis not an easy ting ter do; ta be tellin' people dat dere loved ones are gone. I've had ter do it more n' once. It never gets any easier.' Captain Bloomingdale patted Hanzel on his shoulder.

Hanzel thanked the captain for his good wishes and walked down the gangplank. He waved to his friends as he stepped on the pier. Then he walked off to find a ride to de Witt & Zoon.

When Hanzel arrived at the workshop and home of Master de Witt, he caused some pandemonium as the household came running to meet him in the courtyard. Everyone was happy to see him safely returned. Then it began to dawn on everybody that he was alone. Master De Wit and Master van Dijk were not coming home.

'I managed to get an audience with King James. However, it was to no avail. His mind was made up.' *I can't tell them the king was right. I saw his side of the story. A king can not tolerate people selling arms to his enemies.* Hanzel's eyes began to fill with tears. 'I couldn't save them. They were both hanged for aiding and abetting treason.' He never told them the rest, as the final scene of the execution flashed through his mind, his tears flowing like rivers. The vision of those grisly trophies staring back at him from their bloody pikes brought on further paroxysms of grief. It was all so horrible; so very, very horrible. *And they think themselves, civilized.*

The wives of the dead masters howled with grief, soon joined by the children and staff. Hanzel did not know what more to say, except that, 'it was over quickly. They did not suffer too much.' *When they were hung, it was over quickly. I'll bet they suffered in the dungeons of the Tower. Neither one of them looked fit when they brought them out.*

Eventually the families drifted off to grieve in their private apartments, leaving Hanzel to gather up his things. When he was finished, he gently told Missus de Witt that he was leaving to join the crew of a merchant ship headed for Hamburg.

Missus de Witt thanked Hanzel for his services and gave him a purse with a half pound of silver coins. 'These are to help you find your way Hanzel. I am confident you will do well in life. Your heart is pure and your will is strong.' She kissed Hanzel on the cheek. 'God speed you, Hanzel Sventska. Remember that you are always welcome here.'

Hanzel nodded and thanked her for the purse. She closed the door. His life at De Witt & Zoon was over.

Chapter 17

Hanzel's new life on board the good ship, *Hamburg Swan*, was hard work sometimes. Other times there wasn't much to do, as the leagues drifted by and the wind was steady on gentle seas. Sometimes life on board was pure hell, when a vicious storm blew from the north, for example. It was during one such storm, while sailing to Hamburg from Amsterdam, when Patrick was blown overboard and disappeared beneath the waves. Hanzel saw him go. He could see Patrick screaming, but heard nothing over the roaring of the wind. The crew held a memorial service two days later, when the storm finally blew itself out. It was Hanzel's first lesson regarding the danger sailing presented on the open seas. It was a hard lesson. He liked Patrick.

As time passed, Hanzel became ever more skilled in the art of sailing. Captain Bloomingdale and Mister Swansong, the first mate taught him something new everyday. They taught him about navigation and how to use an astrolabe and read the compass. Hanzel learned about wind and sails; how to set them to gain maximum speed, or what sails to use during storms. Eventually, storms did not bother Hanzel anymore. He began to take them in stride.

The sailors taught him the ropes. Hanzel learned which ropes did what and how to tie them. What was at first a chaotic spider's web, became an ordered arrangement of ropes which made perfect sense. The ropes were no longer a mystery to him.

Olafson taught him how to use a marlin spike to splice the ropes together or stop ends from fraying. 'Ye have ta takes good care a yer ropes,' said Olafson. 'If'n yer lets em fray, dey'll wer out an be no use ter yer. Ropes is xpensive.'

Ignatius taught Hanzel about swabbing decks and otherwise keeping things clean and in good working order. Iggy, as he was called, oversaw the maintenance of the ship. Two mates helped him with his daily work, keeping, *Hamburg Swan* floating.

'A clean ship, that is ship shape, is a safe ship,' said Ignatius, when he was showing Hanzel how to grease a stubborn block which had started squeaking.

Ben, the lone Scot, taught Hanzel how to cook on the little galley stove and how to be careful with fire on board ship. 'If yer no careful be, wid the fire, a boot soch as dis'n will go up n' flames, bafor yer nows it, on account of 'n de wood n' tar.' Ben carefully closed the door of the little stove just as a spark tried to jump out.

Herman taught Hanzel how to speak French and German. 'Da more languages you shpeak, de bedder it goes for you in da wurld,' said Herman in his thick German accent.

Hanzel could not agree more. By the time a year had passed, he was becoming quite fluent in French. The German was still giving him some trouble, in spite of the fact he spoke Dutch.

'Ya, bot, Hollandish ist niet German. Zey are verry different,' noted Herman, when Hanzel expressed his frustration over the formulation of a complex noun.

The quartermaster, Piet van Maas taught Hanzel about scrimshaw and wood carving. 'A man has to have a hobby,' said Piet wisely. 'If a man does not have something to occupy his interest during his leisure times, he will go slowly crazy. Especially during these long voyages, when there really isn't much to do, at times.'

Hanzel realized the truth of Piet's statement and therefore took up wood carving to help pass the hours when his work was done. Piet also taught Hanzel a love for reading, and gladly lent his books to help further the young Hollander's education.

Together, the entire crew taught Hanzel about friendship and harmonic cooperation on board a ship. Under Captain Bloomingdale and First Mate Swansong, *Hamburg Swan* was a well run vessel. Hanzel felt fortunate to have joined her crew. Everyone of his mates was a fine fellow, full of humour and good cheer, even the new man, Johannes van der Kley, who joined the crew in Hamburg.

Because Captain Bloomingdale ran a tight ship, his sailors worked for him gladly and made her sail fast and profitably. The captain was a partner with three other businessmen in Lubbock. They bought and sold necessary commodities and sold them in bulk at various ports where they had buyers.

The farthest south they sailed was London. The farthest north was Oslo. Everyone on board shared in the profits. By the time an other year had passed, Hanzel was 18 and already becoming an experienced sailor. His hands were hardened and his muscles were strong. Captain Bloomingdale recognized Hanzel's potential and had begun to teach him how to be a master of a ship. By the time another year had passed, Hanzel knew what was necessary to be a master and commander. All he lacked was experience. Captain Bloomingdale was going to make sure he got it.

'Fer yer nineteenth, lad, I am promotin' yer ter becomin second mate abor dis ere ship. I ave talked dis over wid me partners in Lubbock, las time we was in port. An I ave discussed dis wid Mister Swansong. Since we're going ter be addin five additional sailors ter work de boat, we needs anuddah officer. Dis ways we all kin git a bit more rest or elp when we runs inta der storms, likes we do from time ter time. Whadaye say, lad?'

Hanzel couldn't believe his ears. *Second mate. That's incredible. I can't believe my good fortune.* He stared incredulously at the captain and the first mate. For a moment Hanzel did not know what to say.

'An besides, de crew likes yer, Hanzel. Dey wuld agree wid our decision an foller yer orders.'

'I am deeply grateful, Captain. Thank you. Thank you very much. And you too, Mister Swansong. I am honoured to stand at the helm with you.'

Hanzel and Captain Bloomingdale and Mister Swansong shook hands.

A package was brought to Captain Bloomingdale by Olafson, who was grinning from ear to ear.

Captain Bloomingdale regarded the package for a moment and then handed it to Hanzel. 'Dis is fer ye, Hanzel. From all on board. Everyone chipped in. Appy Birthday, Hanzel.'

Hanzel regarded the package and looked out at the assembled crew on deck. They were all smiling. When he opened the package he discovered a beautiful blue officer's jacket with silver buttons and piping. There was also a magnificent beaver hat and a new pair of white breeches and buckled shoes. Hanzel carefully set the package down on the deck and took off his old jacket, which he handed to Olafson. Then he reached down and carefully lifted the new jacket and put it on. Then he grabbed the hat. When he put it on his head, the entire crew cheered. Hanzel had become an officer in the merchant marine.

The company who owned the ship was growing and showing good profits, in spite of the hardships imposed on the masses by the terrible conflicts breaking out in the German states and elsewhere. Hence, they decided to add a second ship; a one hundred and thirty foot, armed brigantine. Captain Bloomingdale was offered the job to captain the new, larger ship and Mister Swansong was offered the captaincy of *The Hamburg Swan*. Captain Bloomingdale made Hanzel his first officer on the new ship. The date was, Sunday, April 16th, 1620. It was a week before Hanzel's 20th birthday.

'Well, ow does it feel? First officer of a brigantine?' Captain Bloomingdale regarded Hanzel as they walked up the gang plank of *The New Venture*. He was grinning broadly.

'I am greatly honoured. She's truly a beautiful looking boat. Her lines are sleek. She appears to be capable of some speed.'

'Aye, dat she be, alright. Dat las time we's in Lubbock, when ye an de boys went sightseein, I took er out fer a test run.'

'I can't wait to get er out to sea,' said Hanzel, enthusiastically.

'First we must hire our sailors,' replied the captain.

'Too bad we couldn't have kept the entire crew off *Hamburg Swan*.' Hanzel shrugged. 'At least we kept Olafsen. We'll have an opportunity to hand pick a crew. I'm sure we'll get some fine sailors here. We'll hire what we can and if we still need more sailors we'll stop along the coast and pick them up out of the taverns.'

'Te sail *The New Venture* we are going ter need at leas twenty sailors an one more officer,' replied the captain as they stepped onto the deck of the new ship. 'I let it be known in the sailors' pubs an de various taverns dat we be ere, on board, an lookin for able bodied seamen to come ter de ship.'

'Let's hope it works,' said Hanzel, admiring the sturdy main mast.

'We'll set up a barrel, dere, facin de gang plank. So's as dey walks up the board, we'll git a good look at em, before e speaks. Ye can tell a whole lot about a man from first seein im.' Captain Bloomingdale walked to a barrel sitting beside the main hatch door. 'Ere, Hanzel, elp me wid dis barrel, please, if ye will.'

They rolled the barrel, so that it was sitting directly opposite the gang plank, almost beside the starboard freeboard. Sailors would have to walk sixteen feet toward the barrel behind which the captain and first officer would sit.

'I ave a new log book fer dis ship inter which we signs de new sailors.' Just as he said the words a voice on the dock shouted, 'Ahoy! Is there anyone on deck?!'

Hanzel and Captain Bloomingdale stepped over to the gang plank and looked down at the dock. Three sailors were standing there with their duffel bags.

'Permission to come aboard?' asked the sailor who had first shouted.

'Permission granted,' replied the captain. He turned to Hanzel. 'Please fetch de log book from de great cabin. Remember ter bring a quill an soch.'

'Aye, Captain,' replied Hanzel. He quickly walked off to fetch the requested items.

The three sailors stepped on board and stood before the captain.

'My name is Roland McDonald, this here is my brother, Jock McDonald and our cousin, Mack Pearson.'

Captain Bloomingdale looked the sailors over. They appeared to be able bodied. No one was missing a finger, or a hand. Nobody had a peg leg or an eye patch.

The three men were dressed in typical sailor garb. Dark blue pea jackets, petticoat breeches, flat, felt hats, and buckled shoes. Roland was tall and slender, Jock, of medium height and build, and Mack, somewhat corpulent.

I'll work dat belly off, right quickly. Odder dan dat, dey looks alright. Captain Bloomingdale gestured to Roland, 'What ships ave ye sailed?'

'Merchantmen, mostly.' Roland gestured to his cousin. 'He has been in the navy.'

Captain Bloomingdale regarded Mack. 'What navy?'

'English,' replied Mack. 'I served on a ship of the line.'

Captain Bloomingdale nodded. 'A ship of de line, indeed.'

As he said the words, Hanzel returned with the log book and writing tools; quill, ink, and sand. He set everything on the barrel.

'Dis ere be, First Mate Sventska. Ye will address im as, Mister Sventska.

The three sailors touched their foreheads in salute. Hanzel nodded and regarded the three sailors with a stern expression. *I'd better let them see I'm not to be trifled with.* Hanzel could sense that his gravitas was working. He watched carefully as the three men signed the log book.

And so it came to be. Hanzel and the captain signed thirteen seemingly good sailors in Lubbock. They signed enough sailors to take the loaded ship out to sea. However, thirteen hands was not enough. Albeit, the *New Venture* was a pleasure to sail, she kept everyone busy with little time to rest. When they finally arrived in Edinburgh, having crossed the North Sea in a squall, everyone was bone tired.

'We'll lays over fer a week,' said Captain Bloomingdale to the crew after they were docked and tied to the pier. 'I will give yer some a yer wages, so's ye can have some spendin' money.'

The crew cheered.

'Mister Sventska will make de disbursements,' added the captain.

Hanzel was sitting on a chair with a small table in front of him, on which lay the register and a leather bag of coins. One by one he dispensed a portion of the sailor's wages and had him sign in the book. When they had their money, the captain asked them to do some recruiting. 'We kin use anuddah sebben, maybe even ten more sailors.'

The crew vowed they would keep an eye open as they stepped down the gang plank to pursue the adventures sailors seek in port. Hanzel and the captain supervised the offloading of a shipment of German metal products, flour, lace, tobacco, and ten new spars for a ship that was being built not far from where the *New Venture* was unloading. When the cargo was off loaded, the holds were filled with bales of wool bound for London.

Hanzel and Captain Bloomingdale also did some recruiting, while in port. The two friends went out for a meal and an evening of entertainment, during which time they met three French sailors, who were looking for work. Jacques, Michel, and Pierre were three amiable brothers, who had been to sea for more than ten years. They had served in the French Navy and in the merchant marine. They quit the navy and were not overly happy with the conditions on their last merchantman. The master was a cruel despot.

'Zere is a time ven a man can only take zo much,' said Michel.

'Qui, zat is zo,' agreed Jacques and Pierre, nodding their heads.

'Ve are gute zailers, but ve veel not vurk for no more martinets.' Michel crossed his arms across his chest.

Captain Bloomingdale looked at Hanzel. They communicated in their expressions. The three French sailors accompanied them to the brigantine after dinner and were signed into the register and shown to their quarters. By the time they left Edinburgh, ten more sailors had joined the crew and the sailing became much easier.

The following evening, one of the French sailors asked Hanzel, when they happened to be standing side by side. 'Av you effer fire de cannon?'

Hanzel regarded the cannon Michel was indicating.

'Eet look new. I don theen you fire de cannon. Do you know eet wurk?' Michel tied the rope and looked up at the sail they were adjusting.

'I suppose we should test them, to see if they work,' replied Hanzel; looking at Michel.

'Eet make sense to me,' said Michel.

'I will mention it to the captain. Thank you Michel.' Hanzel smiled and patted Michel on the shoulder before sending him on his way to fix a broken rope. Hanzel returned to the rear deck where Captain Bloomingdale was taking a bearing with his astrolabe.

'Now we have time to see if the cannons work,' said Hanzel, as they were sailing along the north coast of England.

'Opefully we don attracts no attention from no war ships,' replied Captain Bloomingdale.

'Yes, but, given how things are now a days, what with the war and all of that nonsense, we have to train our crew how to defend the ship if we're attacked. As you know, Captain, there are more pirates now, as well. Privateers are beginning to plunder more ships.' Hanzel pointed to one of the five port side eight pounders. 'Let's fire just one. Just so everyone can see how it works, at least.'

Captain Bloomingdale thought about what Hanzel had said. 'It makes sense, I suppose. Night is coming anyway. Alright, let's see how it works.'

So, on a warm Sunday evening, on a calm sea, with a light breeze, after spying with their glasses along the horizon and to the shore, to see if any ship was anywhere to be seen, they fired a port side eight pounder for the first time on the *New Venture*. With the strong encouragement of the three Frenchmen, it became an excuse for an impromptu party and the imbibing of more rum than anyone should have. It was just the wrong time in the wrong place to have fired that gun. The sound alerted some people who were looking for just such a ship as Hanzel was sailing in. The people who were alerted by the sound of the gun were friends of the three French sailors who had joined the crew in Edinburgh.

As night fell, in spite of his inebriated state, Captain Bloomingdale did have the good sense to light the lanterns. He was still in control of his ship, and so was Hanzel. However, the sailors were quite a lot slower in their motions. Fortunately, the sea was calm and a full moon lit their way, once in a while, when it managed to peek through heavy clouds. It was the perfect time for Pierre le Grand and his gang of 37 privateers to sneak up on the *New Venture* from their hideout on the coast. The sound of the gun alerted them to her position.

Pierre had to fall back to using a small sloop, after losing his brigantine in a battle with English privateers. *The New Venture* presented a much better type of ship suited to the pirate's needs.

When the new brigantine arrived in Edinburgh, word was quickly sent along the grapevine to Pierre. Because of the lay over, there was enough time for the pirate to be ready. He knew they were coming.

In the dark depth of night, under a heavy sky obscuring the moon, which barely struggled to peek for a few moments, Pierre le Grand and his men captured the *New Venture* with no blood shed. While most everybody was sleeping, the pirate and his gang snuck on board and overcame everyone. Neither Hanzel, nor Captain Bloomingdale could do anything about it. The large bore pistols held to their chests were very convincing.

The entire crew was brought on deck and appraised of the situation by Pierre, who gave them two choices. 'You can join my gang, or you can go ashore with your captain in the sloop you see tied alongside.'

'Ye are lettin' us go?' asked Captain Bloomingdale, incredulously.

Pierre nodded. 'I need your ship, not your life, monsieur.' He pointed to the sloop. 'The sloop is provisioned with enough to take you back to Edinburgh, or Hamburg, even. Depending on how many of you stay with me.'

'Whot's te advantage of joinin' yer?' asked one of the sailors.

'A life of adventure and the very real possibility of making a whole lot of money,' replied Pierre. 'With this ship, we will sail to find gold in the new world. Hispaniola is where we need to be.'

'Ispaniola? I hoid of dat ploice,' replied one of the sailors, a man named Erik, who signed on in Edinburgh. 'Der's a lotta gold comin' from dat paht o' da wuld.'

'Dah's troo,' said another sailor; a man with a missing left ear. 'I knows de Spaniard gits a loada gold from dere.'

'We shuld goes dere,' suggested Erik to a group of his mess mates. They all agreed it was an interesting proposition.

When it was all said and done, nine of the ten who joined in Edinburgh and five original sailors, including Olafsen, elected to join the pirates and remained on board the *New Venture*. The others climbed over the freeboard and down the ladder to the sloop tied alongside.

'What're ye going ter do wid the wool?' asked Captain Bloomingdale, as he was about to step over the freeboard.

Pierre thought for a moment. 'I think we'll sell it in Le Havre.' Then he laughed. 'Thank you, Captain Bloomingdale.'

Captain Bloomingdale smiled ruefully. 'Thank you for sparing us our lives and for providing us a boat.'

'You are welcome. And God speed you on your way,' replied Pierre.

'And you as well, monsieur,' replied Captain Bloomingdale. 'However, I expect the devil speeds you. And he who would follow the Father of Lies will most surely fall into a trap and become damned.'

Pierre laughed. 'Well, so damned be I. My life is free and a great deal of fun.' He continued to laugh as he watched Captain Bloomingdale climb down the ladder.

When the captain stood on the deck of the sloop, Hanzel began to climb over the freeboard to follow the captain. Pierre stopped him by pointing his pistol at his chest. 'Not you,' he said. 'I have different plans for you, Hollander.'

Chapter 18

Hanzel watched sadly from the rear deck as the sloop sailed off in the direction of Edinburgh. Captain Bloomingdale waved. Hanzel returned the wave. He knew it was the last time he would ever see the man. *A great captain. I learned a lot from him. I will miss him. He was like a father.* He stood for a long time at the rail, watching the sloop until it disappeared over the horizon.

'So, now that you have watched your captain sail off, and you have collected your thoughts, let me tell you, Hollander, what my plans are and why I chose to keep you on board.' Pierre was carrying a decanter and two goblets. He poured wine in a goblet and handed it to Hanzel. Then he poured the other and set the decanter down on the deck. He raised his goblet and held it toward Hanzel, startling him. 'Here's to you, Hollander,' he said.

'This is very good wine,' remarked Hanzel, after savoring a mouthful.

'Only the best. That is how we live. We live for the best in life,' said Pierre. 'Now we can return to serious work with this ship. We'll see how she sails as we go to Le Havre. Then, when we get rid of the wool, we'll use the proceeds to further equip this boat and find a few more men, to round up the number to forty. That way none of us will have to work too hard and can enjoy the voyage to Hispaniola.'

'But, what does any of this have to do with me? I'm an officer of a merchant ship.' Hanzel smiled ruefully. 'This one, to be exact. I'm not a pirate or a privateer.'

'Exactly. You are an officer. You are young,' Pierre leaned closer to examine Hanzel's face. 'How old are you, Hollander?'

'Twenty,' replied Hanzel.

'Twenty? And you're a first officer on a fine new merchant ship?' Pierre smiled. 'That means you know sailing and you are smart. Having experience as an officer, you know what that entails; a certain demeanor. A man is an officer because men respect him and follow his orders. I need such a man on board for the venture I am going to undertake.' Pierre sipped his wine, his eyes twinkling.

Hanzel watched Pierre sip his wine. *What in heaven's name have I fallen into? For a privateer, he appears very civil. I guess they're not all cutthroats. I wonder what venture he has planned.*

'So, are you not curious what the venture is?' Pierre studied Hanzel closely. *I have to be sure of this Hollander. Can I trust him?* He suddenly realized. 'I don't even know your name.'

'Sventska. Hanzel Sventska.'

'Hanzel the Swede?' asked Pierre. 'No wonder you have such white hair.'

'Ya, I suppose that's right. Although I was born in Holland. Not far from Amsterdam. My father was a fisherman,' replied Hanzel. He took a long drink. 'Hmm, this wine is very good, indeed.'

'You can have as much as you like, my young friend,' said Pierre as he reached down for the decanter.

'Oh, I didn't mean it that way,' said Hanzel. 'I like good wine. Captain Bloomingdale taught me about wine.'

'Oh, yes, of course,' replied Pierre, filling Hanzel's goblet. He finished off the contents of the decanter into his own cup. Then he signaled to one of the sailors to take the decanter away.

'It is very rude to hold a person at gun point,' said Hanzel. 'You could have asked me.'

'Would you have stayed?'

'Probably not,' replied Hanzel, taking a sip of his wine. 'So, what is this venture you talk about? Show me how it is worth my while to become an officer on your ship.'

'We are very lucky to get this ship, with an expensive cargo which we can sell to finance a voyage to Hispaniola where the Spaniard has significant interest. I have a very reliable source, as I also do in Scotland, as you know, who told me about the Spanish treasure fleet and where it assembles. He was very certain it was there, in Hispaniola. When I study the charts of the area, it makes sense they would gather there before returning to Spain.'

Hanzel looked at the privateer sharing wine with him. *I wonder how old he is. Probably about thirty or thirty five, thereabouts. What was he doing in a sloop on the north coast of England?* 'How did you come to be in a sloop on the north coast of England? And, how did you know about us?'

'I lost my ship in a battle with some English. We had to steal the sloop and left Michel and his friends in Edinburgh on the lookout for just your type of boat. We've been waiting for some months now. We've existed off the land and the capture of a fishing boat and a small merchant vessel plying the coastal trade. I'd heard that a vessel, such as yours is a new design, made to go fast and in all kinds of seas. It is just such a boat I need to do what I plan.' Pierre stared over his goblet at the handsome young Hollander. 'So, now we need to learn how to handle her. That's another reason I chose you to remain. You're young, strong, and a first officer. You also know how to work this boat.'

'I've only served on her a short while, however, yes, I do know how to sail her. But, to kidnap me, that is a bit much, don't you think? I should be recompensed for that,' replied Hanzel slyly.

'If you will assist me with this plan, I will pay you twenty percent of the swag we capture.' Pierre watched for a reaction, however, he saw no change in Hanzel's expression.'

'With some gold to seal the contract,' suggested Hanzel, cool as a clam.

Pierre paused for a moment. 'Gold, to seal the contract?'

'I want some gold in my hand, to pay a recompense for kidnapping me, and a deposit, so to speak. To prove your good faith.' Hanzel watched Pierre consider his offer. *How in the world do I know he won't kill me once he gets the treasure?* 'And, besides, how do I know you will not kill me when I have served your purposes.'

Pierre's eyes narrowed. 'Kill you? Yes, I suppose you could assume such a thing. However, monsieur, I assure you, I give you the word of a gentleman. I will give you a hundred gold ducats when we sell the wool in Le Havre. If you decide against joining me, in our adventure to Hispaniola, I will set you free in port. You may keep the gold.'

Hanzel regarded Pierre for a long while as he thought it all over. *Twenty percent of a treasure. Who knows, I could get rich very quickly. Or I could end up dead. If he's willing to let me go in Le Havre, if I say no, and he'll pay me a hundred ducats anyway, that sounds like I can trust this man. And he's willing to share twenty percent of a treasure.*

I believe this Frenchman is honorable and telling the truth. This could be an amazing adventure. Hanzel smiled. 'Alright, Pierre, I will accept your offer. I will join you on the adventure to Hispaniola.'

Pierre grabbed Hanzel's proffered hand, and shaking it vigorously enthused, 'That is good news. I am confident we will work well together.' He held up his goblet. 'A toast. Here is to success in Hispaniola.' He and Hanzel clicked their goblets together and drank a hearty drought. Both men knew they would be friends.

By the time they reached Le Havre, Hanzel had earned the respect of Pierre's crew. He had helped them get used to the ship and Pierre had indeed become his friend.

It did not take very long to find a buyer for the wool, which netted them thirty five thousand ducats, much to everyone's surprise. Wool was in short supply, on account of hostilities. Pierre promptly paid Hanzel the one hundred ducats he promised. It enabled Hanzel to purchase some clothing and necessities.

During their third day in port, Hanzel, Pierre, and Michel were sitting together over a meal and drinks, on a terrace overlooking the harbour.

'Why do countries have to make war?' asked Pierre, as he looked out at a French navy vessel anchored at the mouth of the harbour.

Hanzel shook his head slowly. 'It is all so strange, isn't it? People being killed, and property destroyed, over ideas they carry in their hearts and nobody can actually see or touch.'

Pierre regarded Hanzel for a moment. 'Are you talking about religion?'

Hanzel nodded. 'Yes, religion. Roman Catholics against Protestants. Christians against Muslims. Judaists against everybody. Religion and politics are the problem. If everyone was to just think about these things in their own house and not bother anyone else, that is fine. When you get priests and such like taking charge. To my way of thinking, it's all about controlling people. The church wants to control people and the king wants to control everybody, as well.'

'You are a very wise young man, Hanzel,' replied Pierre, smiling. He turned to a young woman, sitting beside him. Giselle Paradise was his girl of choice, when in Le Havre. 'Isn't he wise?'

Giselle nodded her pretty head, but did not really understand what Hanzel was talking about. As Pierre had explained it to Hanzel, before they fetched her, 'She only has twelve brain cells. However, they only work intermittently.'

Hanzel smiled. 'And you have a document saying it's alright to plunder the ships of the English and the Spanish. Your king says it's alright. But, what gives him the right to ignore the rights of others?' He picked up his glass and sipped his wine. 'It's all so strange.'

'Well, I for one am not going to question it. Because I have the Letter of Marque, I am safe in French ports. We at least have safe ports to return the plunder to.'

'If you get to a safe port before the English or the Spaniard finds you,' replied Hanzel.

'That's why I wanted this boat. It's one of the fastest on the water, and just the right size to carry all of us. We can catch slow moving galleons and we have enough men on board to do what we need to do. That's why I bought six more cannons and ammunition.' Pierre pointed at the naval vessel. 'If one of those was sent against us, we would be in trouble. But, sailing such a huge ship, that requires a lot of sailors working around the clock.'

Hanzel nodded. The wine had gone to his head. He smiled. The sun was warm on his face. He was filled with good feelings about the upcoming adventure. *I'll make a point to stay away from war ships.*

The following morning the *New Venture* sailed out of Le Havre with a crew of forty five sailors and three officers; Pierre, Hanzel, and Michel. Everyone was excited by the prospect of Spanish gold. Stories about the success of the Spaniard in the New World were ripe with mention of strange customs and macabre rituals; of bleeding hearts torn from the writhing bodies of living victims, and about severed heads, thousands of severed heads in various stages of decomposition displayed on racks; a most gruesome prospect. However, most of the sailors' stories were about Aztec and Mayan gold, silver, and precious stones, and how they were all going to be rich beyond the dreams of Solomon.

'Zere are huge rooms fool de tresure. Mountains of de gol an de seelver,' said a sailor named Francois; a man with a nasty scar on his right forearm. Hanzel had overheard him talking with an other sailor, a tall, lanky man with a long pony tail.

Hanzel often envisioned mountains of gold and silver in his dreams, as they sailed swiftly across the Atlantic; their ship well provisioned with rum and other essentials. Life on board was pleasant, everyone got along. Hanzel was happy.

They reached the little chain of islands called the Azores two and a half months later. Not one man had been lost. The voyage was completely routine and pleasant sailing. However, everybody was glad to touch land on Pico Island, where they found water and an abundance of the provisions they required in the town of São Roque, a Portuguese settlement. Fortunately several sailors could speak the language, which helped to facilitate the purchase of preserved beef, water, wheat, and wine, lots of wine. They also acquired an abundance of fresh fruits and vegetables, enough to provide everyone with excellent meals during the long voyage to Hispaniola.

When they were ready to sail, everybody gathered on board and Pierre gave the sailors some words of encouragement.

'My dear friends and comrades,' he said with his powerful voice. 'We are about to sail across a wide and treacherous sea. However, if we all pull our weight and perform our duties faithfully, there is a great reward waiting for us. So, let us sail to Hispaniola and may God be with us!'

The crew cheered and threw hats in the air.

'All right, then,' said Pierre, 'Let's cast off and be gone from this place.'

'To your stations, men!' shouted Hanzel. He signaled the boatswain to pipe the command. A moment later a shrill whistle told everyone what to do.

Several islanders had come to wave the ship off. The sun was warm. The sea was calm. The breeze was good. Sea birds screeched overhead. It was a perfect day for sailing.

Several dolphins jumped out of the waves and chattered in their peculiar language.

'They're probably saying, good bye,' said Pierre as they sailed past the chattering creatures, jumping in the bow waves.

Hanzel nodded. 'Whatever they're saying, I think it's good luck when dolphins swim alongside your ship.'

Pierre looked at the dolphins. 'I think that's a good belief. I pray the dolphins are bringing us all the luck we need to carry off our venture.'

'If the treasure galleons are truly carrying such huge loads of gold and silver, and we manage to capture one, you know how tenacious and cruel the Spaniard is.' Hanzel looked at Pierre. 'The Inquisition comes from there. And I'm sure you have heard stories about their methods.'

Pierre nodded, sadly. 'I know of it first hand. The cousin of my uncle's wife was murdered by them.'

Hanzel shook his head. 'I can never understand how it is possible for people to be so cruel to each other.'

'I have always tried to avoid bloodshed. I am praying we will find our galleon and sail her safely home. If the treasure is good enough, we can all retire.' Pierre smiled. 'I'm not greedy. Why push your luck?'

'That sounds good to me,' replied Hanzel, returning his gaze to the graceful dolphins swimming so freely, ahead of the swiftly moving ship. 'Let's find it first. Then we'll formulate a plan to avoid unnecessary bloodshed, if it comes to that. Maybe we'll be able to climb on board and simply steal her from under their very noses.'

'That would be the ideal plan,' agreed Pierre. 'I hope that's how we do it. I don't have plans for an early death. I want to buy a house in the country side, with a forest and a lake, where the Spaniard will never find me.'

'Well, let's pray it happens,' replied Hanzel staring at the dolphins jumping in the waves. 'I also have no plans for an early retirement to the life beyond. I am finding that my life is becoming ever more interesting. I want to live it for as long as I can.'

Pierre looked at the sails and noted the mainsail was not quite set right. He shouted out an order. 'Back to work, eh, Hanzel?'

'Aye, aye, Captain,' replied Hanzel.

Pierre clapped Hanzel on the shoulder. 'Thank you, Hanzel. I'll make it worth your while. Don't worry.'

'I trust you, Pierre. We are friends, are we not?'

'We are friends, Hanzel,' replied Pierre. 'Indeed I have come to like you, young Hollander. I know you will go far in this world.'

'Thank you, Pierre.' Hanzel smiled as he watched Pierre walk back to stand with the helmsman. A moment later Hanzel turned and returned to his cabin, to lie down in his bunk, it being his rest time. As he took off his jacket he began thinking about the adventure he had agreed to.

If we get lucky and find that galleon....Oh, that would be so good. I could send some money to my sisters and brothers and help them out. I wonder how they're faring. Probably still fishing. They could use some gold and silver to better their lives. If Pierre lives up to his word, and I get twenty percent and the treasure is substantial, it could be thousands of ducats. I might even be able to buy my own ship. I will be my own privateer.

Hanzel smiled as he lay back and closed his eyes. He sighed contentedly. Within moments, pictures of beautiful sailing vessels began to glide past as he drifted off into a glorious dream full of sparkling gold and glistening jewels.

Chapter 19

Ten days out from the Azores Archipelago found Hanzel standing with the sailing master, Marcel de Champignon, discussing sailing plans for the oncoming inclement weather. Some miles directly ahead, dark, foreboding clouds were roiling. Lightning could be seen, but the distance was too great to hear the thunder. Waves were already preceding the weather front. The sturdy brigantine began to creak as the hull strained against the increasing volumes of water smashing into her timbers.

Hanzel looked at Marcel, studying the sails. 'It's still some distance away. We should assume it's a big storm. Looking in either direction, south and north, I see no way around it.'

'I've sailed for nigh on twenty seven years. I've encountered many storms. I have survived a shipwreck because of a storm. I've seen dark clouds, of many types.' Marcel pointed at the oncoming darkness. 'I've never seen clouds like that.' He turned to look at Hanzel. 'We had better batten all hatches, tighter than ever and start furling sails and reefing others. I think what we'll try is a single, reefed storm jib and just a tri sail from the top mainmast. There will be just enough sail to keep her into the wind. I suggest we'll use safety ropes on deck.'

Hanzel pointed at the storm. 'Well, let's hope we can keep her stem into the waves and pray they don't harm us too much.' He clapped Marcel on the shoulder and then stepped briskly to the rear quarter deck to discuss matters with Pierre.

'I think Marcel makes the right decision to begin taking sails down and putting some small sails up, to keep us into the wind,' said Pierre. 'We had better get some safety ropes on deck. I don't want anybody flying overboard.'

'I'm going to see about a batten crew,' replied Hanzel.

'Yes, good. Best to double batten the hatches. This storm is giving me a bad feeling.' Pierre frowned and shrugged his shoulders. 'But, what can we do? It looks like we are going to be tested. Nature is like that.'

'I'm sure we'll be fine,' replied Hanzel, patting Pierre on the shoulder. 'We'll get through it. Don't worry.'

Pierre nodded, unconvincingly. He was filled with doubts.

'Alright. I'm off,' said Hanzel. He quickly gathered five sailors and oversaw them batten down the four hatches with double sheets of oiled canvas.

Other sailors were busy changing sails. Two were laying out safety lines for the helmsman and officers of the deck. They also lay out two lines from stem to stern, along the gunwales. Since everyone stood to benefit, everyone working did it well and to the best of his ability. Hence, when they came into contact with the front edge of the turbulent mass, nothing was to be feared, so they thought. The ship rode the waves and the wind shrieked through the rigging, no different than normal storms at sea. However, no one was really fooled, everyone on board was a seasoned veteran of the world's oceans.

An hour passed and then another. Thunder began to reverberate against the masts as flash after flash of intensely bright lightning lit up the tormented clouds and dark, foaming waters tossing the ship ever more up and down and sideways. Rain began to pelt the decks with increasingly more intense onslaughts of stinging, cold water.

Hanzel and his deck mates had put on their oil skins and managed to stay dry. Except for their exposed faces; pelted mercilessly by the stinging sheets of rain, as the men stared bravely into the Maw of Hell. Everyone recited prayer after prayer, hoping that God would intervene and save them. Everyone on board felt they were trapped in something none of them had ever experienced before.

The wind picked up and began to wail and howl, tearing at the sheets and everything else exposed; ropes, tackle, spars, masts, and human beings braving the onslaught on an open deck, to keep the brigantine from succumbing to the diabolical onslaught. The noise was so loud, everyone had to shout to be heard.

'SHE'S HANDLING THE STORM PRETTY WELL!' shouted Hanzel to Pierre, standing right next to him and trying to appear calm and positive; as an officer should in times of adversity. Officers can not show their men that they are scared to death.

'A TRULY WONDERFUL BOAT!' replied Pierre, he also appearing calm and in command of his senses; when, just like Hanzel, he was scared out of his wits. 'WHAT DO YOU THINK, ALPHONSE?! ISN'T SHE A FINE BOAT?!'

The helmsman; holding onto the wheel with all of his strength, grinned. 'THAT SHE BE, ALRIGHT! THAT SHE BE, INDEED! NEVER SAILED ANYTHING BETTER!'

Pierre nodded. *I pray to God we make it through this storm. Please help me God. We are so small and the waves so high. Please, please, please save us.*

The sky lit up with a brilliant flash of blue light. Everything could be seen for an instant in sharp detail, just as an earsplitting clap of thunder shook every board and bone as a giant wave washed over the deck and nearly took everyone off with it. Had it not been for the safety lines, the deck would have been cleared of humans.

The ship slowly rose out of the wave and continued her course for a moment longer, until a forty foot wave hit them broadside; pushing the brigantine to port and nearly tipping her over. Under such circumstances, wooden things can break, and did break on board the *New Venture*. And so it was that the main mast suffered a serious compromise.

CRACK! CRAAACK!

'LOOK OUT!' shouted Pierre, as he pushed Hanzel to starboard.

The top main mast snapped and came crashing down; puncturing the batting of the mid ship hatch. The compromised mast caused ropes and blocks to fly hither and thither in the roaring wind. One of the loose blocks came flying aft, on the end of its rope.

'AAAAAAGH!' shouted the helmsman, as the block came swinging at him. It missed him by inches. The heavy object could easily have taken his head off. It would not have been the first time in the history of seamanship. Alphonse thanked his guardian angels for saving him. He watched as the block stopped and began to swing back.

'THAT WAS CLOSE!' shouted Pierre as he watched the block swing past his shoulder. This time Alphonse was ready for it and neatly ducked as the formidable object whizzed past him.

'WE HAVE TO STOP THAT BLOCK FROM SWINGING!' shouted Pierre.

'JACQUES! MAURICE! AND YOU, ANDRÉ!' shouted Hanzel from the quarter deck to the three sailors tending to the punctured hatch. 'TRY AND CATCH THAT BLOCK! USE A GAFF!'

'AYE, MISTER SVENTSKA!' shouted André. The three sailors quickly attended to the problem by catching the swinging block with a gaff hook. When the block was secured, they shouted for more help to join them on deck. The spar, which had punctured the hatch batting, was too heavy for them to move.

As the sailors frantically worked to fix the hatch, a long, drawn out ripping sound heralded the demise of the tri sail as it tore free and whirled off into the darkness, ropes flying behind. Another piece of the broken spar crashed to the deck, puncturing the batting of the forward hatch, this time. Men scrambled below deck to hold back the water which started to gush in, as waves and rain smashed into the struggling brigantine.

Fortunately the jib remained, enabling the helmsman to keep the brigantine into the wind as cold rain pelted the deck and stung exposed faces.

'BETTER GET ANOTHER SAIL UP THERE!' shouted Pierre to the sailing master. 'I DON'T LIKE THE WAY SHE'S HANDLING!'

'AYE, CAPTAIN!' shouted Marcel. He immediately set about organizing his crew to replan the sails as the ship continued to ride up and down gigantic waves, through rain, howling winds, lightning, and thunder.

And so it went, for hour after hour, as the ship was ever more battered and heaved to and fro. Things broke free and rolled about, ropes and sails kept flying off. Everyone began to think they might be lost and prepared themselves for what they thought was the inevitable. Their death at sea.

In the thirty first hour of their ordeal, the wind stopped and they were once again sailing in calm waters. There was no rain, no lightning, and no thunder, to rattle the very bones of one's skeleton. Everyone heaved a sigh of great relief. The sailors cheered as they came up from below deck, glad to be breathing fresh air and counting themselves amongst the living.

'Well, let's see about cleaning up this mess,' said Pierre. 'Maybe we can repair some of the damage. However, I'm afraid we're going to have to do some serious refitting on land.'

Three hours later, the sailors had managed to fix rope and tackle problems and replan the sails. By the fourth hour they had managed to lift the broken spars out of the compromised hatch covers. Double sheets of oiled canvas were used to batten the hatches anew.

'Batten those hatches well, lads. I think there's more trouble coming,' said Hanzel, staring into his telescope

'We're in the eye,' said Marcel, studying the mainsail.

'The eye?' asked Alphonse, the helmsman. 'What's the eye?'

'The eye of the storm,' replied Marcel. 'The middle of the hurricane.'

'A hurricane? We're in a hurricane?' Alphonse stared straight ahead, his knees quivering with fright.

'Aye,' replied Marcel.

'We're in the eye? Of a hurricane?' Alphonse looked up at the calm sky.

'Aye. We're in the eye of a hurricane.' Marcel regarded Alphonse, staring bug eyed at the roiling clouds, surrounding their ship, two leagues distant in every direction.

'I've never been in a hurricane before,' said Alphonse nervously. 'I hope it doesn't get any worse than what we already went through.'

'Judging from what I see through my glass, we're in for something very powerful. The clouds I see are darker and even more menacing.' Hanzel handed the glass to Marcel.

'I suggest we just put out a storm jib. That way we ease the strain on the main mast,' suggested Pierre to Marcel, who was studying the clouds through the telescope.

'Yes, that's what I was thinking. I think we've got about an hour, or so, before we sail into that swirling mass.' Marcel handed the glass back to Hanzel. 'Well, gentlemen. I wish us all good luck. And may God spare us. From what I saw through the glass, I also think we're facing something even more terrible that what we've already sailed through.'

'May God help us,' murmured Alphonse. 'We're in a hurricane.'

There was no way out. It did not matter in which direction Hanzel looked, they were surrounded by the swirling cloud. As they approached the westerly point of the shrieking storm, the waves grew in size again, and the wind began to whirr and whine through the rigging.

'I hope that storm jib will do it. I did not dare put up anything off the main mast,' said Michel. He was standing on the quarter deck with Pierre and Hanzel, staring at the foreboding clouds beginning to engulf them.

'I think you made the right choice,' replied Pierre. 'What do you think, Alphonse?'

The helmsman nodded. 'I think I can hold er. If I need help, I will ask Olafson.'

'Noted.' Pierre gestured to Hanzel to note the request and see to it.

Hanzel sent word to the midshipman, Jules Riviere to inform Olafson to prepare himself. 'Remind him to put on his rain gear,' said Hanzel.

'Aye, Mister Sventska,' came the reply. The midshipman quickly went below deck to find Olafson.

Meantime the waves were beginning to toss the ship ever more. By the time Olafson reached the quarterdeck, the waves were breaking over the bows and washing the decks. Spray was beginning to sting faces as the wind began to rage and howl.

The cloud whirling around them became darker and darker, until it was no longer possible to see ahead. All they could do was watch the compass and try to keep her on course. As the wind screamed and the waves bashed the timbers of the wooden ship, the men on deck were beginning to shiver with cold and fright.

As more and more of hell's fury was hurled at the tossing ship, even seasoned sailors began to feel queasy in their stomachs. Some of the weaker ones began to vomit. The smell of vomit can lead to other's vomiting. Soon the reek of vomit began to make its presence known below.

'IT'S A GOOD THING WE HAVE THESE SAFETY ROPES TIED TO OUR BELTS!' shouted Hanzel over the raging wind.

Pierre nodded, just as a wave came crashing over them.

'THAT WATER IS COLD!' shouted Hanzel. 'I THOUGHT IT WOULD BE WARMER BY NOW!'

'THIS IS STILL THE *NORTH* ATLANTIC!' replied Pierre. 'THIS WATER IS COLD WHEN IT IS STIRRED UP LIKE THIS!'

Hanzel nodded and braced himself as another wave crashed over the quarter deck.

The sound of the wind and waves became a horrific cacophony, as ear splitting thunder and blinding flashes of light lit up everything for miles and miles. Everyone was afraid they would succumb to the onslaught and began making preparations to meet his Maker.

For twenty four hours they battled the storm, managing to keep the ship more or less on course. Nobody got any rest. Everyone was bone tired. In all the years the crew members had sailed the seven seas, no one had ever encountered such a storm. A horrific storm. The storm to remember and tell tales about, if they survived; something everyone was becoming ever more doubtful of as a mountain of water took away their bow sprit. The storm jib flew loose into the wind, held to the foremast by a single rope. Ropes and tackle swung dangerously. Moments later the top foremast cracked and the jib flew off into the shrieking darkness.

'WE HAVE NO SAILS!' shouted Marcel. He looked frantically at Alphonse, Hanzel, and Pierre holding onto the wheel with all their might.

'I CAN'T SEE WHERE WE'RE GOING!' Hanzel stared forward into the tumbling haze and began to pray, *Oh God, please help us. Help us all. Please save us from this horror. We don't deserve to be lost at sea. What wrong have we done? I haven't done any wrong. I was abducted. Dear God.*

A loud crunching noise and a hard jolt stopped the ship's motion forward. The sound became louder. The ship lurched to starboard as a huge wave crashed over the deck, splintering what was left of the foremast which fell backward onto the quarter deck and crushed Alphonse against the boards. Ropes and blocks smashed into the railing, next to where Hanzel had fallen.

Cracking timbers and smashing waves began to be drowned by the sounds of screaming men below deck as water started pouring in through the ever widening hole in the port bow.

'WE'VE HIT A ROCK!' shouted Pierre as he disentangled himself from ropes which had fallen on him.

'I THINK SHE'S BREAKING UP!' Hanzel looked at Pierre on the opposite side of the spar which had crushed the helmsman.

The ship lurched and began to break in the middle and suddenly the rear quarterdeck was tossed high up and brought hard down on the rocks they had struck. Boards groaned and split, sending deadly splinters flying off in all directions above and below decks. Screams of trapped men increased a hundred fold as they were drowning and struck with needle sharp slivers of tortured oak.

Without warning a wave smashed into the starboard side of the quarter deck, sending Hanzel and Pierre into the tossing waters. 'HEEEEEELLLLPPPP!' is the last Hanzel heard of him as he landed in the waves.

Oh my God! Please save me. I don't want to drown.

When he came to the surface, Hanzel looked frantically for something to help him float. *I have to save myself. I need a plank, a spar, a barrel, anything that floats.*

A large piece of sideboard broke off the ship and crashed into the water. Hanzel saw it come off the ship and swam with all of his might to get to it before the waves took it away. *I've got to get on that plank. Please help me.*

Hanzel managed to get to the large plank just when a wave tossed him and the plank into the air and far away from where the *New Venture* had foundered. The last thing Hanzel heard was the cracking of timber and the screams of men. Within moments the noise was swallowed as the storm pushed Hanzel toward the north coast of Hispaniola.

Chapter 20

Hanzel had no idea how long he clung to the plank, holding on for dear life, and praying he would be saved, before being tossed onto a beach where he lay for a long while thanking God for his deliverance.

Thank you, thank you, thank you....

The storm was still raging, sending massive waves crashing onto the rocky beach where Hanzel lay, gathering his wits. He was shivering and needed to find shelter. He stood up slowly; his joints paining him from having held onto the plank with all of his strength. He stumbled his way to the trees, lining the beach. As he made his way to the forest, a voice shouted,

'Hey there! Is it you, Hanzel?!'

Hanzel was instantly cheered. The voice was that of Pierre LeGrange. 'Ya!' shouted Hanzel. 'Ya, ya, I am Hanzel!'

He quickly headed in the direction of the voice. Pierre and two others were huddled under a huge tree at the edge of the beach. They had watched as Hanzel landed with his plank.

'Now we're four,' said Pierre, happily. 'This way we can help each other and we'll survive.'

Hanzel was glad. 'It's good to see that you survived. Let's hope that the storm quits soon and we can find our way out of here.'

'Let's hope so,' said Pierre. 'I'm cold and hungry.'

'When the storm blows over, we can look around and see if anything from the ship made it to land. If we're lucky, we'll find some kegs with food and drink,' replied Hanzel.

'Let's hope so...' Pierre stared at the waves crashing on the beach, suddenly lost in his own thoughts.

The four men stayed huddled under the tree for the rest of that day and the next, when the storm finally played itself out. The rain stopped much to everyone's relief. The four hungry, dehydrated men quickly extricated themselves from under the tree and walked out onto the rocky beach.

'Aaah, this is much better,' said Pierre, stretching his aching limbs. He pointed to the sky, where the clouds were breaking up and rays of sunshine were beginning to be seen. 'Thank God, it's over.'

Everyone agreed, it was a great blessing to be finally free of the storm's icy grip.

'Let's see what we can find,' suggested Hanzel as he began to walk towards the water line. 'I'm really parched and hungry.'

'Where do you think we are?' asked Jean La Plante, one of the two sailors; a tall, thin man. His clothes were badly torn. He had lost his shoes in the waves.

Pierre shrugged his shoulders. 'I'm not exactly sure. We could be on a small island, or we could be on Hispaniola. I've no idea. I guess we'll find out as we walk.'

'We should leave a marker here, just in case we do walk around an island. That way we'll know,' suggested the other sailor; a man with a thick, bushy beard and a golden ring in his right ear lobe.

'Good thinking, Max,' said Hanzel. 'What can we use for a marker?'

Max pointed to the rocks. 'We can pile rocks.'

'Good idea. We'll pile rocks right here,' said Pierre as he began to pick up a large boulder.

Soon the four men had made a small cairn which would serve to mark where they had been. Then they set off to explore the beach and see if there was anything they could salvage from the ship.

After walking for more than an hour, all that they found was bits of rope, canvas, boards, and smashed up barrels and kegs.

'We don't have any weapons. How are we going to survive? We need to find food,' said Jean.

'And water,' added Max.

'Don't worry, lads,' replied Pierre encouragingly. 'There's got to be fresh water on a place like this. Probably further up the beach we'll find a creek or a stream.'

'Or a brook,' suggested Jean.

'Maybe a river,' added Hanzel.

'Let's keep going and not give up hope. The sun is beginning to warm the air. Soon our clothes will dry and we'll feel a whole lot better.' Pierre pointed ahead and continued on his way along the beach.

As the men approached a rocky outcropping, a flock of sea birds flew off with a noisy flutter.

'We could eat those birds,' suggested Max.

'If you can catch em first,' laughed Jean.

'I've eaten gull,' replied Pierre. 'Not much meat on em and taste terrible. I'm confident there is better food to be had here.'

'Maybe we'll find some nests up there,' said Hanzel, pointing to the top of the outcropping. 'We're going to have to climb over these rocks. Who knows, we might find food up there.'

'Gull eggs?' asked Max. 'What would we cook em in?'

'Eat em raw,' said Pierre. 'Just poke a hole in em and suck out the contents.'

Max screwed up his face. 'A person will do anything to stay alive, I suppose.'

When the four men reached the top of the outcropping a wondrous sight greeted them on the other side. Their ship's long boat was pulled up on the beach and fifteen of their friends were sitting on nice white sand around a large fire.

'Well, I'll be....' said Pierre.

'Unbelievable,' replied Hanzel.

'There's Marcel!' shouted Max, pointing.

'And Olafson,' added Hanzel, overjoyed to see his friend. 'Nothing can kill that big Swede, thank God.'

Pierre laughed. 'We have nothing to fear. With this many of us, and the boat. We'll survive, my young friend. We'll survive.'

'HEY! WE'RE UP HERE!' shouted Jean as he waved his arms.

A moment later their friends came running as Hanzel and his little group stumbled as quickly as they could down the rocky pile to be embraced when they reached the sand. Everyone patted each other's shoulders, shook hands, or hugged, depending on the depth of friendship. Everyone was grateful to be alive and to see so many saved from the wreck.

'How in the blue blazes did you manage to save yourselves with the boat?' asked Pierre incredulously.

'When we hit the rocks, we knew what was coming. So, Olafson managed to open the hatch and we climbed on deck just as the boat went overboard in a wave. We simply jumped after her and got away just before the main mast came down and crashed beside us.'

'Fortunately some of us had time to grab a bag of things, like our tobacco and flint boxes,' added Jacques LaTuque, a sailor from Quebec.

'Good thing,' said Hanzel. 'Now we can dry ourselves and get warm.' He shivered. 'I'm freezing.'

'Yes, it does take a while for the air to warm up again after such a storm,' reflected Marcel.

'Do you think there might be others alive?' asked Pierre.

Marcel shook his head. 'I don't know. Perhaps what we should do is take the boat, now that the waters are calming, and see. The boat has her spar and sail.'

'What about food?' asked Max. 'Did you manage to save any food?'

'Or water?' added Jean.

'There was no time,' replied Marcel. 'We just managed to keep our weapons and a few personal things. That's all.'

'It's a lucky thing you kept your weapons. We can use them to acquire food,' suggested Hanzel.

'So, here we are then. At least we have a boat and weapons. I know we'll survive. Before I wasn't so sure.' Pierre looked at Hanzel. 'Eh, Hanzel. It was touch and go out there.'

Hanzel nodded. 'I must have a guardian angel.'

Pierre paused for a moment. 'I think we all must have guardian angels. Because, here we are. Safe and sound. With a boat and weapons. I know we'll get back to France.' Pierre clapped his hands together. 'Alright, it makes no sense for us to sit here and wait for nightfall to come, with no water or food. We need to take the boat and row along the coast to find a stream of fresh water. We may even find a spring fed pond. Sitting here is not going to get us what we need. Let's go.'

'Aye, Captain!' shouted the men as they began to push the long boat into the water. When the boat was afloat, everyone climbed, one after another, over the gunwales. They rowed with all their might to overcome the incoming surf. Pierre spurred them on. Hanzel held the tiller steady. Fifteen minutes later they were past the surf and rowing on calmer waters.

'I have a feeling we're on the coast of Hispaniola. We were blown west. I think it's the only large island in the direction we were blown.' Pierre pointed north and south. 'Each direction you look, you see land. This is obviously a large island.'

'Maybe we were blown to Brazil?' suggested Max, rowing on the bench ahead of the helm.

'Did you look at charts before we came into the storm, Captain?' asked Jean, pulling on the starboard oar beside Max.

'That's why I think we're off the coast of Hispaniola. The north coast, somewhere.' Pierre pursed his lips and stared north. 'We'll head north and see what we can see. Maybe we'll discover a settlement.'

'Well, I sure hopes there's women in that settlement,' replied Jean.

'I jes hopes they's free coz all me money went down wid de ship,' said Joachim, a grey haired sailor from Le Havre.

Everyone agreed, women would be a nice discovery, indeed. Especially if they were free. Many comments, regarding what and how various sailors would treat the women they discovered in the settlement, stirred much laughter. Eventually the poor women were subjected to more and more outrageous fantasies; followed with ever greater volumes of raucous laughter.

Eventually, everyone broke out into a chanty about women and sailors and how the two should behave with each other in every kind of position known to mankind since times immemorial. Everyone was so happy to be alive and able to contemplate sex with a beautiful woman, it made everybody grin from ear to ear. Each man thanked God deep in his heart for his survival from the terror of the storm.

As the happy privateers rowed, the sea became ever calmer and the clouds evaporated into little white fluffy piles; allowing a glorious warming sun to further brighten everyone's spirits, notwithstanding their growling stomachs and parched throats.

After rowing for several hours, a sailor named, Hugo Waart shouted, 'Look there!' He was pointing toward the beach.

Everyone looked intently in the direction, Hugo indicated. It took a while as their eyes had to adjust to looking at the trees lining the beach they were rowing past. As their eyes focused, each man could clearly see three masts peeking over the tree tops.

'There must be a bay or cove over there,' said Pierre. 'We don't know whose ship it is, so be very quiet from now on. They must not hear us.'

Hanzel pointed to the shore. 'We should land over there and several of us can sneak through the trees and have a look. You never know who might be lurking there.'

'Yes, of course. Good thinking, Hanzel,' replied Pierre. He immediately directed the men to row to where Hanzel pointed. When they made land, Hanzel, Olafson and Pierre ran off to reconnoiter and see if there was anything to fear from the large ship, whose masts they saw when they were rowing a short distance off shore.

The three explorers quickly walked across a narrow beach of sand and stones to a forest of exotic trees and large leafed plants.

'I wonder whose ship it is,' whispered Hanzel. He pushed a large leaf aside and looked for a place to set his foot in the dense undergrowth.

Pierre pointed. 'Look, past those trees. You can see one of the masts.'

Hanzel and Olafson stared through the trees. A moment later they could see the masts moving, as the ship bobbed gently in the water, not too much further on.

The three privateers came to the edge of a small bay, where a crippled galleon was being repaired. A Spanish flag fluttered lazily in the gentle breeze left over from the storm.

'Maybe it's one of those treasure galleons,' suggested Hanzel. 'One of those ships we set out to find.'

Pierre smiled as he removed his spyglass from its holster. 'If it is, then we are in luck.' He put the glass to his eye and studied the galleon. A moment later he handed the instrument to Hanzel. 'See what you make of her. From what I can tell, there are not many sailors on board. They're pretending to be merely a merchant ship, but I think otherwise, judging from how low she rides in the water.'

Hanzel nodded. 'She's carrying a significant weight. There's no doubt about that. I count only five sailors at work fixing the top main and only, one, two, three. Oh, and that one, four. Only four working on the broken bow sprit.'

'There are probably three officers and maybe another dozen below, if that. That's not so many. I think we can take that ship.' Pierre regarded Hanzel and Olafson.

'Ya, I tink ve can do it,' replied Olafson, nodding his head. 'Zo, vhat are ve vaiting for? Les get de boys.'

'We'll do it at night,' suggested Hanzel. 'Then we'll really take them by surprise.'

'Right you are, Hanzel. We'll take em by surprise in the dark of night.' Pierre clapped Hanzel on his shoulder.

The three friends quickly made their way back to the boat and their fellows. Pierre wasted no time and informed the others about the plan to steal the Spanish ship out from under their noses. 'We'll row over there around midnight.' Pierre looked at the sky for a moment before returning his attention on his men. 'Then, when it is good and dark, we'll climb on board and take over the ship. Avoid bloodshed at all costs. There are not many sailors on board, otherwise there would be larger work crews repairing things on board that ship. She's likely a straggler from a convoy.'

'What if they put up a resistance?' asked one of the sailors, a man named Marcello.

'We'll commandeer the officers and demand a surrender. I think it's possible we outnumber them,' said Hanzel. 'So, not to worry. We'll surprise them in their sleep.'

'So, I suggest we all get some rest and prepare for tonight. You will need all of your wits to carry this plan forward. If she is what I think she is, you will all be very happy men when we meet with success.'

'Does she be one er dem royal ships, Cap'n?' asked an old sailor named, Tomas. 'One er de ships we heerd so much aboot?'

'She is flying a Spanish flag from her transom. I could not make out a royal pennant,' replied Pierre. 'Did you see a pennant, Hanzel?'

Hanzel shook his head. 'No. I saw no pennant. But, that doesn't mean anything. Whatever is on that ship, is heavy. There is heavy cargo on board that ship. Since we have a Letter of Marque to take Spanish ships, it is very patriotic of you, to fulfill the king's wishes and deprive the Spanish of their ship and its merchandise.'

Laughter filled the space.

'Hurrah to our captain and Hanzel Sventska!' shouted Marcello.

'Vive le Capitan!' shouted a short, stout sailor who looked like a human version of a pug.

Hanzel regarded the sailor. *I wouldn't want to get into a fight with that one. He's built like a brick.*

'Vive Hanzel Sventska!' shouted others.

Hanzel waved and bowed. 'Thank you. Thank you,' he said. 'I wish us all great success tonight.'

Cheers, handshakes, and shoulder pats followed, as the men wished each other success.

'Well, my friends,' said Pierre, holding his open palmed right hand in the air. 'Since there are some hours before we leave, look to your weapons and get some rest. Capturing that ship is of utmost importance because it is also our only way home.'

'Aye, aye, Captain!' shouted the men as they disassembled and began to make themselves comfortable on the sand.

Pierre and Hanzel watched as the men began to examine their weapons.

'Well, Pierre, let's hope this adventure works for us. I pray that we have no resistance.' Hanzel regarded his friend. A serious expression came to his face. 'What if there are marines or some such military presence?'

'We would have seen them walking about on deck,' replied Pierre. 'Don't you think?'

Hanzel nodded. 'Ya, I suppose so. After spending their time cooped up during the storm....'

'We didn't see very many men on board, did we?' Pierre smiled and his eyes twinkled. 'I'm convinced now. The sailors would want to be outdoors too. That ship only has a small crew. Just enough to sail her.' Pierre pointed where the Spanish ship lay anchored. 'Those Spaniards figured they are untouchable when they disguise their treasure boats and sail in a convoy. However, alone, the treasure ships are helpless.'

Hanzel rubbed his hands together. 'I think we're in for a very pleasant surprise.'

'I agree,' replied Pierre beaming. He clapped Hanzel on the shoulder. 'Well, my friend. I think I will get some shut eye and dream of success with no blood shed.'

'Aye, aye, Captain,' said Hanzel, shaking Pierre's hand. 'Let the angels of success guide us.'

Pierre nodded and smiled. 'So be it,' he said, as he sat down on the sand.

Hanzel watched his friend settle into a comfortable position. Then, he too lay down on the sand and closed his eyes. He realized that he was actually tired. When he began to take note of his body, he realized that his muscles were sore from the rowing. He had used muscles he had not used much before. Officers do not row boats. Sailors row the boats. Officers merely guide them and keep the men on task. Hanzel was an officer.

I hope this adventure works out for us. I don't want to kill anybody. I just want a piece of the gold. Who knows? Maybe I can retire and live happily ever after, when we're done. That would be so good. I could send my brothers and sisters money. I could buy my own boat. I could own a boat, or maybe even several boats and hire captains and crews and start my own business. Oh, that would be so great. I'd be so happy. Perhaps I'll find a good wife...

Hanzel drifted off to sleep. He never heard the snores and farts as everyone else settled into the sand. All of the men were tired and sore from their exertions in the storm and the hours of rowing they performed.

As they lay there sleeping, the weather cleared, revealing a sky full of stars and a magnificent moon, full and smiling. The air warmed slightly and the waves settled down. The hours passed and the sky remained clear and began to warm. A small flock of pelicans flew past, skimming over the water, looking for fish. No one noticed. Some creature growled somewhere in the forest. Not one of the men heard it. By the time midnight arrived, no one stirred on the beach. The nineteen privateers had been pummeled by the storm and were tired down to their very bones.

The first one to wake up was Max. He had to take care of bladder issues. He stumbled some ways away from the sleeping sailors, and began urinating into the sand. As he stood there he noted that the sky was considerably lighter than it should have been at midnight. He directed his gaze at the horizon and noticed that the sun was coming up. A hint of golden glow began to grow larger and stronger. The tiny, wispy clouds near the horizon began to glow orange, red, and pink. Max looked over at his sleeping companions then back at the rising sun, now beginning to glow stronger.

'Hey!' he shouted. 'The sun is rising!'

Nobody stirred.

'HEY! WAKE UP!' yelled Max. 'DAYBREAK IS HERE!'

As he returned his penis to its codpiece, he looked over to see if his shouting had done any good. He smiled as his friends slowly rose from their healing slumbers. They were all a little bewildered it was daybreak already.

Pierre stared bleary eyed at Hanzel. 'We missed midnight.'

Hanzel regarded Pierre for a moment without saying anything. Then he replied, 'It doesn't matter, Pierre. You said *after midnight*.' Hanzel gestured towards the rising sun. 'It is *after* midnight, is it not?'

Pierre laughed. 'Indeed it is. It's after midnight.'

'We didn't see many sailors. Even if they're on deck working, couldn't we overtake them, anyway? We'll just figure a way to get on board and hold them at gunpoint.' Hanzel regarded Pierre to see his reaction.

'Not a good idea. Under cover of night, we take them by surprise. In the daylight we don't have the advantage,' replied Pierre.

Hanzel nodded. 'So, what do you suggest we do here for the day? We need to eat and find water. That ship has both. I know it was my idea to go at night, but I really don't think it matters. Day or night. Your men know what they are doing.'

Pierre looked out to sea and thought about the risks involved. *A daylight raid. In full view. I've no idea how many there are. I'm going on a hunch. I've a good feeling about this. I think we'd be alright. The boys have done it before. Nothing this big, but they've taken on larger numbers.* Pierre looked at his eager crew waiting for instructions. Then he regarded Hanzel and nodded. 'Alright. Why not? We could row into the bay and just tell them we are ship wrecked sailors off a merchant ship looking for help. Since they are not great in number they would welcome the additional crew to help repair the ship and sail her home. Once they're comfortable with us, we overtake them and steal their ship. How does that sound?'

Hanzel smiled. 'I think that's brilliant. Let's do it. We have no choice. We need to eat and drink.'

Pierre turned to regard the other men. 'Hanzel and I have decided we're going to take the ship today.'

'But it's bright daylight, Captain,' said Marcel.

'Aye, Captain, it's daylight,' said several other voices.

Pierre raised his hands. 'Boys, we're going to surprise em. We'll row over there and tell em we're shipwrecked sailors from a merchant ship. We'll ask to come on board for water and food, perhaps to sign on and go home.'

'Thas a gute idea,' said Olafson.

'We should do it!' replied several others.

'Yes, let's go!' agreed several more.

'What are we waiting for?!' shouted the rest.

So, off they went. They dragged the boat to the water and soon were on their way, over the mild breakers to the bay where their treasure lay waiting. They had no idea what they were about to find on board that Spanish ship.

Chapter 21

'Because they steal the gold and silver from the Indians, I have no qualms taking the Spaniard's gold,' said Pierre as they rounded the point and came into the bay where the Spanish ship was anchored.

'Neither do I,' replied Hanzel. 'I think we can do a lot of good with whatever is on board that ship.'

'I hope so.' Pierre looked at Hanzel and smiled. 'I sure hope so.'

'She's a goodly sized ship,' said Hanzel, eyeing her up. 'A fat, Spanish merchantman.'

'See how low she's in the water, boys?' asked Pierre.

The sailors rowing the boat all smiled, understanding full well what, low in the water meant.

'Alright boys,' whispered Pierre. 'No more talking. We need to convince them that we're harmless, shipwrecked sailors.'

The privateers had crept up on a ship before. They knew what to do. The only concern they had; there were only nineteen of them. They had no idea how many Spaniards there really were on board that ship.

A voice shouting in Spanish could be heard coming from the heavily laden merchantman.

'We have been spotted,' whispered Pierre. 'This is it boys. Hide your weapons.'

The men did as Pierre told them. Hanzel watched as the men checked over the few weapons they had; twelve pistols, Hanzel's dirk, a short sword, and five cutlasses. As they approached the Spanish ship, Pierre held up a white handkerchief.

More Spanish voices shouted.

'Ahoy!' shouted Pierre, in perfect Spanish. 'We are shipwrecked sailors! We need help! We lost our ship.'

'We are blessed by the Holy Mother. We only lost some spars!' shouted a Spanish sailor, as he and a companion stood looking over the port gunwale. Hanzel noted there was a stern faced officer standing behind them. Their eyes met. The man stood mesmerized for a moment, as he stared into Hanzel's unique blue eyes. The officer quickly broke eye contact and turned his gaze to the sailors rowing the boat. He watched intently as the boat was tied to the side of the ship.

'May we come aboard?' asked Pierre. 'We need water. And food. We were shipwrecked off the coast. In the storm. This is all that is left of us.'

Hanzel noted that the officer nodded his consent.

'All right then,' said the Spanish sailor. 'Come on board.'

'Our cook will take care of you,' said the other sailor. 'You will all be good as new in no time.' He chuckled.

'All right men. Let's take this ship,' whispered Pierre as the men began to climb up the ship's ladder. 'Hanzel, Marcel, and I will take the officers and the rest of you see to the sailors. Olafson, you and Sven take the fore hatch. The rest of you see to the decks and spars.'

Within minutes the nineteen shipwrecked privateers were standing on the Spanish deck, intently watched by ten sailors holding assorted weapons. Olafson and Sven disappeared down the forward hatch. A moment later, two stern looking Spanish officers stepped out of the aftercastle.

'Who are you? What ship are you from?' asked the captain in rapid Castilian as he surveyed the nineteen new arrivals.

Pierre was about to explain when Olafson and Sven urged six protesting sailors on deck.

'Eighteen to nineteen, boys,' whispered Pierre. 'Pick your man and let's get it done.'

The element of surprise overwhelmed the merchant sailors as the seasoned privateers quickly set about their business. Another moment passed and the crew of the Spanish ship were staring at the points and barrels of lethal weapons.

'We are stealing this ship, senior,' said Pierre politely to the captain. He pointed his pistol at the man's chest and gestured toward the open sea. 'We need this ship to return home, and therefore take her a prize according to the articles of a Letter of Marque from the King of France.'

'The King of France be damned,' replied the captain haughtily.

'I give you a choice. You can come peacefully with us and return to France. Or we will let you take our boat and you can do as you like.' Pierre regarded the two officers.

The two men looked at each other for a moment and nodded.

'We would rather take your boat and take our chances, than accompany you French pigs to your apostate country,' replied the stern faced captain.

Hanzel watched as Pierre's expression changed to a hard, cold stare. 'Take yourselves off this ship. And be quick about it.' Pierre looked at the Spanish sailors held in check by his crew. 'If any of you feel as your officers do, then go with them now. If you stay on board and attempt to retake this ship, you will be killed, sure as Pharisees killed Christ.'

The Spanish captain looked at his sailors. 'If you go with these French swine, by the Holy Mother, you will be damned to Hell.'

The sixteen Spanish sailors discussed the options. Only six chose to accompany the officers.

'You will hang for this crime against the Spanish Crown!' shouted the captain as he stepped over the gunwale of the big ship.

Pierre laughed. 'The Spanish Crown be damned!'

'Damn you all!' yelled the captain as he stepped into the boat.

The second officer stepped over the gunwale. 'May you rot in Hell,' he said brusquely, his eyes staring into Pierre's steady gaze.

'Find a barrel of water and gather up some food for those men,' ordered Pierre. 'And give them a keg of wine, as well.'

'You are most generous, senior,' said a Spanish sailor as he stepped over the gunwale.

Pierre nodded.

The rest of the sailors quickly climbed down to the boat, soon followed by a keg of wine, a barrel of water, two chickens, a goat, a keg of salted beef, a bag of salt, and a bag of flour.

'Give them a knife,' said Pierre. 'They'll need a knife to kill the goat.'

Max, who was standing nearby tossed his knife down to a Spanish sailor. 'He can have mine. I've found a better one.' He held up the magnificent knife he took off one of the Spaniards.

'You will burn in a thousand fires!' shouted the Spanish captain as the long boat drifted away from the big ship.

Hanzel and Pierre watched from the quarter deck as the Spaniards rowed toward the shore of the little bay, to gather their wits and make their plans.

'Well, boys, now we are twenty nine in number. That should be enough to sail this ship home.' Looking up, Pierre continued, 'It looks like most of the necessary repairs are done. What do you think, Hanzel?'

Hanzel nodded. 'It appears to be the case. This ship weathered that storm pretty well.'

'We were lucky to make it into this bay, before the worst of the storm. Those outcroppings protected us. We were not badly damaged and finished the work last night. We were ready to sail when you came on board,' said a Spanish sailor; a tall, slim man with drooping mustaches. Hanzel noted he had a long scar on his right cheek and was missing an eye.

'Well, if you boys will help us get this ship back to France, I promise you will receive a piece of what we have taken.' He looked at his fellow privateers. 'What say you boys? Shall we sail er home?'

'Aye! Captain!' came the instant reply.

Pierre looked at Hanzel. 'Alright, Mister Sventska, let's take er out of the bay and go home.

Hanzel smiled broadly. 'Aye Captain Le Grange,' he said, saluting. Then, turning to the crew he shouted, 'Weigh anchor boys! We are going back to France!'

A great cheer rang out. 'VIVE LA FRANCE!!! VIVE LA FRANCE!!!'

A moment later, ten sailors manned the capstan, others began to set sails. Within twenty minutes the 2000 pound anchor was hauled up and made secure as sails began to unfurl. As the sails began to fill, the big ship slowly moved out of the bay, all the while intently watched by the Spaniards standing on shore.

'Marcel, while you work on your sail plan, Hanzel and I will take a look at the cargo we have taken.' Pierre regarded Max. 'Take the helm and head due north north east.

Max smiled. 'Aye, Captain,' he said.

'Come on Hanzel, let us take a look below.' Pierre smiled broadly as he led the way to the forward hatch and access to the ship's hold.

'I can't wait to see what we captured. I hope it's what you think it is. If it is, we'll all be able to retire on land and live a life of luxury.' Hanzel followed Pierre as they stepped down the ladder into the dark hold of the ship. Hanzel lit a lantern and held it up. When their eyes grew accustomed to the dim light, they saw exactly what they hoped they would see.

Treasure!!!!

Boxes and chests, kegs and barrels, sacks and bags full of gold, silver, jewels, ornaments, statues; all made of gold or silver with precious stones for eyes and decorations. Hanzel and Pierre could hardly believe their eyes as they took stock of the hold full of marvelous surprises. In addition to the treasure, barrels of food, water, wine, rum, twelve goats, six cows, five sheep, sixteen chickens, and two monkeys added their weight and sounds to the heavy ship.

'No wonder she's so low in the water,' said Hanzel.

'We will live happily ever after,' replied Pierre, as he reached into a box and let a handful of red, green, and blue stones fall through his fingers.

'This is unbelievable.' Hanzel opened a sack to find it filled with gold nuggets the size of thumb nails.

'We are all rich beyond our wildest dreams!' Pierre looked wide eyed at Hanzel; a big grin on his weathered face; an odd looking statuette in his hands; its turqoise eyes staring into eternity.

'Hopefully we can get this ship home without being attacked, ourselves,' said Hanzel.

'Yes, there is that, of course. Let's go up and tell the boys the good news. We'll vote regarding how much to give those Spaniards for helping with the crossing.' Pierre looked at a huge chest. 'I'm sure there's enough for everybody.'

Hanzel smiled and nodded. 'I'm sure.'

When Hanzel and Pierre returned on deck, several privateers asked about the treasure. Pierre told them to wait a moment. He would let everybody know at the same time. A few minutes later all hands stood below the quarter deck and listened to Pierre and Hanzel describe what they had captured. Pierre finished by saying, 'So, boys, I will gladly give each of you a tour, four at a time. Not you Spaniards, because we are only doing you a favour to take you back to Europe. We will pay you well for your service. If you betray us, we will kill you. Do you understand? I will shoot you myself.' Pierre paused for good effect. 'Alright then, Marcel, Olafsen, Sven, and Francois, you can come first. Grab the lantern.' Hanzel watched as the five men went below. A moment later he could hear loud whoops and hollers as the men realized what was making the ship ride so low in the water.

Hanzel aimed a telescope toward the beach. As the ship sailed away from the bay, he could see that the Spaniards were watching them and likely shouting insults, judging from the many raised fists waving in the air. He could not hear them because of the surf. It did not matter. Hanzel could well imagine what they were saying. *You steal from them, we steal from you, so, we're even in the total scheme of things. The treasure will spread out, instead of being hoarded by a wealthy few. That's the way it's meant to be. It's like I'm helping to do God's work.* Hanzel took a deep breath. *I'm helping spread wealth. That's a good thing. Like that English fellow. Robin Hood. Take from the rich and give to the poor.* He regarded the sailors. *I'm certain most of those fellows are not going to settle down. They'll spend their treasure on, food, wine, women, riotous living. I'll bet that most of them will be broke in two years. Lots of people will get a piece of this treasure. That's a good thing.* Hanzel stared at the island they were leaving. Sea gulls screeched overhead. *I am to have twenty percent of all of that. That is incredible. I'm so glad I was chosen to come on this adventure. My share of all that treasure makes me a very wealthy man. The question now is, how do I get it back to Holland?*

The voyage across the Atlantic was slow and pleasantly spent sailing the big merchantman in excellent weather. For the twenty nine sailors, there was plenty of food and wine. Many days were spent, pleasantly plastered under a warming sun. Waves lapped at the bows and the wake was gentle. Sometimes everyone had a siesta.

'I think we are in Paradise,' said Pierre, one afternoon, as he and Hanzel were lolling in large arm chairs set up on the quarter deck. 'I pray this weather stays like this the rest of the way to France. This tub wouldn't make it through a major storm.'

'It's the risk we take. I'm just glad we've had so many good days of sailing. And, I'm glad we've got this wine.' Hanzel raised his crystal glass.

'To this wine,' replied Pierre, raising his glass. Then he drank the glass dry in one drought.

'So, how far have we gone, you figure?' asked Hanzel.

'When I did my astrolabe calculations, I think we're past half way home. If we get some stronger winds, we could be home in three weeks.' Pierre poured more wine into his glass.

'Let's pray for some strong winds, then,' suggested Max, who was manning the wheel. 'I'm beginning to get bored with the slow going. I want to get home and spend some of my share of the loot.'

'Don't we all,' said Marcel, the sailing master. 'Let's hope we get er home.'

'So, what do you think, Marcel?' asked Pierre. 'Do you think we should give half to the king?'

'Half to the king? Is that the agreement?' Hanzel regarded Pierre closely.

'That's what it says in the Letter of Marque. The king gets half.' Pierre drank some wine and nodded. 'Half.'

'That's ridiculous,' said Max. 'He did nothing to get this treasure.'

'What's to stop us from taking this ship out of his sight?' asked Hanzel. 'I mean. How does he know where this ship is, unless you take it into a major harbour?'

Pierre regarded Hanzel and scratched his head. 'I've always given a piece to the king. He expects it of me.'

Hanzel gestured towards the men. 'Look at these men. Don't they deserve to share what they captured with their bare hands? The king did nothing. He probably sat on his throne, dreaming of ways to spend the people's wealth on frivolous ends. Wars, for example.'.

'You have a point there. The king really doesn't deserve it, does he?' Pierre stroked his chin.

'Not he,' said Max. 'He don't deserve it.'

'We'll sail her into our little bay. It's a remote spot.' PIerre stood up from his chair. 'Why don't we go have a look at the charts. I'll show you where it is.'

Hanzel smiled and rose from his chair. 'Why not. There's nothing else interesting to do. Might as well study some charts.'

'You coming, Marcel?' Pierre looked at Max. 'Keep her on our present course, if you please.'

'Aye, Captain,' replied Max. He watched as the three officers climbed down the ladder to the main deck.

Hanzel held the door for Pierre and Marcel. Moments later they were standing in the great cabin. Pierre opened a large chart of the coast of northern France. The three men began to look at the coast line and pointed to the place where they could land the ship and make off with their treasure.

'We're going to need wagons,' said Marcel. 'How else are we going to take the treasure away?'

'There are definite logistical problems.' Pierre looked at Marcel. 'We'll need a lot of wagons, and boats to ferry the treasure to shore.'

'We've got a lot to consider. We had better choose our landing place wisely.' Hanzel pointed to a place on the chart. 'What about there?' He pointed to the north coast of France. The name, *Dunkerque* was neatly printed in ink.

'Not there,' replied Pierre. 'Then we'd have to sail along both coasts of England and France, where naval vessels are always on patrol looking for plunder.' Pierre pointed to the south coast, near the frontier between France and Portugal. 'We shall land there. In a little bay we have used before.'

'But, then I'll have to haul my share all the way through France to get it home,' replied Hanzel. 'Where will I get a wagon, there?' He looked closer at the chart. 'What town or village is there?'

'There is no need, my friend. As I said, we have used that bay on many occasions. We have some buildings and assorted conveyances, including wagons.' Pierre laughed. 'But, what would you need a wagon for? I'll sell you one of our pinnaces. You can rent a couple of our friends to help you sail her, until you get a bigger ship. At least the pinnace will get your treasure home.'

'What are you going to do?' asked Hanzel.

'Retire,' replied Pierre. 'I'm going to retire from privateering. Too dangerous. We could have been killed.'

'We're not home yet,' replied Hanzel.

'We're almost home, actually.' Pierre laughed. 'I always tell my men, when we're nearly home, that we're still a long way away. They expect about three weeks. Actually we're five days from our hideout.' Pierre laughed louder. 'It catches them by surprise, every time.' He pointed to the place they were headed. 'Here there are no patrols. And sailing a pinnace along the coast will not attract attention. A pinnace is hardly carrying anything of note. Little do they know what you will actually be carrying.'

'My share is a lot. Are you sure you can be so generous?'

'You helped us learn the boat that got us where we needed to be. Too bad it was wrecked, but I promised it to you, I had no idea we would come across so much treasure.' Pierre opened a bottle of rum and poured it into three cups he had taken off a shelf above the captain's desk.

'If you only gave me a tenth share, it would still be a huge amount of wealth.'

'There is so much. You and I can each retire. The boys, they will have enough to retire, however, I think most of them will piss it all away in a few years or less and end up on a scaffold.' Pierre pointed his thumb to his chest. 'Not me. I am retiring. When fortune pays you a visit, grab her in front, for behind she is bald.' Pierre laughed. 'Do you understand that, my young friend? Behind she is bald.' Pierre laughed more uproariously and repeated the line, "behind she is bald," each time laughing louder until he began to cough.

Hanzel took a thoughtful drought from his cup and thought about the aphorism. *Grab her in front for behind she is bald. Hmm.*

When Pierre finished laughing and coughing, he became philosophical. 'It means that here is a fortune for me to do something with. Instead of second guessing it. I am making the decision to retire and live happily ever after, with no more danger presenting the ever present spectre of death. Seizing upon the opportunity that is afforded me, by virtue of my having a quarter share of the treasure, will take care of me and my loved ones for ever. Me, I'm investing my fortune. They will wish they had by this time next year.' He gestured towards a couple of sailors working a rope. 'Remember what I told you. Behind, fortune is bald. Her pussy is in front. If you don't grab the opportunity to achieve what you really want when it is presented to you, you will always wonder afterwards and never have had the pussy in your hand.' A serious expression spread over Pierre's face. 'Are you sure you want to go back to Holland? The south of France has a much nicer climate.'

'No, I have people I need to bring some happiness to. Some of this wealth can help them live better lives, also.'

PIerre nodded. 'That's a good reason to go back. Helping people is good. I like to help people. I'll help people by building a nice big house and hiring lots of helpers. A cook, a scullery maid, an upstairs maid, a downstairs maid, and a few other maids to do other necessary tasks in a big house, such as the one I plan to build.' Pierre took a long drought of his rum, emptying his cup. 'Ahhhaaa, Hanzel my lad. Lots of maids to help around the house.' He laughed and poured himself another rum.

Hanzel laughed, and then also drained his cup, setting it by the bottle for a refill.

And so it went, for the following three days. Hanzel, Marcel, and Pierre laughed and laughed and drank and drank rum in the great cabin until a cannon blast woke them from their revelries.

'What in the blue blazes?' Pierre stared wideyed at Hanzel whose wide eyed stare reflected back. In an instant the three men ran out of the great cabin just as a cannon ball whizzed by in front of the ship and splashed into the sea a hundred yards away. 'Who is shooting at us?!'

'It's a French navy pinnace. They think we're a Spanish ship and are planning to stop us,' replied Marcel.

'Stop us?' Pierre stared at the pinnace, four hundred yards off the starboard bow. 'That little boat? How many d'you suppose are on board?'

'Looks like no more than ten or twelve. They are trying to intimidate us. They think we're unarmed.' Marcel handed his telescope to Pierre. 'Here, take a look for yourself.'

Hanzel stared at the audacious pinnace beginning to sail towards the big ship. Another cannon shot blasted a ball in front of the big ship's bows.

'Max, come off the wind, if you please,' said Pierre to the helmsman.

'Yes, Captain,' answered Max, steering the big ship out of the wind.

'Luff the sails, Marcel, if you will. We'll pretend to be subservient merchantmen.'

'Aye, Captain.'

'To arms!' shouted Pierre. 'All hands! Grab your weapons, men. I think they mean to board us!'

Everyone quickly set about obtaining their weapons; axes, cutlasses, pistols, and swords. All the while Pierre admonished everybody, including the Spanish sailors, they had to protect their treasure.

Ten minutes later the pinnace luffed her sails as she approached on the port side of the merchantman.

'WE ARE COMING TO BOARD YOU!' shouted a voice through a speaking trumpet. 'IN THE NAME OF THE KING OF FRANCE!'

'Fuck Louis. Let them try and take us. My men will make mince meat of them.' The happy privateer suddenly brightened. 'Hey, there we have the perfect boat for you to take your treasure back to Holland.'

Hanzel laughed as he watched grappling hooks being tossed from the pinnace. 'That pinnace will do nicely.'

The sailors in the pinnace pulled the two vessels together. Everyone watched and waited. They could clearly see onto the deck of the pinnace, six feet below the freeboards of the merchantman. The pinnace was just a little sail boat. And, it only carried fourteen men; armed with pistols and cutlasses. They never suspected they were attacking an experienced crew of privateers who were intent upon protecting what they felt to be rightfully theirs.

The first to step on board were three navy sailors brandishing blunderbusses. Hanzel and his friends held their weapons out of sight. The navy men had no idea what they were facing. A moment later a pompous little officer climbed on board. 'Who is in charge here?' he demanded in a deep voice, totally unexpected from such a short, thin man. Hanzel noted that Max and Olafsen were standing close to the three sailors with the blunderbusses. Jean and Marcel were standing nearby. He could see that they were fingering their hidden weapons. Other sailors were watching from the rigging above. Everyone was anxious for a signal from Pierre to start the adventure.

'I am in charge here,' said Pierre calmly. 'I am Captain Pierre LeGrange. And to whom do I have the honour?'

'I am Lieutenant, Montperpitroi. I am seizing this ship in name of King Louis the Thirteenth of France. We are making her a prize.'

Pierre nodded. 'A prize you say?'

'Yes, a prize,' replied the haughty little man.

'Do you have any idea to whom this ship belongs?' asked Pierre, cool as a clam.

'It matters not, to whom this ship belongs. I am seizing this ship in the king's name.' He turned and gestured toward the mast of the pinnace bobbing beside the port side freeboard. I have thirteen armed men with me. And two cannons. Four leagues distant lies our mother ship, *Nancy*. She's a frigate with 28 guns.' He looked about and sniffed his nose. 'Of which you do not seem to have any, I see.'

'You have only two cannons? You have two cannons? And thirteen armed men?' Pierre smiled. 'We outnumber you. What if I refuse to give this ship to you? What then?'

'We will take her by storm. The lives of your sailors could be lost. Perhaps even your own.' The little officer turned his head as Olafsen adjusted his position.

Pierre stroked his chin. He looked up and regarded the sailors standing in the rigging. 'Well, I suggest you leave us be, or there will be blood spilled. However, it will not be our blood that is spilled.'

'I warn you, monsieur. This is not a frivolous matter. I wish you no harm. I just want to take your ship, in the king's name. If we do not return to the *Nancy* after midnight, she will come looking for us.' The little man puffed himself up to appear somewhat bigger. Hanzel nearly burst out laughing, the officer was so ridiculous.

'I refuse to give up my ship,' said Pierre.

'You leave me no choice.' He pulled his navy sword from its scabbard. As he did so, the three sailors raised their blunderbusses and backed up against the port side freeboard. The tiny lieutenant raised his sword and pointed it at Pierre.

Pierre looked down at the sword pointed at his chest. Then he gently pushed it away. The officer frowned as his eyes followed the point of his sword. It was the clear signal the privateers were waiting for. Within an instant the three sailors were disarmed and the little lieutenant was looking down the bore of Hanzel's pistol. It happened that quickly.

'So, there you have it. Our answer is, *no*, to you seizing my ship. However, we are seizing your pinnace. You have the option of sailing with us, in peace, or we set you loose in our row boat.' Pierre pointed to the ten seater strapped to the deck by the midship hatch. 'Tell your men to stand down.'

'Never,' replied the officer. Then he yelled so that his sailors on the pinnace could hear him. 'Make sail! Make sail!'

Hanzel looked over the gunwale and watched as French sailors began to attempt a getaway. Max, Olafsen, and seven friends swung over to the pinnace with ropes. Eight others quickly climbed down the side of the ship and jumped on board the pinnace to join Olafsen.

'Hurry!' shouted the lieutenant frantically.

It was to no avail. Several pistols could be heard through the sound of clashing steel, as the French sailors on the pinnace put up a resistance. Screams sounded when someone was wounded in the melee. Hanzel smiled as he witnessed the action. The navy sailors were no match for the seasoned privateers. Only a few minutes elapsed when the entire affair was over. The pinnace was taken. Only one man was wounded; a French sailor who lost an arm when he tried to skewer Jean.

'That ends this affront,' said Pierre to the stunned officer. 'You have a choice. Stay in peace, or row your boat to shore.' Pierre stared down at the defeated little man.

'I will never cooperate. Set me adrift in the row boat,' replied the little officer.

Pierre regarded the three sailors who had wielded the blunderbusses. 'What about you? Are you joining your lieutenant?'

The three sailors looked at each other for a moment and then shook their heads. 'No, no. We'll stay with you. We'll help you sail this ship.'

Five sailors from the pinnace elected to join the lieutenant. The row boat was lowered and fifteen minutes later, the little man was facing the sea in a much smaller vessel.

'What a silly little man,' said Hanzel, as the big ship began to pull away from the row boat. The pinnace, with some new crew members from the merchantman, followed.

'Delusions of grandeur,' replied Pierre, watching the row boat bobbing on the waves behind the stern. He turned to the helmsman. 'Take us home, Max. West, west, north west.'

'Aye, Captain,' replied Max.

'I wish all of our battles were so easy,' said Pierre as he and Hanzel walked into the great cabin to toast their victory.

'If it could only be so,' replied Hanzel.

Pierre poured two cups full of rum and handed a cup to Hanzel. 'Here's to your new pinnace. May she take you safely to Holland.'

'I pray she does,' replied Hanzel. 'I pray she does, indeed.' He looked into his cup and then took a long, thoughtful drought. *The seas are full of sharks.*

Three days later they dropped anchor in the little bay on the south west coast of France. The pinnace anchored alongside. Everyone was bone tired and in need of good food, drink, and rest. Food was taken care of with a huge fire over which a pig was roasted. Several barrels of wine and rum were set on racks and the bungs fixed with spigots. Old friends of the gang came from the nearby village to join the party which lasted for three days and nights. When everyone sobered up, they began the task of unloading the treasure.

Chest after chest, bags, and boxes; all went to shore or on board the pinnace, until the pinnace was riding dangerously low in the water. 'That's enough,' said Hanzel, fearful he and the three sailors accompanying him would sink the boat.

'Don't worry, Hanzel,' said Pierre. 'I've sailed heavier laden pinnaces. It can handle the weight.' Pierre clapped Hanzel on the shoulder. "Don't worry. You'll get it home. You're a good sailor.'

Hanzel looked Pierre in the eyes. 'I'll miss you, old friend.'

'I'll miss you too,' replied Pierre.

That night a huge bonfire party was held in honour of Hanzel and the treasure they stole from under the nose of the hated Spaniard.

Chapter 22

Not one to prolong matters, Hanzel set out the next morning, taking Jean, Max, and Olafsen to help with the boat. He also took: plenty of food, drink, a backgammon board, a deck of cards, and coins for buying things along the way. Everything was safely stowed below deck in the copious hold, also protecting the fabulous treasure that was Hanzel's share. Although he did not take an entire twenty percent; only about twelve to fifteen percent, for which Pierre was very grateful. Hanzel realized he had more than plenty. He was not greedy.

One afternoon a few days later, while sailing off the coast of Central France, Max was regarding the keg from which he had just drawn a cup of wine. He set his cup on the table and untied his purse.

'We may have to make port; if we run out of wine,' said Max, counting some of his coins into the leather bag.

'Maybe an overnighter or two, where we can get us some women,' replied Jean. 'I wants wine and women.'

'Ah, wine and women.' Max took a deep breath. 'I wouldn't mind spending some time with a woman.'

'Vimmin and vine ees nice. Bot not too moch vine. An of corse ve need a few songs, too, added Olafsen, who was deep into his cups by now. He broke out into a shanty he made up on the spot.

'Ven I vas bot a yunger boiy

a long time ago

I vas a hellion frum da shtart

dat is zo

Ya, ya, ya, ya, yaaaaaaaaaa

Ya, ya, yaaaaaaaaaaaaaaaaa

Ven I vas a moch ohlder boiy
a long time ago
To sea, to sea, to sea I vent
dat is vhy my back is bent
Ya dat is zo.
Ven I vas aged bot twenty tree
at sea I be, a sea I'd see
An effry vere I'd look to see
A sea I'd see for days at sea
Ya dat is zo
Oh, oh, oh, ooooooh.
Ant on it vent by year by year
to sea I vent, to sea you see.
To be at sea is best for me
I like the sea, you see, you see
Ya dat is zo.
Ant now I am an oldah man
Sailing the sea as best I can
Ya dat is zo.
Ya dat is zo.
Oh oh ooooooooh,
Ya dat is zooooooo!'

When he was done, Olafsen took a long drink from his cup while his shipmates applauded the wonderful song.

'Well done, Olafsen,' said Hanzel, clapping the big Swede on his right shoulder, nearly knocking the inebriated sailor over. Everyone laughed.

As the day went by, the four men learned Olafsen's song and sang it with joyous hearts, inventing various melodies and assorted rhythms on kegs and barrels which they beat with wooden spoons. By night fall the four sailors were gloriously into their cups as they celebrated their adventure and the treasure, safely secured in the hold. Their singing and raucous noise was only heard by shore birds and fish. No humans paid them any attention as they sailed and sang their way north.

A full moon reflected in the placid waters. There was enough light to sail by. They did not light the lamps, choosing, instead, to keep a good watch for lights on the horizon. A starry dome filled the space beyond the moon. Everything was gentle and soft when the men stopped singing and banging on things. When they became quiet, they moved into private thoughts for a while as gentle waves broke across the bows of the sturdy pinnace.

'I want to avoid being seen, as much as possible,' said Hanzel, scanning the horizon with his telescope. 'We don't want to be seen and then robbed by government agents or English privateers.'

'Ya dat is gute. I don vant to be keeled. Dere are scurvy naves oot dere. Nut efry privateer is like Pierre LeGrange. He did not keel. Keeling vas nut vhat he did. He jus took shtuff dat vas alreddy shtolen frum odder pheeple. He's not a cutthroat.'

'Some of those scummy thieves are ruthless,' added Jean. 'Olafsen is right in saying, Pierre was not a cutthroat.'

'Like that villain, Roche Brasiliano, for example.' Jean regarded Hanzel. 'Have you ever heard of him. He's a Dutchman.'

Hanzel shook his head. 'Never heard of him.'

'One of the cruelest pirates I know of.' Jean grimaced. 'I never met him, but I knows about him.' Jean scratched his chin. 'A cousin of mine met him. He was lucky to get away.' Jean paused. 'I'm trying to think if I remember his name. Let me see.' He gestured with his right index finger. 'Yes, I remember. His Hollander name is, Gerrit Gerritzoon.'

'Gerrit Geritzoon.' Hanzel shook his head. 'No. I never heard of him.'

'He apparently burned some captives alive on spits. He ate someone's heart.' Jean shook his head. 'The man is mad. He is a monster. I hope, if it is true, that they hang him soon.'

'Why is he called, Roche Brasiliano?' asked Hanzel.

'Because he lives in Brazil and sails off her coast,' replied Jean. 'He is unbeatable, apparently.'

Hanzel shook his head. 'Nobody is unbeatable. It's a good reason to keep up our practice with weapons, If you have no way of defending yourself from creatures like this, Roche Braziliano character, you are lost. You have no hope to survive. If you have good control of your weapons, you can at least defend yourself.'

Olafsen nodded, 'Yha, dat is zo.'

'What an incredible break, don't you think?' asked Jean. 'Here we are, sailing along, pretending to be a small merchant vessel of no particular note, and yet, here we are carrying a heavy treasure.'

Hanzel smiled. 'Don't worry, we are going to use this wealth to good effect. There is more than enough for anyone of us. Why don't we buy a ship with it?'

'A sheep? *Ve* boiy a sheep?' Olafsen looked at Jean and then back at Hanzel.

'I was thinking,' replied Hanzel. 'We get along so well. We love to sail. And all four of us hate the Spaniard for what he does in the New World. And this, Roche Brasiliano monster, he needs to be taken out. So, since taking the Spaniard's stuff was, in this case, an easy task, I don't think that will always be the case. So, if we stay together, that is, if you decide to join my crew as first mate, boatswain, and quartermaster. Then we four buy a frigate and fill her with as many guns as she'll carry. Then we'll recruit a prize crew everywhere we make port. Eventually, we can take a crew of two hundred, two fifty, say. Since we have more than enough to buy all of that, and pay the sailors. We will arm them to the teeth and train them in the use of everything. Since we can buy the time, we'll be in no hurry. When we're all trained up we'll go after this, Roche Brasiliano and bring him to justice. A man like that gives privateering a bad name. Don't you think?'

Jean looked at Olafsen. Olafsen looked at Max. Max looked at Jean. Then, Max, Jean, and Olafson regarded Hanzel. All at once they responded; 'What a great idea,' 'Tank yu,' 'Sure, I'll sail with you,'.

Hanzel smiled. 'Alright then. Let's make that our goal. We'll buy a frigate and arm her.

Jean, Max, and Olafsen looked at each other and at Hanzel and then all agreed, *why not?*

'How do we sell those things?' asked Max. 'I mean, gold statues, piles of precious stones, gold plate, nuggets, dust. Silver stuff. Don't we need coins?'

'Wood eet be bedder to sell it in Ollant?' Olafsen regarded Hanzel.

'I know people. Wealthy people. People who trade in arms. They do gold plating and silver work. They make fine swords and so on. I want to take the treasure to them. They will know what to do with it and we would not draw much attention there.'

'I hope we get there safely,' said Max soberly.

'Dutch frigates are known for their sturdiness,' added Hanzel.

'Yha, dat is zo,' agreed Olafsen. 'Dey built gute boahts.'

Hanzel nodded. 'Let's to Holland and pray for the best.' He raised his cup. 'Here's to our new company. Hanzel Sventska & Friends.'

'I like the sound of that,' replied Max, smiling.

'To Hanzel Sventska & Friends, may the company prosper.' Jean clicked his cup against the others' and then drank his cup dry.

When the four men had emptied their cups, they returned to their places. Jean and Max on the ropes. Olafsen at the helm and Hanzel with the spy glass ever scanning the horizon.

The pinnace rode low in the water but handled well. Sailing her with four men was no problem for the seasoned veterans of the sea, even though they were gloriously inebriated. The boat was 50 feet long and 20 feet abeam. The bow sprit stuck out another 15 feet from the stem. A main mast supported a double lateen sail and a jib. She carried several other sails in case of inclement weather. Her hold was spacious and crammed with treasure and supplies. Her speed was a mere four knots in the gentle wind. She was not likely to attract much attention, looking like a typical small trade vessel which plied the coast of France. To be certain not to be bothered, a French Fluer de Lis was flying from the jack staff. A blue and gold pennant fluttered from the mast head. Hanzel took all precautions.

One afternoon, six days later, when they were approaching the Channel Islands, Max accidentally sliced Jean's cheek when they were practicing with cutlasses. Blood dripped on the deck. Max immediately handed Jean his handkerchief to stem the flow. 'I'm so sorry, my dear friend,' said Max. 'That wave knocked me off my balance.'

'I understand,' said Jean. 'You couldn't help it. It's just a flesh wound.'

'We're approaching Guernsey. Perhaps there's a doctor,' suggested Max.

'Not in Guernsey,' replied Hanzel. 'There are only a few fisher folk who live there. They're not exactly the people who would know much about things, medical.'

'What do we do with him?' asked Max anxiously regarding the increasingly bloody handkerchief Jean held against his cheek.

'I tink ve shud fust vash de vound mit sea vater,' suggested Olafsen. 'Dat take de dark vapours avay.'

'Alright,' said Jean, unconvincingly. 'Sea water it is.'

'It's going to sting. But it's for the best.' Hanzel regarded the bloodied handkerchief. 'You really got a good slice out of his cheek,' he said looking at Max. 'Save that for the opposition.'

Max nodded. 'I'm really sorry, Jean.'

'Like I said, it's just a flesh wound. It'll heal.'

Olafsen dropped a pail into the sea and drew up the water needed. Jean put the handkerchief into the pail. The water turned red as the handkerchief released its load. When he held the cloth against the wound Jean winced as the salt began its work disinfecting the opened skin. Olafsen tore a piece of cloth off an old shirt and bound the salty handkerchief firmly to Jean's sliced cheek. 'Kip dat on da vound an don toch eet.'

Jean winced as he tried to smile. 'Thanks.'

'Have some rum,' said Hanzel, handing him a cup of the dark liquor. 'That'll make you forget you were wounded.' He chuckled. 'I guess that puts an end to weapons practice for today.'

On the eighth day they reached the narrow Straits of Dover. 'This is where we must be especially vigilant,' said Hanzel, surveying the coast north of Calais. 'We could have trouble with English privateers.'

'Is there an English flag on board?' asked Max. 'If we fly an English flag, they'll leave us alone.'

'Ya bot ve cud den be boddered by French vuns.'

'What about a Dutch flag? Maybe there's a Dutch flag on board,' suggested Jean.

'Let's take a look around. Maybe there are some other flags on board. I never thought about it.' Hanzel headed for the rear hatch leading to the captain's cabin to search in every nook and cranny. Max and Olafsen searched through the hold while Jean manned the wheel.

After searching for nearly an hour, no other flags were found. 'I guess we'll have to take our chances with the English.'

'Why not take the flags down?' suggested Max.

'Then we'll be attractive to either the English or the French,' replied Jean.

'Or Danish, Dutch, German, all kinds of rovers are floating about out here, looking for treasures. Sailing is becoming an ever more dangerous business.' Hanzel smiled ruefully. 'Everyone wants to win a prize.'

'When we have our new ship, we'll win many prizes,' laughed Jean. He suddenly winced as pain stabbed his wounded cheek. 'It hurts when I smile.'

'Vell, shtop shmiling,' replied Olafsen, chuckling.

Jean nodded. 'I will take that advice. So, you three have to make sure you don't make me laugh.'

As the four men were thusly engaged in conversation, the sky clouded over and a cold, north westerly wind began to blow. The waves started to rise. A flash of light on the horizon heralded thunder, which was not long in coming. The shock wave fluttered the sails.

'Looks like we're in for a doozy,' said Max. 'Maybe we should consider making land and waiting this one out.'

'Let's take a look at the chart,' said Hanzel. He and Max went below and studied the chart in Hanzel's cabin. 'Look, there's a small island there.' He pointed to the place. 'We're not far from it. Let's head there.' Hanzel made note of the coordinates and then he and Max returned topside to relay the information to Olafsen who was manning the helm.

Twenty minutes later they could see the hazy shore of the small island, dead ahead. Hanzel sent Max and Olafsen to the bows to watch for rocks and other dangers. 'We'll sail along her east coast and hope we find a place to anchor out of the wind.'

'It is really picking up. I'm beginning to think we should consider taking the main sail down,' said Jean.

Hanzel regarded the large lateen sail. It was holding but showing signs of strain. 'I think you're right.' He shouted to Olafsen to come and give him a hand. A moment later the large lateen sail was furled, leaving the smaller triangular top sail and the jib.

'We'll stay close to shore. That way the wind will be the least troublesome,' said Hanzel to Jean, holding the ever more bucking wheel, as the storm increased its intensity.

Gradually they managed to sail out of the strongest wind on the lee side of the island. Hanzel scanned the coast for sign of a bay or cove. Eventually they did, indeed, find a small bay into which they were able to sail the pinnace and drop her anchor.

'Phew,' sighed Jean. 'This is a whole lot better. Now I can go below and get some rest.'

'Dat's a gute idee,' replied Olafsen. 'Ve kan shleep out de shturm.'

'Alright, go have a rest,' agreed Hanzel. He surveyed the shoreline of the bay. 'I think we're quite safe here. We can all have a rest.' Hanzel yawned. 'I'm tired also.' He watched as his three friends walked to the hatch. Ten minutes later they were all fast asleep and happily waiting out the storm. Nobody on board the pinnace had a care or a worry.

Just after midnight, when the storm was blowing hard and waves were crashing loudly on the rocky beach, a sloop poked her nose into the little bay, also looking for a place to anchor out of the wind. The sloop was difficult to see because she was painted completely black: hull, freeboards, gunwales, spars, sails, ropes, and tackle. The flag flying from the mast was also black, except for a white skull over two crossed femurs.

'Captain, captain,' shouted the lookout, 'there's a boat anchored ahead!'

The sound of the voice woke Hanzel first. He sat up in his bunk and listened. A moment later he could hear sounds of boots on planks and the muffled sounds of voices. Hanzel jumped out of bed and ran to the door. Opening it he shouted, 'Wake up! Wake up! There's a boat coming into the bay.'

Jean, Max, and Olafsen quickly woke up, grabbed their weapons and ran up the steps. Within two minutes the four men stood on deck of the pinnace, straining into the darkness to see the moving black shape coming into the bay.

'Pirates,' whispered Max.

'It's a sloop,' replied Jean.

'Vhat ve do? Dere is only four of uz.' Olafson took a ball from a pouch on his belt.

Hanzel whispered his instructions. 'Remain calm. Load your pistols and hide them. Put the three loaded blunderbusses here and there, where we can grab them. We have nine pistols, so I will take two, you can divvy up the other seven. We all have dirks in our boots, and we have our cutlasses. Let's be real quiet and just watch them. They will have to make the first move. If any one comes on board it's best to kill them with a knife, rather than a gun.'

'It's best to slice their throats,' suggested Max. 'Cut right through the larynx. That way they can't shout and warn the others.'

'As revolting as that is, it may have to be what we do,' whispered Hanzel. 'Let's hope it doesn't come to that. Just let me handle the negotiations.'

The three sailors agreed to the plan.

'You're the captain,' whispered Jean.

'Aye,' agreed Olafsen, barely audible over the sound of wind and rain.

As the four men watched, the dark sloop slipped silently into the little bay and dropped her anchors, effectively blocking the exit. No voices could be heard coming from the black boat blocking the entrance to the bay. Hanzel and his friends watched and waited with baited breath, but nothing further accrued. The night was only filled with stormy clouds, thunder, waves, and wind, no other sounds were heard except the snores of the four watchers who had fallen asleep by the time the storm abated and the sun was beginning to dissolve the clouds.

A splash, not far away, woke Hanzel from a bloody dream in which he was the avenger. He sat up and rubbed his eyes. The rain had stopped. He looked up to a clearing sky where blue was beginning to predominate. The sun was already working to evaporate the water from his clothes. Steam was rising around him as the water changed to air.

Hanzel looked at his sleeping friends. 'Hey, wake up,' he whispered. 'I heard something.'

As he said the words he clearly heard the sounds of boots on planks, the jangle of arms, and muffled voices.

'They're coming,' whispered Hanzel. 'Just remain calm and mind your weapons.'

A moment later they could clearly hear the splashing of oars. The four men crawled to the starboard gunwale and peered over the top.

Six men were rowing towards the pinnace in a small boat. They were trying very hard not to make a sound.

'We'll hide and surprise them,' whispered Hanzel. 'Max and Olafsen, you two go hide in the hold. Jean, you and I will hide in the cabin.'

The four men quickly and quietly scurried off to do as Hanzel ordered.

Four minutes later the row boat bumped against the pinnace and boots were quickly heard thereafter as the six pirates stepped on board.

'There doesn't seem to be anyone on board,' said a voice.

'Search the boat,' commanded an other voice.

Hanzel heard boots clomping about on the boards as people set off to search through the ship. *Englishmen. Their king killed my friends.*

The door to the great cabin opened. Two rough looking men stepped into the room. Hanzel and Jean surprised them and quickly took the men prisoner. They tied their hands behind them, put a wad of cloth in their mouths and locked the two indignant marauders in a closet. They quickly made their way on deck, to discover Olafsen and Max holding the other four men at gun point.

'Tie those men up and stow them in the forward hold,' commanded Hanzel. His three friends set about realizing the command in quick order. When the job was done, Hanzel and his friends waited to see what would happen next. After two hours passed another boat was dropped into the water. This time eight men rowed the boat. 'That makes fourteen so far. I wonder how many there are. Perhaps we should just shoot them as they approach and take our chances.'

'There could be a whole lot more. Maybe they are being cautious,' suggested Max.

A bright flash and a loud boom came from the black ship. The sound reverberated across the bay.

'Down!, Down!' shouted Hanzel as everyone immediately fell face down on the deck. A second later an eight pound ball whizzed over them.

Another flash and powerful boom was followed by another whizzing ball. It buzzed past the mast and took a chunk out of it. The lethal splinters flew along behind the ball. Had there been a man standing there, he would have been sliced in a thousand places.

'What do we do now?' asked Max.

'They'll stop shooting when their men get here,' said Hanzel reassuringly. Just as he said the words they heard a bump against the side of the pinnace. 'Quick. Hide.'

The four men quickly hid themselves together in the hold and waited.

Footsteps on the stairs alerted them to be ready. Three armed sailors stepped into the hold and began to look around. They were quickly arrested with pistols pointed at their chests. One of the sailors was about to yell out. Olafsen put an end to his attempt by snapping the man's neck with an instant movement he learned from a Japanese monk. The sudden demise of the pirate put a scare into the other two. They were quickly tied up with the others in the forward hold. After twenty minutes, two more pirates came down into the hold. They were also caught by surprise and tied up with the others.

'I think that leaves three,' whispered Hanzel.

'Shall we go get them?' asked Max.

Hanzel shook his head. 'No. I still think this place is our best defense.' Just as he uttered the words, footsteps on the stairs alerted them to the arrival of more victims. The remaining three pirates came down into the hold and were dazzled by what they saw. A moment later, they too, were overcome by Hanzel and his friends.

'How many of you are there?' asked Hanzel, regarding a short, pudgy pirate with a patch over his right eye.

The man stared at Hanzel with his single, green eye. 'That's for me to know and you to find out,' he said defiantly.

Hanzel stared at the man. 'I don't want to harm you. I just want to know how many more of you there are on the sloop.'

'I don't care what you do to me. I'm not telling you anything.' The man spat at Hanzel but missed, hitting Max, instead. Hanzel had to hold Max back from lunging at the man and running him through with his cutlass.

'I am giving you a final opportunity to tell me how many of you there are. If you do not tell me, we will torture you to get the answer. Your screams will be heard by your comrades across the bay.'

The man regarded Hanzel with his one eye and laughed. 'Do you really think that you scare me?'

Hanzel looked at his friends.

Max looked at Olafsen, who nodded his head. He pointed to the main mast. 'Tie heem up to de mast. Dat vay his companions can vatch from ovah dere,' he said.

The man was stretched with his back against the main mast. His arms were tied around and behind him. His legs straddled the spar. Max and Jean did a very good job of tying the pirate. 'Rrip off hiz shurt,' said Olafsen.

'Now is this all going to be necessary for us to get some information from you?' asked Hanzel. 'Do you really want to suffer?'

The other pirates who were tied up in the forward hold started shouting, those who could see past the bulkhead into the midship hold where their friend was about to be pummelled. Hanzel and his friends quickly convinced those errant pirates to stop shouting by smacking a couple of them over the head with the butts of their pistols. Unfortunately Olafsen hit his man somewhat harder than required, effectively caving in his left temple. The crack of the breaking skull sobered everyone instantly. The pirates saw clearly their intended victims were taking matters very seriously indeed and were not to be trifled with. They stopped shouting. Hanzel et al returned to the pirate they were about convince he should not withold information.

'I'll tell you nothing. I will not be a traitor,' replied the man, his one eye staring wildly at the knotted cord Olafsen was holding in his hand.

'You have one more chance to save yourself. How many of you are there?' asked Hanzel calmly.

The man pinched his mouth shut.

Hanzel nodded to Olafsen who immediately began to pummel the man with the knotted cord until his chest was a bruised mess, bleeding from numerous abrasions.

'Now are you going to tell us, or do we continue?' asked Hanzel.

The pirate moaned. 'Go to Hell.'

Hanzel nodded to Olafsen.

'Turn heem around,' he said to Max and Jean.

They tied the pirate face first to the mast and Olafsen pummeled his back until the man sank in the knees. Blood was spattered around here and there.

'This is my final time asking you. How many of you are there?' asked Hanzel, his face close to the suffering man's sweating visage.

'Go to Hell,' whispered the man.

'Alright, so be it.' Hanzel looked at Olafsen.

Olafsen shrugged his shoulders. 'Tie hees hands behind his bak an trow heem eento the water.'

'No, no!! You can't do that! Don't throw me in the water!' The man struggled but Max and Olafsen had a good hold of him.

'And, why wouldn't we throw you into the water?' asked Max, pushing the man towards the stairs.

'Because, because, er...' Olafsen prodded the man up the stairs with the point of his cutlass. Back up on deck, Olafsen leaned the man backwards over the transom.

The man looked down at the dark water of the bay. 'Don't thow me in the water. I can't swim.'

Olafsen shrugged his shoulders. 'Zo?'

'Well, my hands are tied. I'll drown. That would be murder,' stammered the pirate.

'What about you and your cronies?' asked Hanzel. 'You came on board this pinnace with weapons, intent upon murder and plunder.'

The man nodded. 'Yes, yes, I must admit. That was the general idea. But not to murder you in cold blood. We thought we'd do a bit o' the swashbuckling. For the fun of it.' He looked down at the water lapping against the rudder of the pinnace.

'Throw him in,' said Hanzel.

The man struggled as Max and Olafsen were about to push the man over the transom of the ship.

'NO! Wait! I'll tell you what you want to know. There are thirty of us altogether. We were sent over to reconnoiter, since we did not see anyone on deck. Your boat is low in the water. You must be carrying something heavy. Since we are pirates, it only makes sense that we came to check you out and see if you have anything worth stealing. That's what pirates do. They steal other people's stuff and sell it, or use it for their own purposes. That's why we're here. On your boat. It was just our luck we had to come into this bay to get out of the storm.' The man nodded. 'That's pretty much it. That's all there is to tell.' He gestured towards the foreward hatch. 'You already have fourteen of us. The question is, how will you handle the other sixteen, when there appear to be only four of you?'

'You're telling me there are only sixteen of you left on the sloop?' Hanzel regarded the man quizzically.

The man looked surprised at Hanzel's question. 'Sixteen *armed* pirates. They have cannons, and pistols, and cutlasses, and, and, boarding axes, and three pikes, and a blunderbuss.'

Hanzel and his friends laughed as they set the pirate down.

'Only sixteen left, you said?' Hanzel stared into the man's eyes. *Is he telling the truth? Or is he lying?* 'Well, if there are only sixteen left, we should be safe.' He looked at his three friends. 'Don't you think so?'

Hanzel's friends heartily agreed.

The pirate sneered. 'You can tie us up in your hold, but we won't be there for long. Our mates will come to rescue us.'

Hanzel laughed. 'How many rowboats do you have on board your sloop?' He pointed over the gunwale. 'We have two of them.'

The pirate stared at Hanzel and sniffed. 'You will have to wait and find out, won't you?'

Hanzel stared at the man as Max and Olafsen coaxed back to the foreward hold to join his friends. *I better keep an eye on him. I don't trust him at all.*

Moments later, Max and Olafsen returned from stowing the man.

'Tough son of a bitch, that last one,' said Max, shaking his head.

'Doze type men, yu kan beet dem an beet dem. Nuffin yu do kin git ta dem. Dey be mor stubern dan a mule.' Olafsen looked back at the hatch.

'He's something alright,' agree Max.

'He said there were thirty of em,' said Hanzel. 'Do you believe him?'

'Not me,' said Olafsen.

'Me neither,' agreed Max.

'I think he may be their leader, actually,' suggested Jean.

Hanzel nodded. 'I think Jean's correct. I don't think there are any more of em. Their ship is only a sloop. Sixteen can sail her easily.'

Max looked out at the black ship anchored in the mouth of the little bay. 'There doesn't seem to be any movement over there.'

A bright flash and a loud boom told a different story.

Hanzel and his friends immediately lay down on the deck. A split second later an eight pound ball whizzed through the jib sail and splashed into the water forty yards off the port bow of the pinnace. 'I think he, or they are sending us a message.'

'They wouldn't risk hurting their own men,' replied Max. 'What shots they send our way, will be over our heads.'

'Yu don teenk dey vill shoodt at our holl?' Olafsen peered at the dark sloop blocking their escape.

A bright flash and loud boom reverberated around the bay.

'Down, everyone!' shouted Hanzel just as a flesh eating string of chain shot tore through the main topmast, sending it down onto the deck with a loud splintering of wood and tackle. A swinging block just missed Hanzel but caught Jean square in the head, sending his brains out of the back of his skull and the smashed remains of it after them. The sight caused Hanzel to vomit.

'Oh, no, Jean!' shouted Max, moving toward the remains of his friend.

'Steady, Max,' said Hanzel, grabbing his shoulder. 'We must get below. They can obviously see us on deck and that we took their pirates below.' They won't shoot at the hull.'

The three men quickly ran to the hatch and went below. Just as Olafsen closed the hatch door another loud boom blasted the silence. A moment later they could hear another chain shot wreaking havoc across the deck.

'Those things can shred many men,' said Max. 'I've seen it.'

'OUR FRIENDS WILL COME TO RESCUE US!" shouted the belligerent pirate from the forward hold.

'What if there are a lot more of em?' asked Max, peering fearfully at the hatch door.

'Eet steel dependz on da number of boats dey got. Ve got too. An ve got fourteen pyrates.'

'YOU HAVEN'T GOT A CHANCE! YOU MIGHT AS WELL GIVE UP!' shouted the belligerent pirate from the foreward hold.

'Do you believe him?' asked Max, regarding Hanzel.

'I think he's bluffing,' replied Hanzel. 'I have a suspicion they only have two boats, maybe three. If there were more of them, don't you think they would shoot several cannons? Not one at a time with long intervals. As in now.' Hanzel perked up his ears. 'I'm wondering if they've stopped shooting.'

'I don vhant to go topzide to find out an end up like poor Jean.' Olafsen looked at the floor.

'I think we should wait down here. Let them come to us,' suggested Max. 'If we stand at the bottom of the ladder. We can kill them as they come down.'

'I am reddie,' said Olafson, brandishing his cutlass.

'GIVE UP, YOU COCKROACHES!' YOU HAVEN'T GOT A CHANCE!!' shouted the pirate.

'Shud I poot a shtop to dat ranting?' asked Olafson. He pointed his sword in the direction of the forward hold.

The other pirates began chanting together, making an ever louder cacophony.

'GIVE UP! GIVE UP! GIVE UP!'

'The English are so annoying,' said Max. 'We should do the world a favour and just shoot them all.'

'Ya reely. Vhat yuse are dey?'

Hanzel shook his head. 'We can sell them in exchange for safe passage.'

'Do you really think we can negotiate with pirates?' asked Max, staring at Hanzel as if the Dutchman was mad.

'Let's just wait and see what happens,' suggested Hanzel. 'i haven't heard any cannons. Have you?'

Indeed, there had not been any more cannon shots. As the three men listened, between the cracks of the constant noise coming from the pirates in the hold, they heard a wooden bump against the hold and muffled voices outside. As they listened closely, they could hear boots climbing up the port side ladder. Boots stepped onto the deck.

'There are three of em,' whispered Hanzel.

A voice shouted. 'Look over here! There's one of em with his head smashed off.'

Boot steps clomped on the deck to where Jean's remains lay in a pool of blood.

'Yes, well, such are the fruits of resistance,' said a haughty voice. 'Let us rescue our brothers.'

The pirates in the hold began yelling and shouting ever more loudly.

The boot steps stomped to the midship hatch, the entrance to the forward and midship holds. When the first man reached the bottom of the step he was immediately seized and subdued. The second man did not suspect a thing. He too enjoyed the same treatment as the first.

'What do you see?!' shouted the third man.

Hanzel looked at Max and Olafsen. Then in a rough voice he answered, 'Come down. We need your help!'

A moment later the third man also found himself at the point of a cutlass.

'How many more of you are there?' asked Hanzel. 'Or are you three the last of them?'

The pirate regarded his captors in the dim light of the midship hold. 'We lost twenty good men in a skirmish, when we attempted to board a merchantman, just before the storm. We lost three more overboard when a wave washed them off the ropes.'

'If all twenty five of you had rushed this boat, you would have taken us,' laughed Hanzel. 'Why did your captain send you as he did?'

'He was being cautious. He didn't see many of you on deck. We thought it was safe to send only six men at first; to reconnoiter.'

'Thank God you were only twenty five,' said Hanzel. He looked at his two friends. 'Well, I suppose we can tie these fellows up, as well.'

'We should take their ship. It's larger and has more cannons,' suggested Max.

Hanzel pointed at the cargo crowding the place they were standing. 'What about that? It would take us three days to unload this. And only with the cooperation of those pirates.' He shook his head. 'I can't see them wanting to help us, do you?'

'At gun point they will,' said Max, brandishing a pistol he took off the third man.

'Let's take a look at that ship,' replied Hanzel. 'Maybe you're right. That ship is larger.'

'Eet need mor men ter sail er,' suggested Olafsen. 'Now dat dere is only tree of us. Eet ees alreddy nut enuff ter sail dis'n, let alone dat shloop.'

'Maybe some of them will come over to us, if we offer them some treasure,' suggested Hanzel.

Max scratched his chin. 'How much treasure?'

'Enough to make it worth their while.' Hanzel smiled. 'We've got a lot of treasure in these holds.

'If none come over, then what are we going to do with them?' asked Max, gesturing toward the forward hold, where the pirates were still raising a ruckus.

Hanzel looked toward the makeshift prison. 'I think I can bribe them to help us. I'll give them a good piece of the treasure.'

'How much of the treasure?' asked Max, thinking he was going to lose out, somehow.

'Half as much as you were each getting before we decided to form a crew and buy a ship. Since the distance from here to Amsterdam is past half way,' replied Hanzel. 'I would offer them collectively five percent.

Max nodded. 'That's fair, I think. The question is, will they agree to it?'

'If'n dey don agree, den vhat?'

'We throw them in the water and they can swim to shore,' suggested Hanzel.

'Their boat is blocking our way out,' observed Max.

Hanzel regarded Max for a moment as he considered an alternative plan. Voices in his mind were offering suggestions. Voices for good and voices for evil. Hanzel had to make sense of the voices in his head. *We need them to move their boat. The only way they'll do that is if we force them. We can let them have their boats but confiscate their weapons and get them to move their boat in gratitude for us being so benevolent. If they refuse you could kill one in front of the others. I hate to have to do that. I don't want to kill anyone. If there is no other way, that'll have to be the way. Hanzel, listen. You have to kill to survive. It is the law of nature, Hanzel. To kill is wrong according to the Bible. What am I to do? Kill, or be killed?* 'We will force them to move their boat. If they refuse, we will kill one in front of the others.'

'Hoo is ta do da keeling?'

Hanzel regarded Olafsen. 'I will do it. I am captain of this boat. It has to be me, so be it. We have to get this treasure to Amsterdam. We can't stay here.'

'Alright, then,' said Max. 'Let's go and talk to them. It wouldn't bother me to kill one. They would have killed us, probably.'

Hanzel nodded. 'Let's go.'

The three men stepped into the forward hold where the pirates were sitting on the floor or on boxes and chests. They were tied with their hands behind their backs and secured to various chains, cargo rings, chests, and a bulkhead. The pirates quit talking when their wily captors walked into the makeshift prison.

Hanzel regarded the pirates one by one. He searched into their eyes to see what was there. When he had looked them over he began, 'My name is Hanzel Sventska. I am captain of this pinnace.' He indicated his friends. 'My mates are Max and Olafsen. Which one of you is the captain of the sloop blocking our way out?'

For a long time nobody spoke. The silence was deafening. Hanzel, Max, and Olafsen looked the pirates over and assessed their capability to effect harm. A number of faces snarled and sneered. Eventually a lanky Englishman spoke up. He was not the belligerent one, which surprised the three friends.

'I am the captain of the sloop, *Black Swan*,' he said, calmly. 'My name is, Edward Steele.'

'Why did you not swarm us?' asked Hanzel. 'There are twenty five of you and only three of us. You killed one of us with a cannon shot.'

'Since I lost a lot of men in a skirmish and more in the storm, I did not want to take the chance that there were more of you hiding below. I have learned to be very careful. When our reconnaissance group failed to return, I thought it best to come over and investigate for myself, leaving those three to fire our remaining forward cannon. To make it appear as if there were many more of us.'

Hanzel smiled. 'You say, *remaining*. What do you mean by that?'

'We were badly shot up. It is hard to tell at this distance, but if you examine her closely, the *Black Swan* is badly beaten up. She is sinking, actually. That is another reason we wanted to take this boat, so we could at least sail home.'

'If she sinks there, in the entrance to the bay, your ship will prevent me from sailing away.' Hanzel stared at the captain.

Edward grinned. 'That is quite correct, I would say.'

Hanzel stared exasperatedly at the pirate captain. 'Then we'll all be stuck here. You included. Then what?'

'I guess that's up to you.' Edward raised his chin and stared down his nose at Hanzel.

'You did not tell me your name.'

Hanzel stared into the man's eyes. *I have to convince him. Stay calm. Stay calm.* You will have to send your men to the *Black Swan* and move her. If they fail to comply, I will kill you.'

Edward stared back at Hanzel. *This bloke is serious. He will kill me. I can see it in his eyes.* Edward averted his gaze and regarded his men.

'Who are your first officers?' asked Hanzel.

'I'm first mate,' said a large, quiet man with mutton chops and long braided hair. He wore a gold ring in his right earlobe.'

'I'm the boatswain,' said a short, pudgy man with a blue kerchief over his bald head.

'I'm the navigator,' said a tall, thin man with shoulder length brown hair and waxed mustaches.

'And, I am the quartermaster,' said a tough looking man. He was wearing an open vest, revealing a hairy chest over which he wore a golden chain with a large pendant.

'I will keep you also. If your men do not comply, I will kill all five of you.' Hanzel paused for a moment. 'I will kill you, one by one, for every hour that we have to wait here after midnight, tonight. That should give your men plenty of time to move your sloop.' He regarded the other pirates. 'Do you want to see these men killed?'

'No!' filled the space. Of course the men did not want to see their officers killed. They were not navy sailors.

'Alright, we will free you to return to your sloop. We will hold your five officers. The twenty of you can take two of the row boats. If you do not have that sloop out of the way by midnight, a few minutes after that you will hear the first splash of a body in the water.' Hanzel eyed the men. 'Do you understand?'

The pirates could clearly see that Hanzel and his men were deadly serious. They all agreed to do what was necessary. Hanzel signaled Max and Olafsen to set the twenty sailors free, one by one, and sent them on their way to effect the desired result.

Hanzel and his friends stayed on deck to attend to Jean, who still lay where he fell. His head sustained a massive blunt force trauma, breaking his skull and taking the top half off. His brains were partly in and partly out of his head. A large spatter of blood formed a sanguine circle around the corpse.

'Poor Jean,' sighed Max. 'He was a good friend. What a tragedy to come to such an end.'

'Ya, he vas a gute man,' agreed Olafsen. 'I vas glad to haf known heem.'

'What should we do with the body?' asked Hanzel.

'We have no choice but to commit him to the deep. Right here. Right here, in this bay,' suggested Max, tears streaming from his eyes. 'I've known Jean for a long time. Since we were children.'

Hanzel looked at Max kneeling beside his dead friend. 'Do you want to say any words over him before we slip him over the side?'

Max looked at Hanzel and Olafsen standing over him. Then he returned his gaze to the lifeless body of his friend. 'Good bye, old friend. May God take your soul and admit you to his bosom.' Max nodded. A moment later he watched as Jean's body disappeared under the dark water. He sat watching the water for a long while after, as he thought about his friend.

Hanzel and Olafsen left Max to mourn as they watched proceedings unfolding with the *Black Swan*. The sloop was listing to starboard. Upon closer examination with the pinnace's telescope it became more evident that the ship had been severely damaged by numerous cannon balls. Her sheets were in tatters and there was a large hole near the water line. She was shipping water every time a wave hit her.

It took the pirates many hours to pump water out of the ship and help her to float better. Since there was not much wind, they had to lighten their boat as much as possible by tossing everything that was not required to sail the hulk, overboard. Soon the waves sent barrels, kegs, chairs, boxes, and sundre other items on a gradual voyage to shore. As the hours ticked by, gradually, puff by fluff, clouds began to gather and darken the sky. A sudden flash of light heralded a thunder storm. Indeed, a minute later, cold rain began to pelt the boats in the bay.

'I don't think they're going to do it,' suggested Max.

'Ve shtill gots tu hours an a arf,' said Olafsen.

'There's plenty of time. I'm confident they'll do it,' replied Hanzel.

'You're putting more confidence in em, than I would,' said Max. 'I don't trust pirates.'

'You're a pirate, of sorts, are you not?' asked Hanzel.

Max nodded. 'Well, yeah, I suppose so. However, there is a distinction. I call myself a, *privateer*. I have a letter from the king.'

'That makes stealing alright then?' Hanzel smiled. 'I despise monarchies, quite frankly.'

'Come to think of it, so do I,' answered Max. 'Wherever there is a government in place, we have no freedom. Governments attempt to rule every facet of our lives and threaten us with incarceration and death if we don't follow their rules.'

'So, we must be pirates, all of us,' said Hanzel, laughing. 'Those fellows,' he gestured toward the forward hold, 'They are our brothers.'

'You never did attempt to bribe them to join us. Why is that?' asked Max.

Hanzel regarded Max and smiled. 'I don't trust pirates.' He regarded his friends with a straight face, then suddenly burst out laughing.

Max and Olafsen looked at each other and then back at Hanzel before joining him in the merriment as a mighty clap of thunder rumbled through the darkened sky.

Chapter 23

When midnight arrived, Hanzel, Max, and Olafsen had fallen asleep in Hanzel's cabin. They had succumbed to the heady rum they were drinking. The five pirates were asleep, also. No one on board heard the rest of the thunder storm as it rolled through the night.

The pirates were heartened because no executions were performed. They thought it was because of the storm. They did not know Hanzel and his mates had drifted off. As the night progressed, moving their sinking sloop became a nightmarish misery. Eventually they realized, the only way for them to move the ship was to tow her with the row boats, every man pulling for all his might to turn the vessel and take her out of the bay.

When the sun rose, the water logged sloop bobbed past the bay's entrance and towards open water. Because the sails were unfurled, the strong winds pushed her out to sea. The tossing water made it impossible for the pirates to catch the sloop. They barely made it back to shore; three miles north of the bay. Hanzel and his friends slept through it all.

The morning brought better weather. Although it was still a blustery day, there was no rain and there was some blue in the clouded sky. When Hanzel woke up he immediately realized it was way past midnight and well into the morning. Sunlight lit up the cabin through the small windows. He regarded his friends. Max was still sleeping in the big arm chair and Olafsen was lying on the floor. Three empty rum bottles sat on the table.

'Max! Olafsen! Wake up. It's morning.'

Not a body stirred.

Hanzel repeated his instructions to wake up.

Max stirred. He suddenly sat upright and rubbed his eyes. Max looked at Hanzel with a surprised expression.

'It's morning?' Max looked at the light coming into the widows. 'I wonder if they moved the sloop?' He peeked out a window. 'She's not there.'

Hanzel rushed to the window and peered out. 'Well, let's get going. We've no time to waste.'

Max nudged Olafsen with the toe of his boot. 'Hey, Olafsen. We're setting sail.'

The big Scandinavian grunted and slowly raised himself off the floor. He stretched and farted.

'Oooh, thanks a lot, ya big lunk.' Max frowned at the big Swede

'Vhat kin I say, exzept, sorrie. Ven yu haf ter faht, yer jes kin nay help it. Dat's natuur.'

'Yeah, well, do it outside. Not in confined quarters,' grumbled Max, opening a window.

Hanzel looked at Olafsen. 'What do you think, Olafsen? Do you think those pirates will cooperate?'

'Led us zee,' replied Olafsen.

Max headed for the door. 'I'm going topside to begin preparations. If you can persuade those officers to help us, things will go quicker and we'll be away from here.'

Hanzel and Olafsen walked to the forward hold. Upon entering the place, the pirate officers immediately began to complain about the bad treatment, they felt they were getting.

'We need to take care of nature's call,' complained Edward. 'And we need food and drink.'

'Please. You must at least let us attend to our toilet,' begged the navigator.

Hanzel realized it was a legitimate request and let Olafsen untie the one in most need; he being the boatswain.

During the following hour, Hanzel let each pirate have access to the head over the port bow. Each man was strictly supervised by Olafsen while Hanzel presented the opportunity to join him and help sail the pinnace to Holland for a small, but lucrative piece of the treasure. The offer was too generous to refuse. The four men who decided to join Hanzel were most grateful for his generosity. They were also greatly relieved to be still alive. Their leader, Edward Steele was the only man who would not join Hanzel and his friends.

An hour later, Edward was accompanied by Max and Olafsen, and his four officers in the row boat. They landed Edward on the north shore.

'I thank you for not killing me, Hollander,' said Edward, as he jumped out of the row boat. 'You are a magnanimous chap. I wish you all the best.'

Hanzel nodded. 'Thank you, Edward. Good luck to you.'

Edward smiled ruefully. 'Thank you, Hanzel Sventska. I won't forget this.' Then he looked at his officers who had abandoned him. 'As for you four traitors. When I find you again, I will kill you.' He stared at each man and then jumped into the water.

The four Englishmen did not say a word.

Hanzel and his friends watched as Edward waded ashore. A moment later they rowed back to the pinnace and began preparations for sailing

Edward was happily surprised, twenty minutes later to see the two row boats with his compatriots land on the rocky beach. The moment he saw the boats land, he ran towards them, waving his arms.

'They're making sail!' he shouted, pointing to the pinnace.

'There's Edward!' shouted Frank, a gnarled old sailor with whom Edward had sailed for fifteen years. 'Are you the only one left?!'

'No, no. They didn't kill any of us,' replied Edward.

'What about the others?' asked Stanley Barton, another of Edward's longer serving crew members.

Edward sneered. 'Those traitors chose to help the Dutchman. I would see them cut in pieces, the scurvy dogs.' He pointed to the pinnace which was beginning to move out of the bay. 'We've got to hurry if we want to catch em. There's only seven of em.'

Frank looked at the pinnace and shook his head. 'We're bone tired. We haven't a hope of catching her.' He looked at his companions. 'Do we lads?'

The other sailors shook their heads and agreed with Frank. They had nothing left.

'We needs ter rest,' said Justin; a young man from Dover.

Edward realized his men were spent and sadly nodded his head as he watched the pinnace sail out of the little bay.

'There goes a whole lot of treasure,' he murmured softly. 'That lucky Dutchman. He's got it made. God help him.'

'God elp im, my arse,' replied a gnarled old sailor named Peter. He shook his fist at the departing pinnace.

'I ope dat fat little runt of a boatswain gets it,' replied Stanley. 'I never liked im. You shoulda never av taken im on board.' He regarded Edward, who shook his head sadly.

'I never thought George would do that. They were lured by greed,' sighed Edward.

'Why didn't you go with em?' asked Justin.

Edward regarded his comrades and smiled. 'I didn't want to leave you, my friends. We are brothers. We will capture another ship.' He smiled ruefully and stared at the pinnace as it steered northward and headed away from there.

On the pinnace, Hanzel stared back at the beach where Edward and his men were standing. He waved, smiling broadly. *Thank God they were so incompetent. If they had come all at once. We would have lost it.* Hanzel turned around and watched as Olafsen directed the four new men in trimming sails. As they caught the wind, the sturdy pinnace picked up speed and sped through the waters at six knots. Hanzel could not be more pleased. *Incompetent pirates, that's what they are. If I was to be a pirate, I'd do a better job of it.* Hanzel paused for a moment. *But, I am a pirate, I think. If stealing from the Spaniards constitutes piracy. After all, it's as Pierre said, the Spaniard steals from the Indians.* Hanzel smiled as he directed his gaze to the forward hatch. *I'll put that gold to better use. I think we will buy a ship. I'll turn the gold into a ship with which we'll harass the Spaniard and redistribute his wealth to those who need it. I like that idea.*

Or, I could retire in a magnificent house and live a happy, comfortable life on land. That's another option. It's a whole lot safer. I could marry and have children. We could go to church together and be respectable citizens. Perhaps I could become an armorer. Hanzel visualized himself in a workshop making a sword. Master de Witt was looking on.

As Hanzel stood staring off into inner space, deep in thought about what he would do with the treasure, a sea gull screeched overhead and dropped a packet on his shoulder, splattering his cheek. The unwelcome present immediately shook Hanzel out of his ruminations and woke him up to reality. He looked up to watch the gull veer off to starboard, screeching. *He's probably laughing. Nice joke. Very funny.* Hanzel frowned as he wiped his cheek with the handkerchief he kept in his pocket. *Nuisance birds, that's what they are. Noisy, nuisance birds.*

'I see you got yourself a little present,' said Max, pointing at the mess on Hanzel's shoulder.

'Damn gulls,' replied Hanzel, wiping the goo off his shoulder.

'Gull. It was only one gull. You can't condemn the entire flock of gulls. That's unfair. It doesn't happen often that gulls poop on you. Maybe this is an omen?' Max pointed to Hanzel's shoulder. 'Maybe that's the poop of good fortune?'

Hanzel laughed. 'Yes, let's hope it is. Let's hope it is truly, the poop of good fortune.' He clapped Max on the shoulder as they laughed over the moment.

During the next two days, the weather carried the pinnace steadily northward. Sun warmed the decks and good cheer prevailed. The boat was easy to manage and without fuss in the pleasant weather. The men got to spend some of the time at leisure, dreaming and talking about the treasure in the holds.

Hanzel's greatest concern became entrance into the port of Amsterdam. He would have to report everything. His cargo manifest would have to be examined. Rules were strictly followed. There had to be an alternative considered.

'We will land in a fishing village instead. We'll make land at Vollendam. That way we'll avoid a lot of prying eyes,' said Hanzel.

'We can probably hire wagons,' suggested Max.

'They use wagons to haul fish inland. Surely they have some not in use?' Hanzel shrugged. 'I guess we'll see.'

'Ve bedder make shure nobudy no's vhat ve are movin.' Olafsen looked down at the chart they were studying. 'Haf yu any experience wid, Vollendam?'

'I've been there and know people there. I'm sure we'll manage to get the cargo to Amsterdam. First I'll go there and make arrangements with the De Witt family. We are going to have to convert a lot of that stuff into bullion. I suppose we could try and sell some of it as curios and art objects.'

'Dat wuld fetch a bedder prize I shud tink.' Olafsen picked up a small golden statue of a strange god, which Hanzel had picked out of one of the boxes below. It had blue turquoise eyes and a large ruby in its navel.

'The trouble is, where does one find collectors who would pay well for those things?' Max regarded the object in Olafsen's hands.

'I'm sure Missus De Witt will know people.' Hanzel rolled up the chart and put it aside.

'How are we going to pay those Englishmen?' asked Max.

'They seem like amiable, reliable fellows. Maybe we should ask if they want to join us in our venture to buy a ship. We're going to have to man her. Maybe these fellows will go along with our plan.' Hanzel smiled. 'Why don't we ask them?'

When Hanzel and his friends did ask them, the four men heartily agreed.

'Privateering is great fun,' said George, the boatswain.

'I agree,' said the tall navigator. 'It is immensely fun to hunt for prizes. Especially if one has a Letter of Marque.'

'I agree with Mister Alexander,' said George. 'Wouldn't you say, gentlemen?' He directed his gaze at his colleagues.

The first mate and quartermaster agreed.

'Privateering or piracy, it amounts to the same thing, really,' said Max. 'We just have permission from one king to rob other kings. It's all such nonsense. The only difference with us is, we are not reporting this haul to any king.' He laughed. 'I think that's wonderful.'

Hanzel nodded thoughtfully. 'I hope we get away with it.'

'Ve joost pretent dat ve are muchants,' said Olafsen.

'Yes, that is all well and good. However, even in little Vollendam, there is someone from the government overseeing what goes on in the harbour,' said Hanzel. 'We have to make up a manifest. We need an official list of our cargo. A list that makes sense. What could we have brought from France?'

'Or England,' said Mister Archer, the first mate. 'You could have come from England.

'What about Scotland? Don't forget Scotland,' replied Mister McMac, the quartermaster. 'Ee coulda come from Scotland.'

Hanzel smiled. 'Who can make up an official looking manifest?'

'I've had a little training in calligraphy,' said Mister Alexander. 'I could write a manifest.'

Hanzel patted the navigator on the shoulder. 'Most excellent.' He pointed to the hatch. 'Come with me.' He led the navigator to the great cabin at the stern. Hanzel looked in a drawer and pulled out a sheet of paper. He laid it on the table. 'Here is paper. There's a quill and ink.' He pointed to the small ink pot and goose quill lying on the cover of the log book. 'We'll need a seal. I don't have one. Nor do we have sealing wax.'

'I can fashion a seal,' said George, who had followed them into the cabin. 'I can make something official looking. All I need is a piece of oak and a sharp knife and a nail. I'll carve us a seal like shape. All we need to do is fake the wax with a bit of a bees wax and some red dye.' He scratched his chin and looked at his friends. 'Trouble is; where do we get the red dye?'

'We're still aways from Vollendam. We can make land anywhere along this coast and come upon a village. Surely we could find some dye, or the sealing wax,' suggested Mister Alexander.

Hanzel nodded. 'That's true. However, the less suspicion we draw to ourselves, the better. We should try and improvise out here; at sea. The fewer places we stop at, the better.'

The three men pondered the problem. *What can we use for red dye?*

A moment later, Hanzel stuck up his right index finger. 'I know where we can get red.' He grinned widely. 'We'll have to powder up a small ruby.'

'A ruby?' asked George. 'Pulverize a ruby?'

Hanzel shrugged his shoulders. 'Why not? We have a keg full of them. What does one less matter?'

George stared at Hanzel. He had no idea how many rubies there were on board. 'Yes, I suppose so. One less ruby isn't going to make much difference.' He looked at his colleague poised to write the manifest and shrugged his shoulders.

'Come with me, George.' Hanzel left the cabin and signaled Max, who was standing beside Olafsen at the helm. 'If you'd be so kind, Max. Please bring up a ruby. You know where they are. Please fetch a small one. We need it to colour wax, for a seal.'

'Colour wax for a seal? What kind of seal?' asked Max.

'We need an official looking seal on a manifest document to show port authorities,' replied Hanzel.

'A manifest document?' Max scratched his right temple.

'We need to pretend we are carrying a legitimate cargo. It will keep the authorities away, I hope.' Hanzel turned on his heels and returned to the cabin.

Max walked off to obtain the ruby as Hanzel indicated. 'Please, Mister Alexander. If you would take a seat we can begin writing the manifest while George fashions the seal and Mister McMac and company procure the wax. What say you?'

The lanky navigator sat down and picked up the quill. He examined the tip. Seeing it was sharp, he dipped it into the ink pot and poised himself to write. 'Ready,' he said, staring at the paper.

Hanzel tapped his right temple and thought for a moment. 'Alright. Write this. At the top of the page write in large, fancy script; Port Authority for the City of Newcastle.' He watched as Mister Alexander wrote the words in large, flowing script with elegant capitals. Hanzel nodded approvingly when the heading was done. 'Now write; Manifest of Goods shipped on,' Hanzel paused and looked at Mister Archer. 'What date is it?'

Mister Archer thought for a moment. 'The date? Well, first of all, I know we are in the year, sixteen hundred and twenty. I also know that we're in the month of August. I have no idea what day it is. Is it the twentieth?'

'Close enough,' replied Hanzel. 'Date the manifest for the tenth. Then, after the date list the following cargo: Ten crates of iron works. Twenty barrels of wine. Five boxes of pottery. Fifteen chests of tea. Twelve kegs of nails.' Hanzel paused and watched as Mister Alexander wrote in neat, tight script each of the items Hanzel listed. He looked over the list and counted in his head. *Ten, twenty, that is thirty, and five that is thirty five and fifteen that is fifty. Fifty, let me see. I think there are more....Oh, yes, of course. I forgot about those other barrels.* 'And twelve barrels of...'

'What about, beer?' asked Mister Archer.

Hanzel regarded the first mate and smiled. 'Okay, why not? Although they're not exactly, beer barrels, we'll list them as, *specialty ale*; brewed for the Royal House of Orange.' Hanzel pointed to the paper on the table. 'Write that. Write, twelve barrels of special ale for the Royal House of Orange. That will encourage the authorities not to be too nosy. If they believe we're carrying something for the royals, they'll be very careful to tamper with us.'

'That's good thinking,' agreed Mister McMac, who was preparing a bees wax candle for the sealing material.

A moment later, Max returned with a small anvil and hammer from the forward locker. When Olafsen set the anvil on the table, Max pulled a ruby from his pocket. The English privateers' eyes bulged when they saw it.

'I asked you to bring a small one,' said Hanzel.

'That's the smallest one I could find,' replied Max. 'I dug around in the barrel.'

Hanzel shrugged. 'Oh, well. Go ahead and crush it.' He could not help but flinch as Max began to break the ruby.

When the ruby had been well pulverized, the red powder was mixed with the wax Mister McMac had prepared.

'That looks perfect,' said Hanzel, admiring the sealing wax they had made. 'That will look official enough if George manages to fashion a credible seal.' He looked up to see George entering the cabin. He was grinning.

'Look,' he said, holding up the seal he had carved from an oak spindle.

'That looks official enough,' said Hanzel. He patted George on the back. 'Thank you, George.' Hanzel pointed to the sealing wax. 'Alright. If you'll be so kind as to apply the wax to the lower right corner of the document,' he said to Mister McMac.

The quartermaster began to melt the wax onto the document by holding a candle to the lump they had formed out of the beeswax and crushed ruby. When there was a sufficient blob of red wax, George carefully pressed his wooden seal into the yielding puddle, which quickly dried, leaving an official looking seal, albeit, illegible. The imprint had the impression of officialdom.

'I think that will work splendidly,' said Hanzel.

'With a document like that, why don't we just go straight into Amsterdam?' asked Max.

'The officials there are much more suspicious and scrutinize things with a fine toothed comb,' replied Hanzel. 'In Vollendam, it is not so. The officials are simple fisher folk.' He pointed to the document on the table. 'To them that will look official. They won't examine our cargo. We'll hire some wagons and take the load to Amsterdam, like I said. After I talk with Mevrouw de Witt.'

'What if she doesn't want any part of this?' asked Max.

'Trust me. I think I know her. Where there is a guilder to be made, she will want to make it.' Hanzel nodded. 'Mevrouw de Witt has many connections.'

'ON DECK! HURRY! COME!' shouted Olafsen from the helm.

The cabin quickly emptied as Hanzel and company rushed outside in time to witness a horrific sight ahead. They had sailed into uncharted shallow water as they rounded the Hook van Holland. Just yards ahead lay the partially submerged wreck of the *Black Swan*.

A loud screeching sound preceded a heavy crunch as the pinnace scraped over the submerged deck of the pirate sloop. In an instant the pinnace halted and swung to starboard as an upsurge pushed the stump of the broken mainmast of the sloop through the bottom of the trapped pinnace, holding her firmly skewered and shipping water.

The sudden jolt threw everyone onto the deck or into each other.

'What happened?!' shouted Max.

'Ve haf crashed into dat sheep!' replied Olafsen. He was still holding onto the wheel, but to no avail. The pinnace would not respond. She was firmly held by the heavy timber piercing her hull. The hapless pinnace began to lean to starboard as waves crashed over her deck.

When Hanzel picked himself up he looked about; his mouth agape and eyes bulging. *We're sinking. We're bloody sinking.* He rushed to the forward hatch, followed by his friends. Lurching it open, he flew down the ladder and stopped midway down. A huge gash in the bottom of the boat was admitting an unstoppable flow of water. 'We're doomed,' he said quietly. 'There's nothing we can do.'

'Can't we at least save some of the treasure?' asked Max.

'If we hurry, we might be able to grab a few boxes and kegs,' replied Hanzel. 'Come on fellows, let's get our long boat over board and save what we can.'

As the pinnace continued to lurch about in the heavy waves, Hanzel and his comrades rushed about, loosing the long boat and managing to launch it overboard. Then, with a mighty effort the seven men saved: one large trunk, containing gold and silver objects, three kegs containing precious stones, and a sack full of gold nuggets before the hull gave up and the pinnace began to sink. The rest of the treasure sank along with the pinnace and the *Black Swan* somewhere off the Hook van Holland. Hanzel and his friends were glad to be alive as they rowed away from the wrecks, partially sticking out of the water and bashed by constant waves.

'I guess we've got to look on the bright side of things,' said Max. 'At least we still got some of the gold. There still might be enough to buy a ship.'

Hanzel gazed at Max and slowly nodded. 'How could we not have known there would be shallows there? We should have veered a wider course.'

'Your charts are old and these coastlines change over time. Those shallows were not on your chart.' Mister Alexander frowned. 'It's not anyone's fault. It's just one of those unfortunate things.'

'Unfortunate, alright. We lost a lot of treasure.' Hanzel regarded Mister Alexander. 'Do you have any idea how much treasure was in our holds?'

'I have an idea. But not really,' replied the lanky navigator.

Hanzel gestured at the chest and kegs. 'That is but a small sample of what was there. Those boxes you saw in the holds were not full of sugar and cigars.' Hanzel sighed. 'We could have done so much with that gold. Now we have just a fraction to share amongst us.'

'There's still quite a lot of wealth here,' said George. 'I'm sure that when we divide this according to our percentages, we'll still have a goodly sum.'

Hanzel nodded. 'Yes, but when we split it up, there won't be enough to buy a ship.'

'Oh, is that what you were planning to do with the money,' said Mister Archer, the first mate. 'Buy a ship?'

Hanzel nodded. 'I told you already.'

'Yes. We were going to buy a ship to use for harassing the Spaniard.' Max acted as if he was swashbuckling with an errant Iberian.

Mister Archer regarded his colleagues for a moment. 'If we four join you, as we talked about, and we seven put this treasure to use and obtain a ship, we might be able to do it. What say you, lads? Don't you rather stay at sea and steal the Spaniard's ill gotten treasure?'

'Aye,' agreed George. 'I thought it was a good idea the first time we talked about it.'

'Count me in,' added Mister McMac.

'What else are we to do? We're privateers. We're not land lubbers,' said Mister Alexander.

Hanzel grinned. He regarded Max and Olafsen, who nodded agreement. 'Well, then, let's swear a pact to each other. We'll buy a sturdy ship and arm her, after which we'll seek the Spaniard's treasure.'

'Aye, Hanzel Sventska!' shouted the Englishmen.

'Aye, aye,' added Max and Olafsen.

'Alright then, it's done,' said Hanzel. 'We seven will procure the ship we need and arm her accordingly. Then we'll recruit a reliable crew and fill the ship with proper libations and victuals. Enough for a six month or year long voyage.'

'Sounds like we'll be looking for a much larger ship than the *Black Swan*. I'm sorry about that, by the way,' said Mister Archer. 'If it wasn't for us, you wouldn't have lost your pinnace.'

Hanzel nodded. 'Sometimes that's just how it is. You win and you lose. The main thing is, we're still alive. That's all that matters.' He adjusted the tiller to steer the long boat into an approaching wave. As the long boat rode over the rising water, Hanzel noted the beautiful colours of the transparent wave as he drifted into a deep meditation regarding his circumstances. *I'm grateful for what I've got. These friends will be a great help. I'm confident we'll find a ship. Perhaps we've still got enough gold and precious stones to buy a frigate. That would be ideal. A frigate with forty guns. But where do we sell those stones and objects? The nuggets are not a problem. But the other stuff. Too bad we couldn't have saved a chest of gold coins.* Hanzel scratched his chin as he stared at the remnants of the great treasure. *I sure hope we can do it.* He watched his friends rowing for a while before diverting his attention to the shoreline off their starboard side. 'Instead of rowing all the way to Vollendam. Let's just put in at any fishing village we come to.'

'Good idea,' agreed George. 'My arms are getting tired.'

'Mine too,' agreed Max. He pointed to smoke rising from shore. 'That smoke probably is coming from a village. Let's row closer to shore and we'll find out.'

'Too bad we lost our telescopes,' lamented Hanzel.

'We'll see what's there, soon enough,' suggested Mister Alexander.

'It's always nice to know what you're coming to,' replied Hanzel. 'I don't know what village that is.'

'I figure we'll get there in another half hour of rowing,' said Max, pulling on his oar. 'What say you boys? Shall we give a final hard pull?'

The other men heartily agreed and together they made it a game to see how fast they could row the long boat. Indeed, within less than an hour, the little group made land at a tiny fishing hamlet of thirty souls, fifteen of whom were out to sea, leaving only six women, four children, and five old people. None of them witnessed the landing. It was mid afternoon and the air was warm.

Gulls screeched insults as Hanzel and his friends unloaded the longboat, setting the heavy trunk and kegs on the pebble strewn shore, beside the rickety wooden pier.

'Now all we have to do is find a wagon,' said Hanzel, wiping his brow. 'So we don't draw too much attention to ourselves, only two of us should go and reconnoiter; to see if there is a wagon to be had in this village.'

'Can we just sit and relax for a moment, Hanzel? I'm pooped, from all that rowing and hauling this treasure here. That chest is heavy.' Max pointed to the trunk.

'Dat's a gute teeng et iz hevie,' agreed Olafsen. 'Dat meenz ve shteel haf zumtin left of all dat ve had.'

Max nodded. 'Yeah. However, I'm still pooped and I want to sit down for a while and get my strength back. All that Hanzel had to do was work the tiller, while we rowed the boat.'

Hanzel nodded. 'Alright. Not a problem.' He looked at the village, past Max's shoulder for a moment. 'I'll go and have a look around. One man alone is likely to draw less attention than three of us.'

'It really doesn't look like anyone is there. The village appears empty,' observed Mister Alexander, peering at a house with an open door, swinging gently in the light breeze blowing in from the north.

'I vill come wid yu,' said Olafsen. The big Swede rubbed his right biceps, 'I am not tired.'

'Alright, Olafsen and I will go have a look around. You stay here and guard the treasure,' said Hanzel.

'Don't worry,' replied Max. 'It'll be here when you get back.'

Hanzel smiled and then he and Olafsen walked up to the roadway fifteen paces away. Gulls screeched and several small shore birds skittered off under the pier. The smell of rotting seaweed and dead marine fauna permeated the beach area. Hanzel was glad to step onto the dirt road, lined by ten houses and several work sheds. Three broken boats lay on their sides on the beach on the other side of the pier. As they walked along the road, the reek of salted fish replaced the odours of the beach.

As the two men came to the end of the road, they looked behind one of the work sheds and discovered a wagon. Unfortunately there was no horse.

'Ve vill haf tu pool dat vagon oursefs,' said Olafsen.

Hanzel regarded the wagon and shrugged his shoulders. 'We couldn't pull that. We're going to need help from the others.'

Olafsen rubbed his chin as he picked up the tongue with his left hand. 'Hmmm,' he mumbled as he grabbed the tongue with his other hand as well. 'Deeze vagon iz nut too heffy.' He pulled and momentarily the wagon began to move.

Hanzel was amazed to see the man's incredible strength. He quickly walked over and began to help Olafsen pull the wagon out from behind the shed. The wheels creaked. Hanzel could tell that the wagon was very heavy. Olafsen took most of the burden. *That man is a giant. I can't believe how strong he is. I'm glad he's my friend.*

'Whaaat dyu teenk yur duuing vit der vaagon?' said an old croaky voice coming from within the shed.

Hanzel and Olafsen stopped pulling and regarded the shed.

A door opened and a very thin old man stepped out of the little building. He was wearing the typical clothes of a fisherman; wooden shoes, huge pants, a vest, shirt, bandana, and typical woolen fisherman's cap.

'Vy aaar yu takin my zun's vaagon?' he asked.

Olafsen looked at Hanzel.

Hanzel looked at Olafsen.

Then they both regarded the old man.

'We need to borrow it for a while,' said Hanzel. 'To take some goods to Amsterdam.

'Dat ees my zun's vaagon. Heee's feesing,' replied the old geezer. He coughed and spat on the ground.

'We can rent it. I'll pay you. We'll return it,' said Hanzel as he showed the man a large golden nugget.

The man's eyes regarded the nugget with greedy eyes. 'Du yu haf mooor of doze?'

Hanzel reached into his purse and extracted a small ruby. 'No, but I have one of these,' he said, holding the precious gem between his thumb and forefinger.

The old man held out his right hand. 'I aaam shure dat my zun vhill aprooof. Yu kan uuse de vagon an breeeng eet bak fer dat gholt un dat rooby.'

Hanzel smiled. 'Agreed.' He handed the precious items to the old man.

'Taank de,' said the man. Then, without further ado, the old skeleton returned to the shed and shut the door with a bang.

'That was easy,' said Hanzel. 'I guess we are meant to take our treasure to Amsterdam.' He picked up the tongue.

'Yu tink ve got de best deal?' asked Olafsen. 'Yu tink diz vagon is vurth dat much. Vun gold nugget an a rooby?'

Hanzel smiled as they began to pull the wagon along the road. 'One nugget and one ruby? We won't even know they're missing.'

Olafsen chuckled. 'I am zoo happy ve vur able to safe sum of da treasure.'

'It's too bad about our pinnace hitting the *Black Swan*. How could that have happened? You were at the helm,' said Hanzel.

'Vhyle all of yu vur beesy mid da official papehs, no vun vas keepin eye open. Ze vaters vere ferry shallow dere. I hat no idea.' Olafsen shrugged his shoulders. 'Dere vas nutin ve culd do.'

Hanzel shook his head sadly. 'Yes, I know. It's just too bad. We lost a lot of gold. We could have had our boat and been rich. Now we'll have a boat, but may not have any money left and will have no choice but to steal from the greedy Spanish.'

'I am shure dere is enuff golt in dat trunk,' replied Olafsen. 'Don vurry, Hanzel. Ve vill get our boat.'

Hanzel smiled at his friend and nodded. 'I hope so.'

Chapter 24

"Oiy! Vere d'ye tinks yer takin der vagon!?' shouted a voice from inside a house. Hanzel and Olafsen stopped pulling the wagon and looked in the direction the voice had come from. A moment later a short, fat woman, wearing a leather apron came rushing out of the house and stood in front of Hanzel and Olafsen. 'Vell?'

Hanzel and Olafsen were momentarily out of words to say.

'Are ye def?' asked the woman. 'Did ye not hears me ask yer vere are ye going mid der vagon?'

Hanzel and Olafsen nodded. 'Yes, yes, we heard you.' answered Hanzel. 'We didn't know exactly what to say at the moment.'

'Vell? Vere are ye going mid my hoosbant's vagon?'

'Your husband's wagon?' Hanzel pointed back to the old man's shed. 'The old man said it was his son's wagon. He rented it to us.'

The woman regarded the shed with a disdainful expression. 'Is zun is my hoosban.' She looked towards the shed. 'Ow mooch did e renter fer?'

Hanzel looked at Olafsen before replying. *If I tell her a gold nugget and a ruby will she be suspicious? The old man couldn't care less. But this one. Hmmm. I don't know. I'll take a chance and see what her reaction will be.* Hanzel scratched his chin and regarded the woman, who was growing increasingly impatient. 'I gave him gold and a gemstone,' replied Hanzel.

'Vhat kind a gemstone?' The woman stared at Hanzel. *Vhat kinda gennelmun carries golt n' gemstones aroun? They's no fisher folk. Dey don looks ta reech, nyder. How dey com by der golt ant gemstones?'* 'Wad Is ye? Is ye pyrates?'

Hanzel stared at the woman and then regarded Olafsen, who shrugged his shoulders. Hanzel returned his gaze at the woman and shook his head. 'No, we're not pirates. We were just lucky and found a treasure. That's why we need the wagon. To haul the treasure we found.'

The woman regarded the two men for a long while and then burst out laughing. 'A tresure?' Laugh. 'Ye foun a tresure?' Laugh. 'I bet ye bin ter Timbuktoo, too.' Laugh. When she was done laughing she turned on her heels and returned to her house, speaking over her shoulder. 'Fine. If'n de olt man lent yer de vagon. Go on. Tis his ter begin wid.' She banged the door closed. Hanzel and Olafsen looked at each other and shrugged their shoulders.

'I gets der opinion dat de peeple in dis plaze is all related,' observed Olafsen as he took note of another old man walking towards them on the road.

As the old man approached he pointed at the wagon with his walking stick. 'Ver der yer tinks yer going wid dat der vagon?' asked the wrinkled skeleton. He came to a stop standing in front of the two privateers. 'Dat vagon belongs to my brodder.'

'If he is the man working in that shed, over there.' Hanzel pointed to the shed. 'He rented the wagon to us.'

The man's eyes narrowed as he rubbed his chin. 'Ow much e charg yer?

'A gold nugget and a ruby,' replied Hanzel.

'A golt noogit unt a rooby?' asked the old codger, rubbing his stubbled chin.

Hanzel nodded his head.

The old geezer regarded Hanzel and Olafsen a long while before responding. He pulled on his right earlobe and cleared his throat loudly. Then he spat an oyster into the hedge they were standing beside. Hanzel felt his stomach move. Olafsen looked away.

'Ee only ask yer fer arf price. De aktool price ter rent der vagon is two noogits and two roobies.' The old man watched for Hanzel's reaction.

Hanzel looked at Olafsen who shrugged his shoulders. 'Do ve ave any more?' he asked.

Hanzel felt in his pocket. 'I just happen to have one more nugget, that's all.' He extracted another thumb sized nugget from his coat pocket and showed it to the wizened old man. His eyes opened widely and a greedy expression came over his face. 'Here,' said Hanzel, handing the nugget to the old man. 'That's all I have.'

'Vat aboot im?' asked the old man, pointing his cane at Olafsen.

'He has nothing,' replied Hanzel.

'Joost like me,' said the wrinkled codger. 'I arf nuttin too. Pleny orf nuttin ter boot.'

'Well, that's all I have. Just one more large nugget. Probably worth quite a lot of guilders. Take it or leave it.' Hanzel stared at the man who was examining the nugget.

'Olrite den. Ur kin take der vagon. Boot remember ter bringer bak.' The old man put the nugget into his coat pocket and continued on his way, a big grin on his wrinkled face.

Hanzel and Olafsen picked up the pole and continued pulling the wagon along the road.

As they passed the last house, across from the pier, next to which the treasure sat waiting, seagulls screeched as the door opened and a bigger, fatter woman, wearing a white apron and white bonnet stepped out. She was carrying a small child under her left arm. The child was squirming and squealing.

'Dat vaaagon is my popa's vagon. How kins it be dat yer be poolin er?' she asked in a high pitched voice.

'Dey's verrry nosy, dese peepel,' observed Olafsen, his eyes on the fat woman walking towards them.

'They're certainly security conscious. They look after each other's things. Can't blame them for that, replied Hanzel.

The fat woman waved her right arm in the air and then pointed at the wagon. 'Hoo ar yu? Vhat yu doin mid der vagon?'

'We are renting it, madam,' replied Hanzel. 'Is your popa the old man in the shed over there?' Hanzel pointed to the shed at the end of the street.

'Ee isn olt. Ees only ferty nine. Ees ad a ard life on der zee fishing fer de errings. Eet preematurly age im, it did.' The fat woman looked affectionately towards the shed. 'Now e spend is time mendin nets an floots.' She pointed to the wagon. 'Wad di e charge yer fer rentin et?'

'So far we have paid, your father and his brother, two gold nuggets and a ruby,' replied Hanzel.

'Golt noogits an a roobie?' The woman stared at Hanzel with widened eyes. 'In't dat a strange vay of payin? I means er dat normuly peepel pays mid der florijns or dem guilders. Maybe a dukat, or sompin like dat. Nebber in golt noogits an der roobies.' Narrowing her eyes she asked, 'Yer ain no piraates or sumpin? Are ye?'

Hanzel smiled. 'No, we're not pirates. We're shipwrecked sailors who managed to save their treasure and now need to take it to Amsterdam.'

The woman regarded her child for a moment and swatted it on its arse. 'Shut up!' she shouted at the child. The stunned child paused its squirming and jabbered something before bursting into louder protestations and wriggling. The woman smacked it again. 'Ur keeps dat up an I'll...' The child stopped just long enough for her to look back at Hanzel and say, 'A tresure yer say? Vere is dis tresure?'

'That is not your business.' Hanzel looked at the sky, which was darkening, it being late afternoon. 'Look, we've got to get going. There are other shipwrecked mariners waiting for us. It is getting late. We paid the rent for the wagon. You can ask your popa or your uncle.' Hanzel looked at Olafsen and nodded. They began pulling the wagon.

'Ees not my unkel,' she said, insulted. 'De udder man is me mudder's kuzin.'

'Who ever he is, we also paid him to use this wagon' replied Hanzel. 'So, if you will kindly excuse us, we have to go.'

The woman stared dumbfounded as Hanzel and Olafsen pulled the wagon down the road, past the pier and down the inclining beach on the other side. She scratched her head. *I mus tell me usbant bout dat ven e gits ome. Eel vant ter knows boot dat fer sure. Tresure? Hmmm.* She turned on her heels and returned to the house.

When Hanzel and Olafsen arrived at the beach, their friends were delighted to see they found a wagon.

'Well done,' said Max. 'We've got a wagon, boys. Let's get er loaded and be out of here.'

'Aye!' agreed the others enthusiastically.

They quickly set about loading the heavy trunk onto the wagon. Loading the kegs was easier. Placing the sack with nuggets onto the wagon only took two men.

When they were finished loading the wagon, they left that place and headed south on the muddy road to Amsterdam. Gulls screeched overhead in the darkening sky. The reek of rotting marine fauna hung in the air as they passed the village dumping ground.

'What a stench,' said Max, pinching his nose.

The men hastened to push and pull the wagon as quickly away from the place before they retched up what little was left in their stomachs. Twenty minutes later they had traveled a few miles inland and far from the stomach turning stench. As the sky darkened and night began to fall, they found themselves entering a forest, where deep shadows were beginning to make the road difficult to see.

'Maybe we should camp here for the night,' suggested Hanzel. 'Here on the edge of the forest. Without a lantern, the forest will be much too dark to continue.'

'I agree,' said Max. 'Better we're on the edge of the woods.' He looked into the forest. 'Who knows what lurks there in the dark?'

'Bears,' replied Mister McMac. 'Brown bears and wild boar.'

'And wolves,' added George.

'And foxes and squirrels.' Mister Archer smiled. 'I like squirrels.'

'A forest like this would probably have lots of mice, voles, rats, you name it. The place is full of creatures,' said Mister Alexander.

'Therefore it's best we stop here. I don't like the idea of wolves coming for us in the night. While we're sleeping.' Hanzel gestured, indicating the place where they had stopped.

'Another danger in there,' said Max. 'It's highwaymen. They like hiding in the dark in forests such as this. Lots of folks have gone missing in places like that.' Max shivered. He did not like forests. Forests were dark, dangerous places for him.

Meanwhile, back at the fishing village, the fleet of five boats returned. The first thing the women of the village did was tell their husbands about the strange men and the wagon. When the word, *treasure* was mentioned, the men grew very interested, indeed. By midnight they hatched a plot and decided to not bother fishing the next morning. They chose, instead, to follow the wagon and see if the women were correct. To steal a treasure from only a few men, was not an immoral thing to do, as far as they were concerned. They were poor fishermen. A free treasure could help them survive a few more years.

When the hour stood in the neighbourhood of three, Hanzel woke up. He was restless and could not sleep. Something had invaded his dreams and unsettled him. He regarded the tree against which he had slept and noticed an ant crawling up the thick bark. Not liking insects very much, being a sea dog, he recoiled and stood up immediately. In the foggy darkness he walked a short distance away from where everyone lay sleeping and emptied his bladder against a huge chestnut tree.

As he stood there, urinating against the tree, he heard noises. When he was done he quickly returned his penis to its codpiece and turned around just as the thirteen fishermen fell upon the sleeping privateers. In the mist, the attacking felons did not see Hanzel, who instantly crouched behind a tree. His cutlass lay beside the tree where he had slept. Hanzel was defenseless, except for the dirk he always carried in his right boot. His heart pounded in his chest. The sounds of struggle came from the camp. Yells and screams alerted Hanzel there was something seriously wrong. When he crept closer he witnessed the fishermen mercilessly murdering his friends with clubs and knives. The screams sent shivers slithering up his spine. He became frozen and did not know what to do. If he jumped into the melee, he would surely be killed also.

It began to rain. There was nothing unusual about that. Rain is normal on the coast at that time of year. Hanzel huddled under a tree and managed to remain dry. In the flash of a lightning bolt, he could see the fishermen leaving with the wagon. There was nothing he could do.

When the fishermen were far enough away from the place, Hanzel crept to the place his friends lay bludgeoned, stabbed, and bleeding on the ground where the wagon had been. He crouched beside each of his slain friends. Max was the last of the friends Hanzel came to. As he crouched down, Max moaned. Hanzel cradled Max's head and looked down at the face of his friend. Max opened his eyes and stared at Hanzel. 'What did we do to deserve this?' he croaked.

Hanzel's eyes filled with tears. 'I have no idea, my friend. I don't know what we did wrong. We paid a fair price to use the wagon.'

'Yes, but did we plan to bring it back?' Max coughed.

'Probably not,' replied Hanzel.

'So, they just took back what was theirs.' Max spit up blood, which drooled out of his mouth and onto Hanzel's lap.

'We paid them a goodly price. The gold was easily worth two wagons. And the ruby one wagon by itself,' replied Hanzel.

Max stared at Hanzel but did not say more. He collapsed into Hanzel's lap and died.

Hanzel tearfully closed Max's eyes and lay him gently down. *I would give my soul to the devil to reverse all of this.* A brilliant flash of blue light lit up the scene, followed by a terrible crack of thunder, which rolled and rolled through the trees; vibrating the very marrow in Hanzel's bones. He was left in the forest, all alone. *I vow I will come back and take what is mine. I will get revenge for my dead friends. May they rest in peace.*

Hanzel remained, huddled under an oak tree until morning, contemplating what had happened. The rain made the temperature drop and Hanzel began to shiver. He did not sleep another wink.

When morning came, a weak sun began to worm its way through the hazy drizzle, Hanzel stood up and stretched. Then, holding his coat close around himself he walked away from that place, into the forest; alone and bewildered.

An owl hooted. Creatures scurried in the brushes and squirrels ran along branches, chattering greetings and warnings. Gradually the drizzle stopped and the sun began to break through the clouds. Hanzel stepped out of the forest onto a better road bordered by cultivated fields and grasslands where sheep grazed and cows chewed their cud. 'This is much better,' he said to himself. Off in the distance he could see farm buildings.

When Hanzel arrived at the farm he stumbled into the courtyard to be greeted by a young, very attractive woman wearing a blue apron and white bonnet.

'Hello,' she said. 'Who might you be?'

'Hanzel. I am Hanzel Sventska,' he replied.

'I am pleased to meet you. My name is Hanna. Hanna van Hooven.' She pointed to Hanzel's clothing. 'You look disheveled. What happened to you?' she asked, examining him closely.

Hanzel looked down at his rumpled clothing. 'Well, to tell you the truth, I am a shipwrecked sailor. A privateer, actually....'

'Oh, a privateer?' she replied. 'I have read about you, *privateers*. Is it true? Is it true what they say?'

'Er, what exactly do *they* say?' asked Hanzel, not having the slightest clue what she meant.

'That you are very virile men who take great risks with your lives in order to steal treasure for the crown.'

Hanzel smiled. 'We certainly take risks. The risk I took was to ship a treasure in a small boat through shallow waters. The risk I took was not to sink a certain sloop. I took a risk telling people about a treasure...'

'A treasure?' The girl flushed. 'A real treasure? You know about a treasure?'

Hanzel nodded. 'I will tell you about my treasure, but first I need water and some food. I have not had either for a long time.'

The girl nodded and smiled. 'Yes, yes, of course. Come with me. I will take care of you.' She took his right hand and led Hanzel through a door into the kitchen of the house. Mouthwatering aromas filled Hanzel's nostrils. The cook was standing at the fireplace stirring a large cauldron hanging from chains. 'Margaret, this is Hanzel Sventska. He's a shipwrecked sailor trying to find his way back to Amsterdam.'

'By the looks of im, ee culd use a bath,' said the cook brusquely. She immediately returned to her work and took no further notice of Hanzel.

'You can sit there,' said Hanna sweetly, indicating a chair at the large table. 'I will get you a bowl.' Hanna reached up on a shelf and took a bowl down. 'Margaret, give Hanzel a bowl full of the stew you're stirring. It smells ready.'

'Oh, so now we're feedin' shipwrecked sailors, are we?' asked Margaret insolently.

'That is not your business, Margaret, who I chose to feed. This man is hungry and thirsty. It is the Christian thing to do. Remember that.' Hanna looked ready to cuff the cook. Hanzel could tell that there was no love lost between the two.

Margaret dutifully spooned the stew into the proffered bowl and handed it back, all the while mumbling under her breath. Hanna pretended not to notice. 'Now cut a goodly piece of bread and give him butter,' she commanded, 'and ale. He needs ale.' Margaret did as she was told and cut a slab of bread which she slapped onto a plate. Hanna returned her attention to Hanzel. *He's so good looking. I would love to run my hands through his hair and kiss those sumptuous lips. Why can't Henrick look like him? Just my bad luck.*

'I really appreciate this, Hanna,' said Hanzel as he sniffed the delicious aroma emanating from the bowl. He picked up the spoon and sipped the hot broth. 'Hmmm,' he murmured as he took a spoon full. 'This is delicious, Margaret. Thank you.'

Margaret did not turn around and mumbled something under her breath, followed by a grunt.

'So, tell me, Hanzel Sventska, what actually happened to you?' Hanna sat down on the bench facing Hanzel across the table. She stared into his eyes and became lost.

'This story begins when I was basically kidnapped by Pierre Le Grange, a French privateer. We became friends and I served him as first mate, in order to pursue a dream of his, to capture a Spanish Treasure Galleon. We actually managed to capture such a ship, except it was disguised as a merchantman. She was damaged after a terrible storm which shipwrecked us. The ship was damaged by the storm and was refitting in a small bay off the coast of Hispaniola. Hanzel paused for a moment as he thought about the details. 'Anyway, we captured the ship which was loaded to the scuppers with treasure. Then we sailed her back to France and divided up the treasure. I was promised a goodly percentage for helping him. I only took about 15 percent, about as much as we could safely stow in a small pinnace. My friends, Jean, Olafsen, and Max helped me sail her back to Amsterdam. Anyway, we were nearly robbed by English privateers and then eventually shipwrecked on their scuttled sloop in shallow waters. We managed to save a trunk load of gold and silver, three kegs of precious stones, and a sack of nuggets before the pinnace went down. Then we rowed the load ashore, to a small fishing village. We rented a wagon and were taking the treasure to Amsterdam when they came after us in the night and killed my friends before my eyes. In the misty gloom of the morning they didn't see me some distance away. They clubbed and stabbed my friends to death and stole the wagon loaded with our treasure.' Hanzel sighed and stared at Hanna. 'I'm lucky to be alive.' He looked at Hanna for a long time as his eyes filled with tears. 'I'm lucky to be alive.'

'What happened to Pierre LeGrange?' she asked, helping to change the subject.

'He took his share and likely retired in the country, on an estate; with servants and a fine coach,' sniffed Hanzel staring into his stew. 'We captured a very large treasure.' Hanzel sighed and wiped his nose on the handkerchief he kept in his pocket. 'Alas, my piece of it lies at the bottom of the sea.'

'And in the hands of fishermen. Do you remember the road to that village?' Hanzel nodded. 'I think so.'

'Just tell the authorities and they'll get it back for you,' she said. 'If you know which village it is. Surely the treasure would still be there. Wouldn't you think?'

Hanzel shook his head. 'No. It is best not to tell the authorities. They will just want most of it. A tax of some sort. You know; a piece for the king. He always gets a piece of the action.' Hanzel smiled. 'It really is extortion, isn't it?'

Hanna wasn't sure what he meant. She just stared at Hanzel's blue eyes and nodded.

'The king enforces his tax with his army. If you don't pay now, you will pay later, even with your life.' Hanzel scooped a spoonful of stew and sipped it slowly. 'I don't want the king to get it. So, I'll see about getting it back. First I have to get to Amsterdam.'

'Amsterdam is still quite a long distance. It will take you three days to walk there,' replied Hanna.

'Then I must go there as soon as possible. Since there is still a long day for me to walk, I must eat and run,' he said.

Hanna looked at the table. 'Why must you leave so soon? It has taken you this long. Why not stay for a while? You can have a bath and clean up. We may even have some clean clothes for you. You're the same size as my brother. He's off to the war.'

'I'm sorry to hear that,' replied Hanzel.

'What do you mean?' asked Hanna.

'That he's off to war. I don't like war. We have too much of it.' Hanzel began to eat the now cooler stew with gusto. *This is really good.* 'You've done an excellent job making this stew, Margaret.'

Margaret looked briefly in his direction and sniffed. 'Nobody else tells me that around here,' she mumbled.

Hanna ignored her and remained focused on Hanzel, heartily eating the stew and butter laden bread. 'You could stay here for a few days and rest up. I think my father is going into Amsterdam on Saturday. You can ride with him. Maybe I'll come along too.'

Hanzel regarded Hanna. She was obviously thrilled to be with him. He could see it in her eyes. *She is very pretty. I really like her voice. What would it matter if I stay here until Saturday? I'm sure she'd be good company.* 'Alright, why not? I'll stay here until Saturday. Are you certain that your father will agree to take me with him?'

'Of course he will. Father will do anything for me. Especially since I am his only other child. Since my brother went to war, he's been especially caring.' Hanna smiled. *I wonder what it would be like with him. I would love to love a man like him. He's so handsome. And so intelligent. He's not like Henrick, that's for sure. I wonder how old he is.*

Hanzel smiled at Hanna. 'Thank you Hanna. I will take you up on your offer. That is, if your father agrees.'

'Don't worry, he will.' Hanna grinned.

Hanzel noted the excellence of her straight white teeth. *She's a healthy girl. Hanzel and Hanna has a nice ring to it. I really like this girl.*

'When you finish your stew you can have a bath. I will go and arrange it for you. Margaret will tell you where to go.' Hanna got up from her seat. 'I will see you in a couple of hours. I have to go to my Bible study.' Hanna laughed and then turned on her heels and left the kitchen through the inner door leaving Hanzel with Margaret who did not want anything to do with him and had a different idea about where he should go. Hanzel essentially ate the stew alone. He dared not ask for another bowl full. When he was done, Margaret told him where to go for his bath. Hanzel was only too glad to leave the kitchen.

Following Margaret's directions, Hanzel stepped outside into the courtyard. He walked across the yard to a bath house; a rare luxury. A large tub, filled with hot water awaited him. A small table beside the tub held a large bar of scented soap. The room was hazy with steam. 'Thank you, Father. I am so grateful.' Hanzel quickly stepped out of his clothes and immersed himself in the water. 'Aaaaahhhhh,' he sighed as he sank back and let the warm water soothe his aching muscles and wounded spirit. Gradually Hanzel closed his eyes and drifted off into a dream of sunshine and warmth. Wealth and gardens. Paintings on walls. Him in love with her. Flowers.....

Hanzel never noticed when Hanna stepped into the large tub, naked, her nipples pink and hard. When she trickled water over his face he woke up with a start, surprised to see her. 'Hanna! What are you doing? What if your parents find out?'

'My parents are at the market. They will not be home until after sundown. The only ones here are you, me, Margaret, Jane, and Henk. Jane is the cleaning girl and Henk looks after our horses. The other workers went with my parents: Henrick, Renee, Ruthy, Miep, and Wim. Margaret and Henk don't know I'm here. I was very careful. I hope you don't mind that I am taking a bath with you. I just couldn't resist. You are so beautiful.'

'So are you,' replied Hanzel, smiling. *This is incredible. I can't believe it. Perhaps I am dreaming.*

Hanna grinned. Then she moved across the tub and pressed her naked body against his. She looked into his eyes and then kissed him long and tenderly. Hanna knew she had fallen in love.

Hanzel felt it when she surrounded him with her feminine warmth; sliding her body over his magnificent erection until they both exploded in a series of pelvic thrusts. The resultant firing of neurons in their brains were like fireworks. When the pyrotechnics subsided they fell into each other's arms for a long while, feeling each other breathing.

'That was unbelievable,' said Hanna grinning from ear to ear. 'I like it with you, Hanzel.'

'I like it with you too, Hanna,' replied Hanzel. He looked deep into her bright, blue eyes which were twinkling. He could feel that his own were doing the same.

The next two days were spent in a loving euphoria. Hanzel had met Hanna's parents and they were most welcoming. Hanna explained Hanzel's circumstances and they were very sympathetic. They were happy to let him sleep in one of the extra bedrooms, the room at the far end of a hall. Hanna's room was at the other end of the hallway and the parent's room was in the middle. Hanna knew how to be very quiet as she tiptoed to Hanzel's room in the middle of the night, when everyone else was sleeping.

The only person on the farm, who was not happy was Henrick. He could sense there was something going on between Hanzel and Hanna, right from the beginning. Henrick knew right away, when he saw how Hanna regarded

Hanzel when she introduced him. Henrick was instantly jealous. *She never looked at me that way. If he takes her away from me, by the Holy Saints, I will kill him.*

Early Saturday morning, Henrick had to get up to tend to the cows. As he crossed the courtyard he noticed light in Hanna's window. He grew instantly suspicious because Hanna never had light on in her window at that time of the morning.

There's a ladder in the barn.

Henrick ran to the barn and retrieved the ladder which reached to just under Hanna's window. He leaned the ladder very carefully against the wall, lest he made a noise and alerted her. Then, with careful steps, he climbed up the ladder. A dog barked. Henrick froze. *I hate that dog. Shut up you mangy mutt. Damn dog...*

The barking stopped and Henrick continued his cat climb up the ladder. The shutters were open, making it easy to see into the room. As Henrick's eyes peeked above the sill he looked into Hanna's room, right next to her bed in which Hanna lay naked with Hanzel. The instant Henrick saw what was going on he immediately reacted, the result of which was his falling backwards off the ladder. When he smacked his head on the pebbled ground he was knocked unconscious.

'What was that?' asked Hanna, looking at the window.

Hanzel shrugged his shoulders. He leaned over her and looked out of the window. Hanna squirmed out from under him and also looked out of the window. When they looked down, there was Henrick, sprawled on the ground, out stone cold.

'It's Henrick,' said Hanna. 'He was spying on us.'

'Then he deserves what he got,' replied Hanzel, suddenly jumping back from the window as Hanna's father came out of the house with a lantern. Hanzel quickly snuffed the candles as Hanna jumped back on the bed with him, just avoiding her father seeing her.

'Hmmm,' mumbled Meinheer van Hooven. 'That is odd.' He looked up at Hanna's window, but all he saw was open shutters and darkness. *She's still sleeping. I wonder what Henrick was doing on that ladder? Trying to elope with my daughter?* He stepped over to take a closer look at Henrick, who was sprawled on his back looking up at the star filled sky. Whether he was actually seeing anything, Meinheer van Hooven could not tell. It did not appear that there was a light on in Henrick's head. He tried to lift the young man up, but, Henrick being over 235 pounds, and Meinheer van Hooven only being 162 pounds, and not all that fit, could not lift the boy. *He'll just have to come to his light on his own. I'll check on him in the morning.* He looked up at Hanna's window. *I'll have to have a talk with that girl. What was Henrick up to?* As he walked back to the door, he looked over his shoulder once more at the scene of the ladder under Hanna's window, and Henrick unconscious at the bottom of it. Meinheer van Hooven scratched his head and stepped back into the house and closed the door.

In Hanna's room, 15 feet above conked out Henrick, Hanna returned to making love with Hanzel. It was their last night together. They made the best of it.

In the morning, after the cock had crowed three times, Hanzel and Hanna woke up. They looked at each other for a long time before speaking.

'My father needs another hand with the horses, I'm sure he would hire you if you asked him,' said Hanna.

'I don't know a thing about horses. I've been at sea since I was sixteen. I'm the son of a fisherman. The sea is my life.' Hanzel regarded Hanna. 'And, I know something about sword making.'

'You could learn. Horses are amazing animals. You'll see. I'll teach you. I've been around horses all my life. You'll come to appreciate them. And that will bring you money from my father, and room and board. I mean, what else are you going to do? You have no home.' Hanna sat up and regarded Hanzel, lying on his back and looking up at her with a smile on his face.

Hanzel regarded Hanna for a long time. He gently stroked her cheek. 'Alright,' he said. 'I'll give it a go. I'll ask your father to hire me. I'll stay here with you. Why not?'

Hanna was delighted and kissed Hanzel with much happiness and love. She was so happy. So, very, very happy.

Hanzel looked at the window and noticed that the sun was beginning to rise. 'I better tiptoe back to my room before your father gets up and sees me coming from yours.'

Hanna realized he was right. He had better not be seen. She looked at the window. 'Maybe you should go down the ladder and come in the front door.' She stood up and stepped to the window to look and see what state Henrick was in. 'He's still lying there on his back. It doesn't look like he's breathing.'

Hanzel came to stand beside Hanna and regarded stone cold Henrick. Then he looked at the ladder. 'I'd better get going. Your father said he wanted to make an early start.' He reached for his clothes and dressed, all the while intensely watched by Hanna. Then with a kiss he left, climbed out of the window, and down the ladder. He looked at Henrick for a moment. His eyes were wide open and staring up. *I think he might be dead.* Hanzel kneeled beside Henrick and felt for a pulse at his neck. He could feel a very faint pulse. *He's alive! But, only barely. He's just unconscious. Maybe a splash of water will wake him.* Hanzel walked to the barn where the horses greeted him. *They seem friendly.* Hanzel stroked the nose of a large horse with long hairs over its hooves. *This horse is huge.* He looked up at the big brown eyes looking down at him. The other horses looked on and made sounds as if they were jealous, except for one, who did not care for strangers.

Hanzel looked about for a bucket. Finding one, he filled it with water from the rain barrel outside. With the full bucket he walked back to Henrick, just as Meinheer van Hooven came out of the house.

'What are you doing?' he asked of Hanzel, who was walking towards Henrick.

'Good morning,' answered Hanzel. 'I'm going to splash water on Henrick, to see if he will wake up.'

Hanna's father came to stand beside Hanzel. He looked down at Henrick and then pointed at the ladder. 'He must have been trying to get into my daughter's room. Or maybe he was trying to elope with Hanna.' He looked up at the open window. 'HANNA!' he shouted. 'HANNA!' A moment later Hanna looked out of the window.

'What is it, Father?' she said sleepily.

'What was Henrick doing with a ladder at your window?' he asked.

Hanna regarded Henrick, as if for the first time. 'What happened? What's he doing down there? I have no idea, Father.'

'You were not trying to elope with him?'

Hanna shook her head. "With Henrick? Don't be absurd. I'm not interested in Henrick. I've told you that.'

'Yes, but he certainly has expressed interest in you,' replied her father. 'Not that I would approve of you marrying Henrick. I have a much better, richer man in mind for you.' He returned his gaze to Henrick. 'Alright, young man, pour the water on him.'

Hanzel upturned the bucket and poured the contents over Henrick's face. They waited but Henrick did not budge. Hanzel reached down and touched Henrick's chest. 'He's not breathing. I think he's dead.'

'Cracked his skull, most likely,' replied Meinheer van Hooven philosophically. 'Maybe he was a peeping Tom. Perhaps he was trying to get a glimpse of my daughter, naked. The pervert.' Meinheer van Hooven prodded Henrick with the toe of his wooden shoe. Henrick did not move. He was dead. Henrick was dead as a plank. So much for Henrick. He was buried the next day. People shrugged their shoulders afterwards. Lots of people died in strange ways in those days. Death was no big deal. Especially the deaths of simple farm hands.

'Well, are you coming with me to Amsterdam? I have to go there to visit my banker and take some things to resupply my market stall.' Meinheer van Hooven regarded Hanzel, who was looking up at Hanna, watching from her window.

'Actually, sir. I was hoping you might be able to give me work with room and board. I understand you are needing someone to look after your horses.' Hanzel shifted on his feet.

'What do you know about horses?'

'All kinds of things. What would you like to know?' *I'll stare into his eyes and appear confident. Hanna said she would teach me. I'm sure it's not ballistics science.*

Meinheer van Hooven regarded the confident young man for a moment. He scratched his chin and then slowly nodded. 'Alright. Since Henrick is dead, I need a hand with the horses, so alright. I will pay you a rijksdaalder a week and let you use the room you are in. You can eat in the kitchen with the staff.'

'Thank you,' replied Hanzel gratefully. 'I will take good care of your horses. How long will you be away?'

'Vrouw van Hooven and I will be gone for five days,' replied Hanna's father. 'Anyway, I must get ready. Welcome to Van Hooven Farm.'

Hanzel smiled.

Meinheer van Hooven pointed to the ladder. 'Please return the ladder to the barn, will you, Hanzel?'

'Yes sir,' replied Hanzel, grinning from ear to ear.

Chapter 25

For Hanzel, life on the farm was interesting and exciting, even. He had learned many things about horses, about their care, how to harness them, how to be firm when needed. Hanna taught Hanzel how to ride horses, as well. Many days were spent working and then, when the work was done, the two lovers rode off for a few hours in the evening. Until winter. In the winter they hitched the two heavy horses to a sleigh. When the weather was mild, there were even times when they made love, while parked on a path only the two lovers knew about.

Hanzel was well liked by everyone working on the Van Hooven Farm. Even, Margaret, grunted less objectionably and more favorably. That made visiting the kitchen more inviting. Eventually, Hanzel was able to come into the kitchen on his own and Margaret did not complain.

The winter blew some bitterly cold winds which made outdoor work very unpleasant. However, the horses still had to be fed and their stables kept clean. Hanzel didn't mind the work. However, it was not the life he really wanted. Hanzel did it for Hanna. He was deeply in love with her.

When Hanzel's third winter arrived at the farm and the year turned 1623, Hanzel was beginning to grow restless. The salt in his blood was pulling him seaward. He began discussing nautical plans with Hanna. To his great surprise, she was receptive.

One winter night in miserable February, Hanzel and Hanna were sitting on the sleigh, watching stars and talking, when Hanzel said, 'Why don't we take our money and buy a sloop. Then we'll recruit some good men and collectively arm the boat with swords, guns, crossbows, whatever we can get. Then we'll get ourselves a Letter of Marque and go privateering. Hanna you would love the life. I think it's possible we could even get ourselves a larger ship and go to Brazil or Mexico.'

'It sounds like a great idea, Hanzel,' replied Hanna. 'We've talked about this before. I'm willing to try it. If that's what would make you happy. I don't want to be without you.'

'You would have to dress like a man,' replied Hanzel. 'Pirates are suspicious about women on board a ship. Brings bad luck, they say.' Hanzel smiled. 'You can be my first mate.'

Hanna laughed. 'Your only mate.'

'I couldn't be happier,' replied Hanzel. Then he kissed her, long and tenderly, and whispered, 'I love you.'

That March the two young lovers left the farm. They did it at night. This time nobody fell off a ladder. And, it was returned to the barn and not left under Hanna's window. Not wanting to inconvenience anyone, they took one of the older, extra horses and no harness. The two able riders rode on the horse together; Hanzel in front. In a purse they carried a heavy collection of coins in silver and gold. The sun was just beginning to rise. The two fugitives were bathed in an orange glow.

'We'll sell Sally on Saturday at the market,' said Hanna. 'That's the day after tomorrow. I'm sure we'll still get some money for her.'

Sally snorted and looked back as if she was thinking, *what do you mean, still get some money for her?*

'I wonder if we could use her as part of the payment on a sloop. Do you suppose a boat seller could use her?' asked Hanzel.

Hanna shrugged. 'I've no idea. Would a boat seller use a horse?'

'For his carriage, maybe?' Hanzel shrugged. 'I don't know.'

'I think we should sell Sally Saturday so we're sure to have the money,' replied Hanna. 'Going to a boat seller and trying to trade her in is not a sure thing, I think.'

'I think you're right,' agreed Hanzel. 'We sell Sally Saturday.' He laughed. 'Sell, Sally, Saturday....

Hanna laughed. The two friends laughed for a long time together. Hanzel and Hanna loved to laugh. The more time they spent together, the more they laughed. When Hanzel made note of it, the mere fact he mentioned that they laughed a lot more together made them laugh all over again.

When they approached Amsterdam, they stopped laughing. They did not want to bring attention to themselves because the milling throng coming and going from the great city contained miscreants, pickpockets, and other vile manifestations of humanity sniffing for easy prey and purses; the fatter, the better.

'Don't worry,' said Hanzel, placing his right hand on the pommel of his cutlass. 'I still have this sword and know how to use it.'

'I'm not worried,' replied Hanna, smiling. She was enjoying the trip. She had only been to Amsterdam a few times in her life. The multitude pouring in and out of the north gate was a wonder to Hanna. On the farm she did not see so many people.

'I haven't been to Amsterdam for a long time. It will take me a little while to adjust and remember exactly how to get to the docks.'

'The docks?' Hanna raised her eyebrows.

'If we're going to buy a boat, we need to be near the docks. We can get a room at an inn on the waterfront and then find a sloop, or a pinnace, or something like that.'

'Are you sure we have enough money?'

'Remember, we're selling Sally on Saturday?'

Hanna nodded.

Hanzel burst out laughing.

Hanna turned to look at him and then also burst out laughing. For some reason the two of them found that business about Sally for sale on Saturday somehow very silly. They had no idea whose attention they attracted with their mirth on the back of the old horse.

'Look loike dose two don arf a care in da woild,' said a voice from a shadow next to the street.

'People who don arf a worry usually gots money,' said another voice from the darkness.

'We should foller dem. Dey don looks loike dey'd be much trubble. Jes a cupla kids,' said a third voice.

'I'd fancy a ride on de loikes of er,' said the first voice. 'Let's foller dem and see if'n we can't get ourselves suma dat pussy an dere money.'

'Aargh!' replied the third voice. 'Les go.'

The three men, to whom the voices belonged, stepped out of the darkness and began to follow Hanzel and Hanna. The first speaker was of medium height and build. He carried a pistol and a rapier. On his head he wore a woolen cap with a red feather. The second man was a beanpole with an emaciated face. He was wearing a long coat. A rapier hung by his side. The third man was built solid and hard. He was about five feet tall. His nose had been broken several times. On his head he wore a Spanish hat with an ostrich feather.

Hanzel and Hanna had no idea they were being followed and continued their merry way into the city alongside a busy canal carrying all manner of boats, some with freight, others without.

'The empty boats are going that way. They're likely going to pick up more freight from the harbour,' observed Hanzel.

'That makes sense,' replied Hanna, looking at the barges floating in the canal next to the street. As she followed a particularly heavily laden boat heading in the opposite direction to hers, she turned around to continue looking at the over loaded vessel. Before she returned her gaze forward she noticed the three men. Hanna noted their peculiar appearance but did not say anything to Hanzel, who was intent on watching ahead.

After they had ridden into the city for half an hour, following the empty boats along the canal the sound of more and more gulls began to fill the air.

'I think we're getting closer,' said Hanna.

Hanzel nodded. 'I can see masts.' He pointed. 'The port is just over there.'

A few moments later the street ended at a perpendicular roadway. Ships of many nations were tied to the piers. A busy hustle bustle permeated the place as thousands of people plied their trade, hauling, shipping, storing, taxing, entertaining sailors, keeping books, mending and repairing all manner of nautical stuff. The port clearly showed why Amsterdam was rich. One of the richest cities in the world.

It was already evening by the time the young couple reached the port. The sky was darkening and the moon was barely visible through gathering clouds. And yet, the hubbub continued, the cries of traders mixing with those of gulls. The port did not sleep. Stevedores hauled cargo, wagons, horses, mules, carts, and people were all busy doing their utmost to wreak whatever bit of extra money they could make to feed their needy families.

'I don't ever want to live like that,' observed Hanzel, gazing at the hard working laborers. 'I much prefer my life at sea.'

'You know that I've never been to sea,' replied Hanna. 'I've always lived on the farm.'

'Don't worry, you'll get used to it.' Hanzel pointed. 'Look, there's an inn. Let's check in there and see if they have a stable for Sally.'

'I'm tired. And hungry,' replied Hanna. 'Plus my backside is sore. I was hoping you'd want to stop.'

Hanzel directed Sally to the inn. He dismounted and tied the horse to the hitching post before assisting Hanna down. The two lovers stepped inside and were met by a young woman.

'Yes, can I help you?'

'We need a room for the night and a place for our horse,' replied Hanzel.

'We have a room available,' said the young woman. 'You can put your horse in the stable out back.'

'What do you charge?' asked Hanna.

'One gulden. If you want hot water and a meal that will be two guilders.'

'We have money,' replied Hanna. 'I am famished and would really like to have a hot bath.'

The young woman pointed up the stairs. 'The room is the second one on the left.'

'Thank you,' said Hanzel, handing the young woman two silver guilders. He pointed up the stairs. 'Go ahead, Hanna. You go up to the room. I'll put Sally away.'

Hanna smiled at Hanzel. 'I'll meet you upstairs.'

Hanzel smiled back, then turned on his heels and proceeded out of the building. As he approached the hitching post, the three miscreants who had been following them were there trying to untie Sally.

'Hey, what do you think you're doing with my horse?' asked Hanzel as he approached the thieves.

The three men regarded Hanzel for a moment before one of them, the man with the Spanish hat, told Hanzel to, 'piss off.' And that it was none of his business.

'What do you mean, it's none of my business?' asked Hanzel incredulously. 'That's my horse.'

The emaciated skeleton pulled a pistol out from under his coat and pointed it at Hanzel. 'If'n youse makes trubble, I'll puts a ball trou yer fore ed.'

'That horse is all we have. If you take our horse, we have nothing. Can't you give a young couple a break?' pleaded Hanzel, carefully eyeing the three misfits. *They don't look overly fit. Maybe I can take them by surprise? But, then , there are three of them, and it looks like they are well armed. Do I dare risk my life over a horse? Is it worth it?* Hanzel fingered the hilt of his cutlass.

The man wearing the woolen cap pointed at Hanzel. 'He's going fer is sword.'

'You watch it,' said the emaciated man pointing the pistol. 'Jes lets us toike yer orse an de'll be no trubble. We don wants ter kill nobuddy.'

I don't trust these slimy cockroaches. They'd as soon throw their mothers in a canal if they could wring a stuiver out of them. Hanzel eyed the skinny man's pistol and then regarded the other two, standing by Sally. They had undone her reins from the hitching post. The man with the Spanish hat was holding the leather straps with both hands. The shorter man was standing beside the horse, attempting to climb on her back.

Without warning, Sally reacted to the stranger trying to climb on her back. She tugged at the reins, which surprised the man who was holding them. The skinny man looked back to see what was going on. In that split instant Hanzel pulled out his sword and with one rapid slice, removed the hand holding the pistol. The man's hand and pistol dropped to the ground as the man emitted a terrible scream. He watched with bulging eyes as his stump spurted blood some distance.

Because the shorter man was trying to climb on the horse, he had no time to reach for a weapon, and the other man's hands were full with the reins of an unwilling horse. The shorter man felt a sharp object slice through his liver and come out through his lower back. The burning object twisted and was pulled back, taking a bit of his liver with it, as it stuck to the blade of Hanzel's swift sword. The man's eyeballs bulged as red hot blood spurted from his mouth, he having bit his tongue clean into two pieces, one of which he spat out just before he collapsed on the cobblestones in a gathering pool of blood.

Hanzel pointed his sword at the man with the Spanish hat. 'Please, I don wan any trubble. We was jes stealin yer orse.' He looked down at his two companions. 'Ur din af ter kill em?'

'I only killed that one,' replied Hanzel pointing to the shorter man lying crumpled up on the cobblestones. 'I just disarmed the skinny one.' He looked down at the emaciated man clutching his bleeding stump with a bloody handkerchief.

'Well, yer mite jes as well av killt im, cuttin is and off like dat.'

'I'm done with people stealing from me,' replied Hanzel. 'This is the last time I'll let anyone try to take something from me, do you hear me?' He threatened the man with his bloodied sword and reached for the reins with his other hand. 'Now give me back my horse.'

The man reluctantly handed over the reins.

Hanzel gestured with his free hand. 'Tie her back to the post.'

Fortunately Sally had settled down, likely realizing that Hanzel had her abductors under control. She happily nudged his shoulder. When Sally's reins were once again tied to the post, the man stood back and looked down at his groaning friend, sitting on the cobblestones holding his stump.

Hanzel picked up the severed hand with the point of his sword. The pistol dropped to the ground as he did so. 'You take this, and your disarmed friend over there and get away from here. If I see you again, I will kill you both, as well.' He shoved the grizzly trophy at the intact man, who had no choice but to accept it. He looked disgustedly down at the gory hand and then at his companion. 'Ees not gona need dis any more.' Without further thought he tossed the hand into the street. Instantly, a couple of dogs who were squabbling over a bone, rushed for the bleeding object. The bigger dog quickly grabbed the horrid hand; it having more meat on its bones and ran off with it firmly clenched in its teeth. 'We won ferget dis, Friesian. Jes ye watch yer back.'

'Ya. Jes watcher back, Friesian. Ye'll pay fer me and.' The mutilated man scowled at Hanzel. His eyes were filled with hatred and the fire of extreme pain.

'Get out of here, you scurvy dogs!' Hanzel menaced the men with his sword. 'If I see you again, I'll run you both through, just like your friend over there.' He pointed to the fallen thief on the ground. 'You just messed with the wrong man.'

The men backed away. Hanzel watched them go. When they disappeared around a corner, Hanzel reached down and picked up the pistol, which he stuck in his belt. Then he untied Sally and took her into the stable behind the inn. The two men returned to their liar; a leaky top floor tenement above a seedy tavern filled with the lowest forms of human life imaginable. Hanzel returned to Hanna, who was anxiously waiting for him.

'What happened to you?' was the first thing she said as he entered the room. 'You're covered in blood.'

Hanzel looked down at his clothes and saw the blood for the first time. He recoiled. 'Oh, no. I hope my clothes are not ruined.'

'Hanzel, never mind your clothes. Tell me what happened.'

'Horse thieves. They tried to steal Sally. I stopped them.' He showed her his bloodied sword. 'Disarmed one and sliced another.' Hanzel smiled. 'The third one was lucky.' He held up the pistol. 'And I got a pistol out of the bargain. A man can always use one of these in his belt.'

'Will we be in trouble with the authorities?' Hanna looked worried.

'Nobody saw anything. I doubt if those horse thieves will go to the police. So, don't worry.'

'Did anyone see you come in with those bloodied clothes?'

Hanzel shook his head as he began to remove his waistcoat.

'Here, let me help you with that,' said Hanna as she helped him out of his vest and shirt. Some of the blood had soaked through and stained his chest. 'Good thing I ordered hot water to be brought up. 'It should arrive soon, I should think.'

Hanzel smiled. Then he kissed Hanna tenderly. *I love this girl. My sweet and lovely Hanna. Her lips feel so good.*

A knock on the door interrupted their moment. 'Just a minute,' said Hanna as she quickly hid the bloodied shirt and vest under the bed. When the clothes were hidden she gestured for Hanzel to open the door. The young woman who had received them was standing in the hallway holding two large pails of steaming hot water. 'Here's your hot water.' She stepped into the room and set the pails down. Then she started towards the bed. 'The wash basin is under the bed.'

Hanna immediately intercepted her. 'Oh, that's fine. I'll pull it out. Thank you very much for bringing the water. Until what hour are you serving food?'

'Food is served at all hours. The tavern is where many sailor folk and travelers come to drink and eat until dawn. Then it starts all over again.'

'Excellent,' replied Hanzel. 'We'll be down for food later. Thank you. You may go now.' He held the door open and smiled as the young woman left the room. He watched her for a moment and closed the door.

Hanna pointed to his pantaloons. They were also spattered with blood. 'It's a good thing she kept looking at your naked chest and didn't notice those,' she said.

'I'm sure it's not so unusual around here for people to have blood on their clothes. Ports are notorious places where people live lives far different from those of genteel farmers like you and your parents.'

'I guess we had better be careful, then,' replied Hanna as she pulled the wash basin out from under the bed. 'Take those bloodied clothes off, Hanzel.'

'What will I wear to go eat, then?'

'I'll have food sent up. I'll give the girl an extra stuiver.'

Hanzel nodded. 'Alright. We can bathe and then I'll wash the clothes in the soapy water afterwards.'

Hanna smiled. 'You're so smart, Hanzel.' She kissed him warmly as she helped him out of the rest of his clothes. Then she poured the hot water into the small tub.

'I think you should have the first water,' said Hanzel.

Hanna smiled. 'Thank you, Hanzel.' She turned her back to him. 'Please help me with my straps.'

And so Hanzel undressed his girl. Then they bathed each other, drying off on a soft towel provided with the room. Afterward they enjoyed a delicious meal of roasted pork, chicken, potatoes, cabbage, carrots, peas, and a flagon of wine. The two lovers satiated themselves and became quite drunk on the fermented juice. Eventually they fell into each other's arms on the soft bed and did not wake until far into the next morning.

Chapter 26

Next morning Hanzel and Hanna woke up excited to get their day started. First thing Hanzel did was to throw open the shutters of the little window looking out over the courtyard where the stable was located.

'Hmm, it smells good out there.' Hanzel took a deep breath. 'The kitchen must be below this room. Breakfast is ready, I think.'

'I'm hungry,' replied Hanna, yawning. She stretched her arms, tightening her magnificent breasts. Hanzel could not help but stare at her. *She's so beautiful. I sure do love this girl.*

'I can't wait to go boat shopping. Not that I expect we'll be able to buy much with Sally and the money we have, but it'll buy us something to start with.' Hanzel looked at the sky. 'I think it will be a nice day today.'

'Why don't you go to De Wittt's and borrow money from them?'

'I just can't go back there. The memories are too painful.'

Hanna nodded. 'I understand. It must have been tough on you to watch your friends...'

Hanzel stared at Hanna for a moment, a sad expression on his handsome face. He nodded slowly. 'One of the saddest days of my life.' Tears welled up in his eyes as he visualized the tragic event at the Tower of London.

To get his mind off the horror he was seeing, Hanna handed him his shirt. 'It's dry now. It looks as if most of the stains are gone. If you button your waistcoat over your chest, nobody will notice, really.'

Hanzel snapped out of the hellish vision and looked at Hanna. He smiled ruefully. 'Thank you,' he said as he accepted the shirt from her. He put it on quickly followed by the rest of his ensemble. Hanna, too, got dressed quickly. When they were done they went downstairs into the tavern and ordered potato pancakes, herrings, and ale.

After breakfast they left the inn by the back door leading to the courtyard and the stable. Sally was happy to see her friends. She snorted and stamped her feet as she saw Hanzel and Hanna cross the yard.

Hanzel stroked Sally's nose and then let her out of the stall. Outside, he climbed on her back and pulled Hanna up behind him. Then they clomped out of the courtyard. As they came to the hitching post the cadaver of the short man was still lying in its pool of coagulating blood. A dog was sniffing at its groin, while another was gnawing on a hand. Flies were buzzing about. Several onlookers were staring at the corpse.

Hanna screwed up her face. 'Euw. Is that the man you killed?' she whispered.

Hanzel nodded discreetly. As they passed the deceased, Hanzel pointed at the remains and said to the people standing there looking down at the victim, 'Someone ought to clean that mess up. Are there no authorities over such matters in this city?'

The people looked up at Hanzel for a moment. They all nodded and agreed with the blond Friesian, but nobody moved to call the police. With no further interest in Hanzel, they returned their gaze to the corpse. One of the men, a tall fellow wearing a tall black hat, prodded the cadaver with the toe of his left boot.

Hanzel shrugged his shoulders and urged Sally on. He and Hanna did not give the corpse another thought. Instead, they turned their attention to the search for a buyer for Sally and a boat for sale.

'Why exactly do we want to buy this boat? You never really said. I mean, I know you want to go back to sea, Hanzel, but why buy a boat and not hire on with a ship?'

Hanzel turned his head and regarded Hanna for a moment. 'With our own boat, if it is big enough, we can convince some honest, brave men to join us to get my treasure back from those fishermen. With our own boat we don't have to answer to anybody else. And, besides, you can come along.' He smiled. 'I don't want to go on adventures without you Hanna.' Hanzel's eyes sparkled. 'I have fallen in love with you. I don't want to go anywhere without you.'

Hanna stared into Hanzel's eyes. Tears began to flow down her cheeks.

Hanzel was shocked. 'Why, what's the matter? You're crying, Hanna.'

Hanna shook her head and hugged Hanzel tightly. 'Oh, Hanzel. I love you too. I loved you the moment I saw you.' As she said the words Hanna looked past Hanzel's shoulder. A collision was imminent. 'Hanzel, watch out!'

As Hanzel jerked his head forward, he saw just in the nick of time that Sally was headed straight into the path of an oncoming wagon stacked with heavy hogsheads. Hanzel jerked her reins to the right, just as the wagon rolled past, nearly taking their left legs with it.

It took Hanzel and Hanna a moment to regain their senses.

'I guess I had better keep an eye on the road,' said Hanzel, much chagrined. 'I think that Sally is blind.' *My God, my God, if we had been hit by that wagon. I have to take better care of my angel. I can't let anything happen to her.* Hanzel straightened up and watched the busy port traffic on the roadway they were clomping along.

The morning air was chilly. It was only March, and winter still had an icy grip on Amsterdam. A cold breeze was blowing in from the sea. The sky was crystal clear. The air was filled with the busy sounds of commerce helping to make Amsterdam even richer.

When they had clomped along the roadway for forty minutes, or so, Hanna pointed. 'Look there, Hanzel. Look at that boat there. Is that not a, FOR SALE sign?'

Hanzel looked to where Hanna pointed. Indeed, there lay a little sloop for sale. From his vantage point the vessel looked ship shape enough, however, without a proper inspection, who knows what problems might have accrued.

Hanzel steered Sally to the boat and dismounted. He helped Hanna down. Then he tied Sally to a cleat on the edge of the roadway, to which the sloop was moored. When he stood up he looked the sloop over. 'She appears to be in good shape.'

'So, what kind of boat is this?' asked Hanna. 'I don't know anything about boats. Except a row boat. I went in a row boat once. On a canal.'

'It's a sloop.' Hanzel pointed at the mast. 'See, it only has one mast.' He pointed to the boom. 'That long spar is the boom and holds the bottom of the mainsail.' He looked around to see if there was anyone they could talk to.

Hanna examined the sign. 'It says here to see Mister Goldman who has a shop just over there. Hanna pointed to a small mercantile establishment on the first floor of a six story building facing the port. 'Let's go talk to him.'

Hanzel nodded. 'Let's go talk to him.' He untied Sally from the cleat and then the three friends walked over to Mister Goldman's place of business. Hanzel tied Sally to the railing in front of the shop and then he and Hanna stepped inside. The powerful smell of expensive tobacco permeated the space which was filled with all manner of nautical supplies; back staves, astrolabes, compasses of various kinds, charts, books, geographer's tools, telescopes…

Mister Goldman was sitting at a desk behind piles of papers, boxes, and assorted miscellanies. A fat Sumatra cigar was just beginning its slow burn in his fat lipped mouth. He was barely there; he not being very tall. His gaunt little face was barely visible in his huge, tangled beard, making his head look unproportionally large under his silk tasseled cap, identifying his religious persuasion.

'Yes, yes. What do you want? What do you want?' asked the man irritably, staring over his thick lensed spectacles.

'We want to inquire about the sloop for sale,' replied Hanzel. 'How much are you asking for her?'

The man eyed Hanzel with a pair of watery eyes. Then he stared at Hanna. 'Who's this? Your wife?'

Hanzel regarded the little man for a moment before replying. He looked at Hanna and smiled.

'Yes, she's my wife. This is Hanna.'

Hanna was grinning from ear to ear. 'How do you do,' she cooed.

'Hmph,' replied the irritated little merchant. 'So you want to buy that sloop, do you?' He eyed the young couple. 'Do you have money? You don't look like you have money.'

'How much do you want for the sloop?' asked Hanzel, once again.

The man rubbed his chin. 'How much do I want for the sloop? How much, you ask?' He opened a thick, leather ledger and turned some pages. 'Let me see. How much do I want for that sloop out there?' He wrote some figures on a piece of paper and did some calculations.' All the while that he was figuring he muttered to himself.

As the boat merchant was figuring, a second little man walked into the shop. Hanzel and Hanna had to do a second take to see they were not seeing double. The second man looked identical to the first man. He nodded to the young couple before greeting Mister Goldman. 'Good morning to you, Joseph,' he said cheerfully.

'Hmmph,' replied Mister Goldman. 'Isaac, what are we asking for that sloop? That dark blue one tied across the road?' He tapped irritably at the ledger.

Isaac stood still for a moment and thought. 'It just came in. We have not had time to really go over it. You must buy it as is. The price is five hundred Florins.'

Hanzel looked at Hanna and she back at him.

'We don't have that much, even with Sally,' whispered Hanzel.

Hanna looked into the purse and frowned. 'What do we do now?'

'We have a horse,' said Hanzel pointing outside.

The two men stared at Hanzel.

'You have a horse,' confirmed Joseph staring over his fat spectacles.

'Yes. We have a horse for sale. Her name is Sally. She's a really good horse. Well bred. Comes from Hanna's farm. She should be worth a few hundred florins, I should think.' Hanzel looked at Hanna, who was nodding agreement to what he had said.

'Sally comes from a long line of very good horses, back to the days of my great grandparents who began the farm,' said Hanna encouragingly.

Joseph looked at Isaac. 'They have a horse. What do you make of that? A horse.'

Isaac shook his head. 'I don't know, Joseph. What do we do with a horse?'

'I am a boat seller. I sell nautical gear and supplies. I am not a horse dealer.' Joseph regarded Isaac. 'Does it look like we sell equestrian gear, Isaac? Is there a sign anywhere near this shop which indicates we deal in horse flesh? I ask you Isaac.'

Hanzel and Hanna realized it was hopeless attempting to deal with Mister Goldman and his twin. 'Let's go,' said Hanzel quietly to Hanna. 'Thank you for your time, gentlemen,' said Hanzel amiably as he and Hanna stepped out of the shop. They could hear Joseph berating Isaac, as if it was his fault. 'They have a horse, indeed. Indeed, Isaac.'

'Well, that was a waste of time,' said Hanzel, regarding Sally calmly standing there looking at them. 'Maybe we need to go to a different place to sell Sally. There has to be a horse market. Let's go find it, then we can come back.'

'What if we still don't get enough for Sally? Five hundred florins is a lot of money. Do you think a horse is worth that much?'

Hanzel thought for a moment as he regarded Hanna. 'It all depends on the horse's pedigree. Maybe we can build up Sally's pedigree to someone who doesn't know much about horses.'

Hanna regarded Sally. 'He would have to be pretty gullible. And don't take this personally, Sally, but, you're not exactly the best looking horse in the land.'

'Well, if worse comes to worse, we'll just steal the sloop.' Hanzel looked towards the blue boat tied beside the roadway. 'She looks seaworthy enough. The two of us can sail her.'

'I've never been to sea, Hanzel. What do I know about sailing? And, besides, stealing isn't exactly a good way to get ahead in life. It could get you hanged.'

Hanzel smiled at his girlfriend. 'Don't worry Hanna. I have a plan. Let's first go sell the horse.'

'As long as your plan doesn't get us killed,' replied Hanna dubiously.

'Don't worry. I know this will work. Let's go find a buyer for Sally.'

The two friends climbed onto Sally's back and rode off in search of the livestock market, which, as it turned out, was not far from where they were. As they approached the place a whole new set of smells attacked their nostrils. Instead of fish, rotting aquatic flotsam, and the mingled smells of tar, excrement, and urine their noses were now filled with the smells of animals; goats, pigs, cows, chickens, horses, cats, and dogs; all of which left their odiferous byproducts to collect in steaming piles in dirty pens. Mud and filth was everywhere.

Hanzel screwed up his nose. 'I don't know which is worse, this place or the port.'

'Oh, I'd say the port is far smellier,' said Hanna.

'Yes, but you come from a farm. You're used to these smells,' replied Hanzel.

'Yes, but never in such concentration as this place. Even I find the air foul. But, it's natural. Animals have to poop, just as we do.' Hanna pointed. 'Look, over there. Horses.'

Hanzel nodded and steered Sally over to the horse sellers. Three corpulent gentlemen farmers were standing by some horses discussing matters pertaining to the horse trade. Hanzel asked if they knew if anyone was looking for a horse to buy.

'Buy the horse you are riding?' asked one of the men, dressed in the black of a reformed believer.

'Vy zat horrs iz nott vurth zending to ze nakkers,' laughed the man who was standing in the middle. He was wearing a tall, black hat. 'I vuldn't giff yu ten florins fer it.'

Hanzel turned and looked at Hanna. 'Now at least we have a price to start with,' he chuckled.

'If you make it one fifty, you have a deal,' replied Hanzel. 'This horse comes from a long line of excellent farm horses, good for work and riding.'

The third man smiled and spat an oyster into the mud. Hanna saw it and cringed. *That's so disgusting.*

'Fifty florins, for that hag is fifty too many,' said the reformer.

'Now we're getting somewhere,' said Hanzel to Hanna. 'Now we've got em at fifty.'

Hanna smiled and gave him a squeeze.

'I'll tell you what,' said Hanzel, looking deep into the men's' eyes. 'Since we're from out of town and we need some money, I'll let you have her for one seventy five.'

'One seventy five?' asked the third man. 'I thought you said one fifty?' His belly indicated that business was good.

'He can easily afford it, by the looks of him,' whispered Hanzel to Hanna.

Hanna smiled and nodded. 'See if they'll bid higher.'

Hanzel regarded the three men. 'So, is it going to be one seventy five?'

'But, but, I thought you said one fifty before,' said the protestant.

'Yes, that was a moment ago, when you had the chance to buy Sally for one fifty. However, the longer you wait, the price goes up. Inflation, you see,' replied Hanzel cockily. 'It eats at our savings like worms feed on corpses.'

The three horse traders looked at each other with exasperated expressions.

'I neffer erd of zucha ting,' said the man with the taller hat, looking from one colleague to the other. 'Haf eider of you?'

The other two shook their heads.

Then the three men looked back at the horse before walking up to Sally, who started back. Hanzel held her reins and steadied the nervous animal. 'She isn't used to strangers,' apologized Hanzel.

'That's alright,' said the third man, spitting into the mud. 'We're used to that.'

'She looks a sturdy horse,' said the first man. Hanna noted that he had a pair of large mustaches and a pointy beard. The man examined Sally's teeth.

Hanna regarded the man for a moment before replying. *By the looks of him, he's worth a few florins. I think he'll buy her.* 'Oh, she's sturdy, alright,' said Hanna. 'Good strong legs. She comes from very sturdy stock. Her dam was *Southern Sunshine Sally* and her sire was called, *Long Wind Storming*. Perhaps you heard of him?'

The three men looked at each other and shook their heads.

'Neffer erd of em,' said the man with the taller hat.

'That's no matter,' said the first man. 'The horse looks in good shape. I'll give you one sixty and not a stuiver more.'

The man with the taller hat looked at his colleague. Hanzel could tell that he was not one to let someone get the better of him. 'I vill gif yu vun zeventie.'

Hanzel frowned. 'I had said one seventy five. Now you are still trying to get Sally for less than I said.' He looked in the sky for a moment. 'Oh, darn. There is that terrible inflation again. Sally is now worth one ninety five.'

The three men looked up to the sky then back at Hanzel.

The man with the tall hat regarded his colleagues. 'Ve need horses. Zat looks like a gute horse.'

'Yes, but do you want to pay more than one seventy five?' asked the reformer.

The three men looked back at Sally and then returned to their huddle.

'Ve neet horses.' The man with the tall hat turned and pointed at the horses in the pen. 'Ve haf only fife horses left.'

'Yes but can we get more than one seventy five for that horse?' asked the third man.

'That's the question,' replied the first man, looking over his shoulder at the horse, still bearing the young couple.

'Horses are in short supply because of the war,' said the third man, spitting another fat gob into the mud.

'Alright, I'll pay you one ninety five,' agreed the first man, untying his fat purse from his belt.

The man with the taller hat looked at his colleague. 'Nott zo vast. I vill giff yu too hunret fife.'

The third man looked into his purse. 'I'll give you two fifteen.'

'Too tventy fife.' The man pushed his tall hat back and stared at his colleagues, defying them to bid higher.

'Two thirty five.' The first man stared at the man with the taller hat, who looked back and forth at his two colleagues.

'Two fifty! I'll give you two fifty for her,' said the third man. 'But, really, that is all we could get for her. So, I'm buying out of the goodness of my heart, to help a young couple in need.'

'You wouldn't even help your dear, old mother if she was in need, Johan. Why would you help two strangers?' asked the first man. Hanzel noticed he had long black hairs growing out of his nostrils, which blended into his mustaches. They quivered as he spoke.

'Well, I am feeling good about life today,' replied the third man, expansively, opening his arms to the world and sticking his ample stomach out.

'Vell, I'm out. I don van ter pay any more dan dat,' said the man with the tall hat. He regarded the first man who nodded.

'I'm out. You can have her, Johan.' The first man clapped his hands together and smiled. 'She's all yours.'

Hanzel looked impatiently at the three gentlemen traders. 'If that is the highest bid, we'll take it and with thanks.' He climbed down from Sally and then helped Hanna. The third man handed Hanzel a leather bag full of coins.

'That's two hundred and fifty florins,' said the man handing over the leather bag.

'Shouldn't I count it first?' asked Hanzel, eyeing the man.

'Count it? Count it? Why, don't you trust me?' asked the third man, taken aback.

'Well, I don't know you, or your friends. What if there is less than two fifty in the bag?' Hanzel regarded the man closely.

'That is how I carry my money here at the stock market. I put bags of two hundred and fifty florins into a strong box. Either I have to add or subtract some. However, two hundred fifty is a fairly standard price for lots of horses that come and go from here. Yours is an average horse. Good natured, I can see. She'll be a good horse for somebody for a good five or ten years, yet. Two fifty is a fair price for me to pay for an animal I may have to feed for a while, before I sell her. Hence, I know I can make a reasonable return on her if I don't have to feed her too long, that is. She'll brush up fine. She may even go to war, who knows?'

Sally whinnied and fussed at her reins.

'I am happy to have come to you,' said Hanzel. He held out his hand. 'My name is Hanzel Sventska and she is my,' he looked at Hanna who was smiling at him. *What is she? Is she my wife? We're not really married. But I want to be with her. She did like it when I agreed with Mister Goldman. Should I say wife, or girl friend, or what? She's my best friend?* 'She's my best friend, Hanna.' He noted that Hanna's eyes continued to sparkle. Hanzel got the impression it did not matter what he called her as long as it was all good. She was in love with him and he was definitely growing ever more in love with her. *But to call her wife. That just doesn't work in our society. But what do I care about that? I don't really care for society. It's all so corrupt and stupid.*

The third man introduced himself as, Johan van der Stroom and his two colleagues; the man with the taller hat was named, Pieter van Pietersdorp, and the first man was named, William de Bakker. Everyone shook hands after which Hanzel and Hanna said goodbye to Sally. She appeared sad but resigned to her fate. Hanzel and Hanna were content she was in good hands. When they were done, they waved a final goodbye to the three horse traders and left that smelly place to replace it for another smelly place; the roadway of the Port of Amsterdam.

'You know what we can do with this money,' said Hanzel as they were walking away from the market. 'We can hire us a few helpers. Since I am no longer concerned about taking things from people anymore; lots has been taken from me, that I'm tired of it. Anyway, I doubt if Mister Goldman is suffering financial ruin. A missing sloop won't be a major inconvenience. He probably has it insured, anyway. So, we hire some helpers and steal the sloop; when the night is dark and it is miserable with hazy rain. We'll slip her moorings and slide her out to sea. If we have enough money we can buy some weapons, as well. Then we can return to that fishing village and get my treasure back; whatever is left of it.'

'Why not just start fresh, with the men and the sloop? Forget about the treasure. Those fishermen have probably spent it long ago on the things the village needed. So it probably went to good, not evil, ' said Hanna wisely. 'Storming that village could get some of you killed. What good would that do?' Hanna indicated the ships in the harbour. 'Look out there. Hundreds of ships; many with precious cargos, come and go from here. Surely we can effect a little local larceny and not have to take such risks.'

'It is true, those merchant ships are generally only lightly manned and armed. And, that sloop looks like a fast sail boat. She'll carry at least twenty.' Hanzel rubbed his chin as he looked at Hanna walking beside him. ' You know, Hanna, I think you have the makings of a pirate in you.'

'I've always thought there was something right about pirates,' replied Hanna. 'I know I don't know a lot about boats and such, but I do know something about pirates. Pirates are generally sailors who live a much happier life on board their ships; the work load is lighter and the potential rewards greater than serving in the navy or merchant marine. I know that much. And, besides, when you think about it. Those wealthy traders basically steal goods for a song from poor people in Indonesia and the Caribbean and sell it here for exorbitant prices, while having paid their sailors with whips and a pittance for risking their lives through waves and weather.' Hanna smiled. 'I guess you can say that I've given it some thought over the years. My great uncle was a pirate and so was his sister. He was eventually caught and hanged, while she, being pregnant at the time, was able to escape the noose and disappeared.'

Hanzel stopped walking and looked at Hanna. 'That's fantastic, Hanna. I didn't know you had piracy in your blood!' Hanzel quickly realized he was standing in a place where he could be overheard. He looked about to see if anyone had been listening. Nobody was paying him or her the slightest mind as people continued on their sundry paths. 'Hanna, I know that you and I are going to make a great team. We'll go to sea and do piracy right. We'll steal from the rich and we'll give it to the poor. What say you?'

Hanna did not say anything. She simply stepped closer and then hugged him for the longest time. Finally she said. 'I can't wait to get started.'

Hanzel, grinning from ear to ear, took her hand and began to walk faster in order to get to their inn and begin talking with prospective Brothers of the Coast. 'I can't wait.'

As they approached the inn a loud voice rang out.

'DERE E IS!' DAT'S IM!'

Hanzel and Hanna looked in the direction the voice came from. Hanzel immediately recognized the tall man from the night before.

'Dat's the murderer. He murdered my brudder an cut my fren's and orf!' shouted the man. He had brought some official looking men with him.

'I think he's brought the police,' said Hanzel.

Hanna looked worried. 'What're we going to do now?'

'Just relax. Let me handle this. After all, they did try to steal Sally.' I was perfectly in my rights. Before I disarmed the pistol holder, he was going to shoot me.'

When Hanzel and Hanna approached the front of the inn, the shouting man pointed at Hanzel. 'Arrest im. E dun it. E cut my frens and orf. An e kilt me brudder.'

'They tried to steal my horse,' said Hanzel calmly.

'What horse?' asked the most officious looking of the three policemen.

'The one Hanna and I sold in the market place this morning,' replied Hanzel.

The officious policeman looked at the people standing around. 'Did any of you see them with a horse?'

Nobody in the crowd spoke up.

'The girl in the inn.' Hanzel pointed at the front door. 'Last night. When we arrived, we asked the girl about a place for Sally. You can ask her. She'll confirm that we had a horse.'

'What is the girl's name?' asked the policeman.

'Vy are ve vasting time mit all dis? E kilt my brudder, and chopt up my fren. E shud ang!' shouted the angry horse thief.

The policeman looked at the man and told him to be quiet. Then he instructed one of the other men to fetch the girl.

The accuser pointed at Hanzel's belt. 'Dere! Look dere! Dat's my fren's pistol. E's got it stuck in is belt! E stole my fren's pistol.'

'I didn't steal it. He dropped it,' replied Hanzel.

'E dropt it bcoz you cut is and orf!' shouted the man.

'He was going to shoot me with it. I acted in self defense.' Hanzel slowly pulled the pistol from his belt.

The policemen reacted and jumped back and reached for their pistols.

'No, no. Relax,' said Hanzel, holding the pistol by the barrel. 'I'm not going to shoot anybody.'

The policemen relaxed and put their pistols back in their belts. 'You have to be careful with those things. Could get a fellow killed.'

'Well, that's what I thought last night when his friend pointed it at me,' said Hanzel.

'An wha bout my brudder? Did yer af ter kill im?'

'That is what happens to horse thieves,' replied Hanzel calmly.

The officious policeman shook his head. 'We can't be taking the law into our own hands,' he said self righteously.

Hanzel stared at the policeman and then glanced at Hanna who shrugged her shoulders. 'Better not argue with the man,' she whispered. Hanzel nodded and returned his gaze to the policeman.

'The girl is not working today,' said the third policeman as he stepped out of the front door of the inn. 'Nobody else knows anything about a horse in connection to those two.' He pointed at Hanzel and Hanna.

'Where is the body of the dead man?' asked the officious policeman.

'It vas rite ere,' replied the accuser. He pointed to the place where his brother had fallen and ran to it. 'See, you can still see a puddel of blud ere.'

The three policemen stepped over to the puddle of blood, followed by the onlookers.

'Dat's vere e kilt my brudder mit is sord.' The horse thief stared menacingly at Hanzel.

'A horse could have been here,' said one of the subordinate policemen. He pointed to a relatively fresh pile of glistening road apples. 'That would have been dumped last night some time.'

'That confirms a horse,' replied the first policeman. 'But not necessarily their horse.'

'You can go to the market and talk to the horse traders. We just came from there,' said Hanna beginning to become frustrated.

'There was a body lying there early this morning,' volunteered one of the by standers. 'I have no idea what happened to it.'

The chief policeman looked at the horse thief. 'Did you remove the body?'

The man shook his head. 'No.'

'Why did you not remove your dead brother's remains?' asked the policeman incredulously.

'I ad ter attend to me fren who was bleedin ter det,' replied the man. 'An beside, I ad ter get elp. I cudn't carry me brudder by me sef and me fren ad only one and on account a im.' He gestured towards Hanzel.

'And what about the hand? You claim that he cut your friend's hand off. Where is the hand and where is your disarmed friend?' asked the policeman.

'A dog ran orf mid da and.' A woman amongst the bystanders gasped. 'An me fren, e's at ome, tendin ter is bleedin stump.'

'Alright, take us to your friend,' said the policeman. He gestured towards Hanzel and Hanna. 'Do not leave Amsterdam. We may have to question you further.' He pointed to the inn. 'Will you be staying here?'

Hanzel nodded.

'Ar you not going ter arrest im?' asked the horse thief. 'I tell you e kilt me brudder.'

'I do not see a body,' replied the policeman as he pointed down the road. 'Come. Let us find your friend.'

Momentarily the two burly police officers took the horse thief by the arms and led him off down the roadway.

'Where did you say your friend lives?' asked the chief policeman as they walked away.

Hanzel and Hanna watched them walk down the road for a moment before entering the inn. Once inside they quickly went up to their room and happily lay down on the comfortable bed.

'I think we should go to a different inn,' suggested Hanna. 'The police know you are here. They may find the body and get more evidence from the disarmed man.' She shook her head with a worried expression on her pretty face. 'I have a bad feeling about this.'

Hanzel smiled. 'I think you're right, Hanna. Let's gather up our stuff and get out of here. We've already paid so we can just leave.'

Hanna nodded and began to organize what little baggage they had. Five minutes later they left the inn and headed into town, away from the port; to find another inn and thusly lose themselves deep within the teeming multitudes of Amsterdam.

Chapter 27

De Dikke Boer was an old run down inn along a busy canal. Noise pervaded the place as boatmen shouted to each other, maneuvering their loaded barges along the narrow waterway. The loathsome smells of rotting things and sewage floated along the water and in the narrow street. The sky had turned grey and portended rain in the near future. The air had become damp and chilly.

'Let's get inside,' said Hanna, shivering. 'I'm beginning to get cold.'

Hanzel looked up at the dreary sky. 'Hopefully they have a place for us,' he replied, returning his gaze towards the inn. 'It looks affordable.'

'Hopefully they have good food,' said Hanna, touching her stomach. 'I could use a meal.'

'Me too,' said Hanzel as he opened the door for her. As the two friends entered the inn, the succulent smells of roasted flesh and cooking vegetables filled their nostrils. 'I think we've come to the right place.'

Hanna nodded. 'It seems to be a popular place to eat, that's for sure.'

The large room was filled with diners; happily eating and babbling about their affairs and schemes, filling the space with enough noise so that Hanzel and Hanna had to raise their voices to be heard.

Hanna pointed to a table at the far end of the spacious room. 'There appears to be two places over there.'

Hanzel nodded and walked over to the place Hanna had indicated. A moment later the two comrades were sitting side by side on a bench at a table. On either side sat several sailors slurping soup and across from them some sleazy characters were deeply into their cups. Their half eaten meals still sitting steaming before them.

A corpulent waiting woman waltzed wearily over to Hanzel. She stood over him for a moment savoring a look at the handsome young man. Then after a long, deep breath she asked, 'what'll it be? D'yer wants ter eat or are yer ere jes ter drink yer fill?'

Hanzel was momentarily stuck for words as his eyes took her in. *The poor thing was beaten with an ugly stick. It is so sad how some people end up looking like that.* Hanzel crinkled his nose. *Not only is she fat and ugly, she smells bad, too.* 'Oh, no. That is, we are not here to drink our fill, as you say. We are here for a meal, a drink, and hopefully a room, or at least a place to sleep for the night.'

The woman snorted and stared down her bulbous nose at the two lovers. 'Oh, so ye'll be wantin' a room, will yer?' She narrowed her eyes. 'Are yer married, den? Let me see yer rings.'

'We don't have rings,' replied Hanna quickly. 'We were married in a civil ceremony at my father's farm.'

'That's one of the reasons we came to Amsterdam,' added Hanzel. 'To buy rings.'

The elephantine woman grunted. 'We arf a room available. It'll cost yer three guilders per nite. If you arf a meal an two drinks each, yer can arf all of it for five guilders a nite.'

'Sounds good to me. We'll need the room for at least a week.'

The woman nodded. 'The weekly rate with the daily meal is twenty five guilders.'

'What's for dinner?' Hanzel smiled as he reached into the purse and extracted twenty five guilders.

'Roasted beef, pork, venison, broiled herrings, kippers, or oysters with boiled leeks, onions, beets, beans, and Brussels sprouts. You can drink ale, Jenever, or wine.' The fat woman huffed and puffed to catch her wind.

'I'll have the pork with white wine,' answered Hanna.

'And I'll have the broiled herrings with ale,' said Hanzel, already starting to salivate at the thought of the meal forthcoming.

The woman nodded as Hanzel handed her the twenty five guilders. 'I will let the inn keeper know that you paid for the empty room.' She pointed to the stair case. 'It's the third door on the left.' Then she shuffled off to process the order.

'I can't wait to eat,' said Hanzel happily looking into the purse the horse trader had given him. 'I wonder how many men we can buy with this money.'

'Are you sure it's the best thing we can do with it?' asked Hanna, looking at the purse Hanzel was holding in his lap; hiding it so others would not see it.

'Hanna. If we can get back some or all of that treasure, we can finance a really interesting future for ourselves.'

'Yes, I understand that, Hanzel. But what if you're killed. Then what?' Hanna looked deep into Hanzel's blue eyes. 'If you're dead, what kind of future will that turn out to be? You'll be gone and I'll still be here, without you. I don't want that. Do you?'

Hanzel regarded his girl friend for a moment before replying. He shook his head slowly. 'Well, no. I don't want to die and go somewhere without you. However, if we have enough men, I can't see there will be any problem. The village is not very large. And, besides, they're just ignorant fishermen. They'll be no match against some hardened sailors with treasure on their minds.' He returned his attention to the contents of the purse. 'You know Hanna, I think that horse seller cheated us. I don't think there's two hundred florins in here, let alone two fifty.'

'Don't forget you just gave that woman twenty five guilders.' Hanna looked in the direction the serving woman had gone. 'You didn't accidentally give her more, did you?'

Hanzel shook his head. 'No, of course not. You saw me give it to her.'

'Well, the only way to tell for sure is to empty the purse completely out and count each coin,' suggested Hanna.

'Empty the purse? What, here? On the table in front of all of these people?' Hanzel stared at the sleazy crew sitting opposite.

'No, not here. When we get upstairs. Hopefully we're not sharing the room with anyone.'

'Let's hope so. For twenty five guilders, the room better be ours alone.' Hanzel looked past Hanna's shoulder. The serving woman was shuffling in their direction with a platter loaded with boards of food and tankards of libations. 'Here comes our food. I can already smell it.'

Hanna turned just as the woman arrived at their table. 'I've gots yer food fer yer. An yer drinks.' She set the food and drinks on the table in front of Hanna and Hanzel, over whom she lingered a bit longer than was required. Hanna wrinkled up her nose due to the unfortunate odours emanating from the corpulent servant. 'Boss says yer fine ter stay in dat room wat is vacant. I'll bring yer a key wen I picks up yer empty boards.' The fat woman snorted and then turned on her heels to deliver the rest of the food on her tray to some boisterous characters sitting at a table behind Hanzel and Hanna.

The food smelled delicious. The two friends quickly dug in. As they ate, Hanzel discussed the issue of the possible short change from the horse trader. 'If it's true, I'll go back there and do him some harm,' said Hanzel tersely. 'I am so sick and tired of people stealing from me.'

'Hanzel, just forget about it for now. When we get the key, we'll go upstairs and count the money. You probably miscounted it yourself. The horse trader seemed honest enough. You thought so.'

Hanzel nodded and then bit off a piece of herring. 'Hmm, this herring is really good.'

Hanna smiled and happily munched on a piece of roasted pork.

When they were done, the fat woman brought them a key. As she began to clear the table, she reminded them that the room was the third door on the left.

Hanzel thanked her. He wasted no more time sitting there watching the serving blob clear the table. He and Hanna quickly headed upstairs and located their room. The key scraped in the old lock. Momentarily the two lovers were standing in a small room with a big bed against the far wall, under the window.

'Quick, open the shutters,' said Hanna. 'It smells stuffy in here.'

Hanzel opened the shutters, flooding the room with the dreary light of an overcast day. 'I think it's going to rain any moment.'

Hanna lay back on the bed. 'Oh, that meal sure stuffed me up. I could fall asleep about now.'

Hanzel smiled as he opened the purse. He peered inside and shook his head.

'Maybe you should lock the door before you spill those coins,' suggested Hanna. 'Just in case. We don't know who might be out there listening. The sound of coins jingling always brings out the worst sort of people, my father always told me.'

Hanzel did as Hanna suggested and locked the door. Then he poured the coins onto the bed and began to count them. When he was done he could account for no more than one hundred and eighty three florins. When Hanna counted them there were one hundred and eighty seven. When they counted the coins together, they ended up with one hundred and eighty five florins. 'That's a whole lot less than two fifty,' spat Hanzel through clenched teeth. 'So help me. I'll run him through, just like I did that horse thief.'

Hanna looked at Hanzel with a sad expression. 'I don't like it when you talk like that, Hanzel. You scare me when you're like that.'

'Yes, well, so be it. I don't mean you any harm, Hanna. I would never hurt you. Don't worry.' He smacked his right fist into his open left palm. 'But damn it, Hanna. I am so sick of people stealing from me. It's not fair. I just want what is ours.'

'If you go back to the market, what are the chances he's still there? If he is there and sees you, he'll disappear. That place is a warren. We'd never find him.'

'Well, maybe we should just count our blessings. We didn't think we'd get a hundred for Sally. So, I guess we did alright. If you add the twenty five the food and room cost us, we still made quite a lot off Sally. For what we have, we should be able to hire some mercenaries for a few days.'

Hanna frowned. 'I don't think we should go after that treasure. From what I know about fishermen, they can be very violent, if necessary. And, besides, it's been how long, since your treasure was stolen? I doubt if there's anything left, like I told you. I think we should just steal the sloop.'

'We'll still need help to do that. And, if we're going to use the sloop to effect some larceny, we definitely will need some extra hands.' Hanzel stared at the coins spread out on the bed. 'I sure like the idea of many more piles of those.'

'Especially lots of gold ones,' added Hanna.

'And jewels; pearls, diamonds, rubies...'

'Emeralds, sapphires, the whole lot. Every gem stone in earrings, pendants, necklaces...'

'You'll have it all Hanna. The world will be our oyster. What do you say? Shall we become pirates?'

Hanna grinned from ear to ear. 'Yes, Hanzel. Let's be pirates.'

'But first I want to lie down for a little while to digest my meal.' Hanzel gathered up the coins and put them back into the leather bag. He laughed and patted the bed. Hanna lay down beside him, her head in the crook of his right arm. He kissed her tenderly. 'You'll make a fine pirate queen, Hanna. I can't wait for us to get started. Pirates we'll be then.'

'Aye, aye, Captain,' replied Hanna, laughing.

Chapter 28

Since the day was overcast and beginning to haze over with a gossamer sheet of rain, Hanzel and Hanna decided to stay in their room and make their plans. There was no sense in going out to seek sailors in port side bars and eateries. By the time they would have gotten to the port they'd be soaked. 'And, besides, Hanna, there might be some suitable men right here. Right here at the inn. Not all sailors prefer to stay port side. Some do come into the city. Who knows? We don't need more than three or four to sail that sloop.'

'And then what? Once we have the sloop, what then?'

'I don't think we should stay in Amsterdam. I'm sure that Mister Goldman will have people out looking for us,' replied Hanzel.

'Where should we go?'

'Rotterdam. We'll sail to Rotterdam. That's a big port. I'm sure we can find some more men and some more of the things we'll need.' Hanzel's eyes sparkled. He could already see an adventure before his eyes.

'Won't they come looking for that sloop in Rotterdam?'

'We'll repaint her and change her name. We can do that on a deserted beach along the way.' Hanzel smacked his fist into the palm of his left hand. 'I think we can do it, Hanna. And we can begin right here. Right here at this inn.' He cracked a shutter open and peered outside. 'It's beginning to rain harder. It'll be cozy downstairs. Let's go down and drink some more ale and get to know some folks. Who knows, there might be the right candidates right under our very noses.'

Ten minutes later, Hanzel and Hanna stepped into the dining hall and sat down at an empty table against the west wall. It was already deep into the evening and the place was full up with people looking for a good warm meal. From where Hanzel and Hanna were sitting, they could see everyone who entered the room. Ten minutes later a blond serving wench stepped over to their table. Hanzel did not see her at first, his attention being distracted by several sailors strutting into the room. The serving wench stopped in her tracks as she approached and stared wide eyed at Hanzel.

'Hanzel Sventska! Is it really you?! I would recognize you anywhere. I always wondered what happened to you.'

It took Hanzel a moment in the dim light to recognize the young woman standing over him. When his eyes adjusted he stood up. 'Angela. Is it really you?'

'When I saw that white blond hair I thought it might be you. When I saw your eyes, I knew it was you. How are you Hanzel? You look well.' Angela's eyes were sparkling.

'I often think of you and wondered what had happened to you.'

'I've had a lot of adventures over the years, Angela.'

'What brings you here?'

'To this inn, you mean?'

Angela nodded. 'Yes. What are you doing here?'

Hanzel regarded Angela for a moment. 'Well, you see. Hanna and I are trying to round up a crew to man a boat. We thought, since this place attracts a crowd, there might be some good candidates here.'

Angela looked over at Hanna. 'Is she your wife, then?'

Hanzel smiled and nodded. 'Yes. Hanna is my wife.'

Hanna grinned and put her hand on his arm.

'I see. How do you do?' asked Angela, her tone more formal and cool.

'Say, Angela, perhaps you could do us a favour. Ask those sailors if they're looking for a ship.'

'Do you want anything to drink?' asked Angela, not pleased that Hanzel was married.

Hanzel looked at Hanna, who nodded.

'Of course, please bring us an ale and a white wine.' Hanzel smiled at Angela. 'It's good to see you Angela. I've got a place in my heart for you on account of what you did for me.'

'It's been a long time, Hanzel. You're all grown up.' Angela smiled and took one more long look at Hanzel. She sighed. 'I've got to be about my work. Perhaps we can talk later.' Then with a quick glance at Hanna, Angela turned on her heel and set about her work.

'She helped me after I ran away from home,' said Hanzel, anticipating Hanna's question.

'She still recognized you after all these years.' Hanna leaned closer to Hanzel. 'It's your arresting eyes. They'll do it every time.'

'Do what?'

'Drive a girl crazy,' replied Hanna as she kissed his cheek. 'They certainly drive this girl crazy.'

Hanzel stared at Hanna and then deliberately crossed his eyes.

'Oh, you brat.' She gently punched him on the shoulder.

As Hanzel and Hanna were thusly engaged, three sailors came to sit opposite them at the table. 'We hope we're not interrupting' anything,' said the taller of the three jack tars. 'But, Angela told us you was looking for sailor men, like ourselves, here.' He indicated his two mates. 'This here be Michael Webb, an that one be Morgan Three Eyes. My name be Henk de Loop.'

Hanzel looked the three sailors over. *They seem honest enough. They certainly appear to be sailors by the look of their sunburned faces and calloused hands.* 'What sort of ships have you sailed on and why are you without a ship now?'

Henk regarded Hanzel, sizing him up. Henk was at least ten years older but he could sense that Hanzel was one of those, *born leaders . This man has charisma. Others will follow this man's command, I think.* Henk sensed there was something very special about this, Hanzel Sventska. 'The three of us just got off a ship two weeks ago. We survived eight months at sea returning from Batavia. It was horrible. So we needed some time off and been laying about this inn. That's how come we know Angela.'

Hanzel's eyes narrowed. 'I need at least five good men to effect a little bit of larceny.'

'What kind of larceny would that be?' asked Henk leaning closer. His friends also leaned closer to hear clearly over the cacophony enveloping them in that noisy room.

'I want to steal a sloop. It's tied along the roadway. Then I want to use it to practice piracy off the coast.' Hanzel sat back against the wall. He watched the sailors' expressions closely.

'Piracy, you say?' Henk leaned closer, assuming a more conspiratorial demeanor.

'Steal a sloop?' asked Michael. 'Isn't that against the law?' His eyes twinkled as he and Hanzel made eye contact. Hanzel immediately picked up on Michael's sense of humour. He smiled, knowing that he was going to like developing a friendship with him; should he choose to join in the proffered adventure.

'Steal a sloop and become pirates?' asked Morgan incredulously.

Hanzel and Hanna nodded. 'Do you know any others who might be interested?'

'Are you planning to pay us?' asked Henk, eyeing Hanzel's purse.

'Yes, of course. A share of whatever swag we capture,' answered Hanzel.

'No money on the table?' Henk eyed Hanzel. 'I mean, why should we go pirating with you and risk being executed? You're an unknown. How do we know you have any experience with pirating?'

'I have experience as a privateer. I was part of a crew which rescued a huge treasure from the Spaniards. Alas, my share was stolen by fishermen.'

'Stolen by fishermen? How can fishermen steal someone's treasure?' asked Morgan, a surprised expression on his weathered face.

'Can you get it back?' asked Henk greedily.

Hanzel shook his head. 'Too much time has passed.'

'There is likely no treasure left,' added Hanna. 'Those fishermen have probably spent it all by now.'

Hanzel nodded. 'I'm so sick of people stealing from me. That's why I want to go pirating and get somebody else's stuff for a change.'

Henk and his friends looked at Hanzel and Hanna but did not say anything right away. They went into a huddle and discussed Hanzel's proposal in whispers.

'What do you think they'll do?' asked Hanna, not taking her eyes off the huddled threesome.

'I think they'll go for it. They look like adventurers,' replied Hanzel.

'Perhaps. But can we trust them?' Hanna glanced sideways at Hanzel and then returned her gaze to the sailors.

'Of that I am certain, Hanna. I can read people pretty well. These men are good, honest sailors, with a sense of adventure. And a sense of humour by the looks of that Michael chap. He already made me smile. He seems a likeable fellow. I have a feeling he could go places with us.'

Hanna nodded. 'I agree, Hanzel. I also have a good feeling about these men. I did not sense anything untoward. They're not the leering type, either; like some men, always trying to look down my bodice.'

Hanzel smiled and looked into Hanna's eyes. 'I can't say I blame them. You have the most beautiful breasts in the world, my dear. Everyone man wants to see them.'

Hanna's eyes twinkled. 'Well, that may be so, but they're for your eyes only.'

'I'm the luckiest man in the world.' Hanzel leaned over and kissed her on the mouth. 'I love you, Hanna.'

'I love you too, Hanzel.'

The two lovers sat staring into each other's eyes for a few more minutes, while the three sailors deliberated over the proposal. When they were done, Henk and his comrades turned their attention back to Hanzel and Hanna. 'Alright, we'll take a chance. If you say you have a sloop we can easily steal, we're in. We need a ship and our chances for a better life are more likely to be found as pirates.' Henk looked at his friends for confirmation.

'Ya we will come with you,' said Morgan smiling. 'We'll take a chance with the sloop.'

'Sounds good to me,' added Michael. "When do we start?'

Hanzel smiled. 'Excellent. That is good news. Now all we'll need is a couple more men. I think seven of us can handle that sloop just fine.'

'What do you mean, seven of us?' asked Henk. 'If you get a couple more than us that would be five of us and you to make six.'

'You're forgetting that there are two of us. Hanna is my partner. She goes wherever I go.'

'She's a woman. Are you suggesting we take a woman on board?' asked Henk, not believing his ears.

'A woman is bad luck on board of a ship,' added Morgan.

'Bad luck and ill omens.' Michael nodded knowingly. 'But, I don't believe it. I like women. The idea of having a woman, or women on board, would make sailing a whole lot more pleasant, don't you think?' He looked at his friends, a big grin on his handsome face.

Hanzel regarded Henk and Morgan for a moment and then burst out laughing. 'You two can't be serious? Those beliefs went out with the dark ages. Hanna is my partner and best friend. I'm not going to leave her alone here in Amsterdam. Who knows what might happen to her? Especially with all these wars brewing all the time.'

Hanna smiled at Hanzel and pressed his arm.

'Well, I don't know,' mumbled Henk. He regarded his friends and then looked back at Hanzel. 'We're going to have to discuss this further.' Henk formed a huddle with his chums and discussed the potential dangers of having a woman on board. Every once in a while one of them would look at Hanna and then quickly return to the huddle.

Hanna looked at Hanzel and frowned. 'Men can be so ridiculous sometimes. Just because I'm a woman doesn't mean I can't learn to sail.'

'That's the spirit, Hanna.' Hanzel grinned and then spontaneously added, 'Will you marry me?'

Hanna stopped for a moment. She wasn't sure she heard rightly. *Did he just ask to marry me? Of course I'll marry him. I love him.* 'Yes of course I'll marry you, Hanzel. I can't think of anyone I would rather marry. I love you.' Hanna put her arms around Hanzel's neck and gave him a long kiss.

'See, that's exactly the sort of thing we're talking about. Instead of captaining our ship, you'll be busy attending to your sweetheart,' said Henk, disdainfully.

'Nonsense. Hanna will learn the ropes and be every bit as good a sailor as a man. She is a farm girl. She has strong hands and arms. I'll bet she'll out walk or out run any of you.' Hanzel put his arm over Hanna's shoulders and pulled her closer. 'She and I are a team. If you don't like it we'll find other sailors. I'm sure there are lots of unemployed sailors looking for a ship in Amsterdam.'

Henk and his pals regarded the young couple without saying anything. Then they went back into a huddle from which Henk finally emerged to say, 'Alright, we'll do it. We'll forget she's a woman if you'll dress her as a swab. We don't want no petticoats or dresses on board ship. If she dresses as a man, it's kind of like she's out of mind, if you get my drift.'

Hanzel nodded. 'Yes, I catch your drift.' He looked at Hanna. 'What do you think? Dress like a man?'

'I think I could get used to that too. Probably a lot more practical on board a ship, I should think, than a dress and petticoats.'

'Alright then. That's that. You three can join us. All we need to do is find a couple more and we'll take that sloop out from under Mister Goldman's big, hooked nose.

'If the sloop is still moored where you said,' replied Henk. 'Could it be that he's sold it since you last saw it?'

'I guess we'll see. If it's gone, we'll find another,' answered Hanzel.

'Alright, then. I think we may know a couple more, like ourselves, who may be interested in joining our party. Life is tough. If we increase our numbers, we have strength and may actually be able to do something,' said Henk wisely. 'We'll go find our friends and bring them back here. Don't go away.'

Hanzel smiled. 'We'll be right here waiting for you. When there are five of you, Hanna and I will buy you all dinner over which we can discuss our plans. What say you?'

Henk smiled. Then he stepped over and shook Hanzel's hand. 'Aye, aye, Captain,' he said happily. Then turning on his heels he said, 'Come on lads, let's go find Pedro the Spaniard and that Irishman, what's his name?'

'Angus O'Riley,' replied Morgan. 'That fiery red head could be a menace, don't you think?'

'He's a fine sailor and one hell of a fighter if need be. He'd make a perfect pirate. Don't worry, I know how to keep him in line,' said Henk reassuringly.

'Alright, then,' agreed Morgan. 'Let's go find em.'

Hanzel and Hanna watched the three men leave and sat back with a sigh of relief. 'It looks like we got ourselves a crew.' Hanzel raised his cup. 'Here's to our new adventure.'

Hanna knocked her cup against his. 'I pray we don't get caught.'

'Don't worry Hanna. We'll do it when it is dark. When the moon is obscured. No one will suspect a thing.' Hanzel looked into Hanna's eyes. 'We'll be fine. Especially with those fellows. I get the impression they've probably done a heist or two before.'

'I'm convinced of it. I thought that the moment I laid eyes on them. Especially Morgan. I wonder how he got the name, *Three Eyes*?'

Hanzel laughed. 'He probably has an eye in the back of his head. That's why he wears that toque pulled over his ears.'

For a moment Hanna paused. 'Don't laugh. I've heard of people having an extra arm or a leg. Why not an eye?'

Hanzel stopped laughing. 'Why not, indeed? There are all kinds of strange anomalies in nature. I do recall that two headed calf born at your farm.'

'How can one ever forget that monstrosity? It's a good thing the poor creature only lived for five days.'

'Do you think we should ask him?' Hanzel took a sip of his ale.

'I can't see any harm in that. But wait until we know him better. We could ask Henk, away from Morgan's ears,' suggested Hanna. 'No harm in asking.'

Hanzel nodded. 'I'm curious. We'll ask Henk. I mean, Morgan Three Eyes, definitely has a story attached to him.'

Hanna did not reply, but rather stared into Hanzel's eyes. Her face expressed a gentle, softness; with a mysterious smile like that of Mona Lisa. Then she spoke in a voice choked with emotion. 'Do you really want to marry me, Hanzel?'

'I can't think of anyone I would rather marry than you, Hanna. You are exactly the right girl I want to share my life with. You have spirit. You have heart. You are smart as a whip. You are strong and you want to go adventuring with me. And, besides, looking at you and being with you makes my heart glad. You are so beautiful, Hanna. I love you with all of my heart.'

'Oh, Hanzel,' cried Hanna as she put her arms around his neck and kissed him long and passionately. Hanzel could taste the salty brine of her tears in his mouth as they flowed from Hanna's blue eyes.

The two lovers remained in their embrace for a long while. Each having grown ever more in love with the other. They were a match made in Heaven. Hanzel knew it and so did Hanna. They had no idea, the Devil was keeping an eye on the details.

'Hey you two, d'you want another drink?' asked Angela, who had walked by on her round. By this time she had already forgiven Hanzel and decided to be friendly. After all, so many years had passed. She knew back then there was no chance of him ever coming back for her. *No sense in blaming her. She seems like a nice girl. She certainly is pretty.*

Hanzel looked up at Angela as the two lovers broke their embrace. Hanna brushed her hand through her hair, straightening it, as Hanzel engaged Angela. 'Oh, Angela.' He looked into his cup. Then he looked at Hanna's. 'Yes, please bring us each another. Wine for Hanna and ale for me. And, by the way, at some time this evening your friends, Henk and his pals, plus two others are coming to join us here.'

'Oh, so you got along with Henk and his friends?' asked Angela. 'I've known Henk for years. He's a good man.'

'What about his other friends?' asked Hanna.

'You mean, Pedro the Spaniard and Morgan Three Eyes? Or do you mean, Michael?'

Hanzel and Hanna nodded.

'I've only known Pedro and Morgan a short while. They seem alright, I guess. I just assume they're alright since they're with Henk. As for Michael, he's every girl's friend. Everybody likes him. He's our Mikey.'

'How did Morgan get the name, Three Eyes?' asked Hanna.

'He has an eye in the back of his head?' replied Angela nonchalantly. Hanna exchanged a glance with Hanzel. 'Actually, I have no idea. He wears that toque pulled over his head every time I've seen him.'

'The mystery of the third eye,' laughed Hanzel, finding the idea suddenly very amusing.

'He has a strange sense of humour sometimes,' said Hanna to Angela in one of those tones of voice only women understand.

'It's one of those men things,' replied Angela, matter of factly. 'My Gerard is the same way. He laughs at the oddest things. I mean, I don't find the idea of someone having three eyes all that funny. I mean, he could only sleep on his sides if he had an eye in the back of his head. He'd be lying on the eye all night if he lay on his back. That would be uncomfortable, don't you think?'

Angela's response made Hanzel burst out in a whole new bout of laughter which was infectious. Within an instant both Angela and Hanna joined him in his merriment; the three friends laughing with great good humour.

When their happy moment had passed Angela excused herself and returned to her work. Hanzel and Hanna returned to their discussion regarding Hanzel's marriage proposal.

With sparkling eyes and a racing heart, Hanna accepted Hanzel's hand and vowed she would be a good wife to him for ever, until death parted them from their life's adventure together. Hanzel could not be happier.

It was in a blaze of glorious euphoria that Henk and his friends found Hanzel and Hanna. The two lovers were embraced and kissing with great passion. They had found each other's soul mate. From then on they were inseparable until death parted their ways. However, that comes much later in the story. For now they were deeply in love and considering themselves married. They were no longer just boy friend and girl friend. They were engaged. 'You are now my fiancée,' said Hanzel grinning from ear to ear.'

'So I am. So I am most gladly,' replied Hanna staring into her lover's eyes.

'See what I mean,' said Morgan as they approached the table where Hanzel and Hanna were sitting. 'If we take her on board those two will be coupled while we do the work.'

When Hanzel and Hanna heard Morgan's voice they came out of their embrace and looked up at five smiling sailors staring at them over the table. Hanzel smiled sheepishly but immediately took command of the situation. He indicated the bench opposite them. 'Please have a seat, gentlemen. Thank you for coming.'

Before sitting, Henk indicated the red headed Irish man and a dark skinned man with waxed mustaches. 'This is Angus O'Riley and he is Pedro. We call him Pedro the Spaniard because it is just easier. Being Spanish he has a very long name. I can't even remember all of the names.' He smiled apologetically at Pedro.

Pedro smiled, revealing three golden teeth. 'Eet matter not. Pedro will suffice.'

'Just out of curiosity,' replied Hanna, 'What exactly is your full name?'

'Pedro Gonzales Mauritius Salvador Francesco Balthasar de Velasqueza.'

'I see why you are called Pedro the Spaniard,' laughed Hanzel. He indicated the chair at the end of the table. 'Please have a seat.'

'So, tell us more about that sloop you mentioned,' said Henk as the five men sat down.

'Before we begin, let me order food and drink. I forgot to ask Angela when she was just over here.' Hanzel searched with his eyes. Angela was delivering a tray of drinks to a group of merchants seated around a circular table. Hanzel caught her eye and beckoned her to come over. Then he asked the sailors what they would like to drink. To a man they ordered rum. When Angela arrived, Hanzel presented her with an order for drinks and a feast for seven. The five men expressed their gratitude.

That's a good sign. They are polite and grateful. Hanzel smiled. *I think these fellows will make for good company.* 'Well gentlemen, let me begin by welcoming you. I am happy now because I believe we seven will be able to form the nucleus of what I hope will become a dedicated band of adventurers who wish to become wealthy in the sweet trade.'

'How do you plan to do that?' asked Angus. 'Do you have a ship?'

'No, not yet. That is why we are here. I want us to steal a sloop which is lying along the roadway,' answered Hanzel.

'Steal a sloop? Steal a sloop?' Angus looked at Henk. 'You didn't say anything about stealing a sloop.'

'Just let him talk, Angus. I'm sure he's got it figured out.' Henk smiled apologetically at Hanzel.

'Alright. But, if there is any danger involved. I don't want to go back to prison this early after I got out,' replied Angus shaking his head.

'I really don't think we've got a thing to worry about,' said Hanzel reassuringly. 'The sloop appears to be well appointed and ready to sail away. All that we need to do is release her mooring cables and sail her out of the harbour in the dead of night when there is no moon.'

'Oose boat ees eet?' asked Pedro.

'The boat seller, Goldman,' replied Hanzel.

'A Jew, eh? Well, I'm a sure e's stolen from more than a few peepel in a ees day.' Pedro smacked his hand on the table. 'I don a mine stealing from a Jew. My contree keek dem out more dan a once when eet was discovered what they were up to.'

'Well, I don't care whose boat it is,' said Morgan. 'If we can successfully steal that sloop and improve our circumstances, count me in.'

The others agreed it was an opportunity worth risking. Hanzel grinned from ear to ear. He could already envision their new career as pirates off the coasts of western Europe and beyond. When dinner arrived the seven new friends dove in with hearty appetites over which many toasts were quaffed, blessing the larceny they would effect against the Jew, Goldman.

'May he burst a blood vessel,' suggested Michael, raising his cup.

'May ee burst several blood vessels, dat usurious maggot,' added Pedro laughing and holding his cup in the air.

Hanzel regarded Pedro for a moment. 'How can you call him that? You don't even know him.'

'Ees a Jew. All Jews are a usurious maggots,' replied Pedro, laughing.

'I've not had many dealings with Jews, so I wouldn't know. He wasn't very nice to Hanna and me, that's for sure. I have no idea what it's worth and what he would have charged. So, whether he practices usury, I don't know. Let's not wish him any ill will. He was just having a bad day. We'll just steal his sloop, that's all.'

'Well, I've had dealings with em,' said Morgan. 'I don't trust em, myself.'

'We learn from experience,' said Henk, wisely. 'But, let's not talk about Jews. We're here to plan a larceny.'

'Indeed, that is why we're gathered here. To plan a larceny. I want to steal Goldman's sloop and use it to venture at sea in the sweet trade. I want to be a pirate.' Hanzel regarded his new crewmates.

Angus burst out laughing. 'I think that is a grand idea. Let us be pirates.' He stopped and looked at his friends and at Hanzel and Hanna. 'But do we have enough man power to be pirates?'

'We'll gather up more men. We just need enough to steal the sloop and get away from Amsterdam. We can sail to Rotterdam and find some more friends to join us,' replied Hanzel.

'You see, Angus. He's got most of it figured out already. I told you,' said Henk regarding his red headed friend.

'So, when should we steal the sloop, do you figure?' asked Michael.

'We could do it tonight, if you feel up to it,' answered Hanzel.

Henk shook his head. 'No. That's too soon. I want to have a look at that sloop first. Besides, I need to clear up some affairs here before I set sail.'

'Aye, me too,' said Morgan. 'I want to have a look at that sloop first. Case the place out. You know. Look around and make a sailing plan.'

Hanzel smiled. *I think I've got me a crew. This is going to work out famously. I can just tell. These fellows know their business.* Hanzel raised his cup. 'Here's to our venture. May it meet with success.'

'To our success!' shouted the others in glorious harmony clicking their cups together.

And so Hanzel's gang had its beginnings at the *Dikke Boer*, that rainy evening in Amsterdam in the year 1623, thirteen days before Hanzel's twenty third birthday. Over a sumptuous feast of roast beef, roasted potatoes with onions and Brussels sprouts accompanied by a glorious thick gravy, they began their planning. Angela made sure to keep the cups full at Hanzel's request. As the evening progressed into night and their many toasts were beginning to wreak havoc on their equilibrium the seven new friends became ever more convinced they were the perfect match up and would make a great name for themselves in the history of piracy.

Chapter 29

The next three days saw warm, sunny weather with only occasional cloud cover. They were the perfect days for scoping things out. Everyone got a good look at the sloop and its mooring arrangements. They were able to plan a route out of the harbour past the many ships anchored there. There was no room for mistakes because the authorities would be on them in an instant. It was another reason why the heist had to be in as dark a night as possible.

'Preferably just a dark night. Not dark and rainy,' said Michael.

'If'n ye can't stand the wet, then ye should not be going out ter sea,' replied Angus.

Hanzel laughed. 'Chances are, it will be raining here sooner than later. It's likely better it be dark and raining. I think we have a better chance of disappearing with the sloop.'

Henk looked at the sky. 'I think we're going to have rain tonight. Maybe we should do it tonight. I'm all packed and ready to go. What about you fellows?'

'I'm ready,' said Michael eagerly.

Morgan nodded. 'No reason for me to stay in Amsterdam.'

Pedro agreed, he was also ready to go.

'I was born ready,' laughed Angus, his round belly jiggling up an down with each guffaw.

Hanzel looked at Hanna. She nodded. 'If tonight is dark, and even raining, let's go. We've all had a good look at the sloop. I don't think Goldman suspects anything. We've all been discreet. So, let's do it. Let's do it tonight.'

Michael held up his cup. 'I toast to our success. We'll do the heist tonight.'

'Aye!' agreed everyone.

And so the plan was hatched. They would meet up at the *Dikke Boer* at eleven o'clock for a drink and final plans. Everyone was to bring their duffel bags, or trunks so that they can sail away and not have to come back for anything.

'Especially, do not forget what weapons and ammunition you have,' suggested Hanzel.

When the meeting was over everyone went about their business of getting ready for the night's work. Hanzel and Hanna used the time they had to shop for some suitable men's clothes for Hanna and rain gear for both of them.

'We better buy some food and a couple of good, leather bags,' suggested Hanna. 'We really don't have anything to carry our belongings in.'

Hanzel agreed. So, the two lovers went shopping.

Meanwhile, in Mister Goldman's shop, Joseph was feeling unsettled. He had a suspicion about the sloop. Some suspicious looking characters had been seen snooping about the sloop for the last few days. Goldman had seen them with his own eyes.

'I recognized that young couple, who were in here a while ago. You remember them, Isaac? Remember the blond couple who wanted to sell us a horse? A horse, Isaac. They came to Goldman & Goldman to sell us a horse. We're boat sellers, Isaac. Boat sellers. Do we look like horse traders? Do we?'

Isaac shook his head. 'No we don't look like horse traders, Joseph. So, you say you saw that blond couple?'

'They were checking the mooring ropes, when I saw them.'

'Maybe they're still interested in the sloop, Joseph. They're careful buyers.' Isaac regarded his brother. 'Did they have a horse with them?'

'No, they did not have a horse with them,' replied Joseph, irritably.

'Well, then. Maybe they have sold the horse and now have some more money to buy the sloop,' suggested Isaac.

Joseph rubbed his chin. 'Well, I don't know. I don't know, Isaac. I think they have something to do with those suspicious characters. I looked out of the window yesterday and saw the woman talking to one of them.'

'You are a worry wart, my brother. I say forget about it. Nobody is stealing that sloop. Let's take a look at those plans for the new ship for the East India Company,' suggested Isaac, taking the drawing out of its filing tube.

Back at the *Dikke Boer* Hanzel and Hanna were enjoying their last hours in the comfortable bed. They spent the time making love, napping, snacking, drinking ale, and laughing. They spent a lot of time laughing. Life was good together.

When closing time came, Joseph said good night to his brother Isaac and pretended to head home. He did not let Isaac know that he, Joseph had a bad feeling about the sloop and decided to board her and sleep there; in order to guard against possible thieves. Joseph had learned to trust his intuition over the years. The fact that he saw unsavory looking characters checking her out had made him sense that the time was coming when the sloop would disappear. Nobody saw him climb on board. He had armed himself with two pistols and a rapier. His hiding place was in the foc'sle.

When eleven o'clock arrived, Hanzel's gang began to gather around a table in the dining hall of *De Dikke Boer*. By midnight the seven conspirators left the place, two and three at a time, carrying their duffel bags or trunks on their shoulders. By twelve thirty they were standing beside the sloop and whispering final instructions before boarding her. Henk and Morgan tended to the mooring lines. The others set about prepping the sails.

In the foc'sle, old Mister Goldman had long ago fallen asleep on some sails which were stored there. He never heard, nor felt anything as he dreamt about piles of gold and sacks of silver.

Fifteen minutes later, as the sloop began to slip out of the harbour, the rain began. Fortunately, the sailors knew what they were doing and managed to maneuver the sloop past the many anchored ships. Nobody took any notice of them; not even a gull watched them go.

Around five in the morning, when the sloop was approaching the Hook van Holland, Mister Goldman woke up. His bladder was urgently suggesting an evacuation order was warranted. In his hurry, and due to bad planning, he had forgotten to take a lantern into the foc'sle. It was pitch dark in there. He could not see a thing. As he stood up, he realized the ship was moving. He could hear the waves against the bows as the sloop cut through the water. Joseph fell over as the sloop suddenly moved sideways in a trough. He hit his head on an oak bulkhead, knocking him unconscious.

That is how and where Hanzel and Michael found the old boat seller; unconscious and sprawled out in the foc'sle, later that day.

'What in de blue blazes?!' exclaimed Michael. 'Dat does not look like a sail.'

Hanzel took a closer look at the old man, holding up the lantern so he could make out his face. 'Mister Goldman. It's Mister Goldman, the boat seller.'

'Is he dead?'

Hanzel touched the old man's neck; feeling for a pulse. 'He's alive. Must have bumped his head.' Hanzel regarded Michael. 'Go get us some water. We'll see if we can revive him.'

The old man heard voices somewhere in a fog. He opened an eye and peeked out. It took him a moment to adjust to the light of the lantern on his face. The man holding the lantern was a silhouette; Goldman could not make out who he was. He rolled his eyeball around in its socket and tried to take in his circumstances. *So, my sloop has been stolen, just as I expected. But, what do I do now? There surely are more than two on this boat.*

As Hanzel turned back to look at Mister Goldman, the wily old man closed his eyelid and continued to pretend he was unconscious. *I need to take them by surprise.*

Michael returned with a bucket of water and was about to pour it over the old man.

'That will not be necessary,' croaked the old man, rubbing the back of his head.

'Oh, so you are awake? What are you doing here?' asked Hanzel.

'This is my sloop. The question that should be asked is, what are *you* doing here?' The old boat seller slowly sat up. Hanzel offered him a hand, to help him. The old man regarded the hand for a moment and then refused it. 'I do not take the hand of the man who has robbed me,' he said defiantly.

Hanzel and Michael stood back and watched as the old man painfully got to his feet. Being a height deprived man, he was able to stand upright in the cramped space. He regarded the two men watching him. Unbeknownst to Hanzel and Olafsen, the wily boat seller carried his pistols under his coat. His rapier lay on the sails.

Hanzel noticed the rapier and stepped over to the pile of sails. 'What's this? A rapier?' He looked at Goldman. 'Is this yours? Or was this here?'

'It's mine,' answered Joseph.

'What were you going to do with this thin blade? Just little old you against seven of us? With a rapier, no less.' Hanzel and Michael laughed.

As the two men stood there, laughing at the old boat seller, Goldman pulled his pistols out of his coat and pointed them at Hanzel and Michael. He cocked the hammers. 'Now we'll see who laughs last,' said the old man, menacing his captors with the armed pistols.

'Whoa, Mister Goldman,' said Hanzel holding up his hands. 'There's no need to get violent. We would not have done you any harm.'

'So you say,' replied Goldman. 'You'd probably toss me overboard and be done with it. Dead men tell no tales. Isn't that how you pirates think?'

Hanzel looked at Michael and then back at Goldman. 'Perhaps there are some pirates that do that sort of thing. We're not cutthroats. That's not what we're about. We just want to raise funds for charitable purposes.'

Michael nodded. 'Ya, ya, that's what we do. We are good pirates. We share our wealth with others.'

Goldman laughed. 'A likely story.' He gestured with the pistols. 'Turn around and walk ahead of me. We are going up on deck.' He pushed a barrel into Hanzel's back. 'Go,' he commanded.

Hanzel and Olafsen thought it better to do as Goldman said. Neither wanted to risk scaring the old man resulting in someone getting shot. *We'll deal with him on deck.* He eyed Michael who winked, just before climbing up the ladder. Hanzel followed him. When Michael climbed out of the hatch, he immediately gestured to Henk, who was standing nearby repairing a damaged cleat. Michael pointed down and then made as if he was holding two pistols. Then he pointed down, once again and put a finger to his lips.

Henk nodded he understood, just as Hanzel climbed out of the hatch.

'And no shenanigans!' shouted Mister Goldman, from below. 'I'll shoot through the boards!'

Hanzel signaled Henk and Michael and pointed to the hatch cover. 'Quick. Help me with this,' he whispered. The three men quickly covered the hatch.

'Oh, so you think you can beat me by covering the hatch? Not a chance!' Instantly an explosion preceded a ball slicing through the hatch cover, which whizzed past Henk's right ear and flew off in a trajectory ending up in the ocean somewhere off to starboard.

'That's one shot gone,' said Hanzel.

'Do we storm him now?' asked Henk.

'Send Morgan and Pedro below through the rear hatch. Make sure they have pistols. We'll try and draw out Mister Goldman. He might use his other shot,' whispered Hanzel.

'He could be reloading,' suggested Michael.

Hanzel nodded. 'It's possible. He could be reloading. I didn't notice if he had a powder horn.'

'What was that shot?' asked Hanna, who had come to join Hanzel, standing to port of the hatch.

Hanzel cautioned her to be careful and to stand back. 'Mister Goldman, the boat seller was in the sail locker. He was guarding the boat. He's armed with two pistols.' He signaled Max to go with Morgan and Pedro. 'They'll soon have the old fellow under control,' said Hanzel confidently. He gently moved Hanna away from the hatch. 'I don't want a shot to come out of there and hit you.'

'Or you,' replied Hanna, pulling Hanzel back.

'That silly Jew. He thinks we're scared of him. Not a chance,' said Henk, smiling.

Hanzel nodded. He held Hanna close and kept an eye on the covered hatch.

A shot rang out. A ball came out of the hatch cover and flew off into the rigging, high above the deck. Then voices and a struggle could be heard coming from below. Another shot exploded below deck followed by a scream. Then all was quiet for a moment. Hanzel looked at Hanna, who stared back at him, a questioning look in her eyes. Two minutes later, Mister Goldman, clutching his left arm stepped on deck from the midship hatch. He was followed by Morgan and Pedro.

'So, you steal my boat, shoot me in the arm, and now you hold me prisoner? On my own boat? How dare you, you, Friesian!' shouted Mister Goldman.

'We didn't shoot him,' said Morgan. 'He struggled when Pedro tried to take the gun away from him. The old man shot himself.'

'That is ridiculous! He shot me in cold blood. Could have killed me,' said Mister Goldman looking at his damaged arm.

'So, what are we going to do with him?' asked Henk. 'We can't take him with us.'

'I wouldn't come with you if this was the last ship off a sinking island,' replied Mister Goldman.

'Well, then. That answers the question what we do with him,' said Hanzel. 'He doesn't want to sail with us so we'll set him down on some remote coast of Scotland.'

'Oh, I know just the place,' said Morgan. 'He'll likely never survive that place.'

'That's a bit rough, wouldn't you say?' asked Hanzel. 'I was thinking a village, or a hamlet, or even a monastery; something like that.'

'He's a Jew. He'd do the same to you, or worse,' replied Henk.

'Yeah, he is a Jew,' agreed Michael.

'That's no reason to kill him,' replied Hanzel.

'Dead men tell no tales,' said Henk. 'Letting him live will give him an opportunity to go to the authorities and have us hanged.'

'That's a better reason to kill him. Not just because he is a Jew. If we kill him because he is a Jew, we lower ourselves to his way of doing things because he would kill you because you are a Gentile. Isn't that so, Mister Goldman?' Hanzel regarded the old boat seller cradling his injured arm.

'I would kill you because you are stealing my boat,' replied Mister Goldman. 'I don't care if you are a Gentile. That is just happenstance. Even if you were a Jew I would kill you for stealing my boat.'

'Isn't that against your law?' asked Pedro.

'What?' asked Mister Goldman.

'For a Jew to kill another Jew,' replied Pedro.

The old boat seller thought for a moment. 'To kill is a sin.'

'And yet, you were prepared to kill us,' replied Hanzel. 'You shot through the hatch.'

'And he tried to shoot me,' said Henk. 'Good thing Pedro grabbed his arm and the shot went up and not into me.'

'So, there you have it, pure and simple,' said Hanzel. 'You tried to kill one or more of us. That is attempted murder.'

'Yes, but you are stealing my boat,' protested Mister Goldman.

'What are we going to do with him, boys?' asked Hanzel.

'Dead men tell no tales. If we let him live he'll turn us in,' said Henk.

'He has not harmed us. He might have a slight chance to survive if we put him down on the coast of Scotland, as I suggested.' Morgan regarded Hanzel for a reply.

'That is a slow, tortuous death,' replied Hanzel.

'Then, the only other option is to kill him, here and now, and dump his body overboard,' said Michael.

'Who is going to do that?' asked Hanzel. 'To shoot the man in cold blood?'

'I'll do it,' volunteered Henk. 'I don't like Jews.'

'Neither do I,' said Pedro the Spaniard. 'I'll do it.'

Hanzel regarded the two volunteers. 'What say you lads? What do we do with Mister Goldman?'

The majority of the men on board voted to kill the old boat seller. Hanna and Hanzel did not want to do it, but they both realized they had no choice. They were now truly committed to piracy. In that world, murders in cold blood happened as a matter of course. Hanzel nodded. 'Alright then. I guess we have come to the conclusion that you must be killed, Mister Goldman. You pose too much of a risk to us.'

The old man regarded Hanzel and then looked at each of the other crew members; except for Angus, who was manning the helm. 'So, you are going to kill me. For trying to protect what is mine. What injustice. I don't deserve this.'

Hanzel realized in order for him to truly be the captain, he had to be the courageous one. He had to be the executioner. As distasteful as that was to him, he knew he had no choice. He looked at Hanna, who had tears in her eyes. She knew what he had to do. Hanzel looked at Henk, who was holding a pistol. 'Give me that pistol, if you please, Henk.'

Henk handed Hanzel the pistol.

'So, you think you are doing the right thing, by killing me,' said the old man. 'Killing me will be a stain on your souls for ever. I was merely trying to protect my property. Wouldn't you do the same thing?'

Hanzel stared at the old boat seller; a million thoughts going through his head. He had to struggle to stay focused on the thoughts pertaining to putting the pistol to Goldman's head and pulling the trigger. BANG! went the gun. Hanzel was not quite clear how that happened, but a split second later, Mister

Goldman crumpled on the deck, a big hole in his left temple. Blood was already forming a pool around his head.

'Well, that's that then,' said Michael. 'We'll throw him overboard for the fishes. Here, Henk and Pedro, give me a hand.'

The three men lifted the frail old merchant and tossed him over the starboard side. No ceremony, no words, nothing. Goldman was just another body; one of millions, lost at sea; unheralded.

'Poor old Mister Goldman,' said Hanzel. 'He should have gone home after work.'

Hanna nodded. 'It's always sad when someone is killed.'

The two lovers stood at the transom for a long time, arms around each other, staring out to sea; out to the waves which had swallowed old Mister Goldman, who only wanted to protect his property and got caught in the wrong circumstances. The old man was the second person Hanzel had killed. Unlike the horse thief, killing the old Jew did not sit well with Hanzel. *Me killing the horse thief would have been no different than Goldman killing me for stealing his boat. Now I've stolen and killed. Armed robbery with a victim. That is already enough cause to get me broken and braided. At the very least I'd be hanged. And there are six witnesses. Hanzel, Hanzel, what have you done?*

'Henk,' said Hanzel, turning around. Henk was standing next to Angus, manning the helm. 'How many men have you killed, so far in your life?'

Henk looked at Hanzel for a long while before answering. 'I've killed probably half a dozen, or so. During my years in the navy and as a privateer.'

'How about you, Angus? Have you ever killed anybody?' Hanzel regarded his chubby helmsman, expecting the man to admit to a similar number or more to that of Henk.

'One. I've only ever killed one man,' replied Angus. 'I've hurt a few. But, I only killed one. And he was a crewmate. I got flogged for it, but wasn't hung because the navy understood the circumstances. They admitted it was really an accident.'

'What happened?' asked Hanzel.

'We got into a fight, down below decks. In our quarters, like. The bastard had been stealing rations from his mess mates; me being one of them. When I caught him at it, he came at me with his dirk. I sidestepped him and gave him a hard shove. He fell on his own knife. It just so happened to catch him in the neck and punctured a jugular vein. He bled out before the doctor could get to him.'

'And they still flogged you?' asked Hanna.

'That's the navy for you,' replied Angus.

'That's one of the things we're not going to see on our ship. Flogging is barbaric. Besides, what would any of us do to warrant a flogging? On our ship? We stole this together. This sloop belongs to all of us,' said Hanzel.

'However, I do think we need a written code. A set of rules, so that everyone on board knows exactly what is what,' suggested Michael.

'I agree,' said Henk. 'All pirate gangs, pretty much, have a written code. As long as the rules are fair, that's the main thing. We all vote on them, so there's no way anyone can complain about them.'

'We should write this code before we recruit any more sailors,' said Hanna wisely. 'This way, the seven of us will have it in place and the new people will swear on it.'

'Hanna is right. We should work on this code before we make port.' Hanzel looked out to sea. 'Where are we going, by the way? We've not determined where we want to begin recruiting.'

'I thought you said Rotterdam. Rotterdam is not far. Let's sail tthere,' suggested Henk.

'Alright, let's sail to Rotterdam. We'll write up a set of articles before we begin recruiting,' agreed Hanzel. 'Once we have our crew, we'll go about our business. I have a good feeling about all of this. I think we'll have money in the kitty before too much longer.'

'Aye, Captain,' came the unanimous reply.

Ten hours later they sailed into the port of Rotterdam. It was early in the afternoon The harbour, like that of Amsterdam, was busy loading and offloading ships of many nations. Shuttle craft, rowboats, longboats, small skiffs, sloops, barges, every floating craft imaginable moved amongst the huge merchantmen and navy ships lying at anchor. As they passed a massive ship of the line, Henk noticed some sailors were touching up the ship's name on the transom with white paint. *De Grote Apple*.

'That reminds me, Hanzel. We need to change the name of this sloop. Her name is on the transom. It will not be long until people come looking for this sloop. When Goldman doesn't return, someone will report him missing; of course the fact that the sloop is no longer tied across the street from the shop...' Michael regarded Hanzel, who was watching the painters as the sloop slipped past.

'Good idea. We will attend to that when we're back out to sea. It will appear suspicious if we change the name while we're docked, wouldn't you think?' Hanzel looked at Michael and shrugged his shoulders.

'I think it doesn't matter. People are always having to paint their boats. I don't think changing a name will be noticed by anyone. Not in this busy place,' replied Michael, indicating the harbour with a sweep of his right arm.

Hanzel regarded his friend. 'What do you suggest we change the name to?'

'Oh, I don't know. How about, *New Adventure*. Something like that,' suggested Michael.

'I like the sound of that,' said Angus, as he turned the wheel to port in order to slide past a huge East Indiaman offloading a cargo from Sumatra. 'A new adventure is what we're in for. Once we have a full crew, we will be off on a new adventure.'

'Another name we could consider is, *Great Fortune*,' suggested Hanna.

'Oh, I like the sound of that,' said Henk. '*Great Fortune* speaks to what we want to achieve.'

'I like it too,' agreed Angus. 'I like the sound of it. *Great Fortune*.' Angus pointed to a place where they could drop anchors. Not too close to other ships and well out of the main channel. 'We should anchor there.'

Hanzel and Henk agreed it was the right place. Ten minutes later the sloop lay at anchor and the seven friends set about making the ship safe and secure. When everything was ready, they gathered in the master's cabin and began writing down some ideas for a code to guide their affairs. It turned out to be an exercise which took most of the day and into the evening. However, when they were done, everyone expressed satisfaction they made up fair rules which made sense.

'This way, we actually have some rules to guide us. It will show the new recruits we mean business and are not some amateurs,' said Hanzel, taking a sip of rum. 'We'll go into town tomorrow morning and see how many we can attract.'

'How many more do we need?' asked Henk

'This sloop will accommodate twenty, don't you think?' asked Hanzel.

'Twenty is a goodly number, however, with a bit of squeezing, we could easily take thirty on board. With thirty we'd be in an excellent position to actually be a threat,' suggested Morgan.

'Let's try for thirty, then,' agreed Hanzel. 'We'll go out first thing in the morning.' Hanzel held up his cup. 'Here's to our success. May we all come out rich and happy.'

'Aye, aye, Captain,' agreed everyone in chorus.

Next morning, everyone was excited about the day's prospects. The morning was already warm and pleasant. Fishermen were leaving the harbour, ready to secure the day's catch. Gulls followed them, squawking over bits and pieces of bait tossed overboard as the fishermen prepared their hooks.

'Two of us will have to stay on board,' suggested Hanzel. 'For security.'

Michael and Pedro volunteered.

'Alright, the rest of us will take the rowboat and go recruiting. We'll bring back some paint, so we can change the name of our sloop,' said Hanzel.

Fifteen minutes later, everyone but Michael and Pedro rowed into town. When they had tied up the rowboat beside the roadway, they climbed up the steps and took a look around themselves, to get their bearings. While they were thusly standing there, Hanzel gave each man some money with which to buy food and drink. 'I suggest you three go together and Hanna and I will go our own way. This way we've got all day to stroll about, visit an assortment of places and likely increase our chances of finding some good candidates. Remember, don't get drunk and carefully screen those whom you want to have join us. We do not want to take chances on some misfits who'll cause us grief.'

'Aye, Captain,' agreed the others. 'We'll meet back here at what time?'

Hanzel looked at Hanna, who shrugged her shoulders and then suggested, ten o'clock p.m.

Everyone thought ten o'clock in the evening would be ideal. That would give everyone fourteen hours to find suitable sailors with an interest in piracy. They set off with a bounce in their steps; each group going a different direction.

'I think we should see about getting something to eat,' suggested Hanna. 'I'm hungry.'

'An excellent idea. Let's go eat. Maybe we'll meet someone in the restaurant.' Hanzel smiled and taking her hand, walked off to find a suitable place to eat. *De Zwarte Kat* was the ideal place. The smells of cooking food permeated the place and made one feel welcome. Several sailors savored soup at a table near the window. Two bawds sat with a couple of shady men at a table in a corner. A lone fisherman sat over an ale at the bar. To the left of the entrance a long table was occupied by the crew of a merchantman on their last day of shore leave before heading back to Indonesia. 'The place is not too busy, just yet,' said Hanzel. 'That's good. We have some choice where to sit.'

Hanna pointed to a table from which they would have a good view of the entire room and the entrance. 'We can see who comes in. I'm sure, as the day unfolds, this place will get busy.'

'I get that impression, as well,' agreed Hanzel.

A pleasantly plump serving girl approached. She was wearing one of those low cut blouses allowing a significant amount of cleavage to be visible. Around her waist she wore an apron. 'Are you here to eat?'

'Yes. Yes we are,' agreed Hanzel. He pointed to the table Hanna had pointed out. 'We'll sit there.'

'Alright,' said the pleasant server. 'I'll come right back and take your order.'

'Thank you,' said Hanzel.

'It smells nice in here,' said Hanna. 'I wonder what's for breakfast.'

'I fancy potato pancakes with some fried eggs and ham.' Hanzel rubbed his belly. I could eat a horse just about now.'

'We serve horse,' said the serving girl, as she approached their table.

'No, I don't really want to eat a horse,' replied Hanzel. 'I just have a big appetite, is what I meant.'

'Have you ever eaten horse?' asked the girl. 'We prepare it in many different ways. You can have it: boiled, broiled, grilled, deep fried, pan fried, ...'

Hanzel held up his hand. 'That's alright. Thank you. We're not here to eat horse meat.'

'Oh, that's too bad. It is one of our specialties. 'Did I mention you can eat it in a stew?'

'I want to eat potato pancakes with eggs and ham,' said Hanzel.

'And I want the same.' Hanna smiled at the girl.

'Two orders of potato pancakes with eggs and ham,' repeated the girl. 'How many eggs do you want?'

Hanzel wanted three and Hanna wanted two.

'Are you sure you wouldn't prefer some horse meat instead of the ham?'

Hanzel looked at Hanna, and she back at him. Then Hanzel regarded the girl. 'Do you have ham?'

'Oh. Do we have ham?' The girl thought for a moment 'I'm not sure. We tend to mostly sell horse. We don't get much call for ham, I don't think. But then, I'm new. I only started yesterday.' The girl looked over her shoulder and then back at the two friends. 'I was told to sell the horse meat. I think the owner got a deal on a horse from a horse seller at the market.'

'I hope it wasn't Sally,' said Hanna, looking fearfully at Hanzel.

Hanzel shook his head. 'The chances of that happening are pretty slim, Hanna. You would have to admit.'

'Who is Sally?' asked the girl.

'A horse we sold in the horse market,' replied Hanna. 'She was a pet.'

'Oh, ya. Of course, I understand. I wouldn't be wanting to eat my pet. Anyway, I'll go and find out if we have ham. I'll be right back.'

'Have you ever eaten horse meat?' asked Hanna, regarding Hanzel, sitting beside her.

Hanzel shook his head. 'I don't think so. I grew up eating mostly fish. We did eat meat at Master De Witt's table and when I was sailing with Pierre and with Captain Bloomingdale. I think it was beef, mostly. Sometimes we ate chicken, if we took some with us in pens. And pork. We ate salted pork. Now, whether some of the questionable meat might have been horse flesh, I really can't say.'

'They say it tastes quite nice, if prepared properly. However, the thought of eating horses revolts me. Don't forget, I have raised horses since I was little. I grew up with horses. We worked with them. We didn't eat them. We ate our cows and chickens. And pigs, of course.'

The girl returned. 'Yes. Yes, apparently we do have ham. You can have it baked, fried, roasted, ...'

Hanzel nodded. 'Yes, roasted.' He looked at Hanna who nodded. 'She'll have the same. And bring us a couple of ales right away. We are both thirsty.' Hanna smiled.

As the young lovers sat waiting for their ales, four interesting looking men stepped into the place. Hanna noticed them first and alerted Hanzel by nudging him in the ribs with her elbow. Two of the men were tall and lanky, one was mid sized, and the fourth one was at least a head shorter than the other three, but of the same build. The tall lanky fellows wore a gold earring in each ear. One had a scarf tied under his leather tricorn. The other had a black patch over his left eye. They all carried two pistols from bandoliers and a cutlass in scabbards hanging at their sides. The shorter man had a gold ring through his right nostril and a silk bandana over his bald head. He wore a thick gold chain around his neck which glinted against his bare chest, visible due to his shirt being open to his navel. All four men wore leather boots.

'Those fellows look like pirates,' suggested Hanna. 'What do you think? They don't look like your average sailors.'

'They could be pirates. Or, they could be sailors from another country. Maybe they're from Russia.' Hanzel regarded his mate.

'Maybe. Those tall ones are very blond. They could be Russians. Or they could be Friesians, like you, Hanzel.' Hanna smiled. 'Maybe they're Friesian.'

'My grand parents came from Friesland. Not my parents. I was born in Holland. I don't speak Friesian.'

'Well, anyway. Those fellows look piratical. Who knows, maybe they're looking for a ship. Perhaps we can get the girl to ask them some questions when she serves them.' Hanna looked over towards the kitchen. Their serving girl was just coming out with a platter containing their breakfast and ales.

'I'm sorry I didn't bring the ales first. But as you can see, we're starting to get busy. Anyway, here are your pancakes with eggs and ham.' She carefully set the trenchers down in front of Hanna and Hanzel. Then she placed the ales beside the boards and asked if there was anything else they needed.

Hanzel beckoned her to lean closer. 'Do you see those men, over there?' Hanzel gestured surreptitiously at the four men. The girl nodded. 'Ask them if they are possibly looking for a ship. Kind of feel them out. What kind of chaps are they? Are they nice and friendly or do you get the feeling that they're bad men?'

'Are they pirates?' asked Hanna, bluntly. 'Ask them if they're pirates looking for a ship. Not to steal one, but to join one.'

'Join one?' The girl looked wideyed at Hanzel and Hanna. 'Join one? What do you mean, join one? Are you members of a pirate gang?'

Hanna indicated Hanzel. 'Meet Hanzel Sventska, The Scourge of the North Sea.'

Hanzel raised his eyebrows and regarded his lover. *Scourge of the North Sea?*

'He doesn't look like much of a scourge to me,' said the girl bluntly.

'Looks are deceiving,' replied Hanna

'Shouldn't a scourge at least have a scar, or something?' asked the girl, staring at Hanzel.

'He's still young. He's only just begun being a pirate,' replied Hanna.

'And he's already a scourge? Boy, he should go far in the pirate business if he's already a scourge.' The girl looked over her shoulder at the four men. 'Should I tell him that you are, Hanzel Sventska, the Scourge of the North Sea?'

Hanzel smiled and shook his head. 'Just ask them if they are looking for a ship and if they are pirates, or what?' He handed the girl two gulden. 'One for the meals and one for you.'

The girl stared at the coins. 'Thank you, sir,' she gushed.

'And sense them out to see what sort of fellows they are?' added Hanna, lifting her tankard.

'Yes. Yes, certainly I will. I will let you know what I find out.' The girl left the table and went about her duties.

Hanzel and Hanna kept an eye on her and the four men. While the two friends were eating, more patrons came in and soon the house was full of people creating a busy hubbub as several dozen conversations were all being carried on at once. Two more serving girls came on the floor. All three were kept busy. It was some time before Hanzel and Hanna's server was able to collect their empty boards and refill their tankards. When she approached Hanzel and Hanna immediately asked, 'So, what did you find out from those men?'

'They're not sailors. And they certainly are not pirates. They wouldn't say, exactly what they do. I suspect they're likely small time criminals. Maybe they are conycatchers.'

Hanzel pursed his lips as he regarded the three men. 'Hmm. Conycatchers or highwaymen, perhaps.' He looked at Hanna. 'We definitely need sailors.'

'Who are friendly,' added Hanna.

The girl nodded. 'I'll keep asking around. I'm sure there's a likelihood at least one man will show up here, who is looking for a ship and fits your needs.' She looked down at the empty boards. 'How did you enjoy your breakfast?'

Hanna smiled. 'Delicious.'

Hanzel nodded. 'Yes, it was very good, thank you.' He indicated the two empty tankards. 'You can bring us a refill, as well.'

The girl picked up the empty boards and tankards. 'I'll be right back,' she said and left their table.

A moment later two sailors stepped into the room. They were laughing over something. Both of them were tall, strong looking men. One had blond hair and the other was a redhead. The redhead wore a beard and mustaches, the blond was clean shaven.

They were both wearing the typical costume of seamen, silver buckled, low healed shoes, striped hose, petticoat breeches, a white and blue striped shirt, red scarf, and a dark blue pea jacket with silver buttons. The blond wore a dark blue woolen cap. The other man was wearing a low, beaver top hat with a silver buckle on the front.

'These sailors look fairly prosperous,' remarked Hanzel, looking them over as they proceeded to walk to an empty table at the other side of the room.

'Why do you say that?' asked Hanna, regarding the two men walking across the dining hall.

'Notice the silver buckles and buttons? And, they are each wearing heavy gold rings in their ears. These chaps have not squandered their earnings, but converted some of it into valuable commodities.'

Hanna nodded. 'Perhaps those two might be suitable candidates? They certainly look as if they could be helpful to us.'

'We have room around our table. Let's see if we can entice them to sit with us. We'll buy them a drink.'

'Good idea, Hanzel. Why don't you go over and talk to them?'

'Alright, I will.' With that, Hanzel got up and walked over to the two sailors and introduced himself. Figuring it best to get straight to the point, he asked point blank, 'Are you gentlemen perhaps looking for a ship?'

The two sailors regarded Hanzel for a moment before replying. As it turned out, they were, indeed, looking for a ship.

'What kind of ship?' asked the blond.

'A sloop.'

'A sloop?' asked the redhead. 'What size sloop?'

'Eighty feet,' answered Hanzel, 'give or take a foot, here or there.'

'An eighty foot sloop? That's not a very big boat. We're looking for a large merchantman or perhaps a ship of the line. Something like that,' said the blond.

'The likelihood is that you'll make much better money with us, than you would earn in either the merchant marine or in the navy,' replied Hanzel. 'Isn't that really the bottom line? Our sloop is a fine, sturdy boat with lots of cargo space. We expect to carry on some significant commerce with this boat.'

The blond raised his eyebrows. 'Oh? So, what line of business are you in?'

Hanzel indicated Hanna, sitting across the room. 'She is my wife, Hanna. She and I, plus our crew of five, carry on a moderate merchant trade in the Baltic region in the summer and along the coasts of England and France.'

'You have a woman on board? That's bad luck, isn't it?' asked the redhead.

'Not in our case. Hanna brings us very good luck,' replied Hanzel, smiling at his sweet friend, patiently waiting at their table. 'We would like it if you would join us so we can buy you a drink, and, if you are hungry, we'll buy you a meal, as well, so we can discuss our needs. Perhaps what we have to offer will be attractive to you.'

'The blond looked at the redhead, who nodded. 'Why not? What have we got to lose? Nothing. And we get a free meal and a drink? Sure, Hanzel, we'll listen to you, eh?' He regarded his partner, who nodded agreement.

A moment later the two sailors were sitting with Hanna and Hanzel at their table. When the serving girl returned with Hanzel and Hanna's ales, Hanzel asked her to bring two more for their new friends, and to add a meal for each man, as well.

While they waited for the ales and food to arrive, Hanzel and Hanna did not discuss their plans, but chose instead to find out who these two men were and whether they would be suitable crewmates. It was not until the men were eating when Hanzel introduced the master plan; to use the sloop for piratical adventures.

'Piracy? A person can be hung, or worse for piracy,' said the blond, whose name was Peter.

'I think you can be broken or beheaded for piracy. I know they cut your head off in Germany,' added the redhead, whose name was Martin. He touched his neck and shivered.

'I believe we are smarter than that. We do not expect to be caught. One must be careful in choosing targets. What we need is man power. With the right number of crew members we can work wonders.'

'Can we bring women on board?' asked Peter.

'Do you have women to bring on board?' asked Hanna.

Peter shook his head. 'No, not really. But if we did, could we?'

Hanzel looked at Hanna, who nodded. 'Of course. Why not? As long as they are willing to contribute if combat is called for.'

'Yes, of course. Warrior women. They would have to know how to sail, as well,' suggested Martin. 'They'd have to be like us, only they're women.'

'Precisely,' agreed Hanzel.

Peter looked at Martin, then back at Hanzel. 'So, I take it there is no wage. We would sign up and be eligible for a percentage of the prizes?'

'That is how it works,' replied Hanzel. 'However, as you well know, the potential is pretty good.'

Peter and Martin nodded. 'We'll talk it over and let you know,' said Peter. Then they excused themselves, in order to discuss the offer. The two sailors left the inn. Hanzel and Hanna watched them go.

'Do you think they'll be back?' asked Hanna.

Hanzel shook his head. 'I've no idea. Maybe we just wasted good money on food and drink.' He frowned and shrugged his shoulders. 'We'll just have to keep trying. Those were only the first two sailors we have talked to. There'll be others. If not here. Then maybe another place. We have to keep trying.

Otherwise we'll not be able to do what we want. With only seven, we're not much of a threat.'

Hanna nodded. 'And, until I learn how to handle weapons, I'm a liability. We actually only have six functioning pirates, at the moment.'

'You'll learn. Don't worry, Hanna. You'll have good teachers. Once we're out at sea, we'll practice everyday.'

'I can't wait until we actually raid a ship,' said Hanna.

'As long as they're afraid of us, and they don't put up a fight, then it is fun and games. If there is resistance, it could get ugly. That is what we'll try to avoid. I don't like seeing people killed.'

'I've never seen anyone dead, except for Henrick and that horse thief, but they don't count. And, Mister Goldman. That was unfortunate. Too bad we had to kill him.' Hanna stared at Hanzel.

'It was not a pretty sight. I will never feel good about that. But, if we're going to be pirates, we have to harden our hearts, to some extent. If we had let him live, he would have turned us in and we would have lost the sloop and our lives. It was either him or us.'

Hanna nodded sadly. 'We've chosen to be pirates. There's no going back now. We have stolen the sloop and killed its owner. The sooner we get a crew together and get out of Rotterdam, the better I'll feel. Word can come from Amsterdam for people to be on the lookout for us.'

Hanzel shook his head. 'Not much chance of that, Hanna. Nobody knows Mister Goldman was on board. Nobody saw us steal the sloop.'

'That is what we hope,' replied Hanna. 'Maybe Goldman's brother knew that Mister Goldman was on board.'

'Even so. Nobody saw us take the sloop.' Hanzel shrugged his shoulders. 'There is nobody who can identify us.'

'Unless the name of the sloop gets here. For the authorities to be on the lookout for that sloop. We still haven't changed the name.'

As the two lovers sat there in the dining room of *De Zwarte Kat* chatting and discussing plans, time drifted by. Hanzel and Hanna had no idea how much time had elapsed by the time they were drinking their fourth tankard of ale and beginning to feel the effects of the heady brew. Whatever the time, it turned out to be a good time when Peter and Martin returned with their duffel bags and twelve more sailors; who had already been filled in on the master plan and were willing to go a roving.

'We brought some friends along. They're all looking for a ship and champing at the bit for adventure. When Martin and I told them about you, they jumped at the opportunity,' said Peter.

'So, now we are twenty one,' said Hanzel happily. 'I wonder how Henk and the boys are making out?' asked Hanzel, looking at his mate.

'If they do half as well as us, we'll have a full compliment. We could go roving tomorrow, or the day after. I can't wait.' Hanna grinned and gestured, as if she was handling a cutlass.

'What is the time?' asked Hanzel. 'Does anyone have an idea?'

One of the new men, a fellow named Bartolemo had a time piece. 'The hour is four,' he said in an unusual accent, Hanzel and Hanna had not heard before.

'We told Henk we would meet up at ten this evening. However, with this many men, ready to go, we'll take you on board now, so you can get set up. This way, Angus and Morgan can come into town for a few hours. I'm sure they would appreciate that.' Hanzel smiled at his pretty wife.

'I'm sure they'll want to spend a few hours on land before we set off,' she replied.

'Alright, then, gentlemen,' said Hanzel, addressing the fourteen new crewmates. 'Our rowboat is tied nearby. Let's go and we'll begin rowing everyone out to the sloop.'

'Hanzel. We must remember to bring paint and some brushes,' said Hanna.

'Oh, yes, of course. I nearly forgot.' Hanzel regarded the new men. 'Does anyone know where we can buy paint?'

A sailor named Jock knew of a shop, not far from *De Zwarte Kat*.

'Alright. Hanna, why don't you take the men to the rowboat and take them to the sloop. I'll go with Jock and buy the paint. I'll meet you on board.' Hanzel touched Hanna's cheek and looked into her eyes for a moment before leaving the room with Jock. A moment later, Hanna led the fourteen new men to the rowboat and they began to row each other out to the sloop anchored nearby.

An hour later, Hanzel and Jock returned to the pier where the rowboat would pick them up. Ten minutes later, Angus and Morgan arrived to bring them the rowboat. Hanzel and Jock thanked them and quickly rowed out to the sloop. Once on board, Hanzel pulled out the articles they had written up and read them to the new men. Then he had each man sign his name or mark on the bottom of the document. Nobody disagreed with the words because they made such good sense. Everyone realized that the ideas expressed would help to keep order in their organization. There was no doubt about the consequences for those who would chose to disregard the rules.

'That is how all law should be,' observed Jock. 'A few rules, easy to understand, with no doubt what happens to transgressors.'

'That is exactly what we wanted to achieve,' agreed Hanzel. 'I'm happy you see it so.' He clapped his hands together. 'Well, that's that. So, welcome aboard, lads. You can go make yourselves comfortable. You will meet the rest of the crew later tonight.'

The new men went about setting themselves up in various places below, where they could hang a hammock and set down their trunk or duffel bag. Eventually, they wandered about the ship acquainting themselves with the ropes.

Meantime, on shore, Angus and Morgan hooked up with their crewmates in a merry bar on the roadway. Henk, Michael, and Pedro were accompanied by seven others; each one of them happily into their cups and laughing uproariously.

On board ship they changed the name of the sloop to, *Great Fortune*.

The following morning when Hanzel and Hanna woke up they found the ship's crew had grown to 24. Half of them were hung over from the previous day's recruiting. Finding good crewmates was hard work; so Morgan claimed when he stepped on deck and Hanzel asked him why he was walking so unsteadily. Hanzel laughed after Morgan had delivered his explanation.

'Hard work, indeed. More like hard drinking, if you ask me,' laughed Hanzel.

When Henk stepped on deck, Hanzel asked him to call all men on deck so that those men who had not yet signed the articles, could do so, before they set sail.

'Is twenty six enough to go roving, Captain?' asked Henk. 'Do you not think we should try to find at least six more?'

'The longer we stay in Rotterdam, the better the chances we could be connected with this stolen sloop, even though we've changed the name. I think we should leave here and do some more recruiting. London is just across the channel. Let's sail there,' suggested Hanzel. 'I'm sure we'll find piratically minded fellows like ourselves.'

'We have enough food and water to take us across the channel. We'll be there tomorrow morning,' said Henk.

Hanzel regarded his new crew. 'What do you say boys? Shall we find some more rovers in London?'

Everyone agreed it was a good idea. Hence, after breakfast, they cast off their lines and sailed out of Rotterdam. A glorious sun warmed the air and lightening everyone's spirits. Gulls followed them for a while, until they were well out into the English channel. The water was choppy but something the sloop was made to slice through. Nobody noticed much of a rise or fall as the ship slipped across the waters, arriving at the entrance to the mighty Thames early the next morning; just as the sun began to rise, bathing the waters in an orange light filtered through a thickening fog; eventually becoming a velvet blanket through which the sun could no longer penetrate.

Chapter 30

'I can't see a thing,' said Angus.

'This fog is really something,' agreed Morgan; standing beside his redheaded friend.

'Better wake Hanzel. We have to have our captain on deck,' suggested Angus.

'Right you are,' agreed Morgan, who ran off to wake Hanzel.

While Morgan was gone, the fog became so thick, Angus became fearful they would not be safe any longer. 'Better get some men out front,' he said to Michael, who had stepped up on the quarterdeck to see if Angus wanted to be relieved at the helm. He agreed spotters were needed and quickly set about organizing the sailors needed for the various jobs.

'And you get up there on the mast and keep an eye for other ships,' ordered Michael as he pointed up the mainmast. The sailor quickly followed his order and climbed up the port shroud. Morgan watched him go. As the man neared the top of the mast he was almost impossible to see in the thickened air.

'Good thing we have lamps,' said Hanzel, as he stepped on deck. 'I've never sailed in such a fog. Maybe we should drop our anchors and wait until the fog dissipates? I don't like sailing in this. We could easily hit something.'

The men agreed that Hanzel was right. They quickly furled the sails and dropped their anchors. They lit extra lamps and posted spotters at the bows, the stern, and on each side of the ship.

'The rest of you can go back to your hammocks,' said Hanzel. 'When the fog has lifted, we'll continue.'

When the fog finally did lift, around ten o'clock, they pulled up their anchors and set their sails to continue sailing up the Thames, making port at Wapping some hours later. The port was teeming with ships of all sizes. Gulls were screaming overhead and pungent smells of human byproducts, dead sea things, and salt filled one's nostrils.

'There is no smell like that of a busy port,' laughed Angus, when Hanna complained of the terrible smells.

'The sailors have to poop somewhere,' observed Peter, who had stepped up on the quarterdeck.

Hanna nodded. 'I'm used to poop. I come from a farm. But to see and smell human poop on the bows of those ships, it's disgusting.' She crinkled up her nose as they sailed past a huge ship of the line. A sailor, just completing his business on the port bow head, looked down at the sloop slipping past. He spat an oyster into the air. It landed with a splash in the discolored water. *I wish I hadn't seen that. Yuck.* She felt her stomach turn. *Euw. Some people are so disgusting.*

A half hour later they found a place where they could drop their anchors, next to a Danish merchantman.

'I'm willing to bet, when we have some more fellows on board, we could easily effect some larceny right here in port,' suggested Martin. 'I mean, look around you. This place is ripe for the pickings. If we find a fat merchantman, ready to set out; we take her under cover of night and slip out of port. We can sell the stuff in France.'

'I think that's a good idea. I'm sure, if we do a little bit of sleuthing, we'll find an appropriate ship, with few hands on board,' said Hanzel clapping his hands together. 'When we go recruiting, keep an ear open for possible candidates, as well. Who knows, we could earn a good start to our business plans here, in Wapping.'

'I suggest we go out, as we did in Rotterdam. Now that there are more of us, we can send out more groups of two or three. Hanna and I will go together. The rest of you can buddy up as you see fit. We'll use the long boat, as well. That way we can all go to shore in two trips.' Hanzel regarded his crew. 'Who volunteers to stay on board?'

Two of the new men, a tall bald man with two golden earrings by the name of Stuwart, and a medium sized man with a big chest and a red bandana on his head, named John, elected to stay on board. Hanzel was satisfied the ship would be in good hands. He handed out some money to those who had none, then they lowered the long boat and rowed to shore.

Hanzel and Hanna were glad to step foot onto the roadway. It was lined with pubs, ordinaries, stewpots, and assorted shops and warehouses dedicated to the marine trade. Gulls squawking overhead, human voices yelling and shouting, snorting horses, squeaking wheels, groaning timbers; all the sounds of a busy commerce filled the space.

'I'm hungry,' said Hanna. 'Let's go find a decent eating place and have breakfast. Maybe we'll luck out, like we did at *De Zwarte Kat* and meet some more sailors. I'm anxious to get out to sea and actually go after a ship.'

'If we can take something here, while in port, we could already have a cargo we can sell in France. Then we can finance a trip across the Atlantic and maybe find another Spanish treasure ship. I'm sure the king would be very interested in us bringing back some treasure for him. He would likely reward us handsomely. And, besides, it is our ultimate goal. If we could find another treasure like we did with Pierre LeGrange, we'd be set for life, Hanna. Just imagine it. We could likely live as well as the king and queen themselves.'

Hanna smiled and hugged his arm. 'I believe you Hanzel. I think we can do it.'

Hanzel pointed. 'Look there. Notice all of those people coming and going from that inn. That looks like it could be the right place to get something to eat. *The Grinning Pig* turned out to be the perfect place to eat and recruit. Within two hours, Hanzel and Hanna had recruited five more interested sailors who brought their duffel bags to the landing where the long boat lay waiting. Hanzel and Hanna and their new friends waited for a half hour when Angus, Pedro, and Henk, arrived with five more sailors.

'Now we're thirty six,' observed Hanzel. 'That is a goodly number.'

'Will our sloop hold that many?' asked Hanna.

'I'm sure our sloop will carry that many,' replied Hanzel. 'They'll be a little bit cramped, but I'm sure we'll be alright. The more the merrier.'

'Ya, Hanna. It's not a problem,' added Henk, stepping into the long boat. 'We've got lots of room.'

As Hanzel was about to step into the boat, he looked back and noticed that Martin and Peter, followed by three other sailors were walking along the roadway, enroute to the boat.

'Now we're thirty nine.' Hanzel grinned. 'We're actually a force to be reckoned with.'

'Aye Captain,' agreed Peter. 'That we are. A force to be reckoned with.'

Eventually, when everyone was back on board ship their number had swelled to 45. The sloop being plenty large enough, was able to comfortably accommodate everyone. Later that evening, Hanzel assembled the crew on deck. They who had not signed the articles were appraised of their import and solemnly sworn into the pirate gang; fixing their signatures or marks next to those of the others.

'Now we are a force to be taken seriously,' said Hanzel smiling. 'You men are in for a real adventure. We'll see about taking something worthwhile locally. Something we can sell in France and then finance a trip to Hispaniola where we will get us a treasure galleon filled with all the gold and silver you will ever want in a lifetime.'

One of the new men pointed to a black East Indiaman anchored next to a navy frigate. 'See that ship? Notice how she is floating low in the water? I was supposed to sail on her; heading back to Batavia with a load of: cheese, pottery, clothing, building material, windows, nails, tools, cows, horses, beer, and other things I can't remember. All things for the colonies there.'

'The further people are from home, the more they want amenities from home,' observed Hanna.

'And they'll pay a fortune for them, too,' added Martin.

'I'm sure that stuff can be sold in France. It won't get us what we'd get if we sailed to Batavia. But who wants to go there? I'm confident the stuff will fetch enough to buy us the food and drink; weapons and other things we're going to need to threaten the Spaniard,' said Hanzel.

'How many crew?' asked Michael.

'Usually no more than twenty, or so,' replied the sailor. 'The owners are cheap, so they use minimum crews. That way they have to pay less.'

'Cheap bastards like that deserve to have their stuff redistributed,' said Angus. 'When are we going to do it?'

'We should wait until it is good and dark. Then we'll dress in dark clothes and row over in the long boat. Then we'll quietly sneak on board and take the crew by surprise.' Hanzel looked at his crew. 'Thirty five of us can go over so we can sail that ship out of port. The other ten can follow in the sloop. What do you think of that plan?'

Everyone agreed the plan was sound.

'Make sure your weapons are ready. If it is good and dark tonight, we'll go tonight. There's no sense in waiting around. Even if it is not totally black, we should still go. I'm tired and so is Hanna, of waiting. It is time to get this show on the road, or, in this case, on the water.' Hanzel laughed. He raised his cutlass. 'To our success, gentlemen!' Then he bowed to Hanna. 'And to our lady, as well.'

Hanna grinned. 'Thank you, Hanzel.' She gave him a big hug and a kiss. The crew cheered.

That night, just around midnight, when clouds obscured the moon, but there was still enough light by which to see where one was going, 25 men in the long boat, followed by another 10 in the rowboat, made their way to the heavily laden merchantman. Quietly, ever so quietly, they approached the massive ship and gently bumped the boats against her hull. The men climbed up the ladders, not making a sound. Nobody on board heard anything. Within the blink of an eye, a pirate took care of the sentry. Another minute later, the pirates began searching about the ship in order to find the officers and crew. Ten minutes later, 20 surprised men stood on deck.

'I will give you a choice,' said Hanzel, facing the captured crew. 'You can join us in this larceny, or you will have to be clapped in irons and eventually dropped off somewhere far from here. If you join us, you will have to sign our articles and become a member of our gang.'

Only the captain and first mate did not want to join Hanzel and his gang. So they were given a cabin to share on board the merchantman; keeping the door locked and guarded by two pirates at all times. The ship was sailed out of the harbour, nobody being any the wiser as to what had occurred on board the big ship. As they sailed down the Thames, followed by the sloop, in the dead of night; there was nobody to challenge them. By morning they were into the channel headed for France.

'Where in France?' asked Angus.

'Le Havre,' replied Hanzel. 'We'll sail there.'

'Good choice,' agreed Michael. 'Been there. They have a good market. I'm sure we'll get rid of this cargo and make a good profit, to boot.'

The trip across the channel to Le Havre was uneventful. All they had to be concerned about was privateers. However, none showed themselves. They arrived in Le Havre the following morning. Several members of the new crew spoke French. They dressed up as well to do merchants, using the last of Hanzel and Hanna's money to buy the proper clothes. Once dressed they set about marketing the cargo. Everyday, boats would come to take another load off the big ship. While they off loaded, the crew took the time to get the sloop and the merchantman ready for an ocean crossing, including changing the name of the merchantman to *Golden Treasure*. It took a week to sell off all the cargo and empty the holds, except for those goods they themselves would need. They got excellent prices, since there was a shortage of some of the goods due to the wars.

'I think it's a good idea to keep both ships,' said Henk to Hanzel as they were watching the loading of barrels of ale, rum, water, and wine. 'That way we'll be much more comfortable crossing the ocean. Once we're in Hispaniola, we can use our swift sloop to chase a galleon.'

'We need to buy some cannons,' suggested Hanzel. 'Now that we have a goodly return off the cargo, we should be able to buy some cannons for the sloop. Eight pounders would do it.'

'There must be an armory here. This is a port. Surely someone has cannons for sale.' Henk looked at Michael, who shrugged his shoulders.

'I don't know how much longer we should be staying here,' said Hanna. 'Word is bound to get here, sooner or later. The big merchantman is easily identified, inspite of our changing the name.'

'Hanna is right,' agreed Hanzel. 'Looking for cannons and getting them installed will take more days. We can likely obtain cannons elsewhere. We should get out of here.'

Henk and Michael agreed it was the right thing to do. So did everyone else, when they were filled in on what was happening. Hence, when the ships were provisioned and ready to sail, Henk became captain of the sloop and Hanzel assumed leadership of *Golden Treasure*. They slipped out of Le Havre mid afternoon on Hanzel's birthday, April 23rd, 1624.

'HAPPY BIRTHDAY!!!' shouted Hanzel's friends.

'Happy Birthday, darling,' said Hanna, giving Hanzel a kiss.

'A toast!' proposed, Michael, holding up a cup of rum. 'To our favorite captain, Hanzel Sventska. May he live a hundred years!'

Everyone on board raised their cup and shouted, 'TO HANZEL SVENTSKA, MAY HE LIVE A HUNDRED YEARS!!!'

Hanzel thanked his friends as presents piled up on the table. He was overwhelmed. 'Thank you, thank you,' he kept saying over and over again. When the crew was done presenting Hanzel with tokens of their esteem he thanked them all once again and then turned the ship over to Michael and Angus, while he and Hanna went below, to the master's cabin, where Hanna made sweet love to her dearest Hanzel in the whole world.

Next day, when Hanzel and Hanna reemerged from their cabin, they had sailed out of the channel and were now ploughing waves in the North Atlantic, off the coast of Brest.

'Good morning, gentlemen,' said Hanzel, taking in a deep breath as he stepped onto the quarter deck.

'Good morning Capitan,' said Pedro. He had taken over the helm from Angus, who had gone to his hammock, having served through most of the night.

'Morning, Hanzel,' said Peter; putting his spyglass down. 'Did you sleep well?'

Hanzel looked at Hanna, who blushed. 'Yes, yes, thank you. We slept well.'

'It's a beautiful morning,' said Hanna, taking in a deep breath. The air is so fresh out here on the ocean. It's so much nicer than the smells of the farm.'

'That is one of the reasons we like sailing,' said Michael, who was standing beside Pedro at the helm. 'It's the fresh air.'

'And the adventure,' added Peter.

'Yes, the adventure, the fresh air,...' continued Michael.

'And the fish. I like the fresh fish we eat when we're at sea,' said Morgan, who was standing at the transom. 'I love fresh fish.'

'You can keep the fish,' replied Hanzel. 'I grew up on fish. Ate fish until I was twelve, when I ran away from home. Give me a good piece of roasted beef, or pork.'

'Aye, Capitan. Beef and pork. That's my choice.' Pedro looked at Hanzel and smiled.

'To change the subject, gentlemen. I have been wondering where we should sail to, enroute to Hispaniola. Should we sail south to the Cape Verde Islands or shall we head to the Azores?' Hanzel regarded his friends. 'The Azores are only eight hundred, or so nautical miles off the south coast of Portugal.'

'I've been there,' said Peter enthusiastically. 'Beautiful. They're the perfect place to stop.'

'I agree,' said Pedro. 'I have been to the Azores a number of times. You will love it. I can't wait to get into a hot spring and soak my creaky bones.'

'What do you say, gentlemen? The Azores?' asked Hanzel.

Everyone agreed it was the best place to go. Not too far away and would provide a good rest stop before the long crossing to Hispaniola. Thus, they set their course to 30 degrees 15 minutes West by 37 degrees 50 minutes north, somewhere smack dab in the middle of the volcanic archipelago.

The voyage to the Azores was easy sailing for the most part, except for a day long squall which amounted to nothing but was enough to bring the dreaded sea sickness to Hanna, who lay miserably in bed for four days. Hanzel, knowing full well what sea sickness was all about, having seen others succumb to that scourge, felt very sad for his dearest friend. Poor Hanna, there were times when she wished she were dead. Hanzel did his best to comfort her; even reading to her from a book they found in the master's cabin. The book was a 1615 English translation of *Don Quixote*. Hanzel's reading greatly brightened Hanna's mood.

On the fifteenth day from the time they passed Brest, the lookout on the big merchantman shouted, 'LAND HO!' Soon thereafter, a gull perched on top of the main mast; the best sign that land was near. Six hours later they sailed into *Ponta Delgada*, the capital of the island of Sao Miguel. It was mid afternoon. The sky had become overcast and threatened rain. The date was May 7, 1624.

The two ships were able to anchor side by side in the well protected harbour. Only three other ships lay at anchor and two were tied to the pier. One of the anchored ships belonged to the Spanish navy. 'We'll keep an eye on that one,' suggested Hanzel.

When all was secure, Hanzel called a meeting on the deck of the *Golden Treasure*.

'What say you men? Shall we sojourn here for a week, or so? We can replenish our supplies and see if we can find out anything about the Spanish treasure fleet. There are lots of Spaniards about in this place, so be careful what you say to them.' Hanzel regarded his crew mates for a moment before continuing. 'Remember the words of a wise admiral of old; "Loose lips sink ships."'

'Aye, aye, Captain! Loose lips sink ships!' shouted the men in agreement.

'Alright then. Lower the boats and let's go enjoy ourselves.' Hanzel grinned as the men quickly set about lowering the boats. Even after only a couple of weeks at sea, the men were eager to step on land and find a tavern to sit in. Perhaps to find a, *girlfriend*. The time spent on shore would prepare them for the long voyage to Hispaniola; a passage which was always fraught with danger.

'What are your plans, Hanzel? What are you and Hanna going to do while you're here?' asked Henk.

'Hanna and I found an interesting book identifying flora and fauna. We're going to see if we can identify some while we're here.'

'We're going on a natural history tour,' added Hanna. 'I'm sure we'll find some interesting things here.'

'Before it rains?' asked Henk, looking at the sky.

'Well, maybe not today,' replied Hanzel. 'First we're going to find a good meal, eh, Hanna?'

'Aye, Captain,' she said smiling as she stepped onto the ladder leading down to the long boat.

A half hour later, Hanzel and Hanna were sitting side by side on a bench against the west wall of a large eating house. From their vantage point they could see just about everyone in the place. Nine members of their crew had also landed in the place and were sitting together at a long table in the middle of the room.

'Should we go and join them, Hanzel?' asked Hanna, watching their crewmates ordering drinks.

'No, Hanna. I just want to be alone with you. We've spent the last couple of weeks with those fellows, with little privacy. I want us just to be with each other. We'll have plenty of time cooped up with those chaps when we sail to Hispaniola.' Hanzel smiled at his partner. They looked into each other's eyes for a long while; deeply in love and praying that their happiness would last forever.

Chapter 31

The following morning, Hanzel and Hanna decided to go exploring. They packed a picnic lunch before going ashore, making sure to bring the naturalist book along. On shore they hired a horse and carriage, asking directions to the hot springs Pedro had told them about. The man who rented the carriage explained how to find a nice, private one. 'Nobody goes there. Very few people know of that one. It is the perfect place for lovers.'

Hanzel and Hanna thanked the man and gave him a little extra money because he was kind enough to share the information about the hot spring.

The ride to the spring was on a road, at first. Eventually they turned off onto a winding track, climbing up the volcano. They arrived at the spring a half hour later. A magnificent private pool greeted them, surrounded by cedar, mahogany, and dogwood trees. The pool was fed with a small waterfall of hot water and a spring. The shore was a riot of multicolored flowers and every shade of green.

'This is Paradise,' said Hanna, taking a deep breath as she regarded the idyllic place with arms outspread.

'The carriage renter was right. This is the perfect place for lovers.' Hanzel began to remove his shirt. 'I can't wait to get into that water. I'm sure it will feel great.'

'Oh, Hanzel. Isn't this glorious? I have dreamt of places such as this. I had no idea they actually existed.'

'Apparently this one does.' He pointed. 'Look. Flat rocks to sit on.'

'This is incredible,' replied Hanna, sitting down on a rock. 'I can't believe how clear this water is. However, I wouldn't drink it. It does have a sulfurous smell.'

'No wonder. We're on the slopes of a volcano. It would make sense that the water would have a sulfur smell.' Hanzel stretched out. 'This sure feels good.'

Hanna moved closer to him and returned to her more intimate explorations. 'And, how does this feel?'

Hanzel smiled and kissed his lover, long, deep, and passionately. 'I love you, Hanna,' he whispered.

'I love you too, Hanzel,' she replied, as she took him into her body and proceeded to move her pelvis in the rhythms of passion.

Birds twittered in the trees overhead. A butterfly settled on a leaf and then fluttered off to land on a yellow flower on the opposite side of the pool. Water splashed on water. A gentle breeze jiggled grasses. Sunlight glinted off droplets. Life was warm and good.

Meanwhile, back in town, the crews of *Great Fortune* and *Golden Treasure* had spread out and were having a happy time in three different establishments. Henk, Michael, Morgan, and Angus found themselves in the *Taverna Madrid*, a busy inn not far from the harbour, where Michael found a lady; a young woman looking for adventure. He and she became inseparable from then on. Her name was Maria Angelina. She had no idea about a family name; having been an orphan; there was no record in the books regarding her parents. She had grown up in Lisbon and was brought out to the Azores by a merchant who purchased her from the orphanage at the age of 12. She had lived in Ponta Delgada for 13 years. Now that she was 25, she had earned her freedom and made her living tending to patrons of the inn. Maria wanted out and Michael was her opportunity.

'I guarantee that you'll like her, Hanna,' said Michael, one afternoon when they were sitting in the great cabin waiting out a rain storm.

'I don't mind having another woman on board,' replied Hanna. 'If she is accepted by the crew, I think it would be wonderful to have another female sailing with us. It would be nice for me, to have a sister on board.'

'The best thing to do is to introduce her to the rest of the crew,' suggested Hanzel. 'Does she know what we do?'

Michael nodded. 'I told her a little bit. She's all for having an adventure. And, she's good and sturdy. I'm sure she'll pull her weight.'

'I suggest you start bringing her on board,' said Hanzel. 'Let the crew get used to her.'

'Angus, Henk, Morgan, and Pedro have already met her and spent some time with us. They like her,' replied Henk. 'If there was something wrong with her, they would have told me.'

'If she joins us, she'll have to sign the articles, just like everyone else,' said Hanzel.

'Of course, of course, Hanzel. And, she's told me that she'll practice learning to use weapons and is prepared to climb ropes, or do whatever is required.'

'Hanna and I look forward to meeting her,' said Hanzel, taking Hanna's hand. 'We are off to do some sightseeing. Hanna discovered a canary like bird yesterday. We think it may be a finch. So, now that the rain is letting up, we're going to see if we can identify it.' Hanzel picked up the natural science book off the table. 'This book might help us.'

'Good luck,' said Michael, standing up from his chair. 'I'm going into town to be with Maria. Perhaps I'll bring her back this evening for you to meet. I'm going to get ready.'

'We'll be ready in ten minutes, or so. We can take the boat together,' said Hanzel.

Michael nodded and left the cabin. Hanzel and Hanna quickly set about organizing themselves for their natural history tour of the beautiful island. In town they hired a horse and carriage and returned to the place where they had seen the bird. Eventually, ending up in each other's arms in a hot pool five miles from town. They never did find their yellow bird, however, they did identify a cliff pigeon and a rainbow trout.

When Hanzel and Hanna returned to the merchantman they were immediately introduced to Maria Angelina. Hanna and she took to each other instantly. The rest of the crew were content to have her on board. Hence, later in the evening, after dinner Maria signed the articles and officially joined a pirate gang .

Three days later they decided they had enough of Ponta Delgada and the Azores. It was time to finish provisioning and head for Santo Domingo on the island of Hispaniola where the Spanish treasure fleet lay waiting; a fleet Angus and Morgan had been told about by two drunken Spanish sailors. When

Hanzel and his gang sailed out of the harbour, Maria pointed. 'Right there. That's where a Portuguese ship blew up a Spanish navy ship. You can still see it under the water. It was over forty years ago in the Battle of Ponta Delgada. It was one of the few victories the Portuguese won over the Spanish. Now the Spaniards are finally leaving, after all of these years.'

'Makes you wonder, doesn't it? Countries make wars and achieve some result, which later on reverses right back to the way things were before,' observed Hanna. 'It's all such a waste.'

Maria nodded sadly. 'A lot of good people have died in wars. I think that might have happened to my parents. They were likely killed. Nobody could tell me at the orphanage, what happened to them.'

'I can't imagine growing up without parents,' replied Hanna. 'I'm lucky. I have good parents.'

'You *are* lucky,' sighed Maria, staring out to sea.

Gulls screeched overhead as the big merchantman sailed out of the harbour and headed for open water, followed by the sloop, sailing close behind.

'Next stop, Hispaniola,' said Hanzel, clapping his hands together. 'Hispaniola and the Spanish treasure fleet.'

'If those Spanish sailors are to be believed,' said Angus, 'the Spaniard has been assembling a fleet in a large, secluded bay along the east shore of the island. They didn't know the exact location, unfortunately.'

'There are a lot of secluded bays along the coasts of Hispaniola,' replied Peter. 'I've sailed along the east shore. I know what I'm talking about.'

'We'll sail along the coast and see what we can see,' said Hanzel. 'As long as our supplies hold out and we have plenty of water.'

'We'll know that when we've made the crossing,' suggested Angus. 'There are places we can find water, but we'll have to look for them.'

'I have a good feeling about this voyage,' said Hanzel, grinning at his lover. 'Eh, Hanna. What do you think?'

'It feels better, now that I'm not getting woozy from seasickness.'

'That's just the worst feeling, isn't it?' agreed Angus. 'When I first went to sea, I got seasick. Lots of people get seasick. It's not normal for the body to be going up and down and sideways all the time.'

'Especially when it is windy,' agreed Hanna.

'Speaking of,' said Morgan. 'Look over there.' He pointed in the direction of the starboard bow. 'Look at those clouds. They're pretty dark. We may get some rain later today.'

Hanna shrugged her shoulders. 'Oh well. Some of us will get wet. That's life at sea. Isn't it?'

The others agreed that being wet was the norm on board a ship. There was always water seeping in somewhere, washing down between cracks in boards as waves crashed over the bows, or just the mist in the air accumulating on clothes and in people's hair. Water was unavoidable at sea.

When the rain came, Hanzel and Hanna went into the master's cabin, leaving Angus to handle the helm, Morgan to handle the watch, and five others to handle sails as needed. Everyone else took refuge below decks, where they played cards, read, wrote letters, drank rum, and talked about treasure.

The storm lasted for three days, as rain splattered the decks and visibility remained poor. However, the storm was nothing severe, hence everyone took it in stride; performing their duties as per normal. Food and drink was plentiful and morale was high. Everyone looked forward to relieving the Spaniard of his treasure.

As the days passed into weeks and the weeks became a month, Hanna and Maria Angelina became excellent friends. They worked hard at learning the ropes and by the time they had been at sea for over a month, the women had become capable sailors who were completely familiar with the operation of the ship. They also became adept at shooting a pistol and harquebus, as well as handling: boarding axes, dirks, marlin spikes, pikes, and a crossbow.

'I wouldn't want to cross one of those ladies,' said Peter to his friend Martin. 'Look at them. Hanna really handles a cutlass well. I was practicing with her yesterday. She has come a long way in short time.'

'She's a farm girl. She has strong arms and legs. Hanna is no pushover,' replied his red headed friend.

'And what about Maria? She can shoot. Did you see her with the harquebus yesterday? She hit every target we threw out there.' Peter regarded his friend. 'I hope I find a good woman like one of those two.'

'Maybe, if we make port in Hispaniola or Tortuga we'll find us some girl friends to bring on board,' replied Martin. 'In the meantime, it doesn't bother me not to have a woman, at the moment. Although, watching those two,' he indicated the two young women, sitting side by side on a hatch cover sewing a flag for their ship, 'makes me jealous of Hanzel and Michael.'

Peter regarded his friend. 'You be careful you don't get no bad thoughts developing in your head. You know what would happen to you if you touched one of those women?'

Martin nodded. 'I know. I signed the articles, same as you.'

'Yes, well, just don't be jealous. Jealousy is a very bad state of mind. It will eat you up.' Peter stared into his friend's eyes.

Martin nodded. 'I know. I know about that. And, I can control it. But, I've heard some of the new men talking. I don't know if it was such a good idea bringing those women on board, as nice as they are; there are some in our crew, who might be potential problems.'

'If anyone touches those women, either the women will chop him into pieces, or Hanzel and Michael will. I don't think we have anything to be worried about. It's just talk. Men talk about doing things with women. That's how we are. I'm sure you've bragged about an exploit or two with some angel, somewhere.' Peter grinned. 'I know I have.'

Martin nodded. 'I hope you're right. I wouldn't want to see trouble of that kind on board. It makes for a bad energy which might bring out the Klabautermann.'

'Yes, that's possible, isn't it. If this ship has one, dark energy will bring it out, that's for sure,' Peter looked over his shoulder, suddenly nervous the ship's kobold was stirring.

Meanwhile, below deck, another conversation was taking place between three sailors who had joined the crew in Le Havre. The three men were discussing women over a bottle of rum. By the time their blood streams were circulating a nearly equal mixture of rum and leukocytes, a man named Bart suggested a plot; a dastardly plot which resulted in consequences most dire and foul. 'Since we three are natural men who need women from time to time; and we've been at sea for over five weeks now, since we left Ponta Delgada, and there are women available; we should see if we can't lure one of em down here; in the foc'sle where nobody but us will know where she is.'

'You mean, we should imprison one of em?' asked Joe, a tall, thin man with a dragon tattoo on his left forearm. 'Imprison her and then have our way with her whenever we want?'

'That sounds dangerous to me,' suggested Karl, a young man with tribal tattoos on his neck and the back of his bald head. 'Surely someone will hear her screaming.'

'We gag her, you dolt. We tie her up and gag her. Then we can do what we want,' replied Bart.

'Which one should we grab?' asked Karl.

'The small one. Maria. She should be easy because Michael leaves her alone quite a lot. If she's not with Hanna, she's in her cabin. We'll grab her out of her cabin and bring her here,' said Bart.

'Someone will see us. To carry her all the way from the back to the front of the ship, someone will see us, for sure,' suggested Karl.

'We'll knock her out and carry her in a duffel bag. If anyone asks, it's laundry,' said Bart. 'Then we'll tie her up in here, gag her, and then we can have our way with her, anytime we want.'

'If we're caught, we're dead,' suggested Karl.

'We're not going to get caught. We'll make it look like she fell overboard. If we gag her properly, nobody will hear her.' Bart took another swig of rum from the bottle.

'Lord help us,' muttered Karl.

'So, when do you plan to do this?' asked Joe.

'Tonight,' answered Bart, licking his pudgy lips.

'Tonight?' asked Karl, surprised it would be so soon.

'Yes, tonight,' answered Bart. 'Michael has the midnight watch. Maria will be alone, and likely asleep in their cabin.'

'Won't anyone hear her screaming?' asked Joe.

'We'll sneak into her cabin and immediately put a pillow over her head. When she passes out, we'll put her into that large duffel bag I have. Since you're the strongest, Karl, you can carry her over your shoulders. Then we'll climb down to the hold. Nobody is down there, at night. We'll simply bring her here and tie her up to that bulkhead. We'll gag her and then do whatever we want.'

'What about food and water?' asked Joe.

'We'll bring her food and water,' said Bart, taking a drink from the bottle.

'I don't know, Bart,' said Karl nervously. 'I have a bad feeling about this.'

'If you want to back out....'

Karl shook his head. 'No, no, Bart, I don't want to back out. But, I have a bad feeling, is all.'

'Trust me. This will work. We'll do it tonight.' Bart licked his lips and took another long drink from the nearly empty bottle.

'Hey, leave some for the rest of us,' said Joe, reaching for the rum.

The three miscreants passed out in the foc'sle, victims of excessive drink. Nobody missed them, since they were not scheduled on deck anyway. Eventually, as the night had passed its mid point and the bell rang two, the three plotters woke up from their drunken sleep. They had no idea what time it was, not sure how many bells had rung. In the darkness they had trouble stumbling their way out of the foc'sle into the bottom hold; a place of rats, worms, cockroaches, and the putrid smells of rotting things and stagnant water.

'This is a foul place,' observed Karl as they bumbled their way to the ladder leading to the upper deck.

'It's the perfect place to bring her. Nobody will suspect she is down there. If she is gagged, nobody will ever hear her,' said Bart.

'How do we pretend she fell overboard?' asked Joe.

'We'll sneak up on deck through the forward hatch. Then we'll toss something overboard which will make a splash. Then we'll pretend we saw her leaning over the railing. When we came running, she had fallen overboard.' Bart scratched his bushy beard.

'You're so smart,' said Karl, admiringly. 'That's why you're our leader.'

Bart grinned. 'Thank you, Karl.'

'One of us better make sure that Michael is on the quarterdeck. I don't want to walk into their cabin and find him there,' said Joe.

'You go,' replied Bart. 'Karl and I will meet you outside her cabin door.'

Joe nodded and climbed up the stairs to the main deck, while Bart and Karl made their way aft to the officer's quarters; four cabins and the grand cabin at the back of the ship. When the two monsters arrived in the officer's quarters Bart could not remember which of the four cabins was Michael and Maria's.

'I don't know which one is hers,' he whispered.

'Try listening at the doors,' suggested Karl.

Bart put his right ear to a door and listened intently. Not hearing anything he moved on to the next door. When he put his ear to the third door, the fourth door opened and Maria stepped out just when Joe stepped around the corner.

'Quick, grab her,' whispered Bart.

Joe tried to put his hand over Maria's mouth as he grabbed her waist. She bit his hand and yelled. Instantly, Bart knocked her on the head with a peg, sending Maria to the floor with a thump. The noise woke up Hanna, who sat up in bed and listened. She nudged Hanzel. 'Hanzel,' she whispered. 'There's something going on in the gangway. I heard a noise.'

Hanzel mumbled something unintelligible as he slowly sat up in bed. 'What is it?'

'I heard a noise. Outside the door. It sounded like something hit the floor.'

Hanzel listened intently. He heard nothing except the creaking of the ship's timbers and the sound of water against the hull. 'I don't hear anything.'

In the gangway, the three criminals had frozen in their tracks and waited for a few minutes before picking up Maria from the floor. As Karl bent over to pick her up, Maria's hand flopped against his jacket, catching a finger nail on a button which was about to fall off. As Karl adjusted his hold on her, so that Joe could lift her legs, the button came off the jacket and fell to the floor; rolling towards Michael's door, unbeknownst to the three kidnappers. Without wasting anymore time they quickly carried the hapless woman down to the hold, where they stuffed her into the duffel bag before carrying her down to that foul little room in the starboard bow. Because it was so early in the morning, nobody was about, except for the officers on the deck, the helmsman and a couple of sailors. Everyone else was snoring in their hammocks. Hanzel and Hanna also returned to their slumbers.

In the tiny room, Karl lit a small lamp. Then the three conspirators extracted Maria from the duffel bag and tied her wrists. Karl pulled the rope through a ring in the ceiling, stretching her arms over her head. She did not regain consciousness during this procedure.

'Now for the fun part,' said Bart lasciviously, extracting a dirk from his boot. He carefully sliced Maria's clothes off, rendering her naked in a few deft strokes. When he was done, he stood back and picking up the lantern, played the flickering light over Maria's body. The three men grunted and began to touch her. Maria moaned.

'Quick. Grab that rag,' said Bart, 'and stuff it into her mouth before she comes to.'

Joe picked up a dirty rag and stuffed it into Maria's mouth. 'There,' he said. 'That'll keep her quiet.'

The three misfits then set about their business in earnest, groping the victim and eventually raping her, one by one. By that time Maria was fully conscious and wriggling. The three monsters preferred it that way.

'Way more fun when she's awake, don't you think, boys?' asked Bart as he attempted to enter her for a second time. Maria jerked away, hurting his quivering unit. Bart did not appreciate that and smacked the poor girl hard across the face, again and again all the while berating her with a litany of, 'You bitch! You cunt! You whore!' When he felt she was sufficiently punished he backed off. 'All right boys. I think it's becoming morning. We had better get out of here. We'll come back tonight and have some more fun.' He stared at the barely conscious girl tied with her arms over her head to the bulkhead. 'Don't you go away, sweetheart. We'll see you later.' Then he laughed in such a way, even Joe and Karl got chills.

The three monsters left that foul place and crawled back, leaving Maria in darkness; her arms going numb as the blood barely made its way to her hands. They totally forgot to throw something overboard, being heavily inebriated. Eventually Maria couldn't feel her hands and arms anymore. She tried to yell, but the disgusting rag was firmly stuck deep into her mouth. There was nothing she could do but try and take the weight off her arms by standing as much as possible, shivering, naked, in the cold bows of the rolling ship.

When Michael came off watch at five bells, he yawned and wished Morgan and Pedro a good night. He quickly climbed down from the quarter deck and headed for his cabin in the officer's quarters. He could not wait to cuddle up with his sweet Maria. When he stepped into the gangway, he noticed the button on the floor outside his door. He picked it up and checked his buttons. Noting it was not one of his own, he shrugged his shoulders and put it into a side pocket of his jacket. Then he entered his cabin. It was dark inside. He did not want to wake his lover and therefore undressed in the dark. He did not notice that Maria was not there until he had fully undressed and climbed into bed. *That's strange. Where's Maria? There's a head in the cabin. Surely she wouldn't be up already. That's not like her.* Michael could not figure out where his girlfriend was.

He lit a lamp and put his clothes back on. Then he left the cabin and went up on deck.

Morgan and Pedro were still standing on the quarterdeck; Pedro handling the wheel and Morgan keeping an eye on things. 'Have you seen Maria?' asked Michael.

Morgan and Pedro regarded their friend. 'Maria? What do you mean, have we seen Maria? Isn't she in your cabin?' asked Morgan, perplexed.

Michael shook his head. 'No. She's not there. That's not like her. She does not appear to be up on deck. Surely she wouldn't be wandering about down below.'

'Maybe she's with Hanzel and Hanna in their cabin. Have you tried them?' asked Pedro.

'I'd hate to wake them,' replied Michael.

'Better go look. You've got to find her. Otherwise we have a missing person, and that's a problem on a ship,' said Morgan earnestly.

Michael nodded and returned to the officer's quarters where he knocked on Hanzel and Hanna's door.

'Now what?' asked Hanzel, looking at Hanna. 'Who is it?'

'Michael,' came the reply from behind the door. 'Is Maria with you?'

Hanzel looked at Hanna and she back at him. 'Why would Maria be with us? At this time?' whispered Hanzel.

Hanna regarded Hanzel with a worried expression. 'There's something wrong.'

'No. Maria is not with us,' said Hanzel.

Michael paused. 'Maria is missing,' he replied at last. 'She's not in bed and not on deck. She wouldn't be wandering around the ship. I don't know what to think.'

Hanzel climbed out of bed and opened the door. He gestured for Michael to enter the cabin.

'Sorry to bother you,' he said apologetically, looking at Hanna, sitting up in bed. She smiled a greeting and nodded.

'So, what's this about Maria?' asked Hanzel, sitting down in a chair. He gestured for Michael to sit down, but he was too anxious, he could not sit down. 'I came off the watch at five bells and went to bed. When I climbed in bed she was not there. I thought perhaps she was using the head. She wasn't there either. I have no idea. Then I went on deck but she's not there. Nobody has seen her.'

Hanzel stared at his friend for a moment and then looked at Hanna. 'What do you think?'

'Maybe, God forbid, she fell overboard. Maybe she'd gone up on deck and leaned over the railing,' suggested Hanna. Then she shook her head. 'You would have seen her. You were on watch.'

Michael nodded. 'So, that's not it. She has to be somewhere on this ship.'

'Do you suppose that she was kidnapped?' asked Hanna. She looked from Hanzel to Michael. 'Remember, I thought I heard something outside our door. Could it be that a sailor, or a group of sailors decided they needed a woman?'

'Kidnapping and rape?' Michael looked horrified. 'Do you really think that's possible? We screened the fellows pretty closely before signing them up. And, besides, they signed the articles. They know what the penalty is for messing with a crewmate's woman.'

'The question is, is that what happened? We don't know.' Hanzel regarded Michael for a moment before continuing. 'We need to search the ship, that's all there is to it.' He clapped his hands together. 'I'll get dressed and meet you on deck.'

'Thank you, Hanzel.' Michael left the cabin and closed the door.

Hanzel tossed off his pajamas and reached for his clothes.

'I'm coming with you,' said Hanna, climbing out of bed.

'The more people searching, the sooner we'll find her, I should think.' Hanzel smiled as he watched his beautiful friend remove her night clothes. 'It's very strange, her going missing like that. Maybe she's having an affair with another man?'

Hanna shook her head. 'I don't think so. I've spent a lot of time with her. If she was interested in someone else, I'm sure I would know about it.'

'So, there we have it. Either she fell overboard, or she's been kidnapped.' Hanzel adjusted his shirt. 'I hope neither are true.'

'Me too,' agreed Hanna, putting on her breeches.

A few minutes later, Hanzel and his mate stepped on deck. The air was bracing and fresh. The big ship was plowing through the waves at four knots.

The sloop was a half league ahead. Overhead the sky was mostly deep blue, with the odd cloud floating here and there. They each took deep breaths.

'Now I'm awake,' said Hanzel. 'Fresh air always does that for me.'

'Me too,' agreed Hanna. 'Especially this ocean air. I am so loving this. I should have been born the daughter of a sea captain.'

Hanzel smiled and looked at his lovely partner. 'Well, now you're the *wife* of a sea captain. That's just as good, isn't it?'

Hanna smiled and gave him a kiss. 'Even better.'

Michael climbed down from the quarter deck. 'As you can see, she's not on deck. I've asked a few crew mates to join us in the search.' He pointed. 'That's them, there. Waiting at the fore hatch. I thought we could do a search, deck by deck, from stem to stern.'

'Alright, let's go,' said Hanzel. He walked over to the sailors waiting at the fore hatch. The four jack tars greeted Hanzel and Michael with a friendly good morning.

Michael addressed the sailors. 'Albert, you and Stewart go down to the hold and search the entire deck. Look everywhere.' The two sailors nodded and climbed down the stairs of the fore hatch. Michael looked at the other sailors. 'Luke, you and Karl will search all the storage lockers and Hanzel and I will search everywhere else.'

The two sailors nodded. Michael noticed that Karl was missing a button off his jacket. *His buttons look like the one I picked up.* He took the button out of his pocket and examined it as the two sailors set off on their mission. *Could be just a coincidence. What would Karl be doing in the officers' quarters?* Michael thought about the button as he and Michael began their search in the great cabin.

The search of the ship woke those sailors, who were still sleeping. By six bells everyone was up and about, searching for the lost woman. After an hour, all hands stood on deck. The search was over. According to the crew, every place on the ship had been searched. Nobody, however, had thought to look in the very lowest, meanest place, the little room in the starboard bow. The three kidnappers were standing together. Bart whispered to his mates, 'I told you nobody would find her there.'

'The only conclusion we can now reach,' said Hanzel gravely, 'is that Maria has fallen overboard sometime during the night. May God grant her peace.' He paused for a minute then dismissed the crew.

Michael shook his head. 'I just can't accept that. It makes no sense.'

'We've searched the entire ship,' said Hanzel.

Michael nodded. 'She has to be here. There has to be a corner where we haven't looked.' He fingered the button in his pocket. 'If she has been kidnapped, and there is a place on board this ship we have not looked in, perhaps this button serves as a clue.' He showed the button to Hanzel. He took the button and examined it.

'Looks like a button off a sailor's coat,' said Hanzel.

'I found it outside my cabin. It must have fallen there in the night, otherwise I would have noticed it yesterday.' Michael gestured towards the three kidnappers standing together near the midship hatch.

'Hanna said she heard noises outside our cabin and Karl is missing a button on his jacket.' He handed the button back to Michael.

Michael looked at Karl. 'He came on board in Le Havre. He seems like a decent enough fellow.'

'He is missing a button just like that one.' Hanzel pointed to the button in Michael's hand.

'Maybe that's what I heard last night, Hanzel. It could have been a button falling on deck.' Hanna looked at her lover. 'I'm not sure what it was, but it could very well have been that.'

'I think we should have us a little talk with Karl,' suggested Hanzel. He signaled the man to come up on the quarterdeck. Hanna excused herself to return to the cabin and get herself properly ready for breakfast.

'You want to see me, Captain?' asked Karl, stepping onto the quarterdeck.

'You are missing a button off your jacket,' said Hanzel.

Karl looked at his jacket. 'Yes, I know. I have no idea where that button went. Must have fallen off somewhere I was working.'

Michael held up the button. 'I found this button in the officers' quarters. It looks like your missing button.'

Karl regarded the button and nodded. 'Yes, it does look my button. But, it can't be mine. What would I be doing in the officers' quarters?'

'That is the question, isn't it? What, indeed, were you doing in the officers' quarters?' asked Michael.

'I wasn't,' replied Karl, a hint of desperation in his voice.

'I wonder how many other sailors are missing a button?' asked Hanzel, looking at Michael. 'We'll call all hands on deck and ask them.' Hanzel looked at Morgan, standing beside Angus at the helm. 'Call all hands on deck.'

Morgan made the call. Five minutes later all hands were gathered top side. Hanzel asked them if any man was missing a button off a jacket or coat. Everyone's buttons appeared to be where they were supposed to be. The ones who were missing buttons, were missing buttons of the wrong size or colour.

'It looks like you are the only one missing a button such as this one,' said Hanzel. 'So, the question remains, what were you doing outside Michael's cabin?'

'I wasn't outside your cabin,' replied Karl defiantly. 'I have no idea how that button got there. Maybe someone is trying to frame me for Maria's disappearance.'

'Why would anyone do that?' asked Michael. 'Who would want to disappear Maria and frame you for it?'

Karl shook his head. 'I have no idea. She seems like a nice girl.'

'Who, indeed, would want to frame you for such a dastardly deed?' asked Hanzel. 'Do you have enemies on board?'

Karl paused to think. *Enemies? If I name anyone, they'll question them. I have to play dumb. I don't have enemies.* He shook his head. 'I don't have any enemies, that I can think of.'

Hanzel looked at Michael and frowned. 'How do we make any sense of this? Maria goes missing in the night and we find his button outside your cabin door. What do you make of that?'

Karl became flustered. 'I have nothing to do with any of this. I have no idea about the button.'

'Who would possibly want to frame you? It makes no sense. None whatsoever.' Hanzel looked at Michael and back to Karl; boring into his brain with his ice blue eyes.

'Not to me, either. I can't imagine that someone would plant someone's button outside my door during a night when Maria goes missing. I think the button was either, pulled off, or fell off when you kidnapped her,' said Michael, staring into Karl's eyes.

Karl became more flustered and nervous. *If I come clean, maybe they'll have mercy on me. They're bound to find out sooner or later. I had a bad feeling about this right from the beginning. Oh, God, I'm so scared. I should never have trusted Bart. They have my button. What can I do?* 'I tell you I have nothing to do with Maria's kidnapping. It wasn't my idea. I really didn't want to do it.'

Hanzel and Michael stared at Karl as they took in what he had just said.

'What do you mean, *it wasn't your idea?* It wasn't your idea? *What* wasn't your idea?' Michael grabbed the man's lapel.

'To kidnap Maria. I really didn't want to go along with it. It was all Bart's idea. And Joe. Bart and Joe. I was never....'

'Where is she?' asked Michael, staring into Karl's eyes. 'So help me. If any harm has come to her...'

Karl stared fearfully from Hanzel to Michael. 'She's in a storage locker in the starboard bow.'

Hanzel and Michael looked at each other for a split instant before jumping into action.

'Hold this man,' said Hanzel to Morgan, who immediately signaled Peter and Martin to take Karl into custody. Hanzel and Michael ran to the forward hatch and practically flew down the stairs. Hanzel lit a lantern and then the two friends proceeded to climb down to the forward hold where they almost had to crawl to get to the locker where they found Maria in a most miserable condition; hungry, naked, dehydrated, and in terrible misery and pain.

'Who did this to you?' asked Michael, carefully taking the disgusting rag out of her mouth before untying his hapless girlfriend.

Maria was barely able to croak an answer. 'Three monsters. I know that one of them is Bart. I don't know the names of the other two. They grabbed me when I stepped outside our cabin because I heard noises.'

'Bart,' hissed Hanzel between his teeth. 'He will pay for this outrage.'

'He is so dead,' replied Michael, gently lowering Maria into his lap. Her arms, having been tied above her head for so long, had lost all feeling. Michael stroked her hair. 'Oh, Maria. My dear Maria. We will avenge this insult.'

Hanzel picked up Maria's clothes which had been tossed on the filthy floor, where vermin had scurried about and left their defecation and urination. 'I'll go fetch some clean clothes. Can you handle this place for another ten minutes?'

Maria nodded. 'Now that I have been rescued and am, once again, in the arms of my lover, I can endure anything.'

Michael managed a tight lipped smile, as tears welled up in his eyes. 'That's my girl,' he said; gently stroking her hair; his tears running down her cheeks.

Hanzel quickly returned topside and immediately ordered the arrest of Bart. He told Peter, who functioned as sergeant at arms, to have Bart and Karl clapped in irons to the main mast. Then he went to his cabin, where he told Hanna what had happened to Maria.

'Oh, my dear God,' replied Hanna, putting her hands to her mouth. 'Poor Maria. How is she?'

'Naked and cold,' said Hanzel. 'She needs clothes.'

'Naked too? Oh, my, what have they done?' She pointed to the door. 'I'll go and get some clothes from her closet.' Hanna quickly left the cabin; returning a moment later with suitable clothes for Maria. She handed them to Hanzel. 'Do you want me to come with you?'

'No, you'd better stay here. That place is not suitable for anyone to be in, let alone a woman. I don't want you anywhere near that rat infested hole.' Hanzel gave Hanna a kiss on the top of her head and left the cabin; returning to Michael and Maria five minutes later. When the three friends stepped on deck, word had already circulated amongst the crew. Everyone knew fairly well what was going on. When Maria walked past the two criminals tied to the main mast she asked, 'where is the other one?'

'The other one?' asked Michael. 'What other one?'

'There were three of them,' she replied, as she scanned the crew to see if she could recognize Joe. 'It was dark when they kidnapped me. I was unconscious for part of it.'

Michael frowned and regarded Bart with an intense stare. 'We'll find out who is the other one.' He grabbed the front of Bart's shirt. 'Who is the third man?'

'A kidnapper I may be, but a snitch I'm not,' replied Bart insolently.

'I admire that,' said Michael. 'I don't like snitches either.' He turned to Karl. 'What about you, Karl? Are you going to tell us who the third man is?'

Karl looked fearfully at Joe, standing with two other sailors by the midship hatch. 'I'm no snitch, either,' he said, trying to sound defiant.

Hanzel regarded the rest of the crew and asked if the third man would come forward voluntarily. Joe stared at Karl; Bart could not see him because he was tied on the other side of the massive spar. Bart was facing the quarterdeck. Joe, however, remained silent; praying he would not be implicated. Hanzel regarded Maria. 'You were not blindfolded. Is it possible, inspite of the dim light, that you are able to recognize the third man?'

Maria looked at the sailors gathered on deck, however, the light and circumstances made it difficult to identify Joe. She shook her head and admitted it was not possible. However, she did put a worm of fear into Joe by saying, 'whoever he is. He will be found out, eventually. I can guarantee that.' When Joe heard that, he nearly peed his pants, but stayed as calm as a cucumber.

'So, Maria. Are these two men, Bart and Karl, two of the three men who abducted you?' Hanzel pointed at the criminals tied to the mainmast.

Maria nodded. 'Yes they are. Those two men kidnapped me and raped me.'

The rest of the crew were shocked to hear what had been done. The men had given their word they would not tamper with a crewmate's woman. Bart and Karl had signed the articles. The articles did not say anything about rape.

'Rape is an even more heinous crime than kidnapping!' shouted Michael. 'I say we cut their knackers off and throw them into the sea!'

'I say we feed them with their own knackers before we throw them in,' suggested Angus from the helm.

'Keel haul them!' shouted Peter.

'Feed em to the sharks,' suggested Martin.

'Hang em from a yardarm!' shouted Joe, trying to ward off suspicions.

Hearing Joe suggest they be hanged riled Bart and Karl. 'You traitor!' they shouted in unison.

'You lousy bastard! You did her, same as us!' shouted Karl. 'It's Joe! Joe is the third man!'

Upon hearing his denunciation, Joe did not know what to do. There was nowhere to run; nowhere to hide.

'Seize that man!' shouted Hanzel. Several sailors immediately grabbed Joe and brought him forward. 'Tie him with those two.'

Joe was tied to the mainmast with Bart and Karl, the three of them facing outward.

Hanzel asked Morgan to retrieve the articles from the grand cabin. When he returned, Hanzel read the clause which clearly stated that tampering with another man's woman was cause for marooning. 'However, we have evidence of rape. That is not in our articles. Should we add it?'

All the men, and the two women agreed to add rape into the articles. Collectively they agreed that death was a suitable penalty.

When Karl heard the sentence he started yelling, 'It was all Bart's idea. I didn't want to go along with it. You can't kill me. I wasn't in my right mind!'

'You were in mind enough to have your way with me, you bastard!' shouted Maria.

'Bart made me do it!"' replied Karl, shaking like a leaf.

'You coward!' shouted Bart. 'I'm not your puppet master!'

'Enough!' shouted Hanzel. 'You are sentenced to death. Now we just have to determine how you will meet your ends.'

'I say you strip them naked and bugger them with pegs before you whip them to death,' said Maria calmly.

Hanna looked at her friend. *That would do it . It would certainly send a message to the rest of the men that we're not to be tampered with.* 'I didn't know you had it in you, Maria.'

'They have to be taught a lesson. A woman's chastity is a sacred thing,' replied Angus.

'I agree,' said Michael. 'These men have done a terrible thing; something which Maria might never get over. If we do not punish them severely, then we are, essentially, condoning their actions. Rape and murder are two of the most heinous crimes on the books. On land, it matters not what country, a rapist is executed.'

When the question was put to the rest of the crew, to a man they agreed with the punishment suggested by the victim. Hence, the three men were stripped naked, tied, bent over, to chairs, and buggered with pegs. The screams were most pitiable, however, nobody had empathy for them. When the pegs were firmly implanted in their bleeding rectums, the rest of the ordeal began as the crew took turns lashing the three men with cats made of hemp rope. After a half hour, Hanna and Maria could not stomach the spectacle any longer and retired to Hanna's cabin, where they tried to drown out the screams of the condemned rapists.

After three hours of constant pummeling, the three criminals were covered from top to bottom with bleeding gashes. The deck was spattered with blood and yet, the men were still breathing.

'It takes a lot to whip a man to death,' observed Hanzel. 'Those three have had at least three hundred lashes each and yet they still breathe. I wonder how many more it will take?'

'I don't care how many it will take,' said Michael through clenched teeth. 'We'll continue to beat them until they have no blood left.' He grabbed one of the cats out of the boatswain's hand and began laying into Bart; opening deep wounds where the knotted cords had already weakened the skin. Bart screamed until he could not scream anymore then he passed out.

'You're a sadistic psychopath,' hissed Joe as Michael stepped in front of him. 'Why don't you just shoot us and get it over with? Do you take pleasure in spattering our blood all over the deck?'

'Yeah. Do you take pleasure in that?' cried Karl. 'Spattering our blood? Why not just shoot us? Please, have mercy and shoot me!'

Michael looked at Hanzel. 'What do you think? Should we just shoot them and get it over with?'

'Throw them to the sharks,' replied Hanzel. 'Why waste good ammunition on them?'

Hanzel faced the rest of the crew. 'What say you, mates? Flog them to death, or throw them to the sharks?'

'They've seen the error of their ways, Captain,' said Martin.

'Aye, Captain. We don't need to be barbarians. Those men are dead men already. Why should we waste any more energy on them?' Peter crossed his arms and spat an oyster into the sea.

Everyone agreed the three rapists were not worthy of more attention. Throwing the miscreants to the sharks was a fitting end to their ordeal. Hence, the three blood smeared rapists were untied and tossed overboard, one, two, three, with no ceremony and no remorse; victims of their own stupidity.

'That takes care of that,' said Hanzel, clapping his hands together. He pointed to the gore. 'Morgan. Organize a crew and clean up this mess, please. Thank you.' As he turned he looked back to where the three kidnappers were still struggling to stay afloat; becoming smaller and smaller dots on the tossing waves.

Chapter 32

One evening, many days after the execution, and the memories were no longer heavy, Hanzel lit the lanterns and bathed his cabin in a warm, yellow light. He picked up the natural history book and set it on the table in front of his chair. 'Come and look at this with me, Hanna. Maybe we can identify some of the birds we saw on Sao Miguel.' Hanna pulled up her chair beside Hanzel's and watched as he opened the book to the section on birds of Europe. As time passed on the long voyage, Hanzel and Hanna had become ever more interested in pursuing their own natural science explorations. 'Perhaps we'll discover a new specie in Hispaniola,' suggested Hanna.

'If we do, we'll name it after you. We'll call the creature, Creaturus Hannanus.' Hanzel laughed and repeated the silly sounding Latin name. 'Creaturus Hannanus. What do you think of that?'

Hanna frowned and gave him a punch in the shoulder. 'We should call it, Hanzelentus Horribilis .'

'Horribilis? Horribilis? Who are you calling horrible?' Hanzel stared at his partner with a big frown on his face.

'You. You are Hanzel the Horrible.'

'Why do you say that?'

'You have been ignoring me for quite a while. You are always so busy being the captain.'

Hanzel regarded Hanna with a serious expression. 'Why haven't you said something before? I don't mean to ignore you, Hanna. You know how much I love you, don't you?'

'Yes, but....'

'It's a big responsibility, running a big ship, like this one. The crew wants me to be in charge, so I have to do what I must. You have to understand that.'

Hanna nodded and looked at the floor.

'However, I'll tell you what. I'll delegate some more authority to Michael and Morgan. Since they are the first officers, they can handle some more responsibilities and we can spend some more time together. How's that?' Hanzel stroked her hair as she looked up at him.

Hanna nodded. 'That would be wonderful, Hanzel. We could play chess, or just talk, or study natural history, or read together...'

Hanzel leaned down and kissed his sweetheart. *Spending time with her is no chore. I love this woman.* 'I love you Hanna.'

'I love you too, Hanzel.'

When the two lovers released each other from their embrace, Hanzel called Michael and gave him orders not to disturb Hanna and he for the rest of the evening. 'And ask Cookie to bring us dinner and a bottle of red wine, please. Thank you.'

Michael smiled. 'Aye, Captain.' He winked at Hanna and left the cabin.

'Is that better, my love?' Hanzel looked at Hanna sitting on their bed.

'Much better, Hanzel. Now lock the door and make love to me. We won't be seeing Cookie for at least forty minutes.'

Hanzel grinned as he locked the door. 'That should be enough time, for now.'

Meanwhile, in Michael's cabin, Maria Angelina was pacing the floor. She was not happy, either. Since coming on board, Michael had hardly paid any attention to her. It was the same story. Both Hanzel and Michael learned; women do not like to be ignored. Hence, Michael also had to delegate some of his work to another man; the man being, Peter. Maria was much happier, and so was Hanna. The other lesson the two men learned was; Happy Wife, Happy Life. Hanzel and Michael smiled and grinned a lot. Life was good on board ship when they stopped ignoring their women and taking them for granted.

Most of the crew were glad the women were on board, not withstanding the affair with the rapists. However, not all crew members were happy. There were still a couple who felt that women were unlucky on board a ship.

'We lost three good men because of a woman. I tells ye that little dark haired one; that Maria, she's a witch for certain. I don't know about the other one,' said Kevin, a small, dark haired man. He was playing cards with two friends, using his trunk for a table.

'I can see that. She has those dark eyes, like a raven's eyes. Eyes like that be the devil's eyes,' suggested Howard, a young, pimply faced sailor, who had only been to sea for two years, at this time. At this time, he was still a virgin.

'Well, whatever ye thinks, I say, stay away from those women. Stop thinking about them. Put them out of your minds. You saw what Hanzel and Michael are capable of. Do you want to end up shark food?' Andrew regarded his shipmates with a stern expression. 'I been te sea for twenty two years. Trust me. I knows what I am talking about.'

Meanwhile, up on the quarterdeck, Hanzel was showing Hanna how to read the compass. 'You see Hanna, we're heading west, south west. Now, if we take a look with our Davis backstaff, we'll know approximately where we are on the globe.' He placed the instrument on his shoulder and stood with his back to the sun. Then he lined up the horizon vane and slid the half cross back and forth until the shadow of its vane fell across the slit in the bottom vane, while the horizon was visible through the slit. When he was done, he looked at the calibration mark and determined that they were at a longitude of 69 degrees. 'I already know our latitude, that being twenty six degrees, give or take some minutes.'

'We're heading into the Devil's triangle,' muttered Angus. 'I suggest we double the watch from now on. Strange goings on occur in this place. Mark my words, Hanzel.'

'I've never sailed these waters. I don't know anything about the Devil's triangle,' replied Hanzel.

'Me neither,' added Hanna. 'What is it?'

'The kraken lives there,' replied Angus.

'The kraken lives there, my arse.' Martin stared at Angus. 'You're so full of crap, Angus. There's no such thing as a kraken.'

'I seen it with my own eyes.' Angus frowned and made a face at Martin.

'What you seen with your own eyes, you Irish carrothead, is a delusion brought on by excessive alcohol. There's no such thing as a kraken.' Martin regarded Hanzel. 'Do you believe in the kraken?'

Hanzel shrugged his shoulders. 'I have no idea what a kraken is.'

'Yes, what is a kraken?' asked Hanna, her curiosity aroused.

Angus regarded her with a fearful expression. 'A most diabolical monster of the deep. It's huge and pale white. It glows with an iridescence under moonlight and can wreck a ship like this in minutes with its gigantic, suckered arms.'

'Yeah, yeah,' laughed Martin. 'And it has a huge, parrot beak which cuts sailors in half at one bite.' Martin regarded Angus. 'You're so full of crap, Angus, you're trying to scare Hanna.'

'Well, he's done a pretty good job of it,' replied Hanna, looking fearfully off to starboard.

'I think the kraken is a myth. It sounds like a myth,' said Hanzel. 'I wouldn't worry about it, Hanna. Besides, we'll keep a good watch out.'

'I say double the watch, Captain,' suggested Angus. 'In the Devil's triangle, you never know what you are going to confront.'

'I think doubling the watch, regardless of the triangle, is a good idea. We're now in waters where other pirates ply their sweet trade and the Spaniard will be present,' said Hanzel. 'Martin, will you see to it, please. Double the watch and have everybody keep an eye open for any abnormalities.'

'Aye, aye, Captain,' replied Martin.

'Will that make you feel more comfortable, Angus?' asked Hanzel, regarding his helmsman.

Angus nodded. 'One can't be too careful here. I've heard of more than one ship to go missing in these waters.'

Hanzel held his telescope to his right eye and scanned the horizon ahead. He could see the mainsail of the sloop, sailing a half league, or so, up ahead. He handed the glass to Hanna and pointed in the direction of *Great Fortune*. 'You can see her mainsail, but that's all.'

Hanna pointed the glass where Hanzel had indicated. She careful scanned the horizon. 'I don't see anything,' she said, squinting into the glass.

'What do you mean, you don't see anything?' asked Hanzel.

'I don't see any sails. I've scanned the horizon, as you taught me, but there are no sails,' replied Hanna.

Hanzel held out his hand. 'Let me have a look. You have to be able to see her. *Great Fortune* is just up ahead of us. I just saw her.' He held the glass to his eye and scanned the horizon where he last saw the sail. 'Hmm, that's strange. They're not there. How's that possible?'

'The Devil's triangle. I told you. We're in strange waters now,' said Angus, a *I told you so* expression on his ruddy face.

'Martin. Call all hands. Put out all the sail we have. We have to catch up to *Great Fortune*. She's likely picked up a wind and sailed below the horizon.' Hanzel looked through the glass again. 'That's so strange,' he muttered, handing the glass back to Hanna.

The crew quickly set out a full parade of sails and the merchantman picked up two more knots. Waves crashed over the bows as the big ship plowed through the water. Dolphins skimmed across the waves in front of the ship, racing the huge boat and chattering, as if they were laughing at the clumsy humans.

After sailing hard for over three hours, they had not caught up to the sloop.

'I guess Henk got tired of being at sea and is racing us to Santo Domingo. We'll meet up with them there,' said Hanzel, putting his spyglass down. 'I don't believe the Devil got them.' Hanzel stared at Angus as he said it.

'It's time for the five o'clock watch, Captain,' said Morgan as he began to ring the bell.

Sailors came down from the rigging and others climbed up. Angus handed the helm over to Peter and Morgan was replaced by Martin. Hanzel preferred to stay on deck for a little while longer.

'I'm going to our cabin, Hanzel. Will you come at six bells? I'll ask Cookie to send supper there. I'd prefer to sup with just you tonight.'

Hanzel regarded his beautiful friend. 'Ask him to send a bottle of wine, as well.' He gave her a kiss on the mouth and she left the quarterdeck.

'She's a fine woman, that Hanna,' said Peter. 'You're a lucky man, Hanzel.'

'They don't come much finer than her,' agreed Hanzel.

That evening, Hanzel and Hanna enjoyed an excellent supper of baked ham with steamed rice in a curry sauce, and boiled onions and peas, accompanied with a robust red wine from Burgundy. After supper the two friends dove into their natural history studies and learned about spiders.

And so it went for the next week; essentially uneventful sailing. They did see sails on the horizon, however, they were so far away, and the merchantman so slow, there was no hope of ever catching up with them. As they neared Santo Domingo, more ships shared the water; they being mostly fishing boats and coastal traders plying a trade between Santo and Tortuga. When the merchantman crept into the harbour, everyone kept a lookout for, *Great Fortune*. Alas, the sloop was nowhere to be seen in the early morning mist.

'That is so odd. Unless Henk decided to chase a ship, or something. But surely, they must be running out of supplies. Perhaps they'll show up later.' Hanzel gazed around the harbour but his eyes did not light on the ship he was looking for. 'As soon as the ship is made fast, let the crew go ashore. We'll need a few volunteers to stay on board to guard against, whatever,' said Hanzel to Morgan.

'Aye, Captain,' said Morgan, who immediately set about expediting the orders.

Hanzel shook his head as he looked at Hanna. 'I wonder where Henk is?'

Hanna shrugged her shoulders. 'I have no idea. Unless Angus is right and we sailed through the Devil's Triangle. Maybe our sloop was taken by the kraken.'

Hanzel looked at Hanna for a moment before replying. 'I don't know what to think about that, anymore. However, we'll see. It's like I said. Maybe they're off chasing something and will show up here in a day or two.'

'I hope so, Hanzel. I sure hope so,' said Hanna.

'I think she's lost. The kraken got her,' said Angus. 'Or something else. After all, many different stories have come from the Devil's Triangle.'

Hanzel looked out at the harbour. He sighed. Henk was a good friend. The sloop was a good boat. 'Well, so be it, I guess. We win and we lose. Our sloop could just as well have gone down in a storm, or been taken over by pirates needing a boat. We better not let it get to us. We'll have to make due with the merchantman, for now. If we don't have to chase anyone, we'll be fine. Who knows, we might be able to take over a ship, like I did with Pierre LeGrange.'

'Let's pray we win our treasure as easily as that,' said Hanna.

Hanzel nodded. 'I hope so.'

'Now that we may have lost our sloop, we are going to have to recruit some more men and or women,' suggested Morgan.

'This time we'll screen them even closer. I don't ever want a repeat of that incident at sea. If the men have wives or girlfriends, encourage them to bring them along,' said Hanzel.

'Aye, that's a good idea, Hanzel. If the men have women on board, they are more likely to fight more tenaciously to defend them, wouldn't you think?' Angus looked at Hanzel for a response. 'And, most certainly, there'll be less chance for a repeat of that horrible incident with Maria. When there are more women on board, the men will be happier. Believe it.'

'Makes sense to me,' said Hanzel. 'So, make sure to encourage the men to look for both men and women.'

'Aye Captain,' said Morgan who passed the information down the ranks.

When all was secure and a watch in place, the crew of the *Golden Treasure* went into Santo Domingo to learn what they could about the Spaniard and his treasure fleet.

'But first I want to eat,' said Hanna. 'I need to sit down in a restaurant and eat a land lubber meal. Something with fresh meat and vegetables.'

'Oh, me too,' agreed Maria. 'A nice juicy slab of beef with roasted potatoes...'

'And fresh bread and butter,' added Michael.

'Not to forget gravy,' said Hanzel, pointing to an inn. 'Do you suppose they have that, there?'

'Let's find out,' said Michael heading for the front door.

When the four friends stepped into the dining hall, they knew they had come to the right place. Beef was being abundantly roasted along with various other species of dripping flesh. The place was filled with mouth watering aromas, conversations, tobacco smoke, and the pungent odours of spirits. A table with four chairs was available by one of the windows looking out on the harbour.

'This is perfect,' said Hanna, sitting down.

'My mouth is already watering,' said Hanzel.

A moment later a buxom wench with buck teeth came to attend to them. She efficiently took their orders and returned momentarily with their drinks. She set the drinks in front of the four shipmates and told them their meals would be ready in about fifteen minutes. Then she left them to their conversation.

'You speak pretty good Spanish, Hanzel,' said Hanna admiringly.

'When I worked for Master De Witt, we had customers from many countries. Spanish customers were plentiful.'

'The war with Spain ended a while ago. And yet, there are still all those Spaniards in Holland. They don't belong there,' replied Hanna.

'The ones I dealt with were typical. Arrogant, short tempered, but still, good customers, in that they bought lots of weapons and armour from us. But, they never paid on time. Master De Witt always had to go after them with his collection agents; Ben and Roelof.' Hanzel smiled. 'When we find out where their treasure is, they'll pay in short order. No waiting around this time.' Hanzel laughed at his own joke.

Hanna smiled. 'I like the idea of an instant payment. However, if we are going to do that, we should keep our eyes open, Hanzel. We really do need more crew, now that Henk and the sloop have disappeared.'

Hanzel regarded Hanna and sadly nodded his head. 'What do you suppose happened to Henk?'

'Maybe they had an emergency and had to put into a bay or cove somewhere. If we stay here a while, perhaps they'll show up. We did say we'd meet in Santo Domingo,' suggested Michael.

'Best thing is to not worry about the sloop and concentrate on interviewing and recruiting,' replied Hanzel.

'Aye, Captain,' agreed Michael. He gestured with his chin. 'Look, there. Those sailors look like Spaniards. Let's keep an eye on them.'

'They probably belong to that navy ship in the harbour. Those certainly are the uniforms of Spanish navy tars,' agreed Hanzel.

As the four friends sat there, sizing up the Spanish sailors, their food arrived. The waitress requested a half peso. Hanzel handed her a silver daalder and told her to keep the change.' The girl thanked Hanzel and left their table.

'Hanzel. Just because you feel confident we'll find treasure, there's no need to go spending our money on tips to bucktoothed waitresses. Don't spend it until we've got it,' warned Hanna.

'Hanna, my sweet angel. I'm tipping the girl because she will be helpful to us. By giving her a little extra, she'll work for us. And, what have her buck teeth to do with this?'

Hanna frowned. 'Nothing. Except in this case, I saw how you admired her tits when she leaned over to place your trencher. I just wanted to remind you, she has buckteeth.'

'Oh, for heaven's sake, Hanna. Are you jealous? Just because hers are bigger than yours?' Hanzel shook his head. 'I love you just the way you are. Your breasts are perfect. You don't want bigger ones. They'll just sag way down when you get older.'

Hanna took a bite of her roasted pork loin and thought about what Hanzel had said. *He always knows what to say. I guess I was just being silly. She did lean over him. He really didn't have much choice to look. It's not his fault she is wearing such a revealing chemise under her bodice, which is cut much to low, in my opinion.* Hanna put her hand on Hanzel's thigh for a moment, unconciously staking claim to her man.

'I think we'll do well in Santo Domingo. Since we've got to wait for Henk and information, we're in no hurry. Let's hire a carriage after breakfast and go sightseeing,' suggested Hanzel.

The others agreed it was a good idea. Hence, after their meal was done, the four adventurers went sightseeing in the Zona Colonial; the first settlement of Christopher Columbus in the new world. They rode along the wall to their first destination, the 84 year old Cathedral of Santa Maria La Menor; a Spanish style basilica sitting in the extreme west corner of the zona. Hanna remarked that the building looked odd, compared to churches back home. 'The single column supporting those two arches over those imposing rectangular doors totally compromises the harmony of the facade. The thing has the appearance of a jumble of styles, sort of tossed together to come up with that.'

'It really doesn't know what it is, I think. Is it a Greekish, Roman, Gothic, Byzantine facade, or what?' Michael scratched his head. 'It's a puzzle, isn't it?'

Hanzel shrugged his shoulders. 'I have no idea. All I know is, I don't really like it. I think our churches, back home, are better designed.'

The four friends decided not to bother looking inside. 'I don't much like Catholic churches,' said Michael. 'The incense makes me nauseous.'

'I think we should go buy some food for a picnic and some wine and go for a ride out in the country side. The fresh air will do us good,' suggested Hanna.

The others thought it was a good idea, hence they bought some provisions and spent the rest of the day, sightseeing in the country side, visiting a sugar cane farm and a tobacco plantation where Hanzel and Michael each bought several boxes of aromatic cigars.

'You know, Hanzel, there is another treasure here which we might want to consider.'

'What might that be, Michael?'

'Tobacco,' said Michael, lighting a cigar. 'Think what this cigar costs in Amsterdam.'

'I have no idea,' replied Hanzel. 'This is the first time I've ever had a cigar.'

'Well, just be careful. Only inhale a very little bit of the smoke. Just taste it in your mouth,' suggested Michael, taking a puff of his cigar. 'A cigar like this costs us a penny. We can sell it for a florin. That's a huge profit. Maybe we should steal a shipload of tobacco and sail her home. It would be easy to do because they wouldn't suspect us going after tobacco. Pirates generally go after gold, do they not? That Spanish navy ship is not here to protect tobacco shipments, it's here to protect the gold. There likely is a treasure ship in port. I know for sure there are several tobacco merchant's ships. A shipload of tobacco would fetch a big enough fortune to finance more significant piratical adventures. One shipload will buy us a well armed, swift sailing brigantine.'

Hanzel regarded Michael for a moment as he thought about what he had said. 'That makes a lot of sense, doesn't it Hanna?'

Hanna nodded as she fumbled with a cigar. 'It makes a lot of sense. Tobacco sure smells nice as it burns.' She held up her cigar. 'How do you light this, Michael?'

Michael showed his friends how to cut a wedge in the tapered end of the cigar and then showed them how to evenly light it. Upon their first puff, Hanzel and the women coughed. Michael had to remind them not to inhale too much and go gentle into that good smoke. Eventually they got the idea and began to enjoy their cigars with a bottle of wine they passed around. It was a gloriously warm day and spirits were high as the four friends began to discuss in earnest, the pilfering of a tobacco laden merchantman.

The two couples returned to the *Golden Treasure* after nine bells. They were tired after a long day outdoors, exploring Santo Domingo and its countryside. They decided to go straight to bed and discuss the tobacco ship next day. The night passed uneventfully. Hanzel dreamt of a new, well armed sloop. Hanna dreamt of children.

Next morning, the sun rose to reveal a glorious day. The golden rays bathed Fortaleza Ozama in oranges and reds. The imposing fort was a reminder to Hanzel and his crew mates, they had better be careful. If the fort were to fire on them, they had little to defend themselves; two small rail mounted cannons.

'Merchantmen are usually not fitted with many cannons,' observed Martin.

'If I was a merchant, I'd arm my ships to the teeth,' replied Angus. 'No bloody way any pirates or privateers would steal my goods without a fight.'

'I would have at least ten eight pounders per side and a couple of chase guns and four eight pounders on the stern. That would do it, I would guess,' said Hanzel.

'Yeah, that would be good, but now you have to add fifty more crew to handle the guns; counting only five per gun,' observed Michael.

'How many are we now?' asked Hanzel.

Michael thought for a moment. 'There's we four, plus Hanna and Maria.'

'And Morgan and Peter, plus the three we picked up in Le Havre and those chaps from Sao Miquel; Anthony, Juan, Harry, George, Derek... I can't remember all of their names.' Hanzel paused for a moment as he counted in his head. There's twenty seven of us. Not a lucky number. We need to recruit more men, before we attempt any larceny here.'

'Too bad about Henk and Pedro and all those other fellows on the *Great Fortune*. We could have used them,' said Michael sadly.

'They might still show up,' suggested Hanzel. 'I'm trying to remain positive. They might have had some rigging problems, or something like that. Who knows, they might be in a cove somewhere along this shore and are refitting.'

Angus shook his head. 'They succumbed to the kraken in the Devil's Triangle. That's my guess.' He regarded Hanzel. 'Remember, you saw the sloop and then when you handed the glass to Hanna, the sloop had disappeared.'

'If there had been a kraken, wouldn't one of us have seen it in the glass? Surely the thing doesn't drag a ship to hell that fast. The sloop was gone within the space of less than a minute,' answered Hanzel.

Angus regarded his shipmates with a serious expression. 'It's the Devil's Triangle, I tell you. The *Great Fortune* would not be the only ship that's ever disappeared there.'

'I say that Devil's Triangle idea is an old wife's tale,' replied Michael. 'I don't buy it. What do you think, Hanzel?'

'I'm not sure. It seems fantastical. However, we know so little about our world, who knows, perhaps there is such a thing as a Devil's Triangle. But, I'm continuing to hope the sloop is fine and we'll see Henk and Pedro very soon.' Hanzel clapped his hands together.

'Enough about that. Michael and I want to discuss a different plan with you. We think we may have come up with a simpler plan, which will still net us a fortune.'

'What might that be?' asked Angus.

'Tobacco, gentlemen. It's tobacco. A shipload of tobacco is worth a fortune back home.' Hanzel pulled a cigar from his waistcoat pocket. 'Look at this cigar. What does a cigar like that cost in Amsterdam? I'll bet at least a florin.'

'Those few who smoke tobacco, usually use a pipe or powder it into snuff,' said Martin. 'I've had snuff a couple of times. That's quite a rush of pleasure, I must say.'

'Wait until you try a cigar. You will love to smoke tobacco that way. It's so much easier than a pipe because it stays lit. And, you don't need to bring a pipe along.' Hanzel lit the cigar and then passed it to Martin.

Martin took a puff from the cigar and immediately began to cough. He handed the cigar to Angus.

'You have to be careful. Don't suck in too much smoke, until you are used to it,' said Michael. 'Just take a little bit into your mouth and slowly suck it into your lungs.'

Angus sucked on the cigar and did as Michael suggested. When he exhaled, he licked his lips. 'Hmm. That feels and tastes really nice.' He took another drag and then passed the cigar to Morgan who had come up on deck. 'Do you have any more of those things?'

'We bought a couple of bundles,' replied Hanzel. 'There are six to a bundle.'

'I think it's a splendid idea,' agreed Angus. 'Tobacco is just beginning to be appreciated. I believe there is a huge market for it anywhere back home; England, Holland, Germany, France...'

'We could likely sell it for profit in any country,' suggested Morgan.

'I have contacts in Amsterdam,' said Hanzel. 'Holland is where we'll sell it. The Dutch love tobacco.'

'First we've got to locate the ship,' replied Michael.

'And recruit. We need at least another ten men and women,' suggested Martin.

'So, that will be our goal, henceforth,' said Hanzel, clapping his hands together. 'We'll make an earnest effort to recruit more crewmates and find out, which of those ships in the harbour are loading tobacco. The sooner we get on this project, the sooner we'll be heading home and making a fortune in Amsterdam.'

'Aye, aye, Captain,' agreed the others in unison.

So, after a quick breakfast of bread and ale, everyone but Hanna and Maria, went into town. The women chose to remain on board because they were not feeling well due to their menstruation. Hanna, in particular, suffered from troublesome cramps. She and Maria spent most of the morning in bed. In the afternoon, they sat on deck, soaking up the healing sunlight.

The men returned to the ship sometime after seven bells. They had to row in three shifts to get everyone on board with their trunks or duffel bags. Fourteen new members had joined the crew; five women and nine men.

'Now we have enough,' said Hanzel happily. 'We can go after that French merchantman. According to the new men, that ship will be finished loading the day after tomorrow. The entire ship is being loaded with tobacco. They have a crew of eighteen. Only half of whom are on board at any given time, while in port.'

'There's forty one of us now,' said Michael. 'We should be able to steal that ship without any bloodshed.'

'That's our objective. We want to sail the ship out of port, without bloodshed,' agreed Hanzel.

'What about this ship? Why sail two ships back? It would be better if all of us are on board the tobacco ship. Just in case it is attacked on the way home. That way there will be more of us to defend our prize,' suggested Peter, wisely.

'We'd have to bring all of our things over to the other ship which will take more time. We need to move quickly. We can transfer everything at sea and then scuttle this ship. We only need twelve to sail this thing out of port,' replied Hanzel.

Everyone agreed that Hanzel's idea was the right decision. Hence, over the next day they scouted out the French ship and made their plans. When the appointed day arrived, the big merchantman hoisted a flag indicating they were making preparations to sail with the tide, the following morning. It was during the night when Hanzel and his crew made their move. They rowed both of their boats over to the merchantman; 14 in one and 15 in the other. Everyone was armed to the teeth with at least two weapons; a pistol and a cutlass, a short sword and a boarding axe, a blunderbuss and a dirk, and so on. The crew of the merchantman did not have a chance. Within minutes of the pirates coming on board, they had captured the captain and a skeleton crew. Most of the crew were still in town on their final hours of shore leave.

'You have two choices,' said Hanzel to the captain and crew of, *La Belle Magdalina*. 'You can join us or you can go back to shore. We prefer to have you join our company, but, it is your choice.'

The French crew knew there was no sense in resisting, since they were outnumbered by armed assailants. The captain and his officers elected to return to town and thanked the pirates for being so magnanimous in letting them live. The 8 sailors elected to join Hanzel's crew.

'We are not blood thirsty cutthroats,' said Hanzel. 'We are gentlemen and women, conducting a slightly different trading system to your own. I assure you, this ship and cargo will be put to excellent use. Many people will benefit.' Hanzel indicated the starboard side of the ship. 'So, gentlemen, if you are ready, your boat is waiting.'

'Even though you have spared our lives, monsieur, you realize that we will have to report you to the authorities. This is an act of piracy and in my country, the penalty for piracy is breaking on the wheel; a very unpleasant way to die.' The French captain stared directly into Hanzel's eyes.

Hanzel nodded. 'Yes, I'm familiar with that,' he said tersely. 'However, we are not worried. We'll take our chances.' He saluted the captain and then watched as he and his officers climbed down the ladder to the waiting row boat. Then, not wasting another second, he ordered the anchor weighed and ship readied for sailing. Fifteen minutes later the merchantman began to creep out of the harbour, followed by the *Golden Treasure* captained by Michael. Nobody took notice of their departure until sometime after the French officers reported the theft to the harbour officials. By the time they could convince the Spanish navy ship to go after the pirates, three hours had elapsed. Hanzel and crew were already away at sea with all sails out.

'The likelihood of that Spanish navy ship catching us are pretty slim,' said Martin, scanning the horizon. 'They are such inept sailors; the Spanish.'

'That's good to know,' replied Hanzel. 'However, in the meantime, we'll keep up a full parade of sails and make as much distance between us as possible. I want to be well out to sea, before we bring our belongings over from the *Golden Treasure*.'

'It's too bad we have to scuttle her,' said Martin.

'We have no choice. In order to protect ourselves and our cargo, we need all hands on this deck. The merchantman served us well enough. It provided an opportunity for a comfortable voyage. Nobody was crowded.'

'On this big ship, with all forty nine of us on board, we'll still not be crowded,' said Martin happily. 'I like lots of room.'

'Me too,' replied Hanzel. He clapped his hands together. 'Well, let's pray we have a safe voyage home.' He turned to the helmsman. 'What do you say, Angus?'

'Aye, Captain. I'll pray we have a safe voyage home. I can't wait to see what this cargo will fetch us.

'Aaargh,' replied Hanzel, grinning from ear to ear.

Hanna put her arm around his waist. She led him to the rear of the ship. As the two friends watched from the transom, Santo Domingo disappeared over the horizon. Hanna turned to Hanzel. 'I love you,' she said. 'This is the best adventure of my life.'

Hanzel grinned. 'Mine too.'

'I love being a pirate. Is it always this easy to steal a ship, I wonder?'

Hanzel frowned. 'No, it isn't. We were just lucky with this one; as Pierre and I were with that Spanish treasure ship. I doubt if we'll ever see a heist as easy as this one.

Hanna thought for a moment. 'Well, perhaps, if we all pray before we go after a ship; maybe God will help us. I mean, after all. We're doing a good thing by taking from some bloated merchants and spreading their wealth around to people who need it.' She turned to Hanzel and laughed. 'That would be, us. We're the people in need.'

Hanzel laughed. 'That would be us, indeed.'

'We can't lose with God on our side.' Hanna's eyes sparkled. Then she kissed Hanzel for a long time.

Chapter 33

'I don't think anyone is coming after us,' said Martin, scanning the horizon from the transom of the French merchantman. I think it will be safe now to transfer the rest of the crew off the *Golden Treasure*.'

'Splendid,' replied Hanzel, clapping his hands together. 'Alright gentlemen, lets bring her to a halt. Luff the sails, if you will, Peter.'

'Aye, aye, Captain,' said Peter. He set about the assigned task. A few minutes later the big ship came to a stop and waited as the other merchantman came alongside and also stopped. Then they set about transferring their goods to the French ship. When they were done, and everyone was safely on board the tobacco boat, Donald and Jake, the ship's carpenters, two men who came on board in Santo Domingo; chopped holes in strategic places in the condemned ship's hull. Peter, who was the explosives expert, used their only three kegs of powder to further hurry the ship's demise.

Just as Peter and the carpenters returned to *La Belle Magdalina*, the explosion went off deep in the bottom of the compromised merchantman. It started with a rumble at first and then suddenly in a massive KABOOM!!! The starboard side amidship blew open, sending bits and pieces of wood flying several hundred yards in many directions. Several large chunks of oak made high splashes as they landed in the water a mere three yards from where Hanzel was standing, watching the spectacle with Hanna at his side. A half hour later it was all over as the *Golden Treasure* slipped beneath the waves.

'She was a good ship,' said Michael. 'Easy to sail.'

'Too bad we didn't have the money to fill her hold. We could have brought two ships back,' sighed Morgan.

Hanzel nodded. 'Perhaps, after we sell this load, and we buy a swift brigantine, we could go after a convoy. Who knows?'

'We'd need even more pirates to do that, Hanzel,' suggested Angus.

'We're stopping in Somers Islands, maybe we'll pick up some pirates there. We'll definitely have success recruiting in Amsterdam. Now that we've proven ourselves to be capable pirates, others will be attracted to join us.' Hanzel looked at his friends. 'Don't you think?'

Everyone agreed, the likelihood of recruiting anyone on Somers Islands was slim, but Amsterdam definitely was the perfect recruiting ground. There was no question of that.

'Set course for thirty two and a half degrees latitude and sixty four degrees longitude where we should find the entrance to a magnificent harbour and a new colony of Englishmen,' said Hanzel.

They entered St. George's Harbour a week later, sailing ever so carefully between small islands and watching out for coral. It was around seven in the morning. Five other ships lay at anchor; two English, one French, and two belonging to the Somers Isles Company. Hanzel pointed to where he wanted to drop anchors. An hour later the ship was made fast and the crew prepared to go ashore.

'I can't imagine there'll be much fun to be had in this tiny place,' remarked Angus. 'Do you think there is an inn or an ordinary?'

'We're only here to refresh our water and buy some fresh food. We'll be on our way again in a couple of days,' replied Hanzel. 'The best thing for us to do is to be quick and efficient.' Then he asked for volunteers to look after various requirements. The women elected to go shopping in the market for food supplies. Fortunately, they had a little bit of money left, plus what they found in a small box in the master's cabin of their pilfered ship.

It was just enough money to buy water and provisions, plus pay for the anchorage fee.

'I don't want to run into problems with the authorities,' said Hanzel, as he paid the harbour master's assistant. 'Now, what do you think, Hanna? Shall we pay the governor a visit?'

'The governor? You know the governor?' Hanna regarded Hanzel, eyes wide.

'No. But, since this is such a small place, I'm sure the governor would appreciate company. No big deal, really. After all, I had an audience with the

King of England when I was sixteen.' Hanzel regarded his partner with a blasé expression and held up a box of cigars. 'I brought these for him.'

Hanna smiled. 'You amaze me Hanzel. I guess that's why I love you so much.'

'You amaze me too, Hanna.' Hanzel gave her a kiss and then, taking her hand, he led her out of the harbour master's office into the glorious sunshine of the morning. Birds twittered in the shrubberies and trees. There were but three tiny clouds in the sky. 'What a great day to be alive, eh, Hanna?'

'Anytime I'm with you, it's a great day, Hanzel,' replied Hanna, adoringly. *I'm the luckiest girl in the world.*

Hanzel blushed slightly. 'I feel the same way. I love you, Hanna. I don't want us ever to be apart.'

When the two lovers finished their embrace, they walked up the street to the beautiful new state house; the only stone structure in town.

'It looks kind of like a big white cube with a door and windows,' remarked Hanna. 'I like how the door is framed by those two unique pillars holding up that lintel and decorated arch. It's all quite symmetrical, isn't it?'

Hanzel regarded his friend. 'It sure does look like a white cube. It's a nicely decorated cube, though.'

'It works. It certainly stands out in this place,' she added as they approached the steps to the front door.' As they walked up the steps, Hanna counted them. 'Sixteen,' she said, when they stopped on the landing in front of the door.

'I counted fifteen.'

Hanna looked back at the steps and quickly counted them in her mind. 'You can't count.' She poked him in the ribs.

Hanzel grinned. 'Alright. I'll let you do the counting from now on.' He laughed as he knocked on the big door.

A moment later a very dark Negro dressed in white livery opened the door and asked in very polite and proper English if he could be of service.

'We are here to pay our respects to the governor,' said Hanzel, holding up the box of cigars.

'Please step inside. I will let the governor know that you are here and wish to see him.' The servant stepped aside to let the two visitors into the lobby. Then he turned on his heels and stepped through a door.

HANZEL SVENTSKA

'Nice place,' said Hanna, looking at the beautiful floor.

'A governor should have a nice place, don't you think?' replied Hanzel. 'If I was a governor, I'd want to live in the best place in town. A governor has to impress people. That is one of the things governors do. Impress people and represent a government.'

'That's not all that they do,' said a friendly voice, stepping into the room.

Hanzel and Hanna turned around to discover the governor. 'Nathaniel Butler,' he said, stretching out his hand.

'Hanzel Sventska,' said Hanzel, taking the governor's hand. 'And she is my wife, Hanna. My dearest friend in the world.'

Hanna and the governor shook hands. 'I am charmed to meet such a pretty lady. Welcome to St. George's.' He bent down and kissed her hand.

Hanna blushed slightly, not having had her hand kissed by a governor, before.

'You'll get used to it,' whispered Hanzel. Hanna smiled and nodded.

'I have brought you a gift.' Hanzel handed the box to the governor.

'What's this?'

'Cigars, your Excellency. Cigars from Santo Domingo.'

'I've heard of these. I've yet to smoke one.' He indicated the door he had come through. 'Please join me in my office and we'll try one of these cigars.' The governor led the two friends to his office where he indicated two comfortable, stuffed chairs for them to sit in as he stepped around his large, ornate desk and sat down in his big, leather chair. He took a cigar from the box and examined it. 'That's a lot of tobacco all rolled up, isn't it? I'm used to taking a pinch of snuff, or a breath of smoke from a pipe. To smoke so much tobacco must take quite a while.'

'That's the joy of it,' said Hanna. 'A cigar is a nice long smoke. It totally relaxes the body and the mind. Hanzel and I have smoked several cigars on the way from Hispaniola to here.'

'I've not heard of too many women smoking the weed,' replied the governor, smiling and regarding Hanna with new eyes. *Obviously not your run of the mill woman, this one.*

'I have no idea how one smokes a cigar.' Nathaniel examined the tobacco tube, not sure which end to light.

Hanzel gently took the cigar from the man's hand and showed him how to cut a wedge out of the smoking end. Then he explained how to hold a match under the other end of the cigar, not quite touching the flame to the tobacco and rotating the tube, in order to get an even heating of the end. Eventually, the cigar burned nice and evenly. 'Now, just be careful not to suck too much smoke all at once.'

The warning came too late as the governor sucked up a lung full and immediately burst out into a coughing fit which lasted several minutes. When he was done coughing, he regarded the cigar warily, hesitating whether to try another puff.

'You have to learn to smoke a cigar,' suggested Hanzel. 'At first, just take some smoke in your mouth and taste it. Then, ever so gently, let a little tiny bit of smoke go to your lungs. Eventually you will learn how much smoke you can breathe in.'

When Nathaniel did as Hanzel suggested he did not cough. Instead, he smiled when he exhaled the smoke. 'Hmm, this tastes nice. I think I could learn to like smoking these. So much easier than a pipe.'

Hanzel pulled two cigars from the inside pocket of his coat and handed one to Hanna. They lit up their cigars and joined the governor in a pleasant hour and a half of conversation in a cloud of aromatic, blue smoke. They talked about the governor's privateering days, his plans for forts, how he managed to get the state house built, and his involvement with the Somers Isles Company. 'He became an admiral, ol' George did. Knighted as well. Quite a man. He died here. His heart is buried in St. George's. They took his body back to England. These islands are named after him. The Somers Isles Company trades between our new colony in Virginia and England. It's quite an operation that is. Maybe they might want to buy your tobacco. It would save you a trip to Amsterdam. I can arrange it.'

Hanzel thought a moment but shook his head. 'No, I don't think so. We'll get a much higher price in Holland than we'll get here. Holland is only a little over a month away.'

'I'm glad I'm not at sea any longer,' replied the governor. 'I'm forty seven and glad to be on land. It was the storms that got to me. I hated storms at sea. Scared the bejeebies out of me. Oh, sure, we get storms here, but I'm on land and not bobbing about in a tub.'

'Who knows, maybe when we get to be your age, we might consider staying on land,' suggested Hanzel. 'I don't know. For now, we like being at sea.'

Hanna nodded agreement. 'I'm a farm girl, who has become a sailor. I now love the sea.' She put a hand on Hanzel's arm. 'Thanks to my Hanzel.'

'Sailing is a young person's occupation. Governing is the occupation of an older man,' suggested Nathaniel. 'Who knows, in this uncertain world, how much longer I may live. Not too many sailors make it past their thirties. Here I am, forty seven already.' He shook his head. 'Where has the time gone?' As he said it, he looked at the clock on his mantle. 'Speaking of time, I must now excuse myself. Today is a busy day. Thank you very much for visiting and for the cigars.' He picked up a book from his desk. 'I also have a gift for you, Hanzel and Hanna. It is a book by a good friend of mine, John Smith. He also is a ship's captain. This book was just published. I bought a couple of dozen copies to give for gifts. It is titled, *A Generall Historie of Virginia, New England and Somers Iles*. You will find it quite interesting, I'm sure. It'll help while away some hours on your voyage to Amsterdam.' Then he tinkled a small bell and the negro servant stepped into the room. 'Please see my guests out, James. Thank you.' The negro servant bowed slightly and held the door open. He graciously showed the couple out. He also thanked them for visiting and told them to, 'come again.' Then he closed the door and the two visitors continued their tour of St. George's.

'That was nice of him to give us this book,' said Hanna. 'I'm looking forward to reading it. Who knows, we might learn some interesting information which could help us in our sweet trade.'

'You never know,' replied Hanzel. 'I've heard some interesting things about Virginia and New England. More ships are going there from Europe.'

'What do you suppose is in those ships?'

'Goods from Europe for the settlers, and tobacco, hemp…I don't know… Lumber. I'm sure this book will fill us in.'

As they approached the end of the street and were back at the harbour, Hanna pointed to an odd contraption sitting beside the water. 'What is that?'

'I have no idea. I've never seen anything like it. Do you suppose it is something used for fishing?' Hanzel scratched his head.

'It's a dunking stool,' said an old fisherman. He was sitting on a chair mending a net, beside the contraption. 'We use it to identify witches and to punish gossipy women. We strap them in that little chair and dunk em under the water. If they float, they're a witch and we hang them. If they drown, then, well, she's not a witch, but her soul gets to Heaven.'

'What about gossipy women?' asked Hanna.

'We don't dunk them quite as long. We just kind of dip em in and out a number of times. It all depends on the seriousness of the gossip.'

'Has it been used recently?' asked Hanna, aghast.

'Just last week we discovered a witch. She didn't drown. She managed to stay alive, so she had to be a witch.'

'Maybe she could just hold her breath longer,' suggested Hanna.

'For three minutes?' The old fisherman regarded the young couple with wideyed wonder. 'Nobody can hold their breath that long. Only a witch.'

'I think that is insane,' replied Hanna.

The old fisherman nodded. 'Yes, I suppose it is. I've often wondered that myself.' He shook his head sadly. 'We live in an insane world.' Then he pointed in the direction of the market. 'Go look over there. You'll see another example of how law breakers are punished around here.'

Hanzel and Hanna looked where the old wrinkle pointed. They thanked the man for his information and walked off in the direction of the market.

'What do you suppose they have there?' asked Hanna.

Hanzel shook his head. 'I guess we'll see.'

When they rounded the corner and entered the market area, they immediately saw what the old man referred to. Two people were standing on a slightly raised platform, with their head and hands clamped between two heavy boards. They had to stand slightly bent over. Some people walking by, taunted them and laughed at their predicament.

'Stocks,' said Hanzel. 'Those are called, stocks. It must be very uncomfortable and hard on the back, being bent over like that.'

'Are they let out for nature's calls?' asked Hanna.

'I don't know. You can ask them.' Hanzel regarded Hanna, who was quite taken aback by the plight of the victims, who looked most discomfited and in distress. 'However, since we are not from here, perhaps we should not interfere by talking with people who have obviously been condemned to this by a court. If someone sees you talking to them, who knows, it could be misconstrued.'

Hanna thought for a moment. Then she turned and asked someone walking past. 'Excuse me. May I ask you a question?'

The woman turned and smiled. 'A question? Certainly. What is your question?'

'Those people over there. Those two in the stocks. Are they released to attend to nature's calls, or....?'

The woman frowned. 'Oh, I think it's barbaric, doing that to people.' She shook her head. 'No, they are not released. Nature calls where she must.'

Hanna put her hands to her face. 'Oh, my. That's just awful.'

The woman nodded. 'Yes, it is. There are some of us in town who are speaking against it, but, we haven't gotten very far. Most people think this is justice.'

'Some people have strange ideas about justice,' observed Hanzel.

'Yes, that is true,' replied the woman. She looked in the direction she was headed. 'Well, if there are no further questions, I must go. I am already late for work.'

'Thank you for the information,' said Hanna.

'At your service,' replied the woman. She smiled and then continued on her way.

Hanzel and Hanna regarded the poor unfortunates for a moment longer. However, knowing that there was nothing they could do about it, they continued into the market, where they found a huge variety of goods for sale; blankets, pots, food, clothes, shoes, sandals, weapons, tableware, sugar, tobacco, rum, wine, ale...everything sailing folk might need on board ship or for trade. Since they did not have a lot of money left, Hanzel and Hanna thought it prudent not to spend too much. Hanna was able to buy a big straw hat, a light weight, cotton dress, and a pair of sandals. Hanzel bought a colourful, silk scarf to wear over his head or around his neck.

When they were done shopping they decided to have a quick lunch at an ordinary along the roadway after which, they headed back to their ship to have a nap. They were both tired from the walking; not doing too much of that on board ship. Midway into their nap, footsteps could be heard clumping on deck. Someone was shouting, 'HANZEL. HANZEL!!!'

Hanzel and Hanna woke up and sat up in bed, listening to the noise. Footsteps clambered down the stairs and into the gangway leading to their cabin. 'HANZEL!' Loud knocking on the door prompted Hanzel to jump off the bed. He opened the door. Outside the door stood two of the new men, Herman and Otto, two Germans who had sailed together for more than twelve years. Inseparable friends. Otto and Dana were a couple, when they came on board. Herman was single.

'What is it, Otto?' he said. 'Why are you waking me from my nap?'

'It's Dana. They've grabbed Dana,' replied the distraught man.

'Who grabbed Dana?' Hanzel motioned for the men to step inside.

'The authorities. The authorities grabbed her.' Otto nodded his regards to Hanna.

'Why? Why did they grab her?' asked Hanzel, puzzled.

'Witchcraft. They've charged her with witchcraft.' Otto looked from Hanzel to Hanna and back. His eyes betrayed his fright.

'Witchcraft? They charged her with, witchcraft? Why would they do that?' Hanzel looked at Hanna and back at Otto. He scratched his right temple and shook his head. 'It makes no sense. Dana isn't a witch.'

'She was seen talking with a black cat. Then, when she walked past this place, the candle in the window blew out. This happened last night, by the way. So, obviously someone reported that to the authorities and they grabbed her this morning, when we were walking to the church, to pay our respects to God.'

'Where is she now?' asked Hanzel, slipping a baldric over his shoulder.

'In the fort. She's in the fort.' Otto pointed to the door.

'Let's go to the fort and see what we can do.' Hanzel regarded Hanna. 'Do you want to come along?'

'Of course I do. Just give me a moment to grab my hat,' replied Hanna, stepping over to where her hat hung on a hook by the door. She put it on and followed the men topside. They quickly clambered down the ladder and stepped into the rowboat. Otto and Herman rowed them to shore. The fort was not far from where they stepped on land, so, within ten minutes the four friends were standing in front of a sergeant; a ruddy faced Scot by the name of Duncan McGrath.

'We have come to fetch Dana Ballantyne, whom you are holding; falsely accused of witchcraft,' said Hanzel, staring into the man's eyes.

'She's a witch, alright. You can tell by looking at her long black hair. She looks like a witch,' said the Scot with a brogue, so thick, one could have cut it with a knife.

'The fact she has long black hair has nothing to do with anything,' replied Hanna. 'How can that make one, a witch?'

'No, that's not what's she's been charged with. I said, it only makes her *look* like a witch. No, she was seen talking to a black cat. And she snuffed out a candle inside a house, when she walked past, outside the house.' The sergeant regarded Hanzel as if it was a foregone conclusion that Dana would be found guilty.

'We need to see her,' demanded Hanzel.

'Habeas corpus does not apply to witches. You can see her at her trial, which is...Let me see,' he looked into a large book on his desk. 'In two weeks from now.'

'Two weeks from now? We need to weigh anchors and continue our voyage,' replied Hanzel. 'We don't have two weeks.'

'Well, so be it,' replied the Scot. 'She stays here. You will have to come back.'

'By the time we come back, she likely will be dead, judging from your detection method,' said Hanna, angrily.

The sergeant shrugged his shoulders. 'Not much I can do about it. I'm under orders.'

'You military people always hide behind orders. It's an easy way to avoid personal responsibility,' replied Otto in an angry voice. He thumped his fist on the sergeant's desk.

Duncan regarded the fist for a moment. 'You know. I could arrest you for doing that.'

Otto stood back and put his hand on the handle of his cutlass.

'I'd be careful if I were you,' said the Scot, indicating the two guards standing by the door.

'Can we at least bring her food and drink?' asked Hanna.

'You can bring food and drink. You can bring her a blanket, as well. She has no blanket in her cell. Gets cold at night,' replied the sergeant, softening a little.

'Alright,' said Hanna. 'We'll be back.' She looked at Hanzel, anxious to get going, assembling comfort and sustenance for Dana. 'Who surely is in great distress.'

As they stepped out of the fort, Otto wondered if there might be a window in Dana's cell. When he looked around the building; whatever windows there were to cells, could not be accessed, since they were placed high up; and too small to look into.

'We've got to get her out of there,' said Hanna firmly, as they walked away from Dana's prison.

Hanzel nodded. 'Let's go talk with Nathaniel. Maybe he can help.'

'Nathaniel? Who is Nathaniel?' asked Otto.

'The governor. He's a friend of ours,' replied Hanzel. 'Hanna and I will go talk with him. You two can go back and work on getting the ship ready. I really want to sail in two days. This Dana business should be concluded forthwith. As soon as we talk with the governor.'

Otto and Herman agreed and headed back to the ship, while Hanzel and Hanna walked to the State House. When they knocked on the door, James opened it. 'Good afternoon. May I help you?'

'We need to see the governor,' said Hanzel. 'This is an important matter of life and death.'

James raised his eyebrows. 'Life and death?'

'Yes. This is urgent. Is the governor in?' asked Hanzel.

James shook his head. 'No, unfortunately. He will not be back for at least two weeks. Mister Butler has gone exploring down the south west coast. He is looking for a suitable place for another settlement. Somewhere that sugar cane will grow and a good harbour available nearby. He left a few hours after your visit.'

Hanzel nodded. 'Is there anyone else we can talk to. Our friend is in your fort, charged with witchcraft.'

'Oh, that is terrible,' replied James. 'A witch trial can only be conducted by the governor. He won't be back for at least two to three weeks,' he said.

'Yes, but we need to sail,' said Hanzel. 'We can't wait here for three weeks.'

James shook his head. 'There is nothing I can do. So, if there is nothing else I can do for you...'

Hanzel nodded. 'No. No that's fine. There's nothing else. Thank you, James.'

James nodded. 'You are welcome. I will let Mister Butler know that you stopped by, upon his return.'

'Thank you,' replied Hanzel. He turned sadly on his heels, as the servant closed the door.

'Now what do we do?' asked Hanna.

Hanzel clapped his hands together. 'We're going to break her out and get out of here.'

Hanna regarded her lover. 'I like the sound of that, Hanzel. We're going to break her out. The only question is, how?'

'We'll get everyone together and discuss a plan. I'm sure, with as many as we are, we can easily overpower the guard in the fort, don't you think?'

Hanna shrugged. 'I have no idea. I guess we'll find out.'

Hanzel nodded. 'I guess we will.'

When the two friends returned to the ship, Hanzel gave orders for all hands to be assembled on deck as soon as possible. Several men went ashore to round up the crew. An hour and a half later, everyone was on deck and Hanzel appraised the men and women what had happened to Dana and began a discussion how they were going to get her out of the fort.

'We can go enmasse and simply overpower the guards,' suggested Michael. 'It appears there is only a small garrison here.'

'I'll bet there are more than thirty soldiers stationed here,' suggested Peter. 'A place that has a governor, would not have fewer than that. Don't you think?'

'We have to treat this just like taking a ship,' said Martin. 'We have to take them by surprise and grab their leaders.'

'There's probably a captain and a lieutenant. And the sergeants, of course. There are likely two sergeants, maybe three.' Michael looked in the direction of the fort. 'The best thing to do is reconnoiter the place thoroughly. Let's find out as much as we can about where the guards are garrisoned and their schedules.'

Hanzel nodded. 'That's what we'll do. Let's be careful we're not too obvious. They've already seen Hanna and I. And Otto and Herman.' He looked at the two Germans. 'Was anyone else with you when they took her?'

Otto shook his head. 'No. Just Herman and me.'

'Alright. Michael, you, Angus, and Peter, go take a look and ask some questions at the fort. Find out all you can. Pretend to be tourists. You are sailors out sightseeing. Do not mention this ship.'

'Understood,' said Michael. 'We'll go first thing in the morning. There's not much point in going now. It will be dark within a couple of hours.'

Everyone agreed to the plan and was fully prepared to storm the fort, if necessary, whether they were outnumbered or not. There was no way they were leaving without Dana.

Next morning the three detectives set out to see and learn as much as they could in and about the fort. The furthest they actually got was the sentries. Since the three friends had to pretend no connection with Dana, they could not provide another name of someone they might have come to visit; hence giving them no valid reason to go into the place. And, when Michael asked how many men were garrisoned there he was told that was classified information.

'Oh well,' said Michael, as they walked away from the fort. 'Maybe we'll have better luck in that public house over there.'

'If nothing else, we can have us a drink,' suggested Peter.

'Now you're talking,' agreed Angus; already visualizing a pint of rum sitting in front of him.

The pub was already full of sailors, three soldiers, five serving wenches, and a lute player. He was barely audible in the noisy place.

'This is my kind of ordinary,' said Angus, licking his lips and rubbing his hands together. 'I'm sure we'll find out all we need to know, in here.'

'I think you're right,' agreed Peter. 'Now, if we can only find us a place to sit down. It looks like the place is full.'

Angus signaled a serving wench as she walked past. 'Is there any place to sit down in here?'

'Sure. You can sit on the floor, over there.' She pointed to the far end of the room, where several others were sitting on the floor. Then she continued on her way with a board full of tankards.

'I think we'll stand, thank you very much,' replied Angus. 'Bring us three pints of rum on your way back, if you please.'

'Three pints of rum,' she said over her shoulder.

'So, what do you think? Shall we go talk to those soldiers?' asked Peter.

'Not so quick, Peter. Let's just stand here for a while and gradually make our way over to them. How much money have you got?' asked Michael.

Peter looked into his purse. 'Not a lot. Let's see. I've got a couple of shillings and twenty pennies. Oh, and a florin.'

Michael looked into his purse. 'I've got some money, as well. What we'll do is buy them a round, and be friendly with them. You know. We pretend to be good, community minded persons with a respect for things military. We compliment them and so on. If we can get them drunk, we may be able to ply the information out of them.'

'Sounds like a good idea to me,' agreed Peter.

The idea, did, indeed prove to be a good one. Angus and Peter gradually made their way over to where the three soldiers were standing, drinking, talking, and laughing. Eventually Angus and Peter helped them lean into their cups some more, and bit by bit managed to get the information they needed. When they decided they had what they needed, Angus, Peter, and Michael returned to their ship and reported what they had learned.

'Thirty five soldiers are garrisoned there. They are commanded by a lieutenant and three sergeants. There is no captain, at the moment. The captain died in an unfortunate accident. They are expecting one to arrive within the month.

'So, that's a total of only thirty nine. We are forty eight without Dana. Those are not the best odds, are they?' asked Hanzel.

'We can do it, Hanzel. If we do it at night. Most of the garrison will be sleeping. We can take them by surprise,' said Michael.

'Does the gate open in or out?' asked Hanzel.

'The doors open outward. They're locked from the inside. The two guards outside the gate have to be let in,' replied Peter. 'There is no man door.'

'Can someone climb over the gate?' asked Hanzel.

Angus and Peter shook their heads. 'The gate goes right up to the arch. There is no space to climb over it.'

'We're going to have to use grapples and ropes and climb over the wall,' suggested Michael. 'We'll subdue the guards in front of the gate and then climb over the wall.'

'The question is, where do we go over the wall and not be detected?' asked Hanzel.

'Did you get into the fort?'

'The guards wouldn't let us in. And, we couldn't claim to know Dana because we would have drawn suspicion,' replied Angus.

'We should send a couple of the women to bring food to Dana,' suggested Martin.

'Yeah, but then, maybe they get charged with witchcraft by association,' replied Hanna.

'That's a definite possibility. We'd better not risk that.' Hanzel looked up at the sky as he thought for a moment, his chin supported on his right hand as he tapped his mouth with his index finger. *It's possible we might not see a moon tonight, if it keeps clouding over like that.* He returned his gaze to his friends. 'It looks like we might be able to do it, by climbing over the wall. We'll send two over, to subdue the guard or guards on the other side of the gate. Then simply open the gate and the rest of us will go in and do what dirty work we might need to do. Keep blood letting to a minimum. If we're lucky, we can do it peacefully, tonight. I think we may have the dark night we are hoping for.'

During the rest of the day, everyone made themselves ready for the night's adventure. They sharpened swords, cleaned and loaded pistols, and planned how they would go about their work; mentally preparing themselves for any contingency. When night fell, and clouds obscured the moon, they were ready.

Around midnight is when they made their move. Everyone was dressed in their darkest clothes. Using soot, they even darkened their faces. All one could see were eyes and teeth, when they smiled. Once, everyone was on shore, they walked in small groups to the fort, trying to stay in the shadows as much as possible. When everyone was assembled a short distance from the formidable building, five men snuck up on the guards and quickly overcame them. The hapless soldiers had no time to cry out. Then, Jake and Markus threw the grappling hooks over the wall. Being expert rope climbers, the two men were up and over within a minute and a half. Anxious moments later the gate opened and everyone rushed into the fort.

'Now that we're here?' whispered Michael, 'where do we go? We never did scope out where the soldiers are sleeping.'

Hanzel looked about the place. There was one large building in the courtyard. A double set of doors led into the place from ground level, and another, more imposing set of doors sat at the top of thirteen steps. 'Alright, you all go through those doors. I suspect that is where you will find the garrison. We seven will go up the steps and see what we see through those doors.' (Hanzel's marvelous seven consisted of: He, Hanna, Angus, Michael, Martin, Peter, and Maria).

Ever so carefully they all set about their dangerous work.

When Hanzel and his group stepped into the building it was dark and difficult to see. Once their eyes adjusted to the dark, they were given three options; a stair going up, one going down, and the floor they were on. 'Down likely leads to the cells. Michael, go with Maria and Martin down stairs. There will likely be a guard down there, so be careful. The rest of us will go up and see if we can find the lieutenant.'

When Hanzel and his friends stepped foot on the second floor, they could see there was a light on in one of the four rooms. 'I'll bet that is where the lieutenant is,' whispered Hanzel. Ever so quietly they crept towards the door, everyone creeping forward on cats' feet, barely breathing. Hanzel put his right index finger to his mouth as he reached for the door handle.

A floor board squeaked.

Everyone froze in their spot and listened; straining their ears to hear if someone in the room might have heard the squeak.

A gunshot rang out from the garrison. And then another.

Hanzel and his group cocked the hammers on their pistols. A moment later the door burst open and the lieutenant ran out of the room, straight into Hanzel's ambush. 'I'll take that pistol and sword,' he said, holding out his hand. The lieutenant, seeing he was terribly outnumbered, did not resist.

'What is the meaning of this?' he asked indignantly. 'How dare you come in here in the middle of the night and take me hostage?'

'You are holding someone who is very dear to us and we are here to take her back,' said Hanzel, accepting the man's sword and pistol.

'The witch. You've come for the witch. Haven't you?' asked the lieutenant as they began to descend the stairs.

'She is no witch,' spat Maria. 'You better not have harmed her.'

'We treated her no different than we treat all women accused of witchcraft,' said the lieutenant in his perfect, upper class English.

'If she has been harmed in any way, I assure you, sir, there will be hell to pay,' replied Hanzel tersely.

When Hanzel reached the bottom of the stairs, Michael and his group were coming up from downstairs, leading a bewildered guard and a much relieved, Dana. 'Did you fire shots?' asked Hanzel of Michael.

'No, it wasn't us. The shots came from outside,' replied Michael. Just as he said the words, two more shots rang out. Then they could hear yelling and commotion in the courtyard. Leading the lieutenant and guard for human shields, Hanzel and his gang carefully stepped out of the building. The sound of steel on steel, yells and screams, greeted them. The garrison had put up a fight and pursued the pirates out of the building, into the courtyard.

Another gun shot rang out. This time the ball whizzed past Hanzel's right ear straight into the middle of Martin's forehead. He immediately slumped forward and tumbled down the steps. Hanzel put a pistol to the lieutenant's right temple. 'Tell your men to lay down their arms or I will put a ball through your head,' said Hanzel calmly. The lieutenant paused.

Hanzel pushed the pistol harder into the side of the man's head. 'I said, tell your men to lay down their arms or I *will* shoot you.'

'You wouldn't dare,' hissed the lieutenant. 'If you kill me, the entire British navy will be after you at sea and the army will pursue you on land.'

'Brave words. Not likely carried out. What would the navy care about a little second rate lieutenant stuck out here in this little port?'

The lieutenant sniffed haughtily. He looked down at the men who were bravely fighting the pirates. 'Alright men! Put down your arms!'

The men kept fighting. Over the noise, nobody could hear the lieutenant.

He tried again. 'Men!! I say, men!! Lay down your arms!'

Nothing changed. The clash of steel continued. A gunshot sounded close by. Michael had to shoot a soldier who was about to skewer Angus.

'LAY DOWN YOUR WEAPONS!!!' shouted Hanzel with his booming voice. The clashing of steel stopped and everyone turned to look at Hanzel and his group standing at the top of the steps leading into the main building and the jails. 'If you do not stop fighting, I will shoot your lieutenant.'

The soldiers looked at each other and back at Hanzel and their lieutenant. As they were thusly standing, wondering what to do, one of the soldiers managed to pull out a concealed pistol and fired it point blank into Jake's chest. That is all it took to effect the horrible outcome of that jail break. Hanzel and his gang immediately sprang into action and pressed the attack with extreme prejudice. Hanzel shot the lieutenant through the temple. Angus stuck his cutlass through the guard. The two men crumpled into heaps like sacks of potatoes and lay bleeding and twitching as Hanzel and his group attacked to defend their friends. Within a few minutes, the soldiers gave up; having lost twenty three men.

'What are we going to do with the rest of em?' asked Angus. 'Do we shoot em?'

Hanzel shook his head. 'No. No, just take them down to the cell where they kept Dana and lock them in there. We'll throw the key somewhere.'

'What about the bodies?' asked Michael.

'Leave them. We have to get out of here.' Hanzel looked at Jake and Martin lying dead at the bottom of the steps. 'Do we have any other dead, or wounded?' he asked of Michael.

'A few cuts and bruises, is all. I guess our practice drills on board ship paid off. The soldiers were no match for us,' laughed Michael.

'Alright. Take what weapons you can carry. Bring Jake and Martin. We'll give them a proper burial at sea.' Hanzel looked to the east. 'It will not be long until morning and all of this is discovered. I'm sure the gunshots must have woken up somebody.'

They left the fort with great haste and returned to their ship. They wasted no time thereafter, weighing anchors immediately and sailing out of Saint George's harbour just as the sun began to peek over the horizon. As they watched the island gradually get smaller, Hanzel and Hanna heaved a sigh of relief. They got out of that place unharmed and alive.

However, totally unharmed Hanzel was not. Shooting the lieutenant through the temple at point blank range and seeing his brains come out of the opposite side of his head, did not sit well with him. Dreams were disturbing for some time afterward.

'I wanted to avoid bloodshed,' said Hanzel sadly one evening, when he and Hanna were sitting in their bed examining their natural history book together.

'You had to do it, Hanzel. They were not going to let us get away. Shooting Jake like that, point blank, set it all off. It was that soldier's fault. Not yours. We had no choice,' replied Hanna, stroking his hair.

Hanzel sighed and nodded his head. 'Yes, I know you're right. It's still too bad. I don't like it when we have to spill blood. Now I have another killing on my conscience. Is it not possible to be a pirate and save lives?'

Hanna shook her head. 'I don't know Hanzel. I don't know if it is possible to be pirates and not kill people. It's a noble ideal to aim for.'

Hanzel shook his head sadly and then fell asleep in Hanna's arms.

Chapter 34

La Belle Magdalina slipped into the port of Amsterdam early afternoon on November first, 1624. It was a cold, miserable day. The sky was overcast and had been threatening snow at any moment. Hanzel shivered in his big woolen cape. He was standing on the quarterdeck overseeing their entry into port. The harbour was full of ships. They had to be very careful as they made their way to an anchorage. When the ship was good and secure everyone went ashore but Michael, Maria, Morgan, and Peter, who elected to stay on board. Hanzel and Hanna went to see the harbour master, pretending to be the legitimate captain of the merchantman.

'How is it that a Dutchman is sailing a French ship?' asked the clerk at the Harbour Master's Office. He was a small, thin man, with nervous movements, much like that of a squirrel. He read everything through a very thick set of lenses perched on the end of his thin, little nose.

'One has to sail for those who will pay him. My masters, as you can see from the manifest, are from le Havre. So, I sail that which provides me a living,' answered Hanzel.

The clerk sniffed and scribbled the information into a big book. He obviously was not fond of the French. Then he assessed the anchorage fees.

'Is it possible to pay those when we have sold our cargo? At the moment, we are totally without funds; having had to use what we had, to buy provisions in St. George's. I'm sure that our tobacco will fetch a good price.'

'All depends on the quality. We've had a lot of bad quality tobacco come here from Brazil,' replied the clerk. He scribbled on the certificate and handed it to Hanzel. 'You are assessed by the day, so, here is your docking certificate with today's date. When you decide to leave port, just bring that in and we'll figure out what is owing.'

Hanzel nodded and smiled at the clerk. *What would stop me from not paying, I wonder? How would he know if we slip out of port and when?* He looked at Hanna. 'Well, shall we go find a tobacco merchant?'

The merchant they found, plied his trade from a small shop in the Jordaan; a place where gypsies, rouges, thieves, conycatchers, whores, and demons laughed it up as if there was no tomorrow. The first merchant they approached was a big, fat man by the name of Kappers. He plied his trade from a cluttered little shop thick with the aromatic fog of burned tobacco leaves. Mister Kappers was the owner of Kappers & Zoon, purveyors of fine tobacco products since 1610. 'Been in business, fourteen years,' said Mister Kappers proudly. 'I was one of the first in Amsterdam to sell tobacco.' He scratched his bald head. 'I still can not understand why people insist, smoking for pleasure is a sin. Once or twice a day I smoke some tobacco and feel good. What is wrong with that?'

'Nothing, as far as we're concerned. But we're sailors and, well, you know the reputation we have with genteel folk. They expect us to be smokers of the herb,' replied Hanzel.

'So, you say you have a ship full? Where is the tobacco from?' The tobacconist looked over his spectacles. His eyes were blood shot.

'Oh, er, well, some of it is from Brazil, some of it comes from Hispaniola. In addition to bales, we also have cigars.' He looked at Hanna for a moment, trying to remember how many cigars, exactly. 'I believe we have ten crates of cigars. They are very good. Hanna and I have smoked some on our voyage here.'

The fat merchant regarded Hanna for moment. 'A woman, smoking tobacco?'

'They're very good, really,' said Hanna. 'As long as you're careful about inhaling.'

'A breath of tobacco is good for the body. Clears the lungs of ill humors. It helps to ward off depression. God knows one gets depressed from time to time, what with all these wars going on all the time. If everyone just would sit down and smoke some tobacco together, all war would stop. I am convinced of that.' Mister Kappers smacked his fat hand on the table and watched for a reaction from his visitors.

Hanzel and Hanna nodded. 'I'm in complete agreement,' replied Hanzel.

'Me too,' said Hanna.

'Just don't be seen smoking tobacco in public. People associate women and tobacco with the lowest of the low. Those hypocritical, sour faced religious, who do not want anyone to have a happy life, will regard you as a minion of the Devil. Just beware of that.' Mister Kappers frowned. 'It's people like that who make people like me fume with indignation. They'll gladly let the apothecary poison them with dubious lotions and potions, but they will call a natural, God made plant, *the Devil's Weed*. If I want to smoke tobacco, that is my business. My business is my business. What you do in the privacy of your circumstances, is your business. As long as you don't hurt anyone else.'

'I totally agree,' said Hanzel. 'As long as you don't hurt someone else.' He looked at Hanna for a moment. *But we've hurt people. Or were we justified to hurt those we did? Mister Goldman for example?* Hanzel looked down and thought about the poor old boat seller; his conscience suddenly troubling him. He dismissed the thoughts an instant later and continued, 'So, what can you do for us, Mister Kappers?'

'I will have to examine your cargo. Take some samples. Try various leaves in my pipe. Then I will know what your cargo is worth,' replied Mister Kappers. 'After that I will have to see if I have enough buyers. I do not normally buy an entire ship load.'

'Do you have the money to buy a ship load?' asked Hanzel, suddenly wondering if they should see another merchant.

'It all depends on the quality of the cargo.' Mister Kappers scratched his beard.

'How long will that all take?' asked Hanna, growing impatient.

'I can come out to your ship tomorrow afternoon. It will take me a few hours to look at the cargo and take the samples. I should have an answer within three to four days after that.'

'Three or four days?' asked Hanna, looking at Hanzel. 'Why so long?'

'Like I told you. I have to find buyers. I can't buy a ship load and not have anyone to sell it to.'

'Alright,' replied Hanzel. 'Come tomorrow and we'll go from there.'

Mister Kappers smiled. 'Excellent. I will see you tomorrow. Do you mind if I bring my assistant?'

'Not at all,' said Hanzel.

'Where are you anchored?'

'Our ship is, *La Belle Magdalina* she's a French merchantman.' Hanzel gave Mister Kappers the directions.

'I will see you tomorrow,' agreed Mister Kappers extending his chubby hand.

Hanzel and Hanna shook the man's hand and left the cluttered shop. The moment they stepped out of the building they were both suddenly aware of the foul smell outside; where all manner of rotting things and filth was scattered about in the narrow lane. Hanzel was nearly doused, as some uncaring low life emptied her chamber pot from an upstairs window.

'Let's get out of here,' said Hanna, suddenly anxious and claustrophobic in the narrow, canyon like alley. 'I want to get back to our ship and smoke a cigar. This place is not a healthy place to linger.' Just as she said it they walked past a crippled beggar; an unfortunate victim of the war. Hanzel tossed him a coin, trying not to look at the man's disfigured face and empty right sleeve.

'Thank ye. God bless yer,' croaked the cripple, as he caught the coin neatly with his left hand.

Hanzel and Hanna nodded and continued their way out of that lane of misery and squalor. When they stepped out of the darkness into a canal street, they both heaved a sigh of relief.

'That is the last place on earth I would ever want to end up living,' said Hanna, noticeably shaken.

'The farm and our ship surely are a far cry from that place. It is too bad that tobacco is still so poorly regarded. I had no idea. Perhaps we stole the wrong cargo and should have taken sugar instead?' asked Hanzel rhetorically.

'Prices rise and fall, Hanzel. Whatever we get, let's use the money wisely. Who knows if everyone will stay together. If the money is not so good, I'm sure we'll lose a few crew members, don't you think?'

Hanzel nodded. 'I'm sure you're right about that, Hanna. We may have to do some more recruiting.'

'We should anyway. That ship will hold a hundred. If we're going to do some more pirating, we need more crew. Look how we lost two, just getting Dana out of prison. And that was a small skirmish. Imagine a battle in which we're greatly outnumbered. Say, God forbid, some country's navy catches us and wants to take us in for trial? What then? If we don't have the numbers, I hate to imagine what might happen, Hanzel. We took a big chance capturing *La Belle Magdalina*. We had no idea, really, how many we would find on board. We could have all been killed, or captured.'

'You're absolutely right, Hanna. We're going recruiting. Let's find a tavern, have some drinks, eat some food, and maybe, just maybe, we'll meet some eligible candidates.' Hanzel smiled and taking Hanna's hand, happily walked to an inviting tavern on the roadway where they spent the rest of the day drinking, eating, and visiting with friendly folk from many places in the world, including Sumatra.

Next afternoon, Mister Kappers and his son arrived on board *La Belle Magdalina*. Being so fat, he had to be lifted on board in a boatswain's chair the crew had to rig up. The son, being equally as fat as the father, also had to be hoisted on board. Hanzel and Michael took them on a tour through the hold and watched as the two chubby traders examined each bale, box, and barrel, taking samples here and there. When they were done, Hanzel handed each of them six cigars, for which the two men were very grateful. Then, utilizing the boatswain's chair, they were lowered to their rowboat with promises to have an answer in a few days.

'He looked impressed, did he not?' asked Hanzel, looking at Michael.

'The younger one certainly was. I think we have high grade tobacco.' Michael stroked his chin. 'I hope we have high grade.'

As it turned out, they did have high grade tobacco and were offered a princely sum for the load. Everyone was pleasantly pleased with their return. It made the voyage worthwhile, greatly encouraging everyone to stay on board. Not one sailor defected; a fact Hanzel remarked upon when he and Hanna were sitting in their cabin, visiting with Michael and Maria.

'So, what's next, Captain?' asked Michael, looking over his glass of wine.

'We need a faster ship. Let's see what we can get for this tub. Maybe we can use the money to buy a brigantine, large enough to accommodate one hundred sailors. If we have money left over, we should buy some guns and weapons for the crew; in case they don't have their own. Then we'll go back to the Caribbean, next spring, so we can take advantage of the summer shipping. Maybe we'll find us a Spanish treasure galleon this time.' Hanzel smiled and raised his glass. 'Here's to our galleon. What say you?'

The four friends clinked their glasses together and repeated in unison, 'Here's to our galleon!'

Ten days later they managed to find a buyer for the merchantman. Since the ship was in reasonably good shape, Hanzel got a good price for it, as well. He convinced the crew to invest the money, instead of sharing it out. 'So we can buy us a faster ship, and really do some roving,' he said to the crew, assembled on deck, the afternoon of the sale. 'I made arrangements with the new owners that we can stay on board until we have a new vessel. However, they only gave us a week, so we had best hurry and find the boat we need.' Then Hanzel sent everyone off to find a suitable ship for sale and, to recruit more crewmates.

Six days after the sale of the merchantman, Hanzel and Hanna were delighted to be appraised of a magnificent brigantine for sale. 'She's named *The Bluerose*,' said Michael enthusiastically. 'Maria and I found her, when we were out on a carriage ride along the shore road. She's berthed in Vollendam. She looks almost brand new.'

'She looks to be in good shape,' said Maria. 'Michael and I were able to board her and look around.'

'Do you have any idea how much they want for it?' asked Hanzel.

'We have no idea. The seller was not available,' replied Michael. 'He has come into Amsterdam, on business. He'll be back tomorrow, according to a fisherman we met.'

'So, it's off to Vollendam tomorrow,' said Hanzel, clapping his hands together. 'We four will hire a carriage and go for a ride. Hopefully the weather is pleasant.'

Alas, the weather was not pleasant. A November storm had blown in and pelted Amsterdam with cold rain and wind; not even hungry rats went out; preferring instead to stay warm and dry in their cozy nests on protruding bricks and ledges in the sewers. The crew of, *La Belle Magdalina* spent the time: drinking, playing games, mending clothing, philosophizing, reading, talking, drinking, sharpening weapons, cleaning firearms, drinking, eating, drinking, talking, singing, and doing what freemen have always done; make love to their women.

'It's a good thing we're saving on hotel bills. It was a good idea to negotiate letting us stay onboard until we find a new ship,' remarked Michael when they were discussing buying the brigantine, while sitting in the captain's cabin. 'I hope we've got enough.'

'We made good on the tobacco sale. I think that Hanna and my share, alone, should bring us the brigantine. We'll use everyone else's money for provisioning and for weapons,' said Hanzel, taking a big drought of rum from his tankard.

Michael smiled. 'Even though it is so miserable out there; it sure is pleasant for me and Maria to be visiting with you in your cozy cabin.' Michael raised his cup. 'Here's to our new ship.'

Hanna, Hanzel, and Maria clinked their cups against Michael's and in unison shouted, 'To our new ship!'

Three days later the weather cleared. Albeit, it was still cold, it being November. It had quit raining and made it possible to take a carriage to Vollendam and see about the brigantine. Which, as it turned out, was easy to see, since it was the largest ship in the little harbour of the tiny fishing village.

'Zo, yu rrr interested in ze brigantine?' asked a man dressed in the traditional garb of the place; wooden shoes, large black pants, embroidered shirt, black vest, and black cap. His klompen clomped on the wooden boards of the pier to which the brigantine lay tied.

'Yes,' replied Hanzel. 'We learned that she is for sale. The question is, how much do you want for her?'

The man sized up Hanzel and his friends. 'I vant vhat iz fairrr. A fairrr prize. Dat iz vhat I vhant. Not a penny lezz.'

'I have no idea what you consider to be a fair price,' replied Hanzel.

'I vant ten dousand silver ducats. Dat iz a fair prize.' The man crossed his arms over his chest.

'Ten thousand? You want ten thousand silver ducats for that old boat?' Hanzel regarded the man as if he was mad. Then he looked at Hanna and the others. 'Do you hear that Michael? He wants ten thousand silver ducats and he thinks that is a fair price for that leaking tub.'

'Dat boot iz zolid az de day it vas made,' replied the man indignantly.

'When was that? A hundred years ago?' asked Michael.

The boat seller pointed to the brigantine. 'Dat boot iz only fifteen years olt.'

'Alright, since it's only fifteen years old and will need some work, I'll give you five thousand silver ducats for her. We'll take her as is and sail her away today.' Hanzel stared into the man's eyes.

'Five dousand? Five dousand. Oh my Dear Mother of God, how iz it pozzible? How can zum wun zink dat boot iz only wurt five dousand?' The man shook his head. Then he walked over to the brigantine and touched her hull. 'Diz boot iz zolid und verrry gute to zail. I haf zailed er mysef.' He scratched his left eyebrow and then pulled on his right earlobe as he thought hard. 'Alrite, I vill gif you a deel. I vill led you haf er forrrr, say, hmmm,' he sucked in a lung full of air and expelled it slowly. 'Nine dousand silver ducats.'

Hanzel looked at Hanna and back at the boat seller. 'Six thousand and not a stuiver more.'

'You reely vant me to go broke? You vant I go to de poorrr house? Six dousand? Dat iz robberrry. I kan't led it go for lezz dan eight dousand five hundret.'

'Just a moment, I will have to discuss this with my partners,' replied Hanzel, pulling his friends away from the boat seller so they could have a private huddle.

'I think he'll go to seven, maybe seven five,' whispered Michael.

'He's come down fifteen hundred. If we show him the money, maybe he'll come down to seven. Let's try that,' suggested Hanna.

'Money talks. Bullshit walks,' added Maria wisely.

'Alright, let's show him the money.' Hanzel and Michael walked to the carriage and extracted two heavy leather bags, each containing four thousand silver ducats. They set the bags at the boat seller's feet. Hanzel opened one of the bags and let silver ducats fall through his fingers. 'Seven thousand. We'll pay you seven thousand. Cash, as you can see.'

The man rolled his eyes. 'You are zo tempting me. Seven dousand iz cloze but…' The man sucked in air and exhaled slowly as he pulled at his earlobe. 'Alrite, make it seven dousand fife hundret und you got a deel.'

Hanzel smiled. 'Alright, done. Seven thousand five hundred.' He and the boat seller shook hands. 'There are eight thousand ducats in those bags. Do you have any weapons for sale? We'll spend the other five hundred with you, if you can supply us with, cutlasses, boarding axes, pistols, pikes…'

'My frent. Hiz name iz Johan. He lifs dere. He haz vepons. Com I vill take you to him und ve kan zee.'

'What about the bags?' asked Michael.

'Ya. Bring dem. Ve kan kount de money at Johan's plaze.'

The boat seller led the four friends to Johan's little house and introduced him as the local arms dealer.

'Do you have any cutlasses? We need cutlasses,' asked Hanzel.

Johan scratched his left temple. 'Hmm, cutlasses you say? Let me have a look.' The tall, thin Volendammer left the house through the back door and went out to a shed. He came back a moment later, shaking his head. 'No, unfortunately I have no cutlasses.'

'What about short swords?' asked Michael. 'Maybe you have some of those?'

The man shook his head. 'While I was in my warehouse, I thought about other types of blades which would be similar to cutlasses, but no, I am all out.'

'Do you have any swords at all, or dirks, perhaps?' asked Hanzel.

'Oh, you might want long knives or very short ones. Hmm. Let me go see. I just assumed, since you are sea faring folk, you would want short blades. I'll be right back.'

'Long blades are not as good in close quarters,' observed Michael.

'Better than nothing. We'll just have to practice with them and learn to use them on board,' replied Hanzel.

The arms dealer returned, shaking his head. 'I looked and looked through all of my inventory. Alas, no long knives. Or very short ones, for that matter.'

'Do you have any kind of sword, or knife, or weapon of that nature?' asked Hanzel.

'A Japanese samurai sword. I have one of those,' said the man.

'Alright, bring us the samurai sword. Also bring us what pistols you have. Or boarding axes,' said Hanzel.

The man nodded and disappeared out the back door. He came back a moment later. 'I totally forgot. I sold the samurai sword last week to a sailor from China.'

'What about the other weapons I asked for?' Hanzel was beginning to grow impatient.

'Oh, I forgot. Pistols, boarding axes... What about pikes? Do you want any of those? Or a halberd, perhaps.'

Hanzel nodded. 'Yes. Bring us what you have.'

The man left the house and was gone for some time. When he returned he was empty handed. He shook his head sadly. 'All out. I am fresh out of pikes, pistols, boarding axes, and halberds. It's because of the wars, you see. They've taken most of my inventory.'

Hanzel looked at the boat seller sitting on a chair watching the proceedings with a serious expression on his face. 'I thought you said he is an arms dealer. It doesn't look like he's got any arms for sale.'

The weapons dealer nodded vociferously. 'I do have weapons for sale. Not so many at the moment, but I do have some things. I have a helmet. And a cuirass and some greaves.' He thought for a moment. 'Oh, yes, I have a pair of scissors. And, let me see, what else was back there?' He shook his head. 'I have so many things back there. Hmmm. Oh, yes, I have a spear. It's a good spear. Comes from Africa. It's a little rusted. But a real marvelous piece of work.'

'A spear is at least something, I suppose,' said Hanzel. 'Alright, bring us the spear.'

'We can use the armour,' suggested Michael.

'Alright, bring the armour, as well. The helmet and such,' said Hanzel.

Johan nodded and rubbed his hands together. 'Alright. I will be right back.'

'A spear is at least one more weapon that we didn't have before,' said Michael.

'The armour will be useful, as well,' replied Hanzel, watching the back door for the man's return.

When the man returned he had an old dented, rusting Spanish helmet on his head and a chipped old spear head on a bent pole. 'There, you see,' said the man happily setting the helmet and spear on the table. 'I told you I had weapons for sale.'

Hanzel and his friends looked down at the ugly old helmet and useless spear. Then they looked at Johan and the boat seller and back to Johan.

'This stuff is useless to us,' said Hanzel. He looked at the boat seller. 'You said Johan is a weapons dealer.'

'He iz. He iz joost oud of shtock ad de momunt. Iz dat not zo, Johan? You arrr oud of shtock.'

'We don't have much call for weapons here in Vollendam; it being a peaceful fishing village,' said Johan. 'I guess I have not been keeping track of inventory lately and did not realize I had become under stocked.' He looked pleadingly at Hanzel and his friends. 'Please excuse me for wasting your time. Come back in a couple of days. Perhaps we'll have some more stock come in.'

Hanzel grunted and stared at the man. Then he grabbed the money bags, turned on his his heels and, followed by his friends, left the house. 'What a waste of time that was. Arms dealer, indeed.' He handed a bag to Michael.

A second later the boat seller came rushing after them. 'Er, ah, vhat aboot de money forrr the sheep?'

'We'll give it to you on board the ship. You have to count it first,' replied Hanzel, not slowing down his pace as he quickly returned to the brigantine and walked up the gang plank. *This ship looks good. I think this is going to work.* When he stepped on deck he said to himself, 'This will do nicely. This will do nicely, indeed.'

When the transaction was completed, the boat seller gave Hanzel a bill of sale. Then they shook hands. Hanzel and his friends returned to Amsterdam to round up their crew and the boat seller went back to visit with his friend Johan, the dubious arms dealer.

The following day, Hanzel and his now much enlarged crew, sailed the brigantine out of Vollendam and set course for Rotterdam, and another arms dealer.

'Hopefully one with actual weapons for sale, instead of promises and hot air,' remarked Hanzel, as he and Hanna were sitting in their cabin, looking out of the transom windows of their marvelous new ship.

'I want to practice with pistols, more. And with the cutlass,' said Hanna. 'Maria and I have been practicing with cutlasses, as you know. Michael and Angus have been teaching us.'

'If we find a suitable arms dealer in Rotterdam, maybe everyone can buy what they need. Now that we have seventy in our gang, we nearly have the numbers I think we should have to sail back to Hispaniola and really get us a treasure. If we can pick up another thirty along the way, we'll be a gang to contend with.'

Hanna smiled and then kissed Hanzel on the cheek. 'Right you are, Captain.'

Gradually Vollendam disappeared in the distance. The day was cool and crisp, it being mid November. Snow was beginning to threaten. Even the gulls were reluctant to do much flying around in the cold air. The sky was overcast and gray. Everyone bundled up and tried to stay warm and dry as best as possible.

'Let us make for southern waters. The sooner the better,' said Hanzel, putting some wood into the little billy stove warming their cabin.

'I can't wait,' replied Hanna, shivering.

Chapter 35

In the Port of Rotterdam, Hanzel and his crew managed to recruit 35 more men and women. Since the gang allowed women on board, twelve of the new men brought their wives or girlfriends. Fifteen of the new people were from Rotterdam and knew several arms dealers. This time there were arms to be bought. By the time *the Bluerose* left port, everyone had a cutlass, a pistol, and a dirk. The ship also carried: ten boarding axes, twelve pikes, nine crossbows, ten English longbows, six halberds, thirty assorted army helmets, twenty five cuirasses, and nineteen chainmail shirts.

'It's a good beginning,' remarked Hanzel as he and Michael examined their arsenal, safely stowed in three lockers amidship. Maybe, when we stop for water and provisions in the Azores, we might be able to find some more.'

'Better to stop there, for sure. We don't want to show our faces in St. George's for a few years, although we would get there a bit sooner,' remarked Michael.

'Indeed. However, since we're on a new ship; we'll likely not be recognized there. Especially now that I'm growing a beard and mustaches. And you, nobody would recognize you from when we were in St. George's. You've changed your shirt.'

Michael frowned. 'At least I've changed my shirt. What about you then?'

Hanzel burst into laughter. 'You know real sailors don't change their shirts. They just let them fall off.'

Michael regarded his friend for a moment and then also burst into laughter. 'We are a filthy lot, aren't we?'

'Disgusting,' laughed Hanzel. 'We're simply, disgusting. No wonder people refer to rovers as, *filthy pirates*.'

'I'll drink to that,' said Michael, raising his cup. He clicked it against Hanzel's cup and together they shouted, 'Here's to the filthiest pirates on the Spanish Main!'

The two friends laughed and laughed as they invented ever more silliness regarding the hygiene of sailors.

The voyage to Ponto Delgada, that being Hanzel's preferred stopover in the Azores, lasted thirteen days; averaging six knots on good days. Not every day was a good day. They encountered some inclement weather off the coast of Brest, which slowed them down for two days, but was not anything the brigantine could not handle; the inclemency being a mere winter squall. The time was spent drinking and getting to know everyone, discussing plans, practicing with weapons, cleaning weapons, drinking, running the ship, playing games, more drinking, partying, and having fun. *The Bluerose* was a happy ship.

'The happier, the better, I say,' remarked Hanzel, one afternoon, when he and Hanna with Michael and Maria were sitting on the quarterdeck, enjoying a warm, sunny day, drinking rum and smoking cigars. 'Our life is the best life. Little stress. Good company. A nice boat...' Hanzel grinned. 'Here's to our new ship. May she bring us great fortune!'

They sailed into the little harbour of Ponto Delgada in the afternoon of December 15, 1624. Three other large ships lay at anchor and two were tied to the pier, offloading cargo from Portugal. One of the anchored ships was a sloop of war belonging to the Spanish navy.

'We'll give that one a wide berth,' suggested Angus, as they slipped past the enemy ship.

'It looks like the Dutch West India Company isn't fooling around. How many guns is she carrying?' asked Hanzel, gazing out at a huge merchantman, riding low in the water.

'Looks like eight per side. She likely has stern guns, as well,' suggested Michael.

'That company nearly owns the world. They can afford to arm their ships, unlike that French tartane over there.' Hanzel pointed to a small French trader.

'Hopefully, we'll capture a ship and get us some cannons. We can use them,' suggested Hanna, who was standing beside Hanzel on the quarterdeck.

'Too bad they're so heavy,' remarked Hanzel. 'If they weren't so darned heavy, we could just sneak on board that merchantman and sloop and steal their cannons.'

'Alas,' agreed Michael, shaking his head.

'Maybe there are cannons for sale, on shore,' suggested Angus. 'If we're going to do any serious pirating, don't you think we should have some cannons. As we are, we don't pose much of a threat.'

Hanzel regarded Angus for a moment. 'It is one way to avert suspicion. We look like simple traders; not a threat to anyone.'

'Yes, but what if we're attacked by pirates, thinking we're traders, carrying something they need? Without cannons, we have no way to protect ourselves,' replied Angus.

'You're absolutely correct, of course,' agreed Hanzel. 'I was just playing Devil's advocate. However, I'm not sure we have enough money to buy cannons. They're not cheap. And, we need the money for provisions when we get to Santo Domingo.'

'We're going to spend a few days here, Hanzel. There are over a hundred of us. Surely we can figure out a way to get us some cannons. Surely ten men can carry a cannon. We just go over to that Dutch merchantman and steal eight of theirs. Eight should do it, don't you think?' Michael regarded his friend.

'By the looks of them, they appear to be eight pounders. That's a perfect size for this boat,' suggested Angus.

'No harm in trying,' agreed Hanzel, as they reached their anchorage. 'Nothing ventured, nothing gained.' Then he set to work commanding the sailors necessary to bring the brigantine to a halt and drop her anchors. A half hour later *the Bluerose* lay safely at anchor and people began rowing to shore.

Later that evening, Hanzel, Hanna, Maria, Michael, and a dozen other couples were sitting at a long table in a restaurant overlooking the harbour. *Casa da Ramboia* served delicious Portuguese quisine and wines from the mainland. Over a fabulous meal and numerous toasts, the sixteen friends hatched a plan to steal the cannons from the Dutch merchantman. When they shared their plans with the rest of the crew, everyone agreed it was a very good idea and proceeded forthwith to put the wheels in motion.

Otto, Peter, Dana, and Carla would go into town the following morning and find out about the number of sailors on board the Dutch ship and how long they would remain in Ponto Delgada. 'When we have that information, we'll know what to do next,' said Hanzel, clapping his hands together. When the two couples returned, the information they presented was as follows: five officers and twenty five sailors. They were scheduled to continue their voyage to Brazil within two days. The owners always let the crew spend a week in Ponto to ready themselves for what was to come.

'That is perfect,' enthused Hanzel, when he, Michael, Hanna, Maria, Angus, Peter, Otto, Dana, and Carla were sitting together in the master's cabin of their brigantine, that evening. 'What we'll do is go and visit the ship, pretending to bring them a farewell party. We have plenty of libations on board. Since they're Dutch, and most of us are Dutch; we'll go over with that keg of Jenever we found below. They'll love it. I'm sure we can get them all drunk and then, when they're all passed out, we steal their guns and sail out of here.'

'But, we're not done provisioning,' reminded Michael. 'We still need to fill our water barrels and get us some more chickens, a couple of goats, a cow, if possible, and wood for the stoves.'

'All right, see to it. We have very little time. Let everyone know what has to be done. We nine will go over and bring the party. They won't suspect us because we're just nine fellow sailors from the low lands.'

'Seeing women will be a novelty for them, I'm sure,' laughed Hanna. 'Eh, girls? We'll help to put them into a party mood.' Hanna adjusted her breasts, thusly enhancing her cleavage. The other women laughed and copied Hanna's gesture.

'If we can't distract them, nobody can,' laughed Dana, her long, black hair glinting in the gentle light of the cabin's lanterns.

'We'll go tomorrow. Since they'll be leaving the day after, everyone will be on board, I would imagine; since they have to make ready to sail to Brazil. The best time likely would be after lunch. We nine, and maybe a few more women, will row over with libations and create a party. Then we'll signal everyone else to bring all of our boats alongside the merchantman and, using the ship's crane, lower their cannons into our boats and row them to *the Bluerose*.' Hanzel grinned. 'They won't remember a thing.'

'Hanzel,' said Carla, pausing for a moment. 'I may have something which could help with their memory loss.'

'Oh? What might that be, Carla?' asked Hanzel.

'Mushrooms. I found mushrooms here. When Peter and I were out walking about in the countryside.'

'What about the mushrooms?' asked Hanzel.

'They are magical. I was taught by my grandmother how to identify mushrooms. These are the ones. They'll make them party very hardy and then they'll pass out and not remember a thing next day.' Carla smiled. 'Peter and I picked a bag full. We thought they would be nice to have on the long voyage to Hispaniola.'

Hanzel grinned. 'That's perfect. We'll spike their drink with mushrooms.' Then he regarded each one in turn. 'We have to drink very sparingly. We can not get drunk. Especially not on the spiked drink.'

'We'll mark a few bottles for ourselves and share them around, to only ourselves,' suggested Hanna.

'Splendid. That's what we'll do. We'll pretend to get drunk with them, but actually be totally sober. I'm sure it will be fun, acting drunk. Don't you think?' Hanzel regarded his friends.

Everyone agreed, the upcoming party with the Dutch sailors was going to be a whole lot of fun.

After the meeting was over, everyone sprang into action. Jenever and other libations, slated for the Dutch sailors, were spiked with the mushrooms. Boats were readied to receive the heavy cannons. Work crews were organized and rehearsed the procedures they would put into effect in order to expedite the removal of the cannons.

'We must remember to grab lots of powder, fuses, and cannon balls,' said Hanzel.

'And ramrods and cleaning supplies,' added Michael.

'We'll empty their arsenal. When everyone is drunk, it should not be too hard to steal the keys. They're likely in the captain's pocket, or in his cabin,' said Peter.

'Right you are then. We'll be ready. I can't wait until tomorrow.' Hanzel put his arm around Hanna's shoulders. He held up his cup. 'Here's to our success.'

'To our success' repeated the others.

An eagle screeched as it flew overhead.

Next morning they lowered the ship's four rowboats and long boat; pretending to be using them to enable sailors to do exterior maintenance on the brigantine. What they were actually doing was readying the boats to carry the heavy cannons.

'Do you think we'll get eight cannons on the boats?' asked Hanzel.

'It'll take a couple of trips,' replied Michael.

'How many cannons can this ship handle?' asked Hanzel.

'Twelve. We can comfortably mount six per side,' suggested Michael. 'Perhaps ten, but then we'd be crowded.'

'What about chase and stern guns?' asked Hanzel.

'Oh, yes, of course. We can probably mount two front and back,' replied Michael.

'That's sixteen. We might as well grab all of their guns. Once the boys have done a couple, the rest will come easier.' Hanzel clapped his hands together. 'I think we'll be ready when we get to Santo Domingo. If we don't capture a treasure galleon, I'll be very surprised.'

'Aye, Captain,' replied Michael, grinning broadly and rubbing his hands together. He could already see himself running his fingers through golden doubloons.

Around three thirty that afternoon, Hanzel and twelve others, including Hanna, rowed over to the fat merchantman with much mirth and banter. They tied their rowboat to the landing platform and were immediately hailed by one of the officers.

'Hello. Is there something I can do for you?' asked the blond haired midshipman.

'Hello. We are fellow Dutchmen and women who have come to give you a proper send off, seeing as how you are leaving tomorrow,' replied Hanzel, happily thrusting a bottle into the air.

The officer stared down at Hanzel and his group with an expression revealing his concern they might be mad. After a long pause, Hanzel spoke again.

'May we come up. We've brought libations for everybody. It's party time!'

'Just a minute. I will have a talk with the captain,' said the dumbstruck midshipman.

Three minutes later the captain leaned over the railing.

'Greetings, Captain. I'm Hanzel Sventska. I captain that beautiful brigantine over there.' Hanzel gestured. 'Since we have an extra keg of Jenever, we thought to bring it over and give you a little send off party; seeing as how you are leaving tomorrow. According to some of your sailors who befriended some of my sailors in one of the ordinaries.'

The captain smiled. 'Jenever, you say? I have not tasted Jenever for nigh on, eight months.' The captain leaned forward. 'You truly have Jenever?'

'Yes, yes,' replied Hanzel. He pointed to the keg. 'That is Jenever.'

'Well, come on up. What are you waiting for? Climb aboard. Welcome. Welcome. Real Jenever, eh?' The captain licked his lips and watched with sparkling eyes as Hanzel and his gang climbed on board, bringing bottles and kegs up with them.

When Hanzel and his pirates were all standing on the deck of the big merchant ship, the captain introduced himself and his crew. Then Hanzel introduced his group. When the formalities were completed, the party began in earnest. Bottles and kegs were opened and the drinking began. None of the Dutch sailors were any the wiser about Hanzel and his gang mostly drinking water. Soon the instruments came out and the band started up, enabling many a jig or a dance with a buxom young woman with a low slung bodice; a sartorial delight the Dutch sailors were very appreciative of.

Gradually, as the hours passed and the sailors became more and more drunk, the mushrooms began to take effect. By the time night fell, the Dutch crew lay sprawled in all manner of strange places and contortions. Two sailors were passed out in a coil of rope. Another sailor was sitting on a hatch cover with his left leg stuck in an empty keg. Three sailors were sprawled out in some bizarre ritual circle, holding each other's left foot with a right hand, while the index finger of his left hand was stuck in the sailor's right ear.

Hanzel could not help but burst out laughing when he discovered the odd threesome. He rubbed his hands together. 'This is splendid. Just splendid. Well done, everybody.' He pointed to a cannon. 'Now let's see about those cannons.'

The cannons were positioned on a specially rigged gun deck and had to be lifted out through the midship hatch. Michael organized the crane gang, while

Hanzel oversaw the removal of the 2500 pound cannons from their carriages. Utilizing twelve men, they were able to lift the cannon off their carriages and carry the them under the hatch. Then, using two slings, they were able to lift the heavy cast iron tubes up and over the port side of the ship to the waiting row boat below. The entire operation to off load one cannon took about fifteen minutes. A rowboat could carry one and the long boat could hold two. As soon as a boat was loaded, four strong men manned the rowboats and eight handled the long boat. A crew of fifteen took care of business on *the Bluerose*. The entire affair was an efficient operation. After three and a half hours, they had managed to steal eleven eight pounders. During that time only one Dutch sailor woke up from his drunken hallucinations. Hanzel quickly convinced him that they were delivering new cannons to the ship and that he, the sailor should help by going below and searching for a very specific cotter pin.

Eventually the process became a routine. As cannon after cannon was lifted out of the merchantman, nobody noticed that one of the slings had slipped partially off the hook. When the heavy metal tube was hanging over the rowboat manned by, Otto and his crew: Derek, George, and Markus, the sling slipped off the hook and the pommel end of the cannon swung down, causing the other end of the cannon to slip out of its sling. The pommel smashed straight through George's head before it plunged through the bottom of the rowboat. When the rest of the cannon followed, one of the trunnions smashed into Derek's chest and tore right through him, spilling his ribs and lungs into the sea. Both men disappeared under the waves. Otto and Markus managed to jump out of the way, into the harbour, where they treaded water and watched the rowboat's pieces bobbing on the bloodied waves. In a couple of seconds, two men were dead, a rowboat was smashed to pieces, and a precious cannon lay at the bottom of the sea.

The noise woke the Dutch captain from his slumbers in Wonderland. 'What's going on here?' he asked in a croaky voice.

Hanzel and his friends regarded the captain for a moment, not immediately able to reply. Everyone was in a daze over what had just happened in the blink of an eye.

'I said, what is going on here?' The captain regarded Hanzel with a strange expression, as if there was something wrong with his eyes.

'We are replacing your cannons with much lighter ones,' replied Hanzel. 'They're not visible, because they are so light weight. They are meant to foil pirates.'

The Dutch captain smiled. 'Oh, that's wonderful. New cannons. Did you hear that, men? We are getting new light weight cannons.' The captain looked about the deck, but in his mushroom induced state, his mind registered nothing abnormal as he wandered off and disappeared through the door beside the quarterdeck stairs.

Hanzel regarded Michael and shook his head. 'We have to get going. The sun will be up soon.'

'What about the carriages?' asked Angus.

'Leave them. There's no time. We'll build new ones on route to Hispaniola,' replied Hanzel.

'With what? We don't have the lumber or the hardware,' suggested Angus.

'Perhaps we can sail for one of the other islands and get lumber?' Michael looked at his friends for a confirmation.

'What about the hardware?' asked Angus.

'There's lots of iron on board. I'm confident that our artists will figure it out,' replied Michael.

'I believe that too,' replied Hanzel. 'What ever we do, we have to get out of here, right now. We have no idea how much longer these Dutch sailors will be sleeping.'

'Right you are, Hanzel.' Michael turned to the others. 'Alright ladies and gentlemen. Let's get out of here.'

Everyone quickly vacated the ship and crowded into the long boat and remaining rowboat. They reached *the Bluerose* just as the sun was beginning to peek over the horizon. The air was fresh and crisp. Several gulls flew over and hurled insults as the eleventh cannon was hoisted aboard. Others began to ready the ship for sailing by weighing anchors, unfurling sails, pulling and tying ropes, and so forth. An hour later, Hanzel and his gang slipped out of Ponto Delgada, their ship more than twenty five thousand pounds heavier.

'Once we have those cannons in place, we'll be a force to contend with; at least for merchant ships. Navy ships are another question,' said Hanzel, examining one of the cast iron cannons, sitting on the deck. 'We'll sail south,

south, east and look for suitable wood on Santa Maria. There's a port on the south side of the island. They may have a lumber mill. Maybe we'll be able to get everything we need. The carriages can be built at sea. It'll give our artists something to do.'

'Aye, aye, Captain,' said Angus, as he turned the big wheel and set the brigantine on course. Seven hours later Pico Alto appeared on the horizon. An hour after that, the shoreline of the small island came into view. Angus steered the ship in order to stay far enough off the coast to avoid whatever rocks might pose a hazard. Three hours later they sailed into the small bay; a perfect harbour supporting Vila do Porto, the second oldest settlement in the Azores.

It was midnight when they finally dropped anchors. Everyone was tired. Only a few people elected to row to shore and partake of libations at one of the two taverns along the roadway. Hanzel and Hanna went to bed and fell into adventurous dreams, entwined in each other's arms.

Next morning Hanzel appointed Angus to oversee the acquisition of lumber from the local mill. 'And see if there is any iron to be had. If there is, buy strapping, carriage bolts, axles, whatever you can find to help with carriage construction.'

Angus nodded. 'Aye, Captain. I'll see what me and my crew can find. Do we have money?'

Hanzel handed Angus a purse he had rescued from the Dutch ship. 'There should be enough in there.'

Angus accepted the bag and then set about organizing his crew. A moment later they rowed to shore with the long boat, loaded with sailors and their women, off to enjoy a pleasant day in town. Hanzel, Hanna, Michael, and Maria took the rowboat, along with some bottles of wine, a cigar, each, and a picnic lunch, to a beautiful white sand beach, where they found a perfect place to lounge for the day. Several large trunks of driftwood enabled them to sit comfortably, as they talked, drank wine, and smoked their cigars. The weather was pleasant and balmy. The sun shone in a cloudless sky. Sea birds pecked the sand at the water line and gulls winged overhead, hoping the humans would toss a crumb their way.

'This is a nice place,' remarked Hanna.

'I would love to sit here in the summer, sometime,' replied Maria. 'This is a beautiful beach. Much nicer than beaches I'm familiar with.'

'We should go for a walk,' suggested Hanzel. 'We can leave that stuff here. I feel like stretching my legs.'

The others agreed that a walk would be pleasant. The sand felt good under their bare feet. The sound of waves crashing against rocks and onto the sand, made for a pleasant white noise in the background. Along the way, the four friends examined some tidal pools and were surprised by the number of creatures living there. When they reached a place where a jumble of rocks and boulders jutted out into the sea, they decided to walk into the forest for a little ways, to see if they could get around the rocks, instead of having to climb over them. As they reached the edge of the forest, Hanna noted there was something sticking out of the sand, beside a tall palm tree.

'Look, there,' she said, pointing to the strange, white, stick like object protruding out of the sand.

When she took a closer look, she suddenly recoiled and gasped. 'It's an arm!' she exclaimed. 'It's a human arm!'

Michael grabbed a stick and dug around the bones. 'I wonder where the hand is?'

Hanzel also took a stick and helped Michael dig around, as the two women stood back, aghast at the horrible object the men were digging up. However, after digging for ten minutes, all they found were the three arm bones; a humorous, a radius, and an ulna, still held together by rotting tendons.

'I wonder where the rest of him is?' asked Maria. 'If there's an arm, there's got to be more, don't you think?'

'Maybe it was someone who was marooned here,' suggested Michael.

Hanzel snorted. 'Then, whoever this was, may have been here a lot longer that a few hundred years. Vila do Porto has been here since the fourteen fifties. Surely, if this person had been put here within the last two hundred years, he could have made it to town, from here.'

Michael examined the bones. 'These bones are not two hundred years old. I don't think these bones are more than ten years old. If these were older, I'm sure those tendons would not be holding them together.'

As Michael and Hanzel examined the bones more closely, Hanna and Maria, curiosity having overcome their fear, scouted about, to see if there were more bones to be found. 'Over here!' shouted Hanna, a moment later. Hanzel and

Michael ran over to where Hanna and Maria were digging into the sand. When the two men reached the place, the two women had dug up a skull attached to the rest of the one armed skeleton.

'Dead men tell no tales,' muttered Michael, as they poked about the decaying carcass for clues.

'Judging from the rags, he was likely a sailor. Those look like petticoat breeches.'

'Whoever put him here, didn't leave him much,' remarked Hanna.

Michael turned the skull over. 'Whoever put him here, murdered him.' Michael pointed to a massive hole in the left side of the skull. 'That hole indicates he was smashed in the side of the head with a heavy, blunt object.'

'Why would someone murder a sailor and bury him on land? Why not throw him into the sea?' asked Maria.

'Unless he was killed to shut him up regarding something that went on here, on land,' suggested Michael.

'Maybe he was part of a crew which buried a treasure and he was shut up to keep it a secret,' ventured Hanzel.

'Now that's an interesting theory. Maybe there's a treasure around here, somewhere.' Hanna stared into the forest.

'Would they kill someone, this close to the treasure? He was likely killed here, but the treasure is elsewhere. Without a map, how would we ever find it?' Michael scratched his left temple.

'It could be anywhere,' said Hanna. 'Indeed, how would we ever find it?'

'There's no harm in us looking around here a bit more intensely. Who knows, perhaps this man was killed on, or near the place. The treasure could be right under our feet, suggested Hanzel. 'Since the bones are not very old, and it's not likely too many people come out here, we should look for a place where the ground appears dug up.'

'If the treasure is buried in the sand, then that would be impossible, since the sands move over time; in wind and surf,' observed Michael.

'They likely would not bury it on the beach, because it could flood in a high tide, or storm.' Hanzel looked into the forest. 'No. If this man was not just a simple murder victim, and there is a treasure he was killed for; it would be buried in the forest. We should look in there and see what we find.'

Hanna regarded the forest and shook her head. 'How in heaven's name do you expect to find anything in there?'

'An unusual mound of dirt, or a cairn of rocks, or something. No harm in looking. We have all the time in the world,' replied Hanzel, stepping into the forest. His friends quickly followed. As they stepped into the twilight of the forest it took a moment for their eyes to adjust. A few seconds later they could make their way through the dense verdure and soon found, what appeared to be, an old trail. It was obvious that some time ago, branches had been hacked away and many feet had trodden down the soil. 'We'll follow this trail. I have a suspicion this might be the path they made to haul something in here.'

Michael examined the trunk of a mahogany tree. 'Look here. Someone cut a slice out of this trunk. A marker, perhaps?'

'There's another over here,' said Hanna, pointing to a palm with a cut mark.

'I would suggest that those cut marks are a dead give away,' suggested Michael.

Ten minutes later, and another hundred yards deeper into the forest, the trail ended. The four friends stopped and looked around, but no mound, or undisturbed place made itself visible.

'Maybe it's just a cigar dream,' said Hanzel. 'That skeleton likely belonged to a simple murder victim. Or a marooning. Animals likely pulled him apart.'

'Why the trail and the markings in the trees?' asked Hanna. 'It's obvious something made this path here. Even though it's all overgrown, it's still visible.'

'It makes no sense that someone would make a trail into this forest, just to have it end here.' Michael shook his head. 'There has to be a reason.'

Hanzel stroked his chin and stared at the trees. Birds twittered and bugs buzzed as the four friends stared into the forest, wondering if there was anything unusual to see.

Suddenly, Hanzel pointed to a large mahogany tree. 'Look, there!' He ran over to the spot and picked up a bone. 'A femur. Now we have two victims. There's got to be another grave around here.'

'Animals likely scattered the remains; just like they must have done with that arm. Pieces of the hand are probably lying about in animal droppings,' suggested Michael.

'I think this is all very creepy,' said Maria, looking anxiously about.

'Two victims,' said Hanzel. 'It's like you said, Michael. Dead men tell no tales.'

Hanna reached into a shrubbery and extracted a rusted, old shovel. 'Here's the grave digger.'

Maria pointed. 'There. See how those plants are much smaller than everything around them. That is all newer growth. Someone cleared some bush and it has grown back since then.'

Hanzel and Michael pulled their cutlasses from their scabbards and began to hack the vegetation back; revealing a mound of soil.

'What do you suppose is under there?' Hanzel began to dig with the shovel.

A few minutes later, he uncovered the rest of the carcass belonging to the femur. The carcass was wearing rotting sailor's clothing. The decaying head was covered with a red bandana. The horror of finding another rotting cadaver shocked Maria, who had to sit down with Hanna, in order to gather her composure.

Michael and Hanzel pulled the corpse out and laid it down beside the hole. When Hanzel resumed digging, the shovel struck something hard. 'There's something down here,' he said, tapping the shovel against, whatever it was under the soil. When he pushed some of the soil away, they could plainly see the top of a chest.

'I think we may have found a treasure,' suggested Hanzel. 'What do you think?'

Michael shook his head. 'I have no idea. However, given we have two dead men, one of which is lying on top of, whatever that is, makes me think, there's something important in that box.'

Twenty minutes later, Hanzel and Michael lifted a heavy chest out of the hole. The chest was made of oak, with metal banding and a heavy padlock.

'We don't have a key,' said Michael, shaking his head. 'Now what?'

'We'll use a rock. That lock is rusted. I'm sure we can break it off with a few good blows,' suggested Hanzel, looking about for a suitable rock to use.

Michael found a good sized stone and began to pound on the lock. Ten blows later, the rusty fastener broke open. He tossed the lock aside and opened the lid. The hinges creaked and groaned.

'What is it?' asked Hanna. 'Is it a treasure?'

Maria had come to join the others, staring into the opened chest.

Inside the box they found a rolled up parchment and a key. When Michael opened the parchment roll everyone gasped; 'A treasure map!'

'X marks the spot,' observed Michael, pointing to the parchment.

'The problem is, where is that X located?' asked Hanzel. 'All we have is a compass orientation, a bit of coast line, what looks like a large rock on the beach, and those two small islands. A small one and a larger one. The map doesn't say if the X is on this island. There's a piece missing.'

'That's a bother, isn't it?' Hanna frowned as she stared at the yellowed map. *There's something about those islands. There are small islands north of here. We sailed past them.* 'Maybe those are two of the islands we sailed past before we got to Vila do Porto.'

Hanzel stroked his chin as he stared at the map. 'You know, Hanna, you might just be right. We should check this map with our chart. Could it be that there is a treasure somewhere on this island, after all?'

'Let's get back to the ship and compare the map with our charts. Who knows, maybe Hanna is right. If she is; the treasure is just north of here.' Michael grinned. 'Now, this is an adventure. Two dead men and a treasure map in a buried chest. It's the stuff of literature. Something worthy of that English fellow; what's his name? The playwright.'

'Oh, you mean, William Shakespeare?' Hanzel regarded Michael.

Michael shook his head. 'No, not him. I think his name is Marlowe, or something like that. When I sojourned in London, some years ago, I saw one of his plays. I don't go to the theatre much. Well, to tell the truth, I've only gone once. When I was in London. Some friends took me. The play was called, something to do with the queen of Carthage.'

'What's that got to do with two dead men and a treasure map?' asked Hanna, regarding Michael with a quizzical expression.

'The play was very dramatic. Finding two cadavers and a buried treasure map is kind of a dramatic experience, wouldn't you say?' Michael grinned, with an expression as if his observation was the most obvious thing in the world.

'Dramatic is one way of putting it, I suppose,' replied Hanna, looking at the human remains lying beside the hole.

'What should we do with him?' asked Michael.

Hanzel pushed at the remains with his boot. They tumbled back into the hole. Then he tossed the chest after him. The box landed on the rib cage. The sound of cracking bones made everyone shiver inside; glad it wasn't their ribcage. 'We'll give him a proper burial,' he said as he began to shovel the soil back into the hole. 'May he rest in peace. Poor lubber, whoever he was.'

'What about the other one?' asked Michael.

'We can use the shovel and dig him a better hole. It's the least we can do. After all, those two died to protect the secret of the map.'

When they were finished filling the hole, they headed back to the beach where they buried the other unfortunate victim.

'May God give them peace, whoever they were,' said Hanzel. He threw the old shovel into the bush. 'We won't need this anymore. Let's get back to the ship and see if we can make anything out of this map.'

'This is exciting, isn't it Maria?' asked Hanna as they walked back towards the large tree trunks, where they had left their picnic.

'Exciting, yes. To find a treasure map. But to find two dead men is disturbing. I've never seen dead people in such a state of decomposition before. I'm scared I'll have bad dreams over this.'

'Don't worry, Maria,' said Michael, reassuringly. 'I'll make sure your dreams will be happy ones.' He smiled into her eyes as he put his arm around her shoulders. He kissed her tenderly on top of her head.

When they returned to *the Bluerose* it was late afternoon. Angus greeted them when they stepped on deck. 'We managed to buy enough lumber to easily make eight, maybe ten carriages,' he said. 'We even found two kegs of carriage bolts and iron strapping. Our artists have assured me they have what they need. They'll be delivering the rest of the lumber tomorrow.'

Hanzel turned to his friend. 'By the time we get to Hispaniola, we'll be a force to reckon with, eh, Michael?'

'Right you are, Hanzel. Right you are,' agreed Michael.

'Well, let's go to our cabin and see what we can find out,' said Hanzel, taking Hanna by the hand. Michael and Maria followed.

When the four friends examined the chart and compared it with their treasure map, it was quickly apparent the islands were those a few miles further north, just off the coast.

'Oh, Hanzel, what if it's true. What if there really is a treasure?' asked Hanna. 'Wouldn't that be exciting?'

'If there's a lock on it, we have the key.' Hanzel laid the key on the map.

'We can look for it tomorrow, while they finish loading the lumber. We'll row out first thing in the morning,' suggested Michael.

The others agreed it was a good idea. Then, feeling tired, Michael and Maria retired to their cabin for a nap. Hanzel and Hanna continued talking about their adventure for a while longer, until, they too, fell asleep in each other's arms; dreaming of treasure. They never heard the dinner bell.

Chapter 36

Morning arrived with a blustery wind and dropping temperatures. The sky was overcast and threatening rain at any moment. The weather was so nasty, not even a gull ventured out. It was no day for treasure hunting, no day for lumber deliveries, and no day for sailing, either. Everyone stayed inside. It was the 17th of December. Winter had reached out from the mainland and gripped the Azores with an icy hand. Some of the new lumber had to be used to stoke the ship's stoves.

The cold weather lasted for three days, during which time the crew spent their hours playing games, dancing, singing, playing music, cleaning weapons, drinking, talking, mending things; the usual things people do on board a ship. Some were also making preparations for Christmas.

'It's only five days away,' said Hanna at dinner on the evening of December 20th. 'I propose, even if the weather improves and the lumber is on board; that we stay in port and celebrate Christmas here, in Villa do Porto. A few more days in port will be good for everybody.'

'I'm sure the treasure fleet can wait. They probably don't want to cross in winter, anyway. We'll catch them in springtime.' Hanzel grinned and held up his cup. 'Here's to springtime and the Spanish treasure fleet!'

'To the treasure fleet!' repeated everyone in unison as they clicked their cups together.

The following day saw much improved weather. The grey clouds had been replaced by fluffy white ones. Glorious sunlight bathed Santa Maria in yellow warmth. It was an excellent day to finish loading lumber and the perfect day to go on a treasure hunt.

Hanzel and Michael, with a couple of the ship's artists, rigged a mast and sail for the other rowboat, thus enabling the four friends to sail leisurely up the coast; ostensibly to do some sightseeing and have a picnic on a beach further north.

'What do you need that shovel for?' asked Angus.

Michael looked at the shovel and then back at the redheaded helmsman. 'It's so we can dig a fire pit. We are going to have a picnic and want to make a fire. Maybe we'll catch a fish or something we can roast.'

The explanation suited Angus just fine. There were no further questions as Hanzel and his friends climbed down to the row boat.

They reached the place where the two islands, indicated on the treasure map, lay opposite a huge rock sitting on the beach. The outline of the rock was exactly as drawn on the chart. They rode the surf in to the beach and dragged the rowboat on shore. Then they followed the instructions to pace 50 yards directly back of the rock, into the forest where there was supposed to be a strange looking tree.

Hanzel and Michael had to hack most of the way through undergrowth as Hanna paced the required steps. Birds twittered and skittered about in the trees adding to the click, clack of beetles and other buzzing insects. When Hanna reached a count of 48 yards they reached a small clearing in which stood an odd looking tree, somewhat like the drawing on the map.

'It's likely been a few years since this map was drawn. The tree is a living thing. It makes sense it would look somewhat different from the drawing,' suggested Hanzel. He regarded the document. 'Alright. Now, if we dig at the base there is supposed to be something to help with the next step.' When they dug where the map directed, they found a small box. The box was locked.

'Try that key,' suggested Hanna.

When Hanzel used the key, the lock clicked open. Inside the box they found another key and the missing piece of the map. 'Now we know where X is,' said Hanzel. He pointed. 'It's over there.'

The four friends walked in the direction Hanzel pointed. Soon they came upon a cairn, as indicated on the formerly missing piece of the map.

'Now we pace ten yards directly west from this cairn.' Hanzel, began pacing the correct number. When he reached the required distance, he pointed to the ground. 'Alright, we'll dig here.'

Twenty minutes later their shovel struck something solid. When Hanzel pushed the last thin layer of dirt aside, they discovered a large trunk.

'Treasure! We've found a treasure!' exclaimed Hanna.

'Madre de Dios!' muttered Maria, her hands to her face. 'We're going to be rich.'

'Now, don't be too anxious, ladies,' cautioned Hanzel. 'There's a trunk. But, we don't know what's in it.'

'Well, surely it's a treasure,' said Hanna, as if it was the most obvious thing in the world. 'Why else would someone have gone to all of this trouble? The map, the key, all of it...'

Hanzel grinned. 'It likely is a treasure. However, remember, what might be one man's treasure might be another man's cast offs.'

Michael nodded, smiling. 'That's pretty much true, isn't it?'

'Well, whatever you two think, Maria and I believe it's a treasure. So, let's get it out of the hole,' urged Hanna.

It took another half an hour to uncover the large box. When they tried to lift the trunk out of the hole, it was much too heavy.

'We'll have to open it and take out some of the heavy stuff,' suggested Hanzel, handing the key to Hanna. She smiled at her lover and then inserted the key into the lock. However, when she tried to turn the key, it did not work. The lock was much too rusted.

'Oh, well,' said Hanzel, taking out his pistol. 'Hanna, my darling, if you would kindly move out of the way.'

Hanna did so.

Then, taking careful aim, Hanzel shot the lock open. 'These things are such handy tools,' he said, looking fondly at the weapon.

'I never leave home without one,' laughed Michael. 'A pistol, next to his woman, is a man's best friend. What else can one use to protect oneself and one's loved ones against rogues and cutthroats?'

'If it ever happens, sometime in the future, when governments take away a man's weapons, people with weapons will create a terrible world where people become victims,' replied Michael.

'I agree with that,' said Hanna. 'However, I think women should also be armed. What do you think, Maria?'

Maria nodded. 'I definitely agree. I'm glad we practice with weapons on board. I don't think there's a woman on board who can't shoot or handle any other weapon we have.'

'That's a good thing,' laughed Hanzel. 'This way I feel much safer, don't you, Michael?'

'Oh, most definitely,' agreed Michael, laughing. He put his arm around Maria's shoulders and pulled her close. 'I love the fact that my woman can protect her man.' He gave her a kiss and looked into her eyes. 'I love you.'

Maria kissed him back. 'I love you too, Michael.'

'So, let's see what's in this trunk,' said Hanzel, working on the lid. 'The hinges are very rusted. I think we're going to need some more strength on this.'

Michael jumped into the hole. Taking a hold of the lid, the two men strained to pull it open. Gradually, with a great deal of creaking and groaning, the lid opened. When the four friends saw what was in the box, they all gasped at once. With eyes widened, they discovered a real treasure.

'It really is a treasure,' said Hanzel, looking at Hanna and back at the bars and coins, pearls, rings, pendants, and chains of gold and silver. Precious stones sparkled in the light beams filtering through the leaves overhead.

'We have actually found a treasure. That is totally amazing,' said Hanna, taking a rope of heavy pearls from the trunk. She turned to Maria. 'Here, Maria. These will look good on you.' Maria grinned as Hanna put the rope around her friend's neck. Maria held the pearls in her hands and admired how beautiful they were. All the iridescent colours of the rainbow shone back at her.

'When we divide this treasure with our crew, everyone is going to be so happy. We'll all look like nobility, decked out in gold or silver, or any of those beautiful rings,' said Hanzel. 'We'll divide this according to our code.'

'Totally agreed,' replied Michael. 'However I move that our ladies be allowed to keep the trinket they have chosen, as a reward for us finding this.'

'Oh, I completely agree,' said Hanzel. 'That will not be difficult to convince our friends of. That really is a given, don't you think?'

Hanna and Maria nodded. 'Oh, most definitely. We most definitely agree, don't we, Maria?'

'Well, let's see how much we need to empty, to get the box out of the hole,' said Hanzel, grabbing a handful of treasure. 'Michael, please lay my cloak on the ground and we'll put the treasure on it.'

Ten minutes later a pile of treasure lay on the cloak. When they tried to lift the chest, it was light enough, but still heavy. With some groaning, Hanzel and Michael lifted the box out of the hole and set it next to the pile of treasure they had removed.

'I suggest we haul the chest to the boat, and then come back for this stuff,' said Hanzel, pointing to the pile of treasure.

Hanna and Maria filled their pockets with as much of the "stuff" as they could hold, and carried more in their arms. Even so, there was still more to be returned for.

By the time they had loaded the heavy chest into the boat, and filled it up again, it was becoming evening.

'The sun will be setting in an hour, or so,' observed Michael, looking at the sky.

'We had better get rowing,' suggested Hanzel.

Because of the added weight, the rowing took much longer. It was dark by the time they returned to *the Bluerose*. When the crew was appraised of the treasure, there was great jubilation and an excellent excuse for a party.

'Light the lanterns!' shouted Hanzel, 'And lay a sheet on deck. We'll divide the treasure right now, ladies and gentlemen!' The pronouncement was followed by hoots and hollers from the rest of the crew.

'AND BRING OUT THE LIBATIONS!' shouted Hanzel over the joyous cacophony.

And so the drinking started and the party got underway. In the gentle light of two dozen lanterns the treasure glittered on the white hemp sheet laid out on deck. Nobody denied Hanna and Maria their little extras. Everybody was happy with what they got, which, if sold, would, 'fetch a pretty penny for sure.'

'More like a pretty pound,' remarked Angus to Michael sitting beside him on the midship hatch.

Michael nodded, grinning. 'A pretty bushel, if truth be told.'

As the libations flowed and people became ever more happy, spontaneous shanties broke out and couples and singles jigged and danced, singing, and laughing; totally enjoying the life of freemen and women, happy in each other's company. However, in a company of a hundred or more, there is always bound to be one malcontent. At this juncture, this person or persons, had not revealed themselves yet. But, you know how it goes. When so many people live in close quarters on a ship, jealousies, petty gripes become festering sores, mole hills become mountains; all of that low level human emotion stuff, tends to manifest and build up, the longer the people are at sea in their floating prison. You know about that. It is called, *human nature*.

'I love the life we're living, Hanzel,' said Hanna, her blue eyes regarding her best friend with a deep love and respect. 'If it wasn't for you, I would never have experienced this. This is really what it means to be free.'

Hanzel laughed. 'Finding that treasure surely helped.'

Hanna nodded, a big grin on her face, as she thought about the magnificent pearl earrings and triple rope of heavy pearls around her neck. 'These pearls were meant for a queen, or at least a noble woman,' she said. 'Without you. I would never have gotten to wear something so splendid and rich. I wonder whose treasure it was.'

Hanzel shook his head. 'I have no idea. There was no note, no calling card, nothing. Judging from the rusted lock and hinges, the box was in the ground for some years.'

'The skeletons were at least two, or three years old,' remarked Hanna, crinkling up her nose and shivering. 'Those things disturbed me. I mean. It's the first time I've actually seen dead people. I mean, decayed dead people. Bones with tendons and bits of muscle and stuff. Yuck.' She crinkled her nose.

'Well, whoever's treasure it was, he will be very unhappy,' laughed Hanzel, holding up his cup. 'HERE'S A TOAST, MY FINE FRIENDS! HERE'S TO OUR UNKNOWN BENEFACTOR! MAY HE NEVER FIND US!'

'MAY HE NEVER FIND US!' chorused everyone else, immediately after which a sailor began a shanty he made up on the spot, not caring whether it rhymed particularly well. It all sounded great when accompanied by the ship's musicians, a pipe, a drum, a sackbut, two viols, three horns, and a coronet, each one doing their best to make some sort of harmonious melody. In their inebriated state, it didn't matter what it sounded like. It was music to their ears.

'There was this man named Hanzel

Together with his bride

Did take the first mate and his partner
And together they did ride
Together they did ride
The waves so blue
In a boat that's new
To find a treasure in the wild
To find a treasure in the wild.
When they came back they called the crew
And said, Look what we brought for you
Lots of gold and silver
And stones and pearls
And chains and swirls
From the treasure, the treasure
They shared with us together
They shared with us together.

'I SAY, HIP HIP HOORAY FOR HANZEL, MICHAEL, HANNA, AND MARIA!' shouted Dana, holding her cup high.

'HIP HIP HOORAY! HIP HIP HOORAY!' shouted the crew. 'MAY THEY LIVE A HUNDRED YEARS!'

And so the party continued through the night and the next day, and the day after that. When everyone woke from their stupor, it was Christmas.

'MERRY CHRISTMAS!' everyone shouted and saluted each other, which gave the entire crew another reason to party. And party they did, through Boxing Day, and the next day, and the day after that. On the 29th of December three people had birthdays which brought further reason to party. When December 31st arrived, and the new year was pending, there was no reason to stop partying, so the party just continued.

'HAPPY NEW YEAR!' shouted everybody, when the time came.

'I love the life of a pirate,' said Hanzel happily into his cups on the first of January, 1625. 'I wish I could be a pirate for a hundred years.'

'That would be nice, as long as we don't get old. I mean, I can't see us being pirates as normal eighty year olds, can you? I don't think that geriatric pirates pose much of a threat to anybody,' replied Hanna.

'It would be slow swashbuckling, that's for sure,' laughed Hanzel. He pretended to sword fight in slow motion as an eighty year old. Hanna laughed. 'Aaargh!' croaked Hanzel with his eighty year old voice. Hanna laughed and laughed. 'Oh, Hanzel. You're so funny. I love you!'

'I love you too, Hanna. I'll love you for ever. I don't ever want us to be apart.' Hanzel gazed into her eyes and then they kissed and hugged for a long time. They no longer heard the music, singing, and raucous laughter, as they listened to each other's breathing. Hanzel and Hanna were a match made in Heaven. They knew it and so did Heaven.

'Hey you two love birds,' said a friendly voice. 'A bunch of us are going into town. It looks like the tavern is open and there is a party going on there. Do you want to come?'

Hanzel looked up at Michael. Then he looked at Hanna, who shook her head gently. *I want him to myself tonight. I want to show him how the new year should be celebrated.* 'No, Michael. Thank you, but Hanna and I would prefer to stay up not too much later. We're both tired from all the partying we've been doing over the last couple of weeks.' Hanzel yawned, to emphasize his point.

'I understand. No problem. We'll see you tomorrow,' replied Michael.

'Good night, Michael. And to you too, Maria. Have fun in town. And be careful,' suggested Hanzel.

'Good night,' replied Michael and Maria in unison. Then they joined Angus and several others in the rowboat, to go to shore and have more fun.

Hanzel and Hanna went to bed, where Hanna made sweet love to her favorite man.

Next morning they were woken up by a loud crying and wailing and stomping on the boards as people returned from their night of partying in town.

Hanzel and Hanna sat up in bed and looked at each other. 'What do you suppose that is all about?' asked Hanna.

Hanzel shook his head. 'I have no idea. Sounds like someone is in great distress. We'd better go see what's the matter.' He and Hanna jumped out of bed and quickly got dressed. All the while the wailing did not stop. 'I wonder if someone is dead?' asked Hanna, as they hurried along the gangway to the stairs. When they stepped on deck a pitiable sight greeted them. There, sprawled out dead as a coffin nail, lay Otto. It was Dana who was doing the wailing. Around the dead sailor stood his comrades, Herman, Markus, and Eldon. Everyone was standing there, dumbfounded.

'What happened?' asked Hanzel.

'A fight. In the tavern. This morning. Some drunken fisherman mistook Otto for someone else and poured an ale over his head. When Otto got up to fight, the fisherman stabbed him with his dirk. Right into the heart.' Herman shook his head sadly.

'What happened to the fisherman?' asked Hanzel, looking over the body. A nasty, bloody stab wound soiled Otto's shirt and waistcoat.

'He ran away. We couldn't catch him,' replied Markus. 'Lord knows, Eldon and I tried. Didn't we?'

Eldon nodded his head. 'Aye. That we did. The fisherman disappeared.'

'Did you get a good look at him?' asked Hanzel.

'That we did. That we did for certain. Didn't we boys?' Herman looked at his comrades.

The others agreed they could recognized the man.

'Then, I suggest you go back to town and find that murderer and bring him here. We can't let a murderer of one of our own get away.' Hanzel pointed towards the town. 'Go get him and don't come back without him.'

'What about Otto?' asked Herman.

'We'll fix him up so that we can have a wake. That way, Otto can be there when we punish his killer,' replied Hanzel, a grim expression on his face.

'Aye, aye, Captain,' replied the others. They immediately jumped to action and climbed back into the rowboat and set off to find the culprit.

'Meanwhile, you get him cleaned up and ready for a wake tonight. Then we'll give him a decent burial at sea. Poor Otto. He was a good friend.' Hanzel regarded Otto's other mess mates; a sad expression on his face.

'Shouldn't we let the authorities deal with the murderer?' asked Hanna.

Hanzel shook his head. 'It would take too long. We'd likely have to stay here for a trial, which could not be for some time. Then there is the possibility, because the fisherman is a local, he might get off.' Hanzel shook his head. 'No, we need to set an example. People can't just up and murder someone and claim a mistaken identity and then we're supposed to let it go at that?'

'So, do you plan to execute the fisherman?' asked Michael.

'I don't know, what do you think?' Hanzel regarded his friend closely.

'An eye for an eye...' replied Michael.

'However, the man, being a simple fisherman, made an honest mistake and thought he had killed someone who had wronged him,' observed Maria.

'That still is no excuse to kill someone in cold blood. To take the law into one's own hands,' replied Hanzel. 'No, he must pay for his crime. Waiting for the authorities to do it is futile, because, like I said, we likely won't see justice done. We, all together, are a community. We'll let our community decide collectively what should be done with the fisherman. We'll hold court at the wake tonight. We'll give the man a chance to defend himself.'

'That's about as fair as it gets,' said Hanna.

'That is the spirit of our code, isn't it? We strive for justice, fairness, honesty, brotherhood. As a community we share everything together. We look after each other,' added Hanzel. 'We are what the Greeks called, a democracy.'

'I like the sound of that,' replied Hanna. 'We're a, *Democracy*.'

'Because our code is truly democratic, my position is not guaranteed. I am not above the code. If the crew collectively decided they do not want me to be captain any longer, they can vote me out.' Hanzel grinned. 'I guess I had better continue to do a good job. Finding and sharing that treasure sure helped with morale.'

'I think it will be a good wake tonight,' said Michael, watching several sailors begin checking lanterns.

'Yes, I'm sure,' replied Hanzel thoughtfully. 'We'll use the occasion to celebrate, the loss of Henk and his crew in the Devil's Triangle, plus, the others.'

'We still don't really know, if that's what happened to Henk,' said Michael. 'We lost track of them. Maybe there was a mutiny. Or perhaps they somehow sailed off course. You know that Henk was not the best of navigators.'

Hanzel nodded his head. 'Ya, that's true. Alright, let's not include Henk. Since we're not sure, let's stay positive. Perhaps they are alive and will find us eventually.'

'Tonight it will just be, Otto and the others.' Michael looked at Hanzel.

'Yes. Just them.' Hanzel looked sadly down from the quarterdeck at the sailors preparing Otto for his party.

Just after nightfall, Herman and his group returned with the fisherman, who was greeted by many jeers, taunts, and insults. Several sailors spat at the man.

'Keel haul him!' shouted a number of sailors.

'Hang him from a yardarm!' shouted others.

'Garrote him!' shouted a voice.

Another immediately answered, 'That'd be too easy on him!'

'Flog him to death! Tear him apart! Break his bones!' were the words from other mouths seeking vengeance.

The hapless fisherman got the impression that his time was near the end. Seeing all of those angry pirates waving weapons in his direction and cursing and condemning him to great pain and suffering, made him piss into his codpiece. When the crew saw that, they laughed and made even more fun of the murderer.

Hanzel held up his right hand. The crew stopped their noise and looked up at their captain, standing on the quarterdeck. 'Set that man down in the chair,' he said. Two sailors sat the man down in a chair from the master's cabin, which had been set up on deck for the purpose. Another chair held Otto. He was dressed in his best clothes. His head was topped with a splendid Dutch hat bearing a pheasant's feather. The dead man stared with blank eyes at his murderer, who sat facing him; furthering the fisherman's distress.

The man squirmed in the chair. 'What are you going to do to me?'

Hanzel regarded the man coldly. 'We are going to give you an opportunity to defend yourself.'

'Defend myself?'

'Yes. You can tell us why you killed our friend,' replied Hanzel, indicating Otto.

The fisherman pointed at Otto. 'He looks just like a sailor who came through here three years ago. He stole my wife.'

'Shouldn't you have first asked if he was the one?' asked Michael.

'I was drunk. I'm still drunk. I didn't think straight.'

'You're not thinking straight cost me a good friend,' replied Hanzel. 'Otto was our quartermaster.'

'Yeah, well, I'm sorry. I'm sorry he's dead. Even now that I look at him, I am sure it's the other man.'

Michael scoffed. 'If you had treated your wife better, she wouldn't have left you.'

The man stared angrily at Michael. 'What do you know about how I treated my wife? You know nothing about that. I treated her good. As best as she deserved.'

Hanzel stared at the fisherman, boring deep into his eyes, scaring the bejeebies out him. His knees shook under Hanzel's icy blue stare. 'So, in your drunken haze you saw Otto in the tavern and decided to kill him, is that correct?'

'No, no, that's not it. He was getting up to do me a dirty business.'

'After you poured ale over his head!' shouted Herman.

'That was an accident. I was bumped. Someone bumped into me.'

'Liar!' shouted Markus. 'I saw everything right in front of me. I was sitting at the table with Otto.' Markus pointed at the fisherman. 'He poured the ale over Otto's head, totally unprovoked. That's why Otto stood up.'

'I confirm that,' said Herman. 'I was at the table, as well.'

'Liars!' shouted the fisherman. 'You're all a bunch of liars. I'm sure it was him.'

Hanzel regarded his shipmates. 'Well, ladies and gentlemen, what do you think? Is he guilty? Yeah, or nay?'

A chorus of voices shouted, 'Yeah!'

Others shouted, 'HANG HIM!!'

Others made threatening gestures toward the quaking fisherman in the chair, as they shouted, 'Hang him! HANG HIM!! HANG HIM!!!'

Hanzel held up his right hand to silence his crew. It took a moment, but silence prevailed once again. He stared at the fisherman. 'We judge you guilty of murder. In our code the penalty for murder is death. You may choose which way to go out of this life. People have expressed some options. Do you want to be hanged? Do you want to be shot? Do you want to be keel hauled and hope you live?'

'BREAK HIS BONES!!!' shouted Otto's mess mates.

'There's another option for you,' said Hanzel calmly. 'You could live up to three days longer if we break your bones. Hanging is actually too good for the likes of you, however it's over fairly quickly. You'll be dead in three to five minutes. Or longer, if we decide to play with you a while.' Hanzel narrowed his eyes. Even the Devil would have cringed at that moment.

The fisherman stared bug eyed at Hanzel and then at the frenzied pirates waving their weapons at him. Suddenly he lunged out of the chair and tried to run to the railing, to jump off the ship, however he was grabbed by a powerful sailor named Albert who put him roughly back into the chair.

'There is no way out of this. You are going to die. Do you want to choose, or do we choose for you?' asked Hanzel calmly.

The frenzied man stared dumbfoundedly at Hanzel. 'You can't hang me? This is not a proper trial. By what right?'

'By the rights granted by our charter. You murdered one of us in cold blood. Hence, you will be killed, in cold blood.' Hanzel stared unflinchingly at the trembling fisherman.

The man did not respond. He just stared at Hanzel, knowing his end was near.

Hanzel waited for a moment longer. Seeing that the man was not going to give him a choice he pronounced sentence. 'HANG HIM!' shouted Hanzel.

The sentence was immediately carried out, to much cheering from the offended crew. Moments later the fisherman was dangling from a rope and dancing his final jig, much to the enjoyment of Otto's mates, who elected to play with the fisherman for a while and prolong his agony. After ten minutes he was dead as a plank. When his final jig was completed the crew toasted his demise and threw the body overboard. Then the party really got started, as toast after toast gave tribute to Otto, and their other friends who were prematurely demised.

'May they rest in peace,' said Hanzel, holding his cup aloft.

'MAY THEY REST IN PEACE!' shouted the crew in unison. Then the band started up and the jigs and reels began. It was party time on the *Bluerose*, once again.

Chapter 37

Three days later, when the party finally came to an end and people had recovered from their hangovers, they came to the realization that all their libations had been consumed. There was not a drop of: ale, rum, wine, or water left in any barrel, cask, or keg. The wake had consumed it all.

'So, now what do we do?' asked Michael. 'We can't go sailing without libations.'

'We're going to have to return to Ponta Delgada. We'll try and buy what we can, here, but I doubt if there's much to be had. Send Herman and his crew to procure what they can.'

'You know, Hanzel. Another thing we still have not done and really should do, before we sail for Hispaniola. We have not careened this ship. If we want this boat to glide through the water, we should clean the hull and tallow it.'

'Of course. You're absolutely correct. Why didn't I think of that?' Hanzel scratched his chin and regarded his friend.

'Since it's winter, and reasonably warm here, this is a good time and place to do it. We can quickly sail to Sao Miguel and obtain supplies. Then we'll sail to that nice beach, just north of here, and do it there.

'How long do you think it will take?' Hanzel regarded his friend.

'It all depends on the encrustation, of course,' replied Michael.

'Yes, of course. Well, we might as well get on with it. Let's call the crew on deck and we'll go over our plan,' suggested Hanzel.

'What we haven't discussed is, what if the Dutch merchantman is still in port?'

'They might use their imaginary cannons on us,' laughed Hanzel. 'Before we sail into port, we can stand off and send a boat in with a small crew to reconnoiter.'

'Alright. That sounds good to me,' agreed Michael.

Hanzel looked out of a window. 'The weather looks perfect for sailing. Shall we to Ponta Delgada?'

'Indeed we shall,' agreed Michael, stepping out of the cabin. Hanzel followed him up on deck. They apprised the crew of the plan and set events in motion. Within an hour, Herman returned with his little group. They had managed to procure three barrels of potable water, one keg of rum, and two of wine. 'It isn't much for a crew of a hundred,' remarked Hanzel, but it will help. Hopefully we'll be able to get what we need in Ponta Delgada.'

Six hours later, off the coast of Sao Miguel, a crew of six, three men and three women, rowed into town to discover that the Dutch West India Company ship was still in the harbour. The unfortunate addition, however, was a Dutch navy frigate.

'Captain Verhooven would have informed them about us. The fact we stole eleven of the company's cannons, makes us major criminals. We hurt the corporation,' suggested Hanzel, gravely. 'The government doesn't like it when people mess with their friends' property.'

'So, what do we do now?' asked Hanna, as they sat in the great cabin discussing their options.

'It'll seem suspicious in such a small port, if we go back and forth with the long boat. They'll wonder, why are those people going back and forth with those barrels and kegs? Is there a ship standing off the coast? Why would they not sail into port and make things easier on themselves?' Michael looked at his friends and shrugged his shoulders. 'I don't know, what do you think?'

Hanzel regarded his friend. 'I think you're absolutely correct.'

'Maybe we could disguise ourselves,' suggested Maria.

'Disguise ourselves? That's not a bad idea,' agreed Hanzel. 'How do you propose we do that?'

'Well, we could change the name of this ship, first of all. Then, perhaps we can rig her differently. Fly another country's flag. We all dress a bit differently. Ideas like that,' said Maria confidently.

'Those are excellent ideas, Maria. Let's do it. We'll get our artists to change the name. From Bluerose to what?' Hanzel regarded his friends.

'What about, *Golden Purpose*? That has kind of a nice ring to it, don't you think?' Herman regarded his friends.

'I like the sound of that,' agreed Michael.

'Or, what about?' Hanna looked at her friends. 'Now, this may seem a bit odd, but, you can decide. It's to symbolize how fast we can sail.'

Hanzel looked at his partner. 'Well, go on. What is it?'

'*Silver Streak*,' answered Hanna.

'That's an interesting name,' replied Michael.

'Yes. I think so too,' agreed Hanzel. '*Silver Streak* certainly sounds fast.' He clapped his hands together. 'We'll put it to a vote.'

When the name change was suggested to the crew, several other ideas were proposed, however, in the end; they all agreed that, *Silver Streak* was the right choice. Then, while two artists took care of that detail, Hanzel and Michael discussed a new sail plan.

'We can leave the square rigging for the top main and take down the lateen sails. Then by simply rigging only the jib, we'll look quite a bit different from what we looked like when we were here last,' suggested Hanzel.

'That's a good plan,' agreed Michael. 'I'll get a crew on it right away.'

'What about a flag?' asked Hanna.

'I think there's a French one and a Danish one in that storage closet in the gangway. It seems to me I saw them in there,' replied Hanzel. 'I think there is also a Spanish flag.'

'And costumes?' asked Maria.

'You and Hanna can organize that with the other ladies. If we get all of this underway, we could be in port by tomorrow morning.

And, so it came to be. Next morning a very different brigantine and crew sailed into port under cloudy skies and a slight drizzle. The hazy moisture further helped to disguise them. Nobody was any the wiser; not even the crew of the West Indiaman. Without wasting a second, Herman the newly elected quartermaster, organized his crew and procured as much food and potable liquids as they could find; which eventually amounted to: enough tallow to coat the hull, six kegs of tar, three kegs of carriage bolts, a barrel of vinegar, a barrel of pickled herrings, two of salted herrings, six kegs of dried beef, five kegs of dried pork, ten live chickens, two goats, a cow, ten barrels of water, two barrels of ale, three of wine, five kegs of rum, a keg of Jenever, two casks of brandy, and a keg of vodka, the crew of a Russian ship had traded with the local merchant.

'I think this will go nicely in fruit juices,' suggested Hanzel as he and Hanna sampled some of the new Russian libation.

Hanna thought for a moment, as she held a little bit of the vodka in her mouth. She sniffed and then swallowed. 'It has a fairly pleasant taste. However, I like wine better. And ale.'

'We'll see what it tastes like in fruit juices, then we'll make another assessment,' suggested Hanzel, taking a cigar out of the small wooden box on the table.

Hanna smiled and then drank the rest of the vodka sample. She licked her lips and then also took a cigar from the box. Hanzel helped her light it. Then the two friends sat back in their chairs savoring the delicious cigars and happy conversation, as they talked about the voyage to Hispaniola and the Spanish treasure fleet.

The morning brought fair skies and breezes. The ship was loaded and everyone was ready to sail back to Santa Maria to careen their ship and make ready for the voyage to Hispaniola. The beach they chose was on the north side of the island and perfect to bring the ship out of the water. The tide enabled the ship to float high up on the sandy beach, where they cable tied the vessel to sturdy mahogany trees. When the tide receded, the ship was high and dry, enabling the crew to scrape the barnacles off the hull and fill cracks with tar, stopping the myriad tiny leaks adding to the ten inches of water which had already accumulated in the very bottom of the ship.

'It'll be nice to get that water out of the ship, as well,' remarked Michael, sitting beside Hanzel; he and their ladies regarding the work being conducted on the hull, as they smoked cigars and drank brandy, while sitting in comfortable deck chairs.

'Once the leaks are patched, we'll pump it all out and go in there with vinegar and clean the place up,' replied Hanzel, puffing on his cigar.

'That'll make the place smell a whole lot better, too.' Hanna crinkled up her nose. 'The deeper one goes in the ship, the smellier it gets.'

Maria frowned. 'And then when you add the body smells of a hundred people...'

'I think we'll organize a cleaning crew,' suggested Hanna. 'We'll get the women together and do a thorough scrub down in there. Too bad we didn't see about some lavender, or rose petals, or something like that.'

Maria looked towards the forest. 'I'll bet we can find aromatic bark and flowers in there.'

Hanna looked where Maria was pointing. 'That's a great idea. It's a beautiful day; let's get Dana and the gang together. I'm sure Angela and Carla would be interested.'

Hanzel regarded his mate. 'That's a great idea, girls. Why don't you take some cutlasses and sacks and go find some nice scents to make our ship smell nice. We'll stay here and supervise the work on the hull.' He smiled at Hanna and then gave her a kiss. He and Michael watched the two women happily set off to gather up their friends and see about making the ship a more aromatic home.

'Our prizes will smell us coming from a league away,' laughed Michael.

'They'll think Heaven has sent a ship of angels,' replied Hanzel, taking a sip of his brandy.

'They wouldn't be far wrong, considering the beautiful women we have on board. Especially Hanna and Maria. I think of them as angels.' Michael regarded his friend as he puffed on his cigar.

Hanzel nodded and smiled. 'I am so blessed. I couldn't want for a better woman than Hanna. She's the best friend I have, female that is. You're my best *man* friend. That's why I'm glad the crew voted you First Mate. And you get a fairly large percentage of whatever treasure we gather. Me, being captain get fifteen and you get ten percent. That's a goodly share, don't you think?'

Michael grinned. 'I like the percentages.'

Hanzel took a long drag of his cigar and blew out three perfect rings. 'Our code is likely the fairest set of laws any community has. When you analyze our code, it's the ten commandments; but elaborated with specified penalties, like in the ancient law codes.'

'An eye for an eye...' mused Michael over his cup. He took a long drought and swallowed it slowly. 'It really is unfortunate that today's monarchs don't live up to those codes. They commit all manner of felonies with impunity, while we, "common folk" suffer horribly for the same crimes. Take us, for example. We're pirates. We admit that. We never went to the king to ask for a Letter of Marque.

We are independent of the crown. Hence, we can be prosecuted for piracy and perhaps even be executed. And, yet, when the king gives some sailors a Letter of Marque, they have royal permission to steal the ships and cargoes of an *enemy*. Even though there is no official declaration of war. That makes the king a pirate also, don't you think?'

'I've sailed as a privateer. But I always thought it was dishonest,' replied Hanzel thoughtfully sniffing his cigar. 'I like what we're doing much better. We are pirates who are going to steal the gold from the Spaniard and not involve anyone else, but us. No crown or other authorities will take what we have earned by our own hard work.'

'Amen,' replied Michael, taking another long drought of his drink. He smiled. 'Hmmm, this is good. I'm really beginning to like brandy.'

'Goes well with cigars, that's for sure,' agreed Hanzel, sniffing the brandy in his cup.

Ten days later the work was completed. The ship's rigging had been restored to its former fore aft configuration with the lateen sails, and square rigged on the fore and top main masts. The hull had been scraped, patched, and tallowed and the interior completely pumped dry, cleaned with vinegar, and scented with thirty large potpourri of aromatic bark, roots, leaves, and blossoms. They undid the cables from the mahogany trees and waited for the tide. When it came, it floated the brigantine and enabled the crew to pull her into deeper water. When the wind arrived, they set the sails and pointed their ship in the direction of Hispaniola, nearly 3000 miles away, across the mid west Atlantic. The date was January 16th, 1625.

Albeit, they were sailing in the Tropic of Cancer, and the temperatures were comfortable, it was winter and cold weather did collide with warm weather from time to time. Over a three thousand mile span, a ship is bound to be visited by at least one storm. Hanzel and his friends were visited by one of those storms during their crossing. It came on January 30th. The problem was, the storm was more like thirteen storms all rolled into one gargantuan diabolical monster which screamed and roared and tore at flesh and tackle, ropes and sheets, slowly, relentlessly consuming the hapless brigantine splinter by splinter, and man by man.

Very few people on board, *Silver Streak* had ever experienced such tortuous weather. Hanna was scared to death, as she was tossed to and fro on her bed, shivering with fear, while Hanzel stood on deck and performed his duties as captain of the ship. *Oh my God, we're going to die,* went over and over in her head. The fact that Maria and Dana were in the cabin with her was no comfort. They too were scared to death; as the three women huddled together trembling with dreaded anticipation of the Grim Reaper at the door. Every time something knocked, banged, or crashed, they jumped with fright. Fortunately, these three women had earned their sea legs already and were not sick as a result of the up and down, this way and that, motions of the brigantine, unlike many others on board the heaving ship. Seasickness grabbed hold of thirty three people, whose vomit began to foul the air below decks. Some were so ill, they begged their mess mates to end it for them with a quick slice across the throat, or a cannon ball on the head.

'Too messy,' remarked Herman as he tended to Albert, who was convinced he was dying. 'Smashing you on the head would send blood and brains spattering all over your hammock. Even slicing your throat makes a big mess. Your blood would spurt all over this place. Likely stain my hammock, as well as your own.' Herman shook his head. 'No, my friend. The best thing for you is to ride it out. You'll see. As soon as this storm is gone, you'll feel fine in no time. And,' he added, raising his right index finger, 'chances are, you won't ever be seasick again. Your body gets an immunity to it.'

Albert regarded his friend through half closed eyelids; a grim expression, tinged with green, on his contorted face. All he could manage was a moan, after which he immediately began to retch. It was a good thing for Herman that Albert had not a drop of anything left in his stomach. All that Albert could do was retch and moan with pain, as his stomach collapsed from the effort, nearly sending it and accompanying intestines up through his throat. Herman shook his head sadly as Albert lay back down. 'Please, just let me die,' muttered Albert.

Up on deck, another story of pain, suffering, and mayhem was unfolding as the ship was being dismantled piece by piece. It began with the top main mast, which so often is the spar to go first in a storm such as the banshee which had gripped them. As the spar splintered away, it took the top trysail along with it, sending ropes and blocks flying. One of those blocks caught a sailor square in the side of his head, sending his head off into the briny foam and his body onto the deck; where it lay for a few seconds twitching and bleeding out until a massive wave hit the ship broadside and washed the gruesome remains overboard for its meeting with Davey Jones and his infamous locker. It all happened so fast, and under such conditions, nobody on the quarterdeck saw it. One of the man's friends saw it. He was never the same again.

'I DON'T KNOW HOW MUCH LONGER SHE'LL HOLD UP!' shouted Hanzel to Michael as he watched the storm jib torn off its ropes with a great tearing sound, barely audible over the wailing of the tortured winds.

'I THINK SHE'LL RIDE ER OUT! THIS IS A STURDY BOAT!' shouted Michael. As he said the words, a blinding flash of light and a mighty crack, like thunder, heralded the demise of the fore mast; it being compromised as the lightning turned the spar to charcoal from the inside out. Within seconds the screaming winds pushed the mighty tree over and sent sheets, ropes, blocks, and splinters flying in all directions. Michael and Hanzel were spared for another day, alas, Harry and Markus were not so lucky.

As the twisted mess came crashing to the boards, Markus, who was tending the helm, got caught by flying ropes, attached to a huge piece of the mast, and sent flying into the tormented foam. Harry, who was standing beside Markus, caught a block square in the chest, effectively caving it in, before sending him flying after the helmsman.

Elsewhere, others were visited by splinters, mangling and maiming their yielding bodies. Screams and moans were not heard over the roaring waves and shrieking winds.

Hanzel and Michael, quickly managed to untangle the wheel from ropes and a piece of a sail, enabling them to turn the stem back into the waves just before *Silver Streak* would have met with a disastrous broadside.

As the seconds ticked by; each of them seeming to be minutes long, and the minutes became hours, eventually, the storm began to lose its battle against those puny men and women floating on the open ocean in their little wooden boat. As the hours passed through a day and the days had become a week, the howling banshee winds gradually changed back to a gentle, caressing breeze of warm air. The black clouds of death were replaced with soft, white downy wisps and cotton balls, lit by glorious sunlight; ringing everything it touched with a soft golden yellow aura.

'What a mess!' exclaimed Hanna, when she and her friends stepped furtively on deck, to take the air and begin to rejuvenate themselves.

'My God!' whispered Maria, sucking in her breath and holding her hands to her face.

Hanzel smiled. 'Well, it actually looks worse than it is. We can replace the foremast and the top main in Santo Domingo. I'm sure we'll be able to mend those sails and replace those we lost. Ropes and tackle are no problem either. What the problem is, we have lost some good men, three have lost a limb, and two have lost an eye from flying splinters. Cookie and his mates are taking care of them. Just as he said it, a scream signaled that the cook had begun to saw off a sailor's right forearm. Hanna shivered and stared wide eyed at Hanzel. He shrugged his shoulders and shook his head sadly. 'Thank God it wasn't us,' he said softly; tears beginning to wet his eyes. He and Hanna hugged each other and stood like that for a long time amidst the carnage the storm had wrought.

'Well, I guess we had better have a discussion with our artists and figure out how best to clear up this mess and begin repairs,' said Hanzel sadly. 'It would be so nice, if just for once, we got a break.'

'All good things worth striving for, sometimes come with hard bargains. Having survived the storm, we have much to be thankful for, and whatever treasure we win, we will have earned it,' replied Michael wisely.

Hanzel nodded thoughtfully. 'That makes good sense to me. Whatever treasure we win, we'll have earned it.'

Michael smiled and clapped his friend on the shoulder. Then he set about gathering the ship's artists together and began organizing the clean up.

Three days later, the ship had been returned to a semblance of order. Albeit, the main mast was missing its top spar and the foremast was gone; they were able to still put out enough sail to keep the ship moving and under control. Below decks had been thoroughly washed and disinfected with vinegar. Smudges and potpourris were used to return a better smell. When Hanzel and Michael figured the ship was orderly, once again; it was time for a, "Thank God We're Alive Party" and a celebration of those who lost their lives; Harry, Markus, and the sailor who called himself, King Solomon. Fortunately, they had only lost two barrels of water, a barrel of wine, and two kegs of rum; when they broke loose from their restraints and crashed into each other when a particularly large wave hit the ship on her starboard side. There were still plenty of libations available to create the necessary liquidity to make a party flow.

And *flow* it did. Copious toasts were drunk in honour of their salvation and those who lost life or limb. By the time night fell, everyone was happily into their cups and enjoying a star filled sky; a pleasant sliver of moonlight helping to add sparkles to the waves breaking on the bows of the damaged ship. However, nobody cared about the damages; not even Hanzel. Everyone knew that their three carpenters and their mates would bring things back to good order. Hence, since nobody cared a whit, nobody thought twice about getting pleasantly plastered with the beverage of their choice. Hanzel and Michael chose brandy. Hanna and the girls chose wine. Most everyone else drank rum and ale.

As was typical of their parties, it continued, hard core, for three days, and then petered out as people began dealing with hangovers and stories about their antics while under the influence of Diablo's elixirs, and still running a ship; a damaged one, at that. It did tend to zig zag a bit more than usual during party time.

'Ooooh,' moaned Hanzel, holding his head as he rose up in bed. 'I've got to stop doing that to myself.'

'Hmfxpblmdpd,' mumbled Hanna, not wanting to open her eyes and face reality just yet. She knew that light would come intensely through her dilated pupils straight into her brain where the rays would exacerbate the intense corpuscular protest going on there. *I have to stop doing that to myself. I feel awful. I don't think I'll get out of bed for a few weeks, maybe never.*

Hanzel sat on the edge of the bed and regarded his lover. *That girl knows how to party. I had no idea a woman could drink that much. What a woman. I love her. I don't know what I'd do without her. I pray we're always together. But we've got to stop drinking so much. One of us could fall overboard one of these days, if we're not careful. We almost lost Derek and Becky during that wild reel. Good thing that Eldon and Gerry were standing by the railing.* Hanzel smiled. *We pirates sure know how to have a good time. I love this life. I want to be able to do this for a hundred years. I don't ever want to give this up.* The image of cadavers of convicted pirates rotting in gibbets on the shore at Wapping came into view. Hanzel stared at it for a moment and then, forcefully willed it out of his mind. *That's not what I have planned. Those pirates were stupid and let themselves be caught. Nobody is going to catch Hanzel Sventska.* He looked at Hanna and smiled. Then he tried to get up. *Ohh, that was a mistake.* Hanzel fell back onto the bed. *Well, since I'm the captain, and we have fair weather, I can chose to stay in bed.* He cuddled into Hanna, throwing an arm around her waist and listening to her breathing for awhile. As his breath eventually coordinated with hers, he drifted off into dreams of conquest and capture; half, ideal visions of Paradise, and the other half, visions of Hell, where he saw himself compromised by a gorgeous, raven haired succubus, who gyrated on his naked body until an unnatural climax seared his soul, instantly waking him; his bed clothes soaked with a cold sweat and milky fluid.

Hanzel shook his head and rubbed his eyes; wondering what had just happened. He looked at Hanna, peacefully sleeping beside him. *She's sleeping.* He looked down at his groin; a massive erection projecting his night shirt into the disturbed silence of his cabin. *What just happened to me?* Hanzel scratched his head. *I have to stop drinking so much. Now I'm having strange dreams. Or is it possible someone spiked my drink with mushrooms? This is really weird.*

He gently moved himself out of the bed, being careful to stay on his back, so as not to wet the sheets with his soaked night clothes. Carefully he slid out of the bed and, holding his crotch with his night shirt, he dried himself off and removed the shirt from his sweat soaked body. As he stumbled about, Hanna eventually woke up. She rubbed her eyes and looked through a hazy fog at Hanzel. 'What are you doing?' she mumbled.

Hanzel regarded Hanna with a guilty expression on his face.

'What's wrong, Hanzel? Why do you look at me like that?' Hanna blinked several times, trying to clear her eyes.

'I had a dream. It was like a nightmare, really. A succubus. I was raped by a succubus.'

Hanna frowned. 'You were raped by a succubus? What do you mean, you were raped by a succubus?'

'It's true. Why else would I be all wet? I came into that succubus. That's what woke me up.' Hanzel grabbed a cloth and moistened it from the water carafe.

Hanna laughed. 'You had a wet dream, Hanzel. That's all. It means I've been ignoring you. Your body just needed to get rid of some extra juice. Your vessels can only hold so much.' Hanna's eyes exhuded 'hearts'. 'After all, my love, you are a very virile man.'

Hanzel shook his head, trying to clear it. 'The dream was so real.'

'I have those.' Hanna regarded Hanzel's night shirt lying crumpled on the floor. 'Looks like you really had yourself a tidal wave.'

'I came and came. It was so bizarre, Hanna.'

Hanna frowned. 'Well, you just stop dreaming about those succubuses. You can only dream about me. I'm your wife, remember?' Then she smiled. 'When you finish wiping yourself off, come here. I'll help you forget about that bitch. I'll make sure she never disturbs your dreams of me, ever again.'

And so, Hanna made sweet love to her man; leaving the disturbing dream far behind him.

As life returned to normal on board *Silver Streak,* work continued apace on the gun carriages and what repairs could be effected on the damaged ship. By the time they made port in Santo Domingo, seven carriages were in place with their guns and a new main top mast had been constructed from mahogany they brought from the Azores. Apart from the fact the fore mast was missing, to an untrained eye, the brigantine looked in good shape.

However, to a trained eye it, 'Looks like yer got sum sturm damage,' said a wrinkled old jack tar watching the brigantine's crew tie her to a pier. 'Got sum wind, did yer?'

'Aye, that we did,' replied Pedro, securing the bow line. 'It's a wonder we got here alive.'

'One of dem sturms, eh? Well, let me tell yer. Ye likely seen nuttin' compared ter de sturm me an me crew sailed thru.' The old wrinkle held up his right index finger and stared at it for a moment, wondering where that came from, before attempting to continue with his story. Unfortunately for him, Pedro had no time for his tale, looking forward to wine, women, and song at the various taverns and inns lining the roadway and streets of the inner city.

'It feels good to be back,' said Hanzel before taking a sip of rum and fruit juice.

'I have a good feeling we'll meet our objective,' said Hanna, smiling. 'Judging from the number of Spanish ships in the harbour; I think there may be a treasure ship nearby.'

Hanzel grinned and held up his cup. 'Here's to Spanish treasure. May it land in our purses, where it belongs.'

Over the next two weeks, Hanzel and his gang spent most of their days and nights in the inns, public houses, and taverns, eating, drinking, and making friends with sailors from many countries. The sailors they were especially interested in were those from Spain. However, the only crewmates who spoke with them were those of other than Dutch descent; considering the historic issues between the Protestant low lands and that bloated Catholic country on the Iberian peninsula. There were way too many reasons for Dutch and Spanish sailors to come to blows.

As time drifted by, Hanzel and Hanna often left town and explored the area surrounding the city; deepening their interest and experience with natural science. They both took a delighted interest in the flora and fauna of the area; making many interesting discoveries just within the first few miles of Santo Domingo. It was on one of those excursions; while the two lovers were sitting on their blanket, enjoying a picnic in a beautiful glade beside a burbling brook, when Hanna presented Hanzel with information which would change his life forever. Just as Hanzel was about to take a sip of his wine, Hanna surprised him; 'I have not had a period for two months. I believe that we're pregnant.'

Hanzel, who had taken the sip, instantly spurted it back into his cup. 'We're pregnant?! We're pregnant, as in, we're going to have a baby?'

Hanna nodded, biting her lower lip.

Hanzel was dumbstruck for a moment as thoughts raced through his head. *A baby? We're going to have a baby? I'm going to be a father? Will this be a good thing? Just when we're going to go pirating? But, then, that's fairly soon. If she's only been pregnant two months... I'm going to be a father. That's amazing. I'll be a much better father than mine was to me, that's for sure. I'm a father? I can't believe it.* He looked at Hanna and grinned from ear to ear. Then he blurted out, 'That's wonderful news, Hanna. We're going to be pirate parents. That's quite something, isn't it? Pirate parents. It certainly is one way to grow our numbers. Maybe the other women will get the hint, once they learn that you are pregnant. Maybe they'll want to make little pirates of their own.'

Hanna beamed. *I'm so glad he's happy. He's going to be a good father, I know it.* Then they hugged each other for a long time before making love, there in that hidden glade; the sounds of gently running water and twittering birds providing an angel's serenade in the background.

When the parents to be returned to their ship, later that evening, a party was in full swing.

'I guess they must know that we're pregnant,' chuckled Hanzel, as they walked up the gang plank.

Hanna shook her head. 'I haven't told anyone but you.'

'What's the occasion?' asked Hanzel, as he stepped on board.

'We managed to get some Spanish navy sailors drunk and convinced them to come back with us,' answered Michael. 'We're going to try and find out what we can. So far we've had no luck. They will not talk about a treasure fleet.'

Hanzel held out his hand to help Hanna step on deck. 'Well, let's keep at em. If they don't divulge anything under the spell of rum, then we might have to use more drastic measures.' Hanzel regarded the Spanish sailors partying with his crew. 'Surely they must know something. Why would there be three navy ships anchored in the harbour? They must be here to protect something, wouldn't you think?'

Michael nodded. 'You'd think so. Unless they're here to escort those merchant ships. Apparently there are more of us out here.'

'What do you mean, there are more of *us* out here?' Hanzel regarded his friend with a quizzical expression.

'More pirates. There are more pirates plying these waters and raiding the Spanish merchantmen.'

'Are they Dutchmen?'

'English, Dutch, Danish, Swedish, French, Portuguese, Arabs… They are more coming as the years pass. According to some people Maria and I spoke to. Some of those gangs have built colonies in the various bays, cays, and estuaries along the coast and on the islands. They have been quite a problem.' Porto Bello is where more of them are showing up, apparently.'

Hanzel nodded. 'Well, I guess we have to be extra cautious. Maybe we're the only ones smart enough to come into port and check things out for ourselves, instead of relying on ships to float by our colony.' He looked at Hanna and then back to Michael. 'Although, the idea of a colony appeals to me. An actual place where we can build houses and have a place to work on our ship.'

Hanna smiled. 'I like the idea of having a house to live in. As much as I like sailing, it would be nice to have a break, now and then. Life on board ship does have its problems.'

'Like being wet most of the time,' grumbled Maria.

'Let's suggest the idea to the gang and see what they think of it. Maybe lots of folks will go along with it. Once we have the money again, we can buy lumber and supplies,' suggested Hanzel.

'Or we might just luck out and capture a ship carrying lumber and supplies,' laughed Michael. 'Either way I can envision it already.'

'We can have a little church...' Hanna looked at Hanzel.

'And flower boxes...' added Maria.

'And a garden...' continued Hanna.

'And *children* playing with cats in the yard...' ventured Maria, closely regarding Michael, who pretended not to notice.

Hanna nudged Hanzel in the ribs. 'Life will be less hard. In a colony everything will so much easier. And it'll all be, because of you, Hanzel.'

Hanzel smiled knowingly and nodded his head. He clapped his hands together. 'Well then. I guess we're resolved to bring this up at tonight's dinner. I have a feeling that most of the crew will go along with the idea. The main thing, for now, is that we manage to raise the funds necessary.'

'And that means, we had better get to work and make our living here,' said Michael. 'We have to stop wasting time.' He looked over at the drunken Spaniards cavorting on the deck with several of the ladies. 'Let's see what they will tell us.'

'Bring them to the grand cabin, one at a time. We'll interrogate them there. Oh, and ask Herman and his crew if they can do the honours. We'll need Juan to help with translations.' Hanzel winced inside as an image of torture flashed through his head. *I really don't have the stomach for it. Maybe we'll get the information without having to hurt anybody? However, if we don't live up to expectations, not too many will stay. It's the sad role a pirate captain must play, I guess. I have to be strong and fearless.* He looked at Hanna. 'I think it's better if you ladies go for a stroll on deck, or maybe visit with your friends.'

Hanna nodded. She had no stomach for torture, either. Neither did Maria. However, both women were resigned to the necessity of it. If they were to continue as a pirate gang, they had to find treasure, or commodities they required; food, clothing, cannon balls, powder, ropes, libations, etcetera. 'I hope it will be worth it,' she said before she and Maria went below to find their friends.

Ten minutes later, Hanzel and Michael were sitting in the grand cabin facing a very inebriated Spanish sailor. Hanzel gestured to a chair. The sailor nodded and sat down, nearly falling off in the process. When the man was settled, Hanzel regarded Juan and told him to ask the sailor, point blank, if they were there to escort any treasure ships. The man shook his head and was adamant there were no treasure ships. They were there merely to escort the merchant fleet. Hanzel gestured to Juan to tell the sailor he should tell the truth because otherwise he would have to extract information in a very painful manner. However, even when the man was shown a very sharp blade, he insisted there was no treasure fleet.

Michael leaned closer to Hanzel and whispered, 'What if he is telling the truth? Maybe there is no treasure fleet and we'll have to content ourselves with stealing a merchant ship. The cargo will be worth something.'

'Then we'll have some of what we need to build a colony somewhere. However, if we have gold and silver, we can buy whatever we need,' replied Hanzel.

'I just got an idea. Maybe we should bring one of the others to watch what we do to this one. Maybe by just watching, the other one might talk.' Michael regarded the drunken Spaniard, who did not seem to comprehend what was happening.

Hanzel nodded. 'That might be worth a try. Why not? It might save us from having to spill too much of somebody's blood.'

'The less the better, always.' Michael gestured to one of Herman's men and told him to fetch another Spaniard.

However, the other Spaniard, who was equally drunk, did not know anything about treasure fleets, either. He did introduce another variable, that Juan translated. 'Even if dere vas a trezure fleet, only de officiers know anytin bout dat.'

Hanzel stared at the two inebriated sailors before addressing MIchael. 'Maybe we need to abduct an officer. What the man is saying makes sense. Loose lips can sink ships. Hence, it makes sense the officers don't tell the crew anything. For all we know, at this point, one of those merchant ships could be carrying treasure.' He regarded the sailor. 'Where are your officers?' Juan translated and the man responded that their officers were having a farewell dinner at *Taverna Madrid*. Hanzel looked at Michael and grinned. 'It's all so easy. Why didn't we ask them that question right from the beginning? Alright, Herman, since you have your mates with you, take the rowboat and find us one of those officers. You can likely kidnap him when he's in the lavatory.'

'Not to worry, Captain. Me and my crew know what to do. We'll be back within two hours, I can pretty much guarantee that,' replied Herman.

Hanzel nodded and wiped his brow. 'We should have thought of that right from the beginning and saved ourselves some anguish.' He gestured to the Spanish sailors to follow Herman out of the cabin. 'Let them continue to party with the others.' Then he regarded his first mate. 'I'm so glad we didn't have to torture those two. Torturing a drunk is not right practice. A drunk is not in his right mind and will likely say anything.'

Michael smiled. 'I'm glad too. I don't like torture. The less we have to use it, the better it is for us.'

'I was quite upset, thinking about watching a man being sliced and diced in my cabin. That creates a dark mood. I'd much rather we achieve our goals with a minimum of bloodshed. We might get lucky and not have to torture the officer, either.' Hanzel regarded Michael with a hopeful expression on his face. 'There's nothing wrong with being nice pirates. As we finish more gun carriages and have all of those guns in place, most prizes will just give up when they see us.'

MIchael nodded and grinned. 'We're going to be the nicest, most successful pirates on the Spanish Main.'

'I'll drink to that,' said Hanzel, grinning and filling his cup.

An hour and a half later Herman returned with his little crew and a Spanish navy midshipman named, Alphonso Raphael da Carcorala. The young man was quite indignant for having been kidnapped. When he saw the Spanish sailors cavorting with the women, he became quite livid; shouting at the dancing men to cease and desist their cavorting and come to his assistance. The inebriated sailors took a long look at the irate midshipman, wondering what to do; visions of severe discipline rushing through their besotted brains. However, they realized that they were already in trouble, so whether they rescued the midshipman or not, it would make no difference. They likely were each facing a flogging as it was. So, they shrugged their shoulders and returned to the jigs and reels. As a member of a pirate gang, life was much more fun than serving on a navy ship.

Hanzel ordered the man to be brought to the great cabin. A moment later, he, Michael, Herman, and his little crew faced the midshipman, now sitting in a chair. He remained defiant and insisted that his abductors would be dealt a painful blow by the Spanish Crown.

Hanzel laughed. 'Who is going to tell the Spanish Crown? Your sailors, enjoying themselves on our deck?' Hanzel leaned closer to the midshipman and stared into his black eyes. 'You?' (He and the officer were roughly the same age). 'If you tell us what we want to know, we'll let you live. If you do not tell us anything of value, we can't risk having you return to your ship. Surely you understand that?'

The Spanish officer stared into Hanzel's eyes with a hateful fire. 'Pyrates! Yu are pyrates! Yu weel all ang for dees!'

Hanzel shook his head. 'I doubt that very much. Nobody will know where you are and you will not reveal us. You might as well get used to the fact, you can not return to your ship.'

'My colleeges weel be meessing me by now. They'll wunder why I lef de taverna withoud sayeeng anyteeng.'

'They'll likely think you were drunk and decided to return to your ship,' replied Hanzel.

'Or you fell off a pier and drowned,' insinuated Michael.

'Things like that happen to drunks all the time,' agreed Hanzel.

The man stared at Hanzel; knowing he was correct. He would not be missed until muster the next morning and, since he was known to have been drinking, falling off a pier was not an unlikely possibility. However, he remained defiant and refused to divulge why the Spanish navy felt it necessary to have three ships in port. 'If your king is so concerned about pirates in these waters, why are your navy ships in port and not out chasing rovers?'

'And why were you and your colleagues having a *farewell* party? Is it that you are planning to leave port to escort a fleet?' Michael glanced at Hanzel, who nodded.

The midshipman did not reply. He stuck his chin out and remained belligerent.

'Show him your knife, Herman,' commanded Hanzel in a stern voice.

Herman held the knife under the man's chin.

'Eef yu keel me senior, yu will sure lee ang. My keeng weel send sheeps to unt you down. All over de wurl.'

Hanzel remained grim. 'Tie him to the chair.'

Two of Herman's crew bound the man's wrists, chest, and ankles to the armchair with cords of hemp. The midshipman wriggled and squirmed, however the sailors assisting Herman were much stronger than the skinny officer; who grew up privileged and did not have to work for a living. Hence, Alphonso was not very strong and was easily manhandled.

Hanzel looked at Herman. 'You know what to do.'

Herman regarded his captain and shook his head slowly. 'Well, I kind of know what to do.'

'What do you mean, you *kind of know* what to do?' asked Hanzel, puzzled.

'Well, I've never actually tortured anybody. I've just seen it done, once. When I served on His Majestie's ship, *Royal Avenger*. And then it was done with a hot poker, not a knife.'

'You mean to say that you have never tortured anybody to extract information?' Hanzel regarded the tall Prussian; a dumbfounded expression on his face. Then he looked at Michael, who shrugged his shoulders.

'Don't look at me. I've never done it, either,' said Michael. 'I wouldn't know where to begin.'

Hanzel shook his head. 'Is there anyone on board who knows how to torture someone?'

Herman looked at his mates. The three men shook their heads. They did not know of anyone either.

'A fine bunch of pirates we are,' grumbled Hanzel. 'How are we going to get this man to talk if we don't torture him?'

'Eet matter not if yu torture me. Yu weel get nuffin frum me. I don haf de eenformation yu zeek.' The midshipman regarded his abductors; a defiant expression on his tanned face.

Hanzel stared at the Spaniard. 'What information would that be? The information I am seeking?'

The midshipman looked surprised by the question. 'Do not pyrates look for trezure? Yu are looking for a trezure fleet. Yu theenk der iz one in diz port.'

Hanzel nodded. 'So? Is there a treasure ship in port?'

The Spaniard shook his head. 'I tol yu. I tell yu nuffin.'

'I don't believe you,' replied Hanzel. He looked at Michael. 'Do you believe him?'

Michael shook his head. 'It makes no sense there are three navy ships in port. I can't see the Spanish navy sending three war ships to seek out the pirates who ply these waters. There are far more in the Mediterranean.'

'What about you, Herman?' Hanzel regarded the burly Prussian.

Herman shook his head. 'I agree with Michael.'

Hanzel nodded and thought for a moment. Then he regarded the Spaniard with cold steel blue eyes. 'Open his shirt.'

One of Herman's crew mates tore the man's shirt open. Then Hanzel took Herman's knife and held it under the midshipman's nose. 'I give you one more opportunity to tell me what I want to know.'

The Spaniard spat into Hanzel's face. 'Yu weel get nuffin frum me.'

Hanzel slowly wiped the sputum off his face with a handkerchief he carried in his sleeve. Without a further thought, he sliced a deep cut across the man's chest.

The Spaniard screamed, staring bug eyed at his tormentor.

Hanzel wiped the blade on the man's shirt. *This is making me sick to my stomach. You've got to be strong. If you're going to remain captain, you've got to be strong. The welfare of everyone on board is at stake here.* He looked at Michael and then back at the panting Spaniard. 'Why are there three navy ships in port?'

'I tol yu. I tell yu nuffin,' panted the hapless midshipman.

Hanzel made another slice in the man's heaving chest.

As before, the man screamed, making everyone wince, inspite of their attempts at appearing to be tough pirates. Seeing the bleeding gashes made everyone else feel glad they were not on the receiving end of Hanzel's blade.

The suffering midshipman looked down at the bleeding gashes in his chest. 'Eef I tell yu, senior, an my superior officers lern of dat, I weel be keeld. Dey weel ang me.'

'They'll likely torture you much worse than we have done,' said one of Herman's crewmates, a man named, Juan. 'I know how cruel you Spaniards are. You kill bulls for fun.'

'You people breed mad monks who pull people apart and burn them alive!' spat Herman. 'You Spanish are a despicable, cruel people.' He spat a gob at the midshipman's head. 'And that's for spitting on my captain, you sorry excuse for a navy officer.'

The midshipman stared at Herman with a tangible hatred. He despised Prussians.

Hanzel and Michael exchanged a smile. They thought Herman's outburst to be funny and out of character for him, he being normally reserved and not so demonstrative.

'If you tell us what we need to know, we'll let you join us, with full privileges, as long as you sign our code. The Spanish Crown will never know that you joined us for a much better life,' said Hanzel, persuasively. *I hope he accepts. I don't want to cut him anymore. I don't like doing this.*

The midshipman took a minute to reflect on Hanzel's offer. The deep cuts were burning in his flesh. He realized that it really was not worth it. Why should he protect stolen gold of which he would not see but a tiny pittance for having risked his life? Why should he be cut up so that the king and his *royal* household can live high off the hog?

'On board our ship, every man and woman has an equal say in how we conduct our affairs,' said Hanzel.

'And we have strict rules to make sure everyone treats each other as equals. Every officer is elected by the rest of the crew,' added Michael.

The bleeding Spaniard regarded the six men watching him, eagerly waiting for a positive answer. He looked down at his wounds; stinging like hot pokers and still dripping blood. Then he nodded slowly. 'I don theen eet is wurt eet for me to reesk my life for de keeng's gol. Eef yu weel let me join yur gang weed full privileges, I weel tell yu wad yu wan a kno.'

Hanzel looked at Michael and handed him a key. 'Please take our charter from its chest and read the articles to Senor da Carcorala. If you agree to tell us what we want to know and sign the charter to join us as an equal member; who will faithfully help us deliver the stolen treasure from the Spanish Crown, we will cut your bonds and cease further torments. What say you?'

The man nodded his head slowly. 'Si. Si. I weel tell yu. Der eez a sheep. She ees call, *Santa Isabella*. She eez carry mucho grande gol, seelver, ana color stones.'

'When is the convoy sailing?' asked Hanzel.

'De day affer manyana,' replied Alphonso.

Hanzel scratched his chin. 'If you betray us, you will surely die a horrible death. You must understand that.'

Alphonso nodded. 'I unerstan senior. I weel sign yur charter.'

'Read it to him, if you please,' said Hanzel to Michael, who had retrieved the precious document from its locked box.

Michael unrolled the document and read the fourteen articles everyone on board had signed. 'Article one. Every man or woman member of our crew will have an equal vote whether to pirate or not. Everyone has equal access to all food and drink. Article two. Nobody will receive a share of a prize who has not participated in its gain. All gains to be distributed according to rank. The captain receives fifteen percent. All officers will receive an equal portion of twenty five percent. The balance is to be paid out in equal amounts to everyone who participated in obtaining the prize. Article three. Any crew member who strikes another in anger will be expelled. In the case of a mutual disagreement, differences are to be settled with swords or pistols. The first to draw blood is declared, victor. Article four. Any member who defrauds the crew of so much as a farthing will be marooned.' Michael looked up from the document and regarded Alphonso, who nodded agreement.

'Everthin so far soun fare.'

Hanzel gestured for Michael to continue.

'Article five. Any man or woman who steals from a colony member will be marooned. Article six. Everyone is responsible to keep their weapons in good working order. Failure to do so will result in disciplinary action at the discretion of the captain and two other officers. Article seven. Any member of the crew who deserts his or her post in time of battle will be marooned. Article eight. Any man who seduces another man's woman will be marooned. Article nine. A crew member who murders another will be subject to the death penalty. Article ten. The first member of the crew who sights a prize will receive his or her choice of the finest small arms found on board the said trophy. Article eleven. Any man or woman who shall lose a limb, or in some other way be incapacitated, shall be provided for by the colony at the same level of all other members.'

'Dat iz mos fare. In de navy yu are luky if yu get anytin for losin a limb,' muttered Alphonso.

Michael looked up for a moment and then continued to read. 'Article twelve. A crew member can only participate in piracy of their own free will. Anyone coercing another to pirate will be marooned. Article thirteen. Married members of the crew are under no obligation to pirate without the consent of their spouse, especially if they have children. However, if one does not participate in the capture of a prize one is subject to article two.

And, finally, article fourteen. Gratuitous violence against officers and crew of captured prizes is strictly forbidden. Any member found to have broken this rule will be marooned.'

'Those are our rules. As you can see, there are over a hundred signatures or marks. Everyone on board has signed this.' Hanzel regarded the Spaniard.

'Yur rules are mos fare. I weel sign. An, I weel be a loyal member of dees crew. I theen I weel like it here bedder dan the navy.'

Hanzel gestured to Herman. 'Untie him.'

When his bonds were removed, Alphonso signed the document and was welcomed on board.

'Take him to see Cookie. He'll tend to those wounds and fix you up, good as new.' Hanzel clapped his hands together and regarded his friends. 'Well, gentlemen. There we have it. We have ourselves a treasure ship. Now all we have to do is figure out how to capture it. Do we do it in port, as I've done before? Or do we take her out at sea? That is the question.'

'We don't have a lot of time to make plans, seeing as how they are leaving the day after tomorrow,' suggested Michael.

'Well then, I guess we had better get to it.' Hanzel grinned. 'This is going to be so much fun. I can't wait to get started.'

Early next morning, Hanzel, Michael, Herman, Juan, and a new man named, Derek rowed about in the harbour to assess the situation. They discovered that the treasure ship was hemmed in by a navy ship. The other navy ships effectively blocked the entrance to the harbour. No ship could enter the harbour now without having to pass by a close scrutiny from the two navy ships.

'There is no way we'll sail that ship out of here,' said Hanzel, as they began to row back to *Silver Streak*. 'We have no choice. We're going to have to take her at sea.'

'It's a good thing we've got most of our gun carriages built. At least we can use eight of our cannons if we have to,' replied Michael.

'It's not much, but at least it's something,' said Hanzel, looking up at the Spanish navy frigate they were rowing past. 'We're no match for this thing.'

'We're going to have to do some fancy sailing, if we're going to snatch that treasure ship out from under the noses of these navy ships. If they come after us, our cannons are nothing compared to their twenty pounders,' suggested Herman.

Hanzel scratched his chin as he pondered the problem they were facing. How in the name of the saints were they going to capture that treasure ship? He only had until tomorrow to figure it out. *It's a good thing there are more minds at work on this puzzle. How do we capture her at sea?*

When the scouting party returned to their ship, planning began in earnest. 'With a guard of three navy ships and the other ships likely forming a ring around the treasure vessel, approaching her is going to be nigh on impossible,' suggested Michael.

'At least we're not going at it blind. We know which vessel is the treasure ship,' replied Hanzel. 'Since our brigantine is lower in the water and faster than any of the Spanish ships, we should be able to sail into the convoy at night; in the dark. We'll douse our lanterns, so that we won't be seen. Then we'll take the *Santa Isabella* and sail out of the convoy with her.'

'If we fly a Spanish flag, as well, nobody will be any the wiser what we're up to. They'll just think we're another merchant seeking a safe crossing in a convoy. That's pretty normal,' suggested Michael.

'Right you are, my friend. We'll fly a Spanish flag,' laughed Hanzel, rubbing his hands together. 'I can see the treasure already.'

Chapter 38

Seven Spanish ships sailed slowly out of the harbour during high tide the next morning. The seven ships consisted of two navy frigates and five merchantmen; one of them being the *Santa Isabella*; strategically placed in the middle of the pack. An eighth ship sailed after them later that day, also flying a Spanish flag; a much faster ship; a ship mostly filled with Dutchmen intent upon adventure and some grand larceny. As they sailed out of port, Hanzel and Michael were sitting in deck chairs enjoying cigars and brandies on the quarterdeck.

'Why would they be leaving one of their frigates here?' asked Michael.

'They'll likely be deploying that one to take care of local matters. Hispaniola is Spanish territory, after all,' replied Hanzel.

'Ya, that makes sense. They don't need three frigates to escort only five ships.' Michael took a sip of his brandy.

'With only two frigates guarding the *Santa Isabella* it makes things easier for us. We can slip in and out of that convoy with relative ease.'

'As long as they're not sailing too close to each other,' suggested Michael.

'We'll take our time and plan this out very carefully. We've got several months if need be. However, I would prefer to take her here in the Caribbean. That way we can escape to any one of dozens of islands. I really don't want to do this in the mid Atlantic.'

'We'll catch up with the convoy by this evening. We already know which ship we're after, so it could even happen tonight.' Michael regarded his friend as he took a long puff of his cigar.

'Tonight?'

'Sure, why not? There's not going to be a moon tonight.'

Hanzel regarded his first mate for a moment before replying. 'The question is, are we ready?'

'All we need to do is give the word. Everyone is raring to go. We've spent too many days at sea and in port. It is time to put ourselves to the test. That's why we came out here.'

Hanzel nodded thoughtfully. 'You're right. Let's get everyone together and we'll begin our planning. I want this to go smoothly with a minimum of bloodshed.'

'How many do you suppose are on board the *Santa Isabella*?' asked Michael.

'Let's ask Alphonso. He'll likely know.'

When Hanzel asked the Spanish midshipman the answer he received was a wonderful surprise. Their treasure ship was manned with only thirty three sailors and seven officers. 'Dey are relyin on de navy sheeps an de odder sheeps to protec de trezure sheep.'

'Why are there so few men on board the treasure ship, I wonder?' Hanzel regarded the Spaniard quizzically. Then he looked at Michael, his eyebrows raised.

'To conserve space and weight?' suggested Michael.

'The more sailors on board, the more weight and the less space for the treasure. Makes sense. The manpower is concentrated on the navy ships.' Hanzel scratched his chin. 'Their strategy in based on the idea that pirates would approach from outside the convoy. They have not thought it possible that pirates would be sailing amongst them under their own flag.' Hanzel laughed.

'I'm beginning to get the impression that the treasure ship may be a richer prize than we imagined,' replied Michael, grinning.

Hanzel clapped his hands together. 'This is going to be a wonderful adventure, I can just feel it.'

'Me too,' replied Michael, lifting his cup. He took a long, thoughtful drought. *Me too. I pray none of us gets hurt.*

'I have a plan,' said Hanzel, snapping his fingers. 'What we're going to do is rig six large barrels with a mast and sail, and three lanterns. Then, when we've taken the treasure ship, we'll put the raft in the water with a man to light the lanterns, when we douse the treasure ship's lanterns. The raft will be set to sail on course with the other ships, while we sail ourselves and the treasure ship out of the convoy with our lamps blacked out.'

Michael regarded his friend. 'That's brilliant. That is bloody brilliant, Hanzel. They will never suspect their treasure ship has left the convoy and only discover our ruse at day break.' Michael grinned from ear to ear. 'That is so bloody brilliant. I love it.'

'I can't see it not working,' Hanzel took a drink from his cup, a big grin on his face.

Michael nodded. 'Me neither. I think we've going to have a great success.'

The two friends clicked their cups together. 'Here's to our success,' the said in unison, and laughing with great good cheer.

Just before sunset the convoy was spotted half a league in front of *Silver Streak*. The brigantine's Spanish flag was flying. Nobody in the convoy had the slightest idea they were being infiltrated by pirates, assuming the brigantine to be a merchant's ship, taking refuge within the convoy. Nobody thought anything about the brigantine taking a position off the port side of the central ship; *Santa Isabella*; thinking it fortuitous another ship was there to help protect the treasure. Nobody on board the navy frigates took any notice of the brigantine; it being dark by then, and there being no moon to throw light on any of what was to follow.

What Hanzel and his crew did not see is that there were three sloops sailing directly towards the convoy from starboard. Three slippery sloops topped with black flags on which a skull and two crossed femurs fluttered. Nobody noticed them. The night was much too dark for that.

Onboard *Silver Streak,* work was nearing completion on the raft and everyone was making ready with their weapons: grappling hooks, boarding axes, knives, swords, cutlasses, pistols, crossbows, blunderbusses, cannons, and dirks. Several of the men had even managed to obtain Swiss halberds. Collectively they were a force to reckon with.

When the gang was gathered together on deck, Hanzel gave everyone final instructions before sailing ever closer to the treasure ship. The advantage they had was that the brigantine, being fore and aft rigged, was able to pull quite close to the merchantman without becoming entangled in its rigging. Nobody on board the merchantman was any the wiser. Nobody on any Spanish ship heard the boats being lowered, or people rowing the ten yards left between the two ships. Nobody on board any of the ships saw or heard the raft being dropped into the sea, behind the brigantine.

Ever so quietly, forty five pirates, led by Herman and Juan, climbed ever so quietly onto the merchantman and immediately disabled the watch and helmsman. Meanwhile, the boats were rowed back to ferry another thirty pirates, including Hanzel and Hanna. Michael and Maria remained behind; Michael taking command of *Silver Streak*.

A shot rang out. Then two more. Then shouts and screams and clashing steel began to fill the air as the Spanish crew put up a fight to protect their king's treasure.

'What stupidity,' sighed Hanzel. 'Why bother putting up a fight? Is it worth it to be killed for the king's ill gotten gold?'

'Some people just don't get it,' replied Hanna as she began to climb up the ladder of the merchantman.

Hanzel followed her, each of them brandishing a pistol in their right hand and a knife in their teeth. Hanna had tied her hair back in a long braid and wore a silken scarf over her head, to keep hair out of her eyes. Her breeches were tucked into high leather boots. She wore a tight fitting shirt under a buttoned up waistcoat. Over her right shoulder she wore a baldric from which hung her cutlass and two more loaded pistols across her chest. A powder horn and a ball and wadding pouch hung from her belt. The moment she stepped on board, a Spanish sailor came rushing at her, brandishing a scimitar.

'HANNA!' shouted Hanzel. 'WATCH OUT!'

Hanna turned and faced the oncoming Spaniard. Her pistol discharged with a loud pop, and a large ball of lead tore into the man's chest, neatly coming out of his back and plunging into the man, swashbuckling with Herman. The man crumpled to the deck; joining the first man already bleeding out at Hanna's feet.

Hanzel regarded his courageous woman. 'Good shot! Two in one!' he shouted happily. *What a girl. She's the perfect wife for me, that's for sure.* Herman was grinning from ear to ear.

'So, now what?' she asked, looking around to see if there was any more danger. However, the battle was over. Five surviving officers and 27 Spanish sailors were herded up on deck, where Hanzel told them their rights. Either join him or be put to sea in boats. Two officers and twenty sailors elected to join Hanzel. The others were put into a boat and pushed off. Then the lanterns were doused and the raft's lanterns lit at the same time. The brigantine also doused her lanterns. They set course away from the convoy and slowly, quietly sailed away in another direction. The only ones who saw what had happened were those on board the sloops. Nobody on board the brigantine or the merchantman noticed that the sloops were following them in the darkness and quiet of the open sea. The dead Spaniards were simply tossed overboard without ceremony.

'A few less Spaniards in the world is a good thing,' remarked Hanzel, clapping his hands together. 'They've killed a lot of our countrymen over the years.'

Herman nodded. 'Including my father and an uncle.'

'Bastards,' muttered Hanzel.

'So, I don't feel badly about us killing a few of them. The good thing is, we didn't lose anyone and only suffered a few minor cuts and bruises,' continued Herman.

'We're good at what we do,' replied Hanzel. 'We got what we wanted, with minimum blood shed.' Then, rubbing his hands together, 'Let's go below and see what we've captured, shall we?'

Meanwhile, as Hanzel and his friends examined the fabulous wealth they had captured so easily, the three sloops approached ever so slowly and carefully; also with lanterns doused. The three pirate vessels were forty footers, small, swift, and manned by twenty five pirates each. When the sloops were close enough they pulled up alongside the merchantman. It was only then when someone noticed the sloops and shouted, 'PIRATES! HANZEL!!! HANZEL!!! WE'RE BEING ATTACKED!!!'

When Hanzel and his friends heard the alarm, they ran, weapons drawn, up the stairs to the main deck. Herman was the first to burst out of the door and was immediately shot through the head. He tumbled backwards into Hanzel, who had to let him down gently as he died. Hanzel immediately shouted, 'TAKE COVER!'

The door burst open and several pistol shots rang out as two pirates shot into the darkness of the gangway. Hanzel and Hanna discharged their pistols. Instantly a moan indicated they had hit someone. The other pirate ducked behind the open door. It was then that Hanzel and his friends stormed on deck, immediately being engaged in a vicious game of swords and pistols in the darkness. Shouts, screams, curses, and the clang and clash of steel on steel filled the space; the occasional pistol or blunderbuss shot being the only sound to be heard over all of the others. Eventually the sounds stopped. An eerie silence enveloped the scene, pierced by moans, screams, and curses.

Hanzel and Hanna crouched side by side, their backs against the aftercastle wall. 'This is not something I was ever expecting,' whispered Hanzel, when they had a moment to look at each other. 'I can't see a thing. How does anyone know who is who?'

'I have no idea. I think it's best we stay here and not venture further out on deck.' Hanna looked east. 'It should be daylight soon. When the dust settles, we'll see what's what.'

Hanzel nodded. 'Strange. The fighting has stopped. Is everyone dead?'

Hanna shrugged her shoulders. 'I have no idea. Whatever the situation; we'd better be very quiet and stay crouched here. The open door gives us some cover, at least.'

Twenty minutes of moans and screams later, the first rays of a glorious sunrise began to throw light on the scene of carnage and mayhem. What the light revealed was a number of motionless, bloody corpses strewn about the deck and hatch covers. Several dead sailors hung upside down in the rigging; shot by well aimed pirate harquebuses. Injured pirates moaned, behind spars, barrels, and hatches. It was difficult to tell who was who. However, both Hanzel and Hanna got the impression, many of the moaning and the dead were members of their gang.

A deep, snarling voice shouted. 'WHO IS YOUR CAPTAIN?!'

Hanzel looked at Hanna and she back at him. Then they both looked in the direction the voice had come from. 'He's above us, on the quarterdeck,' he whispered.

'What should we do?' replied Hanna, whispering into Hanzel's ear and trembling with fright.

'I'm not sure, at the moment. Let's wait and see what unfolds. Best thing to do is reload your pistols and be ready when they come.'

'IF YOU ARE STILL ALIVE. OR IF ANY OF YOUR OFFICERS ARE ALIVE, REVEAL YOURSELVES! IT IS HOPELESS FOR YOU! THE

BATTLE IS OVER AND YOU HAVE LOST!' The gruff voice coughed for a full minute afterwards, the strain on his vocal cords being too much for him.

It was then when Michael unleashed four cannons into the starboard side of a pirate sloop as he maneuvered the brigantine away from the scene. He let go another broadside as he passed a second sloop. Neither sloop shot back because most of their sailors were on board the treasure ship. However, since only a skeleton crew remained on his ship, Michael had to be very careful how he maneuvered, while those few remaining on board the brigantine reloaded the cannons for another volley into a sloop. The, seemingly, victorious pirates, did not bother to send a boat after them; being totally focussed on the treasure they had stolen out from under the noses of another pirate gang.

'When they come down the stairs, we'll shoot who we can,' whispered Hanzel. 'We've each got three pistols, so, have one ready in each hand.'

Hanna nodded. She had regained her composure but was still mightily frightened. She could well imagine what might happen if they were captured.

Footsteps creaked on the stairs.

'Here they come.' Hanzel gripped his pistols and made ready. The moment the footsteps hit the deck, he and his courageous woman jumped out from their hiding place and shot directly, at close range, into three men. One was killed outright with a ball through the heart. The other two were wounded. One in the stomach and the other lost his right ear lobe. The wounded men were not pleased. One more shot finished the man with the stomach wound; Hanzel's ball blasting through the top of the pirate's skull as he bent over to clutch his wounded gut. Hanna's shot hit the other man's right hand, the one wielding a pistol he had pointed at her forehead. The man's pistol fell to the deck. Within a split instant, Hanzel extracted his cutlass and drove it into the man's chest. The man followed his pistol to the deck and lay there as an ever larger pool of his blood began to stain his clothes and deck.

Hanzel looked at Hanna and she back at him. 'Are there more?' he whispered.

Hanna leaned out to look up to see if anyone was looking over the railing of the quarterdeck above. A shot blasted the air. A ball whizzed by, missing Hanna by an inch and thudding into the deck. Hanzel grabbed her arm and pulled her back against the wall of the aftercastle.

'That was close.' Hanna looked wideyed at Hanzel. 'I was nearly killed.'

'YOU BETTER GIVE UP!' shouted the gruff voice. 'YOU HAVE NO HOPE!'

It was at that moment when Juan and thirty other friends stormed out of the midship hatch, firing pistols and blunderbusses up at the quarterdeck. A trampling of feet above them signaled to Hanzel and Hanna they could duck back inside the aftercastle and close the door.

'I get the impression we may have won this, after all.' As Hanzel spoke, he and Hanna could hear a number of boots running up the stairs to the quarterdeck above them. Shouts and curses could be heard through the boards above their heads. He held the door open and Hanna took a furtive look outside.

'HANZEL! HANZEL!' shouted Juan. 'THE QUARTERDECK IS SECURE!'

Hanzel and Hanna stepped out of the aftercastle and climbed the stairs to discover seven pirates cowering under the swords and pistols of Hanzel's gang members. Four pirates lay dead and two were sitting on the deck, clutching bleeding wounds.

'That one is their leader,' said Juan, indicating a nasty looking cutthroat with large moustaches and a gold earring in his left earlobe.

'What's his name?' asked Hanzel.

'Gerritt, something or other,' replied Juan.

'Gerrit Gerritzoon?' asked Hanzel, suddenly taking an even greater interest in his attacker. He stepped over to the man and confronted him directly. 'Are you the one who calls himself, Roche Braziliano?'

The man stared into Hanzel's eyes with an evil intensity which gave Hanzel a cold chill up his spine. He had never seen such a look in anyone's eyes. What he saw was something unique. It was a glimpse into the abyss; a glimpse into the total darkness that is the Pit of Hell. Hanzel could not prevent the shiver which traveled throughout his entire nervous system. He was looking into the eyes of a monster; a man capable of roasting people alive and eating their bleeding hearts.

The pirate refused to answer Hanzel's question. He was not about to reveal himself. He knew that amongst pirates, he had a bad name. Some of the things he had done, to provoke terror, were not regular practice amongst Brethren of the Coast. Roasting people alive, or eating their bleeding hearts was not something civilized pirates did. Some could be cruel, to be sure; but cutting someone's heart out and eating it, that was beyond the pale.

One of the pirate's minions, a man clutching a bleeding arm and thinking he might be spared from Hanzel's wrath volunteered that, indeed the man was the one called, Roche Braziliano.

'At last we meet, face to face,' hissed Hanzel. 'I've been wanting to meet you for a long time. I vowed I would bring your miserable life to an end, someday. Now, finally I have the opportunity. The question is, how do we kill you.'

'Kill me?' The feared pirate stared dumbfoundedly at Hanzel. 'You can't kill me? You have to bring me to the authorities. You have no right to kill me in cold blood.'

'Oh? You and your men have killed and wounded many members of my gang. Do you really think that I would trust your demise to the, *authorities*? You've probably paid them off.' Hanzel shook his head. 'No, we can't let you get away. You will pay for your crime.'

The feared pirate stared bug eyed at Hanzel. 'You mean to execute me? Me, Roche Braziliano?'

'Hanging is too good for the likes of him,' muttered Juan.

'We should cut out *his* heart,' suggested Anthony.

'Too bloody. That would make such a mess on deck,' replied Derek. 'Remember who'd have to clean it up.' He shook his head. 'No, we should just hang him, but prolong it.'

'We could break him first. That's not too bloody.' Anthony thought for a moment. 'Well, there would be some spatters and bone chips, but easier to clean up.'

'Breaking is a good idea,' agreed George. 'From what I heard about that monster, he deserves it.'

Hanzel cringed inside at the thought of a breaking. Images of his father being broken on the wheel flashed through his head. *Be strong, Hanzel. The man deserves a painful death. Yes, but is it up to you to do it.? Remember it does say we should not kill? Yes, but, you are a pirate and that man does deserve death. You can't let him get away.*

'If you kill me, you'll pay in Hell for it.'

'We'll be rewarded in Heaven for it,' replied Hanzel.

'Heaven?' scoffed the pirate. 'Don't bring that claptrap into this conversation. There's no Heaven to reward you. Satan overcame all of that. Remember who was hung on a cross. It wasn't him.'

'To save us from our sins,' grumbled Juan.

'Save you from your sins. What a pile of crap. Do you actually believe there is somebody who is going to punish you after you're dead, for things you do here?' The dreaded pirate stared out at his captors. 'You're all deluded if you think that.' He gestured at the gory remains lying on the deck. 'Look about you. Where do you see any sign of Heaven in any of this? Hell, that is what you see operating here on Earth. Everywhere there are wars, there is carnage and destruction of property. Day after day, year after year people die in gruesome ways to feed Satan's lust for blood and screams. I don't see much of Heaven in any of it.' Roche stuck his chin out. 'Tell me. Where do you see anything of Heaven in this world?'

Hanzel indicated Hanna. 'I see Heaven every day in Hanna's eyes. I see how her belly is beginning to fill with our new child. I see how every day is a miracle that we're even alive.'

Roche hung his head and nodded. 'Yes, it's a miracle, alright. A miracle we lost. We should have beaten you.' He looked at his men. 'Are these all that are left of sixty who came on board?'

Juan and his friends laughed. 'There are at least thirty tied up in the hold. Some of them are wounded, but there are only five or six dead ones down there.'

Hanzel looked at Juan; a surprised expression on his face. 'You captured thirty?'

Juan nodded, smiling. 'We tied them up. It's possible they might join us. A couple of them expressed some disgust with their leader.' Juan indicated the heart eater.

'We'll deal with them later. First we must figure out what to do with him,' said Hanzel, indicating the pirate.

Anthony pointed off to port. 'Look, there's Michael. He's probably wondering what is going on.'

Hanzel smiled. 'That's some good sailing, to come around like that. The sloops wouldn't see him as easily; this big ship obscuring his approach.' *Well done, my friend.* 'Signal him that we're alright.'

Derek carried out the order by climbing the port side main shroud and waving to the brigantine, using his trademark red bandana.

Fifteen minutes later, Michael and Maria joined Hanzel on the quarterdeck of the treasure ship. In the meantime Roche had been tied to the mizzen mast. He peppered Hanzel and his friends with a constant barrage of verbiage, until, finally, Hanzel authorized that the man's mouth be gagged.

'Congratulations,' said Michael, taking note of the scene, as he stepped on board; having been rowed over in the brigantine's boat. 'Too bad so much blood had to be spilled.'

Hanzel nodded sadly. 'Ya, that is so.'

'How many did we lose?' Michael prodded a dead pirate with the toe of his left boot.

'We haven't taken count yet. We were surprised to discover that their leader is non other than, Roche Braziliano.'

Michael's eyebrows lifted. 'Roche Braziliano? The pirate who eats hearts?'

Hanzel gestured toward the man squirming in his ropes.

'What are we going to do with him?' asked Michael.

'We're going to execute him, of course,' replied Hanzel.

'Execute him?' Michael nodded. 'That's reasonable, I think.' He regarded the pirate. 'You don't want to turn him over to the authorities?'

Hanzel shook his head. 'Not really. They might not execute him. Or he could be rescued. I don't want to take that chance. When I first heard of him I wanted to find him and strangle his scrawny neck. He gives piracy a bad name. Makes us all look like a pack of rabid hounds; like we're all cutthroats.' Hanzel stared at the pirate. (If looks could kill, Hanzel would have been dead on the spot). 'No. We've got to do it. The question is how?'

'That's simple. Tie a rope around his neck and hang him. Bing, bang, it's done. No mess, no fuss,' suggested Michael.

'Hanging is too good for the likes of him,' repeated Juan.

'Yes, but, if we do something really dastardly to him, would we not be stooping down to the level he is alleged to have fallen to?' Michael regarded Juan.

Juan thought a moment and could not help but agree with Michael. The death had to be humane and swift, not drawn out and cruel. If the latter, they would be no better than the monster they were doing away with. 'Alright. I agree we should just hang him. Be done with it.'

'What about his gang members?' asked Anthony.

'They can join us, or return to port in a rowboat,' replied Hanzel. He regarded the pirate with a cold stare. 'Alright, let's get on with it. We've wasted enough time with this monster. Take that gag out of his mouth and we can hear his final words.'

The pirate squirmed in his ropes as the gag was removed. 'You can't! You can't just hang me without a trial.'

Hanzel regarded the squirming pirate. 'Yes we can.'

'You can't take the law into your own hands,' spat the pirate.

'We do it all the time,' replied Hanzel. He gestured to Juan and Anthony. 'Untie him from the mast and put that noose around his neck.'

'You can't! You can't hang me, Roche Braziliano! I'm the most feared pirate in these waters!'

'Not any more. Not after we're done with you,' replied Hanzel. 'Bring his men up on deck. I want them to see this.'

Minutes later, all of the pirate's men had been assembled on deck. They watched unemotionally as their captain berated his executioners and pleaded for mercy, like a frightened child. Braziliano's men quickly realized that the feared pirate was actually a coward and not worthy of respect by anyone there. After the deed was done, and the pirate had stopped his deadman's dance, everyone cheered, including his own men, who were all glad to sign Hanzel's 14 articles, afterwards. Then the terrible cleanup began and a large funeral committed the many dead to their final resting place at the bottom of the tossing sea. It was at this time that someone on one of the Spanish frigates noticed the raft and the missing treasure ship. All hell broke out there, whilst on board the *Santa Isabella*, Hanzel and his friends were celebrating their success as they sailed five ships to a secret lagoon; Roche Braziliano's former headquarters.

Hanna smiled as she regarded Hanzel. 'Well, my love. How does it feel to now be the leader of a gang with five ships, a huge treasure, and the beginnings of a colony?'

Hanzel grinned from ear to ear as he looked at his amazing wife, already beginning to fill out with their child. 'I am the happiest man in the world.' He leaned over and kissed her, placing his right hand on her belly.

A little foot kicked back.

'We've got a little pirate in there, that's for sure,' laughed Hanzel.

'Takes after the father,' laughed Hanna. Then she hugged her man for a long time; so proud to be the mother of his child.

Roche Braziliano's head quarters turned out to be the perfect location and the beginnings of what Hanzel and his gang envisioned they could build there. The lagoon was deep enough to float the merchantman and large enough to effectively hide all five ships. One large house, with twelve rooms, sat at the head of a large, open yard, facing the lagoon. Twelve huts were scattered about behind the house, in amongst the trees. A large ramada covered a quarter of the yard and provided a shady work area. A long, wooden dock ran out into the water, enabling the three sloops to tie up there. The merchantman and brigantine had to be anchored in the middle of the placid, turquoise harbour. The entire place was only accessible by a narrow channel cut through the many hued corral lining the coast. It was a very good pirate hideout.

'With some work, it'll be perfect,' enthused Hanzel, after they had examined the place and discovered the happy circumstances which Braziliano had accumulated in the twelve rooms of his house. 'We'll become quite comfortable here, wouldn't you say, Hanna?'

Hanna grinned, as she tested the pirate's comfortable four poster bed. 'I assume this will be our room, on account of you being captain?'

Hanzel nodded. 'Indeed, this is the Captain's Cabin in this place. Wouldn't you say, Michael?'

Michael nodded. 'Of course. That goes without saying. The other big bedroom will be Maria's and mine.'

'I like that just fine. Being officers has its rewards, to be sure,' replied Maria, a broad smile on her pretty face.

When Hanzel and his friends stepped outside, they called everyone together and delegated: the unloading of the treasure ship, organized a party to divide the loot, and divided the huts and four other bedrooms in the house to the other officers and coupled crewmates. Single men chose various cabins and places on board the ships; eventually building cabins and huts of their own. By the time three months had passed, the new colony saw tremendous growth. Thirty huts were now scattered throughout the forest, all of them decorated with gold and silver objects; bits and pieces of the share they acquired at the party celebrating their arrival at the lagoon and division of the treasure. By the end of the fourth month, there were forty huts, a second pier, and an acre of cleared, tilled land, ready to receive a garden. Hanna was seven months pregnant by this time and Maria had become pregnant, followed by Dana, Katherine, and Carla, in that order.

'Well, it'll be good for our little pirate,' observed Hanna, one morning, while she and Hanzel were sitting on the verandah of the big house, sipping coffee. 'Now that we've got a little gang of baby pirates on the way, ours will have friends to play with.'

Hanzel smiled as he envisioned five little pirates playing in the yard.

By the end of the fifth month at the lagoon, supplies were running out. They needed to resupply their colony with victuals and libations.

'And seeds and bedding plants for the garden,' added Hanna, when they were seated together in council, putting together their shopping list.

'Maybe you'll get lucky and capture a merchantman or two,' said Michael. 'If you get one coming to Hispaniola, you may find a lot of what we need, and not have to expose yourselves by going into Tortuga or Santo Domingo.'

'I'm sure the Spaniards have navy ships out looking for us,' laughed Hanzel. 'That was no mean treasure we stole from them.'

'Right under their noses,' laughed Hanna. 'You are amazing.'

Hanzel shook his head. '*We* are amazing, Hanna. Don't forget, I didn't do it alone.'

Hanna nodded. 'We are amazing, then.'

'So we are,' agreed Michael, putting a final notation on the list they had prepared. Everyone got an opportunity to request things they needed. 'If you don't find a fat ship to plunder, you'll likely be able to get everything in Tortuga; it being closer.'

'And, less likely to have Spanish navy vessels in port. Its not a very big place,' suggested Juan.

'Smaller than Santo Domingo, that's for sure,' agreed Anthony. 'However, what if Tortuga doesn't have everything we need?'

'Then you'll have to take a chance and go to Santo Domingo. Go with the brigantine and fix her rigging, like we did before. We could add two yardarms, one on the fore and one on the main mast. Then we'll square rig two sails and take down the lateens. You'll not look quite so different from the other ships in port, they being mostly square rigged merchantmen. It's the fore and aft rigging that gives us away so easily,' suggested Hanzel.

'And fly our Spanish flag,' added Michael.

'Nobody will be any the wiser,' laughed Hanzel. He raised his cup. 'Here's to a successful voyage to Tortuga.'

'To a successful voyage!' chorused his friends, clicking their cups together.

Since Hanzel and Michael were rich beyond belief, they were able to send the gold necessary to buy the things they and their women needed, since neither of them wanted to go sailing, given that their women were not desirous of riding the tossing waves on account of them being pregnant and not always feeling too well. Hanzel and Michael felt it was better to stay close to their wives, much to their relief.

Silver Streak sailed out of the lagoon with a crew of 45, on November 1, 1625. Juan served as captain and Anthony as first mate. The remaining 20 people came out to the shore to wave goodbye. When the ship was well out of sight, everyone returned to their homes and continued work improving their living circumstances, and enjoying their lives in what, to many of them had become, Paradise. Nobody gave the brigantine another thought, other than to wish they would return quickly with the libations so needed in a pirate colony.

'It wouldn't be much of a pirate colony without some rum to fuel the imagination, wouldn't you agree?' asked Hanzel, one afternoon, when he and Michael were enjoying their last brandies and cigars on the beach.

'Life would not be quite so relaxing and pleasant,' agreed Michael. He and Hanzel were watching Hanna and Maria examining a tidal pool, looking for flora and fauna to examine. Both women were pregnant; Hanna almost eight months and Maria five. 'So, how does it feel, now that you'll soon be a father?'

Hanzel took a long puff from his cigar and thought about Michael's question. After a moment he replied thoughtfully, 'I'm really not sure how I feel. On the one hand I think it's great. But, on the other hand, will having a baby interfere with my work as captain of this crew?'

'That's the question, isn't it? I feel the same way, to tell you the truth,' replied Michael. 'Having the responsibility of a child and serving as first mate on a pirate ship, a service in which one could easily be killed, or maimed, makes one think twice about pirating and more about settling down in a cottage somewhere and becoming a landlubber.'

Hanzel looked at Michael and studied his face for a moment. 'Settling down and becoming a landlubber? I'll bet you would grow tired of that within a year, or less. Life at sea is a much more free life style, and more interesting when you factor in the piracy part, don't you think?'

'I think what I want to do with my treasure is go back to Amsterdam and go into the fine clothing trade.' Michael examined the ruffle of his left sleeve. 'Maria likes the idea of having a shop to sell high fashion, expensive clothes to the rich women there. I think we could make a fortune and be really happy. We thought we'd call the shop, *La Belle Mode*.

'Yes, but you already have a fortune,' replied Hanzel, blowing a smoke ring.

'With no place to really enjoy it. Amsterdam has restaurants and many, varied entertainments. We don't have that here.' Michael stared into his cup. 'We miss that.'

Hanzel shook his head. 'I've never really experienced any of that. I'm the son of a fisherman. You're the son of a professor at the University of Leiden. There's a big difference.'

Michael nodded. Indeed there was a wide gulf of difference in the class conscious Dutch society he and Hanzel were born into. It was only in a circumstance, such as their pirate colony, that people from such different levels of society were able to be friends. To the Dutch, for the son of a professor to be friends with a fisherman's son was akin to a Hindu Brahman associating with an Untouchable. He took a long sip of his brandy and thought about what Hanzel had said. He looked over at his friend. 'Well, I for one am glad to be a pirate, so that we can be friends.'

Hanzel looked at his comrade and smiled. He clicked his cup against Michael's. 'That goes for me too. If we had not gone to sea the way we did, you and I would not ever have met. What a loss that would have been, for me, that's for certain.'

Michael grinned. 'Me too.'

'With the fortune you have from the treasure ship, you could easily set up shop in Amsterdam for many years before you would have to make a profit. If that's what you and Maria want to do, then why not take one of the sloops and sail to Amsterdam? You can take some of our friends for crew. I'm sure Carla and Dana would want to go.'

'I know. However, the problem I have is, we'd be leaving you and Hanna.'

'You can always come back, if Amsterdam doesn't agree with you,' replied Hanzel. 'You could sail to Amsterdam and consider it a vacation. Personally, I have no desire to go back there. Neither does Hanna. Hence, we'll both be here, unless we're off roving somewhere. We'd still be coming back here, now that our house is becoming what it is; our wonderful home.'

Michael nodded. 'I think what I might prefer to do is travel on a merchant ship out of Santo Domingo. Maria would prefer an easier passage. On such a ship, we'd be seen as a merchant couple returning home from a sojourn in the New World. We'd eat well enough and not have to make it ourselves.'

'How would you carry all that treasure with you? Surely it would be discovered, wouldn't you think?' Hanzel looked quizzically at his friend.

'I was thinking we could melt down some of the larger pieces, to conserve space in the chests and use more, rather than fewer chests, to distribute the weight of the gold and silver under piles of clothing which we can buy in Santo Domingo.'

Hanzel nodded. 'That's actually not a bad idea. It shouldn't take us too many weeks to put that all together. Why don't we take a little cruise tomorrow to Santo Domingo and go buy some chests and clothes? I'm sure the girls would like to do that. We'll take one of the sloops. The one we renamed.'

'That's a good idea. It'll be be fun. We can stay in Santo Domingo for a few days. We'll likely run into *Silver Streak* heading back here, on the way there.'

'Surprise everybody,' laughed Hanzel. He looked over at the tidal pool and watched Hanna pull a large crab out of the water. 'So, do you plan to sail before or after your baby is born?'

'It's November. A winter crossing is not very pleasant for anyone, let alone a pregnant woman. We have about three and a half months to go. I think I would prefer to wait until after the baby is here.'

'It's only three and a half months more. By then Hanna and I will have met our little pirate already.' He laughed at the thought of a baby pirate.

'It'll be quite a Christmas celebration this year, that's for sure.' Michael looked at Hanna holding up the big crab. 'Your baby could even be a Christmas baby, given that is a month away.'

Hanzel nodded. 'I guess we'll find out when the time comes.' He took a long drag off his cigar and slowly circled the smoke in his mouth; letting it out a moment later in five perfect rings. He let out a long, contented sigh. 'Life is good.'

Michael grinned. 'Life is good,' he repeated, taking a sip of his brandy.

Chapter 39

A month later it was Christmas. The day after, Hanna gave birth to Hanzel junior; who made sure to let the entire colony know that he had arrived.

'That boy has lungs!' laughed Michael, raising his cup to toast the new arrival.

'Like his father,' laughed Anthony, who was standing with Michael and Juan, on the quarterdeck. Hanzel had run off to his cabin the moment the first howl came through the boards. He and his friends had been impatiently waiting, drinking, pacing, drinking, pacing, and drinking. By the time Hanzel stumbled off to meet his son, he was already three sheets to the wind and leaning to starboard.

Little Hanzel was welcomed into the colony with a happy party which lasted right into the new year. Heaps of presents were given by the generous crew. A baby pirate was something new, they all thought. But, then, they did not know everything there was to know about pirates. Baby pirates were not abnormal, at all. Many pirates were the children of pirates. Most of the colony members were under thirty. None of them were what one would call, *seasoned* pirates. Hanzel's group was just very lucky at an early stage in their careers in the sweet trade. It certainly whetted many appetites and encouraged loyalty to Hanzel and each other. Of course, nothing in this world is absolutely perfect. And so it was in the colony, as well. When a number of adults live together in close quarters, there are bound to be grumblings. People muttering amongst themselves. In Hanzel's colony, several jealous women nattered at their men and regularly stirred things up. It is always like that, no matter where one lives, throughout the ages.

Three and a half months later, Maria gave birth to a beautiful baby girl, whom they named, Maria Michaela. Two weeks later, Katherine gave birth to a girl they named, Kat. Dana's baby came a few days later. Unfortunately the baby was stillborn. They buried him in a little box not far from the garden. Carla's baby, another boy, arrived at the end of May. This little pirate's name was, William.

On May 15th, Michael and Maria, with little Michaela left Porto Domingo on a Dutch merchant vessel bound for Amsterdam. Copious tears had been shed by the women. Hanzel and Michael had exchanged many toasts of success the night before. Hanzel and Hanna watched the ship until it disappeared below the horizon. They each sighed a deep breath.

'I'm going to miss them,' said Hanna, wiping tears from her cheeks.

Hanzel wiped his nose with the handkerchief he kept up his left sleeve.

Hand in hand they walked back to their boat, each one deep into their own thoughts about life without a favorite friend.

Four years later, after many swashbuckling adventures stealing from the Spaniards and Portuguese Hanzel and Hanna had amassed a considerable fortune in gold, silver, and precious stones. Their wardrobes were filled with rich clothes. Food and drink was plentiful Life was good as successful pirates on their little colony hidden somewhere in the Caribbean; a place marked with a Maltese cross on the map Hanzel and Hanna had drawn, based on their sundre natural history explorations.

However, as time passed, life was becoming dreary. Hanzel and Hanna missed their friends, Michael and Maria. So, one fine day in spring, Hanzel and his family sailed away from their island on a ship bound for Amsterdam. It was time to see what their favorite friends were up to. Life on the island without Michael and Maria was just not as much fun, and less interesting; they being their very best friends.

Hanzel and Hanna's ship was a newly painted sloop they had captured off the coast of Brazil. She was sleek and fast; a war sloop which had belonged to the Portuguese navy. Hanzel renamed her, *Lieve Hanna*, much to his wife's delight.

'I've never had a ship named after me!' she exclaimed, clapping her hands together, as they broke a bottle of good claret over the sloop's bows.

Sailing with the happy family were many new people who had joined the colony over the previous four years. For a first mate, Hanzel had selected a seasoned sailor whose parents named him, Melchior. The second mate was his brother, Jeston. The master's name was Mister Padrone, the quartermaster was Pontelo, and the cook's name was, Martyn. Master at arms was ably performed by Johan van der Meer, a pirate if ever there was one, with a hook and a peg. Poor bastard.

All in all, there were 75 people on board, five goats, ten chickens, three ducks, and Doctor Allan's pet monkey named, Funk. Doctor Allan was the surgeon. He also cut people's hair during the voyage; those who preferred to have shorter hair, that is. Most everybody tended to have long hair. It really was only the balding ones, who did not look very good with long, straggly hair. After all, these pirates liked to look good. Their clothes, their grooming, their boots and baubles signified, *"well off pirates,"* not some starving buccaneers looking for a cow to roast. Hanzel and Hanna and their son especially looked like pirate royalty each and every day; their long blond hair stirring in the wind as they sailed their merry way into the Atlantic.

The sloop was equipped with ten swivel guns mounted on the railings fore and aft, each a five pounder. On the gun deck, below, they were able to run out seven guns per side, these being 18 pounders and very effective at close range. Everyone was armed according to his or her particular skills. All persons on board were always ready, just in case they came upon a fat prize along the way.

Such a prize came their way, twenty days out.

She was a slow moving Spanish tub, plowing heavy waves. It was obvious to everyone on board *Lieve Hanna,* that she was loaded up with something heavy.

'Gold from Mexico, perhaps,' suggested Melchior, when he and Hanzel were eyeing the Spanish ship through their looking glasses.

'The Spaniard wouldn't be shipping gold in an unaccompanied old scow like that,' scoffed Jeston. 'He'd be using a treasure galleon. And there'd be some other boats, with lots of guns.'

'Could be that they want you to think that. Maybe they think that pirates wouldn't be bothered, thinking it is only filled with sugar and lumber. We don't need sugar and lumber. Where would we put it?' Hanzel lowered his looking glass and collapsed it into itself.

'What if it is filled with gold. Maybe it is, and it is, like you say, a ruse,' replied Melchior avariciously. 'I mean, just think, Hanzel, we could have one marvelous time in Amsterdam if we go after them and we do find gold.'

'Hanna wants to visit Amsterdam and see Michael and Maria. So do I. I don't know. If we go after them, someone could get hurt. Even though the ship looks as it does, it could have a lot of soldiers on board. We don't know.' Hanzel stared at the ship a league ahead off the port bow.

'Let's take a chance, Hanzel. It'll be fun. Something to do on a nice day like this. It'll be easy. Nobody's going to get hurt. Everyone is itching to pirate. None of us have done anything for over seven months,' pleaded Justin. 'It'll be good for morale.'

'Morale seems to be pretty good,' replied Hanzel. He looked at several men engaged in sharpening their swords.

'Yes, but Hanzel, remember, we're pirates. Even though we look like rich patricians. Like, somewhat eccentric, merchants, we are still pirates under these fancy clothes,' continued Melchior. 'I really want to take a chance. I'm curious what's on board that ship. She sure is deep in the water and moving slowly considering how many sails it has out.'

Hanzel regarded Hanna, who was standing nearby, looking at the Spanish ship. 'What do you think, Hanna. Should we try and go after her?'

Hanna looked at Hanzel and then back at the ship they were slowly approaching. 'If she is laden with gold, that would surely make life even more wonderful in Amsterdam, Hanzel. We could use a little extra gold. You never know. It could be worth it. She does not appear too heavily armed, if at all. From what I can see through this glass.'

Hanzel smiled. *That's my Hanna. Always ready for adventure.* Hanzel locked eyes with his wife. He knew she wanted him to make a decision. It was not to be on the side of caution. 'Alright,' he said. 'Let's sail closer and see who is on board.'

Melchior clapped his hands together. 'Alright boys and girls, let's go find out what's on board that Spaniard! Are you ready to pirate?!'

A great cheer filled the ship as everyone enthusiastically waved their weapon of choice in the air.

'Alright,' said Hanzel. 'Run up our battle flag, Mister Padrone, if you please.'

'Run up the colours!' shouted Mister Padrone to two pirates standing ready to perform the running of the colours at the mast head. A moment later, Hanzel's red and black battle flag unfurled in the breeze a red skull on a black ground and a black skull on a red ground.

'Sound the trumpets!' bellowed Mister Padrone to the musicians assembled on the fore deck. Immediately two bagpipes, three coronets, a hunting horn, and three drums began to create a cacophony which would have scared the bejeebies out of the Devil himself.

'I think they're on to us,' remarked Justin, as he gazed through his looking glass. 'They're running out more sail.'

Hanzel grinned as he looked through his glass. 'Even with all of his sails out, there's no way he'll out run us. What do you say, Mister Padrone?'

The old master looked up at the mainsail. 'Wind's good. Sails are full. I expect we'll overtake her in two hours, or less, with our present plan.'

Hanzel nodded. 'Very good. That'll give everybody plenty of time to prepare.' He stepped over to his wife and put his right arm around her waist. 'Well, Hanna, my darling. You are going to enjoy this. Are your pistols ready?'

'Armed and ready, my dear.' Hanna patted the ivory handles of her custom made flintlock pistols hanging from the blue bandoleer she preferred, it being the most comfortable of the three she had. It was also her finest, with a filigreed silver buckle.

'You look ready,' replied Hanzel, smiling. 'Are you sure you want to go ahead with this?'

'I'm curious what's on board that ship. Who knows, it could be something we can use. Perhaps some more chickens, even. Some we can roast. I relish a nice roasted chicken for supper.' Hanna grinned.

'Hmm. Roasted chicken. That does sound inviting.' Hanzel gazed at the ship they were chasing. 'Let's hope there are some chickens on board. We'll go on a chicken raid.' Hanzel looked at his officers standing on the quarterdeck. 'What do you say, boys? Shall we go on a chicken raid?'

'Aye, captain! Roasted chickens here we come!' they shouted back. A moment later everyone was laughing as they chanted, 'Roasted chickens here we come!' over and over, as they stamped their feet, making the boards rattle.

Ninety minutes later Hanzel ordered a chase gun to shoot a five pound ball ahead of the Spaniard's starboard bow. The ball splashed thirty yards ahead of the ship. However, it was to no avail. The Spanish ship did not slow down.

'There are only seven on deck, from what I can see,' said Hanzel.

'I counted ten, a moment ago,' replied Hanna. Then she pointed. 'It seems like they're dragging something behind the ship.'

Hanzel stared through his looking glass. 'I think it's just an odd wake. That boat is a tub. It doesn't slide through the water like this fine sloop.' He looked at Melchior. 'What do you think, does the ship have an odd wake, or is it dragging something?'

Melchior stared into his glass, then shook his head. 'I think it's just an odd wake. By the looks of that ship, it isn't in the best of condition. It's a wonder they would risk sailing that pile of rotten timber.'

'Well, let's hope this is going to be worth it. I pray nobody gets hurt. This is supposed to be a pleasure cruise to Amsterdam,' replied Hanzel.

'At any rate, there are not so many on board, it seems. Why would they take a chance and keep running. Surely they can see that we can out sail her and we outnumber her.' Melchior looked at Hanzel.

'Put a ball into her transom, Mister Monk, if you please,' said Hanzel calmly.

'Aye, aye, Captain,' replied the gunner, happily signaling to his mates.

A loud boom filled the space between the two ships, now only three hundred and fifty yards apart. A moment later a loud crack heralded the arrival of the ball into the Spaniard's great cabin, where it nearly decapitated the captain, who was discussing their options with his first mate. The sudden appearance of a five pound ball in the splintered bulkhead of his cabin stirred him to action. 'Release the hogsheads and inform Captain Battaro to get ready. Those Dutch pirates will be boarding us within the half hour, I suspect. Tell the sailing master to luff the sails and the helm crew to heave to. We are going to teach these pirates a lesson they'll never forget.'

'How do you know they're Dutch pirates, sir?' asked the Spanish first mate.

'Their battle flag.' He pointed out of the window at the fast approaching sloop. 'That is the battle flag of the infamous, Hanzel Sventska. He's a prize worth having.' Captain Giez rubbed his hands together. He stared narrow eyed at the floor as he thought of ways to humiliate the Dutchman and see him tortured and hanged. 'When I bring him before the king, I will surely be awarded a nobility. Perhaps count, or baron.' He looked up at his first mate with a regal expression, as if he saw himself already knighted.

'Hanzel,' said Hanna, pointing towards the Spaniard's transom. 'Take a look at those ropes. I think they *are* dragging something behind their ship. Why else would those ropes be there?'

Hanzel stared through his looking glass. When he put it down he nodded. 'They are dragging something. I think they're up to something. It is as I suspected. A ruse. They are deliberately slowing themselves down, making it look like they are loaded down. What do you think, Melchior.'

'I think you're right, Hanzel. I think we're being set up,' replied the first mate, staring through his looking glass.

'Hard to starboard!' shouted Hanzel. 'Run out the port guns, Mister Monk, if you please!

On board the Spanish ship, a sailor approached the sailing master and informed him as to the captain's wishes. Then he picked up a boarding axe and began hacking away at the ropes holding the twelve water filled hogsheads dragging behind the ship. As he was thusly proceeding to cut the ropes, marines stormed on board and began shooting at the sloop veering away to starboard. As Hanna watched through her glass, to her horror she saw that the Spanish ship's side was camouflaged and ten heavy guns were rolled out. A moment later their terrific thunder heralded the near instant arrival of Spanish iron balls which sliced and diced their diabolical paths through sheets, shrouds, railings, and the forward hatch of the unfortunate sloop. Alas, Herman was climbing one of the shrouds when the balls arrived. There was not much left of him but bits and pieces of bleeding flesh and quivering organs, some of which splattered on deck.

Hanna, seeing what happened to Herman, instantly retched the contents of her stomach over the starboard railing just as Mister Monk's gunners fired the sloop's seven eighteen pounders, the balls crashing into the Spaniard's quarterdeck and great cabin. From the screams which followed, Hanzel was confident they had disabled some Spaniards, at least.

As the sloop veered away to starboard, Hanzel ordered her to fall back and to fire into the Spaniard's transom with the swivel guns mounted on the fore deck railings. The five pounders were more for harassment sake, doing not much damage but breaking windows and smashing up the cabins behind them.

The Spanish marines kept up a withering fire, which made life on the sloop's deck a serious hazard. Hanzel ordered that the sloop fall back, to get out of range of the marine's guns. Alas, just before they fell back enough, a ball, with not much velocity left, neatly took out Mister Padrone's left eyeball; the ball lodging in the socket, but not punching through the bone into his brain. The remnants of his eyeball oozed onto his coat. Seeing that, Hanna went below to see how the children were faring. Her stomach felt ready to jump out of her throat.

'Ease the sails, if you please Jeston, and someone take Mister Padrone to see Doctor Allan,' ordered Hanzel.

'Aye, Captain,' replied Bart, one of the sailors standing nearby. He carefully took a hold of Mister Padrone's arm and guided him off the quarterdeck to the midship hatch.

'I want to come up behind her and see if we can disable her rudder. Even though she is now much lighter and we have seen what she is, let's teach them a lesson they won't soon forget. What say you?' Hanzel looked at Jeston

'I'm with you, Captain,' replied Jeston as he set about organizing the bombardment.

'Get those chase guns ready, lads!' he shouted to the forward gunners manning the five pound swivel guns on the fore deck, on either side of the bowsprit.

'We've got to lie close to the deck. Some of those marines are pretty good shots,' cautioned Melchior.

'Our five pounders have a longer range than their muskets. We'll stay out of range of their guns and just keep shooting at their rudder.' Hanzel smiled. 'I knew there was something not right about that ship. Now we've lost a good friend and we have a damaged ship. I sure hope it's worth it. And then there are all of those Spanish marines to deal with. Maybe we should just get out of here and leave them be. We can still out sail them, and make repairs at sea. We're not that badly shot up. What do you think, Melchior?'

'We have lost Herman and Mister Padrone's eye. And they have all of those marines. If we go after them we are going to lose more people. That ship looked heavy because of those hogsheads they had dragging in the water. That ship isn't carrying gold or anything of value, it was a lure, like you said. They have more guns than we have.' Melchior regarded Hanzel and then looked at his brother.

'We can out shoot them. Even if they have a few more guns than we have. We are lower in the water and can hit their water line. They mostly shoot over us.' Jeston regarded the Spanish ship, now about five hundred yards off their port bow. 'Maybe we can sneak up on them in the night? What do you think of that idea?'

'If they have their lamps on,' replied Melchior.

Jeston regarded the sky. 'There's a moon tonight. Winds are likely calming. We might just have the circumstances we need. If the wind quits, we'll row over to them with our boats, quiet as,' Jeston scratched his chin. 'Quiet as… goose feathers.'

Melchior looked at Hanzel and then at his brother. Both of them immediately burst out laughing. Pontelo, who had joined them on the quarterdeck also burst out laughing.

'Quiet as goose feathers, that's a way to describe pirates about their work?' sputtered Melchior, immediately bursting into a whole new round of laughter with his friends.

Eventually, when their laughter subsided, Hanzel shook his head. 'Boys, take a look at our boat. We have holes in sheets and shrouds. The fore hatch is shot to pieces. Herman is dead. Mister Padrone lost an eye. I think we should just forget it. There are women and children on board. Let's just go to Amsterdam and take a vacation. We'll go after the Spaniard another time, when the pickings are easier. I don't really want to do battle with that ship. Especially not now that she is revealed for what she is.'

Melchior nodded his head. 'I agree with Hanzel. What do you think, Pontelo?'

'I think we could have a whole lot more casualties if we go after that ship. It would be foolishness. They have stern guns, likely twelve pounders, to our five.' Pontelo shook his head. 'I say we sail away from here and reset our course for Holland.'

Hanzel nodded and ordered a change of course, north east by east, hastily sailing away from that sneaky, dangerous Spaniard.

Later that night, in their cabin, just Hanzel, Hanna, and little Hanzel sleeping contentedly in his little bunk, Hanzel discussed the day's events with his wife. They both agreed it was the right decision to retreat.

'Just because we declared battle with our flag and then ran away, to fight another day, that's not dishonorable. That's wise. Who knows, a ball might have smashed through our cabin and hit little Hanzel in his bunk. I don't want to pirate a war ship.' Hanna sat back in the plush pillows of their bed.

'I'm glad we decided to leave them be. Doesn't bother me. We've learned a lesson. Never trust a Spaniard.' Hanzel regarded his beautiful wife. 'What if the ball had found you, my dear Hanna. If I lost you, I don't know what I'd do.'

Hanna smiled. 'Oh, you'd probably go find another girl in the next port.'

Hanzel laughed. 'There wouldn't be a port in the world where I would find another you, my love.'

Hanna nodded. 'Sure, sure. You're just saying that because you want sex. I know you, Hanzel.'

Hanzel regarded his wife with a totally innocent look. 'No, really. You're one of a kind, Hanna.

'Oh, so you don't want to make love to me?' Hanna crossed her arms over her chest.

'No, er, yes, of course I do. I'm just saying, if I lost you, I would likely be lonely the rest of my life.' Hanzel lay down beside Hanna and smiled into her eyes.

'Well, let's pray that we'll always be together, because I feel the same way about you Hanzel. If I lost you, I would be lost. I'd probably have to enter a convent.' Hanna, keeping a straight face watched Hanzel's face for a reaction.

'Enter a convent?! Why on earth would you do that? I wouldn't join a monastery, if I lost you. A convent? Isn't that a bit extreme? And you're not even a Catholic.' Hanzel regarded Hanna, wondering if she was being serious.

'Yes, I'd have to become a nun. No more sex with any man. Just me with mother superior and my sisters. All covered up in black and white. Tending our gardens and ministering to the poor. Occasionally we beat our selves with scourges.'

'That's a bit extreme don't you think? I mean, surely you can find another man who would be every bit as good to you, if not better,' replied Hanzel.

Hanna pulled Hanzel into her arms. 'No Hanzel, there is only you in my world.' Then she kissed him for a long time.

A loud boom broke them from their reverie. An instant later a twelve pound iron ball crashed through a window of their cabin and smashed through the door into the bulkhead at the end of the companionway. A piece of glass found Hanna's left cheek, blood stained her pillow. Little Hanzel woke up with a start, then turned over and went right back to sleep. Hanzel and Hanna quickly jumped out of bed and scooping up their little boy, they rushed out of the cabin just as another loud boom preceded an iron ball smashing through another window of their cabin. It splintered the table and a chair, coming to rest in the door post, splinters following Hanzel and his family, fleeing down the gangway. A large chunk of wood caught Hanna and sliced deep into her left calf. She stumbled into Hanzel, who did not see immediately why. He instinctively grabbed her by the waist and pulled her into Melchior's cabin. As he let her go she stumbled to a chair and as she sat down, little Hanzel remarked, 'What's wrong with your leg, Mama?'

Red blood stained her breeches, where a long, three inch thick splinter stuck out.

'DOCTOR ALLAN!' shouted Hanzel as he rushed from the cabin. He shouted up through the afterdeck hatch. 'DOCTOR ALLAN! COME BELOW! HANNA'S BEEN HIT!'

Another loud boom rent the air. A moment later a ball whizzed through the mainsail.

'MAN THE AFTER GUNS!' shouted Melchior from the quarterdeck, just as Hanzel stepped on deck. Sailors were already running out the guns, but in the darkness it was difficult to see the ship which was firing at them from behind.

'DOUSE THE LANTERN!' Hanzel looked at Melchior with a puzzled expression.

'It's the Spaniard, I think. Now that he is no longer dragging those water filled hogsheads, that ship, we thought was a tub, can actually catch wind and sail with some momentum,' suggested Melchior.

'Well, one of his shots splintered wood and caught Hanna. Where is Doctor Allan?'

Hanzel regarded his first mate, a look of desperation in his eyes.

'He's below, getting ready,' answered Melchior. No sooner did the words leave his lips than Hanzel ran off to find the surgeon.

The sloop's three rear guns roared, answered a moment later by two twelve pound balls, one landing twelve yards to starboard and the other right into the back of Pieter Spierenburg, a young sailor who had joined the colony after Hanzel had plundered his ship two years ago. The cold steel broke the man in half, sending one piece into the sea and the other half continued with the ball and mashed into the remains of the forward hatch.

'Hard to port!' shouted Melchior to the helmsman. 'We have to outmaneuver them. PUT OUT MORE SAIL! he yelled to Mister Padrone's two mates, who passed the order down the line.

'Now that the lamp is extinguished, he won't have such an easy target,' suggested Jestin.

'How did he catch up to us with nobody seeing him?' asked Melchior.

'We weren't looking behind us. Nobody suspected the Spaniard would come after us.' Jestin looked back at the barely discernible ship following a mere six hundred yards behind.

Meanwhile, below deck, Hanzel found Doctor Allan getting the surgery ready. 'Come quickly, Doctor Allan. Hanna. It's Hanna. She's been hit in the leg with a big splinter.' Hanzel was frantic.

More cannon shots rattled hardware and shivered timbers as Doctor Allan followed Hanzel to Melchior's cabin, where Hanna lay moaning with excruciating pain. The moment the surgeon examined the wound, his face turned pale. He looked at Hanzel and then at Hanna. From the look in his eyes, Hanna feared the worst. 'Can you save my leg?' she asked, hoping and praying he would say yes. Doctor Allan looked at Hanzel and back at Hanna, who began to cry, which upset little Hanzel, who also began to cry as he hugged his mother.

Doctor Allan shook his head sadly. 'I will do the best I can. You'll have to bring her to the surgery,' he said to Hanzel. Then he left the room and walked back to where the grizzly business was to be attended to.

Meanwhile, Melchior ordered evasive maneuvers, causing the sloop to bump and grind her way through the waves, this way and that; movements not favorable for delicate surgeries.

'Do you have anything for her pain?' asked Hanzel, looking about the surgery for something, anything to dull the pain, causing Hanna's face to contort.

'Laudanum. You'll find a bottle of it on the middle shelf of that cabinet.' Doctor Allan pointed to the medicine cabinet built into the wall beside his desk.

Hanzel rushed to the cabinet and found the bottle. He uncorked it and instantly reacted to the smell which emanated from the vessel. He handed the bottle to Doctor Allan, who proceeded to pour some of the liquid into a glass of water. He stirred the drink with a spoon and helped Hanna to drink the milky drink. Droplets of sweat covered Hanna's face. A look of fear filled her eyes. Hanzel held her head in his lap and stroked her hair.

'How long for this laudanum to work?' asked Hanzel, all the while not taking his eyes from hers. *I pray you'll be alright, my love. Please God, help her. Please don't take her leg.*

Agonizing moments later, Hanna passed out. The laudanum had done its work.

'Can you save her leg?' asked Hanzel, sweat dripping from his brow.

The ship lurched to starboard. Doctor Allan fell backwards, hitting his head on the medicine cabinet. He fell down just as a loud roar, like thunder in a barrel, reverberated the boards as Mister Monk and his crew unleashed seven cannons directly into the bows of the oncoming Spaniard, splintering the bowsprit. Then the sloop veered hard to port, as Melchior effected another evasive maneuver. As soon as he could, Hanzel stepped over to Doctor Allan to see if he was alright. The man was unconscious, but breathing. Hanzel looked frantically at his wife and back at the surgeon. *Maybe if I throw some water in his face.* Hanzel poured water from a small keg into a cup which he emptied on the surgeon's face, but it was to no effect. The man was out. *Now what do I do? Poor Hanna.* He watched for a moment as Funk came to sit beside the unconscious man's head and began gently patting Doctor Allan's cheek.

Seeing that there was nothing he could do for the surgeon or for Hanna, at the moment, he rushed up on deck to see what was going on. Just as he stepped from the hatchway, a ball of merciless Spanish iron came roaring by, missing him by two feet, but taking the starboard corner off the hatch and neatly removing Marvin's leg; he being the hapless pirate who happened to be standing in the wrong place at that time. Marvin's scream was immediately followed by two more as the terrible ball continued on its destructive path.

'We've got to outrun her!' shouted Hanzel to Melchior, who was standing on the quarterdeck beside Victor Demochuck, the Ukrainian helmsman from Kiev.

'I've been trying,' replied Melchior. 'It seems that old tub is actually not a tub at all, but a pretty fast ship, now that he's thrown off all of his camouflage.' The first mate looked up at the sky. 'It'll be completely dark soon. He'll be shooting at shadows. Hopefully this breeze keeps up and we can sneak away in the darkness.' Melchior regarded his friend, 'What's wrong with Hanna?'

'Caught a huge sliver in her leg. Doctor Allan is unconscious. Hit his head when the ship lurched. I think he'll be alright. We gave her laudanum. She is sleeping, but we've got to get that sliver out of her leg.' Hanzel regarded Melchior, a pleading, helpless look in his eyes. 'Is there anyone else on board who can perform surgeries?'

'Martyn. The cook has had some experience, I think. He's good with a knife, that's for sure. What do you think, Jestin? Can Martyn do it?' Melchior looked at his brother, who was watching the Spanish ship through his looking glass.

'Do what?'

'Perform surgeries. Such as taking a sliver out of Hanna's leg,' replied Melchior.

Jestin thought for a moment and then nodded his head. 'Ask Martyn. He's helped Doctor Allan before. Remember when that Jamaican fellow was impaled on that spear, Martyn helped Doctor Allan take the spear out.'

Hanzel nodded. 'Yes, I remember. Didn't the man die a few days later?'

'Well, yes. But he had lost a lot of blood and the spear pierced his liver,' replied Jestin. 'That was not Martyn or Doctor Allan's fault.'

'Alright, I'll find Martyn.' Hanzel looked up at the mainsail. 'Can we put out more sail?'

'It's all we've got,' answered Melchior, just as a loud boom signaled another ball headed in their direction. The projectile splashed harmlessly in the sea, thirty yards behind the sloop. In the encroaching darkness, all anyone could see anymore of the Spanish ship was the flash of cannon fire. Only twice more did anyone see such flashes, the balls landing with loud splashes in the water behind the sloop. Then silence prevailed, except for the creak of wood and ropes and the flap of sails and murmurs of men, wondering if they will come out of this alive.

When Martyn arrived in the surgery, Doctor Allan was sitting up and rubbing the back of his head. He was totally disoriented. Hanna was moaning softly on the bed, a puddle of blood soaking the sheet and floor. Cold sweat covered her contorted face. In spite of the laudanum, she was in a lot of pain. Hanzel was frantically looking on as Martyn assessed the situation. 'It looks pretty serious,' he said, not looking up from his examination. 'What do you think, Doctor Allan?'

The surgeon looked cross eyed at the wound. 'We won't know anything until we remove the sliver. Then we'll know.' He regarded Hanzel, whose face was white as snow.

'Oh, please. Please save her leg, Doctor.' Hanzel knowing there was nothing he could do, except be in the way, he left the surgery and stepped back on deck, drawing in deep lung fulls of air to clear his head. The wind had died, leaving the ship becalmed. *All the better the ship isn't moving, for Hanna's sake. I'd better go check up on little Hanzel. I'm sure he's sleeping through everything.* Hanzel headed down the rear hatchway and soon entered Melchior's cabin, where they had left little Hanzel, before taking Hanna to the surgery. Tina, Melchior's wife was sitting in the cabin, fearfully looking out of a window. 'He hasn't stirred,' she said to Hanzel, trying to be calm. 'I'm sure he's alright.' Hanzel nodded and left the cabin, returning on deck a moment later.

'Now that we're becalmed, do you suppose those sneaky Spaniards might try and row a boat over here in the middle of the night?' Hanzel regarded Melchior.

'We'll post a double watch,' replied the first mate. 'I wouldn't put it past them.'

'Maybe we should row a boat over to them with enough explosives to blow them to kingdom come,' suggested Jestin.

'They'll have sentries posted. No way anyone is sneaking up on anybody,' replied Melchior.

'Well, then, perhaps it's time for some of you to get some sleep. I think we're going to need our energies come morning, I have a feeling,' said Hanzel.

'I think you're right,' agreed Melchior. 'We'd better be ready.'

'See to the watch. Make sure there are always enough men on deck to repulse an attack, should one take place. I'm going back to the surgery.' Hanzel returned to the hatchway and quickly climbed down the ladder. Just before he entered the infirmary, Hanna screamed. Hanzel nearly fainted. *Oh, my dear Hanna.* When he stepped into the room, Martyn had just extracted the splinter from Hanna's calf muscle. Upon examining the wound, he discovered more fragments which had to be removed. As he groped about in the tissue he discovered that her tibia was broken and the fibula shattered into a number of pieces, none of which could be put together again.

'We are going to have to amputate her leg. There is nothing we can do. Do you agree, Doctor Allan?' Martyn regarded the good doctor, who had returned to his senses. Doctor Allan rubbed the back of his head and nodded, then he looked sadly at Hanzel, whose eyes were filling with tears. He kneeled down by her head and looked at her closed eyes, dreaming the deep sleep of opium. *My dear Hanna. How I wish I could save you. Why did this have to happen to you, one so undeserving. Don't worry, my darling. I will love you just the same.*

'We're going to have to proceed quickly, Hanzel. In this humid climate, the heat will bring on gangrene very soon. We have no choice. She will lose her leg below the knee. With a proper prosthesis, she'll be able to walk,' said Doctor Allan reassuringly. 'With a cane, of course.'

Hanzel nodded sadly. 'Yes, of course. With a cane.' *My poor, dear Hanna.*

Then, without further hesitation, while Hanzel stroked her hair and helped to keep her calm, Doctor Allan and Martyn the cook sawed off the damaged half of Hanna's leg, five inches below her left knee. Even though she was under the blanket of laudanum, her body convulsed and stirred as the teeth of the saw sliced through her bones. Hanzel struggled to contain the contents of his stomach.

When the operation was completed and her stump sewn up, they bandaged her with clean linen soaked in alcohol and then bandaged the whole thing up with lots of soft material to lessen the pain for Hanna as much as possible. Then they carefully carried her back to the captain's cabin and laid her gently into the bed she shared with Hanzel. Everyone but Hanzel and Hanna left the cabin. Hanzel's tears stained his cheeks. *My dear Hanna. Why did this have to happen to you? Why did you let his happen? You should never have agreed to go after that damn Spaniard in the first place. I had such a bad feeling about it, right from the beginning.* Hanzel sunk his face into his hands and shed a flood of tears. *My dear, dear Hanna. What I would not give to change this. I'd give my soul to the Devil, even, if that would bring back your leg. Oh, my darling girl. What a terrible pain you are about to face.*

Chapter 40

KABOOM!!!

A moment later, a loud splash, forty yards from the sloop's transom let everyone on board know that it was morning and the Spaniards were awake. They were already attempting to maneuver their ship in order to effect a broadside. Fortunately there still was no wind. Everyone's sails were hanging slack in the yards.

Down below, in Hanzel and Hanna's cabin, Hanzel managed to make Hanna drink more laudanum, so that she was able to continue her sleep, while he dealt with matters topside. Hanna was still not aware of the fact, half of her left leg was missing. Hanzel dreaded the moment when she would learn of her injury.

'It looks like the Spaniard is still trying to get at us, even though we're out of range,' said Melchior to Hanzel, as he stepped onto the quarterdeck.

Hanzel looked up at the luffed sails. 'We have to keep an eye on them. Don't take our eyes off them, not even for a second. And pray for wind. Pray we catch the wind before they do. We have to out sail them.'

'That we can do,' said Mister Padrone. His empty socket was covered with a black patch, the sail maker, Jock McMullen had made for him. 'We'll out sail them. But the question is, how do we do it without wind?'

'Why don't we lower the boats and lets tow her further out of range? I don't like the fact I can see people moving about on that ship. They're much too close for my liking. And, who knows, if we tow our ship, we might meet a wind,' suggested Johan.

'That's not a bad idea. Do we do it in broad daylight? Or should we wait until nightfall?' asked Hanzel.

'If we do it, we should do it now. The sooner we're further out of range of their guns, the better I will feel,' suggested Jestin.

Hanzel nodded. 'Alright, lower the boats. Let's row ourselves out of this predicament.'

'Aye, Captain,' replied Melchior, who immediately set about organizing the towing project. An hour later, their three row boats, each manned by eight rowers and a bosun began pulling the sloop away from the Spaniard. Hanzel could see that the Spaniards were obviously perturbed because a flurry of activity began to take place, as marines started climbing the shrouds with their muskets over their shoulders. Soon they began shooting, but it was a waste of time and lead. They tried shooting their cannons, but only their chase guns were pointed in the right direction, and their range was compromised, now, further so.

The men pulled hard on their oars and after two hours of steady work, they had pulled the sloop a league further away from the Spaniard, but still there was no wind. Not even a whisper. They were becalmed, but so were the Spaniards. The question asked on both ships was, *"What now?"*

Later that morning, Hanna realized what had happened to her when the laudanum wore off. The pain was unbearable. She could not help but scream with pain and sorrow. Hanzel rushed immediately to her side. Little Hanzel was crying, he being scared and confused. Hanzel scooped him up and sat him on his lap as he lowered himself to a chair beside the bed. 'Oh, my dear Hanna. What can I say to you?'

'My leg, Hanzel. You let them cut off my leg.' Hanna stared with tear stained eyes at her husband, whose eyes were also filled with tears.

'There was no choice,' he croaked.

'There was no choice? What do you mean, there was no choice?'

'The bones of your leg were so badly broken up, there was no way they would ever set properly. Doctor Allan and Martyn and I concurred. There was no way to save your leg, Hanna. They had to do it.' Hanzel looked into Hanna's eyes and tried to help her understand. He spent a long time just looking into her eyes, neither one of them saying anything.

Three days later a wind blew up from the south east. Mister Padrone's mate, Sylvester Swackenburg was the first to notice it. When he notified Mister Padrone, full use of the saving breeze was made with every sail they had. The boats were hauled in and within a half an hour they were well on their way.

It was just before sun up. Before the Spaniard got under sail, the sloop was already another league and a half closer to her destination; Amsterdam.

As the day passed into the next, the Spaniard gave up the chase and headed back to the Caribbean, where there were other pirates to pick on. Hanzel let out a sigh of relief as he watched the sneaky Spaniard sail away. 'I'm not sorry to see him go,' he said to Melchior standing beside the helmsman.

'I'm glad not more harm came of it. We lost two good men, Hanna lost a leg, and Mister Padrone lost an eye. Plus all of the damage to our ship, it was not a good encounter.' Melchior sighed. 'How is Hanna faring?'

'She's starting to get used to the idea of losing a leg. Of course she's in a lot of pain. It could have been worse, is how she is thinking now. She could have been killed.' Hanzel looked off to sea. 'I don't know what I would have done if she'd been killed.'

'I know what you mean. It's how I feel about Tina, most of the time.' Melchior laughed. 'Sometimes she drives me crazy.'

Hanzel smiled and nodded his head sadly. He was thinking of Hanna, and how her life had changed so suddenly.

By the time they reached Amsterdam, Hanna's stump was healing very well. It had been a month and a half since the accident. Her bandages were no longer bloody. She was beginning to look forward to having a wooden leg fashioned for her. Hanna was at peace over the loss of her leg. 'It could have been worse,' she told people when they asked about how she was doing, and so forth.

Sailing into Amsterdam took some doing, since the harbour was very busy with all manner of shipping. Huge Dutch east and west Indiamen were off loading expensive cargoes along wharves, piers, and from their anchorages, as were the ships of a number of other trading nations, surprisingly, a Chinese junk with seven masts. Hanzel had ordered that enough lookouts were stationed around the ship to keep them from bumping into anything; a rowboat, perhaps, with a woman and a man selling their meagre wares; some cabbages, carrots, and cucumbers, or perhaps some leeks, onions, and potatoes. They were everywhere, small rowboats with two people going about selling their goods to sailors who were stuck on board ships.

'We'll stock up on some fresh produce, right liketty split,' said Martyn. He was leaning over the port railing and watching the busy vegetable commerce.

'That will be nice. Fresh vegetables. Can't wait. Hopefully there'll be fruit, as well. I fancy a nice crisp apple, or a juicy orange from Spain.' Mister Padrone adjusted his eye patch. 'But the first thing I'm going to do when I step into Amsterdam is get me one of those glass eyes. That way I don't have to keep wearing this patch over my eye. Makes me look like a pirate.'

Martyn regarded the old sailing master. 'But you are a pirate.'

'Well, that may be so. But, I don't have to let everyone else know that. Pirates depend on a certain amount of subterfuge. We are respectable gentlemen, purveyors of the sweet trade. There is nothing dishonorable in what we do. Kings do it too. Banks do it. The merchants who own those huge merchantmen do it. The whole world is built on piracy of one kind or another. I'm happy to be a pirate. But I prefer to look like a gentleman. Hence, I need to find a purveyor of glass eyeballs.'

Martyn frowned. 'Hopefully it stays in its socket. I wouldn't be wanting to see your glass eyeball fall into your bowl of soup or something like that. When the ship heaves, in a storm, or someone bumps you from behind, like. What if the thing fell out on deck and someone stepped on it? Could be a serious accident.'

Mister Padrone regarded his young friend. 'Don't worry. The eye won't fall out. I'll buy a good one.'

Martyn smiled. 'Do you want some company, to go looking for your eyeball?'

Mister Padrone nodded. 'Sure, that would be fine.'

'Maybe Doctor Allan will come with you,' suggested Martyn.

Mister Padrone looked surprised. 'I thought you meant, you. I thought you would come along.'

Martyn shook his head. 'No. No, I can't go. I've got to supervise purchasing some victuals for those who are staying on board, while in port.'

'Oh. Well, that's alright. I can go on my own. I'm sure I'll find an oculist in this huge place.'

'Good luck,' said Martyn, giving Mister Padron a pat on his right shoulder, before proceeding to hail a victual vendor.

Meanwhile on the quarterdeck, Hanzel was directing Melchior to chose an anchorage beside a gargantuan merchantman belonging to the Dutch

East India Trading Company. Their flags and banners were all over the yards. Judging from what was flying in those yards, the ship had seen seven journeys to the far east already. Most ships did not last past five; the worm, or storms usually the cause for their early demise. Or pirates.

'Someday we'll take one of those when it's on its way back from Sumatra or some other exotic place in the East Indies. It looks like that one is well armed. How many gun ports do you count?'

'Sixteen. And judging from the size of the ports, they're likely big guns. At least twenty pounders or more,' suggested Melchior.

'Sixteen per side. Thirty two cannons and swivel guns on the railings. We'd have to come in with more than one ship. Taking one of those monsters would take some serious planning. The corporation does not let go of its stuff too easily.' Hanzel stroked his chin as he looked up at the massive ship they were anchoring beside.

When the anchors were secure, Hanzel, carrying Hanna, stepped from their cabin, followed by little Hanzel. With great care, Hanna was gently lowered into the long boat and made comfortable with pillows. Moments later Hanzel, stepped into the boat and sat beside his son, facing his beautiful wife. The family was dressed in their very finest clothes; silks and brocades, soft leathers, silver, gold, and glowing jewels.

'A finer example of high class pirates can not be found in all of Amsterdam, or anywhere else on the globe, I reckon,' said Jestin to his brother as they watched Hanzel and his family being rowed ashore, along with Mister Padrone, Doctor Allan, and Pontelo and his wife Elizabeth.

On shore, Hanzel hired an open carriage, seeing as how the day was warm and sunny. He gently lifted Hanna into the conveyance and then hoisted little Hanzel up on the step so that he could climb into the carriage by himself. When he had settled into the comfortable leather seat, he asked the driver where merchants of fine clothing were located.

The driver thought for a moment, then he snapped his thumb and middle finger. 'I know where,' he said. He slapped the horse with the reins, and off they went, in search of Michael and Maria.

'When Michael and Maria first began talking about leaving the colony to return here, they mentioned what they would call their shop. Do you remember that?' asked Hanzel.

Hanna thought for a moment and shook her head. 'That's over four years ago. They only mentioned it a few times. It was French, that I remember. And it had the word, *Belle*, I think. I remember hearing, Belle. Belle something.'

'Driver, does a shop's name have the word, Belle, in it. A clothing store that you are aware of?' asked Hanzel.

The driver scratched his head. 'No, can't say I know of a shop with, *Belle* in the name.'

'Maybe we'll just have to ask at a few of the shops. Perhaps someone knows of them,' suggested Hanna. 'Go to where the best shops are. Where the wives of filthy rich merchants and artists buy their clothes.'

'Yes, Madam,' answered the driver.

After some swerving and swaying along the busy streets lining the canals, they eventually ended up on a street where several, very expensive clothing stores were located. The finest satins, the most exquisite velvets, unbelievable brocades, and silks like no silks seen on earth except in the court of the Chinese emperor himself or the Shogun of Japan, were proudly displayed in showcase windows.

'Stop here,' commanded Hanna.

The driver stopped the carriage.

'Hanzel, go into this shop. I have a feeling they might know something.'

Hanzel looked at his pretty wife and then at little Hanzel. He shrugged his shoulders. 'Your mother has a hunch.' Hanzel stepped out of the carriage and up the steps of Wapponzoon van Drenkenstein, Purveyors of Fine Fashions.

'What can we do for you?' sniffed a very pompous young fop, looking down his nose at Hanzel.

Hanzel's immediate impulse was to draw his foil and run the man through, but he resisted the desire and remained civil. 'I'm looking for a fine clothing shop with, *Belle* in its name.'

The fop regarded Hanzel for a long pause, as if he was not sure what to make of this man, dressed in the fashion of five years ago. He sniffed and then shook his head. 'No, I have not heard of anything with, *Belle* in it. Perhaps if you go to the gypsies. They have a market down by the Jordaan. Some of their shops have foreign names.'

Hanzel stared at the man, so wanting to thrash him for his arrogance. However, he kept his calm and thanked the man for his suggestion. Then he turned on his heels and left the shop, fuming. *What an arrogant young fop. I should have smacked him to an inch of his life. How dare he? He has no idea to whom he was speaking. After all, I am Hanzel Sventska, the Scourge of the Seven Seas.* Hanzel mumbled under his breath as he stepped into the coach.

'I take it they didn't know?' asked Hanna.

'I should go back and run him through,' mumbled Hanzel. 'To suggest that Michael and Maria might have a shop amongst the gypsies. How dare he?'

'Calm down, Hanzel. We'll just go to another shop. They can't all be like that.' Hanna smiled and gestured to the driver, to move on to the next emporium.

Jacob Golden & Zoon, Fijne Kleeding Behandelaar was the next stop where Hanzel politely asked a clerk if he knew of a shop with, *Belle* in the name.

'Dat zounds like a French name. Dere iz a French quarter. Maybe itz in dere,' suggested the bespectacled clerk. 'Oderwize I haf no idea. Iz dere somezing else I can help you wid? Perhaps a new vaistcoat. A ruffle perhaps? Ve haf zoots for all occasions.

Ve haf zoots for veddings, funerals, barmitzvahs, vhat you vant? Did I tell you, the artist Johannes Torentius shops here.' The man pointed to a painting on the wall behind a cluttered desk. 'That's one of his still life paintings. It's for sale. For the right price, that is. Who knows, he might become famous someday.'

Hanzel shook his head. 'No, thank you. Not now. I have to find my friends, whose shop I am looking for. I know it has, *Belle* in the name.

'Could be, *La Belle* perhaps. La Belle something,' suggested the clerk, adjusting his skull cap.

Hanzel snapped his fingers. 'Yes, yes, that's it. La Belle, something. That gives me more to work with. Thank you. Yes, indeed, La Belle something or other. I'm sure we'll find them.' Hanzel walked out of the store and happily stepped up into the carriage. 'It's, *La Belle* something. The clerk in there helped me remember. Now, if only we can remember the rest of it.'

Hanna stared at Hanzel, trying to remember. She kept repeating, *La Belle* in her head. 'Let's move on to another shop.' She gestured to the driver. A moment later they were parked in front of, Cooper, Pali & Hofstader, Haberdashers.

'This place looks very posh, don't you think, Hanzel.' Then she leaned over and asked little Hanzel, 'What do you think? Doesn't this place look posh?'

Little Hanzel nodded his head but really had no idea what he was agreeing to and could care less. He was more interested in the dog defecating on the sidewalk.

'I'll be right back.' Hanzel stepped out of the carriage and carefully circumvented the dog turd. He ran up the steps and walked first into an odour; that of copious rolls of old and precious cloth, and then into a sensory overload, as he took in the actual place; a huge room filled with thousands of rolls of cloth of every description imaginable. Mannequins stood here and there, draped in cloth in various stages of assembly into garments for wealthy people. Ten talking tailors told each other tales in Italian, as they worked on clothes fit for kings.

'Are you here for a fitting?' asked a tall, thin clerk.

Hanzel shook his head. 'No, I am here to find out if you have heard of a clothing store with the name of, *La Belle* something.'

'La Belle Something? Have I heard of, La Belle Something?' The clerk shook his head. 'No, I can't say I've heard of that store.'

'No, no. It is just, *La Belle,* and then there is something else, which I can't remember,' replied Hanzel, a hint of frustration in his voice.

'Oh, I see. You expect me to be a directory service to help you find our competitor?' The clerk snorted and turned away.

Hanzel left the shop; a wish list starting to accrue in his mind of prematurely demised haberdashery clerks.

And so it went, all day. Every fancy clothing store Hanzel visited, he became no wiser as to the whereabouts of his friends. However, he did become wiser to the ways of shop keepers for the rich and famous. That night, after a filling meal and several cups of ale, Hanzel and Hanna fell into a deep sleep on their bed in the cabin of their sloop. Little Hanzel was curled up in his bunk. That night Hanna and little Hanzel were at peace, while Hanzel dreamed of things he would do to store clerks.

Next morning greeted Amsterdam with an overcast sky and scudding clouds. Rain was in the wind. It was not a nice day to go looking for Michael and Maria's shop, if there even was one. Hanzel and Hanna had no way of knowing.

'Maybe they're not in Amsterdam,' suggested Hanzel over breakfast. 'For all we know they could be in Leiden, or Amstelveen.'

Hanna shook her head. 'They were adamant they were coming here. This is the place to be. Look at how many expensive clothing stores we stopped at. That was only a portion of them, according to the carriage driver. We'll find them, don't worry. We have to try and remember the entire name of the shop. La Belle, La Belle, ...'

'It's got to be another French word. Maybe something to do with clothing, or fashion, or something like that,' suggested Hanzel. 'What's a French word for fashion?'

'Ask, Jacques LeBlanc, he speaks French. I think he's on board. I was talking with his wife, Natalie, when we returned on board after our tour of Amsterdam yesterday,' replied Hanna.

'Alright, I'll go ask him. He's probably in his quarters.' Hanzel smiled, then bit into a slab of freshly baked bread. 'Hmm, Martyn surely does bake an excellent bread, don't you agree, Hanna, my love?'

Hanna agreed, as she also took a big bite out of a slab of the dark brown bread Martyn had baked in the little oven, in the sloop's galley.

After breakfast Hanzel sought out Jacques LeBlanc, who was, indeed, in his quarters discussing plans for the day with his wife. The word for clothing, or fashion, which he suggested was, *mode*. When he said the word the name instantly came to Hanzel. *La Belle Mode*. 'That's the name. I should have thought to ask you first and saved ourselves a long day being insulted and belittled by clerks in clothing stores. La Belle Mode. That should be easy to find.' Hanzel thanked Jacques and rushed back to tell Hanna.

'It was that easy?' asked Hanna. 'La Belle Mode. That surely rings a bell. Now all we have to do is ask at the City Hall where that business is located. We should have asked Jacques before and saved us a lot of trouble yesterday.'

'Yes, but we wouldn't have seen so much of Amsterdam, my darling.'

'Well, we really didn't see much. Just the rich, hoity toity section,' replied Hanna. 'We could have used the time to find me a leg.'

'We'll go today, my love. We'll go today and find you a leg. Then we'll continue our search for Michael and Maria.'

Hanna nodded. 'Yes, that would be good. I really need to begin walking again. Being carried and so on, is all very fine, however, it crimps my independence.'

'I understand. No problem, really. We'll hire a carriage and go to City Hall and I will ask where there is a purveyor of prosthetic legs and if they know of, La Belle Mode.'

'Try and get the same driver. I liked him. He was patient.' Hanna smiled at her handsome husband. *I'm such a lucky girl to have him in my life.*

Around ten thirty, Hanna was lowered down to the boat and she and Hanzel were rowed ashore, along with seven other ladies and gentlemen from the ship. They left little Hanzel to play with his friends. Going ashore were, Jacques le Blanc and his wife, Natalie, Balthazar, a black pirate who joined the colony when they raided a farming enterprise in Brazil, Gertrude, who called herself, Cleopatra, Jestin, Mister Padrone, who was still looking for an eye, and Kat, also known as Kate the Queen of the Valkyries, a fiery redhead with hair to her waist and big blue eyes, who could out cuss any sailor in any port of the world, including Chinese ones.

As it so happened, the carriage and driver, whom Hanna favored were available for hire. The driver was flattered they sought his services a second time.

'We are looking for a leg,' said Hanzel to the driver, whose name was Gus van der Moolen.

'A leg? You are looking for a leg for your wife? A prosthetic leg?'

'Yes, yes. Do you know a place?' asked Hanzel.

'Best place to find out is to go to City Hall,' suggested Gus.

'That's what we thought. Please take us there,' said Hanna as Hanzel settled himself into the soft, leather seat. Twenty minutes later they were parked outside City Hall. Hanzel quickly mounted the steps and went into the building. He spoke with a clerk who pulled out a large book from a shelf and laid it on the counter. The book's pages were faded to a yellow tint.

'Look in there.' The clerk pointed to the tome. Try looking under, *prosthetics*. The listings are alphabetized. Every legitimate business in Amsterdam is listed there.

Hanzel regarded the book's yellowed pages for a moment and then began his search. Indeed, halfway into the book was a listing for prosthetics.

Doctor Hugo P. van Vliet & Co.

Prosthetics Research and Development

Glass eyes, Lifelike Ears, and Noses, Arms, Hands, Legs.

We don't charge an arm and a leg for our products.

12 Prinze Gracht

Amsterdam

Hanzel memorized the address. *I'll tell Mister Padrone. Maybe there's the eye he's been looking for.* Then he looked for clothing stores and found a long list but no listing for, *La Belle Mode. Now what? How do we find Michael and Maria?*

Hanzel left the building, wondering what other means he could employ to locate his friends. When he climbed into the carriage he directed Gus to take them to 12 Prinze Gracht, which the driver proceeded to do, forthwith. Fifteen minutes later they parked in front of Doctor Hugo P. van Vliet & Co. Hanzel entered the premises and was immediately amazed by the plethora of prosthetics displayed on the walls, on shelves, against cabinets, on cabinets, on desks, tables, and chairs. Shelves of eyeballs glared back at him, blue ones, brown ones, green ones, even a violet one. Noses and ears sat in velvet lined boxes. There were even several hands. Hanzel stood and stared at the life like hands lying in their polished wooden boxes, one of them indicating a lewd gesture with its middle finger.

'It's my partner's way of having fun,' chuckled a short, pudgy man, stepping out from behind a shelf where several dozen prosthetic legs and arms were displayed.

'This is quite a collection of body parts you have here,' said Hanna, admiringly.

'For those unfortunates who lost one in the war,' volunteered the little man. His pince nez dangled precariously on the end of his nose; a nose he constantly wiped with a lace handkerchief he pulled out of the left sleeve of his old, moth eaten coat. The man smelled of glue and varnish. 'Is there something I can help you with?'

'I need a leg,' replied Hanzel.

'No you don't,' replied the man. 'I saw you walk in here.'

'It's not for me. It's for my wife.'

'Oh. I see. Is she with you?'

'Yes. Outside. In our carriage.' Hanzel pointed to the door.

'Well, let's fetch her in, shall we?' The man shouted to several fellows working on eyeballs in the back of the shop. 'Come and give us a hand, will you.'

A moment later two old men, one tall and wiry, the other tall and bulbous, came out of the shop and together with the help of the driver, they carried Hanna into the shop and set her gently down on a chair the short man had set there for her.

Hanzel asked the driver to wait for them outside. The old men returned to their work and the short, pudgy man asked to see Hanna's stump. When she lifted her skirts and revealed what was left of her left leg, Hanzel noted the man's eyebrows raised. The man nodded and gently touched the wound. Hanna flinched.

'Yes, yes, a prothesis will work for you, but it is still much too soon. Your wound will need at least another six months to heal before we can consider a leg for you to stand on. In the meantime, I suggest crutches. You will be able to get around much easier, while your stump heals some more.' The man pointed to a wall were several types of crutches were hanging. He promptly picked a pair purposely built for someone with Hanna's problem. He brought them over to her and with Hanzel's help placed the crutches under her arms and assisted her in learning how to walk with them. It did not take her long to get used to them.

'How much do we owe you for the crutches?' asked Hanzel.

The man named his price and Hanzel gladly paid it. Then he took the man's card and assured him they would be back. 'Oh, and by the way. I'll be sending you our sailing master, Mister Padrone. He is looking for an eye.'

'Eyes we have, as you can see.' The little man gestured towards the shelves containing the assorted eyeballs which stared at Hanzel when he first came into the shop.

'I'll give him your card,' assured Hanzel. Then, bidding the man good day, he and Hanna walked out of the store. He had to steady her going down the steps, and gently lifted her into the carriage.

'So, where to now, guvnor?' asked Gus.

'Did you find out where La Belle Mode is?' asked Hanna.

Hanzel shook his head. 'There is no listing in the directory.'

'Maybe they chose a different name. Maybe you should look under proprietors' names. Look to see if you can find their names. What is Michael's family name?'

Hanzel shrugged his shoulders. 'I've always known him as, Michael. I don't think he ever told me his last name.'

'He didn't, but his friend did. Do you remember, Henk de Loop?' Hanna regarded Hanzel's face.

'Henk de Loop? I vaguely remember him. Didn't he introduce Michael to us? What did he say his name was?'

'Webb. Michael Webb. His family name is Webb. Let's go back to City Hall and see if you can find his name in the registry,' suggested Hanna.

'It's a big book, Hanna. I could be in there for a while.'

'Gus will keep me company. Don't worry. Go see what you can see,' urged Hanna. She signaled Gus to return to City Hall where a half hour later, Hanzel began paging through the directory and found Michael Webb to be the proprietor of a tobacco shop. And it was not far away. Just two streets over. Hanzel and Hanna went there right away. When they arrived at the shop, they were greatly disappointed. Michael and Maria were on a buying trip to Java. The shop was left in the hands of Jarvis Axelrood, who was no help with information as to when they would be back.

'Well, since I can't be fitted for a leg for six months, we might as well remain in Amsterdam. Perhaps they'll be back by the time I get my new leg, or sooner. We'll check back here from time to time, now that we know where their shop is,' suggested Hanna, when Hanzel had returned to the carriage.

So it was decided, they would remain in Amsterdam for as long as was necessary for Hanna's stump to heal well enough for a good prosthesis. Hanzel only wanted the best for his wife.

Over the next few weeks the weather began to turn colder. Autumn had set in and winter was not far away. It was getting harder to keep the sloop heated. Everyone began to spend more time sitting in public houses, sipping on toddies. Gradually, colony members began to drift away; tired of hanging out in Amsterdam and itching to get back to southern seas and sunnier skies.

'Not too many of us left, Hanzel,' remarked Melchior one December evening over a game of cards. 'We don't have enough men and women to man this sloop, should we be going back to sea.'

Hanzel nodded. 'I know. But what's the worry? Come spring, we'll recruit some more.'

'Yes, but we lost some really good people,' added Mister Padrone.

'Some of them will be back. When they realize how much better life is with us, they'll be back.' Hanzel threw an ace of spades on the table.

By the time Christmas arrived, Hanzel, Hanna, and little Hanzel had taken rooms in a hotel some distance from the harbour. The increasing cold and the concentrated smells of so many ships and their effluent had become too much to bear. Tar, excrement, urine, rotting food, dead fish, all of it producing an odiferous presence which eventually drove Hanzel and his family away to get some fresh air.

The hotel was on the outskirts of the city, on the edge of a forest. The air was pure, and fresh. It was the refuge Hanzel and his family needed and the perfect place to stay warm during the cold winter months ahead. Food was excellent. Wine and ale was plentiful. Rum toddies were there when needed, on those particularly cold days, when Hanna's stump ached. On those days Hanzel spent all of his time with her and little Hanzel, sitting by the fire, he reading to both of them; little Hanzel curled up in his mother's lap. They were a happy family.

On warmer days, sometimes Melchior and Jestin would come for a visit. One time they brought Mister Padrone and Doctor Allan. Mister Padrone had followed Hanzel's advice and sought out Doctor van Vliet. His new prosthetic eye looked entirely real, except for the fact it did not move like his other eye. Sometimes, if one forgot which was the real one and which one wasn't, one did not know at which eye to look. Hanzel kept forgetting and never really knew if he was looking at the right eye or the wrong one.

During some warm days in February, Hanzel and Hanna left little Hanzel in the care of the Hotel's proprietors, with whom they had become friends. Their daughter, Elizabeth, had a little son, the same age as little Hanzel. They had become good friends, so little Hanzel did not mind being left , while his mother and father went searching, once more for their friends, Michael and Maria.

In February the snow lay thick and heavy on the roads. Hence, travel was by open sleigh. Hanzel and Hanna were covered in heavy fur blankets, under which they held hands for most of the way to Amsterdam. The entire ride was a very romantic experience, especially when big flakes of pure white snow came drifting down, soon covering the occupants of the sleigh with another, heavier blanket. They shared a long kiss under that white blanket and told each other how happy they were together.

The road approaching the city gate was slushy mud and made travel by anything but sleigh, almost impossible, hence travel into the city was slow going, because of the number of bogged down wagons, carts, and other wheeled conveyances. When Hanzel and Hanna finally entered through the gate, it was evening. They directed the sleigh driver to take them to a hotel where they spent a pleasant, romantic night, while the snow continued to fall, covering the city with a thick blanket, through which nothing could move. Hanzel and Hanna used the opportunity to make love, eat, drink, make love, sleep, eat, drink, and make love, until waking slightly groggy three days later and intent upon venturing outside.

Walking outside was out of the question, since the snow was still thick and slushy on the streets and sidewalks. Coaches were able to traverse the muck, so Hanzel and Hanna hired a coach.

'Where shall we go?' asked Hanna.

'Let's go look at import shops?' asked Hanzel.

Hanna thought a moment and nodded. 'Why not? Let's go and look at import shops.'

'Oh, they're all over. It'll take days to find them all,' suggested the coach driver. 'I don't know where they all are. I know a few of them. I'll take you there.'

Ten minutes later they stopped in a street lined with import shops, art galleries, tobacconists, a musical instrument store, two ale houses, and a flower shop. Since they had not eaten breakfast, Hanzel and Hanna first stopped at one of the ale houses; the one from which the most noise emanated.

'Must be good food in that place. By the sounds of it, they are busy.' Hanzel lifted Hanna down from the coach and carried her into the ale house. The fact he was carrying her stopped people talking for a moment, as they took in the scene. However, a man carrying a woman is not all that strange. Within a flash, the people resumed their conversations and noise, once again, filled the space. Hanzel sat Hanna down on a bench at the far end of the room. Fortunately, there was space for him, as well. A moment later a wench came over to take their order. Hanzel ordered, coffee, with toasted ginger bread, a boiled egg, two smoked herrings, cheese, and rolls. Hanna ordered tea, two boiled eggs, and two rolls with butter and jam.

While they were enjoying their breakfast, Hanzel and Hanna looked about the room to watch their fellow diners. Hanzel watched five men sitting at a round table, eating and talking. The men were dressed in expensive clothing. As Hanzel watched them, one of the men began to seem familiar. Something about the way the man moved his hands as he spoke reminded Hanzel of Michael. He remarked on it to Hanna, who also noticed a similarity. Neither could clearly see the man's face.

'Why don't you walk past them and take a better look. Maybe he is Michael. You never know,' suggested Hanna.

When Hanzel did walk past the men's table and he took a good look at the man in question, the recognition was immediate. There sat Michael Webb, back from Sumatra.

'Hanzel!' exclaimed Michael, standing up and rushing to his friend.

'Michael,' replied Hanzel as they hugged. 'We've been looking for you.' Hanzel indicated Hanna sitting at the other end of the room. 'We came to Amsterdam to visit you and Maria.'

'I'm so glad to see you,' replied Michael. 'Gentlemen, I would like to present my best friend in the world, Hanzel Sventska.'

The other men each stood up and shook hands with Hanzel. Then Michael excused himself from the group in order to come over and greet Hanna. When Hanna revealed that she could not stand to give him a hug, Michael was greatly shocked to learn of her accident. He was immediately sympathetic and expressed his deepest regrets. Hanna, being by this time, totally adjusted to her situation, thanked him for his concern, but did not dwell on the issue to make anyone uncomfortable. 'We went to all of the fancy clothing stores but we couldn't find, *La Belle Mode*,' she said, to change the subject.

'Then we discovered that you are now a tobacco merchant,' said Hanzel.

'Yes, tobacco. We are selling tobacco,' replied Michael. 'When we came to Amsterdam and looked into starting a clothing business, we discovered there was a lot of competition. However, in tobacco sales, there was hardly anyone. So, Maria and I decided to invest in tobacco. Now we are very rich.'

'It's a lot safer than piracy,' replied Hanna.

'Yes, but we are plagued with pirates. One of my shipments from Indonesia was stolen. We lost a lot of money, but insurance covered some of it, so it wasn't too bad a hit.' Michael regarded Hanzel, grinning. 'Maybe I should hire you to guard my shipments.'

Hanzel laughed. 'Pirates to protect you from pirates. That's a very funny idea.' Hanzel regarded Hanna, and then looked back at Michael. 'However, given what's happened to Hanna, I'm having second thoughts about the sweet trade and maybe giving up the sea all together. Who knows, maybe next time she might be killed, or me. We've got a little boy to consider, as well.'

Hanna looked surprised. 'You've never expressed those thoughts before, Hanzel. Give up the sea and do what?'

'Well, maybe we should invest in tobacco, like Michael and Maria. It would be a lot safer.'

'But I like it at sea. And I like the piracy part, as well. So what if I lost a piece of a leg. Once I get my peg, I'll be good as new,' replied Hanna. 'I'm not sure I want to live here anymore. Too cold in winter and too much snow. I like our Caribbean island.'

'Yes, well, that's all fine and good, my love, but here we have all the amenities, which we don't have on our island. Restaurants, museums, theatres, book stores...'

'We really don't need any of it.' Hanna frowned. 'We've done without any of it all of our lives, really. Why would we need any of it now?'

Hanzel regarded his wife and nodded. 'You have a good point there, my darling. But, we can discuss this all later.' Then, looking at Michael. 'When can we come to visit with you and Maria?'

'You can meet her right away. She is at the shop. I will say goodbye to my friends and we can go there,' replied Michael.

Fifteen minutes later they were sitting in the luxurious smoking lounge of, *M & M Webb & Co. Fine Tobacconists*. Maria was overcome with emotions; over reuniting with her friends, but also because of Hanna's plight. Again, Hanna made everyone totally comfortable over her situation and all concern regarding her lost limb was quickly gone from the group. Soon they were reminiscing and laughing like old times over glasses of Jenever for the men and wine for the women.

'A lot has happened over the last four years. As the colony grew and we had accumulated so much stuff from ships and towns we raided, we went out fewer and fewer times. Over the last year, or so, we've pretty much stayed on our island and enjoyed a very pleasant, relaxing life. There are over four hundred pirates living on the island now. One hundred and twenty are women. There are a couple of dozen children. We even built them a school. Life is good on the island. Maybe you should consider returning with us?'

Hanna took a sip of her wine. 'Hmm. This is good wine.'

'Nothing but the best,' replied Michael, offering Hanzel and Hanna fine cigars from a beautiful rosewood box, before taking one himself.

'Well, it is true we don't always have the best wine, or have cigars on the island, we have everything we need. There is no hustle bustle, like here. And it smells better, the water is cleaner...' Hanzel examined the cigar.

'And there is no snow,' added Hanna, cutting a wedge into her cigar with the small knife she kept at her belt.

'It does sound inviting.' Michael struck a match and began to warm up his cigar.

'Well, perhaps we can make a trip and visit them,' suggested Maria. 'It would be nice to go south next winter. Perhaps if we leave here in September, when it starts to get cold, we can be in the Caribbean by November and stay through the winter and come home in the spring. Gerritt and Marijka can look after the shop.'

'Who are Gerritt and Marijka?' asked Hanna.

'Our manager and his wife. She is very good with the books,' answered Michael.

'Oh, I don't know what we'd do without them,' added Maria.

'It does seem like a pleasant thought, to spend the winter in a warm place,' agreed Michael. 'But, we'll have to see.'

'So, now that they're here in Amsterdam, we'll have to take them to the theatre,' suggested Maria. 'What do you think, Michael? There's that play by that English fellow, what's his name? Michael, you know who I mean. Everybody's been talking about it.'

Maria looked at her husband for an immediate answer. When none came she continued.

'Oh, never mind. It doesn't matter. That English fellow has written a play that's all the rage. We'll have to go see it together. Michael you can get tickets, can't you? Ask your friend, Kristofel. Doesn't he own the theatre?'

'I'll see what I can do.' agreed Michael taking a long drag on his cigar.

'The theatre. That'll be wonderful,' agreed Hanna. 'I've never been to a play before. Not a professional one, that is. Some of our colony members have made up plays, but that was just on our island. Not in a real theatre building with professional actors.'

'We actually have a little theatre group on the island,' added Hanzel. 'There's about thirty ladies and gentlemen who get together and make up entertainments for the colony. Some of their shows have been quite spectacular. They even enacted a play we found in a captain's library we plundered. It was something called, *The Merchant of Venice*. Quite a good story. I especially liked how poor old Herman, God rest his soul, played the old Jew, Shylock, I think he was called.'

'What happened to Herman?' asked Michael.

'When those sneaky Spaniards attacked us, on the way here, one of their cannon balls hit Herman when he was climbing a shroud,' replied Hanzel. 'When they came after us, another lucky shot got a young sailor named Pieter. Pieter Spierenburg. To lose two good men like that. For nothing. It's very sad.'

'He was a good actor,' agreed Hanna.

'Who?' asked Hanzel.

'Herman,' replied Hanna, momentarily reliving the moment, as her mind flashed an image of Herman being blown away. She shuddered involuntarily.

'That's too bad,' replied Michael. 'It's amazing they managed to camouflage their ship so well.'

'Spaniards are sneaky bastards. They also took Mister Padrone's eye,' added Hanzel.

'Poor Padrone. How's he doing?' Michael took a sip of Jenever.

'Better, now that he's got a glass one.' Hanzel took a drag on his cigar. 'You know, Michael. I really dislike Spaniards. Look how they are here. Look what they've done to our country. I want to go back to sea and find those scum and really teach them a lesson. But you can't do much with one sloop and only seventy pirates on board. We need at least two more sloops and just as many on each. Where are we going to find another hundred and fifty people wanting to plunder the Spaniard?'

'Not to forget a couple more sloops,' added Hanna looking curiously at her husband. 'I thought you just said we should stay here and get into the tobacco business?'

'I was just kidding. I wanted to see your reaction,' replied Hanzel, grinning.

Hanna frowned and slapped his thigh.

Michael took a long drag of his cigar. He looked at Maria and then at Hanzel. 'Why don't you buy a couple of sloops?'

Hanzel smiled. 'That would take more money than we have with us. Couldn't we steal a couple of sloops?'

'Yes, but you still need one hundred and fifty more people. Where are you going to hide the sloops until you have completed your recruiting? You will need the sloops to house the people you recruit,' replied Michael.

Hanzel nodded. 'Ya, that is true. So what do you propose?'

'I'll buy a couple of boats for you and arm them. You and Hanna can then go out and do the recruiting. Are there any people left who came with you?'

'Mister Padrone, Melchior, his brother Jestin, Doctor Allan, and some of the others,' replied Hanzel.

'They can help with recruiting. I'm confident you'll easily find a hundred and fifty people here in Amsterdam who'll gladly go to sea and teach some Spaniards a lesson.' Michael finished his drink and poured himself another. He held the crock up to Hanzel who finished his drink and held his glass for Michael to pour some more of the heady distillation.

'Don't you miss Jenever on the island?'

Hanzel looked at his glass and examined the clear liquor. 'We'll make sure to take a few cases back with us.'

'So, what do you think, Hanzel? Would you like me to buy the boats? If not sloops, I'm sure there are some suitable vessels for sale.' Michael looked at his friend.

Hanzel grinned. 'Well, what can I say? Sure, why not? But, are you sure we'll find the people to man them?'

'Oh, trust me,' replied Michael confidently. 'I am sure you'll find what you need. There are lots of people who hate the Spaniards. I mean, *really* hate them. They've done a lot of harm in the united provinces. Killed a lot of people.'

'Well, they killed two of ours and maimed two more.' Hanzel looked at Hanna before continuing. 'I am motivated to get even. It would be amazing if we ran into those sneaky devils again. They I want to teach a lesson, especially for what they did to Hanna.'

'What are the chances of finding them?' Hanna regarded her husband. 'On that huge ocean.'

'Ya, I know. I'm not obsessed with finding them. We can take revenge on any Spaniards. They're all the same, where I'm concerned. However, it's possible, if those sneaky bastards are still cruising about in the Caribbean, we might run into them. When we do, and we have three boats and two hundred pirates, I'll send them to the bottom of the sea.' Hanzel took a long drag of his cigar. 'So help me, God.'

Maria nodded her head and smiled. 'With Him on your side, surely you'll vanquish the Spaniard.'

'Yes, that's true,' agreed Michael, 'However, the Spaniard believes he also has God on his side. So, on whose side do you think God will be on?'

Hanzel blew out a smoke ring. 'I don't think God takes sides. How can He? We are all God's children.'

'Well, whatever the case may be, I just pray that you're successful in taking down some Spaniards. You should talk to the king, maybe he'll give you a letter of permission and may even help fund the enterprise,' suggested Maria.

'That's not a bad idea. You're so brilliant, Maria,' said Michael, looking at his wife with adoring eyes. 'We can go to the king. We can get a letter and possibly even enough money to buy some cannons, or perhaps pay for an entire ship. Who knows. If he likes the idea, he might be really helpful. I know he likes my cigars.'

Hanzel raised his eyebrows. 'You sell cigars to the king?'

'Oh, yes. I've been selling him cigars for about a year and a half. Isn't that about how long, Maria?' Michael regarded his spouse.

'Oh, yes, that's about right. It's nearly coming on two years, actually,' answered Maria happily.

'Do you actually get to see the king?' asked Hanzel.

'Sometimes. We have sat and enjoyed a few cigars together, right here in this very room. He is a splendid chap. You'll like him. However, he, like we, is a busy person, so he mostly just sends his valet,' replied Michael.

'So, how do we get an audience with the king?' asked Hanzel.

'I'll ask the valet. He's a nice chap. The king is probably due for another box or two, wouldn't you say, Maria?'

Maria nodded. 'He'll likely be here tomorrow or the day after, I think.'

'We'll ask him then,' said Michael, taking a long drink of Jenever.

And so it came to pass. Michael did ask the valet who did ask the king who did agree to an audience and listen to Michael's proposal. When the appointed day came, Hanzel and Michael, dressed in their finest clothes, rode in Michael's coach to the palace and announced their arrival to the very valet by whom the audience was obtained. Fifteen minutes later they were introduced to the king.

His Majesty was sitting in a comfortable chair beside a huge fireplace with an inviting, crackling fire consuming a huge tree trunk. Other chairs were pulled up by the fire, into two of which, Hanzel and Michael were invited to sit. The king was smiling and offered his guests Jenever. Then he snapped his fingers and his master of the cigars brought forth a box of Michael's finest.

'These cigars are simply divine, Michael. You know how to choose the right leaves. I have never been disappointed,' said the king, offering a cigar to Hanzel.

'Thank you, Your Majesty,' replied Michael as he also took a cigar from the box. He examined it as he spoke. 'The outer leaf comes from Sumatra. The inner leaves are from Java. That is, in these particular cigars. I also have some cigars with leaves from Brazil, from Mexico, and Hispaniola. I tend to prefer these Indonesian blends.'

Hanzel regarded his friend. 'You're quite the connoisseur. I had no idea.'

'That is what my business is all about. Providing a variety of the best tobacco leaves available in the world. I also buy tobacco from South Africa.' Michael lit his cigar.

'Yes. That is the reason I chose you to be my tobacconist, Michael,' said the king. 'You have quality and variety. I also liked those Hispaniolan cigars you had a few months ago. Those were a pleasant smoke.' The king lit his cigar.

'Thank you Your Majesty,' replied Michael, taking a drag from his cigar.

'So, what is it you want to talk to me about?' asked the king, taking a sip of his drink.

'We want to buy and provision three ships to plunder Spanish shipping in the Caribbean,' replied Michael.

The king raised his eyebrows. 'You are a tobacco merchant, Michael. What do you know about sailing?'

'Before I became a tobacconist, I sailed for a number of years. In fact, Hanzel and I sailed together. I was his first mate.'

The king regarded Hanzel. 'So, you're a sea captain?'

'Yes, Your Majesty,' replied Hanzel, totally at ease in the presence of the king. 'I have sailed the seven seas since I was a teenager. I have my own sloop. It's anchored in the harbour.'

The king regarded Hanzel closely. 'And you have experience in the plundering of ships?'

'I have, Your Majesty.'

'How many ships have you plundered?' The king took an other sip from his crystal glass.

Hanzel thought for a moment. 'I think I've been involved in somewhere around eighteen or twenty. Maybe a few more. I would have to look in my log book. I can't remember exactly.'

'Whose ships did you plunder?' The king sat up in his chair and rested his chin in his right hand.

'Oh, er, let me see. Portuguese, French, English, Danish, Spanish, and one German vessel when I sailed in the Baltic. I was about eighteen or nineteen at the time.'

'Never our ships?' asked the king, a hint of insinuation in his voice.

'Never, Your Majesty. I'm a Dutchman. As tempting as the ships of the East and West India companies are, I've never plundered them.'

'That is a good thing. If you had, you would have stolen from me.' The king finished his drink. 'I am heavily invested in those companies.'

'I'm sure those investments are paying a good dividend,' said Michael. 'I've bought some shares in them, as well.'

The king smiled. 'Good thinking, Master Webb. I'm confident those shares will make you a richer man.'

'They already have, Your Majesty.' Michael let out a perfect smoke ring.

'So, you want to obtain some boats, and take a small flotilla after the hated Spaniard?' The king took a drag on his cigar and blew out a couple of perfect rings. Then he turned to one of the gentlemen standing nearby; a tall, emaciated looking old codger who functioned as the exchequer 'What do you think, Robert? These gentlemen want some assistance with obtaining and equipping some ships to plunder Spanish shipping.' The king turned to Michael. 'I'll take forty percent.' Then he turned back to Robert. 'Can we afford it?'

Michael looked at Hanzel. 'Forty percent, Your Majesty?'

'That is if you want me to provide boats and such. I need to see a good return for my investment. What if you get shot up and you end up in Spanish prisons, or worse? I could lose my entire investment in one fell swoop. Forty percent is reasonable, don't you think so, Robert?'

'Oh, yes. Yes, yes, Your Majesty. Yes, forty percent is most certainly reasonable. Considering your investment in ships and such,' muttered Robert; 'That is, if you actually do invest in Master Webb's proposal.'

The king regarded Michael and Hanzel as he took a drag of his cigar. After a moment he blew out three perfect smoke rings. He nodded his head and looked at Robert. 'I think

I will invest in your proposal.' He turned to Robert. 'Provide these gentlemen with the funds necessary to purchase,' he turned to Michael, 'how many boats did you say you need?'

'Two, Your Majesty. We need two boats in addition to the one Hanzel already has,' answered Michael.

The king continued, 'provide the funds to purchase two,' he turned to Michael again. 'What types of boats?'

'Sloops, Your Majesty,' replied Michael.

The king turned to Robert once again, 'provide them with the funds to purchase two sloops and equipment as needed. Also provide funding to provision said ships.'

Michael and Hanzel stood up. 'Thank you Your Majesty. I am confident we'll bring you a good return.'

'Yes, thank you, Your Majesty,' chorused Hanzel, happily.

'You are welcome,' replied the king. 'Now, if you have no further business, I must ask you to leave me to mine. Robert will draw up the requisite papers. Stop by tomorrow and you can sign them. Then you can go shopping for your boats.'

'Thank you, Your Majesty. I am confident you will not be disappointed.' Michael made a deep bow. Hanzel did the same. Then they walked backwards out of the king's reception room, bowing the whole time. Once outside the room, the doors were closed and they quickly left the palace. Once outside they exchanged a glance and then they both whooped with joy. 'That calls for a celebration, eh, Hanzel? What do you think?'

'I'd say we are going to have a celebration. Dinner and drinks are on me tonight,' replied Hanzel, grinning from ear to ear.

Early the next afternoon, Hanzel and Michael traveled to the palace and met with Robert. They signed a document in triplicate attesting to their voluntary compliance with the king's request for 40% of all goods and stores plundered from Spanish shipping. They also signed a document promising to take good care of the ships and accouterments to the best of their abilities. When the documents were signed, Robert presented Michael with a letter which they could take to merchants assuring them of payment by the crown.

When Hanzel and Michael left the palace, Michael exclaimed, 'Let's go shopping!'

However, by the time they stepped outside, the sun was setting and darkness was already on its way.

'If we hadn't drank so much last night, we would've got a much earlier start and had those papers done by nine,' complained Hanzel, when they were driving home in Michael's coach.

'What is one more day?' asked Michael.

'Ya, that is true. What is one more day. It is one more day closer to death.'

'That is a morose thing to say.' Michael regarded Hanzel, sitting beside him.

'Well, it's true. Not to suggest I am wanting death to call. It is an observation of how our lives travel along a continuum from birth to death. Each mark on that scale is a day.' Hanzel smiled. 'I don't know why I was thinking of death, just now. Don't worry about it Michael. It's not a premonition, or anything.'

'That's good. You had me worried there for a minute.'

'Tomorrow I'll round up Melchior and the others. They can help pick out the boats. I'll have Melchior captain one. Do you want to captain the other?' Hanzel looked at his friend.

'Captain the other? Are you serious? I have a business to run. I don't have time to go to sea.'

'Michael, once you step foot aboard a ship, you'll be wanting to go back to sea. I can see it in your eyes. You crave adventure and are not finding much adventure in the tobacco business.'

'What about Maria and Michaela? I don't want to leave them here in Amsterdam while I go off to sea, for who knows how long,' replied Michael.

'We'll take them with us.'

Michael shook his head. 'Too dangerous. Look what happened to Hanna. And what about Mister Padrone?'

'That was an aberration. We had no idea that merchant ship was something else. We had no idea those sneaky Spaniards would camouflage a ship. I've never encountered that before. Have you?'

'No, I can't say I have,' replied Michael. 'But, whatever. I'm still not going to sea. I enjoy my life in Amsterdam. Maria and I go to concerts and plays. We eat in good restaurants.'

'Speaking of, that was a good restaurant we ate in last night,' agreed Hanzel.

'You don't eat like that on board ship,' replied Michael.

'We need to find better cooks, is all. There is no reason we can't eat like that on board ship. I am going to make that one of my first orders of business when we are recruiting; to find some good cooks.' Hanzel smiled at Michael.

'How will you know if they're good cooks?'

'I'll audition them. In the galley of my sloop. If they can cook up some excellent dishes, then I'll hire them. Since you have become such a gastronome, perhaps you can help with the auditions. You can be a taster. What do you say to that?' Hanzel regarded his friend; a big grin on his face.

'I know what you're trying to do. Get me involved with your ship and next thing you expect is that I am going to join you. Go back to sea. Well, let me tell you, my friend, you can try, but I'm not going. Forget it. I'm staying in Amsterdam with Maria and Michaela and my tobacco business.'

Hanzel nodded. 'We'll see.'

The coach arrived at Hanzel's hotel.

'Let's get an early start tomorrow. How about picking me up at eight o'clock. Then we'll go down to the harbour and send a message to the crew of the sloop to come meet us somewhere, and then we'll go from there, looking for boats and people.' Hanzel shook Michael's hand and then stepped out of the coach. 'See you in the morning.'

'Yes, I'll see you at eight.' Michael smiled and then tapped the roof to let the driver know he was ready to go. Hanzel watched the coach drive away before stepping into the hotel. When he entered their room, Hanna was sitting on the bed, waiting for him.

'Hello, my love,' he said as he entered the room. 'How are you feeling?'

'Oh, much better now that you're home,' she replied. They kissed and Hanzel lay his cape over a chair. 'How did everything go?'

'Splendidly. Michael will pick me up in the morning, at eight. Then we'll round up the boys and girls, who are still in town, and go boat shopping. I'll send a few to go do some preliminary recruiting.'

'Oh, I wish I had my leg and could come along. I can't wait for May to get here.' Hanna looked down at her stump. 'If there was only some way to speed up the healing.'

Hanzel pulled up a chair beside the bed and looked gently into her eyes. 'May will come soon, my love. Don't worry. Once you have your leg, you'll be nearly good as new.'

Hanna smiled. 'As long as I have you at my side, I'll be alright.' Hanna leaned over and kissed Hanzel for a long time. When they gently broke away, she was smiling. A moment later Hanzel realized that little Hanzel was not there.

'Where is our son?'

'He is sleeping over at Michaela's. They like each other. Maria has lots of room in her house. He is totally at home there. She figured it is better for him to stay there, than here, with us, in this hotel suite, with nobody to play with.'

'Quite so,' replied Hanzel. 'I'm sure he'll be a lot happier. Michaela seems like a nice girl.'

Hanna nodded. 'Yes she is.'

'So, let's order up some food and drink, or would you like me to carry you down to the dining hall?'

'Let's order in. I don't feel like going anywhere. My stump is aching a bit. It feels good to sit here in bed.'

'Alright,' agreed Hanzel. 'I'll be right back.' In a flash he was out the door and down the stairs, through the lobby, and into the restaurant, where he ordered dinner and drinks to be sent up to his suite. Then he returned to his wife and they spent the rest of the evening happy in each other's company. Sometime later in the evening they made sweet love and fell into deep, contented dreams about the sea and successful plunder. For Hanna, those happy dreams became her journey throughout the night. For Hanzel, his dreams evolved differently.

By the time the third hour had passed, Hanzel was visited by the raven haired succubus, who rode him for all he was worth, leaving him heaving and panting for breath, his bedclothes soaked, once again, in sweat and semen. He sat up abruptly; waking Hanna.

'What's wrong?' she asked, dreamily.

Hanzel looked down at his wife, half asleep, with her back to him. 'Nothing,' he said. 'Go back to sleep. It's nothing. I just had a bad dream, is all.'

'Did she come to you again?'

'Who?' asked Hanzel, a guilty tone in his voice.

'She did, didn't she?' Hanna turned over to look at Hanzel, sitting upright, looking perplexed at his wet sleeping shirt; his erection still firmly pushing up fabric. 'That succubus, that's who. She came to you in your dream again, didn't she?'

Hanzel regarded his wife and slowly nodded his head. 'It's so bizarre, because the dream is so vivid. Like I'm actually there.'

Hanna looked at his stained night shirt. 'Well, she sure knows how to get the most out of you. I don't know if I should be jealous.'

'Jealous? Of a dream? You can't be serious.' Hanzel stared at his wife.

'Well, she sure has an effect on you. I don't leave you dripping like that, do I?'

Hanzel smiled sheepishly. 'What about that time in Ponto Delgada? And, there was that time at the hot spring...'

Hanna frowned. 'You've got to stop dreaming about her. Am I not fulfilling you, somehow?'

Hanzel shook his head. 'Oh, no, Hanna. Don't think that. I love you. You know that. I have no control over the dream. Do you have control over your dreams?'

'Well, no. I suppose not. But, I don't end up dripping because of some incubus penetrating me in the middle of the night.' Hanna frowned. 'Something's gotten a hold of you, Hanzel. Maybe you should talk to Doctor Allen. Maybe he can give you something to prevent the dream from recurring.'

'What could he possibly give me to stop dreams? Come on Hanna, be reasonable. There's no such thing.'

'You never know, Hanzel. With all of the advances in modern medicine, nowadays, you never know. An apothecary may have already discovered some concoction to prevent people from dreaming.'

Hanzel frowned. 'It's called, rat poison.'

'That's not what I meant, Hanzel. I mean, some kind of a laudanum, or a tincture of some kind.'

'Well, whatever, Hanna. I've got to get out of these wet clothes and dry off.' Hanzel carefully extracted himself from the bed, as Hanna held the blankets and sheets up for him; to avoid contact with the wet clothes. She watched as he cleaned himself off. Hanzel returned to bed, his naked body in a fresh, dry night shirt. Hanna immediately snuggled up to him and made him forget all about the demon who had tormented him.

Chapter 41

Next morning, right at eight o'clock, Hanzel sat waiting for Michael in the lobby of his hotel. He was still 'hung over' from his unsettling encounter with the succubus. *I can't understand how can a dream do that to me. It's so bizarre. And why for a second time am I dreaming of that black haired witch?* Hanzel shook his head, trying to make sense of the dreams.

At eight fifteen, he was still waiting. Michael finally arrived at eight forty three. His servant came into the lobby to fetch Hanzel. Michael was waiting in his coach. A light drizzle hung in the air. Hanzel shivered as he stepped outside. The servant put the step down and Hanzel climbed into the conveyance.

Michael helped pull Hanzel into the coach. 'I am terribly sorry to be so late. Morning issues at home. Nothing to worry about, though.' Michael grinned. 'How are you? Ready to go boat shopping?'

'Ya, let's hope we find what we're looking for. First we'll go down to the harbour and fetch my crew. You can see my sloop. We took her away from some Spaniards who didn't deserve her. She's outfitted very nicely. We still have some repairs to do on her, but that can wait until spring.'

When they reached the harbour, Hanzel hired a boat to take Michael and him to the sloop. When they climbed on board, Melchior was on deck to meet them.

'Good morning, Captain,' said Melchior as he helped pull Hanzel onto the deck.

'Good morning, Melchior, replied Hanzel, reaching down to help pull up his friend.

When Michael stood on deck, Hanzel introduced him to his first mate. 'Michael was my first mate up until four and a half years ago.'

Melchior regarded Michael. 'So, are you thinking of coming back to sea?'

Michael shook his head. 'No, I don't think so. I have a successful business to run here in Amsterdam.'

'We're going boat shopping, Melchior. The king is financing the purchase of two more sloops. We're going after the Spaniard with a Letter of Marque,' said Hanzel enthusiastically.

'If we obtain two more ships, we're going to need a lot more crew. There are only seven of us left on board. They are all sleeping it off. We had a bit of a party last night on account of it being Kat's birthday yesterday,' replied Melchior.

'I want you to wake everyone up. I want you to come shopping with us. Some of you can begin recruiting. This sloop can hold seventy, so we'll begin by filling her. In the meantime we'll find two more boats and by that time we should have lots of candidates lined up.' Hanzel turned to Michael. 'Come, I'll show you below.'

While Hanzel showed Michael around the ship, the crew roused themselves from their slumbers and slowly set about getting themselves ready to go to town. An hour later, they lowered themselves into the sloop's long boat and rowed to shore as Hanzel organized them into two groups of two for recruitment purposes. 'Melchior will come with Michael and me. We'll meet back here at five o'clock and see where we're at. Good luck.'

With that, they split up, the recruiters heading for the nearest pubs and Hanzel, with his two friends, set out to find a boat seller. It did not take very long. There were several boat sellers within a street of each other. The first one they stopped at was, Johannes de Vries & Company, Ship Sales.

'Do you have any boats for sale?' asked Hanzel when asked what he wanted by Johannes, himself.

'Of course I do. This is a boat seller's shop. I don't sell cabinets.' The boat seller gave Hanzel a look to suggest he might be insane.

'We need two sloops,' replied Hanzel, not giving Johan's expression any thought. *So what if he thinks I am crazy?*

Johannes looked in a big book, which had been lying under a pile of papers on his desk. 'Sloops you say?' He shook his head. 'No, I don't have any sloops for sale.'

'How about a couple of small brigantines?' asked Hanzel.

Johannes looked through his book. 'No brigantines.'

'Do you have a large ketch, perhaps. Something around sixty feet, or so?' Hanzel looked at Melchior, examining a beautiful model of a yawl.

'No, sorry, no ketches in stock.' Johannes looked over at Melchior examining the model.

'What about one of those yawls, like that model.? Do you have yawls for sale?'

'It is possible. I might have a yawl. I had a brigantine, I know I had one of those. And I had a caravel. But, you wouldn't have wanted her. Old. She was pretty old. About sixty five, or so. It was a wonder she still floated.' Johannes continued to look in the book. 'A yawl, you say? It is possible my partner might have sold it. I was away for a few days.' Johannes dragged his right index finger down another page, then shaking his head, he apologized. 'Sorry, no yawls.'

'It doesn't appear that you have any boats for sale,' said Hanzel, a hint of frustration in his voice.

'Oh, we have boats, but just not the kind you are looking for,' replied Johannes.

'What do you have for sale?' Hanzel pointed at the book.

'Oh, lots of boats. Name a boat.'

'Cog.'

'No, sorry. No cogs.' Johannes looked at Hanzel with an odd expression. 'A cog? Why would you be wanting a cog, anyway? Those went out of fashion over a hundred years ago.'

'Galleon.'

Johannes regarded Hanzel with one of those, *are you kidding* expressions. 'A galleon? Where would I get a galleon?'

Hanzel frowned. 'What about a frigate?'

'No.'

'A ketch?'

'A ketch? Let me see. Johannes ran his bony finger down the page of the book. 'No, sorry, no ketches.'

'A pinnace?'

'Sorry.'

'Do you have a long boat which can be fitted with a sail?' Hanzel was becoming frustrated and began eyeing the door.

'A long boat? Fitted for sailing? Hmmm.' Johannes thought for a moment before excusing himself to go to the back of the shop. Hanzel and his friends could hear him talking with someone, who was obviously hard of hearing. 'Do we have a long boat which can be fitted with a sail?!' he asked in a loud voice.

'A long boat?' croaked a voice. 'A long boat you say?' Then, after a long pause, came the answer. 'No. No long boats.'

Johannes returned to inform Hanzel and his friends there was no long boat to be had.

'What kind of a boat seller are you? You have no boats for sale,' said Hanzel beginning to walk to the door.

'Oh, I assure you, we have boats. Name another boat. I probably have it,' replied Johannes. 'The problem is the wars. All the time, war, war, war, and the need for boats goes up.'

'Alright. I'm willing to compromise. Do you have a merchantman that is in good shape?'

'Alas, we just sold the last one yesterday.'

'A barque. Perhaps you have a barque we can outfit?' Hanzel looked at Michael and Melchior. 'We can use a barque, couldn't we?'

Melchior nodded. 'We would have to change the rigging a bit. Get some more speed out of it.'

'Alright, what about a barque? Surely you have one or two of those. They are a popular design,' said Hanzel.

'I had a barque. In fact, we had three of them. You should have come last week. In good shape, too.' Johannes pointed to an entry in the book. 'Right there. Three barques.'

'We are done here, gentlemen,' said Hanzel curtly. Then he turned on his heels. 'Good day to you.'

'Wait, wait,' said the boat seller. 'I have other boats.'

'What about a snow?' asked Hanzel.

'Sorry. I had a snow two months ago.' Johannes stared down at the book and pointed to an entry. He chuckled. 'It was kind of funny when we sold it. It was covered in snow. A snow, covered in snow. The buyer thought it was funny.

I remember him laughing.' Johannes stared off into space for a moment as he reflected on the funny moment.

'Alright, what about a pink?'

The boat seller shook his head.

'What about a fluyt? Surely you must have half a dozen of those?'

'I did have. We had eight of them. If you had only come here four days ago, I still had two left.'

'Do you, in your dubious boat sales shop, have a caravel?'

'A caravel you say? Let me see.' Johannes took a look through his book, turning several pages. He scratched his chin. 'Just a minute. I'll ask my colleague.' The boat seller went to the back of the shop and consulted the croaky voiced partner. He came back a moment later, shaking his head. 'No can do. No caravel. We haven't seen one of those for a while. Not much call for them up here. I had an order from Portugal for the only one we had.'

'Do you have a carrack, a collier, perhaps? Maybe a lugger, or a tartane?'

'I saw a lugger recently. But it was not in good shape. We scrapped it.'

'We are wasting our time here, gentlemen,' said Hanzel to his friends. 'Good day to you.'

'Wait. I'm looking here in my entry book and it looks like there is a galiote available.' Johannes pointed to an entry in his book. 'A galiote would serve you well.'

'Alright, a galiote it is then. Where is it?' asked Hanzel.

'Oh, sorry. I'm so sorry. There is a notation from my partner. It says it was a stolen boat and had to be returned to its rightful owner. We had no idea it was stolen. We bought it in good faith from an honest privateer by the name of, Max de Kapper.'

Hanzel looked at his friends, an exasperated expression on his face. Then he returned his gaze on Johannes the boat seller. 'You say you have boats, but yet I've named more than a dozen and you don't have a single one. Not even a fluyt! How can you call yourself a boat seller?'

'We sell a lot of boats. You just caught me in an off time,' replied Johannes. 'On account of the wars.'

'An off time? An off time?' Hanzel leaned closer to the man. 'I'll tell you about time. You wasted a lot of mine. Come on boys, we're out of here.'

Across the street was another boat seller. Goldman Zaks & Company, Purveyors of Fine Marine Vessels.

'Goldman. Goldman. That rings a bell,' said Hanzel as they stepped up to the door. 'I knew a Goldman once, a long time ago.'

'Maybe someone you sailed with?' asked Melchior.

Hanzel shook his head. 'No, I don't think I sailed with a Goldman. The name is familiar, is all. I've heard it before. Never mind. Let's go in and see if we're more successful here.'

The shop was cluttered with all kinds of marine memorabilia; models of ships, three ship's bells, five shark jaws, back staves, astrolabes, compasses of various kinds, geographer's tools, telescopes, charts, drawings, books, assorted floats, a six foot tall anchor, a stuffed cayman, and a desk covered with drawings of ships, record books, a pot of ink, a stand of quills, and a mantel clock. The clerk at the desk stood up and welcomed Hanzel and his friends to the shop.

'Mister Goldman will be right back. He just went out for a quick errand,' said the clerk.

'We are looking for two sloops,' replied Hanzel.

'I'm not sure what is available right now. Mister Goldman can help you with that,' said the clerk, fidgeting with a goose quill.

'You don't know if he has sloops for sale?' asked Hanzel.

'I really don't know the inventory very well. I only just started working here a few days ago,' answered the clerk.

'How long do you think Mister Goldman will be gone?'

The clerk looked at Hanzel for a moment. 'Oh, I think he'll be right back. He just went to the bakery down the street.'

'Alright, we'll wait,' replied Hanzel. 'He pointed to some chairs. We'll sit over there.'

'Yes, yes, that'll be fine,' said the clerk, returning to his work at the desk.

Five minutes later the door opened and in walked a stooped old man. The moment Hanzel set eyes on him, he turned white as a ghost.

'These men are looking for two sloops, Mister Goldman,' said the clerk.

'Isaac Goldman,' said the old man, introducing himself.

HANZEL SVENTSKA

Hanzel looked at his two friends and then back at Mister Goldman. 'I've changed my mind. We must go,' he stuttered as he headed for the door.

'He acts like he has seen a ghost,' said Mister Goldman to his clerk as they watched the three men leave the store; the blonde one in the greatest hurry.

'What's wrong?' asked Michael, quizzically regarding his friend.

'Now I know why Goldman rang a bell. That man in there is the spitting image of his brother,' replied Hanzel, looking back at the store he just left.

'So, what does his brother have to do with this?' asked Michael.

'Don't you remember? We murdered his brother, years ago, when we stole that sloop from him. I've never felt good about it. Now, seeing his look alike twin, I just can't do business with him. There are other boat sellers.' Hanzel pointed to a sign hanging from a building down the street. 'We'll go there.'

'Now that you mention it, that old man does look like that Goldman we threw overboard. I remember now,' said Michael as they walked to the other boat seller's shop. 'I guess, eventually it would have dawned on me. I would have felt badly doing business with him, as well. Like doing business with someone from the grave.'

'Exactly,' replied Hanzel.

A moment later they were standing outside the premises of another boat seller. 'Welcome to Fastbinder & Zoons, New and Used Marine Craft,' said an oily sales clerk, as Hanzel and his friends stepped through the door. The clerk had thin, waxed mustaches and yellow teeth. He wore older, slightly frayed clothes, indicating that business may have been better some time in the past. 'My name is Willhelmus Fastbinder. And your name is?'

Hanzel regarded the oily sales clerk. 'Sventska. Captain Sventska. These are my associates, Mister Webb and Mister Mancuso. We are looking for two sloops in the eighty to one hundred and twenty foot range.'

'Two sloops you say?' Willhelmus rubbed his hands together. 'Let me have a look in the book.' He opened a big book on a desk and looked through it, turning several pages. 'I have a very fine brigantine of one hundred and twenty three feet. There's a very nice pinnace of sixty feet. Let me see. Oh, yes, here is one. A six year old sloop, not bad condition. An eighty footer. Needs a little work. Priced to sell. A fixer upper, as they say.' Willhelmus jabbed at another entry. 'There's this really beautiful yacht. Let me see. Yes, it's eighty five and a half feet. I also have two decommissioned merchantmen. They're both one hundred and twenty two feet from stem to stern. Might any of those ships work for you?'

'What do you think, gentlemen?' asked Hanzel.

'The sloop and the yacht might fit the bill,' replied Melchior. 'Let's go and have a look at them.'

'They're tied up not far from here.' Willhelmus pointed in the direction where the ships were berthed. 'I'll come with you.'

Twenty minutes later they were standing on the deck of the sloop. Hanzel was frowning. 'I thought you said this sloop is eighty feet. It's not a foot over forty seven.'

Willhelmus scratched his head. 'I could have sworn it said she was an eighty footer in the book.'

'Alright. Let's see the yacht,' said Hanzel, not amused his time was being wasted again.

Willhelmus pointed. 'She's right there.' Indeed, the yacht was tied up next to a pinnace which lay tied next to the boat they were standing on. And she looked a fright. Her sails were worn, her ropes were frayed, and many were missing. What paint might have been there at one time was long gone. When they stepped on board, Hanzel nearly went through the deck because of a rotten plank.

'She's a bit of a fixer upper,' said Willhelmus, pretending not to notice the rotten board.

'A fixer upper?! A fixer upper!? This tub should have been condemned years ago. I thought you said it was, "really beautiful"? It is nothing of the kind.'

'Yes, well, you know how advertising works. It can be misleading at times. I did not write the entries in the book. That is the work of my father. He's a bit of an optimist.' Willhelmus nervously rubbed his hands together. 'We can give you a really good deal on her. Cut the price in half.'

Hanzel shook his head. 'No, thank you. I'm sure we'll find what we're looking for, eventually.' Looking at Michael and Melchior he said, 'come on boys. We're off to the next one.'

'Wait. Please wait. There are other boats for sale. These are the ones you chose,' said Willhelmus pleadingly.

Hanzel regarded the little man. 'You told us these boats were in good condition. You called this, "a beautiful yacht". I can't for the life of me think why you would call this a beautiful yacht. I wouldn't risk taking this old bucket around the harbour, let alone the seven seas.'

'What about that pinnace over there? It's in good shape,' said Willhelmus with his oily voice.

'Too small,' replied Hanzel, curtly. Then he simply turned on his heels and left the ship, followed by Michael and Melchior, leaving Willhelmus standing on the yacht wondering what his father was going to say.

Their next stop was a boat seller several streets further on. He was sitting beside a bridge over a canal, one of dozens, with a simple sign painted on a board proclaiming, BOATS FOR SALE.

'Let's ask him,' suggested Hanzel as they stopped at the bridge.

'His sign does say he has boats for sale. Maybe just row boats and such like,' suggested Michael. 'He probably doesn't have what we're looking for.'

'Ya, but he might know someone who does,' replied Hanzel, stepping out of the coach.

'Good afternoon, my good man. We are looking for two large sloops, preferably in the one hundred foot range. Do you know anyone who has such boats for sale?'

'You've come to the right man, guvnor,' replied the boat seller, standing up. 'I know someone who as exactly what you're lookin' for.'

'And who would that be?' asked Hanzel.

'You're lookin' at im,' replied the man. 'Barong van Dam, at your service.' The man doffed his cap and made an elaborate bow.

'You have two hundred foot sloops?' Hanzel regarded the man more closely. He was about thirty three years old with long, curly black hair. He was clean shaven. On his left cheek he bore a three inch scar; likely from a knife or sword. Both of his ears were pierced with golden rings. *Gold rings. He is not a poor man, obviously. Those rings must weigh at least half an ounce each.* 'Where are these sloops?'

'Oh, they're tied up to a pier not far from here.' Barong pointed towards the harbour two streets away.

'Can we go to see them?' Hanzel looked in the direction the man pointed at.

'Tomorrow. You can see them tomorrow. We've got to get them ready for you to see. I only just acquired them a few days ago. They belonged to a local importer. Used them to trade in the Baltic. Went out of business and now he has these sloops for sale.' Barong smiled. 'Meet me here tomorrow morning.'

Hanzel regarded his friends in the coach. 'What do you think? Should we trust him and come back tomorrow, or do we keep looking?'

'We've been at it all morning. I'm ready for lunch. Let's go find a good meal. We can come back tomorrow. What is one more day?' replied Michael.

Hanzel assured Barong they would be back in the morning as he climbed into the coach. 'We'll be here at nine o'clock,' he said through the open window.

'Right you are, guvnor,' said Barong, bowing slightly and rubbing his hands together.

Hanzel nodded. 'Alright, then. Tomorrow morning at nine o'clock. And, I warn you. You better not be wasting my time.' He tapped on the roof and the coachman set the vehicle in motion, on the way to find lunch.

Barong, the boat seller, took his sign and got to work rounding up his gang and procuring two large sloops.

Next morning Hanzel and his friends arrived at the bridge where they were to meet Barong. They were obviously early because the boat seller was not there. He arrived a half hour later, just as his customers were about to leave.

'Terribly sorry, guvnor,' said Barong. 'I was delayed on account of a late night working and sleeping past the cock.'

Hanzel assured Barong all was well. 'So, let's go and look at those sloops you promised.'

'Yes, er, that is, well, they're not ready for viewing yet. I have my crew working on them. Nothing serious. We're replacing a couple of sails and some ropes,' answered Barong. 'Can you come back tomorrow? I mean, I want the boats to look as ship shape as possible.'

'Tomorrow?' Hanzel looked exasperatedly at his friends in the coach.

'What's one more day, Hanzel?' asked Michael.

'Yes, what is one more day?' repeated Melchior.

'Come back at this time tomorrow,' said Barong.

Hanzel slowly nodded his head. 'Alright, tomorrow. We'll give you one more day. Saves us from driving all over town.'

'We can go to the theatre this afternoon,' suggested Michael. 'We'll take Hanna and Maria. What about you, Melchior. Do you and your wife want to join us?'

Melchior agreed that it was a good idea. Hence, instead of continuing the boat hunt, the three friends took their wives to see *Hamlet* by "that English fellow," the Bard from Stratford.

Next morning, Hanzel and Melchior went to meet Barong, who was a half hour late and again full of excuses. 'The sloops are just not ready for you to see yet. We discovered a few problems and are fixing those. Remember, they are previously owned. One is eight years old and the other six.'

'I see,' replied Hanzel, not hiding his disappointment.

'Come back tomorrow and everything will be hunky dory.'

'Hunky dory?' asked Hanzel, never having heard that expression before.

'It means everything is good. Things are good to go. It's an expression I learned from my father. I think he brought it back from the East Indies. Or maybe Brazil.' Barong thought for a moment. 'No, it was Halifax. He brought it back from Halifax. Hunky dory. I remember it as if it was yesterday.' Then he paused with his right index finger in the air. 'No, maybe it wasn't Halifax. I'm not sure, now. Anyway, just come back tomorrow and I'm sure all will be good with the sloops.' Barong held his hands out, palms up. 'Come back at this time, tomorrow.'

Hanzel nodded. 'Alright. We'll give you until tomorrow. Otherwise we'll go somewhere else. I'm sure there are others with sloops for sale.'

'Oh, not in the size you're looking for. What with the wars and all that, sloops are in short supply. We're havin' trouble steal, er fixing these two up because parts for sloops are in short supply, so many having been shot up and needing to be repaired. But don't worry, we'll have two sloops for you by tomorrow morning.' Barong smiled ingratiatingly; rubbing his hands together.

Hanzel regarded Barong for another moment and then climbed back into the coach. They left Barong standing by the bridge. The moment the coach was out of sight, Barong walked quickly away from that place and met up with his gang to finalize the details pertaining to the clandestine acquisition of two sloops they had scoped out; one an 85 footer and the other 110.

Next morning Hanzel and Melchior met Barong by the bridge, as before.

'So, do you have the sloops?' asked Hanzel.

Barong nodded. 'Indeed I do. They're tied up near Vollendam.'

'Vollendam? Why there?' asked Hanzel, perplexed.

'That is where our main base of operations is. I advertise here in Amsterdam, but our shop is there, in Vollendam. We save a lot that way and can offer our customers a better price.'

'And, what exactly is the price for these sloops in Vollendam?' asked Hanzel.

'For the two of them we're charging, twenty four thousand.' Barong rubbed his hands together. 'One is an eighty five footer and the other is one hundred and ten feet from stem to stern. Both are in fine condition and ready to sail. You'll need about twenty sailors on each.'

'Twenty four thousand? We'll have to see. Sight unseen can not finalize a price for me,' replied Hanzel. 'Let's go to Vollendam and we'll take a look at these sloops of yours.'

Barong nodded. 'You mean, go there now? To Vollendam?'

'Yes, of course. Let's go now. In the coach. My friend has lent it to me for the day.'

Hanzel held the door open for Barong to climb in. 'I'm anxious to see those sloops.'

'Oh, ah, er, that is, well, you see, I wasn't prepared to go to Vollendam today. I just wanted to make arrangements for you to view the ships. We have the sloops, but I have other appointments for today. There are other people buying boats from us, you see.'

'Just tell me where the boats are tied up and we'll go to Vollendam and take a look at them,' replied Hanzel. 'I have all kinds of time.'

'Oh. Yes. That is an idea. However, it is better I come with you. The people at the shop are a bit suspicious of people poking around our boats without me or one of the other sales representatives being present. The people at the shop are just workers. They worked on your sloops.'

'So, when are you available to go see these ships?' asked Hanzel.

Barong scratched his left temple and thought for a moment. 'The earliest day I can go to Vollendam is next Tuesday.'

'Next Tuesday?! Next Tuesday? That's three days from now!' Hanzel threw his fists into the air in a gesture of extreme frustration.

'We've waited this long, Captain,' suggested Melchior. 'It'll give us more time to enjoy some of the amenities of the city. Perhaps we can go see another play. I quite enjoyed that show yesterday.'

'Alright. Next Tuesday it is. We'll meet you here at this time next Tuesday,' said Hanzel, his temper boiling under his shirt.

'Agreed.' Barong offered his hand which Hanzel gripped for a longer time than normal, putting some extra crushing power in his grip to let Barong know that he, Hanzel Sventska was very strong and quite capable of breaking bones. 'Oh, er, I hate to ask, but I need a deposit. There is not much I can do, in case someone else sees the boats and buys them, I have no way to hold them.'

Hanzel looked at Melchior sitting in the coach and looking out of a window. Melchior shrugged his shoulders. 'A deposit is a reasonable request Captain.'

Hanzel turned his attention back to Barong. 'Alright, how much do you want?'

'How much do you have with you?' asked Barong, holding his right hand out.

Hanzel looked in his purse. 'Here, you can have this.' Hanzel took out five gold coins. 'Five ounces of gold.' He reached into the purse once more and pulled out six silver coins. 'And six ounces of silver. Will that do?'

Barong examined the coins in his hand. 'Yes, that will do nicely.' He put the coins into his purse.

'Alright. I expect to see you here on Tuesday morning. If you do not show up, I assure you that we will find you, and you will repay my deposit, even if I have to take it out of your hide.' Hanzel stared into the man's eyes and then turned on his heels and climbed back into the coach. He looked back at the boat seller, who was cradling his crushed hand with the other. Then Hanzel signaled the driver to go. Twenty minutes later he and Melchior arrived at the roadway where their sloop was anchored.

'Let's see what our friends have achieved with their recruitment program,' said Hanzel, stepping out of the coach.

'It'll be interesting, I'm sure. Tina and I haven't been to the sloop for three days. We also took a hotel. For a break from the sloop. The smells coming from those merchantmen is repulsive to her, especially.' Melchior pointed to a hulking East Indiaman tied up nearby.

The two friends quickly walked down the pier and obtained the services of a dingy man to row them out to the sloop. What they found there was a very pleasant surprise. There was a party going on.

As they climbed on board, they were welcomed by Mister Padrone. 'Welcome on board, Captain. We've been recruiting and have nearly filled the ship. There are sixty five people on board.'

'What are you celebrating?' asked Hanzel.

'The fact that we have sixty five people on board,' came the reply. 'We found quite a few of our own, with no ships and no prospects. When we laid it in front of them that we were acquiring more ships and sailing under a Letter of Marque, many of them saw that they had a better opportunity to continue with us. Well, if you'll excuse me, I'm returning to my new sweetheart.'

'Your new *sweetheart*?' Hanzel raised his eyebrows and stared at his sailing master with a surprised look on his face.

'Yes. I recruited her. She's over there.' Mister Padrone pointed towards a pleasant looking woman with curly red hair. 'Her name is, Lucinda, but everyone calls her, Lucy. Would you like to meet her?'

'Yes, yes, of course,' replied Hanzel as Mister Padrone led him to his new found love.

'Lucy, I would like you to meet our captain, Hanzel Sventska.' Mister Padrone, looked fondly at his new girl friend.

Lucy was immediately smitten by the handsome captain. 'I am so happy to meet you, at last. Pasquali has told me much about you. You are a legend in your own time,' she gushed.

'Only in my own mind,' chuckled Hanzel. 'I am pleased to meet you, Lucy. Welcome on board.'

'Thank you, Captain,' she said, making a slight curtsy.

Hanzel smiled and then excused himself in order to meet more of the new crew members. The rest of the day was thusly spent, meeting and greeting the new ladies and gentlemen with whom Hanzel would wreak his vengeance on the Spaniard; hoping someday he would meet the one who shot off Hanna's leg.

On the following Tuesday morning, Hanzel, and Melchior rode the coach to the bridge and met up with Barong, with whom they drove to Vollendam, in order to view the sloops. When they arrived in the fisherman's village, there were no sloops to be found. When they stopped at the shop, supposedly Barong's operation center, nobody there knew anything about two sloops. Barong acted exasperated. 'I don't know what to say. It seems that the sloops have disappeared.'

Hanzel held out his right hand. 'I will take back my deposit.'

Barong stared wideyed at Hanzel. 'Your deposit back?'

'Yes, I want my deposit back. We are going to look for a different boat seller. One who can deliver.'

'But I can deliver. It's just not so simple, you see. I am working with partners. They're not looking after their part of the bargain. I gave them the money you put on deposit to get the sloops and all, but it looks like they never arrived here, like they are supposed to,' said Barong, his hands outstretched, palms up, a pleading look in his eyes.

'I thought you indicated the sloops were being fixed up here, at this shop. Now you tell me they had to come from somewhere else?' Hanzel stared into the man's eyes. He was not amused that his time was wasted again.

'Well, to be honest, I wasn't sure where they were and what repairs were being made. I'm just the salesman.'

'Well, Mister Salesman, I want my money back.' Hanzel was growing angry.

'I don't have it,' replied Barong.

'What do you mean, you don't have it?' Hanzel was beginning to lose patience.

'I told you, I gave it to my partners. To get the sloops here. Maybe they've run off with it? I don't know what to tell you.'

'Do you have any idea with whom you are doing business? I am Hanzel Sventska.'

'I've never heard of you before,' replied Barong.

'You've wasted my time and stolen my money.'

'I haven't stolen your money. I told you I gave it to my partners. If anyone stole your money, it would be them.'

Hanzel pointed to the coach. 'Get in.'

Barong hesitated. 'Get in?'

'Yes. We're going back to Amsterdam. There is nothing to see here in Vollendam,' replied Hanzel, just barely disguising the rising anger he was feeling. As Barong continued to hesitate, Hanzel gripped his belt from behind and with his other hand grabbing the man's collar he literally heaved the boat seller into the coach. Then he climbed in and told the driver to head back to Amsterdam. Twenty minutes later Hanzel told the driver to stop the coach where the road cut through a small forest. He told Barong to get out of the vehicle.

'What are you doing? Are you leaving me here? It will be night soon. I can't stay here in this forest in the dark. There are wolves and bears.' Barong looked fearfully out of the window at the dark shadows beginning to form amongst the trees.

'Get out of the coach,' demanded Hanzel, pushing the man towards the door.

'What if I tell you I'll get you your money back?' pleaded the boat seller.

'Just another story. I am tired of your stories. You have wasted my time and you have stolen my money. I am the wrong man to do that to. Now, get out of the coach!' Hanzel pushed the man out of the door and quickly followed him. Hanzel pushed the man into the forest.

'What are you doing?' asked Barong fearfully. 'Why are you taking me into the forest? Are you going to tie me to a tree, or something?'

Hanzel did not say anything as he pushed Barong behind a large oak. Then he took out his pistol and shot the boat seller through the front of his skull, right between his eyes at close range, blowing the man's brains out of the back of his head, splattering the tree trunk with blood, bone, and cerebral matter. Barong crumpled to the ground and Hanzel returned to the coach. 'Let's go,' he said curtly to the driver. 'And not a word about this to anyone, do you understand? Or you'll end up the same way as him. Dead.'

'Oh, don't worry about me guvnor. I won't tell a soul. He probably had it coming,' said the driver, the quiver of fear in his voice.

'Now go!' demanded Hanzel. A moment later they continued on their way to Amsterdam. 'I hate it when people waste my time and steal my money. I think he never had any sloops to begin with. It was all a scam.'

'It's a wonder that he thought to get away with this. I mean, he did come with us to Vollendam. Surely he would have realized you would be bothered by him not having the sloops and not being able to repay the deposit,' replied Melchior, as if what Hanzel did was normal. However, Melchior felt suddenly ill at ease. The summary execution was not characteristic of Hanzel. There was something obviously wrong.

'What kind of simpletons did he think we are?' asked Hanzel, shaking his head. 'Now we're back to square one. Is there someone who has two sloops for sale?'

'There must be. Surely in a port the size of Amsterdam, you'd think there'd be sloops for sale,' suggested Melchior, looking out of the window at the trees they were passing. For the rest of the way to Amsterdam the two men rode in silence. Hanzel and Melchior were each into their own minds; Hanzel worrying about obtaining sloops, and Melchior about Hanzel's sudden, uncharacteristic behaviour. Normally Hanzel deliberated, sometimes for days, before he ever executed anyone. And that was only thrice in five years; on the island when they had to adjudicate two serious breaches of their code. Melchior had never seen Hanzel just take someone out and shoot him, except in the case they were pirating a ship and there was resistance. But that was different. That was killing of armed opponents in a battle. It was never done in ice cold blood.

When they arrived back in Amsterdam, Melchior wanted to be dropped off at his hotel. He needed to be with his wife and his thoughts. Hanzel bid him good evening and returned the coach to Michael, who gave Hanzel and Hanna, who had been visiting with Maria, a ride back to their hotel. They promised to meet up in the morning to continue their search for sloops.

Next morning Michael picked Hanzel up from his hotel at nine o'clock. However, when they went to fetch Melchior, he claimed to be under the weather and declined to come along. Hanzel shrugged his shoulders and wished him well. Then he and Michael set off to find a boat seller who actually had what they were looking for.

At ten thirty they arrived at the far end of the harbour where they found a couple of large sloops tied up in an obscure little bay. 'There are the sloops we need!' exclaimed Hanzel enthusiastically. When the coach stopped he jumped out and almost ran to the shore to take in the full magnificence of the two sloops. 'I wonder if they're for sale?'

'Perhaps not,' suggested Michael.

'Then, either we steal them, or expropriate them in the name of the king. Simple.' Hanzel put his hands on his hips and looked defiantly at the two sloops. 'Let's go find out what the story is.'

Michael pointed to a shack with an open door. 'Perhaps there is someone in there who knows something about those sloops.'

Indeed, in the shack was a friendly man who worked for the man who owned the sloops.

'He uses them to trade assorted goods for furs in Oslo and tin goods in Edinburgh, mostly,' said the man, when Hanzel asked him about the sloops.

'Do you think he might consider selling them?' asked Hanzel.

The man shook his head. 'I doubt it. He's getting ready to make another voyage into the Baltic next month. We're going to begin preparations this very afternoon. Have to replace some ropes and sails. Replace some paint, that sort of thing. Mister Koopman is traveling at the moment, picking up lace goods from Belgium and ceramics from Maastricht.'

'I see,' said Hanzel, tersely. He looked at Michael for a moment and then returned his gaze to the man. 'Do you know of anyone who might have a couple of sloops for sale. Similar to those two. I need them to be at least eighty feet, preferably in the hundred foot range, like those.'

The man shook his head. 'Not off the top of my head.'

'When will Mister Koopman be back?' asked Hanzel, beginning to foment a plan.

'Oh, not for at least another two or three weeks,' replied the man. 'We're to begin getting the sloops ready. We'll likely begin loading supplies in the next couple of weeks. We're scheduled out of Amsterdam in early March or April.'

Hanzel nodded and regarded the man for a moment longer before thanking him for the information. Then he regarded Michael. 'Come, let's go. Perhaps we'll find other sloops somewhere.'

'Have you tried Rotterdam? I believe there are a whole lot of boats for sale there. I'm not sure about sloops, though. They're in short supply because of the wars. Privateers prefer them because they are easy to handle and quick.' The man gestured towards the two sloops tied up across from the shack. 'That's why I like sailing those boats. They handle so beautifully up there in the Baltic. Not too large, maneuverable, and quick. They slip through the water like a knife through butter.' The man stepped out of the door and took a deep breath of air. Hanzel and Michael followed him outside. 'Yes sir, those sloops are a couple of the nicest sailing boats I've skippered.'

'Oh, so you're a captain, are you?' asked Hanzel.

The man; nodded proudly. 'Yes, I am. I've skippered boats since I was twenty three. I've been to sea since I was a boy.'

Hanzel glanced at Michael and exchanged a look. Michael could read his mind and nodded almost imperceptibly.

'What sort of money does Mister Koopman pay you to skipper his sloop?' asked Hanzel.

The man regarded Hanzel quizzically. 'Why do you want to know that?'

Hanzel smiled. 'I'm not only looking for two sloops, I'm also looking for another captain to skipper one of the sloops. Perhaps you might be interested to make easily twice, if not three times what Mister Koopman is paying you.'

The man rubbed his chin and regarded Hanzel. 'Two to three times what he pays me?'

Hanzel nodded. 'Easily.' He looked at Michael. 'What do you think, Mister Webb?'

'Oh, easily.' MIchael gestured towards Hanzel. 'With him I made a fortune. And I was first mate, not a captain.'

The man looked at Hanzel for a moment. 'Alright. He pays his captains in English pounds stirling. I get twenty four pounds per annum with a bonus at Christmas, depending on how well we did that year. My bonus was three pounds this last Christmas.'

Hanzel shook his head and looked at Michael. 'Twenty four pounds per annum, Michael. 'Can you believe that? The skinflint pays a skilled man like,' Hanzel leaned towards the man, 'what did you say your name is?'

'I didn't,' replied the man.

'Well, what is your name?' asked Hanzel.

'Grotenberg. Marvijn Grotenberg,' replied the man.

'Alright, Mister Grotenberg, the point is this. Twenty four pounds per annum, plus a piddly bonus at Christmas is not enough for a man with your years of experience at sea. How long have you been to sea?'

'Well, I went to sea when I was ten years old. I believe that I am forty three. So, about thirty three years,' replied Marvijn.

'Thirty three years. And he thinks that twenty four pounds is adequate compensation. Well, Mister Grotenberg, I can assure you that if you were to work for me you would make a whole lot more than that. My guess is you would at least make a hundred pounds per annum with bonuses exceeding that. We sometimes have paid out bonuses five times per year, wouldn't you say, Mister Webb?' Hanzel looked at his friend.

Michael nodded. 'There were a couple of years when we managed to pay dividends five times.' Michael thought for a moment and smiled. 'Yes, those were good years. In fact, I recall one year we had ten. Remember that, Hanzel? Ten in one year!'

Hanzel smiled at the thought. 'Yes, ten. That was a very good year.'

Marvijn watched the two, obviously wealthy gentlemen, reminiscing and was becoming increasingly intrigued. *These men know how to make money, I get the impression. Maybe I would be better to join forces with these two. If I can make a hundred pounds or more per year, I'll be set up and can consider buying a house.*

'Well, what do you say? Are you going to join us, or stay with Mister Skinflint?' Hanzel watched Marvijn giving it another thought and then, holding out his hand, he agreed to join Hanzel and Michael.

Hanzel grinned as he took a golden florijn from his purse. He handed the coin to Marvijn. 'This is to show my good faith.'

Marvijn smiled and thanked Hanzel. 'So, when do I start?'

'You will begin immediately. Continue to oversee the refitting of the ships. Then, when they are ready, we'll steal them from Mister Koopman under a letter of expropriation from the king. He needs the sloops for privateering ventures against the Spaniard in the Caribbean.'

'Oh, I don't think Mister Koopman is going to like that,' replied Marvijn.

'I am willing to bet on that,' agreed Hanzel. 'However, since there are few sloops for sale, and these two will do, we have no choice. You say Mister Koopman will not be back for two to three weeks?'

Marvijn nodded.

'Alright. Here is the plan. I will pay you some more up front. Get the sloops ready in two weeks and we'll take them out of here after that. The king will compensate Mister Koopman.' Hanzel reached into his purse and extracted two golden ducats and another florijn. He handed them to Marvijn, who very gratefully accepted them. The coins represented more than a month's wages. 'We'll check back with you in two weeks. Then we'll go from there.'

Marvijn agreed that he would see to having the sloops ready in two weeks. Hanzel and Michael shook hands with him and then stepped into the coach. 'Alright then. We'll see you in two weeks.' Hanzel regarded Marvijn standing beside the road through the open window of the coach. Marvijn saluted as they drove away.

'Mission accomplished,' said Hanzel, happily. 'Those sloops will fit the bill very nicely. I am so looking forward to the upcoming adventures. Pirating is great fun and like Christmas everytime we take a prize. We never know what we're going to get.'

'Like a box of chocolates,' observed Michael.

Hanzel regarded his friend. 'A box of chocolates?'

'It's the latest thing.' Michael smiled. 'Chocolateries in Amsterdam make these marvelous creations out of cocoa from Brazil. My friend, François de Chevalier has a shop. What a terrible oversight on our part that we never introduced you to his chocolates yet. I will tell Maria when I get home and we'll arrange to go to his shop. You have to try them. They are delightful.'

'What are they, exactly?' asked Hanzel, not being familiar with chocolates. 'I've tasted the chocolaté drink in the Caribbean, but don't care for it much. It's too bitter.'

'No, no. Chocolates are a hardened form of that substance. François mixes the cocoa with butter, sugar, and cream. Then he wraps the chocolate around cherries, or almonds, peanuts, candied confections. I never know what I'm going to get. Everyone is a surprise.' Micheal grinned. 'I can't wait for you to try them. You should bring Hanna a box of chocolates. I guarantee, you will make her day.'

'Well, let's go visit François. I can't wait to try them,' replied Hanzel, happily taking a cigar from the box proffered by his excellent friend.

Over the next two weeks, Hanzel oversaw recruitment since Melchior claimed to be not well and had decided to seek a warmer climate for the rest of the winter. He and Tina, accompanied by Jestin and his girlfriend left for Italy with a wagon and two horses. Their goodbye was cordial but cool. Hanzel did not understand why his first mate and his brother acted as they did, however he wished the three a safe journey.

'I'm sad to see them go,' said Hanzel to Mister Padrone and Michael. They watched from Michael's coach as their friends drove away from Amsterdam through the south gate, headed for Tuscany, where Melchior and Jestin had a brother and two uncles involved in the building trade. 'Something came over him a few weeks back. I don't know. Ever since we stopped doing business with that boat seller we met at the bridge, Melchior began withdrawing his affections. Perhaps he didn't like the way I did business with that fellow.'

Michael shrugged his shoulders. 'Perhaps. Maybe he just needs a break to spend time with family.' Michael shivered. 'However, given how chilly it is here in the winter, I don't blame him for wanting to go to Tuscany. Maybe we should consider that ourselves?' He rapped on the ceiling signaling the driver to head back into the city.

'I told you Michael, we're taking these sloops back to the Caribbean. We'll sail from our island and raid the Spaniards coming from Central America. They're stealing the Indians blind. And look how they've treated the people of these low lands. We can work, make money, and be in a warm climate.'

'Yes, but Hanzel, you have to understand, I have a business to run here. I can't just up and leave. Besides, I don't think Maria would want to go. She is so settled here, now.

You know how passionate she is about the theatre.'

Hanzel nodded. 'Yes, I know. But you are stagnating here. There is no adventure. You work. You make money. You go to the theatre. You go to concerts. You hobnob with the hoity toity, but there is no adventure. You're a man who is made for adventure. Not for becoming a fat old businessman in Amsterdam.'

Michael looked at Hanzel and nodded slowly. *He's right. I am starting to get fat. And there surely isn't any adventure in my life, that's for sure.* 'That's likely why Maria and I like the theatre so much. It replaces the adventures we could otherwise be having. We live something of a vicarious life through the plays we watch.'

'It's not real life. As time has passed, while Hanna and I have had to wait here in Amsterdam, we're both becoming anxious to return to our island and the pirate way of life. As soon as she has her new leg, and we have our boats ready to sail, we are getting out of here. The sooner the better. We're missing out on adventures we could be having. I can't wait to get after those Spaniards.' Hanzel rubbed his hands together.

'I must admit, since you've been here, I've thought about sailing more and more. I do miss our life on the island and the adventures. I miss raiding ships and towns. It's all great fun. And, I do like the easier life. Amsterdam is busy and hectic. It's true.' Michael shrugged his shoulders. 'But, then, life is safer here.'

Hanzel snorted. 'That's not true. There are lots of cutthroats, thieves, cutpurses, and such like roaming about in Amsterdam. Every night there are homicides. Life at sea is likely much safer. Unless we are attacked, or we meet up with belligerent prizes, or we run into an aberration like that camouflaged Spaniard. And there is always the chance we meet a bad storm, or we fall ill, catch rhueme, or aspyrixies, or some such thing. Maybe rotten food gets you. There is always that, of course. But we're pretty careful about screening the victuals we take on board. Martyn does a good job of that. I think he's still with us. Good cook. Makes the best roasted chicken I've ever tasted. And his Italian cuisine is delightful. Nobody does a better eggplant parmigiana than him. If we have the right cheese. It's not so good if you don't have the right cheese.' Hanzel looked away for a moment as he thought of Martyn's eggplant parmigiana, a dreamy expression on his face.

'You're making my mouth water, Hanzel. And bringing attention to the fact it is lunch time. My stomach is saying, "Michael, it's time to eat." Let's go to the *Witte Engel* for lunch. Their herring soup is unbelievable. And mussels, like you've never tasted in your life. Not to forget their fresh bread, sausages, cheeses, and rollmops...' Michael's mouth was beginning to water. 'Come, let's fetch our wives and children and go for lunch. I am feeling like that is the right thing to do for the rest of the afternoon. Don't you, Hanzel? What about you Mister Padrone?'

'Yes, I could stand a bite to eat,' agreed Mister Padrone. 'It'll just be me.'

Hanzel nodded. 'Ya, it is time for lunch. However, given all that we're about, right now, I would rather lunch just with you two, so we can talk and go over details. I want to take those sloops out of here as soon as Hanna has her new leg, which, given how well she has healed, I think she'll be good to go sooner than May. She'll likely be good to go at the end of March or mid April.'

'Are you sure of that? You don't want to rush it. If her leg is not quite healed right...' suggested Michael.

'Yes, Hanzel,' agreed Mister Padrone. 'I know of someone who tried to rush matters and ended up hurting himself.'

'Yes, well, so be it. The experts at the leg place know if it'll work, or not. I'm taking her there at the end of the month,' replied Hanzel.

'I found Doctor van Vliet, most helpful,' agreed Mister Padrone. 'My new eye feels good.'

'Looks good too.' Hanzel smiled at his sailing master, not quite knowing which eye to look at. 'Too bad about that, though.'

'Could have been worse,' suggested Mister Padrone, philosophically. 'Look at your poor wife. I'm sure she'd much rather have lost an eye than a leg.'

'Oh, I don't know. I'd miss that eye. Hanna has beautiful eyes. I love her eyes. However, you are probably right. To lose a leg, especially for someone as active as Hanna is, is likely the worse option of the two. I just wish neither had happened.' Hanzel suddenly assumed a fearsome expression which surprised his two friends. 'If we ever catch that Spaniard, I will personally rip the captain's heart from his chest and feed it to his crew.'

The vehemence by which Hanzel expressed his hatred of the sneaky Spaniard took Michael and Mister Padrone by surprise. They glanced sideways at each other and then back at Hanzel, who sat silent and fuming, looking out of the window of the coach as they rode past a flower shop. 'Stop the coach!' he shouted.

Michael told the driver to stop. No sooner had the coach stopped than Hanzel jumped out and ran to the flower shop, emerging five minutes later with a massive bouquet of flowers. When he stepped into the coach his mood had returned to normal and smiling, he asked to be taken to, François de Chevalier, Chocolaterie et Patisserie for a box of chocolates and fresh croissantes before going back to his hotel. 'I am sorry gentlemen. I will pass on lunch. I need to spend the rest of the day with Hanna. I'm sure you understand.'

Michael and Mister Padrone agreed that Hanzel had likely made the right decision.

'She'll like the flowers,' said Michael when they dropped Hanzel off at his hotel. 'And I already know she likes François' chocolates.'

'Ya, I think so too.' Hanzel nodded as he smiled at the bouquet in his hand. Then he wished his friends a good day, turned on his heels and entered the hotel. Moments later he surprised his happy wife with the beautiful bouquet, much to her delight.

'They pale in comparison to you, my darling,' he said, before kissing her gently on her mouth. 'Where is little Hanzel?'

'Oh, Maria came by and she and Michaela basically kidnapped him. He's staying over there for a sleep over. We have the suite all to ourselves.' Hanna smiled as she watched Hanzel place the bouquet in the water pitcher.

'Good thing there's water in there.' He set the bouquet in the center of the table, beside which Hanna was sitting.

'Thank you Hanzel. They're lovely.' Hanna leaned over and smelled the flowers before opening the box of chocolates. Her surprised expression indicated that François had once again, come up with something new.

'I'm hungry. What about you?' asked Hanzel.

Hanna nodded.

'I'm going down to order up a big lunch. Do you want wine or ale?'

'Wine, please,' replied Hanna, smiling happily. *He's such a good man. I love him so much.* 'Remember butter for the croissantes.'

Forty minutes later, Hanzel and Hanna were enjoying a fabulous meal after which they gratefully reclined on their bed and napped before making love for the rest of the afternoon and into the evening. When they felt hungry again, Hanzel dressed casually and walked down to the kitchen to order dinner to be brought up. He also ordered two more bottles of wine and a bottle of rum with a pitcher of water. An hour later, much to Hanna's happy surprise, Hanzel had ordered a feast. Fresh oysters with lemons, sautéed haddock with roasted potatoes and steamed leeks with onions, slices of roasted beef, two small roasted stuffed hens with rice and vegetables, and for desert Hanzel had chosen Hanna's favorite; chocolate torte and coffee. The torte and coffee was brought up to the room an hour and a half after the main courses had been delivered to their suite. When their appetite for food and drink was finally sated, they lay on the bed, looking at the ceiling of the room. They both sighed at the same time. 'Ah, life is good,' said Hanzel, grinning from ear to ear.

'I totally agree with you. Life is good. Even if I lost a leg. I wouldn't trade my life with you for anything, Hanzel.' Hanna looked into Hanzel's eyes. Then she leaned over and kissed him.

Hanzel smiled. They were a happy couple and happier still, knowing they would soon be returning to the sea and their life as pirates in the Caribbean.

Chapter 42

Two weeks later the time came to see about the sloops. Hanzel had acquired a letter of expropriation from the king's secretary, in the event the owner would not sell the boats. 'But he likely won't be there, anyway. What did Marvijn say? Mister Koopman wouldn't be back for two to three weeks. It has only been two weeks since we contracted with Marvijn. So, we'll just leave Mister Koopman this letter. He can collect directly from the king's exchequer.' Hanzel held up the letter. 'It is marvelous how a piece of paper like this can be exchanged for two ships.'

'Sure does make life simple, doesn't it?' replied Michael, smiling broadly.

At the far end of the harbour where the boats lay tied, Marvijn saw them arrive and waved. The first thing Hanzel asked when he stepped out of the coach is, 'are they ready?'

Marvijn agreed that the sloops were ready. 'However, there is a slight complication. Mister Koopman is arriving this afternoon. I think he may put up a fuss. He is planning to use those sloops next month to begin his trade in the Baltic. I imagine he has many wagon loads of stuff coming back from Belgium, France, Italy, and Switzerland, not to forget several loads of ceramics from Maastricht.'

Hanzel held up the letter from the exchequer. 'I have a letter of expropriation from the king. Mister Koopman has no choice. He has to give up the sloops for the king's service.'

Marvijn looked at the letter in Hanzel's hand. 'You can be the one to give it to him. I know how he'll react. Mister Koopman is not exactly a gentle soul. I think he may even have been a pirate at one time in his life.'

Hanzel stroked his chin. 'A pirate, you say?'

'Rumor has it. I don't know for certain. He's never mentioned it. But he surely has a piratical sense about him. If you know what I mean.' Marvijn regarded Hanzel and Michael.

Hanzel shook his head. 'A piratical sense about him? What do you mean by that?'

Marvijn collected his thoughts for a moment. 'Well, by piratical sense I mean, he talks like a pirate. He has a parrot he likes to carry about on his shoulder, when he's at home. He wears gold earrings in his ears and has a scar, on his cheek. From here to there.' Marvijn drew a line from his right eye to the bottom of his chin. 'When he gets angry, watch out. I'm convinced he's committed some homicides, or has had some committed. And he's very rough around the edges. Quite boorish, in fact. And he drinks, like a fish. And womanizes. I'll bet he's been with every whore in Amsterdam and likely one in every town he spent a night in, back and forth from Sweden to Switzerland.' Marvijn thought for a moment. 'He's quite the irascible character, ol' Mister Koopman.'

'I'm confident he'll want to do business with us,' said Hanzel. He winked at Michael. 'I've dealt with pirates before.'

'You've dealt with pirates? What exactly is it that you do? Why do you need these sloops? I remember you mentioning, privateering?' Marvijn regarded the two men standing beside their coach.

'We aim to take three sloops into the Caribbean and investigate Spanish shipping on behalf of the Dutch Crown. The king is completely agreed to this. I have a Letter of Marque.' Hanzel smiled at the recollection of how easy it all was. 'The king really detests the Spaniard, as I do.' *I think he must have seen it in my eyes.* 'The king knows I will make good on his investment.'

Marvijn regarded Hanzel and Michael for a moment before replying. 'You want me to captain one of the sloops, you said. But, I've no experience with privateering. I've just skippered one of those sloops to trade in the Baltic. I've never boarded a ship and taken her a prize. Nothing like that. Not in the war. Never.'

'It's nothing to be scared of,' said Michael. 'I've been on a number of adventures and you get used to it. It's not really dangerous because most merchant ships are not armed and have but small crews; not more than thirty, forty, tops. They're not trained in combat. Usually, once they've seen my battle flag, and heard the roar of one of my cannons, they capitulate right away and we can take what we need.' Michael looked at Hanzel for him to corroborate what he just said.

'It's true. It is likely more dangerous living in Amsterdam, especially around the harbour, than privateering. Trust us, you'll enjoy it. It's great fun.'

'And the rewards are potentially incredible. As first mate I was able to amass a small fortune with which I have built a very lucrative tobacco business,' added Michael.

Hanzel looked at his friend and smiled. *I'm beginning to think ol' Michael is beginning to consider coming back. He certainly sounds enthusiastic.*

Marvijn scratched his chin. 'Well, what have I got to lose. Why not. And, besides, I'll be doing something good for my country and king. I despise the Spaniard.'

'Well, that's a start,' agreed Hanzel. 'It makes plundering them all the more easy, when you despise them.' Hanzel put his hands on his hips and looked out at the two sloops lying tied up nearby. 'So, without wasting anymore time, we'll round up the crew and we'll sail these beauties out of here to arm and victual them. We should be out to sea within the month, I am hoping.'

'That's probably still too soon for Hanna,' suggested Michael.

'Yes, I know. I'm thinking of paying the good doctor, or one of his best trained specialists to come with us to sea. Then he can look after Hanna and we can make certain she gets the very best care. To have a second doctor on board is also a good idea. With three ships and two doctors, we should be alright.' Hanzel looked to Michael for a response.

'That's a good idea, Hanzel. I'm sure you can dangle a big enough carrot to attract another doctor,' agreed Michael.

'Exactly,' said Hanzel turning to step up into the coach. 'Come, let's fetch the crew.'

An hour later Hanzel and Michael were standing on the deck of the sloop, *Lieve Hanna*. Altogether 83 people were presented to Hanzel by the sailing master, Mister Padrone. Hanzel welcomed them on board. Then, without wasting any more time he informed them of their immediate duty, that being the expropriation of two sloops tied up at the far end of the harbour. Over there.' Hanzel pointed in the direction where the sloops lay tied. He looked over at Michael. 'Do you want to captain one of them? Just to take her out of there and bring her over here?'

Michael looked at Hanzel for a long moment before replying. Then he slowly nodded his head and agreed he would do it. 'But just to bring her here. I'm not going back to sea.'

Hanzel smiled. 'Ya, ya, I know. It's just so we have someone in command on each sloop. I'll let Mister Grotenberg captain the other one. I'll likely be busy dealing with Mister Koopman if he shows up while we're maneuvering the sloops out of that cul de sac they're in.' Hanzel looked out over the assembled crew. 'Alright. I expect you each to do your duty. Be efficient and listen to the officers I am appointing for now. Mister Webb and Mister Grotenberg, whom you shall meet over there, will be your captains. They will each chose their first mates. Other officers are not necessary, yet. Once we have all three sloops together, we'll victual them and get them ready for sea. While that is being done, the rest of you will go recruiting in earnest. I want at least eighty people on board each ship.'

'Aye, Captain!' shouted the assembled group.

'Alright, let's be about our business,' replied Hanzel.

Instantly everyone began to organize rowing people to shore, which was completely effected within a half an hour. With Hanzel and Michael leading in the coach, the crew followed them to the place where the sloops lay waiting. Unfortunately, Mister Koopman had returned in the meantime and was standing in the middle of the road. Behind him were seventeen other men, each one brandishing a weapon of some sort. Mister Koopman was holding a pistol in his right hand. Marvijn was nowhere to be seen.

'I've come for the sloops,' said Hanzel, stepping from the coach.

'Well, you might as well turn around and go back where you came from. These here sloops are not for sale.' Mister Koopman spit an oyster into the water. It landed with a plop.

'I have a letter of expropriation from the king,' replied Hanzel, holding up the letter.

'You can stick that letter up your arse. I don't give a tinker's damn about a letter from the king.' Mister Koopman brandished his pistol in Hanzel's direction.

Hanzel did not react to the pistol as Mister Koopman had anticipated. Hanzel stood his ground and stared into the man's eyes. 'If you look, you'll see eighty five people coming this way. They're my crew. They're coming to sail these sloops to our anchorage where we can get them ready for a voyage to the Caribbean to lay waste on Spanish shipping.' He tried to hand the letter to Mister Koopman.

'I'll not honour that rag by accepting it into my hand.' Mister Koopman spat another gob, this time at Hanzel's feet.

Hanzel looked down at the gob and then back at Mister Koopman. His expression remained ice cold as his eyes bored into those of Mister Koopman. 'You have no choice. If you do not relinquish these sloops, for which you will be recompensed, the king will send his troops down here to enforce the letter. He needs these ships for his service.'

'If you try to board these sloops, there will be trouble. My men are prepared to put up a fight.'

'There are only eighteen of you. There are eighty seven of us. You are greatly outnumbered,' said Hanzel calmly.

'I see there are women in that crowd. My men are seasoned fighters. Have to be. There are a lot of miscreants robbing travelers, especially those with loaded wagons.' Mister Koopman gestured towards his men. 'As you can see, my men are armed, as well.'

'Why must it come to this? Why fight and cause harm and suffering? For what? Two sloops which the king will get regardless? You just have to face the fact. I have a letter of expropriation. The king wants me to fight Spaniards in the Caribbean. We need three sloops to do that properly.'

Mister Koopman regarded Hanzel quizzically. 'But there are only two sloops.'

'We have another one. She's anchored in the harbour.' Hanzel pointed in the direction where the sloop lay bobbing on the gentle waves of the great port. 'We're going to sail these two over there and then outfit and victual them at the same time.'

Mister Koopman raised his eyebrows. 'Outfit them? How exactly are you outfitting them?'

'We're going to add guns to these two. The king has requisitioned thirty two twelve pounders; sixteen per sloop, plus bow and stern guns. The other sloop is already fitted this way. She just needs to be victualed,' answered Hanzel.

'So, when exactly are you planning to leave Amsterdam?' Mister Koopman lowered his pistol as he began to take a greater interest in what Hanzel was saying.

'I hope to leave by April first at the very latest. Preferably we leave in early March,' said Hanzel. 'It will take some time for the carpenters to effect the changes necessary for accommodating the guns.'

Mister Koopman scratched his chin. 'So, you're planning to do some privateering in the Caribbean, eh?'

Hanzel nodded. 'That is the general plan.'

'You know, I've done some, *privateering* myself, nod nod, wink wink,' replied Mister Koopman, conspiratorially. 'Perhaps me and my men should go along with you. It would do us some good. Get some exercise, as it were. It would be a nice change from sailing the Baltic all spring and summer and fall.' He looked back towards a number of loaded wagons sitting by the pier, where the sloops were tied. 'I suppose I could sell that merchandise in Amsterdam. If we don't sail until March, early April, that would give me lots of time.' He looked back at his men. 'What do you say boys? Do you want to sail in the sunny south and wreak havoc on the Spaniard? Or do you want to sail in the cold Baltic and carry on a boring trade?'

Mister Koopman's crew looked at each other and murmured their ideas. The consensus they reached was, *yes*, they would love to sail in the sunny south, but were concerned whether they would make the same money, or not.

Hanzel assured them they would make considerably more money coming with him.

The crew agreed to go south.

Mister Koopman nodded as he regarded Hanzel. 'I'll come with you on one condition.'

'And that is?'

'I am master of my own ship.' He pointed to the blue sloop. 'That would be her. *De Blauwe Tulip*. I've had her for near ten years.'

'What about Mister Grotenberg? I had paid him to become master of one of the ships.' Hanzel looked beyond the group of men to see if he could see Marvijn. He was nowhere to be seen. 'What have you done with him?'

'Mister Grotenberg? He unfortunately met with an accident. I don't know how it happened. When he went over to inspect one of those wagons over there, a barrel full of pewter ware fell on him and crushed his ribcage. He's lying in that building.' Mister Koopman pointed at the structure. 'We're waiting for the coroner.' Mister Koopman shook his head sadly. 'It's a funny thing. One minute a person is alive and negotiating deals with strangers and the next minute they're dead and dealing with the devil.' Mister Koopman stared into Hanzel's eyes, making sure he got the point. He, Mister Koopman did not treat disloyalty kindly.

Hanzel stared back, not flinching a mote. *Even though this man is obviously no push over, and ruthless, he could be a great asset. He has the sense about him of a pirate. And, he likely does have experience in the sweet trade. He didn't get that scar from sitting on his arse in an office. Could be from the wars. If I keep a good eye on him maybe he'll work out. I could certainly use his men. And to have another experienced skipper, that is absolutely necessary.* 'Alright. If you join us, you can be master of your own ship. I expect that you will sign the articles of our organization and comply with them.'

'Depends on what they are. I don't sign anything I have not read.'

'I will show them to you when you're on board my sloop, *Lieve Hanna*. In the meantime, let's get on with the business of moving these sloops where they're more accessible to my carpenters and the king's armorers.' Hanzel pointed to the sloops and gestured for his people to get to work.

'Will you have a drink with me in my office?' Mister Koopman pointed towards the building where Marvijn lay in state. Then he stuck out his hand and introduced himself. 'Bertus, Jacobus, Koopman.

Hanzel took his hand. 'Hanzel Sventska. Captain of the, *Lieve Hanna*. I named her after my wife and mother of my son.'

'I am pleased to make your acquaintance and glad to do business with you,' replied Mister Koopman.

'This is my dearest friend, Michael Webb. He was my first mate, now he is a tobacco tycoon.' Hanzel grinned as he watched Michael and Mister Koopman shake hands.

Hanzel looked at Michael. 'Since you're one of the captains, I guess you will have to oversee one of those sloops.'

'My first mate is looking after *De Blauwe Tulip*,' said Mister Koopman. 'He knows what he's doing.'

Michael looked at the sloop and then back at Hanzel. 'Well, I think I can remember what to do.'

Hanzel touched Michael's shoulder. 'Don't worry. As soon as you stand on deck, you'll know what to do.'

'I take it he hasn't sailed for a while,' observed Mister Koopman, gesturing towards Michael.

Hanzel nodded. 'Not for at least four, nearly five years.'

'Don't worry, you'll remember what to do,' said Mister Koopman over his shoulder as he and Hanzel walked towards the building. Michael took a deep breath and then walked towards the gathered crew and began organizing their distribution on the two sloops.

Meantime, Hanzel and Mister Koopman stepped into the office building and sat down at a table groaning under the combined weight of reams of papers, books, assorted merchandise samples, a pot of ink, and a holder full of goose quills. A crock of Jenever sat on top of a ledger. Mister Koopman obtained two pewter cups and poured a generous portion of the clear liquor into each. He handed a cup to Hanzel. Then he held up his cup and said, 'Here is to successful adventures together. May we wreak vengeance on the Spaniard for what he has done to the United Provinces, and may we become rich in the process.'

Hanzel grinned. 'An excellent toast, my new friend.' He clicked his cup against Mister Koopman's.

'So you say you have a letter of expropriation from the king? May I have a look at it?'

Hanzel retrieved the letter from a pocket and handed it to Mister Koopman. He opened the parchment carefully and read the contents of the missive. When he was done reading he grinned from ear to ear. 'Not only will you have the sloops, my friend, the king is going to pay me for them. There is no mention in the letter that me and my men can't sail on those boats. The letter says that I am to present my invoice to the exchequer at the palace. So, while you and our crews get those boats to their new location, I will go to the palace with this letter and my invoice. Then I can pay my men some money and they can buy what they want to take with them to the south seas. I can further use that money to make my sloop as comfortable as possible.' Mister Koopman rubbed his hands together. 'Yes, she'll be right fine by the time I'm done.'

'So, where is Mister Grotenberg?' asked Hanzel looking towards a curtained doorway.

'He's behind those curtains in another room. Do you want to see him?' Mister Koopman gestured towards the curtains.

'Well, since I did hire him, I should at least pay my respects,' replied Hanzel draining his cup.

Mister Koopman nodded. 'Yes, of course, of course.' He got up and held a curtain aside to facilitate Hanzel's access to the room. There, on a table, lay the outstretched corpse of Marvijn Grotenberg. Hanzel went over to it and gave the body a cursory examination. He touched the ribcage and ascertained that it was, indeed, crushed. As he was thusly touching the cadaver's chest, he noticed two pistol balls had also been put into service to effect the premature demise of the unfortunate skipper. *Probably shot after they tried to crush him. He likely didn't die from the pewter barrel so they had to finish him off with two shots to the head. I had better be on my guard with Mister Koopman. I'm sure he'll make a good ally when it comes time to dealing with the Spaniard. I don't want to be on his bad side.*

When Hanzel returned to the other room, Mister Koopman just finished pouring another round of Jenever. 'Well, what do you think? He's quite dead, yes?'

Hanzel nodded his head slowly. 'Yes, he certainly is dead, alright. Poor fellow.'

'Yes, it is one of life's tragedies, how a simple accident can snuff a man's life, just like that.' Mister Koopman snapped his fingers. Then he drained his cup and grinned. 'Aargh, that's much better.' He poured more Jenever into his cup and held the crock, offering more to Hanzel, who declined. When Mister Koopman drained the cup, he let out a long sigh and then farted mightily. 'So, can you take me to the palace in your coach? Then we'll have us a feast tonight.'

Hanzel nodded, trying hard not to breathe through his nose. 'Ya, we can go now, if you like.'

'Yes, let's go now. While the day is still young,' agreed Mister Koopman. 'First I must write up an invoice for the king.' He reached for a quill and grabbed a piece of blank paper. 'What are those sloops worth? Let me see. I paid twenty for *De Blauwe Tulip* and fifteen for the other one. That's thirty five altogether. But that was a few years ago. But then, I've put money into them over the years to maintain them. So, they really are worth thirty five, still.' He dipped the quill into the ink pot and began to write on the paper. When he was done, he stood up, scratched his groin, and walked out of the building, invoice in one hand and the letter in the other. Hanzel followed, happy to step back into fresh air.

As he climbed into the coach, Hanzel could see that the crew of *the Blauwe Tulip* were already raising the mainsail. 'Shouldn't take them long to get out of here.'

Mister Koopman nodded as he read over the invoice he had cobbled together in such short order. 'Yes, thirty five should do just nicely.'

An hour later Hanzel and Mister Koopman introduced themselves to a page at the palace and asked to see the exchequer.

An hour later they were still seated in an antechamber of the palace waiting for the exchequer to take care of Mister Koopman's invoice. Two hours later they were still waiting. When the clock indicated they had been waiting for four hours, Mister Koopman was becoming impatient. 'I know things work slowly in government. But surely someone should have come to talk to us by now.'

'Ya, it is strange. Maybe we should approach somebody and ask where the exchequer is,' suggested Hanzel. 'I'm not as familiar with how things work here as my friend, Michael.' Hanzel looked at the clock on a mantel across from where they were sitting. 'They likely are anchored by now and wondering where we are.'

'Well, dag nab it! I am bloody sick of this sitting around. Someone had better come and talk to us or by the cod piece of Jupiter, I'll break something!' Mister Koopman looked for something to break.

'I didn't know Jupiter had a cod piece? I thought he went without one. Au nuturelle, so to speak,' replied Hanzel, thoroughly amused by Mister Koopman's histrionics.

'Oh, I don't know if he does or doesn't. It's just something I say, when I'm frustrated.'

Hanzel pointed. 'Look, here comes a courtier, let's ask him.' Hanzel signaled the man to stop. The man did so, indicating in his demeanor that it was a great inconvenience.

'Do you have any idea where the exchequer is. I believe his name is Master Robert.'

The man looked down his long nose at him. 'That would be his grace, Robert van der Bilt.'

'I only know him as Robert,' replied Hanzel.

'He has likely gone to his suite, or he may have left the palace altogether and gone to his country estate for the weekend.' The courtier looked at the mantel clock. 'Yes, he is usually gone from his office by now.'

'What?! Gone from his office?! What do you mean, *gone from his office?*' Mister Koopman was instantly standing beside the courtier with a threatening expression on his face, ready to run him through with his rapier.

The courtier backed up, quivering in his expensive Italian shoes. 'Er, ah, that is how it is. Nothing I can do about it. His grace comes and goes at his pleasure. I have no say in any of his comings and goings. Perhaps you should make an appointment with his secretary.'

'And who by the blue knackers of Bucephalus is that?' thundered Mister Koopman.

The man stared at Mister Koopman with a puzzled expression. 'Er, ah, let me think.' *Blue knackers of Bucephalus?* 'I think you need to speak with the Count of St. Petersberg.'

'Where is he?' asked Mister Koopman impatiently.

The courtier shrugged his bony shoulders. 'I have no idea. He's probably gone home, by now. It's after five o'clock. And it's a Friday. Perhaps it would be better if you came back on Monday. Come back on Monday morning.'

'Come back on Monday morning?! Come back on Monday morning?!!' shouted Mister Koopman. 'By the thunderbolts of Zeus, I'll, I'll break something! Maybe your head!' He reached for the courtier's head, a mad expression in his eyes. The man was so frightened he ducked and ran off, likely to change his undergarment.

When the courtier was well out of ear shot, Mister Koopman laughed. 'Those palace people are such wimpy non men, don't you think?' He looked at Hanzel with a big grin on his face.

'If that one is an example of palace people, I suppose you're right. However, you do present a frightening appearance. The poor man probably thought you would run him through, or tear his head off.'

Mister Koopman nodded. 'So, what do we do now?'

'I guess we go home and come back on Monday,' answered Hanzel. 'Let's go check on the sloops. Then I'll drive you home. Unless you want to stay on board *De Blauwe Tulip*?'

'We'll see when we're there. The boat has been sitting for three months while I was off trading in Switzerland and thereabouts. She probably needs a good airing out.'

'I told Mister Grotenberg to get the sloops ready, two weeks ago. I think an airing out would have been part of that.'

Mister Koopman nodded. 'Well, then. Shall we go?'

'Yes, shall we?' Hanzel gestured towards the doors leading out of the palace. Ten minutes later they were sitting in the coach and headed for the harbour.

When they arrived at the place where the three sloops lay tied, they found that, *Lieve Hanna* was still anchored off shore, but, *De Blauwe Tulip* and *De Heilige Vrouw* were tied to a pier leading out from the roadway on which their conveyance was parked. When Hanzel and Mister Koopman had stepped from the coach, Hanzel pointed to his sloop. 'That's my sloop, over there. And yours you recognize. I see the carpenters are already busy.'

'You waste no time, do you?' observed Mister Koopman, as they began strolling towards the pier.

'My people are well trained. However, most of them are new recruits. It is a good thing that those, who are left of the crew who came with me to Amsterdam, are excellent at teaching others. Because we have pretty regular turnovers in our colony, it is imperative that newcomers be trained quickly.' Hanzel smiled as he put his hands on his hips. He rocked on his heals. 'Ya, my people are the best in the business. That's why we're as wealthy as we are.'

'Oh, so you're pirates, are you?' Mister Koopman regarded Hanzel with great interest.

'I did not say that. I'm a privateer, according to the Letter of Marque from the king. A privateer, not a pirate. I am licensed to plunder Spanish shipping, as long as I give the king forty percent. After all, he is buying your sloops and arming them. Forty percent is reasonable, I think.'

Mister Koopman nodded his head. 'Forty percent? Not a bad deal. For how long will you owe the king forty percent?'

'As long as I sail under his Letter of Marque.'

'If it is true that fortunes can be made in the Caribbean and Central America, at some point you may want to free yourself of your obligations to the king. After a few successful raids, you may very well have paid off everything the king has put into this venture. You can buy him out, if necessary.' Mister Koopman spat a fat gob of goop into the water. He must have scared a gull because one squawked immediately and flew out from below the pier. It flew up and cursed Mister Koopman with a volley of screeches and squawks. before flying off to go sit on a post sticking out of the water ten feet away.

'Ya, there are fortunes to be made out there. If one is smart about it. I have some years of experience and am considered very successful. Compared to most privateers, or pirates out there, I am one of the richer ones.' Hanzel regarded Mister Koopman with a self satisfied countenance.

'You didn't get wealthy like that under Letters of Marque. Come on, tell me the truth. Are you pirates? Have you engaged in the sweet trade?'

Hanzel looked around himself, and then leaned in closer to Mister Koopman. 'Ya. I am a pirate.' He winked and then looked straight ahead with no change in expression.

'I knew it. I think we'll get along famously.' Mister Koopman glanced sideways at Hanzel and nodded. 'Yes, most certainly we'll get a long famously.' He rubbed his hands together.

A gangplank was leaning against *De Blauwe Tulip*. 'You have not seen this sloop, other than from dock side?'

'She looked good from there. I could tell she was in good shape,' said Hanzel. 'I needed to find two sloops. I prefer sloops for our business. They're easy to sail, quick, and maneuverable. These can hold a crew of eighty and carry guns. By the time we're done, your sloops will look quite a lot different when the guns are in place. When we have three, we can carry the cargo of a merchantman and easily overpower them with our numbers.'

When Hanzel and Mister Koopman stepped on board, Hanzel's people saluted him, as did Mister Koopman's men salute him, as well.

'Now that it is getting quite dark out, I suggest you all quit your work and retire for the day,' said Hanzel. 'You can stay on board, if you like, or go elsewhere.'

'Thank you Captain,' answered the crew. Then they dismissed and went their various ways.

'Come, I'll show you my cabin,' said Mister Koopman, heading for the rear hatch.

Standing in the captain's cabin, Hanzel could clearly see that, even though Mister Koopman was uncouth in his behaviour and rough around the edges, he was not an illiterate, uncultured boor. His cabin had a bookshelf with lots of books, and several beautiful paintings graced the walls. A bust of Cicero sat on the desk, which also held several charts, navigation tools, a pot of ink, a jar of quills, and three large, leather bound books.

'Who'se portrait is that?' asked Hanzel, pointing at the bust.

Mister Koopman shrugged his shoulders. 'I have no idea. Some Roman I think. It looks good on my desk.'

'And what about the paintings?' Hanzel walked over to a luminous urban landscape painting of a family sitting in front of their house.

'That one is by some fellow from Delft. Don't know his name. You can read his signature on the lower right, but it is not very clear.'

Hanzel leaned closer but could not make out the signature either. He shrugged his shoulders and then sat down in an ornate chair facing the desk. Mister Koopman retrieved a crock of Jenever and two cups. He poured liquor into each cup and handed one to Hanzel.

'Since the sloop appears to be ship shape and my cabin clean and fresh, I will stay on board. Can you give me a lift to the palace Monday morning?'

'I think it'll be possible. Michael likely will lend me his coach again,' answered Hanzel.

'I can pick you up from here by nine o'clock, I think. It all depends on how soon I can get the coach from him.'

Mister Koopman nodded. 'I'll be ready, whatever time you get here in the morning. I'm an early riser and prefer to get at it. The sooner we get to the palace, the sooner we may get paid for the sloops. Then I'm going to add some more books and nice covers and sheets for my bed. I also think I'll get me a very nice cage and stand for Pedro, my parrot.'

'We have a monkey on board my sloop. His name is Funk. He belongs to Doctor Allan. You'll meet him eventually, that is, if he decides to return with us. He may have decided to stay on shore, I'm not sure. I have not seen him for a while.' Hanzel drained his cup. 'Well, I think I should be going. Hanna is likely hungry and wondering where I am.' He stood up and thanked Mister Koopman for the drink and welcomed him into his gang. 'We'll do a formal induction when we're all ready to sail; when we have a full compliment of crew.'

Mister Koopman nodded. 'Yes, of course. I understand.'

'Right you are,' replied Hanzel as he headed for the door. 'I will see you Monday morning.' Then he left the ship and rode the coach to the other sloop in order to retrieve Michael, who was somewhat hesitant to go.

'There's still so much that needs to be done,' said Michael as they were walking towards the coach.

Hanzel grinned. 'There is always tomorrow.'

'Yes, but I have a business to look after. I can't do both. Captain a ship and conduct my tobacco business.' Michael regarded Hanzel with an exasperated expression.

'At any rate, do you think I can borrow your coach Monday morning, to take Mister Koopman to the palace, so he can get paid for his sloops. If you decide to oversee matters here, we can drive here first, drop you off, and then I'll fetch Koopman and take him to the palace. When he gets his money for the sloops he'll use that to do what is needed on his ship. He's going to give some of the money to his crew, so I'm sure we'll be well equipped by the time we leave port.'

'You can use the coach. But, I'm not sure about my further involvement in your project. If I were to decide to join you, I'd have to clear it with Maria first. I'm not sure she'll go along with it.' Michael shook his head. Hanzel could tell that he was torn and was highly motivated to come back to sea. Hanzel could tell that Michael enjoyed his brief stint as captain of a ship, even if it was for only a short distance.

Michael dropped Hanzel off at his hotel where he joined his wife and little son for a pleasant family evening in their cozy suite. Later that evening, rain started soaking the Port of Amsterdam, not letting up until late Sunday night. Hanzel and his little family stayed dry and happy in their luxurious hotel, eating superbly cooked food and drinking the best the house had to offer.

Monday morning, instead of just sending his driver to pick up Hanzel, Michael personally came to pick him up.

'Does this mean you're going down to the sloop to oversee renovations?' asked Hanzel, surprised to see his friend.

Michael nodded. 'I have good managers. And since you want to go sailing by April, at the latest, I thought I would help you out and donate some time to renovating and outfitting the ships. It's the least I can do to help fight the Spaniard.'

Hanzel smiled and patted his friend on the shoulder. 'Most excellent, Michael. Thank you. Your contributions will be noted and duly recompensed when we return with a treasure.'

Michael nodded. 'Thank you Hanzel. I appreciate that. However, it doesn't matter. I'll consider it like a hobby. I've grown tired, and bored. I spend too much time in the shop and the warehouse. A man needs variety.'

'I heartily agree,' said Hanzel. 'Variety is the spice of life.'

'And so it is,' agreed Michael. 'And so it is, indeed.'

Chapter 43

By mid March the sloops were completely ready. Mister Koopman had been paid by the king, not quite what he was asking, but enough to pay his crew and contribute to making the sloops extra comfortable. Thanks to him, the ships' larders were stocked with excellent fare; the highest quality of everything: pickled herrings, salted herrings, pickled cucumbers, sauerkraut, smoked beef, smoked pork, salted beef, salted pork, salted mutton, fresh potatoes, fresh onions, fresh leeks, cabbages, carrots, beets, dried peas, beans, flour, rice, apples, pears, oranges, lemons, coffee, tea, tobacco, barrels of brandy, ale, wine, rum, and Jenever. Thanks to Michael, Hanzel also had an excellent supply of cigars and tobacco for the pipes of his crew. Michael brought enough for himself and his crew, and Mister Koopman bought what he needed. Each ship also had two live cows and a dozen chickens for fresh milk and eggs. Water was stored in twelve barrels on each ship.

Some of the women fashioned copies of Hanzel's battle flag for the other two sloops. They also sewed three each of, English, French, Netherlands, Spanish, and Swedish flags. 'You never know under what flag you might want to sail to avoid problems with other ships at sea or in ports. There are a lot of pirates and privateers out there. Some are better at it than others. Me, I'm considered to be good at it. Piracy, that is,' answered Hanzel when one of the women asked why they were sewing the flags of other nations as well as their own. She was but sixteen, and inexperienced in the sweet trade.

Much to Hanzel and Hanna's delight, her leg had healed well enough to attempt fitting her for a prosthetic, which Doctor van Vliet was able to fashion for her. By the end of March, much to her great delight, she was able to walk on her own with the aid of a crutch. Doctor van Vliet recommended a doctor to take care of Hanna on board ship. Doctor Winderkint was glad to come along, looking forward to fortune and adventure.

When April 3rd arrived the three sloops left the port of Amsterdam under fair skies and helpful winds. Each ship was crewed by eighty people and captained by, Hanzel, Mister Koopman, and much to Hanzel's great joy, Michael had chosen to come back to sea and captained the, *De Heilige Vrouw*. Maria chose to stay in Amsterdam and oversee their tobacco business. She was completely at peace with Michael's decision, since he promised to return within a year. 'It's just something I need to do one last time, before I completely settle into Amsterdam and become just another wealthy burgher and member of the city council,' he had said to her. Maria heartily agreed. She saw him off with their entire staff and extended family.

Sailing the English Channel passed with no ill winds or ill will from anyone, not the Gods, nor humans intent upon plunder. When they reached the North Atlantic, a squall blew up, necessitating battening the hatches and reefing sails. Routine sailing procedures for the seasoned sailors manning the three sloops. The neophytes were learning their ropes. Not one was lost in the storm. A number did attract that horrible scourge of the unseasoned sailor, sea sickness. Of those green faced victims, several asked to be put out of their misery, making them the brunt of jokes from their more seasoned crewmates.

They anchored in Las Palmas, in the Cape Verde Islands on the first of May. As the three sloops maneuvered to find anchorages, Hanzel sailed past a ship which looked familiar. He mentioned it to Mister Padrone, who agreed he had also seen the ship before. When Hanzel pointed the ship out to Hanna she immediately identified it as the sneaky Spaniard who had shot at them en route to Amsterdam.

'What a splendid coincidence,' said Hanzel rubbing his hands together. 'Now we'll get the chance to get even with him.'

'If they're paying attention, they may have identified us, as well,' replied Hanna. 'We never changed the name of our ship.'

'I doubt if he'll recognize us. We look like an ordinary sloop, like hundreds of others. It's Mister Koopman's, painted blue like that, that makes his stand out. If we don't pay undue attention to their ship they won't be suspicious as to why we're staring at them.' Hanzel returned his gaze to the task at hand, namely guiding the ship to an anchorage. Hanna kept watching the Spaniard.

Later that afternoon, while most of the crew had taken shore leave, Hanzel held a war council in the great cabin of his sloop. Present at the meeting were:

Hanzel, Hanna, Michael, his first mate, Kate, Mister Padrone, Pontelo the quartermaster, Mister Monk, the gunner, Miep, the cook, Mister Koopman, boatswain, Jacques LeBlanc, Mister Koopman's first mate, Norack Waldenstein, Doctors Allan and Winderkint, Gertrude van Hollenhern, quartermaster of *De Blauwe Tulip*, Josephine Mulberry, surgeon's mate, and the gunner on Michael's sloop, Jock McMac. Balthazar served the coffee.

'A great good fortune has presented itself. We have the first opportunity of this voyage, to do something against the Spaniard. We can take revenge on a sneaky bastard who hid himself behind camouflage to entrap us, resulting in terrible effects; Hanna lost a leg, Mister Padrone lost an eye, and two excellent men, Pieter Spierenburg and Herman van der Eisel, an actor of some talent, who entertained us on our island, were killed. We revealed who we were, but they did not reveal that they were an agent of the Spanish crown. Had we known who and what they were; essentially Spanish sea police, we would have stayed clear of them and never lost anything. It is because of that, is why I want to teach those lizards a lesson. I want to show them no mercy. None!' Hanzel banged his fist on the table. 'We do not want such subterfuge to continue on the sea. They must be taught. What do you say?' Hanzel regarded his friends and colleagues, a look in his eyes which could have killed a Spaniard at fifty paces.

'I agree with Hanzel,' said Kate. 'I was there. It's true. Had we known what those cockroaches were, we would never have come within five leagues of them. Think about it. Why would we go after a fully armed navy ship? We wouldn't. They tricked us and we lost two good men and two good people lost pieces of themselves. I agree with our captain. We must teach those Spaniards a lesson they'll never forget. They must be taught to be honest and forthright on the sea. No camouflaging ships.'

'Hear, hear,' said Mister Padrone, nodding his head and tapping his cup with a coffee spoon.

Others followed suit and tapped their cups with spoons.

'Now, the problem is this,' interjected Doctor Allan, 'we could try and board that ship. However, I don't think they leave her unguarded. Knowing something of the Spanish navy, I doubt if many of their sailors or marines have shore leave in any great numbers at a time. Most of the crew would be on board. Given that scenario, we could end up with a lot of casualties; injuries, maimings, and deaths. Is it really worth it? The revenge, I mean. We really don't have anything tangible to achieve. They're not carrying anything of real value to us. We have everything we need, other than treasure. That ship is not carrying any treasure.'

'Doctor Allan is right,' said Gertrude. 'Risking a lot of casualties for nothing is just not worth it. Even though they did what they did, I think we're better serving the king by plundering ships which are carrying precious cargoes. Killing a bunch of Spanish pigs is dangerous. Those swine have sharp tusks.'

'Maybe there's a way we can do something about that ship, without risking any lives or injuries,' suggested Hanna. 'We have explosives experts. Surely we can blow the thing up using subterfuge against them.'

'What do you mean, *subterfuge against them*?' asked Hanzel.

Hanna regarded her husband and smiled. 'We have people on board who speak Spanish. I'm convinced those Spaniards are looking for sailors to replace dead or ill ones. For a navy ship that's a constant problem. They are always having to recruit people. So, we send three or four Spanish speaking people to sign up with the Spaniard. Then, when they're on board, they find out where the powder room is and how it is guarded. When they have the opportunity they rig the place and run a fuse down the side of the ship through an open gun port. Since they're in port, the gun ports are open to air out the ship. Nobody would be on the gun deck because there is no reason to be. It should be a fairly easy task to run a fuse down the side of the ship and then we take our long boat and row alongside that Spanish scorpion and light it and return to our sloop to watch the fireworks.'

Hanzel looked at his wife with admiration in his eyes. 'That sounds like a good plan. If our people can get into their powder stores.'

'Their powder stores are likely guarded,' suggested Mister Koopman.

'Not necessarily,' offered Norack. 'They're in port. There really is no danger.'

'Well, actually, I disagree,' replied Doctor Allan. 'It is likely to be more guarded while in port, than out at sea. It is precisely in port that there is the risk of people doing just as Hanna suggests we do. Those people are paranoid to begin with. Surely they must be concerned there are enemies all around them. There are not too many nations who love the Spaniards, especially not those from *northern* nations.'

'There are ways and means of taking out a couple of marines guarding a locked door,' suggested Hanzel. 'What if we poison them?'

'How would we administer the poison?' asked Doctor Winderkint.

Discussion came to an abrupt end for a moment while everyone pondered the question. How, indeed, would anyone administer poison to a couple of marines guarding a locked door to the powder stores of the Spanish ship?

Miep broke the silence. 'What if we don't bother with poison and simply conk them on the head? Think of it. The powder room of a ship is usually in the bowels where few people have any business. It probably would be easy to sneak down there and knock them on their noggins, break open the door and plant the fuse.'

'Then the question arises. Are any of our Spanish speakers explosives experts?' asked Michael. 'It's all fine and dandy if they succeed in breaking heads and a door. If they don't know anything about explosives, how can we expect to go the next step?'

'We train them beforehand. It doesn't take much to show them what to do,' said Mister Monk. 'I can have them fully trained within an hour.'

'Well, then, that looks like our best plan. Let's approach the crew tomorrow morning, when they have slept off their day in town, and ask for volunteers amongst the Spanish speakers, and then Mister Monk can train them. Hopefully, in the meantime, I hope the Spaniard doesn't leave port. The sooner we get on this project, the sooner the world is rid of those sneaky bastards.' Hanzel clapped his hands together and closed the meeting with a toast. 'Here's to our success!'

'TO OUR SUCCESS!!!' chorused his friends.

Next morning, bright and early, Hanzel visited each sloop and spoke with the crews explaining their plans and asking for volunteers. By noon, four Spanish speaking people were selected from twelve volunteers out of the sixty who could speak Spanish. The four who were chosen, were already trained in the handling of explosives, hence, the plan was immediately put into effect. The four sailors presented themselves to the Spanish ship that very afternoon and were immediately taken on board and given tasks to perform.

Then the waiting began.

It took several days before one of the Spanish speaking sailors, a man named Juan, discovered the powder stores and found they were not heavily guarded at all. Only one marine sat on a chair outside the heavy, locked door. Three days after that, a marine went missing from the ship. He was on duty at nine o'clock in the evening and went missing sometime before the guard change at seven the next morning. Juan and Pedro, one of the other Spanish speakers, managed to break the man's neck and took the key from the deceased before carefully lowering the body overboard through the rear starboard gun port. They made sure to weigh the man down with several cannon balls. When they gained access to the powder stores, they found a keg with a long spool of fuse. They placed the fuse in a keg of powder in the middle of a large stack of kegs and carefully concealed the fuse out of the room and down the side of the ship through the same gun port they lowered the body through. The fuse was difficult to see unless one were to look very closely. When they were done, the powder room was locked and the key thrown overboard.

The next morning, the officers and crew were perplexed. The guard to the powder room was missing, along with the key to the lock.

'De man as gone absento without a leave,' said Captain Battaro to the ship's captain. 'Eef we fine eem I weel mayka an example of eem. Ee wasa guardin de powder room.'

'Did anyone break into the room?' asked the ship's captain, Edwardo Giez. There was fire in his eyes. He was not pleased.

'Not as fara asa we can tell,' replied Captain Battaro. 'De room wasa locked.' He was embarrassed that one of his men had left a sensitive post. 'Wenna I catcha eem I weel whipa de skin ofa ees back. Eel weesh ee wasa nevera born!'

'Search the ship and send a team of scouts to shore and have them search Las Palmas. Have them inquire along the roadway if anyone has seen him. Now go!' ordered Captain Giez

'Si, senior,' replied the captain of the marines. He saluted and then left the cabin, closing the door behind him.

Captain Giez stared at a pistol lying on the table and thought about the strange situation. *Why would the guard to the powder room be gone? Was he murdered? Or did he, in fact, jump ship?* Some minutes later he got up and went down to the powder stores with a second key to the lock, which was kept in his cabin.

Meanwhile, Juan, Pedro, Alberto, and Alfonso, the four members of Hanzel's crew, who rigged the fuse, had to get off the ship, which they neatly effected the next night. The following morning, after that, they were reported missing to Captain Giez. Considering those sailors had only been on board for nine days, it was a puzzle to the captain. Five people missing from his ship and nobody saw them go.

Back on Hanzel's sloop the four Spanish speakers were congratulated for their successful efforts with a gift of gold ducats.

Hanzel clapped his hands together. 'Well, there we have it. The fuse is ready. When shall we light it?'

'The sooner the better,' replied Michael. 'The longer we wait, the more chance they will discover the fuse. We have to do it today.'

'I agree with Michael. We should do it tonight. We'll row over to the gun port and light the fuse. Fireworks are always better at night, don't you think?' Mister Koopman took a sip of Jenever.

'Right you are,' agreed Hanzel. 'We'll do it tonight.'

Unfortunately, that night the weather chose to turn.

Heavy clouds rolled in from the northwest. By later afternoon the sky was completely obscured by roiling clouds which by nightfall began to dump their massive loads of water, driving everyone indoors. Even the gulls took shelter under whatever place they could. Howling winds and torrential rain became the order for the night. All hopes of lighting a fuse were rendered absolutely impossible. And, besides, the Spanish ship had closed all of her port holes. In the process of lowering the gun port door where the fuse was, the fuse was discovered. When Captain Giez was appraised of that anomaly, he quickly put two and two together, to come up with the four who were likely responsible for the plot to connect fire and gun powder and produce a tremendous explosion which might have killed him and his entire crew. Captain Giez was not amused. 'It makes no sense, otherwise. Four men willingly sign up to serve this ship. Then, all four go missing a week later. Now we find there was a fuse hanging down out of the starboard rear gun port. They were going to blow us up!'

'Who ina dis a port woulda wanta blow us up? We dona look like a navy vessel. We a looka like ana armed merchantman?' Captain Battaro, stroked his long, pointed beard. 'I a theen dat a de four who a lef de sheep, are a responsible for a de meesing marine.'

Captain Giez regarded his friend and nodded. 'Of that, there is no question. As soon as the rain quits I want this port searched top to bottom. I want those men found. They will very much regret what they have done.'

'We a will fine dem. Don yu worry, Edwardo. I weel fine dem.' He saluted curtly and gave Captain Giez a tight lipped smile. Then he turned and left the cabin, where Captain Giez thought of ways to exact revenge.

In a thoroughly Spanish evolved mind, and he, Edwardo Manuello Giez de Moesas, coming from many generations of Spaniards, the levels of cruelty which traveled through his imagination were so abominable, that eventually, even he had to turn it off and think about something else, like, who is behind the plot to blow him up? *Someone in port recognized this ship for some reason. Why would a Spanish merchantman be targeted? Unless someone knows we are not what we appear to be and wants to exact revenge. We have lured in three pirates already. One we scuttled. So it has to be the other ones. One was shot up pretty badly before they got away. I doubt if they could have repaired that sad old wreck. They're not likely to be here. But, then, who knows? Maybe some of those pirates managed to find their way here.* Captain Giez stroked his right eyebrow and thought and thought. Eventually he came to an epiphany. *The sloop! Those pirates we lured, thinking we to be a fat prize. It's him. That Dutch pirate. Hanzel Sventska! He is the one. He is in port. I will tell Battaro to find him. If he's here, I'll recognize his boat.* He rubbed his hands together as he peered out of the port side window of his cabin wishing the rain to quit right now!

By the following afternoon the weather abated and life came back to normal in the little port. By two in the afternoon, Hanzel was confronted by a Spanish marine sergeant who had climbed on board *Lieve Hanna* with two companions. When Hanzel asked them their business through one of his interpreters, the sergeant asked for Hanzel Sventska.

Hanzel regarded the marine and told him he had no idea who Hanzel Sventska was. He looked at his friends and then back at the sergeant. 'My name is Jan ver Bruggen.'

'Ee ees a pyrate. Ee ees a Dutch pyrate. Sails in de Caribbean,' replied the sergeant. 'Ee saila sheep wheech looka lot like dese one.' He gestured, indicating the sloop they were standing on.

'There are a lot of sloops on the seven seas which look like this one,' replied Hanzel. 'So, if you will kindly get off my ship, we can set about our work. I want to sail on the next tide.'

'Whad ees your destinatione?' asked the sergeant.

Hanzel eyed the man for a moment before answering. 'Why is that any of your business?'

'We are authorized to get de informasione fora every sheep een port. These islands belong to a Espania,' replied the sergeant haughtily, thinking himself infinitely superior to a mere ship's captain. Especially a Dutch one.

'Well, for your *informasione*, we are heading to the Gold Coast,' replied Hanzel. 'Now, if you will kindly get off my ship we can continue our work.' Hanzel gestured to the port side ladder. 'And, next time, ask permission before boarding my ship.'

The sergeant stared at Hanzel. If looks could have killed someone, that look could have killed Hanzel. The Spaniard was not used to being spoken to like that. Several of Hanzel's crew gathered around, quickly making it apparent to the sergeant and his companions, they had better leave because otherwise they might not ever leave anywhere again. The three Spanish marines quickly climbed down the ladder and rejoined the crew of the longboat. Hanzel and his friends watched them row over to *De Blauwe Tulip*. Hanzel laughed. 'Just wait until they run into Mister Koopman. I'm sure he'll give them a piece of his mind for even approaching his boat.'

When the marine sergeant finally returned to his ship he had to report to Captain Giez. He was asked to describe every ship's master he had spoken with. When he came to the description of Hanzel, Captain Giez sat bolt upright. 'That's him. That's the Dutchman. Hanzel Sventska.' He turned on the sergeant. 'Why didn't you arrest him?'

The sergeant stared dumbfoundedly at the captain. 'I din a no oo e was. E calla a heemsef, ver Bruggen. Jan ver Bruggen.'

'He fits the description of the pirate. He likely made up that name, ver Bruggen.' Captain Giez stroked his right eyebrow as he thought about what to do. A moment later he stood up and told the marine sergeant to go back to the sloop and arrest Jan ver Bruggen.

'Ee as a large crew. I don theenk dey weel joost let us take eem,' replied the marine sergeant.

'Take a ten marines. Shoot ata anyone who a reseest,' ordered Captain Battaro. He regarded Captain Giez, who nodded his assent.

The sergeant saluted and left the cabin to round up his little company.

'I theen I will a go wid dem,' said Captain Battaro. 'I don wanna any mistakes.'

'Neither do I, my friend. Neither do I.' replied Captain Giez. 'Make certain of it.'

'I weel. You can rest assured.' Captain Battaro saluted and then left the cabin.

Captain Giez rubbed his hands together and stared into space, thinking of ways he would be rewarded by the king, and what the king might do to Hanzel Sventska.

Thirty minutes later the Spanish marines were climbing up the sides of *Lieve Hanna*, uninvited and aggressively wielding muskets with bayonets. Hanzel was in his cabin enjoying time with his family. Mister Padrone was in charge on the quarterdeck. Thirty six pirates were lying about on deck, the others were below and in town. Nobody saw the Spaniards coming, it being dusk, and nobody was expecting company. It was not until four marines had climbed over the gunwale when Mark first saw them.

'What are those marines doing here?' he asked, looking at his friend, Elizabeth.

Elizabeth stared through a thin rum induced fog. She rubbed her left eye and focused on the marines. 'They're not supposed to be here.' She nudged Gertrude. 'Someone better alert Hanzel we have company.'

Gertrude stared through her fog and focused on the marines climbing over the gunwale. She shouted, 'AHOY! What are you doing here?!'

Others jumped up and started shouting to call all hands on deck.

'What is all that commotion?' asked Hanna.

Hanzel tried to listen but could not make out what people were shouting. 'I'll go have a look. I'll be right back.' Hanzel got up from his chair and quickly stepped out of the cabin and climbed up the stairs. When he stepped out on deck, he was surprised to find ten Spanish marines, a sergeant and a captain pointing weapons at his crew. 'We are ere to arrest de pyrate, Hanzel Sventska!' shouted the captain. Then he pointed at Hanzel and told the sergeant to cease him.

'I told you people, I am Jan ver Bruggen,' said Hanzel calmly, looking directly at the sergeant.

'You feet de deescreeption of de Ollander, Hanzel Sventska. Captain Giez wanta talka a you,' replied Captain Battaro. He gestured to the marine sergeant to arrest Hanzel.

'You have no right. I am a Hollander. I have done no harm in this port.' Hanzel stared with his ice blues at the shorter man, who did not appreciate having his authority questioned.

'Cease eem,' ordered the captain.

Three marines rushed toward Hanzel. Just before the first one was able to put a hand on him a shot rang out. It was Mister Padrone who shot his pistol into the air. However, the marines did not realize it was a shot into the air, having their attention firmly directed on the arrest of the famous Dutch pirate, Hanzel Sventska. They instantly reacted by shooting off their muskets, just at the same time Hanna and little Hanzel were coming out of the hatchway to join Hanzel and find out what was happening on deck. The moment the shooting started, pirates began wielding what weapons they had, while others came storming out of the forward and midship hatches. The ensuing melee became more serious as people were maimed and slaughtered.

Eventually, the pirates overcame the marines. When the smoke began to clear somewhat, and the battle was over, there were six dead marines and four dead pirates, and much to everyone's sorrow, little Hanzel had been shot through the heart and Hanna received a ball in her abdomen. She lay bleeding in Hanzel's arms, her dead son in her lap. Tears streamed down her cheeks, which mingled with those pouring from Hanzel. Even the marine captain was moved, but tried not to show it. Killing women and children was not something he took any delight in.

As Hanzel sat there with his dead son and dying wife, a million thoughts flashed through his mind, mostly how he was going to get even with the Spaniard. He was going to tear them apart. He was going to roast them alive. He was going to feed them to the sharks. *Why did they have to shoot them? Why God? Why did you let them be killed? What have I done to deserve this?* Hanzel looked down at his dead son. *Poor little Hanzel. He's much too young to be dead.*

Hanna coughed. Blood came from her mouth.

'DOCTOR ALLAN!' shouted Hanzel. 'Oh my God, Hanna. Don't die. Just hold on. Doctor Allan is coming.' Hanzel looked frantically through the drifting haze of the battle. He could not see through the mist clouding his eyes. 'Oh, Hanna, my sweet Hanna. Please don't die.

Hanna looked at Hanzel through clouding eyes. She coughed twice. Then she spoke with a voice filled with pain and sorrow. 'I'm sorry, Hanzel.' Tears filled her eyes as blood trickled from her nostrils. She coughed twice. 'I will always love you.' She coughed once more and became still. The light slowly faded from her eyes. Then she was dead.

Hanzel stared down at his dead wife and son. He sat like that for a long time. Then he calmly and gently lay his wife down on the deck, their son next to her. He slowly raised himself and taking his pistol in hand, shot Captain Battaro through his forehead, scattering his brains out of the back of his head. Then he shot the sergeant with his other pistol. Right through his forehead. The ball burst out of the back of the man's head and spattered cerebral matter all over two marines who were standing frozen with eyes bulging. Then Hanzel ordered the summary execution of the rest of the marines. Bang, Bang, BANG!

When all twelve Spaniards were good and dead, they dumped the bodies over the side into the Spaniard's longboat. Hanzel ordered the Spanish sailors to row their dead back to their ship and to tell their captain, that if he so much as breathes in the direction of Hanzel's sloop, he would come and tear the captain's lungs out. The sailors got the message and quickly rowed away with their grisly cargo. Hanzel returned to his wife and son. Everyone knew to leave him alone and tended to their own dead and wounded. Hanzel eventually sat in a puddle of tears and blood.

'I'd give my soul to the Devil if I could get them back,' he muttered.

A moment later a brilliant flash of light lit the sky, and was instantly followed by a terrible clap of thunder. Within another, torrential rains poured down on the blood stained deck.

Hanzel did not move.

Chapter 44

'So, he will tear my lungs out, will he? Tear my lungs out?!' Captain Giez stared at the two sailors who had come to bring him the news of what happened on Hanzel's sloop.

'Twelve dead! Twelve dead! The impertinence! Why I'll see him drawn and quartered. I'll see him broken into pieces!' He dismissed the sailors with a cursory gesture as he sunk down in his chair to ponder his next move against the pirate he, Edwardo Giez was now obsessed with hunting down. 'Twelve dead,' he muttered as he pulled on his right eyebrow.

The commotion and shooting on board *Lieve Hanna* alerted Michael and Mister Koopman's crews. Within short order Michael and Mister Koopman were rowed over to Hanzel's ship. What they discovered was a most terrible situation.

'We have to get out of here,' said Mister Koopman immediately after Mister Padrone had filled him in on what had happened. 'Those Spaniards will be sending more over here in short order. Now that we've killed twelve of theirs, they will want blood.'

'I want blood,' said Hanzel softly. Then louder. 'I WANT BLOOD! They will pay for killing my wife and son! I will tear their hearts from their heaving chests! I will tear them to pieces!' Hanzel had a wild look in his eyes which Michael had never seen before. 'We are going to go after the Spaniard, right here, right now, right in this harbour.' He stood up to his full height and shook his fist at the Spanish ship.

'If we storm that ship, Hanzel, we could end up with many more deaths. What good would that do us?' Michael regarded his friend.

'However, they are not likely expecting us to do that. And, if you look at it, we outnumber them. We are over two hundred. That ship likely has no more than a hundred on board,' suggested Mister Koopman.

'Two to one,' said Norack Waldenstein, Mister Koopman's first mate. 'If that is correct. We don't know how many are on that ship. Do we really want to take the chance?'

'I want them dead,' hissed Hanzel. 'I want to see the captain boiled in oil. I'll pluck his eyes from his head and break all of his teeth.'

'If we are hell bent on storming that ship, I think we should first give her a good bombarding. Broadside her from both sides,' suggested Mister Monk, the gunner. 'They won't expect that and we can likely kill and maim a lot of them. What might be left could be dispatched by hand.'

Hanzel regarded his gunner with an ice cold stare. He put his right hand on Mister Monk's shoulders. The gunner cringed slightly, noting the new look in Hanzel's eyes. 'Good thinking, Mister Monk. That is how we shall proceed.' He turned to his friend. 'Michael, you'll sail around the harbour and come up along his port side. And you, Mister Koopman, will take a position on his starboard. Since he doesn't suspect either of you, it will appear to be an innocent repositioning. If they ask, you are taking better positions in order to facilitate an exit from port in the near future. We will remain where we are. If we move, he'll suspect something. Anyway. When I see that you are in position I will signal you with two lights; off, on. Then let them have it as many times as you can manage before they can bring any guns out. Hopefully you will have shot up most of their gun placements.'

'Then what?' asked Michael.

'Then what, what?' asked Hanzel.

'After the bombardment?'

'We storm the ship and kill every Spaniard we find. We take what we need and then burn the thing to ashes.' Hanzel slapped his hands together. 'Now get to it.'

Michael looked at Mister Koopman and then back at Hanzel. He nodded. 'Alright, let's get em.'

Mister Koopman smiled. He was looking forward to a good fight.

Twenty minutes later the captains were back on their ships and began organizing the adventure.

Hanzel returned to Hanna and little Hanzel. Several of the women were gathered around her, crying. They helped Hanzel bring the bodies back to his cabin where the women took over and prepared them for burial. Hanzel sat outside the cabin; his head in his hands and tears flowing non stop for the next hour or more. When he was called up on deck, he dried his eyes and returned to his duties as captain.

The other sloops were beginning to take positions on either side of the Spanish ship. It did not appear that the Spaniard expected anything. Just two sloops, flying Swedish flags, maneuvering for a different anchorage. When Hanzel saw they were in position, he ordered his battle flag run up and the signals to be lighted. However, the moment the flag flew from the mast head, cannons began unleashing 18 pound balls into the sides of the Spanish ship. *I guess we didn't need the lights.*

The cannons kept pounding, a ball from every cannon every minute and a half, splintering the gun ports and sides of the bigger Spanish ship. They never had a chance to run out a cannon. Soon the ship was a splintered mess with several holes at her water line. Then, before the Spaniards could retaliate in any manner, the sloops began to drift closer to the sides of the ship. Spaniards began shooting muskets at the sloops which resulted in another bombardment at closer range. In the smoke that filled the narrowing spaces between the sloops and the Spanish merchantman, pirates began to disgorge from their ships and made their way onto the prize. They met with resistance necessitating swashbuckling action at close quarters. The sound of clashing steel, pistol shots, screams, and shouting filled the air.

'We are going over,' said Hanzel, as he gestured for people to fill the boats. Twenty minutes later Hanzel and his crew joined the battle. However, by the time he got there, the battle was pretty much over. All that was left to do was to extract the captain from his cabin. He was most reluctant to come out, knowing what likely lay in store for him.

Meanwhile, people gathered on the roadway by the dozens and watched the spectacle. The port authorities were at a loss for what to do. No Spanish navy vessel was in port and the authorities only had a small skiff with no weapons to speak of. They just had to stand idly by and watch as the pirates overcame the strange Spanish ship where Hanzel was having some trouble extracting the captain from his cabin.

'It will do you no good staying in your cabin with the door locked,' said Hanzel through an interpreter. 'You will eventually run out of powder and balls and we'll bust your door down. Why prolong the agony?'

The captain responded by shooting a ball through the door. The projectile whizzed past Hanzel's left ear and thudded into the wall behind. Again Hanzel pleaded for the man to come out. Again he was answered with a pistol shot through the door. This time a splinter caught Jacques LeBlanc in his right cheek. Fortunately it was not a serious wound and only drew a little blood. Hanzel signaled for him to blow the door lock off with his musket. A moment later a loud boom filled the narrow space. The lock of the door was mangled and the wood holding it in place was splintered into several dozen pieces. The door swung inward. They could not immediately see the Spanish captain.

'He must be behind the door,' whispered Hanzel. He pointed his pistol at the door and let off a blast. The ball went through the door. An instant later a groan indicated the ball made contact.

'You'll never take me alive,' muttered the captain behind the door. Hanzel put another shot through the door with his other pistol. This time he aimed lower. A moment later Captain Giez collapsed, having been hit in the shoulder with the first shot and now his left knee. Hanzel gestured to Jacques LeBlanc to push the door open with his musket. He could only open it a little bit more. There was a noise behind the door, but no shot ensued. Jacques pushed his way in and found the captain on the floor, blocking the door and trying to reload his pistols. Jacques pointed his musket and gestured for the captain to put the pistols aside.

'You can come in now,' said Jacques to his companions.

When Hanzel stepped into the cabin, Captain Giez stared at the handsome Dutchman. 'So, it is you. The famous Hanzel Sventska. Too bad the tables are turned the way they are.'

'Yes, indeed. For you it is too bad,' agreed Hanzel.

'What are you going to do with me?' asked Captain Giez, his eyes wide open and his breath coming in gasps, as searing pain interfered with his normal functioning.

Hanzel stared down at the man and did not reply for a long time as he thought what, indeed, was he going to do with Captain Giez. Hanzel took a deep breath. 'First you caused my wife to lose a leg. And now your men have killed her and my son.'

'I never ordered your wife and child to be killed,' replied Captain Giez. 'I do not condone the killing of women and children.'

'Never the less, there you have it. How would you react if the tables were turned?' Hanzel pulled a chair close to the captain and sat down.

Captain Giez stared up at Hanzel. 'If someone killed my wife and child, I would want revenge. However, as I understand it, you executed the entire marine squad I sent over to your ship, including Captain Battaro and his sergeant. Did that not serve your need for revenge? I did not order your wife or child's death.' Captain Giez looked pleadingly at Hanzel and his companions.

'He does have a valid point, Hanzel,' agreed Mister Padrone. 'If he did not order it, he can't be held responsible for Hanna's death.'

Hanzel looked at his sailing master and paused for a moment before nodding. 'Alright, take him over to my ship and have Doctor Allan take a look at him. We'll figure out what to do with him later. Give the Spanish sailors the opportunity of joining us. Those who don't will be let ashore.'

'What should we do with this ship?' asked Jacques LeBlanc.

'Take what is of use to us then we'll scuttle her at sea. No sense in making a mess here in this nice harbour,' replied Hanzel. 'Alright, boys, take him away. I want to take a look around this cabin and see what there is of use.'

Jacques LeBlanc and Mister Padrone, with the help of two shipmates, carried the Spanish captain topside and ferried him over to *Lieve Hanna* where Doctor Allan tended to his wounds. Hanzel took a quick look around and took note of useful things. Then he left the room and instructed three of his men to take the charts, clothing, books, a painting of a madonna, navigation instruments, the ink pot and quills, the man's sword and pistols, and anything else that caught their eye. 'Bring all of it to my cabin,' he told them. Hanzel returned to his ship and immediately went to his cabin where the women had laid out Hanna and his little son. The moment he set foot in the room the tears welled up in his eyes. He asked the women to leave as he collapsed beside the bed where his wife and son lay, cold, and unmoving. He stayed with them through the rest of that day and night, only coming out of his cabin the next morning. It was time to arrange the funeral.

With the help of Hanna's women friends, Hanna and little Hanzel were carefully lowered to the long boat. Then with the help of twenty friends, they rowed their bodies out of the harbour and around to the south, where they found a suitable beach. They prepared a foundation for a cairn and laid the bodies on the platform. The women gathered flowers and sprinkled them on the bodies as the men began to pile stones over the lifeless remains. With a heavy heart and copious tears, Hanzel did his best to help pile stones over his precious wife and beautiful son. When the bodies were completely covered and a six foot cairn built over them, Doctor Allan read meaningful words from the Book of Psalms about the Lord leading one into good pastures and keeping one from want. Hanzel was convinced Hanna and little Hanzel had gone to a better place. However, in his heart he wished more than anything to have them back. If the Devil had the power, Hanzel was prepared to make the bargain.

Most of the remaining Spanish sailors and marines wanted to join Hanzel's gang, thinking that is how things worked with pirates. They were of the opinion that pirates gave captured sailors the opportunity to spare their lives by becoming members of the colony and swearing allegiance to their articles of cooperation Hanzel had different ideas and had them all clapped in irons and stowed in the forward hold of the Spanish ship. He felt like shooting them, right then and there. Mister Padrone and the other officers, tried to convince Hanzel otherwise, when he and they met in the master's cabin for a war counsel to decide the mens' fate and that of Captain Giez.

'There's been so much blood shed. Is it necessary to spill more?' Mister Padrone regarded Hanzel, knowing full well what he was going through.

'I say we hang em,' suggested Mister Koopman.

'Too much trouble,' suggested Pontelo. 'Then we need to make nooses and all that. It would be easier just to shoot them and toss them overboard.'

'I don't want to kill them.' Doctor Allan stared at Hanzel. 'They are just simple sailors and marines. They were just doing their jobs under orders. That's no different than our own navy sailors.'

'I agree with Doctor Allan,' said Michael. 'I think we've killed enough and enough of our own have been killed, including your wife and son, may they rest in peace. We're privateers sailing under a Letter of Marque. We're not cold blooded cutthroats. We're in the business of plundering Spanish merchant ships for the mutual benefit of the king and us. We're not mass murderers.'

'They killed lots of ours,' said Norack Waldenstein, Mister Koopman's first mate.

'And maimed lots of others,' added Josephine Mulberry. 'Lord knows we had to do some amputations. That's never a good thing.'

'Yes, well, such are the casualties of war. And so will be those Spaniards. They will be casualties of war,' hissed Hanzel, staring at his fists; the knuckles white.

'So, what do you think we should do with the sailors and marines? We've got to do something with them,' suggested Mister Padrone.

'We maroon them, but give them at least a chance to survive,' suggested Michael. 'I can live with that.'

Hanzel stared vacantly at his friend and nodded. His mind was not on anything but Hanna and little Hanzel. Everyone there understood and gestured to each other to leave the cabin and leave their captain to his meditations. Everyone knew it was the right thing to do. Hanzel had enough. As they left the cabin, each one bowed slightly to Hanzel before they walked out of the door.

Over the ensuing five days, Hanzel ate but very little. He did not take part in much; preferring to stay in his cabin. When he finally came out of his cabin he ordered the Spanish ship to be taken out of the harbor and scuttled at sea, which was done forthwith, over the screaming protests of the imprisoned sailors. Everything of use had been stripped from the ship. Captain Giez was allowed to watch and listen to the screams of his sailors as holes were blown into the hulk with a mighty cannonade. The ship slipped under the waves within twenty minutes. Captain Giez wept.

'There,' said Hanzel coldly, pointing to the sinking ship. There you have it, as you requested, Mister Padrone. No blood spilled. Just simple drowning. What's more befitting for Spanish sailors, but to be drowned like rats?' Then he shot Captain Giez through his right temple, blowing the man's brains out to sea, immediately followed by his quivering body. It landed with a splash, soon followed by several ravenous sharks who quickly reduced the corpse into chopped meat and bloody remnants. Hanzel smiled coldly and then directed they set sail for Hispaniola and the Spanish Treasure Fleet.

Chapter 45

By day thirty seven they were becalmed. The wind just stopped. Not a huff or a puff of air moved. No clouds appeared in the sky. The sun was relentless. Each sloop had slung sails for canopies under which the ladies and gentlemen of the colony enjoyed themselves with games, music, dancing, and lots of drinking and smoking of tobacco and hemp. They also used the time to clean and sharpen weapons. Not that anyone was desirous of using them. The events in Las Palmas were still heavy on some people's minds and hearts, especially the heart and mind of Hanzel Sventska.

As the days went by, he spent more and more time alone in his cabin, brooding and talking to God and the Devil. The loss of his wife and son did not make sense to Hanzel. In his mind's eye he did not think he had done so many wrong things, notwithstanding a few incidents where he killed someone. 'I'm not the best of men, but I'm not the worst of them, either,' he said to whomever was listening; The Father, or His errant son, Lucifer, the apostate Archangel and subtle deceiver of men and women on Earth.

In the 13th night of their becalming, Hanzel received another visit from the succubus, who rode him hard and put him away wet and chilled to the bone, leaving him wanting for more and more and more. The rest of that day, Hanzel remained in bed, refusing all food and company. Everyone on board spoke in quiet tones, when in the gangway between the officer's quarters, respecting Hanzel's privacy and the fact their captain was in deep mourning over the loss of his beloved wife and son.

The ravenous succubus returned in the 16th, 17th, and 18th nights; riding Hanzel ever harder and faster; her ink black hair flying out from her head as she became a whirling storm in that wooden cabin, in the middle of that placid sea.

On 20th morning of their becalming, Michael came over for a visit. He encouraged Hanzel to come up on deck to sit under the canopy and share a few drinks and cigars. After much pleading, Hanzel reluctantly came out of his cabin and followed Michael up on deck. His presence on deck caused a bit of a stir. People had not seen him for many days. In the light of the glaring sun, he looked terrible. He had not shaven his face for days. His long hair was unbrushed and disheveled. Large bags hung under his eyes. His clothes were a rumpled mess; having been slept in for all those nights. Several made note of the dried stains on his chemise and pantaloons.

After they had consumed a couple of pints of rum, Michael decided it was time to try and straighten his friend out. 'Hanzel, you have to come to terms with their deaths. You can't go on moping and mourning alone in your cabin day after day. The people need you. You are the leader of this colony of privateers. Others have lost loved ones and they have gone on with their lives. None of them are letting their loss ruin the rest of their days. Surely they mourned, but not this long. You've not been yourself since we left Las Palmas and gotten worse since we were becalmed. This is the first day you've been out of your cabin in ten days.'

Hanzel stared into his cup; a sad expression on his face. It took him a while before he spoke. 'I miss them so much. You have no idea how my heart aches. Everyday is a chore to stay alive; to remain here on Earth, while they are in Heaven. I so want to join them.'

Michael regarded his friend. 'Hanzel, you still have so much to do here. Hanna and little Hanzel will be waiting for you. You'll get there soon enough. There is no need to speed it up by committing suicide.' Michael thought for a moment. 'And, besides; a suicide doesn't get to Heaven, I think.'

Hanzel nodded. 'Yes, I think that is how it goes. So, I'm stuck here to wait it out until we're reunited.' He shook his head sadly. 'I pray I don't have to wait forever.' He took a long drought of rum and slowly let it seep down into his stomach as he thought about Hanna, his beautiful friend and lover; the mother of his son. 'If I could reverse what happened by selling my soul, I'd do it, Michael.' He regarded his friend. 'Truly. If it were possible that an actual Devil exists, and one can make a contract with him; if my soul would bring Hanna and my son back, I'd dip a quill in my own blood.'

Michael thought about what Hanzel had said. He shook his head slowly. 'I don't think it's such a good idea to make a pact with the Devil. He's the King of Liars. You can't trust the Devil. Now, whether he actually exists, or not. I don't know. I think it's just a story priests made up to scare people. So, promising to sell one's soul is likely a waste of thought and breath. You just have to face the fact. As sad as it is to say, Hanna and little Hanzel are dead. They're not coming back.' He took a sip of his drink and watched Hanzel for a reaction. However, none came. Hanzel had drifted into his thoughts.

In the 52nd day out from Las Palmas, the wind returned. Jacques LeBlanc noticed it first when strings on the sails began to flap. He shouted to everyone the wind was back, which instantly stirred everyone to action. It was time they got underway. Everyone was bored stiff and needed to feel the wind in their sails. The return of the wind brought Hanzel back on the quarterdeck. He immediately took command with a steely presence which everyone noted.

Michael and Mister Koopman also organized their crews and within the hour the three sloops were under full sail and back on course to Hispaniola and the port of Santo Domingo. The entire way there, they never saw one sail, not a single one on the horizon, until they neared the port and encountered fishing boats a few leagues off shore. Winds being unfavorable, they stood off shore for two days until they were able to sail into the harbour with the aid of a pilot they hired. The three sloops were able to anchor side by side, next to a Spanish navy vessel; a galleon with sixty guns.

The harbor was larger and busier than Las Palmas. Two dozen ships lay at anchor and another nine were tied up to piers jutting out from the roadway. The town was growing constantly and had, by this time, become a very busy place. Wealth abounded. Gold and silver was everywhere. The taverns were full and the ladies were busy. If one played their cards right, one could become rich in Santo Domingo, where everything could be had for a price and for many, price was no object. Pirates, in particular, spent a lot of money in Santo Domingo. Hanzel's people were no exception.

On the evening of the third day in port, Michael and Mister Koopman managed to convince Hanzel to come out on the town with them. Even though the weather was threatening a storm, it did not matter as far as Hanzel's friends were concerned.

'So what if we get a storm. It doesn't matter. We'll visit some taverns and a good restaurant. Maybe meet some girls. Who knows? Let's just go, spend some money and have some fun,' said Michael. 'It will cheer you up.'

'I hear the women in Santo Domingo are some of the most beautiful in the world,' added Mister Koopman.

Hanzel looked up at his friends and nodded. 'Yes, I think you're right. It's high time I got off this boat.' He stood up from his chair and regarded his face in the mirror on the door of his armoire. 'Give me an hour to get cleaned up and put on some fresh clothes.'

'Excellent. We'll go up on deck and wait for you,' said Mister Koopman. He turned on his heels and, followed by Michael, left the cabin.

An hour later, Hanzel stepped up on deck, dressed in a fine suit of clothes. He looked every inch the wealthy pirate that he was.

'Now, that's better,' said Michael. 'I'm glad I got you that waistcoat. It does look good on you.'

'I'm sure he'll attract a woman or twelve,' said Mister Koopman, smiling at Hanzel.

Hanzel thanked his friends for the compliments. Then they descended the ladder and seated themselves in one of the ship's boats, where they were joined by seven others, going ashore for some fun and games. Twenty minutes later, Hanzel and his friends were sitting in a tavern quaffing their first ales of the day.

Sailors from many countries filled the place. And those spaces where there were no sailors, there were women. Women of all descriptions. Tall ones, short ones, skinny ones, fat ones, noisy ones, and the quiet, silent types. Some with big tits, others with not so much, it did not matter. In *Las Toros d'Oro* all women were welcome and much appreciated by the sailors who displayed their appreciation by spending all of their money on them. There were not many women who did not eat and drink well in Santo Domingo, if they were willing to share their charms. All of those women, who were in the tavern, were more than willing. In a far corner a sailor was being shown how appreciative his women were, as one sucked on his private member, while at the same time he was fondling the bared breast of the other wench. In his free hand he held a bottle of rum. Several other inebriated sailors stood by and watched, all of them leaning precariously and urging the wenches on.

As Hanzel and his friends sat there drinking their ales, the place suddenly went very still, as the door blew open and crashed against the wall with a loud BANG!

Hanzel, having his back to the door, turned around to see what everyone was looking at. His eyes nearly popped out of his head and his heart began to race. In the doorway stood the most beautiful woman in the world; the indigo haired succubus; the nemesis of his erotic nightmares!

She stood in the doorway for a few moments and scanned the tavern to see who was there. When her eyes locked on Hanzel's icy blues, electricity traveled up and down his spine and lit his brain on fire. Without invitation she walked directly toward him, not taking her eyes off him for one instant. When she stood beside his chair, she looked down at him with her raven eyes. She reached out a hand and with a sultry voice, deep like a tiger's growl, told Hanzel to come with her. Resistance was futile. He accepted her hand and let her lead him out of the tavern and into a black coach with purple curtains. The coachman, dressed entirely in black with a violet band around his black hat, closed the door behind them. The coach leaned slightly, as he climbed up on his seat. With a crack of his whip, he urged the four black horses to proceed. The coach jerked forward and disappeared in a flash of light and roar of thunder.

An instant later, the coach jerked to a stop in a moon lit glade, not far off the road, about five miles from Santo Domingo. It was then that the succubus released her icy grip and let go of Hanzel's hand. She gestured for him to get out of the vehicle. Hanzel climbed out and was immediately followed by his mysterious abductor. She pointed to a circle of rocks, in the middle of which sat a large rectangular slab of granite, supported on four large boulders. 'Come,' she said, taking his hand. She led Hanzel to the slab and gestured for him to sit down. Then she stood before the mesmerized Dutchman. A flash of light lit the scene, instantly followed by a horrific clap of thunder.

Hanzel looked fearfully at the succubus. 'Who are you? What is all of this about? How did you become my night mare?'

The woman smiled, revealing a perfect set of white teeth. Hanzel had never seen such perfect teeth. *This woman is perfect. I've never seen such a beautiful woman except in the dreams. Not even my Hanna was as beautiful as this demon.*

'My name is Mephi. Mephi Stofoleas.'

Hanzel relaxed a litltle. 'Oh, you're Greek. That explains your black hair.' Hanzel thought a moment. 'Stofoleas.' He nodded, beginning to relax and enjoy the experience, thinking it to be another version of his succubus dreams. 'Definitely Greek.'

Mephi smiled. 'Yes. Greek. Surely it must be Greek. It sounds Greek.'

Hanzel stared into her eyes and did not know what else to say. She made him speechless. What furthered his inability to speak was her removing her clothes, slowly, erotically, until she was completely naked. Moisture droplets covered her flawless flesh. Her breasts were large and firm, crowned with a pair of magnificent nipples, hard as the granite he was sitting on.

Hanzel became instantly hard. Then she kneeled down and helped Hanzel out of his clothes. When he was also completely naked, she climbed up on the slab and invited Hanzel to make love to her from behind, 'The way animals do it,' she said. Hanzel looked over towards the coach, but the coachman was nowhere to be seen. *Probably sleeping.* Mephi looked over at Hanzel. 'Well, are you going to enter me, or are you going to stand there?'

Hanzel was startled out of his stupor and realized he had a massive erection. Not giving things another thought, he mounted the grinning succubus, there on that granite slab, in that dark, damp forest, on the outskirts of Santo Domingo.

Much to his continual delight, she fit him so perfectly; like a hand, firm, and warm, her vagina was made exactly for him.

An owl hooted nearby.

A raven answered.

Then, just as he came into her, she let out a loud cry as she reached her climax. A flash of lightning lit the skies and illuminated the strange scene in the forest glade. As the pair convulsed on that stony altar, thunder rumbled and rain began to fall in torrents, drenching the pair in seconds. Neither cared, as they remained coupled for a long time after their orgasmic finish, panting like animals.

After what seemed an eternity, they separated and gathered up their wet clothes.

'Come,' she said. 'You'll dry off in my coach.' She took his hand and led him to the vehicle, almost invisible in the dark. She thumped on the door.

'Wake up, Mister Bub. Come on, it is time to go.' A moment later the coachman pulled a curtain aside and peeked out. Lightning lit the skies.

'It's raining,' said the coachman through the closed window.

'Get out here right now or so help me, I will tan your miserable hide,' replied Mephi, pulling the door open and reaching into the coach. In a moment she had his coat in her clutches and physically pulled him out of the vehicle. 'Now get to those horses and take us back to town.'

Mister Bub bowed and scraped as he backed away from his employer. Hanzel looked at Mephi, surprised at her power and strength. *This woman is something else. She's not like any woman I've ever met before.* He held out his hand and helped Mephi step up into the coach. He admired her perfect buttocks as she stepped up. *My God, she is magnificent!*

When they were seated in the coach, Hanzel closed the door and Mephi thumped on the ceiling to signal Mister Bub, to go. As the coach began to roll, the inside of the coach began to warm up. Mephi opened the lid under the seat beside her and pulled out two thick, warm towels. 'Here,' she said. 'Dry yourself off.'

As Hanzel began to dry himself he could no longer restrain himself. He had to pump her for answers. 'Why me? How did you come to single me out? We don't even know each other, and yet you have fucked me silly for so many steamy nights.'

Mephi stared deep into his eyes. 'Do you remember making a pact with the Devil? You have done it three times. Three times you have called upon my Master. The latest time was just after Hanna was killed. Do you remember that?'

Hanzel stared dumbfoundedly at his companion. His mouth was open, but he did not know what to say. He nodded weakly.

'Do you remember?' demanded Mephi.

'Yes. Yes, I remember the last time. I don't know about the other times. That is probably a long time ago,' replied Hanzel.

'Let me refresh your memory,' replied Mephi, drying her hair. 'The first time was when you were still a teenager. It was not long after your friends were hanged. You were robbed by conycatchers who took your money in a dice game. When you were lying in the alley behind the ale house, all muddy and beat, you were prepared to sell your soul.' Mephi moved the towel over her breasts, gently drying her rock hard nipples. She watched him staring at her. 'The second time was after your treasure was stolen by fishermen and all of your friends were killed. You wanted to make a bargain then, as well.' Mephi lifted her left leg, opening her vagina slightly, as she continued to towel dry herself. Hanzel could not help but stare at that magnificent vulva surrounded by soft, black fur. He was again hard like a rock. 'The third time was after Hanna and your son were killed. So, the way it works is, when a human pledges his or her soul three times in their lives, we come to make a deal, in person. My boss sends you an envoy; who is me, in this case. He first warms you up with dreams before he sends a representative. Now I am here to close the deal.'

'We come to make a deal? What do you mean, *we* come and make a deal?' asked Hanzel, putting on his shirt.

Mephi came to sit beside Hanzel and reached down, taking his hard erection in her right hand and squeezing it. 'I am a representative from Lucifer, my Master. I have come to make a deal with you.'

Hanzel moaned softly as Mephi began to stroke his quivering phallus. 'You mean you can bring Hanna and my son back from the dead, if I promise you my soul?'

Mephi stared into Hanzel's eyes. 'No, I can not do that. Hanna and your boy are in Heaven. We have no jurisdiction there.'

'So, what can you promise me, then?' Hanzel shuddered as Mephi squeezed harder and stroked faster.

'Prolonged life. We can promise you prolonged life,' replied Mephi.

'How prolonged?' asked Hanzel having trouble controlling himself as she continued to play with his rod and testicles.

'One hundred years. We can prolong your life for one hundred more years. How does that sound? That way you will have a long time to get even with Spaniards for killing your wife and son. One hundred years will give you a life of abundant riches, as you will be able to plunder many, many vessels over the years.'

'But, will I stay young, or will I become a wrinkled old skeleton by the time I'm a hundred?'

'You will remain as you are,' she said, as she bent down and took his erection into her mouth and brought him to a climax.

Hanzel's eyes rolled into the back of his head as he moaned with pleasure. He sank back into the plush seat and thought about nothing but the sensations she had brought to his body. As he sat there, semi conscious, Mephi continued drying herself and dressed in a set of fresh clothes she retrieved from a storage bin under her seat. When Hanzel came back to reality he regarded the stunning emissary for a long time before replying. 'Do you come along with the bargain?'

Mephi shook her head. 'Alas, no. I am just here to give you a taste of what will lie in store for you when you pirate for a hundred years. With the wealth you reap, you can afford women like me. Trust me. I have many sisters. All of them are beautiful.'

'Alright, I'll do it,' said Hanzel.

'You'll do what?' asked Mephi.

'I will sell my soul to the Devil so that I can pirate for a hundred years,' he said firmly.

'Is that your final answer?'

'That is my final answer,' repeated Hanzel.

'Alright then. Mephi reached into a pocket on the side wall of the coach. She pulled out a document. She opened the parchment and laid it on the seat in front of Hanzel. 'All you have to do is sign this and give us a drop of your blood.' Mephi indicated where to sign and where the drop of blood was to go. She handed Hanzel a quill and a small pot of ink. He dipped the quill into the ink and signed his name with a flourish.

'How do we get the drop of blood?'

Mephi bared her teeth and then picked up his right hand. In an instant she bit his index finger and drew blood, sucking up the extra flow with great pleasure. 'There. Now drop some blood right here.' She pointed to the place and Hanzel did as he was told, dropping blood above his signature.

'So, what happens after a hundred years?' Hanzel looked at his bleeding finger.

'I come and collect your soul. It's as simple as that.' Mephi smiled, revealing her blood stained teeth.

A flash of lightening illuminated the coach. It was immediately followed by a huge crack of thunder rocking the coach and rattling the windows in their panes.

Mephi handed Hanzel a strip of white cotton. 'Here, bind your wound. You are dripping on the furniture.'

'Sorry,' replied Hanzel, apologetically.

Mephi returned the parchment to the pocket in the side wall. Then she straightened herself and watched as Hanzel continued to dress. She giggled as he tried to place his cod piece over his, still hard as a rock, erection. *That woman has a powerful effect.*

When they returned to the tavern, it was raining hard. The roads had become slippery, muddy streams. 'Will I see you again?' asked Hanzel, as he reached for the door handle.

'In one hundred years,' she replied.

'I don't know if I can wait that long.' Hanzel looked admiringly at the gorgeous creature with whom he had such an incredible encounter. He wanted those encounters to continue for ever.

As Hanzel stepped out of the coach his boots landed in a puddle. The moment he closed the door of the coach, it pulled away and disappeared in a strange cloud which suddenly formed within a wall of rain.

Hanzel stared for a long time at the place where the coach disappeared. He scratched his head, wondering if he was dreaming the entire episode. When he turned to enter the tavern and return to his friends, he stepped on a dog turd. He knew it was that from the way the object squished under his left boot. *We should shoot those animals. All of them. Shitting everywhere. It's offensive.* He tried his best to scrape as much of it off on the boot scraper by the front door. However, the odor remained on his boot.

When Hanzel returned to the table, where he and his friends had been sitting, he found out that they were long gone.

'In fact, they were here yesterday. I haven't seen them today,' replied the wench who Hanzel queried.

'Yesterday? How can that be? I was just here, not more than three hours ago.'

The wench shrugged her shoulders and repeated what she had told him. His friends were there two days ago and that he, Hanzel, was mistaken.

Hanzel shook his head as he left the tavern. He could not come to grips with his situation. The whole thing was a mighty puzzle. He figured, therefore, the best thing to do was to return to his sloop and go to sleep. Perhaps an answer would present itself in the morning.

He was lucky to find someone who would row him to his boat at that time of night in the pouring rain. It cost more, but so be it. When Hanzel climbed on board *Lieve Hanna*, nobody was up. Everyone was tucked in and doing their best to stay warm and dry. Hanzel made his way to his cabin and immediately fell into bed. It only took a minute for him to fall into a deep, disturbing dream about making love with the Devil.

Chapter 46

The following morning Hanzel woke up groggy and ill at ease. He was still fully clothed. When he looked in the mirror, he looked a mess, and a bad odour emanated from one of his boots. However, since he was not quite feeling himself, he decided not to bother cleaning up and left the cabin for the quarterdeck. As soon as he stepped on deck, he was queried as to where he had been.

'You left the tavern with that stunning creature and disappeared. Where were you?' asked Michael, who had come over from his sloop to see if his friend was alright. 'We haven't seen you for two days.'

'This being the second day?' asked Hanzel.

'Yes. We were in the tavern two nights ago. That woman came into the tavern and brought the entire place to a standstill. She came straight over to you. Took your hand and you left with her. We haven't seen you since.' Michael looked at his friend and noted his disheveled state. 'You're all rumpled. That's not like you, Hanzel.' Michael fussed over a crease on Hanzel's waistcoat. 'You shouldn't sleep in these clothes, Hanzel. They get all wrinkled and difficult to press back to normal.' He wrinkled up his nose. 'And, what is that smell?'

Hanzel grinned apologetically.

'How many times do I have to tell you? These clothes are not for sleeping in.' Michael sniffed.

'Listen, Michael. You have to do me a favour and come with me. We're going on a little trip a few miles out of town. I want to show you something.' Hanzel looked around to see if anyone else was listening. He looked up at the sky. 'Since it's nice out, we're going for a ride into the forest, west of town.'

'Why? What's there?' asked Michael, his curiosity piqued.

'I'll tell you on the way. I just don't want anyone else involved. Just you and me,' replied Hanzel.

Michael nodded. 'Alright. Sure. I was coming to visit anyway. We can visit in a carriage or on horseback. How do you want to go?'

'We'll hire a couple of horses,' said Hanzel as he walked toward the ladder leading to the long boat bobbing in the water below.

'Aren't you going to clean up first?' asked Michael. 'Put on some clean clothes?'

'No time. We have to get going, while my memory is fresh.' Hanzel climbed over the gunwale.

Michael shrugged his shoulders. 'Alright. If you're in such a hurry. It must be important.'

'Trust me, it is,' said Hanzel, as he climbed down the ladder.

When the two friends were standing on the roadway they went in search of a carriage or horses to rent. The fourth person they asked knew of a place, just three streets further on. So, they headed there. Sure enough, a horse rental agency was established in that location, providing transportation for locals as well as people visiting and wishing to go sight seeing.

Hanzel and Michael rented two horses with saddles and tack and set off for the forest road. As they rode, Hanzel filled Michael in on what happened after he left the tavern with the woman. 'Her name is Mephi. Mephi Stofoleas,' replied Hanzel when Michael had asked her name.

'Sounds like she's Greek,' observed Michael.

'Ya, that's what I think so, too. She agreed her name sounded Greek. She never said if she actually was Greek. However, that's not the point. The point is, she claimed to be an emissary from the Devil himself. She enticed me to sign a contract for my soul.'

'Sounds like you had one of those dreams again.' Michael looked at his friend with a big grin on his face.

'She had me make love to her in the rain on some sort of altar here, in the forest. It was dark when we were there, but I think I can remember the place. Because of where we parked the coach. I figure it's about five miles from town.' Hanzel pointed ahead.

'Well, if it's true, then the altar should be there, I suppose,' said Michael, thinking his friend was losing his mind. 'An altar, you say?'

'Ya. A large granite slab sitting on four large boulders. She stripped naked and then she climbed on the slab and took a position on her hands and knees. Then she enticed me to make love to her like an animal. Right there on that altar.'

Michael laughed. 'It sounds to me like an erotic fantasy. Did you have a wet dream?'

'No, really. It's as I tell you. You'll see. We'll be there fairly soon.' Hanzel urged his horse to go a little faster.

When they reached the place where the coach had parked beside the road, in a small clearing, Hanzel pointed out the marks made by the vehicle's wheels. He climbed off his horse and took a closer look at the tracks. 'See, those are the wheel marks.' Hanzel pointed to the ruts in the soft mud.

Michael climbed down from his horse and took a cursory look at the wheel marks. He shrugged his shoulders. 'Could be anyone's marks. They're not conclusive evidence. Let's go see this altar you were talking about. That's what interests me.'

Hanzel walked along a path, as he remembered it. He was all excited to see the altar again. However, much to his chagrin, when he and Michael reached the little glade where the altar had stood, there was nothing but a mound of soil with three trees growing on it. One could see there were some sort of large stones under the mound, but it had to have been there for a thousand years or more. Hanzel rubbed his right temple. 'How can that be? There was a granite slab, sitting on four large boulders.'

'I can see two boulders, kind of sticking out there.' Michael pointed to the boulders. 'Maybe if we dig into the mound, we might find something resembling a slab. The mound is kind of flat on top, don't you think?'

'It was here. I swear it was here. I humped that woman right there. But it was a slab of stone, not a mound of soil with trees growing out of it.' Hanzel was completely perplexed.

'Maybe it is as you say. She was an emissary from the Apostate Prince of Darkness, then it may be she enchanted this place and got your seed. What do you suppose she is going to do with that? If it is real, that is.' Michael kicked at some soil. His boot stopped short as his toe collided with something very hard under the dirt. 'There certainly is something hard under there,' he said, touching the toe of his boot and wondering if he did not break a bone.

'She wasn't like any woman I've ever been with. Not to suggest I've been with that many women. I was with Hanna for a long time. Before that there were only three others, I think. I can't remember.' He was thinking of Mephi and how she fit like a glove. 'Mephi was perfect, Michael. She is the perfect woman. What I forgot to tell you is, when she left me at the tavern, she rode off in her coach. I watched her go. Suddenly, she disappeared in a haze of rain. The coach disappeared, Michael. Literally. One moment I could see it clear as the rain would allow, and then, in an instant, the coach was gone.'

Michael nodded. 'I think you had one of those dreams, Hanzel. The question is, where did you sleep that night and where were you the next day?'

Hanzel scratched his head. 'I have no idea.'

'Well, the whole thing is pretty weird, if you ask me.' Michael pulled some rotten tree material off the mound and then used a stick to poke more dirt off the pile. 'Grab a stick, Hanzel and help me scrape some of this soil away. I'm curious to see what's under here.'

After an hour of digging and scraping, a piece of a flat slab of granite was exposed. It was obvious it sat on boulders; more of a third one having come to light, as well.

Michael stood back. 'That's really weird, Hanzel. You describe a flat granite slab sitting on boulders. Here you have, what appears to be your altar, but it hasn't seen the light of day for a long time.'

Hanzel stood dumbfounded. He scratched his head and shrugged his shoulders. 'Maybe it was all a dream, after all. However, you did see me go out of the tavern with that woman, did you not?'

Michael nodded. 'Yes, we all did. We discussed her and you for sometime afterward. Lots of people, who saw her approach you and take you away from there, asked about you and her. We had no idea what to tell them, other than she was an old friend of yours.'

'Yeah, she was some friend, alright. I've never experienced such heightened sexual pleasure before. She was something special.' Hanzel's face assumed a dreamy expression.

'Well, I don't know what to say, Hanzel. Your story is very strange. And you say you signed a contract for your soul?'

Hanzel nodded. 'I contracted my soul in return for a hundred more years of life.'

'Oh, so you get to live until you're a hundred and thirty? That's wonderful. A hundred and thirty year old, wrinkled skeleton with a pirate flag. That's some bargain.' Michael frowned.

'No, no, it's not like that. I am not going to age. I get to stay like I am,' replied Hanzel enthusiastically.

Michael frowned and looked at Hanzel's wrinkled clothes. 'I hope you at least get to change your clothes. You don't want to stay as you are.'

Hanzel smiled. 'You're a funny man, Michael. Of course I will change my clothes. I had no idea that wrinkled clothes are such a bother to you.'

'They are, if the clothes were given by me, and made of the best quality.'

Hanzel smiled and nodded. 'Ya, of course. Of course. I completely agree with you, Michael. I shall take better care of my clothes. However, I had no control over how events unfolded. She took her clothes off when it was already starting to rain. Well, what am I supposed to do? Here I was, in this private forest place, with an absolutely gorgeous naked woman asking me to make love to her. I didn't care that it was raining, or that my clothes were becoming wrinkled. What would you have done?'

Michael thought for a moment. 'I would have taken my clothes off in the coach and carefully laid them on the seat.

Hanzel pursed his lips. 'Sure you would. You would have kept her waiting, naked and ready on that altar, and you would have taken your time laying out your clothes?'

'Well, if truth be known. I wouldn't have had to bother, because I am married and loyal to Maria. You, on the other hand, have lost a wife two months ago. You are not married any longer.'

Hanzel hung his head and looked at the ground. 'Is two months an adequate amount of time or did I jump the gun?'

'Nature takes its course the way it does. I can't blame you for making love to that woman, she being naked and all.' Michael shook himself. 'Now you've got me talking as if it was real. I tell you Hanzel, it was a dream.' He pointed at the mound. 'That altar, or whatever it is, has been under the dirt for a long time. That soil is the remains of a lot of dead leaves and trees. I'll bet that, whatever is under there, was built here by natives a eons ago. Maybe to conduct some sort of blood sacrifice. Who knows?'

Hanzel stared down at the mound. 'Well, whatever the story, I guess we'll see over the next hundred years whether I age, or not.'

'What if someone tries to kill you?' asked Michael.

Hanzel paused. 'I never thought to ask her that. Will she protect me over the next hundred years. Am I also invincible?'

'I guess we'll see. If you can stop a pistol ball or a musket shot. Or if you ward off spears and swords, arrows and darts, we'll know that you are invincible. With that kind of power, you really could go places in a hundred years.' Michael looked at Hanzel, wondering if it could all be true. 'If it is true, I hope that selling your soul was a reasonable price.'

Hanzel nodded. 'I hope so too, my friend.'

'Unless one doesn't believe in a soul. That's another matter altogether. I mean, what does it actually mean? You signing a contract for your soul so you can pirate for a hundred years and not age. For a hundred years you can be as you are and then she comes and takes your soul and then you're dead? Surely you won't, after the hundred years are over, then continue aging normally so that, if you live out a normal lifetime, would make you...' Michael looked at the mound as he calculated the numbers. 'You'd be a hundred and thirty plus, say another forty years, if you live a normal seventy year, possibly longer lifetime, making you a hundred and seventy years, or older when you die.' Michael regarded his friend and smiled. 'When you think about that, if that is what it turns out to be, you would learn so much and be able to do so many things. I would love to be able to live that long. As long as I have my health, that is. I could watch the development of clothing styles over a long period. I can't imagine what people will be wearing a hundred years from now. The way things change, every three years there is something different. A new ruffle, a new pattern, a hem line an inch lower or higher; one never knows what the designers come up with.' Michael excused himself as he walked off into the trees to pass water.

Hanzel stared at the mound and scratched his right temple. 'This is really weird, Michael. Maybe it was all a dream. But if it was, how did I come to find this place? Why would I dream of this place? I've never been here before she brought me here.'

Michael responded from behind a nearby tree where he was passing water. 'It's a mystery. I have no idea. Were you dreaming, or did it happen? We all saw the woman. So there is no doubt about her being real. Everyone in the tavern saw her take you out of there. Everyone talked about it for a good half an hour afterwards. Lots of people came to ask us about you and her.'

Hanzel nodded and smiled, as he stared dreamily at the soil covered altar. 'Ya, I must admit, Mephi is gorgeous. I have never seen a finer looking woman in my life.'

'Me neither,' replied Michael stepping out from behind the tree and doing up his cod piece. 'So, we are agreed, she is real. But this business of the altar, that's obviously not real.' Michael snapped his fingers. 'Unless, she somehow influenced your mind while you were with her in the coach. Somehow she put the ritualized coupling on the alter into your head and you think it is real.'

'How do you explain the coach tracks back there?' Hanzel pointed to the clearing along the road where their horses were tied.

'Any coach will make those marks, as I said before,' replied Michael.

'How could I have come here, straight from town, to this place, where there obviously is an altar of some sort in the forest, just as I remembered it?' Hanzel looked at Michael, who shrugged his shoulders. 'Like I said, I have no idea.' Michael looked in the direction of the clearing. 'I've seen enough. Shall we go back to town? I'm getting hungry and really could use a nice cup of rum.'

Hanzel nodded. 'Ya, I've seen enough, as well.' He looked back at the mound and shook his head. Then he followed Michael back to the horses. An hour and a half later they were back in town and enjoying a cup of rum in a local tavern as they waited for a sumptuous feast of roasted beef with sautéed vegetables in a wine sauce.

After dinner, Hanzel and Michael remained to quaff several more cups of rum until they were both leaning into the wind. It was time to return to their respective ships to sleep it off, in order to be alert the next morning, to weigh anchors and leave port to go roving off the coast of Cuba.

Chapter 47

Twelve nights later, Hanzel woke up with a start. She had been in his bed! As he cleared his eyes and brought himself back into the real world, he realized it had been another dream. It had been one of *those* dreams. It was so real, the other pillow was indented as if a head had lain there. Hanzel stared at the pillow, salty brine breaking out of his pores. He shivered as his cold sweat and drenched bed clothes cooled him off instantly. *What in the hell is going on?* When he pulled the covers back, the matress beside him was indented as well.

Hanzel jumped out of bed, as if it was infected with something. He stared at the pillow as he backed up and escaped out of the door of his cabin, eyes bulging. He staggered up the stairs and stepped out of the rear hatchway. The bright sun blinded him as he stepped on deck. He looked about himself as if he had never seen the place before. Pontelo's wife Elizabeth, who was standing beside her husband on the quarterdeck, first noticed Hanzel standing on the deck, looking dazed and confused by the rear hatch.

'Hanzel!' shouted Pontelo from the quarterdeck. 'What's the matter?'

Hanzel looked up at his friend standing beside the helmsman. The bright light made him squint and shield his eyes. He could barely see Pontelo because he was mostly in silhouette. He blinked and took a deep breath as he realized where he was and who was addressing him. Hanzel shook his head and snapped back at the friendly quartermaster, 'Nothing! There's nothing wrong! I was just momentarily blinded by the light, is all!' He gathered his wits and climbed the four steps up to the quarterdeck. Mister Padrone was standing by the port side rail watching the sails. He regarded Hanzel with his good eye but did not say anything. He did note that the captain was acting strangely and appeared not to be himself.

Hanzel took a deep breath and then asked Mister Padrone why there were not more sheets out.

'I didn't know we were in a hurry to get somewhere,' replied Mister Padrone. 'I was under the impression we were cruising these waters hoping to run into a Spanish treasure fleet, or some fat merchantman. If we actually have a destination, I can put more sheets out.'

'Put more sheets out. We're going to Vera Cruz,' replied Hanzel. 'That's where the Spanish treasure fleet is.'

'That's a long way. Do we have enough provisions for that? What if we run out of food, or water?' asked Mister Padrone, his glass eye staring off in a different direction. 'Besides, we never discussed or voted to go to Vera Cruz.'

'That's right,' agreed Pontelo. 'We never voted to go to Mexico.'

Hanzel regarded his friends. 'Trust me. Vera Cruz. That's where the gold is.'

'What if the crew says no?' asked Mister Padrone.

Hanzel glared at his sailing master. His face turned red and his eyes filled with fire. 'I am the captain!' he shouted. 'The crew will do as I say! Or by Satan's horns I'll have em marooned for going against the captain's orders! By all of Diablo's minions I'll have any dissenters stripped of their rights and flogged to within an inch of their lives. They'll wish they never joined this colony, by Lucifer. I'll make an example of them so that anyone else contemplating mutiny will quickly forget it and put on a smiling face. Vera Cruz is where we are going and that is that. What do you think of that, Mister Padrone?' Hanzel's rant took his friends completely by surprise. They had never seen Hanzel like that. He was someone else.

'Set a course for west south west. I will give you the particulars when I have worked them out in more detail,' said Hanzel calmly to the helmsman, as if he had never ranted and all was normal, further mystifying those on the quarterdeck. 'Signal Mister Webb and Mister Koopman about our change of plans. I'm going below to work out the exact course. Meantime, keep an eye out for a prize. It would be excellent for morale if we take a prize on the way.' Then Hanzel turned on his heels and returned to his cabin, to work out the navigational details of the voyage to Vera Cruz across the Gulf of Mexico.

As was typical, under the circumstances, people grumbled. They really did not want to go to Vera Cruz. They were happy just to cruise off the coast of Hispaniola, so that they could return to Santo Domingo to resupply, instead of spending another month or more in a big sea where they might not see a ship the whole time they sailed there. Eventually, as the days stretched into weeks, supplies became less and less available. First to go was the rum. Then it was the last of the fresh beef. The egg laying chickens had all died of some malady and the salted meat had developed a strange, green mold, making it unpalatable. Unfortunately, by the time it was discovered, seven people had died and nineteen were sick with extreme abdominal cramps and vomiting. Doctors Allan and Winderkint were completely perplexed and did not have a clue how to solve the problem, except to give the ailing crew members opium. Five days later, six more died.

As the days passed, life on board *Lieve Hanna* became ever more hostile and unpleasant, as people began to blame Hanzel for the deaths of their loved ones. 'If he had not insisted we sail to Vera Cruz, none of them would have died. If we weren't sailing to Mexico we'd still have enough food to eat and rum to drink,' became the litanies whispered and spoken in the nooks and crannies of the ships; well out of ear shot of Hanzel, who appeared to be acting ever more erratically. People became scared of him. There was a new look in his eyes.

The look could be explained by the fact that Hanzel was not sleeping well. His dreams were filled with strange visions of suffering beings being ripped, torn, and prodded, interspersed with images of Mephi and he making love in all manner of strange places and in all sorts of different positions. As time went by, the love making became ever more violent. What he was experiencing with Mephi was diametrically opposite of how he and Hanna enjoyed their conjugal pleasures. With Hanna, love making was always gentle and pleasurable, with Mephi it was rough and painful. The dreams were so real it felt as if he was actually there and being worn out by an over sexed vixen with the drive of a Grecian nymph. Every time he woke up he was a mess. As time passed, he became ever more neglectful of his personal toilet. He walked about in a daze, rumpled and unshaven, his rumpled clothes, stained and soiled.

'Ever since he met that woman in Santo Domingo, he's been behaving differently. Have you noticed?' asked Michael of his first mate, Kate Montgomery, after they had an officer's meeting on *Lieve Hanna*, and he and she had returned to the captain's cabin on their sloop, *De Heilige Vrouw*. 'He is more curt with everybody and he is so impatient.' Michael thought for a moment. *Why would he be impatient, if he's got a hundred years?* 'I've known him for some years and have never seen him act the way he does. And his clothes...' Michael cringed.

'Well, you have to understand. He's probably still grieving, and this is one of the ways he is trying to cope with it. He lost his wife and son. And yet, he still has to be the captain of a pirate gang,' replied Kate.

'*Privateering* gang. Just to set the record straight. We're privateers. Not pirates. We have a Letter of Marque, from the king. We have a legal right to plunder Spanish ships,' replied Michael.

'That's not how the Spaniards see it. They say you have no right to steal their stuff,' replied Kate.

'That's just how it is. They steal from us and we steal from them.'

'So how does that make us different from pirates?' asked Kate.

'They don't have a Letter of Marque.'

Kate shook her head. 'So, if a Spanish privateer has a Letter of Marque from his or her king, that makes it alright for them to steal from us?'

'Only as far as the Spaniards are concerned. As far as we're concerned, they're stealing our stuff and should be prosecuted if caught.' Michael grabbed the rum bottle which was sitting on the top book of a small pile of books obscuring a piece of the chart lying on the table. He poured two cups of rum and handed one to her. Michael liked her company, because she was intelligent and friendly, and beautiful to look at, with her long red hair and flashing green eyes.

'If they catch us, they'll likely hang us, Letter of Marque or not. I don't really see what good the Letter of Marque does. I mean, all it does is make us liable for a portion of our prizes to the king. The king takes a percentage.' Kate took a sip of her rum.

'He did finance the purchase of two sloops, provisions, and guns. It's only fair he gets a percentage. Don't you agree?' Michael sipped some rum and sat back in his chair, tasting the sweet amber liquid as he rolled it about on his tongue.

'How much of a percentage?' asked Kate, eyeing Michael.

'Forty. He gets forty percent.'

'Forty percent?! Forty percent?!' Why that's outrageous!' Kate nearly spilled her drink.

'Yes, but he did pay for the sloops and stuff.'

'So, let's just pay him back with some interest and be done with it. I mean. Think about it. We do all the work. We risk our lives. Some of us are maimed or killed to get stuff and then give the king forty percent for sitting on his fat arse on a throne not risking diddly squat. He doesn't earn any of the money he spends. It's all stolen to begin with.'

Kate took a long drink of rum. 'Hmm this is good rum.'

Michael nodded. 'Yes it is. I'm glad we found that Spaniard's liquor cabinet.'

Kate laughed. 'Some cabinet that was. More like a small warehouse.'

'I think el Capitano was something of an alcoholic,' laughed Michael. 'Good for us. All three captains still have excellent rum and wine, as a result.'

Kate held up her cup. 'And so it should be, my captain.'

Michael filled Kate's cup and his own. Then they clicked their cups together.

'Here's to success in Vera Cruz,' said Kate.

'To Vera Cruz,' replied Michael. He smiled at Kate and then took a long sip of rum.

Kate smiled over her cup, her eyes sparkling.

'But, we've got to get there soon. We're scraping the bottoms of barrels. Everybody is getting grumpy and blaming Hanzel.' Michael thought about his friend.

'Well, it is his fault. He changed plans while we were at sea and did not reprovision for this long voyage to Mexico. Thank God we haven't been becalmed out here. We'd be eating our boots if we don't catch enough fish,' replied Kate.

'By my reckoning, we're about five days away. Let's pray that everybody can hang on long enough. If we make port, we can buy food again.'

'And rum,' laughed Kate, holding up her cup.

Meanwhile, onboard *De Blauwe Tulip* Mister Koopman was not pleased. 'By the Thundering Testicles of the Minotaur!' he shouted. 'What in the cesspool of life is going on?! Three dead?! Three more!' He stared out of the centre transom window of his cabin. The Caribbean sea was all there was to see. Heat waves shimmered in the air.

'It's the heat,' replied Norack Waldenstein.

Mister Koopman looked at his first mate. 'The heat? It's the heat?'

'Wakes up evil humors. They seep up from the bilges. Maybe it's time we did a good airing out of the ship.' Norack sniffed. 'Even this place could use an airing out, no offense.'

'Yes, well, we need to do something. We've already lost six good people on this ship. He thinks we're going to get rich in Vera Cruz.' Mister Koopman shook his head. 'We should have stayed off Hispaniola. That's where the Spanish treasure fleet will be.'

'I've heard stories about the riches of Vera Cruz,' replied Norack. 'It's a place where the silver and gold of the Mexicans is brought. It has a port.'

Mister Koopman nodded. 'Well, I guess we'll see. Let's pray no more come to grief out here on this accursed sea, in the meantime. If we don't make land soon and find food, we'll be eating our belts.'

'Signals from *Lieve Hanna* and *De Heilige Vrouw* indicated this morning they have each lost another, as well.'

'We lose three today and they each lose one.' Mister Koopman rested his chin on his right fist. 'There obviously is something wrong with this ship. Tell everyone to open every hatch and port. Then tell everyone to scrub down everything with vinegar. And get those bilges pumped out.' Mister Koopman paused for a moment as he thought of what else. 'Oh, and please be so kind as to send me another bottle of rum.'

'Aye, Captain,' replied Norack as he got up from his chair. 'Anything else?'

A sly smile crossed Mister Koopman's lips. 'If you see Alison, maybe you could suggest she come by my cabin. The captain would like a word.'

Norack smiled. 'I'll tell her, if I see her. Good luck with that.' He turned on his heels and left the cabin, leaving Mister Koopman wondering if Alison will come to see him and share some rum.

Two days later, one of Hanzel's crew members had stirred up sixteen of his mates to confront their captain and demand he step down. They blamed all of their misfortunes, while sailing the Gulf of Mexico, on him and he should pay for the loss of their loved ones and their own suffering due to a lack of food and drink. The disgruntled leader of the pack, a man named Jacop van der Sween, waved his cutlass in Hanzel's face.

'It's all because of you. You changed course without consulting anyone. Now we have no food, no rum, hardly any wine, no eggs, no chickens! Five of our crew, dead!'

'Yeah! Five dead!' shouted the others. 'And more on the other boats.'

'If you don't step down, we'll,' Jacop turned around to seek reassurance from his coconspirators.

'You'll do what?' asked Hanzel, taking a pistol from his belt.

As Jacop turned back to face Hanzel, Hanzel shot him point blank through his forehead. As the back of his skull exploded outward, blood with bits of bone and brain spattered his mates. A shocked silence followed as Jacop's friends watched him collapse to the deck. Hanzel took another pistol from his belt and pointed it at the stunned group standing in front of him. 'Is there anyone else who wants to challenge me?'

The shocked group looked at each other and back at Hanzel, each one of them shaking their heads and murmuring that they accepted him as captain and would make no more trouble.

Hanzel continued to point his pistol at the rebels. 'Each of you will be marooned on the first deserted island we find. What possessed you to think you could just walk up to your captain and challenge him. I should have you all flogged for participating in this sordid affair. Thank your lucky stars I don't have each of you thrown to the sharks.' He turned to Pontelo. 'Throw these mistaken mutineers into the forward storage locker. Bread and water only.' Hanzel frowned and wondered why he was being so lenient. 'Marooning is too good for those vile cockroaches!'

As Pontelo, with the help of Jacques LeBlanc and several others began to herd the sixteen errant crewmen, one of them, a man named, Robert Bean, pushed Pontelo aside and then sliced at him with the dirk he'd drawn from his boot. The moment that happened, the other mutineers began to resist their arrest and a scuffle broke out. Hanzel waded into the midst of the battle and shot Robert Bean through his left temple. The sound of the gunshot stopped everybody instantly. Now a second member of their group lay dead. As more and more of the crew members gathered on deck, to see what was going on, they surrounded the trouble makers and forced them to lay down their arms. Now Hanzel was really angry. This time there was not going to be any mercy.

When the remaining fifteen mutineers were subdued and on their knees facing their furious captain the sentence was instantly pronounced. 'One by one you will be flogged to within an inch of your miserable lives. Then, when you are covered in gore, you will be thrown overboard, where you can feed the fishes with your mutinous hides!'

And so it was that the sentence was carried out. Each man was flogged until his entire backside, from top to bottom, was cut open and bleeding; the flesh rendered into pulp. Then the screaming man was thrown overboard as Hanzel's supporters cheered. The executions took place over three days. After that, nobody contemplated mutiny ever again.

Hanzel clapped his hands together. 'So, that's that then,' he said as the last man splashed down into the warm azure waters of the Gulf of Mexico, all the while cursing Hanzel and his progeny until eternity. Hanzel shrugged his shoulders and returned to his cabin and a cup of rum from his special stores, as he thought about Hanna, still so fresh in his mind. However, as soon as images of Hanna came into his mind, Mephi appeared, dressed in a provocative red and black outfit which revealed more than her cleavage. Her raven hair was thrown over her shoulders and her emerald eyes bored into his. Hanzel shuddered as he snapped her out of his mind. He looked into his cup, thinking it might be the rum that was giving him visions. Her face stared back at him.

Three days later they arrived off the coast of Mexico, three leagues from Vera Cruz. Food had run out and water was down to drops per person. It was not a moment too soon. Everyone prayed they would make port as soon as possible. Alas, it was not to be. Nature would not give them relief. The wind turned and stormy clouds rolled in. They had to stand off shore for three days. By that time everyone was starving and dehydrated. When they were able to finally put in to shore, they were nowhere near Vera Cruz.

'We have to row to shore to find water and food,' said Michael at the officer's meeting Hanzel had called, when the ships lay at anchor off a rocky beach, onto which moderate sized waves were breaking. 'With the slight swell and moderate waves, we can put boats ashore and surely water will be available. There have to be pools, or a creek, or something.'

A loud stomping of feet and creaking rigging could be heard outside.

Hanzel looked up. 'By the sounds of it, our friends are not waiting for our orders. Everyone is desperate to get to shore. So, let's watch them go and pray they find water. Food likely is no problem. Those kind of forests are full of edible things.'

'That is true, Hanzel. But we must be careful. Those forests are full of poisonous things, as well,' replied Doctor Winderkint. 'I hope to study some of them, while we're here.'

Hanzel nodded. 'Very well, then. Let's get on with the business at hand. If we don't find water soon, a lot of people will be in very severe straights.'

As everyone left the cabin, Hanzel, for the first time in a long time, took a look at himself in the mirror. The man who stared back at him was a disheveled mess; akin to the appearance of an impoverished man with no master. *When we get back, I'm definitely shaving and changing my clothes. You look a mess, Hanzel. What is wrong with you?* He quickly joined his friends on deck and watched, as people rowed ashore in their long boats.

The first people ashore, sent the boats back with rowers to pick up others. And so they ferried everyone who was able to get out of their hammock and had the energy to move, to shore, where they fanned out and began their desperate search for food and water. The officers were the last to step on shore. A few people were sitting on rocks; exhausted skeletons waiting for water or death. Hanzel looked over at them for a moment and then engaged Michael in a conversation about haberdashery.

'So, Michael. What do you think?' Hanzel adjusted his cod piece. 'Will the cod piece ever be replaced? Do you suppose men will sew these parts together, somehow, and still leave a means of relieving oneself, without having to take down one's pantaloons?'

Michael regarded his friend for a moment. 'Hanzel, half of our people are near death from dehydration and some even from starvation. And here you are talking about cod pieces?'

'Well, there really isn't anything we can do about the water and food, until we find some, so we might as well talk about something which has been on my mind. I find the cod piece is a rather cumbersome affair.' He adjusted the strap holding his in place.

'Hanzel, I am in no mood to talk about cod pieces,' replied Michael tersely.

'What about waist coats, then. What about them? Do you think waistcoats will ever go out of style?' Hanzel watched a man struggling with a gull over a decomposing fish which had lain, washed up under a rock for a week. Hanzel laughed. Michael walked off with Kate and began to organize a search party.

'What do you think, Mister Koopman. Do you think waistcoats will ever go out of style? Or what about cod pieces?' Hanzel sat down on a rock and adjusted the ruffles of his soiled sleeves.'

'By the Blistering Barnacles of Neptune! Why are you talking about clothes when we should be organizing the crews to look for water and food?' Mister Koopman studied Hanzel for a moment and then shook his head as he watched him, like a fop, fuss over his disheveled clothing. Without further words, he walked off, followed by Gertrude van Hollenhern, his quartermaster and several other members of his crew. Soon Hanzel could hear Michael and Mister Koopman ordering people into groups. As groups set off into the forest and in each direction along the beach, Hanzel remained seated on his rock examining his clothes for imperfections.

Some hours later a group stumbled back to the beach. They had found nothing.

Twenty minutes later another group found its way back to the beach. They also had found nothing. Hanzel took no notice because he was busy studying a tide pool.

Mister Koopman returned an hour later, but he and his group also had found nothing. No water and no food.

By this time it was nearing late afternoon. The sun was already low on the horizon and nobody had found food nor drink. Everyone was depressed and weak from hunger. Nobody had the strength or will to row back to the sloops. Since the sky appeared to be clear and the air was warm, everyone just curled up in a fetal ball and lay there amidst the rocks and rotting kelp.

Just before dark, Michael and his group returned from their reconnaissance. Everyone was smiling. They appeared healthy and full of energy. Hanzel looked up from examining a starfish in a puddle.

'We found a small settlement. The people gave us water and bread. They were very kind to us. We told them we were shipwrecked and were trying to get to Vera Cruz, which is north of us, by the way. We're about twenty miles south.' Michael pointed north. 'Anyway, there's about twenty five or thirty people there who have established a ranch. There's a whole herd of cattle to be got.'

Hanzel rubbed his hands together and looked greedily in the direction from which Michael and his group had come. 'So, there's a settlement, you say. With lots of cattle to feed the entire crew? What do you say, Mister Koopman? Do we pay for our food, or do we raid the place?'

'They're Spaniards, are they not?' Mister Koopman looked at Michael.

'They speak Spanish. But they were very nice to us,' replied Michael.

'Well then, by the Thundering Phallus of Zeus! Are we pirates, or are we meek, merchants who pay for their way? What does our Letter of Marque say? We are admonished to pillage, plunder, and wreak havoc on Spaniards, no matter where they are. Is that not so, Hanzel?' Mister Koopman looked at Hanzel who looked over at Michael.

'That is what the Letter says,' replied Hanzel. 'I say we raid the settlement and get ourselves fattened up so we can take on what bigger Spanish prize might be waiting for us in Vera Cruz. Where is this settlement?'

Michael pointed. 'Come, we'll show you.'

Hanzel gestured to the people lying about on the beach. 'Come, you mangy dogs! Bring your weapons. We're going to raid a settlement. Tonight we'll have ourselves a feast!'

Those who were able, gathered themselves together and followed Michael and Hanzel, to raid a settlement which had given succor in a time of need. Michael did not feel good about it, however, he realized the necessity. Either the crews of the three sloops died from dehydration and malnourishment, or they took control of the settlement and procured what was needed to bring everyone back up to working strength.

The path to the village was through some dense jungle, filled with the sounds of insects and animals, lizards and arachnids. Many of the crew members were not used to jungles and the thought that a snake might coil around them at any moment heightened their fear. After an hour of pushing and hacking their way through the dense verdure, they came upon open fields and buildings. Indeed, there was a small village and substantial agriculture. When everyone was assembled, Hanzel and his gang numbered 86; 53 men and 33 women. All of them desperate for fluids and sustenance. When they all showed up in the village, the people were reluctant to extend their hospitality. They had no idea what a bad idea that was.

'Round all of them up and gather them here in the square,' demanded Hanzel. He turned on the village head man. 'Do you have any idea who you are refusing?' Hanzel looked at one of his Spanish speaking crew mates, a man named, Juan Marchesas, to interpret for him.

The headman had no idea and told Hanzel he could sell him a cow, if that would help matters.

'Do you have gold, or silver?' asked Hanzel.

The headman shook his head. 'No, senior. We don't have silver or gold.'

Hanzel eyed the man. 'A likely story.' Hanzel turned away and watched as the twenty seven people, who comprised the village, were rounded up and gathered before Hanzel and the headman. Hanzel had a chair brought out for him to sit on. Then he told the people to sit down. Ten pirates with weapons kept an eye on the group while the rest set about the village looking for food and drink. Eventually Kate Montgomery brought Hanzel a cup of rum to drink.

'Thank you,' he said, taking the cup. He took a sip and swallowed slowly, all the while not taking his eyes off the gathered villagers. 'The headman tells me he has no gold or silver,' said Hanzel, looking up at Kate standing beside his chair. 'What do you think of that?'

Kate stared at the headman. 'I think he's lying.'

'Where is your gold and silver!' shouted Hanzel at the gathered people.

Juan Marchesas interpreted the question.

Nobody said anything.

'I will torture your headman if you do not tell me,' replied Hanzel.

Juan Marchesas interpreted.

Nobody said anything.

'Kate, tell Jacques LeBlanc, Doctor Allan, and Mister Koopman to come here.' Hanzel gestured towards the buildings where the friends in question were likely searching for things they could use.

'Aye Captain,' replied Kate. She turned on her heels and quickly set off to find the people Hanzel wanted to see.

When the three crewmates joined Hanzel, he commanded that the headman be tied to a chair in front of the assembled people. When this was done, Hanzel ordered that Doctor Allan oversee the torture, in order to prevent vital organs from being damaged, or for the wrong veins or arteries to be opened. 'I don't want him to bleed out,' said Hanzel. 'I want him to feel his pain.' Hanzel shouted to the people once more. 'Where is your gold and silver?!'

Juan Marchesas interpreted but nobody replied.

'One hundred slices,' demanded Hanzel.

Immediately the two men who had tied him up, tore the headman's shirt off. Then Jacques LeBlanc began slicing the man's chest with a sharp knife. The man gritted his teeth but did not utter a sound. By the tenth slice, the man's chest was covered with blood. Jacques looked at Hanzel.

'Where is your gold and silver?' asked Hanzel. By this time his gang had found what they needed for rehydration and joined the gathering to watch the torture; all of them anxious to learn if there was gold and silver to be had. 'If you tell us, no more harm will come to you.'

Juan Marchesas interpreted but again nobody said anything.

This time Hanzel stood up. He was enraged. A fire came into his eyes. He ordered the man's fingers cut off.

As Jacques cut off the man's right little finger, the man groaned and yet, he said nothing about gold or silver. The people began to stir.

'Cut off another finger!' demanded Hanzel, cold as ice.

Jacques cut off the man's right ring finger. This time the man began to sweat and groan. However, he still said nothing about gold or silver.

Hanzel nodded and a third finger was cut off. Again nothing was said. *This is not working.* Hanzel took out his pistol and shot the man in the head. Just like that. BANG!

The man fell forward and lay bleeding in front of his villagers.

Hanzel sat down on his chair and pointed to a beautiful dark haired woman. He demanded she be brought on her knees in front of him. 'Where is your gold and silver?' he demanded.

The woman shook her head.

'STRIP HER NAKED!' demanded Hanzel, nearly hysterical with an anger his shipmates had never seen before.

The two crew mates who tied up the headman performed the task, big grins on their guant faces. They stripped her naked and pushed the woman back onto her knees. 'Tie her to the chair,' said Hanzel calmly. When she was tied to the chair Hanzel again demanded where the treasure was, but nobody responded. 'Heat up some implements.'

A brazier was brought forth and a fire was lit. A small sword, a sharp poker, and tongs from the blacksmith's shop were heated up. In the meantime Hanzel kept asking where the treasure was hidden but the people remained stoic. When the time came, and the implements were white hot, Hanzel demanded that the tongs be applied to the woman's nipples. When the first nipple was pinched with the white hot tongs, she screamed at the top of her lungs. Hanzel laughed at her for screaming. 'WHERE IS THE GOLD!' he shouted.

Nothing.

Hanzel nodded and the other nipple was pinched and fried. Again the woman screamed until she was out of breath and could scream no more.

'DO WE HAVE TO TORTURE ALL OF YOU BEFORE YOU TELL US WHERE YOU GOLD IS?' Hanzel was growing impatient. He grabbed his other loaded pistol and shot the woman point blank through the top of her head. Then he pointed to a child; a young girl of about five or six. 'That one,' he said cold as ice.

As the child was grabbed, her mother screamed. 'NO, NO! NOT MY CHILD! I'll tell you where the gold is.'

'Finally,' said Hanzel with a sigh of relief. 'This torture business is much too time consuming.' He looked at the woman. 'Alright, woman, show us where your treasure is.'

The woman pointed to a house. Then she led Hanzel, Michael, and Mister Koopman to a trap door in the floor of the kitchen. The door had been hidden by a rug. When they opened the trap door, a stairway led to the basement where several large boxes stood. They were filled with gold and silver coins, bars, and objects; some of them encrusted with precious stones.

When the boxes were brought out of the house, the treasure brought cheers of joy from Hanzel's crewmates. They all shouted, 'HURRAY FOR HANZEL SVENTSKA!'

Hanzel smiled; an ice cold light emanating from his intense blue eyes.

'So, what do we do with the villagers?' asked Michael.

Hanzel looked down at the kneeling people. 'They're Spaniards. Feed them to their own hogs.'

'You mean you want us to kill them? To kill all of them? Even those children?' asked Michael.

Hanzel nodded. 'They're Spaniards. We can't leave them alive. Dead men tell no tales, my friend. I don't want to sail into Vera Cruz with this crime hanging over our heads, because someone from here told the authorities.'

'You have a point there,' replied Michael. He looked at the assembled villagers with a sad expression. 'Alas, such is life in the privateering business. Sometimes we must be harsh, I suppose.'

Hanzel narrowed his eyes and slowly stroked his right eyebrow. 'Do we shoot them? Do we burn them? Do we hang them? Do we tear their hearts out? How should we dispose of those Spanish vermin? That is now the question.'

'It would be simpler just to shoot them,' suggested Mister Koopman, regarding Hanzel with a sideways glance.

'Hanging. We could hang them,' said Kate.

'Too much trouble. It is simpler to just shoot them.' Hanzel signaled to several of his crewmates wielding a pistol or a musket. 'Go ahead. Fire!.'

'You said no harm would come to us if we told you about the treasure!' shouted the woman who led them to the trap door.

Hanzel stared at the woman, his eyes mad with blood lust. 'I lied,' he said and then laughed in her face.

And so the killing began. It was all over in five minutes. The villagers lay dead or mortally wounded on the ground; every man, woman, and child. Hanzel clapped his hands together. 'Well, that takes care of that. Alright, boys and girls, you may loot the place and when we're done, burn it to the ground.' Hanzel laughed diabolically as he grabbed a bottle of rum out of Kate's hand and took a long drink. 'It feels good to be back to work,' he said, laughing with a banshee voice which unsettled everyone who heard it; including those villagers feeling their lives seeping out of the holes in their tortured flesh.

That night a huge feast of roasted beef filled the empty bellies of Hanzel's crews. Enough wine, ale, rum, and brandy was available to give everyone a pleasant glow in their cheeks. After five days of eating and drinking, everyone was back to strength.

Fortunately, a road led from the village to a pier leading out into a small bay from whence the local fishermen could launch their boats and head out to sea.

'Bring the long boats into the bay,' ordered Hanzel.

When the boats arrived, a lot of useful plunder was already waiting on the pier. Within two days the village was cleaned out, the chickens and what beef they could salt and store, were taken onboard the three sloops. But, instead of burning the village, Michael persuaded Hanzel that the smoke would likely be visible for a long way. It was not a good thing to so herald one's arrival in Vera Cruz and alert the Spanish navy, or marines, who might be stationed there.

'It is best we sail into Vera Cruz under various flags. I think it might be a good idea if we rename our ships. I would not be surprised if word about our caper in Las Palmas has reached the navy here in Mexico. They might even be on the lookout for us.'

Hanzel scratched his chin. 'That is a good idea. We rename our ships. Each crew can vote on what they want to name the ship they're on.'

And so it was done. Hanzel's sloop became, *The Blue Whale*, flying an English flag. Mister Koopman's ship became, *Le Roi d'Or*, flying a French flag, and Michael's fine boat became, *Glistening Dolphin*, flying the flag of Sweden. They each arrived separately into the harbour at Vera Cruz. The false flag ruse worked famously. Nobody suspected they were three sloops belonging to one privateering gang. And so, Hanzel's crew mates were able to infiltrate the town and seek out information regarding Spanish treasure.

Days stretched into a week, the week stretched into two weeks and then a month. All anyone heard were rumours about treasure but nobody knew where it was. Hanzel and his crew were running out of money and desperately needed to find a large pile of gold and silver coins with which they could obtain the things necessary for further adventures at sea. Privateering with two hundred people is not an inexpensive enterprise. It costs money and lots of it. Fortunately, morale was high again amongst Hanzel's crew mates. Many expressed regrets to Hanzel for having doubted him. The raid on the settlement did a lot to boost people up and give them new hope a Spanish treasure fleet was close at hand.

One day, after spending 33 days in Vera Cruz, Hanzel was having dinner with Michael, Mister Koopman, their first mates, Kate Montgomery, and Norack Waldenstein, Doctors Allan and Winderkint with their mates, Josephine Mulberry and Maxine Martin. They were enjoying a wonderful meal of roasted red snapper, mixed sautéed vegetables with a chili sauce, deep fried sweet potatoes, stuffed peppers with rice and beans, fried battered chicken, and lots of ale, rum, and wine. Outside the skies were roiling. Rain had already begun, when an inebriated monk, wearing a black robe came weaving and swaying into the tavern. It was difficult to tell what he looked like because his face was obscured by the shadow of a deep cowl. He was carrying a heavy crucifix in his right hand. His loud and obnoxious behaviour was noticed by everyone as he shouted absurdities about Christ, and His Mother and Father.

As the mad monk stumbled about in the tavern he bumped hard against Hanzel, spilling the wine he was about to drink. A large red stain soaked his expensive silk shirt. Hanzel looked down at the stain and then at the crazy monk, who stood defiantly waving the crucifix in his face. Instantly Hanzel pushed his chair back and pulling out a pistol from his belt, pointed it at the monk. The crazy monk raised the crucifix above his head distracting Hanzel, who looked up. The monk, with his other hand, pulled a stiletto from under his robe and thrust it deep into Hanzel's abdomen. Hanzel's eyes bulged and opened wide as he bent forward, pulling the monk's cowl aside and revealing the grinning face of Mephi Stofeleas.

'I thought you said I could live a hundred years in exchange for my soul,' groaned Hanzel, the pain in his stomach overpowering his body.

'I lied,' laughed Mephi.

'I signed a contract,' muttered Hanzel as he felt his life ebb from his senses.

'This will teach you. DON'T MAKE CONTRACTS WITH THE DEVIL!'

Mephi laughed and laughed, louder and louder, reaching a climax; a shrieking banshee demon sent by Lucifer himself!

And then, in an instant, Hanzel and she disappeared in a flash of light, leaving a sulfurous humour which permeated everything; food, clothing, and drinks.

Everyone in the place wondered, *What the hell just happened?* as they stared dumfoundedly at the place where Hanzel and the witch had disappeared. For surely she was a witch, there was no doubt about that. Nobody believed the Devil can also be a woman. And that smell, it surely came from a witch's cauldron...

As the patrons and staff stumbled outside to get out of the reek, a flash of blue light blinded everyone for an instant as a horrific clap of thunder followed.

Nobody was the same after that.

THE END